"I SAW THEM, T'CHEBBI! SAW CARRIE AND KAID WHEN THEY LINKED! J'KOSHUK MADE ME WATCH!"

Agony coursed through Kusac now. He lashed out at the monitor, hoping to dissipate his anger with a different pain. His fist contacted, smashing the screen which promptly exploded with a loud bang, showering him with shards. Pain lanced through his hand as he staggered back. But it had worked, the anger was gone leaving only agony in his hand.

"You're bleeding," said T'Chebbi calmly, getting up. "Come with me, I'll dress it."

"I'm all right. Leave me alone." He backed off, then turned and headed for the door, shocked by the violence of what he'd done.

His head was throbbing as badly as his hand when he tried to examine it. He was still bleeding copiously. He wrapped a towel tightly round it. T'Chebbi was right. His continued presence was only causing Carrie and Kaid problems. It would have been better for all concerned had he not survived.

He pulled out a small bottle of spirits from the cupboard. Sitting down, he fished in his pocket, pulling out the tablets he kept there. Ten still remained. He washed them down one at a time with the alcohol, knowing that he was doing the right thing. With him dead by his own hand, there'd be no guilt for them. He couldn't go on like this anyway, living with the constant pain caused by the implant whenever he felt anger; living without Carrie and their Link.

J'koshuk had won in the end, he thought. . . .

Stronghold Rising

Lisanne Norman

DAW BOOKS, INC.

DONALD A. WOLLHEIM, FOUNDER

375 Hudson Street, New York, NY 10014

ELIZABETH R. WOLLHEIM

SHEILA E. GILBERT

PUBLISHERS

First Printing, June 2000
3 4 5 6 7 8 9

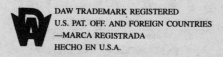

DEDICATION

This book is for the friend I have known longest, Sherry Ward. In these books I craft a vision we both share. And for Jean. Thank you both for your friendship and help over the years.

ACKNOWLEDGMENTS

As always, I have had help from friends providing me with essential knowledge I don't possess. I'd like to thank them here.

Brotherhood Research and Development—Merlin, aka James Chorlton, and Helen Lofting.
Sholan Medical Advisers—Dr. Michelle Harris at the Lawrence General Hospital in Lawrence, Mass, USA.
Alliance Ship Designs—Josh Eastridge, John Phillips, and Martin J. Dougherty
Brotherhood Science Officer, Anchorage—Hanno (Hurga) Foest
Alien Relations—Marsha Jones, Pauline Dungate, MaryAnn Hollingsworth, Lynn Edwards, Ken Slater, Tony Rogers
Sholan Cartography and Architecture—Mike Gilbert

Thanks must also go to members of The Sholan Alliance Fan Club for helping me with my research in fields as diverse as space station designs, weapons, and medicine. People like Greg Hofer and Mary Ann Hollingsworth. Also other members of the medical section at Lawrence General Hospital in Lawrence, Mass. USA.

The Sholan Alliance Fan Club can be found at http://www.sholan-alliance.org

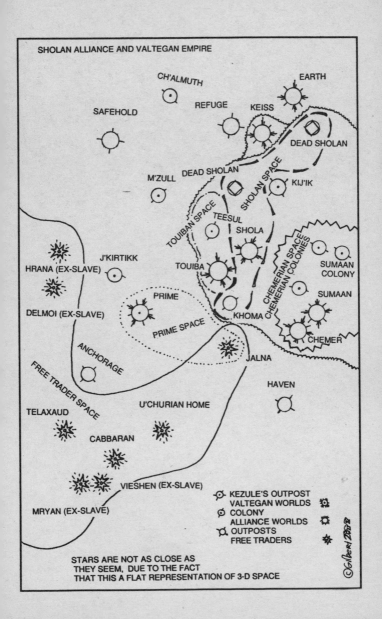

SHOLAN ALLIANCE AND VALTEGAN EMPIRE

CH'ALMUTH

EARTH

SAFEHOLD

REFUGE

KEISS

DEAD SHOLAN

DEAD SHOLAN

M'ZULL

KIJ'IK

SHOLAN SPACE

TOUIBAN SPACE

TEESUL

SHOLA

CHEMERIAN SPACE

CHEMERIAN COLONIES

SUMAAN COLONY

J'KIRTIKK

HRANA (EX-SLAVE)

TOUIBA

SUMAAN

DELMOI (EX-SLAVE)

PRIME

PRIME SPACE

KHOMA

CHEMER

ANCHORAGE

JALNA

FREE TRADER SPACE

U'CHURIAN HOME

HAVEN

TELAXAUD

CABBARAN

MRYAN (EX-SLAVE)

VIESHEN (EX-SLAVE)

⚙ KEZULE'S OUTPOST
VALTEGAN WORLDS
◊ COLONY
ALLIANCE WORLDS
☆ OUTPOSTS
✳ FREE TRADERS

©Gilbert 2002

STARS ARE NOT AS CLOSE AS
THEY SEEM, DUE TO THE FACT
THAT THIS A FLAT REPRESENTATION
OF 3-D SPACE

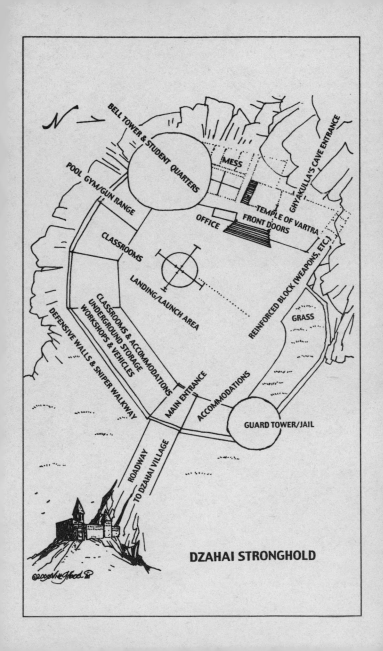

DZAHAI STRONGHOLD

PART 1

Dreaming

CHAPTER 1

Stronghold, Zhal-S'Asha (Month of
Approaching Darkness), 18th day, 1551
(October)

THE door behind him opened and closed. Ignoring the soft
footfall, he continued to stare out across the Dzahai Mountains.

"I thought I'd find you here."

"If you've come to persuade me not to go, you'll fail,"
he said shortly, trying to contain the anger that had been
building now for several days.

"There's no need for it to be you, surely. Since you came
back from Haven, your—health—has not been good. Lijou
and Rhyaz don't even know that the message is genuine.
Are you positive someone else couldn't . . ."

"I'm going," he interrupted, the other's slight hesitation
not lost on him. "As head of AlRel, you know why I was
asked for specifically."

There was a short silence. "At least delay it by a day
or two, Kusac. It shouldn't make any . . ."

"I'm leaving at dawn, when I know Carrie's had their
cub," he said coldly. "To delay any longer would be disastrous."

"Preparations aren't complete. They haven't found a way
to access the ship to reprovision it yet. Rhyaz says we risk
everything if you leave so precipitously."

The tenuous control snapped and he spun around, ears
lying flat and to the side, tail visibly lashing beneath the
purple-bordered black tunic he wore. "*You* risk nothing!

Have you *any* idea what these last few months have been like for me, cut off mentally from my Leska Link with Carrie, and from Kaid?"

"I can imagine . . ."

"You *cannot*! Now get out of here and leave me alone! You've had my answer! I'm leaving as soon as their cub is born! You know I have to!" He spun back to face the window, his gesture an obvious dismissal to the other black-pelted male.

He waited for the sound of the door again before allowing his shoulders to slump in exhaustion. The life he'd lost during his captivity with the Primes was almost within his grasp again, and they were asking him to turn his back on it. More, this venture, which had no guarantee of even being worthwhile, would cost him his reputation: he'd be outcast, branded a traitor by his own kind, unable to return until the outcome cleared his name—if it ever did.

He leaned his head against the glass, welcoming its coolness against his face and hands. Winter was barely three weeks away. Nearly five months had passed since he'd returned from Haven after his release by the Primes, and still he'd not come to terms with what had happened to him. Certain events must be resolved, like the scents only he could smell that had lingered on the message. He had to leave Shola now, before it was too late for him to get the answers he had to have.

Frustration and anger rose in him again and as his hair and the pelt beneath his tunic started to rise, he began to growl. The torc that circled his neck started to vibrate warningly. Ignoring it and the subsequent brief flare of pain the strong emotion still occasionally caused, he lifted his head, letting the growl become a full-throated roar that echoed round the room. Those who still remained in the almost empty halls of Stronghold understood its cause and, shivering, turned to each other for reassurance.

As the echoes died away, he shuddered, trying to shake off the remaining discomfort, and returned to looking across the moonlit landscape, far beyond Dzahai village, to where Kaid's home lay. Like images on an entertainment comm, memories of his time on Haven began to form before his eyes.

Haven, Zhal-Zhalwae (month of the Sun God), 22nd day, 1551 (May)

With a jolt, sweating and shaking, he was suddenly awake. Strong hands gripped his arms, holding him firmly down on the bed. Terror surged through him as he imagined himself back in his cell on the *Kz'adul*, held once more by the armored Prime guard. The scent of his jailer, J'koshuk, the Valtegan torturer-priest, was strong in his nostrils. Fear kept his eyes tightly shut as he braced himself for the next blow from the electronic animal prod.

"Kusac, you're safe on Haven with us," said a quiet voice in Sholan. "You had a bad dream."

He opened his eyes; by the dim light in the IC unit, he could see a vaguely familiar tan-pelted face looking down at him. The bed to one side of him moved. Confused, he slowly turned his head, aware of a stabbing pain in his neck as he did. All he could see was an indistinct figure leaning over the night table until the room began to brighten: he recognized her long blonde hair instantly. Memory returned in a rush then. He was no longer the Primes' prisoner, he was on the Brotherhood outpost of Haven, located far from Shola, on the borders of Chemerian space.

Carrie leaned over him, gently caressing his cheek. "You can let him go now, Kaid."

The pressure on his arms was lifted as Kaid, still watching him carefully, sat back. He opened his mouth to speak, but only a faint croak came out.

"I'll fetch you some water," said Carrie, getting up.

Reaching for Kaid's arm, he grasped it, using his friend's strength to help him sit up. The sudden movement made him aware of a dull, throbbing headache. When Carrie passed him the glass, he drained it while she piled pillows behind him.

"How long have you been here?" he asked Kaid as Carrie urged him to lean back.

"I came up after the talks broke for the night." Kaid nodded toward the chair not far from the bed. "I slept there. We're a Triad, Kusac. Where else would I be but here with you and Carrie?"

Even as feelings blocked off for too long by the Primes' implant began to well up inside him, he felt the warning tingling at the base of his skull. Instinctively, he retreated behind the mental barriers that had given him some little protection from the tortures J'koshuk had inflicted on him. Then Carrie was hugging him, her warmth and scent driving the last remnants of the nightmare away. With one arm, he clumsily returned the embrace, his other hand reaching for Kaid, needing to touch them both.

"I've never been alone," he whispered. "I've always sensed others around me. Now there's nothing. I'm mind-dead." It was a statement of fact, like he might say his pelt was black. He felt numb, as empty of emotions as he had on the Prime ship.

"Your psi Talent will come back," Kaid reassured him. "Until it does, we'll never be far from you. Getting you back to full health is our priority."

"You're not mind-dead," said Carrie forcefully. "You just need time for your mind to heal now that the implant's been deactivated and removed."

He remembered the implant and felt just under his jaw for the dressing that circled his neck. Like his head, it had begun to throb. He ignored it; compared to the unremitting pain J'koshuk had inflicted on him, it was nothing. "How much damage did it do?" he asked, trying to remember what Kaid had said the night before.

"Damage isn't the right word," said Kaid. "It was—invasive. With Valtegans who volunteer to become soldiers, its normal purpose is to take over the brain's hormone production and release. It does this by growing tendrils that create their own neural connections in the brain. They're not functioning now the control unit's been removed."

"He's just awakened, Tallinu, it's too soon to go into all these details," Carrie said.

"I need to know," he said, glancing at her. "What are these tendrils? Could they become active again?"

"Without the external unit, they shouldn't be able to become active. The TeLaxaudin bioengineered the implants for the Primes—they're part device and part a living tissue that bonds with the host. You're being kept in IC for the time being until the physician is sure your own system has stabilized and is functioning properly again. And in case you have another seizure," Kaid added, hand tightening round his.

He'd forgotten about that. "Have they found out what caused it yet?"

"Them," corrected Kaid gently. "You had more than one. No, we don't know, but you haven't had one since the unit was removed twelve hours ago, which is encouraging. Kzizysus, the TeLaxaudin physician, helped remove the implant. He's taken copies of your scans and medical data back to the Prime ship to study, to see if he can discover what caused the seizures."

"Chy'qui implanted me, he should have some idea," he said sharply, his ears folding in the beginnings of anger.

Kaid glanced briefly at Carrie. "Kzizysus didn't actually see you having the first seizure, Kusac. Doctor Chy'qui only called him in to adjust the implant. The subsequent seizures could have been caused either by a failure of the implant to take completely, or by it trying to adapt to your alien physiology. It wasn't designed for Sholan use after all, only for the Valtegans."

"Are you saying that there's some doubt about whether I needed an implant at all? That this Chy'qui could have been lying?" He felt anger surging through him, bringing with it the familiar wave of pain. J'koshuk had inadvertently taught him how to cope with pain. After being cut off from his emotions for so long, it was almost a relief to feel anger, no matter the cost.

"It's a possibility," agreed Carrie, reaching out to touch him reassuringly. "We were only able to find out as much as we have because of Annuur, leader of Captain Tirak's Cabbaran navigators. He was able to translate what Kzizysus said for us. The Cabbarans are old allies of the TeLaxaud—they have a natural talent that allows them to communicate with the TeLaxaudin more accurately than any other species."

"Why did he do it?" he demanded, pulling his hand away from Kaid's and sitting upright. "Why implant me if I didn't need it?"

"To experiment on you and Carrie," said Kaid. "Chy'qui knew you were a Leska pair, but he didn't know about me until after Doctor Zayshul had operated on Carrie. He was the one responsible for keeping the three of us apart, and for letting J'koshuk torture you."

His anger grew, exacerbating the dull aches in his head and neck. As his pelt and hair rose, so too did the pain level until he felt as if every nerve in his body was on fire. "I want to see

Chy'qui now," he snarled, shaking his head in an effort to re-lieve the pain as he tried to force himself back to calmness.

Kaid put a restraining hand on his arm. "No. It's over, Kusac. Chy'qui's been arrested by the Primes, not only for ordering J'koshuk to torture you, but for using you to try and kill Prince Zsurtul. He'll be dealt with, believe me. I'm going to demand I be allowed to scan his mind later today. I want to know why you were implanted as much as you do."

Thrusting Kaid aside, he flung the covers back, attempting to get up. "I want to see him myself. Dammit, Kaid!" he snarled angrily, fending off his sword-brother's efforts to prevent him from rising, "Let me go! If not him, then Doctor Zayshul! I need answers!" In the distance, he could hear the faint sound of an alarm.

"I can't allow you see any of the Primes while you're in this state, Kusac."

The door slid open, a blue-coated physician rushing over to them as Kaid used his full strength to force him back against the pillows.

"I told you he was to be kept calm!" snapped the physician.

His rage spiraled out of control, leaving his body racked with pain. As the physician leaned over him, he caught sight of the hypodermic. Though every movement, every touch was agony, he twisted to one side, trying to avoid the medic's hand while redoubling his efforts to escape from Kaid's grasp.

"No sedatives! La'quo, they gave me la'quo, Kaid!" Then he felt the chill of the hypo nozzle touching his skin. "No!" He was frantic now, but as he felt the sting of the pressurized drug being injected, he knew it was too late. Even as he flinched, it began to take effect. He collapsed back on the bed, his limbs robbed of their strength as the drug swept quickly through him. As it did, the pain began to recede.

"Don't want to sleep," he said with difficulty, fighting to keep his eyes open as Kaid released him. "Dreams—always bad dreams."

"There won't be any, Kusac," said Kaid, reaching out to run gentle fingers across his jawline. "The physician knows about the la'quo. This sedative won't activate any still in your system. I understand your anger at what Chy'qui's cost you, but you have to let it go. Nothing can undo what you've been through, but he will be punished for it, you have my word. Rest easy now, we'll stay with you."

As he lost his battle to stay conscious, Kaid's voice began to fade.

Stronghold, Zhal-S'Asha, 18th day (October)

Again he shuddered, pulling his thoughts with difficulty away from the past. That had been the beginning of his realization that even though he'd killed J'koshuk, in death the Valtegan priest still continued to torment him. As he turned away from the darkness outside the window, the artificial brightness of the lounge momentarily dazzled him. The room seemed to lurch, and as he staggered toward the table in the center, he was once more back on the *Kz'adul*, reliving his first meeting with J'koshuk . . .

the *Kz'adul*, Zhal-Zhalwae, 4th day (May)

The smell of unfamiliar antiseptics was strong in the air. Had they reached their rendezvous so soon? It seemed like only the night before he'd gone to sleep. Automatically, he reached for Carrie with his mind.

Pain exploded at the base of his skull, coursing down his spine then out to his limbs and tail. As spasms racked his body, he yowled in fear and shock. He was falling but, back arched and limbs rigid, he was unable to move to save himself. He slammed into the floor, the impact knocking any remaining air from his lungs. Wave upon wave of fiery agony surged through his body as he lay there barely able to gasp for breath. It seemed to last forever, then as suddenly as it had begun, it stopped and his body went limp. But the pain remained.

Whimpering softly, he attempted to move his trembling limbs, tried to curl himself into a ball. Every movement, no matter how small, hurt; where his body touched the floor, where his limbs touched each other, it felt as if he were still being consumed by the fire that had surged through him.

He heard footsteps approaching and slowly tilted his head to-

ward them. He knew fear as a scent he'd never thought to smell
again filled his nostrils. Blurred images were all he could see because of the tears in his eyes; he blinked in an effort to clear
them. The shapes resolved themselves into the hem of a red robe
above a pair of booted feet.

"Your name is Kusac, and you're my prisoner," the Valtegan said, his Sholan overlaid by a faint lisping hiss as his
tongue tried to form the alien sounds. "You have just had your
first lesson in the futility of using your mind powers. Unless
you enjoyed the experience, I suggest you don't attempt it
again. If you do, the collar you wear round your neck will respond by delivering the pain you just experienced. It also sends
a signal to my wrist unit. I will then administer more pain.
I control the amount, the severity, and its duration. In short, I
control you."

He tried to speak but his throat was so dry and sore that he
began to cough, sending fresh agony lancing through his body.
When the coughing ceased, he pushed himself up on his hands
until his head and chest were clear of the floor. Reptilian yellow
eyes regarded him dispassionately from a pale green face. On his
wrist, the Valtegan wore what Kusac recognized as a control
bracelet.

"What do you want from me?" he whispered. "Who are you?"

"I am Inquisitor Priest J'koshuk, lately in the service of General M'ezozakk, Planetary Governor to His Imperial Highness,
Emperor M'iok'kul, *may His name be revered for all time.* Now
I serve the Primes." He indicated the guard standing several feet
behind him.

He looked, and the sight made the knot of fear in the pit of
his stomach swell. The guard stood like a statue, a pistol trained
directly at him. Over the suit of black, nonreflective battle armor
was a white tabardlike garment. He looked higher, seeing the almost rippling surface of the faceplate. Nausea welled up inside
him and he looked away quickly. Where had the Valtegans gotten these allies from?

"Why am I a prisoner? Where are my companions?"

"I have told you all you need to know. Stand up," J'koshuk
ordered.

The pain was beginning to subside at last, and as he slowly
pushed himself upright on his still-shaking limbs, he realized just
who the priest was. M'ezozakk had been the Governor of Keiss,

the Human colony world where Carrie had lived before the Sholans had liberated it from the Valtegans. J'koshuk had been the one responsible for torturing Carrie's twin sister to death in an effort to gain information about the Human resistance movement there. How the hell had they gotten hold of the *Profit* and all aboard her? And what of Carrie, and Kaid—and T'Chebbi? Were they still alive? Carrie must be, despite her injuries, because otherwise—he'd be dead too. Yet he couldn't sense her at all.

Pain gripped him again, felling him to the floor. His nerves already inflamed by the previous punishment, this time it felt a thousand times worse. He lay there, keening his agony, unable to stop because somehow, it helped lessen the pain. Finally it ceased.

"You took too long," said J'koshuk. "Now get up."

Every muscle in his body shrieked its objections as, still hypersensitized, he tried to move. Hands slick with sweat slipped on the tiled floor, unable to gain purchase. He clawed at the gaps between the tiles, finally managing to get a grip and lift his head and shoulders. J'koshuk was reaching for his wrist unit again.

"No! For pity's sake, no more," he gasped, pushing himself up onto his haunches. "I'll never stand if you do it again!"

"Pity?" said J'koshuk, thoughtfully. "An interesting concept. I have none," he said, his voice suddenly cold. He pressed the button, releasing it again almost instantly.

This time, when the brief jolt of energy from the collar surged through his nervous system, his body arched upward and he found himself staggering to his feet.

"See how quickly you learn?" the priest said, turning his back on him. "You'll follow me to your new quarters."

"Wait! Where am I? Tell me what it is you want!"

J'koshuk stopped, looking over his shoulder. "I won't tolerate curiosity in my captives," he said, brow creasing. "I will not be so lenient next time. You have been told all you need to know for now. As for what I want, you'll find out later, when you fully realize how dependent on me you are." With that, the priest gestured to the guard. "Take charge of him."

The guard stirred, then moments later another, wearing only the black armor, entered. Slinging his rifle over his shoulder, he strode toward Kusac.

His mind seemed to freeze as, swaying slightly, he waited for the guard. It was only when the gloved hand closed round his arm, pressing tightly into his flesh, that his mind began to function again. Powered armor. The Valtegans had had nothing like this on Keiss. What the hell was going on here?

He was afraid, mortally afraid, but as he was dragged staggering out of the medical area, Kaid's training came back to him, giving him something to focus on other than his fear. With difficulty, he pushed it to the back of his mind and concentrated on his surroundings. The corridors told him nothing—they could be anywhere—a space station, a ship, or even a building complex on some world. The air was odorless, scrubbed clean by recycling plants.

Then J'koshuk and the white-robed Prime stopped at the open door of a small room, waiting for them. As he was led inside, he saw it contained only a bed and basic sanitary facilities.

The sound of an electronic translator speaking Sholan startled him, and he twisted around in the guard's grasp to stare at J'koshuk and the Prime. As he did, the grip on his arm tightened viciously and he was jerked back.

"I will examine him before leaving you to your work," it said. "I want to check that the drug levels are adequate."

Drugs? What kind of drugs? He didn't feel drugged.

"As you wish," replied the priest.

Abruptly, the guard released him, turning him round before stepping back and unslinging his rifle. He took up a position in front of the still open door.

"Sit," said the Prime, unclipping a small unit from the belt that circled his tabard.

The fear came rushing back despite his efforts to remain calm. The smallness of the room was amplifying it, making him feel even more trapped and powerless.

"I'd prefer to stand," he said.

The next moment, he was staggering backward, his face burning from the force of J'koshuk's slap. Colliding with the side of the bed, he found himself abruptly sitting down.

"When you are given an order, you will obey it instantly," said the priest, his skin darkening with anger as he displayed a mouth full of needle-sharp teeth. "You will not speak unless given leave to do so. Do you understand?"

Too shocked by pain and the speed with which the Valtegan had moved to answer, he merely nodded.

J'koshuk's hand lashed out again, to be caught in midair by the Prime. "Later," he said. "I wish to examine him now."

"He didn't answer me," said J'koshuk angrily, pulling his arm free.

"You did not give him leave to do so," the translator said. The Prime reached out to take hold of him by the jaw. "I wish to examine the implant on your neck. You will sit still while I do this."

Involuntarily, his hand went up to pull away the Prime's. As his fingers curled round the gloved wrist, the Prime moved his grip until the thumb and index finger pressed deep into the soft tissue under his jaw, forcing his head up.

"Do not presume to touch me. You are not indispensable. We can get what we want from one of the other members of your crew. You will release me and you will sit still while I examine you, otherwise the priest will use the pain collar again."

He let go, sitting there while the Prime put a small scanning device up to the left side of his neck. At least he'd gotten some information out of the alien. He now knew that they had everyone from the *Profit*. A wave of dizziness swept through him, blurring his vision and making him light-headed. By the time it had passed, the Prime had left and the door was closing, leaving him alone with the priest and guard.

The side of his neck began to itch and he put his hand up to investigate. He was shocked to find a hard, regular—*something*—attached to the flesh just under his left ear. As he probed it carefully with his fingertips, he began to feel sick. Immediately he stopped touching it, the nausea disappeared.

"That's the implant," said J'koshuk, his tone conversational. "The Primes control it, and their drugs control your mind. Already your ability to communicate mentally with other members of your crew is being destroyed. It won't prevent you from trying, but when you do, it will alert the collar. Every time you feel any emotion but fear, it will trigger the collar and my wrist unit. You know what happens then. Pain."

He tried to take in the enormity of what the Valtegan was saying, but his mind seemed to have shut down again and he could only stare blankly at his tormentor.

"You asked what I wanted from you. It's not what I want, but what the Primes want," J'koshuk said, moving closer. "Information about your people's involvement on the Human world of Keiss. And the female they found in a cryo unit like yours."

That roused him. They'd found Carrie. He prayed she was still in cryo because if she was, then it would be easier for him to face their inevitable deaths. "I'll tell you nothing," he said.

Another blow to his face sent him sprawling sideways across the bed.

"I didn't give you leave to speak. Make no mistake, you'll tell me everything I want to know. Eventually." J'koshuk hissed quietly. "Especially if you want news of your Human female."

As he pushed himself upright again, he realized what was wrong about this whole situation. J'koshuk had known his name. More, he knew about telepaths, and that Carrie was mentally linked to him. How had he found out? Surely none of the others would have told him?

"So she's a telepath too?" The Valtegan's voice was silky quiet.

He looked up sharply, realizing even as he cursed himself that he must have spoken aloud. What kind of drugs were they using on him? "She's nothing to me," he said, bracing himself for the pain he knew would come.

When it finally stopped, he lay there panting, waiting for the agony to subside.

"You lied to me," he heard the priest say coldly. "I know that she's your mate, that you're linked mentally. You hurt only yourself by lying."

"Then why ask me?" he gasped.

"Why did your people come to Keiss?"

If you're taken, don't try to play the hero, Kaid had said. *There's no one alive that can't be broken, Kusac. All it takes is time and the right levers. Tell them what you can, what will do us the least damage. That way you might survive long enough to escape. It's a game that you can only win by escaping or dying. Put a few lies in with the truth. Misinformation will help us, but be careful what you say because if you get it too wrong, they'll kill you. They'll know they can't trust your answers, and you'll no longer be of any use to them.*

They mustn't find out that Shola hadn't been destroyed, that was what mattered here, not him, not Carrie. Their species' survival was at stake.

"We were off-world when you destroyed our planets. We were looking for more of our kind when we found Keiss," he said. He'd barely stopped speaking before the pain started again.

He felt disembodied, unable to concentrate on what the priest was saying as his hearing and consciousness kept fading in and out. Gradually he became aware of a throbbing in his face as he felt it being repeatedly slapped in an effort to bring him round. Eventually he found the strength to lift an arm to try and fend off the blows.

"We came to find missing crew," he repeated slowly. "I told you, we didn't know about the Humans."

"How is it that you're able to connect mentally and even breed with them?"

That was easy. "Vartra did it. He made us compatible."

"Vartra? Who is this Vartra?"

"Our God. He did it. A blessing for some, a curse for others, to be Linked to a Human," he mumbled.

"Was he your ruler? Did he die when we destroyed your worlds?"

He began to laugh as he squinted up at the priest. It hurt, but he couldn't help it. Here he was, telling the literal truth, and no one in their right mind could possibly believe him.

"He's dead all right, died over a thousand years ago!"

Pain exploded through his body again, but this time, mercifully, he passed out.

Stronghold, Zhal-S'Asha, 18th day (October)

He came to with a start, looking wildly around the room, needing to touch the table, then the chair on which he sat, before he could believe he was really in the Senior lounge at Stronghold rather than on the *Kz'adul*. A shiver ran through him as he tried to dispel the memories of the pain and humiliation he'd suffered at the hands of J'koshuk.

In a way, he was grateful to the priest for stripping away the last of his illusions. Up until then, he'd led the privileged and protected life of a telepath, been sheltered from the harsher realities. He now knew the only constant in life was pain, everything else was transitory, a break or brief diversion, like his Link with Carrie. While they'd been Leskas, he'd been freed from the debilitating pain ordinary telepaths experienced if they tried to fight—their own and that of those they hurt. That respite had gone, replaced by something worse—the inability to even try to use what remained of his psi abilities without experiencing the agony brought on by the filaments left embedded in his brain by the Primes' implant.

Sitting up, he scrubbed at his face then ran his hands over his ears and through his hair, pulling it back from his face. Episodes like this one had been lessening recently to the point where he'd thought they were finally over: he should have known better. He looked at his wrist comm; barely an hour had passed. It had seemed longer. Dawn was still four hours away.

Resting his arms on the table, he lowered his head to rest on them and closed his eyes. He needed some sleep before he left for the spaceport, but he couldn't sleep, not while Carrie was in labor bearing the cub she and Kaid shared—the cub whose very conception had saved the lives of all three of them.

The mixture of drugs and the neural disruptor in the collar he'd worn on the *Kz'adul* had isolated him completely from his Leska Link with her. She'd not been so lucky. Awakened long before him, the time bomb that was their compulsion to mate every fifth day had been ticking away slowly from the moment they'd brought her out of cryo to operate on the near-fatal wound she'd received on Jalna. Only the fact they'd kept putting her back in a reduced stasis field had enabled her to survive.

As soon as they'd awakened him from cryo, because of their separation, their deaths would have been inevitable had it not been for the fact they were a Triad. Unable to reach him mentally, Carrie's mind had subconsciously found Kaid's and begun to bond with him. He'd been there when time had finally run out. Pairing with him wouldn't have been enough; what had swung the balance was her fertility because of the Primes' removal of her contraceptive implant. He owed his life to this cub, he had to wait till she was born, not least because as her Triad-father, he felt responsible for her.

He remembered when Carrie had given birth to their daughter, Kashini. She'd been so afraid, and in such pain. He remembered it well because he'd shared it through their Leska Link. He should be there now, sharing her pain with Kaid—he needed to be there! Anger and resentment flared as he thought of the message that had arrived at Haven a week ago. Damn them! All he'd wanted from life was to raise cubs with her and run his estate, instead of which, there she was with Kaid doing just that while he was the one heading off alone on a mission that was probably nothing more than an elaborate trap!

The torc around his neck began to vibrate gently, warning him. He clasped his hand to it, forcing himself to take slower breaths and turn his thoughts inward to the litanies, trying not to think of Kaid, the sword-brother who had taught them to him a lifetime ago. Slowly, very slowly, he became calmer and the vibration ceased.

Dawn was lighting the sky when he heard the door open again.

"Word's just come from Noni. The cub's been safely delivered and Carrie's fine. It's a daughter," said Rhyaz.

Tiredly, Kusac lifted his head to look at the Brotherhood Warrior Master. His night's vigil, haunted as it had been by memories, had exhausted him. "I know. Are the others ready?"

"They're at the spaceport, yes, but we still haven't got access to the *Couana* yet."

"Then get Captain Kisha onto it," he said, pushing his seat back from the table and getting to his feet. "If you can't do it, I'm sure he can find an excuse to get Shaayiyisis out of the *Couana* long enough for your people to get my crew and supplies on board. Someone's going to have to so we can take it. Just make sure it's fully fueled. Three-day jumps drain the reservoirs."

"We've a day's margin yet, Kusac. There is no need to accelerate the mission like this."

"I'm leaving now," he said, ignoring the censure in Rhyaz's tone as he brushed past him into the corridor. He stopped, turning round to look at the Brotherhood Warrior Master. "Do you really want to run the risk of Carrie's mind automatically Linking to mine again now her cub's born? You're the one who insisted I go on this mission in the first place!" He put all the anger and sarcasm he could into his tone.

"That's a million to one chance, Kusac," Rhyaz said uncomfortably, refusing to meet his gaze. "If you're going, you'd better leave now. I'll speak to Captain Kishasayzar. The disruptor will only give you a two hour window in which to launch the *Couana* without being tracked and followed by the Forces."

"I thought as much," he said, reaching out to place his hand on the Guild Master's chest. Slowly he extended his claws and grasped hold of Rhyaz' tunic. "You owe me for this, Rhyaz, and I'll be back to collect, no matter what happens. Remember that."

Shola, Zhal-Zhalwae, 22nd day (May)

"You didn't have me brought all the way out to Stronghold for a social chat, Lijou. I think it's time you told me what this is about," said Konis as he settled himself in the easy chair. "It can't be bad news or you'd have given it to me at home."

Lijou handed him a mug of c'shar before sitting down opposite him and placing his own mug on the small table beside them.

"We've had news from the *Profit* about your son."

Konis sat up, hands clutching the chair arms, ears flaring wide to catch every nuance. "Get on with it, then!"

"I couldn't tell you sooner because, until last night, we only knew that Carrie and Kaid were safe," he began, but his friend interrupted him.

"Not Kusac? What happened to him? Is he all right? Where was he?" His questions came tumbling out in a rush.

"Konis, please hear me out," said Lijou reaching out to touch him briefly. "When I've finished, you can ask all the questions you want, even speak to Carrie yourself."

"Dammit, Lijou! Get to the point! How is my son?"

"He's safe. We got him back last night during an exchange of hostages."

"Hostages? They were captured then?" His friend's voice was hushed now, and laced with fear.

"The *Profit* flew into a Valtegan trap just before it was due to go into jump. Then, barely a day later, both ships were taken by another craft that had been watching the Valtegans." He stopped, wondering what to say next. "To cut it short, Konis, it turned out this larger ship belonged to another faction of Valtegans, the Primes, from the world that spawned them originally. They were on their way here seeking a treaty with us against the Valtegans that destroyed our two colonies and took Keiss from the Humans."

"There are two worlds of Valtegans?" Konis asked faintly.

"More, four in all, but we can discount the fourth. Since their Cataclysm, it's stayed at a technological level similar to that of the Jalnians. The Valtegans we encountered at Keiss are known as the M'zullians, and they're at war with those from J'kirtikk, their third world. The ones that took the *Profit* and the Valtegan ship are very different from them. For a start, they don't have a psychotic hatred of us."

Konis blinked in confusion, obviously making a visible effort to absorb what Lijou was saying. "It was the Primes who took them and held them prisoner?"

Even as Lijou flicked his ears in an affirmative, he realized he was not making a good job of this explanation. "Yes and no. As far as the Commander of the *Kz'adul* was concerned, the crew and passengers of the *Profit* were guests kept confined to their quarters. It was the M'zullian Valtegans who were the prisoners."

"Then how did my son come to be a hostage?"

"It seems one member of the Prime crew, a Dr. Chy'qui, the medical officer in charge of some of our people, had other plans. An adviser to their Emperor, he was against this hoped-for treaty with us. He used his privileged position on the crew to imprison and antagonize our people to the point where he hoped the treaty would be impossible."

"Antagonize? How? And how did this result in Kusac being a hostage?"

"It's complicated, Konis. Carrie was brought out of cryo and healed of her injuries but Kusac was awakened much later and kept separate from everyone."

Konis closed his eyes. "Their Leska Link! How did they survive?"

"The only way they could, just like Mara and Josh did when Zhyaf died. Because of their Triad, Kaid was able to form a Leska Link with Carrie."

"And my son? What about him? You said he was alive. Zhyaf had to die for Mara and Josh to form their Link." His ears were folding back against his skull and his fear was an almost palpable presence in the room.

"Kusac is alive, Konis, I assure you of that. He was kept separate from them because, according to this Physician Chy'qui, he had a series of life-threatening seizures as they revived him. He took the drastic step of implanting Kusac with a TeLaxaudin device in the hope that it would stabilize him. Apparently it did."

Konis sat there as if carved in ice while everything around him seemed to slow down. Little things suddenly became vital to him, like the sound of birds cooing, the chirping of their chicks, and the ray of sunlight that suddenly fell on Lijou's face, highlighting the streaks of white in the hair and pelt framing his face.

"Implanted where?" he asked finally in a hushed voice.

Lijou realized Konis had already guessed the answer. "In his brain. They saved his life, Konis," he said quickly, leaning forward. "But it seems as if he's lost his Talent."

"You mean he can't . . ." Konis stopped, unable to say the words.

"It's as if he's mind-dead," said Lijou quietly. "I'm sorry, Konis. I wish the news hadn't been so dark, but at least we have him back alive."

"Without his Leska and his Talent, he might as well be dead," said Konis numbly, looking away from his friend. "What kind of life is that for him, Lijou?"

"It may not be permanent. During the exchange there was an incident, an attempt on the life of our hostage, Prince Zsurtul. One of the M'zullians was controlling Kusac through the implant to make him aggressive. Kusac—neutralized—him by drawing on the energy of our other telepaths and triggering that gestalt he and Carrie have."

Konis looked up at Lijou. "Neutralized? You mean killed, don't you? Perhaps he suffered a backlash, or maybe fear of what he did is blocking his Talent."

Lijou could hear the hope in his friend's voice. "This is my thought, and Carrie's and Kaid's. With the help of the TeLaxaudin physician, the implant has been removed and Kusac is no longer being controlled by it, but it has left components in his brain. Components that even the TeLaxaudin physician can't remove, though he's working on it for us. We're doing everything we can for him, Konis, but we don't have any Telepath medics at Haven."

"Then there's still hope," said Konis, his ears beginning to rise again. "We have the best Guild Physicians on Shola available at Valsgarth, Lijou. If anything can be done, they're the ones to do it."

"They are. We've had some good news, though—the TeLaxaudin home world has contacted us. They'll meet us at Jalna in a few days' time to sit at the negotiating table. That means a treaty with them, and an exchange of ambassadors. Which also means an official channel through which to ask them to continue their research into helping Kusac regain his Talent."

Konis leaned forward to take hold of his mug, taking a sip from his drink. "They had a three-way Link, Lijou. One far stronger than Mara and Josh had with Zhyaf."

"I know, Konis. That Link's what saved them."

"There's always a chance that when his Talent returns, his Link with Carrie will reestablish itself."

"There is," said Lijou, hoping his friend was right. To have had a love so closely bound to oneself that you knew her thoughts from moment to moment, then to lose that Link . . . He hoped they'd be able to keep Kusac sane for long enough to help him; he hoped that the same thought didn't occur to Konis or Rhyasha.

"I want to speak to him, Lijou," said Konis decisively, putting his mug back on the table.

"That isn't advisable, Konis," he said. "Talk to Carrie or Kaid. They can tell you more than Kusac at this time."

Konis frowned. "Why not Kusac? What haven't you told me, Lijou? Surely there can't be worse to come?"

"He was only operated on last night, Konis. He's still under sedation in the IC unit to make sure he has no more seizures, that's all."

"That's not the whole truth, Lijou. I can tell you're keeping something back. And you said these Primes were after a treaty with us. As head of Alien Relations, why wasn't I informed?"

"Because we had no word on Kusac," said Lijou quietly. "I couldn't tell you that Kaid had led a successful escape, unaware that Kusac was still alive and on the *Kz'adul.* By the time they contacted us, they'd found out about him from their hostage. The blame is mine for keeping that information from you, but I couldn't see you live in hope your son was still alive only to have it dashed if he wasn't."

"Just how long have you known that Kusac was alive?"

"Five days, but we didn't know what state he was in."

"State? I want the rest of the truth now, Lijou," said Konis, his voice deepening in anger. "Kusac's not mentally impaired in any other way is he? You said he'd been kept separately. What else was done to him? I had your word you'd tell us the moment there was news of him—I trusted you to do that, now I find you waited five days!"

"His mind is sound, Konis. I told you as soon as *we* knew the state of his health," said Lijou. "Till then, we only had a vision of Brynne's, or the word of the Valtegan Prince Zsurtul to depend on. Frankly, as I've already said, I didn't want to tell you he was alive on the strength of either of those. You'd have done the same to me had our positions been reversed, Konis, you know you would. I was only trying to spare you pain if the worst had happened, which, thank Vartra, it didn't."

He'd known his well-intentioned deception would come out into the light of day, and at the time had prayed that his friend would understand. He wasn't yet a father, but he would be in a very few weeks. He knew what his delay had cost Konis, but he also knew what he had spared him.

"As to what else happened to him, he hasn't been debriefed yet, we don't know any details. Look into my mind and see if you wish, Konis. I only meant it for the best," he said quietly. He didn't want to lose this friendship. People like himself, a Guild Master of both the Brotherhood and the Priesthood of Vartra, had few friends. Every one he had was precious.

Konis sighed, his anger evaporating. "I don't need to, Lijou. I know you intended the best. Vartra forbid it, but if there ever *is* a next time, tell me immediately! What about Carrie and the others? Haven't you debriefed them?"

"Yes, and I have their report with me, along with the proposed treaty between us and the Primes. I need you to take over the negotiations, Konis. I'm sorry to have to ask you at a time like this, but you don't need me to tell you what's at stake right now. You're our best negotiator."

"Who's been handling it up till now?"

"We have, through Kaid. An interim nonaggression pact has been agreed upon. We need you to go over the treaty proposals before we can send them to Kaid for signing. The Primes want our help against the other two Valtegan worlds. They lost their Warrior caste during their equivalent of our Cataclysm—their Fall. The Valtegans have three genetic strains, or castes: the Intellectuals, the Warriors, and the Workers. The Primes have no Warriors at all, only volunteers who are implanted with a device similar to that used on Kusac to boost their aggression levels. Now that Jalna has been discovered by the M'zullians, they fear that it won't be long till their world is found. Then they will need all the help they can get to protect themselves."

With an obvious effort of will, Konis asked, "What of their own allies? Presumably they must have some."

"The TeLaxaudin are slender, fragile beings, totally unsuited to any kind of conflict. What use they are to the Primes, we don't yet know. As far as we're aware, the Primes have no other allies. Let's face it, in the days of their empire, they were busy enslaving other races: they must have made a lot of enemies. Now they use large craft like the *Kz'adul* to intimidate anyone they meet. So far, it's worked, mainly because they keep themselves to themselves."

"What's their involvement with Jalna? And what do they want from us? Military aid?"

He flicked his ears in agreement. "Yes, in return they'll give us technology which would enable us to break the Chemerians' stranglehold over all the Alliance. I wouldn't like to guess how much more advanced the Primes are than even the Chemerians. They didn't lose their technology during their Fall the way we did because it was mainly based in their walled Imperial city and survived their own global civil war virtually untouched. As for Jalna, it's beginning to look like the Primes were heavily involved in setting it up as a trading port for the Free Traders, probably to ensure those species have no need to venture further into their space."

"Give me the debriefing report now," said Konis gruffly. "Once

I've read it, I'll talk to Carrie, then call Rhyasha and tell her about Kusac."

Lijou picked up the comp reader from the table and handed it to him, aware of how close to breaking down his friend was. Only the importance of the task he'd been given was holding him together right now. "Would you like me to leave you on your own for a while?" he asked quietly.

"Yes, thank you, I would," said Konis, blinking rapidly as he looked up at him. "I'm sure you appreciate that this has all been rather a lot to take in. When do you intend to go public with this? You realize you're going to need a very strong campaign to sell the idea of friendship with these Valtegan Primes to our people in view of the destruction of our colony worlds by the other Valtegans."

"We'll start the campaign as soon as we've gotten the treaty sewn up as tight as the proverbial demon fish's arse," said Lijou with a slight attempt at levity. "If we call them Primes and paint them as also being victims of the M'zullian Valtegans, it will help considerably." He got to his feet. "Send to me when you're ready to contact Haven and I'll arrange it. Can I get you anything? Some food, perhaps? I know you came straight from the Palace and missed second meal."

"No. I couldn't eat right now, Lijou."

Lijou left the room, closing the door quietly behind him. Outside, Tamghi, an En'Shalla Telepath from Kusac's clan was waiting for him.

"I sensed you were finished," the young male said, falling into step beside him. "Master Rhyaz wanted to know how it went."

"I'm on my way to join him so I'll tell him myself," said Lijou tiredly. "I appreciate your personal concern in this matter since your Clanspeople are involved. I succeeded in getting him to handle the Prime treaty for us. He'll send to me when he's ready to call them on Haven."

"The last few months have been a dark time for him and his family," said Tamghi. "At least events ended happily for his daughter, Liegena Kitra. I pray it works out as well for our Clan Leaders."

"So do I," said Lijou with feeling.

Haven, the same day

Carrie watched as the physician placed his hand against Kusac's throat, checking his pulse while watching the bio-monitor readings on the screen above his bed.

"I told you I wanted him kept calm," said Vryalma angrily, glancing at her and Kaid. "Overstimulation now could cause another seizure."

"If he's going to have one, better he has it now," said Kaid. "He needed to be told what we know about his condition. Leaving it until later wouldn't have changed anything."

"He was a telepath. They're protected, aren't used to handling the harsher realities of life."

"He's a Brother and a Warrior now," said Carrie before Kaid could. "He wanted to know."

"That's debatable," said Vryalma, moving away from the bed, obviously satisfied with the readings. "I have my doubts as to how much of his early training you've actually affected. Deep down we remain what we were when we left childhood, and he was a telepath." He waved them toward the door. "You might as well leave. He'll sleep for the next five or six hours."

"I'm not leaving him alone," said Carrie.

"I'll stay," said T'Chebbi from the doorway. "Am here to relieve you for first meal anyway."

"This is the intensive care unit, not a gathering place," growled the physician. "There's no need for anyone to remain with him, and certainly no justification for more than one of you even when he's awake."

"We're a Triad," said Kaid. "When he's awake and I'm free, we'll both be here."

"That's enough, Physician Vryalma," said a new voice. "You've been briefed about their Triad, you know it's imperative they be together whenever possible."

Carrie went to greet L'Seuli as, muttering under his breath, the physician left.

"I'm still not used to your new rank," she said, touching the gold insignia on the Brother's uniform jacket.

"I'd hoped to find Kusac awake," said Commander L'Seuli. "What happened? Not a seizure, I hope."

"No. Kaid told him the full implications of the implant," sighed Carrie. "He got angry, wanted to leave the sick bay and see

Chy'qui. Then he—" she nodded in the direction of the door Vryalma had gone out— "came in and sedated him."

"To be fair, it was needed," said Kaid. "Kusac's not himself, Carrie. He told me the implant had robbed him of every emotion but fear. Now all the others are rushing in on him as he realizes what's actually been done to him. It's not surprising he should be angry and want to see Chy'qui for himself."

"No one will be seeing Chy'qui, I'm afraid," said L'Seuli. "When I contacted Commander Q'ozoi about your request to have Chy'qui scanned, he told me that when they reached the *Kz'adul* last night, the counselor had been found dead in his cabin on the shuttle. He committed suicide, apparently."

"Very convenient," said Kaid dryly. "Now we'll never know exactly what he was up to. Why the delay in telling us?"

"Autopsy. They found poison in his stomach and bloodstream, and a capsule on the floor by his body. Commander Q'ozoi is bringing a copy of their findings for us."

Kaid grunted, nodding at T'Chebbi as they reached the door. "You've eaten?" he asked her.

She flicked her ears in an affirmative. "Take your time. I be fine here. Both of you look like you got little sleep last night. You need a break. Take it now while he's drugged. Maybe not get much chance later. Besides, you got treaty talks soon."

As they walked down the brightly lit corridor to the mess hall, L'Seuli handed Kaid a sealed document. "Father Lijou contacted Konis Aldatan to give him the news of your rescue and update him on the state of Kusac's health. He's agreed to work on the treaty with us. His amended copy of your proposals should be with us shortly. To give you an idea of his recommendations, here's a draft copy of what he's compiled."

"That's good news," said Kaid. "The nonaggression pact and basic trading agreements I put together are pretty standard, but the military issues need to be formalized by Master Konis and the Sholan High Command. I can only advise. Has Q'ozoi questioned Chy'qui's staff to see if they know anything about his experiments on Kusac?"

"Under way. Again, he's bringing a report of what they find out with him." L'Seuli stopped, taking Kaid briefly by the arm. "Tragic as what's happened to Kusac is, Kaid, it has put them at a severe disadvantage. They owe us because of it. Use it for all it's worth. For all you and Carrie suffered too."

"I already have," said Kaid, his voice emotionless. "It's what will secure us the Outposts we currently hold. We'll have our own private treaty with them before the day's done, L'Seuli."

"Well done."

"The Outposts were Valtegan," L'Seuli said to Commander Rhyaz, adjusting the comm angle so he was looking directly at his Guild Master. "Part of a defense network that surrounded their empire."

"Did Kaid discover the location of any more from them?" asked Master Rhyaz.

"No. They brushed his inquiries aside, saying they weren't concerned with issues dealing with their old empire. They did admit to recognizing the *Va'Khoi*, though. They aren't interested in reclaiming either the four outposts or the ship and agreed to sign a private agreement with us acknowledging them as ours. Kaid also managed to get them to accept that the outposts— Haven, Anchorage, Safehold, and Refuge—mark a buffer zone between Alliance and Free Trader space and themselves—a neutral area that the Brotherhood can guard and police against the raiders that occasionally attack Trader craft. More importantly, now that we know the locations of the two warring Valtegan worlds that attacked our colonies, and the Prime home world, we can monitor their every activity."

"At last we know where to find our enemy," said Rhyaz with satisfaction. "How did Kaid manage to get so many concessions for us?"

"By repeatedly reminding them his Triad had all suffered at the hands of Chy'qui, and that Kusac might still face the rest of his life mentally crippled."

Rhyaz nodded. "At least some good has come from his suffering. Have you spoken to him yet?"

"I went up to sick bay this morning but he'd been sedated. He won't wake till nearer third meal." L'Seuli's wrist comm buzzed briefly. "I have to go now, Master Rhyaz," he said. "We'll have finished discussing all the points in the treaty by second meal and be ready to sign it when we reconvene for our final session afterward."

Jeran and Manesh looked up as Sheeowl and Mrowbay approached their table in the mess. "Captain wants to see you on the *Profit*, Giyesh," said Sheeowl, putting her mug of c'shar down before grabbing a seat from the adjacent table.

"I thought they were still using the landing bay for the Treaty talks," said Giyesh, eyeing Mrowbay's plate of assorted cakes and pastries. "You'll get too fat to sit in your seat on the bridge if you eat that lot."

"I'm just making up for the weight I lost on the Prime ship," said Mrowbay, a pained expression on his face as he picked up a pastry. "It's months since I had any nice nibbles."

"Talks have moved into a room at the back of the bay," said Sheeowl, taking a swig of her drink. "Captain's overseeing a team of Sholan mechanics checking the Prime repair to our hull."

Giyesh got to her feet. "I'd better be off. See you later," she said to Jeran.

Jeran waited for her to move out of earshot before speaking. "What is it you want to say to me that Giyesh can't hear?" he asked the two black-pelted U'Churians.

"You Sholans," said Manesh, shaking her head. "It's impossible to keep anything from you."

"It's about Giyesh," said Sheeowl. "She says you're coming with us when we leave. That true?"

"Yes. I've got nothing, not even a home to go back to. The Valtegans destroyed everything."

"Is that what Giyesh wants, or just you?"

"Of course it's what she wants." He frowned, surprised at her question. "You think I'd want to stay if she didn't . . ."

"How serious are you about her?" interrupted the engineer. "I don't have the time to be polite. In a few minutes, she'll find out the captain didn't send for her."

Jeran fought to keep his ears from folding sideways in anger. "I'm serious enough, but what business is it of . . ."

"Because if you aren't serious, then don't come with us. If she goes back alone, no one needs to know about you," said Sheeowl.

"Why's it so important that no one knows about me?" he

demanded angrily. "I know she should have stayed on Home and taken her first mate rather than come on this mission, but . . ."

"She took you as a lover," said Mrowbay, licking his fingers. "That's the problem. Because of you, none of the males on Home will have her as a mate."

"That's ridiculous!" he exclaimed. "She told me you take lovers between mates!"

"Between," agreed Sheeowl, "but not before the first mating."

"I know that, but what difference does it make? I'm not even one of your people!" He stopped, eyes narrowing. "Or is that the problem?"

"That makes it worse," agreed Mrowbay, picking up another pastry.

"She'll be an outcast, Jeran," said Sheeowl. "Believe me, none of the males will take her as a mate. Ever."

Jeran looked from one to the other of them. Were they lying, saying this in an effort to persuade him to stay with his own people? "She said nothing to me about this, and she was the one who suggested I stay on the *Profit* with her."

"Is it worth the rest of her life?" asked Sheeowl.

"That's unfair, Sheeowl," said Mrowbay, glancing over at her. "You can't expect him to be responsible for her for that long. His people don't choose a partner for life any more than ours do."

"Look, I don't know what all this is about," said Jeran, beginning to get angry. "But if you think you're going to persuade me to leave her . . ."

"Not leave her," said Mrowbay. "She can't take you as a mate, but you can take her. Humans and Sholans do it, why not a U'Churian and a Sholan?"

"You *want* me to take her as a mate?" he asked incredulously. This was the exact opposite of what he'd expected.

"If she goes back with a mate, it would be seen differently," said Sheeowl. "Then she hasn't taken a lover, only chosen her first mate."

Puzzled, he again looked from one to the other. "But I'm still an alien."

Mrowbay sighed. "We're trying to tell you that alien isn't as big a problem as her not having a mate. It's a matter of her honor. If you come back to Home with us and you aren't her mate, then obviously you care nothing for her honor. As for being alien," he shrugged. "You're so like us, most people won't see you as alien. Except for the color of your pelt, you could pass as one of us."

"Giyesh should have told me," he muttered.

"She wouldn't," said Sheeowl. "She's young, but she's a good taiban. She wouldn't want to put pressure on you to do anything you didn't want to do. It's up to us as her family to look out for her."

"Your people have a contract for mixed matings," said Mrowbay. "Must have. Look how many have Human mates."

"Bondings, and not all get bonded," murmured Jeran, not sure this was what either he or Giyesh wanted.

"Kaid is. Byrnne too."

"Rezac and Jo aren't," he countered. "Bondings are a legal and social contract for those wishing to share their cubs, nothing more."

Sheeowl snorted derisively. "Rezac and Jo would bond instantly if given the chance!"

"If they did, it would only be because they're expecting a cub. There isn't anyone here who can conduct bondings anyway."

"Any of the Brothers currently attached to the religious side of your Brotherhood can. I asked."

Jeran began to growl as he got to his feet. He'd had enough of them sticking their noses into his business.

Abruptly Sheeowl rose too. "I'll see you later," she said as Mrowbay reached out to catch Jeran's arm and prevent him leaving.

"Jeran, wait," the U'Churian medic said. "We'll talk now she's gone."

"I think you've already said more than enough," he snarled, really irritated now. He objected to being put on the spot like this by them.

"Not yet. You spent months imprisoned on Jalna, isolated from your own kind, yet you're ready to come with us because of Giyesh. What's so difficult about a entering into a recognized mating with her? That's a smaller step than the one you plan."

"Everyone I cared about has been destroyed, snuffed out like a candle, Mrowbay! I'm not ready to risk that kind of commitment to another person in case it happens again! She's a soldier, dammit! She takes risks for a living!"

"We all are. And so will you if you're with us," the medic said calmly. "This is only another small risk, of not much matter to you. Take one of your contracts for a year. That would be enough. A year of your life in return for her being able to look our family in the eyes when she returns Home with you beside her. She's prepared to stand by you without it. Can you do less for her now that you know what it will cost her?"

Angrily, he jerked his arm free. "I'll think about it," he snarled as he left.

"Don't take too long! We leave the day after tomorrow," Mrowbay called out after him.

"He has to be debriefed, Sister T'Chebbi," said Vriuzu, refusing to be intimidated by the tabby gray-pelted female blocking the door into the IC unit. As Stronghold's chief telepath, on Brotherhood business, he knew his orders outweighed anything she could say. "What happened to Kusac is unlikely to be of much use to us, but for his sake, he needs to talk about it, get it out of his system and realize his mission is over. You should know that."

"Kaid did that last night. Commander has his report," she replied, staring fixedly at him.

"That wasn't a formal debriefing. This is being done on Master Rhyaz' orders. Now stand aside and let us enter."

T'Chebbi gave a small hiss of displeasure as she caught sight of Doctor Zayshul behind Dzaou. "Why are Primes involved if only a debriefing? You got no jurisdiction over us, we're En'Shalla, in the hands of the Gods," she growled, holding her ground.

"The Brotherhood as a whole is En'Shalla." He was trying hard to remain patient, but Vartra knew, she wasn't making it easy for him.

"Only we are En'Shalla Clan. Kusac is our Clan Leader, you know that."

"The mission was for the Warrior side of the Brotherhood. It's in your contract, Rhyaz has jurisdiction. Stand aside,

T'Chebbi, or I will have to authorize the use of force." Behind him, he heard Dzaou powering up his gun.

T'Chebbi's lips pulled back, exposing her teeth in a snarl. "I move when Clan Leader Carrie arrives and tells me to," she said, raising her arm to use her wrist comm.

"Hold it right there," said Dzaou, stepping past the telepath priest, his pistol trained on her. "I'll take your comm." Imperiously, he held out his free hand. "There's no need for anyone else to be present."

As Vriuzu watched, the hair not captured by T'Chebbi's long plait began to bush out in anger. He was glad he'd brought the Brother with him.

Snarling her fury, T'Chebbi held out her arm for Dzaou to remove the comm.

"I'll take your gun while I'm at it," he said, pocketing the wrist unit and reaching for the firearm that hung in the holster at her waist. "Your Liegena is sleeping right now. Circumstances are hard enough for her without disturbing her rest." He gestured to everyone to precede him into the IC room.

"Not fooling anyone with this fake concern over my Liegena, Dzaou! You're too xenophobic to care for anyone but Sholans!"

"Bring him round," Vriuzu instructed Physician Vryalma, as he accompanied Doctor Zayshul over to Kusac's bed.

"Is this necessary?" asked Zayshul. "Surely this could wait until he awakens naturally."

"My orders are to wake him, Doctor," Vriuzu replied firmly.

Carrie woke abruptly, knowing instinctively something was wrong. Her conversation with her bond-father Konis some half an hour before had not been easy. That on top of her lost night's sleep, had thoroughly exhausted her. With Kusac still sleeping, she'd let T'Chebbi persuade her to take a much needed nap.

She lay there, wondering what had awakened her when suddenly a wave of excruciating pain exploded from her neck down her spine and out to her limbs. It was gone almost instantly, leaving her with the sure knowledge that Kusac was in trouble. Reaching out mentally, she sensed immediately what Vriuzu was trying to do.

Even as she threw back the covers and scrambled from the bed, Kaid sent a questing thought in her direction.

Vriuzu's attempting to scan Kusac against his will, she replied, grabbing her shoes and stuffing her feet into them. *I've dealt with him and am on my way there now. He's got Dzaou holding T'Chebbi at gunpoint.*

Rezac's on his way as backup. He's met Jeran and is taking him too. Get Kusac out of there—take him to our room. Guard him from everyone but us. I can't leave this meeting yet. His mental tone was one of suppressed fury.

She left the room at a run.

The anteroom was guarded by Ngio, one of Dzaou's people. She slowed down, approaching him as if to talk, lightly scanning his surface thoughts all the while. When the door behind her burst open to admit Rezac and Jeran, it gave her the opportunity she needed: he never saw the blow that laid him out.

Rezac gave a grunt of approval as he and Jeran drew their guns before flinging open the door into the IC room. Unexpectedly, it was Vriuzu, ears flat against his skull, who was being helped to his feet by the physician. The stench of fear—Sholan and Valtegan—filled the small room. Carrie remained near the door, guarding it as the two males moved in to secure the room and disarm Dzaou.

"You bastard!" Kusac snarled at Vriuzu, as, holding onto the chair beside his bed for support, he tried to stand. "You had to force me, despite what I told you about my mental blocks. Now you know what a Valtegan punishment collar does when you try to use your Talent!"

"I had my orders, Kusac," Vriuzu said, his voice unsteady. "We needed to know what you're hiding behind those blocks. Now we do. There's not a damned thing wrong with your Talent! How else could you have attacked me . . ."

"Shut up, Vriuzu," Carrie snapped, going over to help her mate. "*I* made sure you experienced the pain you caused Kusac. You had no right to do that! You violated his privacy—put his health, possibly his life, at risk! Even we don't dare touch his mind!"

"He's a security risk! We don't know what else Chy'qui programmed into him!" exclaimed Dzaou as he, along with Vriuzu and the physician, was herded to the far side of the room under the watchful eyes of Jeran and T'Chebbi.

"That's not true," interrupted Zayshul. "I've examined the tape. Chy'qui was only interested in killing Prince Zsurtul, nothing more. Kusac is no threat to you. Had my request on behalf of my TeLaxaudin colleague to give him a postoperative examination been granted, I could have told you that. There was no need to subject him to this treatment. I shall be telling Commander Q'ozoi about this!"

"Your objection is noted, Doctor," said Vriuzu, still holding onto the Sholan physician for support.

T'Chebbi meanwhile, treated Dzaou to an openmouthed Human grin as she held out her hand. "I'll have my comm back, too," she purred.

Angrily, he reached into his pocket and gave it to her.

Carrie turned to look at the Valtegan female, noticing that her usually light green skin had darkened considerably. "What are you doing here anyway? I thought you were involved in the Treaty talks down on the flight deck."

"Our respective Commanders decided I should be at the debriefing so I could make a full report on what Kusac said." She hesitated. "And explain what I could of the events to him."

"And did you?"

Kusac's hand closed on Carrie's wrist. "There wasn't time. Vriuzu did the scan almost as soon as I woke."

"The bastard!"

"I want this debriefing, Carrie. I need to know what happened to all of us, not just me. But not with him . . ." he indicated Vriuzu with a flick of his ear. "Not with him or the others here."

"Let Vriuzu stay," said Rezac unexpectedly, keeping his eyes as well as his gun trained on the Brotherhood Telepath. "He has to or the debriefing won't be official. I'll see he doesn't step over the line again. I know a trick or two that will make sure he doesn't." He gave a gentle laugh that held no humor.

Kusac looked at her and she could tell by his expression that he was asking her mutely if they could trust him.

Her heart went out to him as she leaned down to whisper in his ear. "That's Rezac, remember, Kaid's father? Yes, we can trust him. He's like us now, En'Shalla, and part of a Triad with Jo from Keiss. Remember, Vartra said he was one of the first telepaths that he enhanced." She hesitated, then standing up said more loudly, "Kaid wants us to leave the debriefing and take you to our room so we can keep the likes of Vriuzu away."

"There can be no debriefing without me present and able to vouch for the truth," said Vriuzu.

"You're experienced enough to know the feel of the truth without actively scanning," said Carrie, glancing over at him. "And you can drop your link with Jiosha: she's no business being involved. Tell her not to bother sending reinforcements. It would hardly do for Kaid to disrupt the peace talks over this internal matter, would it?" She had the satisfaction of feeling his shock at her knowledge of the link.

"I want to know what just happened to me, why I felt the pain from the collar again," said Kusac, leaning heavily on Carrie as he started to sway. "It comes at other times. When I'm angry."

Zayshul began to move toward them but brought herself up short as Rezac swung round, gun aimed at her. Carrie snapped out a reminder that they were now allies and he dipped his ears in apology and lowered his gun.

"Sorry, Doctor," he mumbled. "Old habits." He turned back to Vriuzu.

"He needs my help," said Zayshul, still keeping a wary eye on Rezac as she came closer. "I think I know what happened, Kusac. The collar Chy'qui put on you wasn't a regular punishment collar. It was one modified to inhibit telepathy as well. He must have brought it with him from the City of Light. We haven't used them since the days before the Fall. I can only assume he must have gotten it from a museum."

"I remember them," said Rezac with a rumble of anger. "The pain they caused whenever you used psi abilities was excruciating. Like fire coursing through your veins."

"Just so," Zayshul agreed. "When Vriuzu tried to push past those blocks, you probably responded automatically, using those areas of your brain where your abilities were. You expected pain, therefore you felt it."

Kusac groped for the bed behind him and sat down.

Carrie could see his nose creasing in pain as he put his hand carefully to the side of his neck. "You can conduct the debriefing if Doctor Zayshul says he's fit enough," she said to Vriuzu. "You," she said, turning to Vryalma. "Some physician you are!

What happened to your oath of healing, to putting the patient first? You were the one who wanted him kept calm to prevent any more seizures! Get out of my sight! And see the ventilation is turned up in here. The place stinks! T'Chebbi, go with him. Bring what drugs you think we might need."

"Aye, Liegena," she said.

"Take them outside," said Zayshul, indicating the group T'Chebbi was guarding. "I can't conduct a medical examination with them in here."

"You heard the doctor," Carrie said.

"You, too," added Zayshul.

Carrie's eyes narrowed as she looked up at the Valtegan female. "No," was all she said.

Kusac's hand tightened round hers. "Please."

She hesitated, torn between what he wanted and what her instincts told her was wise. "I'll wait by the door, but I won't leave," she said. "If I hadn't been persuaded to rest, this never would have happened."

"The debriefing was inevitable," said Kusac, his voice full of pain as he gently massaged his neck. "It wasn't your fault."

"Debriefing be damned! This is an official inquiry!" she said angrily. "They had no right to hold one with neither Kaid nor myself present!"

He squeezed her hand again as T'Chebbi returned, carrying a tray for Zayshul. "Go, I'll be fine. It'll only take a few minutes. Zayshul was the one who helped me on the *Kz'adul,* remember?"

"I'm not leaving the room," she repeated mutinously, returning the squeeze before reluctantly letting him go and following T'Chebbi to the door.

"I've been hoping to see you," Kusac said in an undertone as Zayshul placed herself between him and Carrie's line of sight.

"You mustn't touch the wound," she said, her voice equally quiet as she moved his hand aside and began unwrapping the bandage around his neck. "It will take longer to heal if you keep disturbing the dressings."

"No one must know that you came to me the night before the exchange of hostages."

She continued unwrapping the bandage before replying. "I told you, it wasn't me, Kusac," she said, laying it aside. Bending over him, she lifted the dressing off. "They did a neat job. Not much swelling. It should heal quickly."

As she reached for the fresh dressing, he caught hold of her wrist. "Why are you lying? I know it was you, I recognize your scent!" Her behavior confused him.

"Be quiet!" she hissed. "Let me go now, before your mate sees you!"

"Why are you lying to me?" he demanded. "I know why I'm hiding it from my people, but why won't you at least admit it to me?"

She froze, green eyes blinking slowly at him, the ridges surrounding them meeting in the middle of her forehead. "That's why the mental blocks, why you don't want to be scanned," she whispered. "That's what you're hiding from them!"

"What's wrong?" Carrie called out from the doorway.

Kusac dropped Zayshul's hand as if scalded, noticing as he did that her nonretractile claws were much shorter than J'koshuk's had been. "Nothing," he said loudly as Zayshul straightened up and reached for the dressing pack and a new bandage. "She says it will heal quickly, that's all."

Once more, Zayshul bent over him, placing the dressing over his wound. She began to wrap the fresh bandage over it. "You recognize my scent?"

Her voice was barely more than a whisper and he had to strain his ears forward to hear her. He made a small, exasperated noise, noticing her skin had paled. "How could I not? You came into my bed, Zayshul. I may have been drugged and tortured, but I'm not stupid, despite appearances at the time!"

"I know you're not," she said, sealing the end of the bandage to itself. She took a small flashlight from her pocket, reaching out to take hold of his chin with her other hand. Briefly, she shone it into each eye. "I've said nothing, nor will I," she whispered, letting him go. "I've no wish for anyone to know about the . . ." She faltered briefly. "Our night together." She placed her hand against his neck, feeling for his pulse. "You're in pain." She took hold of him by the chin again, turning his face into the light. "Quite a lot of pain."

He sighed with relief. "You admit it, then."

She reached for the hypodermic, checking the vials of drugs on the tray before choosing and loading one. "It isn't easy for me," she said, administering the shot. "That should take care of the pain. No matter what you've seen the M'zullians do, we Primes do not have a recent history of cross-species—liaisons. When did you last eat?" she asked in a more normal tone.

Kusac blinked in surprise, taken aback by the sudden change in topic. "I haven't been awake long enough for them to give me anything." As he said it, his stomach growled in hunger.

Zayshul looked across at Carrie. "He's weak because he needs food. The last meal he had was on the *Kz'adul,* a day ago. Have something light brought for him. Once he's eaten, the debriefing can go ahead."

Carrie pushed the door behind her open and spoke to T'Chebbi.

As Zayshul replaced the hypodermic on the treatment tray, she noticed her hand was shaking slightly with a mixture of anger and fear. How could that damned female N'koshoh have been stupid enough to scent-mark him? It wasn't as if she could have been under any illusions that he'd be kept on the *Kz'adul.* Everyone had known they were exchanging the hostages the next day. What insanity had prompted her to do that?

A surge of satisfaction that N'koshoh was dead, likely at the hands of Chy'qui, flooded through her, shocking her with its intensity. She wasn't normally a vindictive person, but for N'koshoh to go to Kusac in the night, callously drug him into compliance, then virtually rape him, just to further Chy'qui's mad scheme to breed hybrid Sholans, was morally unforgivable. Even worse was the fact that she'd been unable to find a trace of the samples she knew had been taken. Now that she knew for sure what had happened, she'd have to tell the Commander.

N'koshoh's marker could be turned off, but not here and now with all his family around them. Besides, she wasn't sure she could be that intimate with him, even if the opportunity had presented itself. At least the changes scent-marking instigated in males did lessen with time. He wasn't remaining among her people, he was returning to his own world, likely to live out the rest of his life there now that he'd lost the telepathic skill that had made him so invaluable to his own kind—unless the TeLaxaudin came up with some cure. The thought wasn't as comforting as it should have been as she remembered that he'd already been subtly altered by the implant. There was no way she could check what effect the pheromone transfer would have on him in the long term, unless they confessed the whole matter to the Sholans. And there was no way they could do that without risking the treaty.

Alerted by Jiszoe, Commander L'Seuli was prepared for Kaid's anger when the latter requested a ten minute recess.

"Just what the hell kind of stunt was that, sending Vriuzu in to force a mental examination on Kusac?" Kaid demanded in a low voice, grasping him by the arm and pulling him out of earshot. "He's got neural damage, dammit! The physician's still trying to assess how much, and we're being warned that getting him agitated could trigger a seizure! Now you go and do this!"

"It had to be done, Kaid," said L'Seuli calmly, avoiding eye contact as he extricated himself from the other's grasp. "And for exactly the reasons you were given."

"The order came from a higher level, didn't it? Who?"

"Master Rhyaz."

Kaid's voice was icy. "He hasn't the right. Our En'Shalla status supersedes any but Master Lijou's orders."

"I don't intend to argue protocol with you here, Kaid. Better Kusac had a seizure than he attacked the Primes or attempted to destroy Haven and plunged Shola into a war we cannot win. He's hiding something behind those shields of his, we know that much. Why else would he have them? And we need to know what."

"Don't give me that! His shields are natural, no different from those he had before the Primes took us!"

"Except now he has no Talent! He should be as transparent as a window! Dammit, Kaid," he said, exasperated. "He did what only a few rogue telepaths have *ever* done—killed, using only the power of his mind! We all felt it when he linked into the telepathic web Carrie built at the hostage exchange! There's something alien, not Sholan, or even Human, about him now! If he'd done this six months ago on Shola, he'd have been designated a rogue Talent and you'd likely have been sent to destroy him!"

He watched Kaid very obviously bite back his immediate reply. They both knew the alien quality was due to the filaments that had embedded themselves in Kusac's brain.

"When you've had your official inquiry into what happened to Kusac, leave him to us and the telepath medics back home," said Kaid coldly. "Mark me well, L'Seuli, I will not tolerate any further interference. It's because of him we have leverage over the Primes and it will not go down well back home if anything should happen to any of our Triad. And you can tell Rhyaz that!"

Stronghold, the same day

Lijou had been with Rhyaz when the call from Vriuzu came in, otherwise he'd not have heard anything till later—much later. He suppressed his anger as he listened to Vriuzu give his report to Rhyaz.

"I sensed an anger and a violence within him that should not exist in one brought up as a telepath," he was saying.

"Did he react with anger to your probe?" he asked Vriuzu abruptly.

Startled, Vriuzu turned his head, trying to see him on his comm screen. "No, Father, but I could feel it . . ."

Lijou let his disgust be heard. "You violated his mental privacy, I'm not surprised he was angry! That he concealed it at all is a credit to his training, considering what he's been through. How else did he react to your probe?"

"He seemed to be in great pain, Father. Then Liegena Carrie interfered."

"How?" he asked sharply. "What did she do?"

"She blocked me, making it impossible for me to reach Kusac's mind, then set up a feedback from him to me so I experienced his pain," he said angrily. "Where did she learn to do that? I thought it was a technique only used by the ablest of our Truth-sayers and medics."

Lijou smiled inwardly. Vriuzu had suffered no more than he deserved. To forcibly scan one so recently released from torture was a betrayal of everything Vartra's Priesthood stood for. And for Rhyaz to summarily commandeer one of *his* priests for such a task without asking him first went beyond the bounds of acceptable practice! He would have words with Rhyaz about this later, strong words.

"But I know he was concealing something, Father! I felt it in that instant before the pain hit me!"

"Supposition and conjecture!" Lijou snorted. "You'd have us believe his shields were so strong you had to force a contact, yet you managed to penetrate them *as* the pain hit you? I think not. And you wonder he felt anger toward you for causing him this distress and agony?" He stopped abruptly as he felt Rhyaz' hand close on his knee, claws extending warningly.

"Where is Kusac now?" asked Master Rhyaz.

"He's in the sick bay, eating. Doctor Zayshul examined his wound and said we could proceed with the debriefing after he'd eaten. Carrie has T'Chebbi, Rezac, and Jeran helping her guard him from *us*! I'm lucky she let me out to contact you!"

"Conduct the debriefing normally, Vriuzu. Leave the rest to us. We'll look into it further when they return to Shola."

When the screen went blank, Lijou turned on him. "You had no right to set Vriuzu—one of my priests—on Kusac! You've overstepped your area of responsibility, Rhyaz! When did I ever interfere in your realm of operations? The En'Shallans are mine! My priests, my concern, my responsibility! How dare you have Kusac's person violated in this way! Hasn't he suffered enough?"

"Peace, Lijou. I've achieved what I wanted," said Rhyaz. "I didn't expect to be able to probe his mind but Kaid and Carrie will guard him so closely that should there be any secondary programming, he won't get the opportunity to cause any harm either to the treaty or Haven."

Stunned, Lijou watched Rhyaz get to his feet and walk over to the hot plate for a mug of c'shar.

"You put Kusac through a forced mental contact in his condition, risked triggering a seizure, just to have him guarded by his own people?"

"Can you imagine the outcry from his Triad partners and friends if I'd put guards on him?" Rhyaz asked, spooning the sweetener into his mug. "This way, though Kaid will still be angry, he'll have no option but to do what I want."

"I had the matter in hand! Thanks to you, they'll have lost their trust in me!"

"I doubt it, Lijou. They know the orders came from me, not you."

Lijou got to his feet, his rumble of anger filling the room.

"Next time, consult me before you take matters concerning my priests into your own hands! I could have achieved the same outcome without any ill feelings!" He stormed out of Rhyaz' office, tail flicking angrily beneath his black priest's robe.

CHAPTER 2

Haven, Zhal-Zhalwae, 22nd day (May)

"TROUBLE," observed Manesh, jerking her head toward the approaching figure of Giyesh. "Looks like Jeran's been talking to her."

Sheeowl looked up, taking in their young comm operator's bushed-out mane of black hair and her lashing tail. "I did it in her best interests," she said defensively, watching the Sholan Brothers and Sisters in the crowded mess hurriedly parting to let her through. "The rest of you can back me up on that."

"No," said Manesh, the security officer, unequivocally. "I told you to keep your nose out from the first. You got her riled, you can deal with it. I'll only interfere if it comes to blows, and then only so the Sholans don't have to get involved."

"Same here," agreed Nayash. "They needed each other on the Prime ship, and they obviously want it to continue. Why make more of it than that?"

Giyesh stormed over to their table, and stopped, hands on hips, glowering down at the engineer. "You had no right to go running to Jeran with scare stories, Sheeowl," she snarled, tail flicking angrily. "How d'you think that made me look?"

"We were only thinking of you, taiban," said Sheeowl calmly. "Sit down, let's talk this over quietly."

"The time for that was before you went to Jeran! And that's another thing! Stop calling me taiban! I'm not a child, dammit! If I was, we'd not be having this conversation!"

"Did he offer?" interrupted Mrowbay.

She rounded on the medic. "What option did you leave him? Yes, he did, and I refused! You think I want a contract with him under these circumstances?" she asked scornfully. "How could I accept, knowing he'd asked because of your interference? You ruined it for me!"

"You fool!" exclaimed Sheeowl. "This is serious, Giyesh, not something your mother can sweep into a corner. This'll affect the rest of your life!"

"You think I care?" Giyesh swung back to her, leaning forward and placing her hands on the table. Her mouth widened, displaying her teeth in a humorless smile. "I have now with him, and that's enough. I don't have a burning need to mate and increase the Family! Who knows? In a year, I may ask to work on a Sholan ship. I can pursue a career with them. For the first time, I have an acceptable option. I only came to warn you and Mrowbay to stay out of my affairs from now on, or take the consequences." She pushed herself upright and stalked off.

"You should have respected her decision not to tell him," said Sayuk quietly. "Captain Tirak did."

"Shut up," snarled Sheeowl. "It never occurred to me that she'd be stupid enough to refuse him."

"It should have," said Mrowbay. "She's strong-willed, just like her mother. A real Rryuk. The Matriarch won't be pleased, though. I should never have agreed to talk to her." He shook his head sadly and reached for a cookie on the plate in front of him.

Sheeowl slapped his hand away. "Leave it," she snapped. "Giyesh is right, you're getting fat."

He looked hurt as he tucked his hands beneath the table out of her reach. "Don't take it out on me," he said. "It wasn't my fault it turned out the wrong way."

"You agreed I was right at the time!"

"You're both wrong," said Nayash, leaning back in his seat. "I think the Matriarch will be pleased Giyesh was able to attach Jeran and bring him to Home. It'll add to our status, not only on the Council, but among our military allies. We Rryuks made First Contact with the Sholans, and now we're bringing one of them back, one bound to us alone. And as for mating contracts, I think that the Matriarch will make sure that it's considered a mere technicality that Giyesh and Jeran aren't formally mated. There'll be more than a few males willing to measure themselves against Jeran, prove they're better than a Sholan. I think she'll have her pick of the males in our allied families—if she wants a mate at all considering what she's just said."

"You could be right," agreed Manesh. "I reckon Jeran'll not lack for lovers either, should he wish to look elsewhere. Apart from that light pelt of his, he's almost indistinguishable from us. It isn't as if he were really alien, like one of the Sumaan or a Chemerian, or even a Human."

"I just hope the Captain isn't going to want our hides," said Mrowbay morosely. "If he believes our interference has driven his niece away from any kind of mating with our people, we'll be in for a hard trip home."

"You're just so damned optimistic these days, aren't you, Mrowbay?" snapped Sheeowl, getting to her feet. "Well, I'm not sitting around waiting for Captain Tirak to come and yell at me over this. I'm going down to the *Profit* now. I've got work to do, and so have the rest of you if we're going to leave on schedule tomorrow."

The debriefing had been a long process, taking several hours for Vriuzu's questions to slowly draw the details of his captivity from him. But he'd not told the telepath everything. He'd managed to keep one or two incidents, like his night with Zayshul, locked deep away.

The experience had been intensely painful, and he'd been glad that he'd refused to allow Carrie or T'Chebbi to remain. Rezac had stayed with him, keeping a watch on Vriuzu and encouraging him when the memories became too painful to describe. He felt drained and exhausted, unable to even look Rezac in the eyes.

When it was over, wearing the fresh black robe Carrie had fetched for him, he let himself be led from the sick bay to a private bedroom nearby. Glad though he was to be leaving there, after the quietness of the sick bay, the noise and bustle of the corridors was almost too much for him. When loud voices, followed by the sound of running feet broke out, he began to panic.

Two small white shapes streaked around the corner, heading straight toward him, obviously closely pursued by several people.

"What the hell?" began Rezac, instantly hauling him to one side as he reached for his gun.

Unable to stop in time, the lead figure collided with T'Chebbi, almost knocking her to the ground. As the others rounded the corner, they managed to dodge aside at the last moment.

"Hi, Carrie, Kusac. The jeggets, where did they go?" demanded Brynne, sliding to a stop on the stone floor.

"They didn't," said Jeran, looking down the corridor behind him. "They're still around here somewhere."

"Sorry, T'Chebbi," said the other male Human as he untangled himself from her. "Belle and Scamp suddenly decided to go run-about." Now upright, Kris reached out to help her straighten her jacket.

She batted his hands away, frowning at him. "Haven no place for animals. No business bringing them here in first place," she grumbled, returning her gun to its holster.

"Had no choice. You know I took him with me to Jalna," Kris replied, crouching down to look along the floor.

As Rezac released him and put his gun away, he leaned against the wall, trying to gather his wits together after the shock of the encounter.

"Hello, Kusac," said Brynne quietly, abandoning his search. "It's good to see you in the flesh at last. How're you feeling?" He extended his hand, palm up, in the telepath's greeting.

He looked at Brynne mutely, knowing he should respond but unable to do so.

"It's all right, I understand." Brynne withdrew his hand, clasping him briefly on the shoulder instead. "Must be a hell of a shock after what you've been through to suddenly have us descending on you like this." Brynne glanced down at Kris. "You can stop looking, Kris, I found them." He turned back to Kusac, mouth widening in a grin. "Seems our jeggets have taken a fancy to you, Kusac. They're hiding behind your robes."

Pressing himself back against the wall, he stared wide-eyed at the Human. J'koshuk had shown his teeth in the same way when he'd smiled. He shuddered, remembering what the Valtegan's smile had meant. Anger, quickly suppressed, flared briefly. Dammit, why was he so afraid of something as simple as a Human's smile?

Brynne's smile vanished instantly and he turned his head to glance uncertainly at Carrie.

Stooping, she pushed aside the hem of Kusac's robe. "They're here," she confirmed, reaching behind him.

As she stood up, he got a momentary glimpse of white fur,

a pair of tiny, shining black eyes and a pink, whiskered nose. The creature began struggling, and as it leaped free, Carrie let out an exclamation of surprise.

Instinctively, he grabbed for it, finding himself eye to eye with the jegget. A twist, and it escaped his grasp to scramble up onto his shoulder, dive under his hair and wind itself round the back of his neck, chittering gently.

"Sorry, Kusac," said Brynne, reaching out for her. "She's quite tame."

The creature's long tail began to snake round his neck and tighten. Putting his hand up to stop her, he was surprised by the softness of her pelt.

"Belle, don't do that," said Brynne. "Come on, girl. Time to come back."

"I don't think she wants to," he said, finding his voice as the small, pointed head pushed insistently against his hand, nosing it away from her tail.

"I see you've found one of them at least."

The unfamiliar voice drew his attention away from the jegget. A pair of gray eyes, set in a round face framed by a mane of multicolored tabby hair regarded him steadily. "You must be Kusac. I'm Keeza," she said, leaning against Brynne.

He watched the way Brynne's arm went round her waist and how the Human's body automatically moved to accommodate hers. Then he noticed the broad silver bracelets they both wore on their wrists. Life-bonded? Brynne had life-bonded with a Sholan female?

"Kusac, could I get Scamp?" asked Kris from where he still crouched on the floor.

Holding onto Belle with one hand, Kusac bent down and searched beneath his robe for the other jegget. Grasping him by the scruff, he pulled him out and passed him over to Kris. As he stood up, he tried to unwind Belle's tail from his throat. She'd have none of it and snaked round to the back of his neck, tail well out of reach, chittering even more loudly.

"She seems to want to stay with you. Perhaps you should keep her for a little while," Brynne said. "She's rather special: a gift from Vartra."

Vartra? What had the God to do with jeggets? He gave up trying to remove her and glanced back at Brynne.

"Carrie can—call me—on her comm when you've had enough of her," he heard Brynne say.

He gave the barest of nods, more aware of the feel of tiny paws on his neck and shoulders than of what the Human was saying.

As the two Humans and Keeza began to move away, Carrie took hold of his arm.

"Let's get you settled in our room," she said, gently tugging him on again.

Later that afternoon, when T'Chebbi came to relieve him from guarding Kusac, Rezac made his way to the rec room where he knew Kaid was waiting for him. During Kusac's debriefing, he'd been able to piece together a timetable of events. Now Kaid wanted to be updated. Though the rec was busy, somehow Kaid had managed to ensure they had a table to themselves.

Kaid sat silently, listening while Rezac told him the details.

"So Carrie was moved from cryo to one of their stasis units as early as four days after the Primes took us," he said, keeping his voice low so as not to be overheard. "And Kusac? When did you say he was awakened?"

"Fourteen days later, when they implanted him—four days before you and Carrie were reunited," Rezac said quietly. "When Vriuzu finished the debriefing, while Kusac was recovering, I took the opportunity to speak privately to Doctor Zayshul. She said given what they knew about Leska links, she was sure the timing was significant, that your bond to Carrie had been growing since they'd taken her out of cryo. When she began to weaken after they operated on her, they had to put her in a reduced stasis field. It's looking more and more like the implant wasn't needed at all and that Chy'qui's story of Kusac's seizures was a lie so he could experiment on the two of them. Then you became the jegget in his barn when it became obvious that every time they took Carrie out of stasis, you collapsed in agony."

"Initially Chy'qui may have lied," agreed Kaid. "But we know Kusac's had at least two seizures. Unless Doctor Zayshul . . . ?"

Rezac shook his head. "She only saw those two. As to the abductions of the rest of us, that was done on Chy'qui's orders. Jo and I were obviously taken because we were injured and needed treatment. Kate and Taynar because they provided a healthy specimen of each of our species so Doctor Zayshul could study them before operating on Carrie."

"And Jeran and Giyesh because they were the only U'Churian and Sholan pair."

Rezac nodded. "And you know why you were taken. Our drugs couldn't control the pain you were suffering because they weren't strong enough. The Primes needed to give you more powerful analgesics, and Chy'qui wanted to find out how you were able to sense Carrie's pain despite the fact you were obviously not her Leska. You'd drawn so much attention to yourself and Carrie, he was able to keep his experiments with Kusac secret. Even so, if it hadn't been for Prince Zsurtul haunting Doctor Zayshul's medical labs with the natural curiosity of youth, Chy'qui would likely have succeeded in keeping you and Carrie apart."

"Youth has its advantages, as you know," Kaid said dryly, raising a sardonic eye ridge at his father.

Rezac's mind spun briefly as he remembered that the male sitting opposite him, though some thirty years his senior, was in fact his son, both of them exiles in this time, fifteen hundred years in their future.

Kaid broke the silence. "Does Doctor Zayshul have any new theories as to what caused Kusac's convulsions?"

"No, but she says the TeLaxaudin Kzizysus is convinced it was his system rejecting the implant. If it had been left in, he'd have suffered more frequent and violent seizures until either he died, or Chy'qui put an end to him. Implant rejection isn't common, but it does happen, and there's no cure. M'ezozakk, Captain of the *M'ijikk,* died that way. Kusac is the first person to have survived the removal of a control unit. That's why Zayshul wanted to examine him today."

"Better a swift end than a lingering one," Kaid murmured, realizing that they'd cheated death more than once with the Primes. "He's out of danger now, that's what matters. If it hadn't been for our Triad, all three of us would be dead. At least now we understand why events happened the way they did."

"Kaid, nothing was said to Kusac about neural damage. I know what those collars do. How could they miss it when they knew he was tortured to the extent he was?"

"They know, but I'm having it kept from both Carrie and Kusac for the time being, at least until we know the extent of it," he said.

"I suppose they don't need the extra worry right now. What about the treaty? How're the negotiations going?"

Kaid sighed, resting his elbows on the table. "We're in the last stages now. We've taken a break so copies of the final agreement on the trade and training issues could be sent to our home worlds. I'm told the TeLaxaudins have been in touch with President Nesul, asking for a duplicate of the Primes' treaty for themselves, with the exception of the clauses concerning the young Prime warriors."

"So we're actually going to train some of their precious young warrior caste?"

"Only a token number—twenty to be exact, and only up to Forces skill level, not beyond. They'll come to Shola with the Prime Ambassador in about a month's time."

"Hardly a token number, that's half of them! Are they really that trusting of us?"

"Yes, as far as I and any of the other telepaths can tell, but we're only able to get their surface thoughts, nothing more, without drawing attention to ourselves. They do have more warriors, but they're a full five years younger than this group. Apparently they waited five years to see how the original forty turned out before breeding any more half M'zullian males. They wanted to be sure they'd eradicated the worst of their phobias from their racial memory of the Fall."

"And how did they check they won't go as psychotic as the M'zullians the moment they smell us?" Rezac asked.

"They use chemical scent stimulants and holographic images of us created from their data files to finish their conditioning, but it takes time and doesn't work for all of them. That's why they wanted Kezule. He's pre-Fall, with none of those psychoses." His wrist comm buzzed gently and he pushed himself up from the table. "I have to get back now. L'Seuli sends that they're ready to reconvene. It'll be late when I finish. If you can find a way to discreetly tell Carrie I'll sleep in the dorm tonight, I'd appreciate it. She and Kusac need some time alone."

"Is that wise?" asked Rezac, getting up. "After hearing what J'koshuk put him through, I'd say he's walking too narrow a trail right now to be left alone with her."

"I walked that trail myself not long ago, Rezac. I've no reason to keep them apart. The sooner he's normalized, the quicker his recovery will be. The bio-monitor on his wrist will trigger either mine or T'Chebbi's alarms if there are any abnormal changes in his telemetry and we'll be there instantly."

Rezac grunted softly. "I've had personal experience of J'koshuk's interrogation methods, though obviously not for as long as Kusac. I think it's too soon to leave them alone, especially when he could take the view that you've betrayed him with Carrie."

Kaid's ears folded briefly sideways before righting themselves. "He won't. We don't acknowledge jealousy the way your culture did. He knows why our Link happened. I do intend to leave someone on duty outside his room overnight. I hate playing into Rhyaz' claws like this, but if I don't keep Kusac guarded, Rhyaz will get Vriuzu or Jiosha to try probing him again, and I won't risk him having another seizure."

"I don't think Vriuzu would be that stupid after the pain he experienced. Or Jiosha," Rezac said, accompanying him to the door.

Stronghold, Zhal-S'Asha, 19th day (October)

The wind howled round the towers of Stronghold, gusting through the courtyard to whip his hair about his face as he crossed to the aircar. Fighting to hold his Brotherhood uniform jacket closed, he attempted to buckle the belt one-handed. Already dawn brightened the eastern sky, illuminating the roiling clouds overhead. He was committed to leaving now, there was no turning back. Today would be stormy in more ways than one.

Takeoff needed his full attention, but once he was high above Stronghold and heading for the spaceport, the air currents grew calmer and he switched on the autopilot. His thoughts soon began to wander back to Haven.

Haven, Zhal-Zhalwae, 22nd/23rd day (May)

He hadn't been aware of falling asleep, let alone being undressed and put to bed, but when he woke, the room was quiet and the light had been dimmed. A quick glance around had shown him

he and Carrie were alone. He lay there for some time, just listening to her soft breathing, and that of the jegget curled near
the foot of the bed. Since they'd brought him to this room, either T'Chebbi or Rezac had been with them, trying every now
and then, like Carrie, to draw him into some conversation, but
there was nothing he wanted to say. All he'd wanted was to be
left alone with Carrie.

Among the belongings she'd given him back from the *Profit*
were his wrist comm with the psi-damper he didn't need any-
more. To please her, he'd put it on next to the bio-monitor the
physician had given him. He supposed it would provide him with
some mental protection, meant he didn't have to rely on his natural shielding alone. His torc, like Carrie's, was lost, taken from
them by the Primes. Its loss seemed symbolic.

Turning round carefully, he raised himself on one elbow so
he could watch her. Her face was relaxed in sleep, the taut lines
that had creased her forehead all day were gone now. Realization that he was no longer a captive hit him. He was free, free
to do what *he* chose.

Reaching out, he picked up a lock of her blonde hair, rubbing
it gently between his fingers. It was as soft as he remembered.
Letting it fall back to the pillow, hesitantly he touched her face,
running a gentle fingertip across her cheek. Her skin felt like one
of the fruits from her world, soft, and covered with a very faint
down. He could smell her scent now, and it brought back memories, painful ones, of pairings the like of which they'd never
share again.

He slipped his hand round the back of her neck, tears momentarily blurring his sight. As he blinked them away, her eyes
flicked open—Sholan eyes, the pupils narrowing to vertical slits
as the light from the lamp fell on them. Suddenly, he wanted her
very badly.

Closing the gap that separated them, he leaned across her, lowering his face to hers, catching hold of her bottom lip with his
teeth. He looped his free hand under her back, pressing her close
against·his belly and groin as he began to nip at her face.

Her hands pushed against his chest, trying to ease him away.
He ignored her, clenching his hand in her hair, pulling her head
back to arch her throat toward him. His breathing was uneven
now as the muscles in his lower belly and groin began to contract. With a grunt of discomfort, he loosened his hold on her

body, moving back slightly to allow his genitals room to descend. Releasing her mouth, he began to nip and lick his way down her arched throat.

"Kusac!"

In the unaccustomed heady rush of sexual arousal and freedom, he barely heard her. It had been so long since they'd paired! When he'd first woken to J'koshuk and the world of the *Kz'adul,* he'd been sure that they'd all die. Then the priest had dragged him to the stasis area, shown him her and Kaid pairing. He'd known then that somehow they'd become Leskas and she no longer needed him to survive. But he needed her so badly.

His mouth touched the neckline of her uniform. It was a barrier, preventing him from going further. As he stopped, reaching for the fastening, her hands batted against his chest.

"Kusac! You're hurting me!"

Again he ignored her, his need to have her outweighing any other consideration. The seal parted instantly, exposing her naked flesh and surrounding him with her warm scent. His purr of pleasure was nearer a growl.

She twisted away from him, and surprised, he used his body weight to pin her down. He lapped at her skin, tasting her before closing his teeth on the nearest breast.

A sharp tug on his left ear made him flick it in irritation, but it wasn't till her hand closed, far too tightly, on a sensitive part of his anatomy, that she got his undivided attention.

With a yelp of pain, his hand covered hers, trying to ease her fingers apart. "Not so tight!" His voice was strained, tears springing to his eyes as he tried to roll clumsily off her.

"You're hurting me," she repeated. "What's wrong with you, Kusac? You were never this rough before."

"Let me go," he said, his claws extending just enough to prick her fingers warningly. "There's no need for you to grab me like this."

"Take your claws out of me first. You were ignoring me, it was the only way I could get your attention."

With a rumble of annoyance, he retracted his claws and she released him. "You were never so reluctant before," he muttered, clutching his abused anatomy.

"I'm not reluctant, Kusac," she said. "You were too rough. You know how much stronger than me you are."

He rolled onto his back and stared at the ceiling, the mood

utterly gone. "I wasn't being rough, I just got carried away, that's all. It's been so long . . . I thought you'd be as willing . . . Forget it." He felt her hand touch his chest but ignored it. How could they continue in any kind of relationship when she squealed the first time he laid hands on her? He'd been no more rough than usual. She'd never complained before.

But before, they'd had their Link. He'd known from moment to moment exactly how his touch felt to her, whether he was being too rough. All that was gone now. Dread filled him as he wondered if he was afraid to pick up where they'd left off, afraid he was no longer able to be the lover he'd been before their Leska Link was gone. If he left it like this, he'd never know.

"I am willing," she said softly.

He turned back to her: she was his life-mate, the mother of their cub, the person who mattered most to him, the one he'd tried to protect from J'koshuk. His mind a confused jumble of fear and desire, he let her take the lead, almost afraid to touch her lest he miscalculate his strength again.

The way she ran her hands across his body, her fingers pushing through his pelt to find the skin beneath, brought back so many memories, as did the feel of her blunt teeth nipping their way so gently across his neck and chest.

More confident now, he encouraged her, trying not to think of what was lacking or to remember his last insane night on the *Kz'adul* with the Valtegan doctor. He wanted to forget it completely, as if it had never happened: he needed desperately to pair with her to wash away that memory. As they joined, he felt the brief touch of her mind against his before she remembered.

Fiery pain swept through him then was gone. Like the night with the doctor, in its wake, every sensation was heightened, but this time, because he hadn't triggered it, it was much shorter lived. Enough to bring him to the verge of climax, it left him poised there in limbo. What little self-control he'd been able to exert, vanished. Frustrated and impatient, his hands clenched round her hips as he tensed, readying himself for the initial pain he'd feel when he tried to reach mentally for her.

Then the jegget was there, her tiny clawed feet climbing across his shoulders and back, her insistent wet nose snuffling at his ear as she tried in her own way to join in. The shock of it was enough to tip him over the edge without the need for the pain.

* * *

He'd feigned sleep, waiting till Carrie slept before slipping from the bed and pulling on his robe. Silently he padded to the door and opened it. T'Chebbi sat outside, unsurprised to see him, or with his request. She remained silent as she escorted him up to the observation room. Huge and sullen, the nearby gas giant filled the viewport, bathing the room with its baleful, orange glow.

For several minutes, he stood there, looking out at it without seeing it. "How do you stand it?" he asked suddenly, looking round at her. "To feel nothing with your mind when you pair?"

"Telepaths are few. How should we know what you feel? What we have is good enough," she replied.

He made a sound of exasperation and turned away. "It's pointless when your mind isn't involved," he said at last. "It becomes nothing more than a physical release."

"What's wrong with that?" she asked, moving closer to him. "Many things are done only for pleasure and exercise, why not pairing?"

"If you believe that, why were you celibate until recently?" he countered. "You told me you were trained as a Consortia. Why'd you change your mind?"

"We weren't high-class qwenes," she said quietly. "Pleasing clients sexually was our choice, not theirs, you know that. Was trained to be a hostess, not work for a living, until the Fleet pack took me. You have your life, and your Triad, be grateful for that, Kusac, instead of angry at what you can't change."

"Without our Link, it's pointless, a—travesty—of what we had! I've a right to be angry!"

"Anger like this destroys you. You aren't the only one to lose something you value. Others deal with it, so must you. When we paired, you never had a problem."

"You don't understand. When you and I were together, I could sense something from you, but I could *feel* them—Carrie and Kaid. Now there's nothing at all! I'm trapped alone in my own head, unable to reach beyond myself, unable to sense anything from her!"

"It may come back in time, that's what they say, isn't it? Only been one day, Kusac. Give it time."

"You don't understand," he repeated, hands clenching on the viewport sill. "You're mind-dead to start with! Captivity and the torture, they pass. How could you possibly know the joy of sharing every feeling, every sensation with the one you love, to the point where you actually *become* one being? Chy'qui and J'koshuk, they took what I am, took my very soul away from me! So don't give me any of your platitudes, I don't want them!"

"I heard enough," she growled, turning away from him. "You think you the only one ever to suffer, to lose something! When you're done with self-pity, I be outside!"

"Look, I know you had it rough when the Fleet took you," he began.

"You know nothing!" she spat, backing away in a crouch, tail swaying jerkily. "I lost everything but my life that night! Fleet killed my adoptive father and took me as their prize to frighten other merchants into paying protection money! I was used as pack qwene by them, then the Claws—until Kaid came back for me!" Angrily, she turned her back on him, stalking toward the door where she stopped briefly.

"Wasn't till we nearly lost Kaid to Fyak and Ghezu that I knew I had to tell him what I'd felt for him for all those years. Think on this, Kusac Aldatan. Had you not lost your Talent—temporarily or otherwise—you and Carrie would both be dead, maybe Kaid as well. Is small price to pay for three lives." She turned to look at him as she opened the air lock, eyes glittering with a hardness he'd never seen before. "I'd pay it. Don't call me till you want to go back to your room."

When Carrie woke in the morning, she found herself alone. Lifting her head to look around, she saw Kusac asleep in the other bed. She was about to get up and check on him when she felt Kaid's presence in her mind.

Leave him sleeping, Carrie. Banner's on duty, he'll sit with him while we talk. Join me in the mess. Don't worry about the jegget, she's back with Brynne.

Curious, she sat up and reached for her clothes, wincing as the scratches on her hips hurt. A sense of disquiet filled her, made worse when she noticed the bruise on her wrist where Kusac had grabbed hold of her the night before. She'd had the odd scratch or bruise in the past from him, but nothing like these. She'd need some of the Fastheal salve they kept on their shuttle in the *Hkariyash*, otherwise Kaid would see them.

What's up? came Kaid's thought.

Nothing. I'm on my way, she replied, tucking her worries safely to the back of her mind where he couldn't access them.

The smell of food made her realize how hungry she was. The queue was short, and as she could see Kaid sitting nearby with Captain Tirak and several of his crew, she grabbed a tray and joined the line. Minutes later, he joined her, ordering a drink, then steering her toward an empty table when she was handed her plate of food.

"What do you want to talk about?" she asked as she sat down.

"We're leaving today," he said, putting his own mug on the table. "The treaty is signed and sealed, and Kusac's fit to travel."

"You needed me on my own to tell me this?" She picked up her fork. Much as she wanted to be home with her daughter, she was dreading their return trip, and the homecoming.

"The worst's over," said Kaid quietly, leaning across the table toward her so the general buzz of conversation around them wouldn't drown his voice. "I called Konis and Rhyasha myself last night to give them the details about Kusac. I told them about our cub. You've no need to fear meeting them when we return. Neither of us has done anything we should feel ashamed about."

"I'm not," she said, swallowing a forkful of eggs. "Everyone knew our Triad was a legitimate bonding among the three of us, that it would entail you and I sharing cubs one day. What I feel is more complex than that. It's as though I somehow feel responsible for what happened to Kusac."

"Chy'qui was the one responsible, not you," he said, watching her closely. "Even if J'koshuk hadn't known your twin, Chy'qui was determined to get information from Kusac about us and Keiss. When he realized we were a Triad, he wanted Kusac tortured to the limit to see if either you or I responded to his pain."

As she put her fork down to reach for her mug of coffee, Kaid took hold of her wrist, making her yelp in pain.

"I thought so," he said, carefully pushing her sleeve up. "You were favoring that arm. What happened?"

She snatched her wrist away but not before he'd seen the livid finger marks. "It's nothing," she said, picking up her fork instead and hurriedly shoveling some more food onto it.

He gave a low growl of annoyance, ears flicking briefly. "Kusac? I was afraid of that. I knew I shouldn't have let you close your mind to me last night. When you've eaten, we're going to the sick bay."

She stared at him, blinking her eyes once, very slowly, letting him know he'd overstepped the bounds. "It's nothing. Just a couple of bruises. He was—enthusiastic, that's all."

"That isn't enthusiasm, Carrie. You might be half Sholan now, but you can still be infected by our claws. If you have any scratches, they need to be treated."

"Dammit, Kaid!" she hissed, leaning toward him angrily. "What do you think he is? Some kind of monster? He'd never hurt me deliberately, any more than you would!"

He regarded her steadily, refusing to back down. "You're being too defensive. What happened last night, Carrie? Did he force you?"

"Let's end this conversation right now, Kaid," she said, her voice icy as she resumed eating, praying he wouldn't notice she was trembling.

He was silent for a minute or two. "The *Kz'adul* left last night," he said, changing the topic. "Tirak's ship is scheduled to leave in just over two hours. We leave after them. Captain Kishasayzar is getting the *Hkariyash* ready now."

"What about Brynne and the others?"

"Captain Shaayiyisis is readying the *Couana*. We'll travel back in convoy with her."

"Interesting though this is, it could have waited, Kaid."

"I wanted to see how you were after last night."

"I told you that topic was dead."

"You asked me why I wanted to see you on your own," he said reasonably. "T'Chebbi was concerned for you. Kusac asked her to arrange for him to travel back in the *Couana*."

"What?" Her fork clattered to the table as she stared at Kaid in shock.

He leaned forward to retrieve it. "The journey home will take about two weeks, and we have Link days now," he said gently, handing it back to her. "It's a perfectly understandable request."

"But I thought . . . I've only just got him back . . ." She stopped, eyes narrowing as a suspicion crept into her mind. "Why, apart from that, was T'Chebbi concerned for me? When did she talk to Kusac?"

"He left you sleeping to go up to the observation lounge. He spent most of the night in there alone."

"Did he say something to her?" she demanded.

"If nothing happened, why are you so concerned?" he asked, taking a drink from his mug.

She studied his face, checking the angle of his ears and head, the position of the eye ridges above the dark brown eyes, as well as opening her mind to his every surface thought. He hid nothing, letting her feel his concern that by leaving her alone with Kusac the night before, he'd exposed her to danger from someone still mentally unstable.

"What did happen last night, Carrie?" he repeated quietly, putting his mug back on the table.

"Nothing. I told you, Kusac would never intentionally hurt me," she said slowly.

"Unintentionally then."

She looked away, pushing her plate aside, no longer hungry. "He was enthusiastic, that's all. Forgot his own strength," she muttered, a bitter taste in her mouth.

"He's been relying on your Link. Now it's gone . . ." Kaid ground to a halt. "Apart from those bruises, what else? Tell me, Carrie. Our next Link day is only three days away. I'd rather not find out then."

She pushed her chair back and stood up. "I need some Fastheal salve," she said. "I'm not going to discuss this any further, Kaid. I feel like I'm betraying him. He's never been anything but gentle and loving with me. I know you think you shouldn't have left us alone, but . . ."

He rose, reaching out to grasp her shoulder. "Carrie, I'm not criticizing him, believe me. Remember, I know what it's like to come suddenly from captivity to the arms of your lover. You were there for me when they brought me out of Ghezu's dungeon."

She remembered only too well, and couldn't stop the comparison that came immediately to her mind. Kaid had behaved so differently from Kusac, and it had been their first time together, his first time with a female for thirty years because he'd been afraid to reveal he was a telepath. He'd been hesitant at first, then grown more confident. Even though he'd known nothing of Human lovemaking, nor how fragile they were in comparison to the furred Sholans, he'd known his own strength. And he'd not known then how to use his Talent.

"Maybe it was my fault," she said hesitantly. "I forgot and

reached for his mind like Vriuzu did. I think I triggered that awful pain."

"What?"

"Only for a moment," she said hastily as his hand tightened on her shoulder in concern. "That's when it happened. A reaction to it, I think. Thank Vartra the jegget was there!" She gave a slight smile of amusement, locking away these new worries. Kaid had made her examine the happenings of the night before more closely than she would have wished, and she didn't like the conclusions she was drawing.

"The jegget?" he asked, moving closer, obviously confused. "What did she have to do with it?"

"She jumped on his back. Everything was fine after that. They do that in the wild, don't they? Well, they do on our estate. We shared a cave with them once." She saw his look of utter confusion and added, "They're drawn to pairing couples, Kusac said. Something to do with them being telepathic too."

"Ah," he said, realization dawning. "Yes, I'd heard that," he murmured. "The sick bay has some Fastheal. We'll get it from there, then you can keep some on hand to treat those scratches."

Two hours later, she met Kaid and T'Chebbi as arranged at the elevator down to the flight deck. As the doors opened, she saw Captain Kishasayzar in the middle of the group at the bottom of the *Profit*'s loading ramp. Kate and Taynar, the young Leska couple the U'Churians had rescued, were already there.

"I thought Kisha'd be on the *Hkariyash* now," she said.

"He came over to finalize a trade deal with Tirak. Stronghold just bought his ship contract from the Chemerians. He owes us the money, but he's free to choose his customers and cargoes now."

"Good for him. I know he'll be as glad to see the back of Assadou as I was." She sniffed the air. "Sure smells better than last time I was here. What did they do with J'koshuk's body?"

"I wondered when you'd ask. They had to expel it into space to put the fire out," said Kaid, glancing at her. "Seems that the bolt of energy Kusac used to kill him started a fire smoldering deep within his body."

Shocked, her steps would have faltered had Kaid not caught her by the elbow and drawn her onward. "Officially, he shot the priest with a gun he took from the Valtegan guard. Unofficially, only Doctor Zayshul and those of us involved in the telepathic web at the hostage exchange know what happened. She dropped the gun to cover his tracks, though Vartra knows why."

"And our people?" she whispered. "They won't prosecute him for using his Talent to kill, will they?"

"It's being kept quiet, Carrie, don't worry," he reassured her.

"But Rhyaz and Lijou must know."

"It was a freak incident, a one-time event," he said, lowering his voice even further as they approached the *Profit*. "The Brotherhood needs us too much to have the incident made public. Back home, the authorities are hailing him as a hero because he didn't take the *Kz'adul* to Shola, he brought it here, to us. Besides, I won't let anything happen to him, trust me."

"I do," she said as he gave her arm an extra squeeze before letting her go as they stopped beside Kishasayzar and T'Chebbi.

The Sumaan's long reptilian neck snaked round toward them, lowering his head till his face was level with Kaid's. Lips pulled back from his mouth, exposing the huge teeth and thick pink tongue in a grin that would have been disconcerting had they not known him.

"Novelty it is for our people being in right place to make good trades," he said. "Thanking you for introduction to Merchant Tirak I am, Kaid. The word I be spreading among my kind for news of drug smugglers both your peoples wish to apprehend. Bad trade for all Alliance that is." He grimaced, wrinkling his snout.

"Glad I could help," said Kaid.

"I go now. Docking we are once *Profit* leaves. *Venture* returns then for you to embark."

Carrie watched their bulky Sumaan captain turn and pace off toward the shuttle parked by the landing bay entrance. His thick tail barely touching the ground, Kishasayzar moved with an ease and grace that was belied by his size.

She turned back to Tirak and his crew, feeling slightly awkward at this leave-taking. Having spent most of her time with them either in stasis or a cell, she didn't know them as well as Kaid and T'Chebbi did. Then she caught sight of Jeran, his light sand-colored pelt standing out amid the universal black of the U'Churians.

"We speak to them," suggested T'Chebbi.

Skirting round the edge of the group, they made their way over to him and Giyesh.

"Take care, you two," Carrie said. "It's not easy trying to become part of another species' culture, Jeran, so when you feel weighed down by how little you know, just remember how much you've already overcome to be together."

"We will," said Giyesh, grinning widely as Jeran put his arm across her shoulders. "Knowing it worked for you and Jo gave us hope."

Carrie shrugged. "Remember, it takes time, and don't let anyone else decide what it is you want, you make your own decisions. Kus . . . We did."

"We intend to. I learned that one already," said Jeran, with a sideways look at Giyesh. "Talking of Kusac, where is he?"

"In our quarters," she said. "He didn't feel up to saying good-bye and sends his apologies."

"He'll find it difficult getting used to such large, open areas again, and so many people," said Jeran. "I'm still finding it strange."

"Takes time," agreed T'Chebbi. "Least you still on ships."

"He'll be fine," reassured Carrie, inwardly praying he would as Tirak made a move to catch her attention. She turned to the U'Churian captain. "I never really thanked you for coming to our rescue the way you did," she said to him.

"No thanks necessary," he replied. "I had to know what you were up to. Your group was too good at frustrating most of my efforts to find out!"

"It's the Brotherhood training," she said lightly.

"You may well hear more from me in the future regarding that," he said. "I have many recommendations to put in front of the Rryuk Family council—starting with improving some of our basic skills." He turned to Kaid, extending his hand to him, Human style.

Kaid held out his and found his forearm grasped firmly.

"A warrior's handshake for you," Tirak said. "We'll be in touch, for trade reasons if nothing else."

"You're continuing to pose as a trader?" Kaid raised an eye ridge at him in amusement.

Tirak grinned, then scratched his ear in embarrassment. "Till we met you, it worked. Yes, we'll be keeping our cover for now. I told you, I have plans. You *will* be hearing from us in the future, but as for now, we must leave. They're giving us an escort back to Jalna."

"So I heard," said Kaid. "At least you can be sure this trip will be uneventful."

"Say good-bye to Annuur for us," said Kate. "And give him these." She handed Tirak several packets of candy. "Sorry I took over your mind like I did on the Chemerian station."

"Is all right, taiban," he said, ruffling her hair. "Without that, think of the excitement we'd have missed!" Chuckling, he turned for the *Profit*'s ramp, gesturing his crew to precede him. "You'll be Annuur's friend for at least a week because of the candy!" he called over his shoulder.

Carrie had been aware of a growing gulf between her and Kusac when she'd returned to the room after first meal, so she was surprised when Banner called her on her wrist comm as they were on their way back up in the elevator, telling her that Kusac wanted to talk to her.

"You go," said Kaid. "I have some business to attend to. It won't take me long. I'll meet you in our room in an hour or so."

Sitting on the bed, she watched Kusac pace the length of the room several times before stopping in front of her. Crouching down on his haunches, he reached out a tentative hand to her knee.

"I'm sorry about last night," he said, his ears folding back against his skull in embarrassment. "I'm finding it . . . difficult . . . to relate to everything right now. I hadn't realized I relied so much on my Talent when I was with you. Without it, it's as if I'm blind and deaf. I need some time alone. I don't want what happened last night to happen again. That's why I'm going back on the *Couana,* with T'Chebbi."

She reached out to touch his cheek, aware of the pain she could see in his amber eyes. "Kusac, talk to me. Whatever it is, we can work it out together. Don't try to do it alone."

"When I know what I want to talk about, I will. I have to get used to being alone, Carrie," he said, breaking eye contact with her.

"But I've just got you back!" She tried to keep the pleading tone out of her voice.

"It's only for two weeks," he said with finality, getting up and going to the door to open it. "Our world has changed for all of us. I have to learn to accept we're no longer Leskas, and that will be impossible on a ship the size of the *Hkariyash.* I'll see you again at Chagda Station, when you transfer to the *Couana* to go down to Shola."

"Kusac," she began.

"Don't ask me to travel with you, Carrie, I can't," he said, face creasing in distress before he abruptly left the room.

Shola, Lygoh Space Port, Zhal-S'Asha, 19th day (October)

Leaving her like that had not been easy when every part of him cried out for her company. It had been the first of many such decisions he'd had to make, in every area of his life.

Ahead, he could see the spaceport, the landing lights on the active bays visible despite the driving rain. He pushed his memories aside; time to focus on the task at hand. He reached for his wrist comm, keying in the code that linked him to his team.

"I'm overhead now. Everything ready?"

"Yes, Captain. The *Couana* is ours, fueled and waiting for you."

Dzaou's voice sounded strained. Doubtless he'd find out why soon enough. "Problems?"

"None, sir. Captain Kishasayzar's diversion worked. Port Control assumes we're still running engine checks, so we're ready to lift off immediately you're on board."

"Meet me as arranged in fifteen minutes," he said and cut the connection, dismissing the matter from his mind as he fought the turbulence to bring his aircar down into the parking lot. Now came the difficult part—being noticed enough to be remembered, but not enough to be prevented from planting the signal disruptor.

Powering the vehicle down, he pulled his card from the ignition slot, unlocked his seat, and swung it round to face the rear. His personal kit was already on board the *Couana*, taken there by Banner. All he needed was the bag that lay on the rear seat.

Standing up, he grasped his coat, pulling it on and sealing it closed before grabbing the bag. Slinging it over his shoulder, he stepped to the door, pressing his palm to the lock. It slid back, letting in an icy blast of rain. He jumped down to the ground, hitting the close button as he did. Flattening his ears and leaning into the wind, he began to head toward the main terminal building.

The automatic doors slid back, enveloping him instantly in a cocoon of warm air and bright lights. He stood there for a moment, dripping onto the absorbent mat before shaking his head and walking on. Pushing the damp hair back from his eyes, he headed for the departure lounge for scheduled flights to Chagda Station. Despite the weather, it was quite busy and he had to elbow his way through the milling crowd of assorted species standing beneath the flight information screens.

Reaching the corridor lined with various small stores and eateries, he picked the quietest and, opening his coat so the Brotherhood emblem on his jacket was visible, headed for the counter to buy a mug of c'shar. As he joined the small line of customers waiting to be served, he made sure he jostled the male in front.

With a growl of annoyance, the traveler turned round. "You want to be a bit more careful . . ." He stopped as soon as he caught sight of the distinctive black uniform and badge.

"Apologies," Kusac murmured, inclining his head.

The male said nothing, merely turned back to the counter, but the incident had the desired effect of drawing all eyes to him. A group of people who'd been standing quietly drinking moved away, joining the steady stream of those making their way to the departure area. The assistant behind the counter leaned forward and called out to him.

"Can I serve you now, Brother?"

Kusac kept his sardonic thoughts to himself as he indicated those ahead of him. "I'll wait, thank you. I'm not in a hurry."

"No trouble. I'm sure no one will mind if I serve you first. You'll be wanting to be on your way." The tone was firm. He wasn't offering to serve him, he was insisting. But then, he'd counted on this response.

"C'shar," he said, reaching into his jacket pocket for some coins.

The sense of relief from both the stall holder and customers as he left with his disposable mug of c'shar was
palpable, even to him. Sipping it, he headed for the Chagda
Station lounge.

Once there, he made for the sanitary facilities, tossing
his empty mug into a bin on the way. Plans of the complex had shown him that if he placed the disruptor in the
air-conditioning duct, it would have the desired effect. Out
of the corner of his eye, he saw a dark-clad figure get up
from one of the nearby seats and follow him. Dzaou.

The sanitary facilities were empty, which simplified matters considerably. "You watch the door," he ordered, hauling the nearest bin toward the air vent high above the
washbasins.

Taking the lid off, he upended it, letting the wastepaper
spill onto the floor. Climbing on top, he pulled a small span-
ner out of his jacket pocket and began undoing the bolts.

"Someone's coming," said Dzaou, a few minutes later,
pushing the door shut and leaning on it. "Hurry up. I can't
keep them out for long."

He grunted, letting the third bolt drop to the ground.
Reaching for the bag, he unfastened it and pulled the
disruptor out. The size of a pack of stim twigs, it fit easily into the aperture when he swung the cover aside on
its remaining bolt. Letting the grille fall back into place,
he leaped down, kicking the loose bolts away with his
foot.

"Done," he said, picking the bin up, righting it, and placing it against the nearest wall. Turning, he saw Dzaou suddenly release the door, letting the male outside stumble into
the room.

Glaring at him, the Sholan was about to complain when
he realized they were both wearing the Brotherhood blacks.

"Damned door," said Dzaou. "Sticking like that. They want
to get it seen to."

"And get this place cleaned up," said Kusac disdainfully
as he followed him out. "Disgraceful the way they're letting
hygiene standards fall like this."

Side by side, they headed back up the corridor to the
central area then made their way toward the military exit.

"Now tell me the problem," he said in a low voice.

Dzaou glanced at him, face pulled into a scowl of annoyance. "Security's been increased since yesterday. Raiban's lot. Wasn't easy for me to come in from the field and find a place to change into this uniform."

"You managed," he said shortly, seeing the barrier ahead of them manned by one of the Intelligence Corps as well as the usual two Allied Forces personnel. "My cover should be enough for both of us."

"What if they want ID?"

"You're my aide, you're returning here after escorting me to the *Illshar*," he said, continuing to walk toward the checkpoint.

He stopped, took his ID out of the bag and handed it to the Sholan guard. "Brother Kusac Aldatan, bound for the *Illshar*," he said.

The Intelligence officer leaned forward and took the card from the trooper to examine it. "Bit out of your league, isn't it?" he asked. "A supply ship?"

He reached for his card, deftly flicking it out of the officer's hand. "I'm captaining it," he said. "It's bound for Haven."

"Ah, Haven. The Brotherhood hideaway. What's happening out there, then?"

He smiled, a Human one that exposed his teeth and made the two troopers back off. "Check the flight schedules," he said softly, a low growl underscoring his words. "It's a regular delivery. Since Raiban started her budget cuts, we see to our own supplies. Dzaou, open the barrier. We're late already."

Dzaou stepped forward but the officer held his arm in the way. "ID first," he snapped. "No one goes through without ID."

"You questioning my staff?" he asked, raising an eye ridge. "He's not coming with me, merely picking up a copy of the manifest for Master Rhyaz. Do you really want to delay us further and take the matter up with the Guild Master at Stronghold? Or are you going to let us through?"

The officer's eyes narrowed. "I'll be waiting for him," he snarled. "Ten minutes is all you got!"

"It's all we'll need," he said silkily as he and Dzaou passed through the narrow gate.

As they walked down the corridor to the exit, Dzaou began to increase his pace. "Don't rush," Kusac hissed. "Take your time."

"I want to be out of here," the other muttered as he slowed down.

He glanced at Dzaou. "They obviously trained you differently back then."

Dzaou threw him a look of pure anger. "What would you know about Brotherhood training? You were brought up a Telepath!"

"Leave those attitudes behind right now or you'll come to grief on this mission," said Kusac coldly. "I won't tolerate them." He pushed the door at the end open and stepped out into the rain and wind.

The *Couana* stood alongside the *Illshar.* Both ships had their engines running, ready for immediate takeoff. As they made their way across to them, Kusac reached into his bag, pulling out the control pad for the disruptor.

"Let's hope this works," he muttered as he activated the unit. Tossing it onto the ground toward the other ship, he began to run toward the *Couana.*

As soon as they'd boarded and the landing ramp was closed, he hit the ship's comm. "Get us out of here," he ordered. "Jump as soon as we reach an acceptable altitude and velocity."

"Aye, sir," came Banner's reply.

The deck began to vibrate beneath his feet as he raced for the elevator, Dzaou close behind him. Acceleration was rapid, and he had to grasp the grab rails to prevent himself from being pushed to the floor. He hit the switch and they began to rise. They only had one level to go, then they were tumbling out for the adjacent elevator platform up to the bridge. The short distance from there to the bridge air lock seemed to take them forever.

Once there, he flung himself into the Captain's chair and began checking the console. Dzaou ran past him to his own post.

"Weapon ports open and on-line," said Dzaou, quickly routing them from Comms to his station.

"Set jump coordinates from my data," he said, inserting a data crystal.

"Receiving data. Coordinates locked in," said Khadui.

"Jump engines on-line," said Chima. "Necessary velocity and height achieved, Captain."

"Jump," he said. "Is Control tracking us?" he asked the comms operator as the familiar pulse of energy from the jump engines pushed them briefly back into their seats.

"Jump engines initiated," said Banner.

"Communications from Control ceased before you boarded, sir," said Jayza. "Long-range scanners detected nothing prior to jump. I'd say we made a clean exit."

"What's the penalty for stealing a private yacht like this anyway?" inquired Chima quietly.

"You don't want to know," said Jayza.

He began to unwind slightly as the inertial dampers cut in. Three days, then he'd find out whether this mission was a trap or only too genuine. He didn't know which he feared more.

"When are you briefing us, Captain?" asked Banner, turning round to look at him.

"In three days," he said, putting his hand up to rub his forehead. A headache, not helped by his lack of sleep, was starting to build. He got to his feet, retrieving the data crystal and putting it back in his pocket. "Stand down weapons, Dzaou. Banner, take over. I'm going to my quarters. Call me when it's time to eat," he said abruptly.

Kz'adul, Zhal-Zhalwae, 23rd day (May)

"To prevent General Kezule from waking from his laalgo trance, we've kept him in a reduced stasis field," Zayshul said to Medical Director Zsoyshuu. "I plan to start revival procedures today."

"What of the necessary fluid samples? Have they been taken? General Kezule represents the last of the line of the late Emperor Q'emgo'h, a perfect fusion of the Warrior and Intellectual castes," he said, staring intently out of the comm screen at her. "Whether or not he chooses to mate cannot be left to chance. We need his genes, untainted as they are by the madness of the M'zullians and J'kirtikkians, for the basis of our new Warrior caste."

"Kzizysus and Chy'qui had it done, Director," she said, wishing this interview were over.

"Good. Then see that you initiate the breeding program instantly. I want at least a hundred eggs implanted and put into accelerated development."

"What about the latest M'zullian ones Chy'qui started last week? There must be a couple of hundred of them."

"Terminate all but fifty, Zayshul. Chy'qui shouldn't have started so many. We do need ordinary troops, but without those we'll breed from Kezule with the intellect and forcefulness to control them . . ." He shook his head. "It's a risk neither the Emperor nor I are prepared to take, Doctor."

"But they're almost at birth maturity," she objected. "I'd be terminating viable hatchlings."

"I'm sorry, Doctor Zayshul, it must be done. It's the quality of our future warriors that's important, not the quantity. Unless you can change the gender at this stage? If so, you can keep another fifty."

She hesitated. It was worth a try, though ideally they should have been maintained at a higher temperature from the first. "I'll see what I can do," she said. "What about the new batch? Any females?"

"Twenty should be sufficient. We don't need as many of them. You have to realize we're creating a new caste, Zayshul, upsetting the balance that we've had in our society for the last fifteen hundred years. It must be done carefully, introducing them slowly to ensure they don't take advantage of our weaknesses to overthrow the stability we've built over the last millennium and a half. As the last true Warrior male related to Q'emgo'h, Kezule himself could pose a threat to our Emperor. In the hands of any faction so minded, he could be used to pull down our Lord of Light Himself. We must be very sure of his loyalty."

"I understand, Director. I have adapted the sleep programs you advised me to use on him. He should waken fully adjusted to our culture, and his own innate sense of duty and responsibility should ensure his loyalty to Emperor Cheu'ko'h."

"His gratitude for being liberated from the Sholans should be enough, I hope," said Zsoyshuu dryly. "Very well, Doctor Zayshul, you have your orders. Report back to me on your arrival at K'oish'ik and I'll have the breeding units collected by royal guards."

She sighed as she cut the connection and got up. It pained her to have to terminate the M'zullian pre-hatchlings in the breeder, but Director Zsoyshuu was right, they couldn't afford the risk. When they were eventually taken from the growth tubes, they would be young adults, pre-programmed by the sleep tapes to enable them to live effectively within the strata of society being created for them. But their basic natures could not be known until later. They would need to be adjusted individually, once their personalities had been discerned by those living and working with them. Now that they had Kezule, it was safer all around to rely on him.

She headed for her research lab, surprised to find her assistant Na'qui already there in the company of a steward. Frowning, she let the door close behind her. "What are you doing here, K'hedduk?" She wasn't sure why, but his presence here made her feel uneasy.

"I've been reassigned to you, Doctor, now that you're once more Head of Med Research," he said smoothly. "I was ordered to report to you and was told you were here."

She jerked her head toward the door. "You've done that. This area is off limits to all but my medical staff."

"Your assistant let me in," he said. "If you wish me to stay out, then I will, of course, comply. In the meantime, would you like a midday meal brought for you?"

"Yes, for both of us. We'll be here all day. Now go."

Inclining his head, he left.

"You shouldn't have let him in," she said, moving over to the computer interfaces. "I want him kept out of here in future."

Na'qui gave her a surprised look. "You don't usually react so strongly to people, Doctor."

"He was Chy'qui's steward, I don't trust him."

"I'll see he's kept out, then. What have we got on that's going to keep us so busy in here today? I thought you planned to wake that General of yours."

"He isn't mine," Zayshul said, sitting down at one of the vid screens. "I'll have to postpone that for now. Zsoyshuu wants me to terminate most of the M'zullian pre-hatchlings and start up a hundred from General Kezule's samples." She placed her hand on the desk interface and waited while it verified her identity. "We're keeping only fifty, but if we can change their sex, I got a reprieve for another fifty."

"This late on?" said Na'qui, bringing a chair over to sit beside her. "We normally separate those designated female after a day, never mind nearly a week."

"I need an exact start date and time for them," she said, calling up the data on the screen. "Perhaps they weren't all initiated at once. See there," she pointed. "There's ten. They've only been in two days. I can designate those as female. Chy'qui set them up to start automatically so he probably intended to do the same." Her claw tips hit the depressions in the desk, swiftly changing the environment and thus the gender of the embryos from male to female. She continued to scan the data from the breeder units.

"The rest are all too old, Doctor," said Na'qui. "He did start the rest at the same time—see, one hundred and seventy-two hours ago—six and a half days. Even introducing hormones at this stage won't do more than give you males with secondary female characteristics."

"Time is the problem," Zayshul said, clearing the screen to punch in some theoretical data. "If I reduce the stasis field around them, slowing their development down to less than half normal, then introducing the requisite hormones into their placental fluid at a normal rate might reverse the male characteristics. I can increase the field again and let them develop as females. It isn't as if we don't have plenty of time for that. They won't be coming out of the birth tubes for several months."

"Their chances aren't high," observed Na'qui. "You'll have to either breach the seals on the unit to physically check that they're developing properly, or scan them, introducing another element of risk into their environment."

"I'm going to have to transfer them into another unit anyway because of the temperature differences. So do I terminate all one hundred and fifty?" she asked, looking at her. "Or take this chance of keeping them alive and risk compromising the fifty males?"

Na'qui lifted her shoulders in a shrug. "I think your only chance is with the two-day-old ones. They're already in a separate unit. But try, why not? At worst they'll be terminated anyway, at best, some may be successful. We can do a last minute visual scan before they're birthed from the growth tubes."

The ridges round Zayshul's eyes met in the center of her face as she frowned. "I don't want to even think of terminating them at that late stage."

"How about using the purge function to transfer those forty

embryos into fresh tubes in another unit? It would save you having to enter the breeding area and risk contaminating the fifty males."

"Good thinking, but not the purge, it's too violent. The birth expulsion sequence. We'd have to supervise each transfer manually, though. The system is only set up to purge or birth them, not transfer."

"Then let's start with purging the others first. I'll do that while you set up a fresh unit," said Na'qui. "Will you key in my station, please?"

The purge had only just begun when an alarm went off. "Unacceptable energy level fluctuations in stasis unit three-seven," droned the computerized voice.

"Damn!" Zayshul was on her feet instantly as the door into her lab slid open.

Framed in the doorway was assistant medic Zhy'edd. "Kezule," he said succinctly.

"I heard," said Zayshul shortly as she rushed toward him. "Take over here. We're in the middle of purging one hundred and ten of the M'zullian embryos. Tell me you know the procedure!"

"I know it," he said, heading for her vid. "I'll continue monitoring for you."

"Na'qui," she snapped. "With me!"

Left alone, he waited until the door was sealed behind them before pulling a small card from the top pocket of his white coveralls and slipping it into the reader slot on the desk. Then he pressed the inter-ship communicator on his wrist.

"K'hedduk? You should have the feed from her station now," he said quietly. "You were right, she'd just changed the temperature on the hybrids."

"I'm reversing it now. It shouldn't have harmed them. You activate the M'zullian backup container, I'll see to concealing the presence of the hybrids from the data banks," came the crisp reply. "When you're ready, let me know, then I'll transfer your unit to the position occupied by the hybrids. She'll never know the difference."

"What if they get back before we're finished?"

"They won't. I made sure the General will awaken now."

*   *   *

Deep in a shielded room on the lower lab level, automated machines rolled forward to move a sealed unit containing ten breeder tubes. To the naked eye, they would have appeared empty apart from a small, tethering device. But K'hedduk knew exactly what they held, as did Zhy'edd.

A medic was already working frantically at the controls of Kezule's stasis unit, but the electric blue energy field that surrounded the General's body was slowly fading. Zayshul pushed him aside, turning off the alarm, then systematically checked each system that showed a warning light.

"What happened?" she demanded, switching to the auxiliary control system in an effort to bypass the problem and reactivate the field. "I don't believe it," she muttered as the stasis field continued to falter. "The backup as well? Was there a power surge? Did something short out?"

"I don't know," the medic said. "Zhy'edd and I'd just come on duty and were at the other side of the room running the standard shift checks when the alarm suddenly came on."

"Warning. Warning," intoned the computer. "Critical malfunction in stasis field generator. Patient life signs returning to normal levels. Initiate shutdown procedures."

"We're going to have to sedate him," she said, switching off the stasis field. Abruptly, the remaining faint glow of energy faded and died. "Jikulay, get a recovery room ready for him. Na'qui, I want a floater over her now. And call security. Get two guards dispatched here immediately. This patient's a true warrior, he could wake fighting mad!"

Keeping one eye on the General's still form and the other on her controls, she began to lower the cradle that held him down onto the bed below.

"What about the breeding program?" asked Na'qui, running for the floater as she activated her comm link to call for the guards.

"Zhy'edd can cope, the system's automated." The cradle came to a stop, nestling itself into its recesses on the bed. Leaving the controls, she headed for the drug cupboard. "I'll try sedating him. We've got to do the transfer now. I don't have time to revive him." She loaded the pressure gun, then moved over to the supine body of General Kezule.

"Get maintenance onto this unit immediately we're clear of here," she ordered, bending over the General and placing the gun against his neck. "I want to know why it and the backup systems both failed."

Consciousness returned. Instantly alert, his system went into overdrive, senses extended and feeding him information on many levels. Someone was bending over him, pressing a cold object to his neck. He smelled drugs, and the scent of females of his own species. His hand snaked out, grasping hold of her wrist as he leaped from the bed.

As his feet hit the floor, his legs buckled under him. He grabbed for the side of the bed, feeling suddenly sick and dizzy, confused that his body was failing to respond as it should. As if in slow motion, he heard the sound of a metal object hitting the floor and bouncing several times before coming to rest. A wave of light-headedness swept through him but he managed to keep hold of his captive and lever himself upright.

He'd obviously been unconscious for longer than he'd thought. When his vision returned, he found himself staring into the face of his female captive. Shock and fear flooded through him. Abruptly, he let her go, attempting to back away. He was in no fit state to fight a female.

He could hear his blood pounding in his ears—his heart rate was way too high—if he didn't control it, he was going to black out. He risked a quick glance around the room. This looked like no breeding chamber he'd ever seen. More, these females were clothed, and he was naked. He hoped they'd realize that in his present condition he posed no threat, but he doubted it. Females weren't known for their intelligence, only their ferocity toward males.

His legs buckled under him again and as he clutched at the bed with both hands, the females suddenly sprang to life.

"Help me!" called the one beside him as she grasped hold of him.

"I'll get the sedative," said a male voice.

"No! He's no threat to us like this. There's no need to sedate him," he heard her say as she began to support him. "General Kezule, you're safe among your own kind again. Do you remember the Sholans telling you about us?"

He hadn't the strength to resist them as they hauled him upright before forcing him to lie down on the floating bed. He did have vague recollections of several such conversations, but he'd paid little attention to them. He lay quiet for now, only thankful these females and their owner hadn't turned on him.

"Put a blanket over him, Na'qui," the one in gray ordered. "We're from K'oish'ik, General. From the City of Light. You're among your own kind," she repeated as a blanket was put over him and the floater began to move. "You've been unconscious for several days. While you were on Shola, there was a cave-in. You were hit on the head by rubble and went into a laalgo trance to heal. I'm your doctor, and I'm taking you to a recovery room where you'll be monitored for a few days. Do you understand?"

He stared up at her, his mind still trying to cope with the fact that she'd spoken intelligibly. "You're Valtegan?" he asked, trying to sit up. "A female?"

"Yes. I'm your doctor," she said, gently pushing him down again. "We've come a long way since your time, General Kezule. Females are no longer segregated from society and kept half-feral in breeding rooms. You are in no danger from us, I assure you. Just rest for now, everything will be explained to you shortly."

"Seniormost," said Na'qui quietly, trying to catch the doctor's attention. "Your other work, what shall we do?"

"Let me settle the General, then we'll continue. Get a lab assistant to fetch him one of those meals I programmed into the food distributer for him."

"Yes, Seniormost," Na'qui said, falling back slightly.

As they passed out into a corridor, he heard the sound of running feet. He turned his head toward it, trying to see but found his view blocked by her.

"You took your time," she was saying sharply. "The crisis is over. I want you on guard outside his room. No one but myself or Na'qui is to enter or leave. If anyone even asks, you will take them into custody and contact me immediately, no matter what the hour. Is that absolutely clear?"

"Yes, Seniormost Doctor Zayshul," came the reply.

The voice was deeper, the scent male, but subtly different, even from that of the male in the room where he'd wakened. So her name was Doctor Zayshul, and if the title Seniormost meant anything, she had a high rank.

He caught a glimpse of the two guards as his floater passed between them and into the room. Tall, dressed in black, they carried rifles the like of which he'd not seen before. Then he was inside. The floater was brought to a stop beside another bed, then pushed against it till they were flush with each other.

"I can move myself," he said, sitting up to slide across. The one in green, Na'qui, reached out to pull the covers back for him.

The bed had narrow, rigid sides level with the surface of the mattress. More shocks were in store for him as he put his weight on it. He hissed sharply as it gave slightly under him before immediately molding itself to his body and beginning to radiate warmth into his cold limbs.

"It isn't actually alive," reassured Na'qui as she replaced the covers over him. "But it does have a biological component that responds to your physical comfort. The TeLaxaudin designed it for us."

This female was slightly shorter than the other, with the look of those from his time, but like the doctor, she was far slimmer. Confident now that he was in no present danger from them, he began to relax a little. It seemed they intended to treat him well, for now at least. Gently, the bed beneath his upper body began to rise. The doctor handed a remote controller to him.

"Press this when you're at a comfortable level," she said, "and the one next to it when you want to lie down again. You're weak because you've been unconscious, General. You need rest and food to build your strength up again."

"Why the guards outside if I'm not a prisoner?" he risked asking as he stopped the bed.

"For your protection," she said, reaching up to the wall above him. "We have had a few—problems—over the last two or three days. They involved dissidents. We don't want to take any risks with your safety. Once you've recovered, you'll be allocated your own quarters and taken to meet our Captain. You'll even be shown round the *Kz'adul*."

"Am I on a warship?"

Finished, she stood back where he could see her. "No, we're a survey and science exploration vessel. Don't you remember being told that?"

It was a deep space survey craft, its emphasis on medical and scientific research. "I remember," he said slowly. "You have a treaty with the Sholans, and it was threatened by a faction from the City of Light. A faction that involved one of the Emperor Cheu'ko'h's personal advisers."

She nodded her head once. "Yes. As a member of the military caste, and a distant relative of your own emperor, I know you'll appreciate the need for us to protect you."

He said nothing, wondering instead how he remembered all this, when he'd been told it. If he'd been unconscious as they said . . . The door opened, drawing his attention. A female entered, carrying a tray. Had his world become one populated and ruled by females? Were males in the minority? Then he knew that it wasn't so, it was only that the females had finally taken their rightful place as equals alongside the males.

"I know you're used to raw food, General," Doctor Zayshul said, taking the tray from the white-clad assistant, "but we have it cooked. Your stomach can cope with it, but to help you get used to it more quickly, I've made a calmative herbal drink for you."

She put the tray in front of him, taking the cover off the plate and handing it back to the assistant. Several pieces of thickly cut meat, obviously lightly cooked, flanked by a small pile of green vegetables, lay there. Beside it was a widemouthed cup filled with a transparent pale green liquid. The combined scents wafted up to him, appealing despite the fact the food was cooked. A fork and knife were also on the tray. Metal ones. They were either extremely foolish, or they trusted him.

"You'll find you no longer have a need for the la'quo plant," she said, moving away from his bedside. "I have work to do, I'm afraid, General. If you should need me, press the red button on your remote. It will page me. Otherwise, I'll see you presently."

He watched them leave, then returned to contemplating his meal. He picked up the knife, feeling the edge. Sharp, and pointed at the end. He placed it back on the tray. There was so much that was unanswered, including why he wasn't weaker than he was. Then the answer came to him, just as it had before. They'd fed him intravenously. Was everything he needed to know already there, in his mind, waiting for him? No, but there was enough to allow him to cope with this new time, and to reassure him, as a warrior, that he was an honored guest, not a captive.

Hunger growled in his belly, making it tighten into a knot. He picked up the drink first, aware it could be drugged. He sniffed it, then let the tips of his tongue touch the warm liquid. Nothing overt at least. It even tasted quite pleasant when he drank it.

Putting the cup down, he took up his fork and speared a piece of meat before cutting it in two. Lifting the chunk to his nose, he sniffed it before committing it to his mouth. He'd had cooked food before. It was a prerequisite when one received an invitation to the Palace, and he knew why. Raw meat fed the warrior caste's aggression. Each time he'd been summoned to the City by the Emperor, his adjutant had started preparing cooked meals for him several days before they reached K'oish'ik. It was possible to control one's aggression with the judicious use of powdered la'quo, but that had always been an inexact way of doing it, and a device known only to the most senior officers. In its various forms, the drug was used in the food and water supply to control the troops. And the females at mating time. No wonder the use of la'quo had been at the least restricted, if not banned, in this time.

Cooked meat had always tasted flavorless to him so he chewed the chunk briefly, swallowing it as quickly as possible. But the aftertaste it left in his mouth was not as bland as he'd feared. Curious, he chewed the next chunk more slowly, finding it actually enjoyable.

Turning his attention to the room, he saw it was very simple. A small table stood beside his bed, and off to one side was a doorway which presumably led to the sanitary facilities. The door leading out to the corridor was opposite him.

The walls were plain and unadorned, save for the one behind him where the monitors for his bed were displayed. As he twisted around to see them properly, he felt the bed resist him slightly, then, as his movements became more persistent, it gave, pulling away from his limbs and allowing him to move freely. When he stopped moving, it closed around him once more. He was impressed. It was a definite improvement on anything they'd had in his time. He especially liked the fact that it was heated.

Above him, the display panel listed his vital signs and showed their current levels against the norm. His were elevated, but acceptable for a warrior. The writing was still the same, he noted absently, turning back to his meal. With surprise, he saw that he'd eaten everything but the vegetables. When he tried them, he found they were still crisp and had a refreshing flavor. If all his meals were as good as this, maybe there was something to be said for cooked food after all.

As he put his fork down, he suppressed a yawn, palming his

knife under the pillows. Either the food or the drink, or both, had
been drugged, but then he'd expected that. He'd have done the
same had the positions been reversed.

Lifting the tray, he placed it onto the unit beside him and lay
back. His hunger and his curiosity satisfied for now, he was content to let the drug do its work.

"Burn it, but he had me scared back there," said Na'qui as
they stopped just outside Kezule's room. "Weren't you terrified?
I was."

"Not really," Zayshul said, her mind on other matters. She
called the lab assistant over. "I see you're training as a medic. I
want you to take General Kezule his meals from now on. If anyone, especially the steward called K'hedduk says they'll do it,
you're to refuse."

Surprised, the lab assistant looked at her. "But that's steward's
work."

"Not this time. I need someone like you to stay with the General while he eats, answering any questions he might have. When
do you go off shift?"

"I'm due off in half an hour."

"Good. Come to my lab then and I'll give you a sleep tape
to use. It'll brief you on what you need to know about his background, the subjects you can and can't discuss with him. As of
now, you're working with us, and I'll ensure it counts toward
your next grading. Think of it as expanding your clinical observation skills."

The lab assistant narrowed her eyes, the rainbow-colored skin
around her eye ridges creasing. "Are you still concerned over
Doctor Chy'qui's staff? I thought Commander Q'ozoi had had
them all questioned and those loyal to the Adviser were in the
brig."

"Let's say I'm being cautious, Khiozh. It is Khiozh, isn't it?"

She nodded. "Yes, it is. I'll be there. But why would anyone
want to harm the General?"

"I didn't say they did, but he is the last Prime alive who bears
any of the true Warrior caste genes, and we need those."

A touch on her arm from Na'qui drew her attention. "Our
other work," she reminded her. "The purge should be over by
now."

"Na'qui, would you . . ." she began.

Na'qui sighed. "Yes, I'll go and edit Kezule's tape for Khiozh."

Zayshul turned to the guards. "Amend your orders to permit Assistant Khiozh to enter General Kezule's room," she said.

"Yes, Seniormost."

CHAPTER 3

Shola, Zhal-Zhalwae, 23rd day (May)

GENERAL Raiban exploded out of her office at the Governor's Palace, yelling for her aide. "Myule! Where the hell are you?" She looked around the deserted corridor, seeing only the Warriors on ceremonial guard duty outside her door. She turned to one of them.

"Find Commander Rhyaz and bring him to me," she snarled, spitting the name out like it was a bitter snow berry. "Bring him here. I don't care what he's doing, don't return without him!"

"Yes, General," said the Warrior, backing off before turning tail and fleeing down the corridor.

When he'd gone, still fuming, she stalked back through the small inner office usually occupied by Myule to her own room, slamming the door behind her. She hadn't missed the guard's look of panic at being sent to fetch the Brotherhood Warrior Master.

Where the hell was her damned aide? Surely second meal was over by now? She checked the clock and realized Myule had only been gone for a quarter of an hour. Her hand hovered over her wrist comm, but she decided to let Myule finish her meal in peace. A guard had been sent, he'd find Rhyaz.

It was another half an hour before she heard a scratching at her door. "Come in," she called out, knowing from the sound that it wasn't Rhyaz, or Myule. "Well?" she demanded. "Where is he?"

The Warrior stood at attention before her desk, eyes averted from her face. "Commander Rhyaz isn't in the Palace, General. He left."

"Left? He can't have left! He was here an hour ago! What the hell do you mean left? Get him on his personal comm!"

"I can't, General," he said, concentrating his gaze on the wall behind her. "He's left Shola."

"What?"

"He's left Shola, General. His personal comm won't respond at that distance."

"Where? Where's he gone?" she demanded.

"I don't know, General. No one could tell me more than that he'd been met outside the Palace by a speeder and taken to Lygoh Spaceport where a Striker was waiting for him."

"One of my own fighters," she muttered to herself. "One of the two he stole from me!" Then she remembered the Warrior. "Dismissed!" she snapped.

When he'd left, she called Stronghold. Staring at the Brotherhood symbol of the nung flower amid three ceremonial swords only served to anger her further. They were part of the High Command now, they should be showing that symbol, not their own.

The symbol cleared. "General Raiban," said the elderly Brother on duty. "May the sun shine on you this day. How may we help you?"

"Get me Father Lijou," she said without preamble, cutting across his greeting.

"I'll see if he's available, General." The screen blanked to display the symbol again.

When it finally cleared, she was through to Tutor Kha'Qwa. "General Raiban, I'm afraid . . ." she began.

"Get me that damned mate of yours! Five minutes I've been sitting waiting for him! He obviously has time to waste, I haven't!"

"He's not available right now, General . . ."

"Has he left Shola with that misbegotten jegget, Rhyaz? I want to know what the hell's going on, Kha'Qwa! Why did one of my Strikers—stolen, incidently, by you—meet him at the spaceport, then take him off-world without so much as a by your leave to me? I've been more than patient! I said very little when he took the ships I'd agreed to lend and left my crews stranded at Chagda Station and elsewhere. Now on top of this, I discover he's got an alien destroyer class ship, the existence of which he's purposely concealed from me! So just what the hell is going on?"

"Father Lijou hasn't left Stronghold, General," Kha'Qwa said patiently. "He cannot be disturbed right now, that's all. As for the rest . . ."

"I want to talk to him *now*!" Raiban snarled, ears tilting forward as she let her short hair rise in a display of anger. "I don't care what he's doing! I need to know—the High Command needs to know—why he didn't turn this ship over to us for examination long before now!"

"He cannot be disturbed, General," Kha'Qwa said firmly. "As for the ship, I have no idea what you're talking about."

"I'm talking about the ship that escorted the U'Churians back to Jalnian space! And if you continue to prevent me talking to Lijou, by all the Gods, Tutor Kha'Qwa, you'll have me arriving on your doorstep . . ." She stopped dead, her eyes narrowing as she regarded the younger female in the comm screen. "You're lying. He's gone with Rhyaz, hasn't he? They're on their way to Haven, aren't they? What's happening out there?"

"Father Lijou is here . . ." Kha'Qwa began.

"Then fetch him to the damned comm!" she roared. "Prove to me he's there, before I dispatch a unit to bring him to the Palace on charges of aiding and abetting the theft of Forces' property, namely my two Strikers, and of concealing for personal use ships and resources in a time of global crisis . . ."

"General Raiban!" Kha'Qwa interrupted loudly. "Father Lijou is in the temple. He'll be finished shortly. I will get him to call you then."

"It'll take more than prayers to get him out of this," snapped Raiban.

"The Guild Master will call you shortly," said Kha'Qwa, and cut the connection.

The call from Raiban worried Kha'Qwa. She knew some of what was happening, but not all. With their cub due in just over two weeks, Lijou—and even Rhyaz, Vartra bless him—had tried to create an atmosphere of calm around her by protecting her from the details of the ongoing crisis.

Rhyaz had indeed left Shola for Haven, hoping to return before the ships carrying Kusac and his people arrived home. With the treaty now signed and so many of the Brothers gathered there, he was determined to speak to them before they were reassigned. Until now, his presence had been needed on Shola to coordinate the Brothers during the Prime crisis, and help in the defense of their home world had events not ended peacefully. Now was the time for him to be with those who had stood on the front line.

Still shaking from the shock of Raiban's threats, Kha'Qwa pushed herself up from the chair and got to her feet. Her lifemate was in the temple, working on one of the more dangerous meditation techniques. He was not to be disturbed under any circumstances, the guards at the temple doors would see to that. But they would let her in, and her presence there would be enough to bring him to consciousness again.

She turned around too sharply, unbalanced by the weight of the cub she was carrying. Stumbling, she clutched at the desk, her hand landing on a pile of books and papers instead. They gave instantly under her weight, pitching her forward to the floor. Crying out in shock, her outstretched hand hit the ground first, sending a stab of pain up her arm. As she landed heavily on her side, something hard struck her head from above.

the Haven Belt, the same day

In the heart of one of the smaller asteroids in the Haven Belt, the Instructor sat in his quarters contemplating the small incense burner sitting on the floor before him. The meditation had brought him peace, as it always did, though he wished he was home at Stronghold, amid the halls where Vartra had once walked. It had been his own choice to deny himself the comfort of his fellow Brothers and Sisters as a penance and nine years still remained. His reason for being during the coming years was to continue guarding and training those who Slept here at Haven.

A chime sounded, alerting him to the arrival of Lieutenant Dzaou and his unit. He sighed, and reached out for the lid to seal the incense burner. Time to greet them and give them their new orders. Dzaou, for one, would not be pleased. He sighed again. Brother Dzaou was not adjusting quickly to the new circumstances of this era, which was why Master Rhyaz had decided the unit should remain awake for an unlimited tour of duty on Shola. Hopefully, they could be stationed on the Valsgarth Estate, Brother Kusac's home, to get close firsthand experience of the aliens, and the telepaths, living there. Dzaou needed to rid himself of the prejudices that were crippling his outlook or he'd be of no use to the Brotherhood now or in the future.

* * *

"Under T'Chebbi!" exclaimed Dzaou in stark amazement.

"I know about the incident in the sick bay," said the Instructor calmly. "Sister T'Chebbi can rise above it. Can you? You've all been reassigned to her command until you reach Chagda Station. There Brother Kaid's party will transfer from the *Hkariyash* to the *Couana* for the journey down to Shola and their estate. You will then be under his command until further notice."

"Why? Why T'Chebbi and Kaid?" Dzaou asked, interrupting the Instructor again.

The Instructor frowned, eye ridges meeting and ears slanting sideways in a show of annoyance.

"Not that I'm Challenging your orders," Dzaou began hurriedly.

"Of course not. We in the Brotherhood outgrew the need for the Challenge system long ago, didn't we, Dzaou? Suffice it to say that the En'Shallans and their estate are virtually autonomous. Kaid and T'Chebbi were the first to take on the roles of guardians to Carrie and Kusac Aldatan, then the rest of their clan of altered Human and Sholan telepaths. They therefore see to the disposition of personnel on the estate. As I said, it is Master Rhyaz' hope that you will be able to remain there for several months."

"Why are we being kept awake so long this time, Instructor?" asked Zhiko, sitting back in her chair. "With the treaty signed, I'd have thought we'd be Sleeping again. Not that I'm complaining. With all these new alien allies, this looks to be an interesting time."

"Master Rhyaz wishes to reassign some of the Brotherhood personnel currently at the estate out to Haven for training. Within a month, the Prime Ambassador and his party will arrive at the capital, Shanagi. Those who've had dealings with them here will be useful at the Governor's Palace in those first few weeks. There is no better place to become accustomed to dealing with the different Alliance species than on the Valsgarth Estate. These are challenging times," he continued, looking at each of the five sitting round the briefing table with him. "As you have discovered, we have alien Brothers and Sisters now. One, the Human Brynne, is even training at Stronghold under Father Lijou. We must learn to accept them because of their differences, because of the strengths they bring to our people."

"Will we be allowed to visit Stronghold?" Ngio asked, breaking the silence that followed.

The Instructor glanced at him. "Of course. You will each be allowed two weeks' leave to use as you wish. I suggest you spend some time in one of the towns, or the capital, Shanagi, and see for yourselves the people whose lives and liberty you are protecting. You'll be better equipped for whatever the future holds after your next Sleep."

"What if we change our minds and choose to remain awake?"

He turned to look at the only other female present. "You apply to Stronghold for reassignment, Taeo. That decision rests with the Guild Masters and the Chief Instructor." He glanced around the small group once more. "Are there any other questions?" When none were forthcoming, he inclined his head to one side in a Sholan nod. "Then, Brothers and Sisters, I bid you fare well, till we meet again. When you return to Haven, report to Sister T'Chebbi on the *Couana*. You leave in two hours."

"So this is where you're hiding out these days, Tanjo," said a lazy drawl from behind him. "Nice little speech you gave Dzaou. I was impressed, but I don't think it'll work."

At the unaccustomed sound of his name, the Instructor froze. "You shouldn't be here, Tallinu," he said quietly, turning to face the robed figure that lounged by the entrance. "In fact, you shouldn't even be aware of this facility."

"I've known about it for years," said Kaid, unfolding his arms and pushing himself away from the doorway. "Was a time you'd have heard me coming and been waiting for me."

Tanjo wasn't deceived by the younger male's apparently relaxed manner. As he watched Kaid draw closer, he slipped his hands inside the wide sleeves of his robe, signaling his wish to keep the meeting peaceful. "You overrate my abilities, Tallinu. You were always my best student, far better than I was."

Kaid stopped some ten feet away, resting his hand on the back of one of the chairs that surrounded the briefing table. "Ghezu's dead. I killed him at Chezy."

"I heard. Stronghold does keep me fully briefed. I also heard what Ghezu did to you. If only I'd . . ."

"This is the last place I'd have expected to find you, Tanjo," said Kaid, cutting him short as he made a point of looking round the rather austere room. "When I heard you'd left Stronghold, I always imagined you living in more comfortable surroundings. What happened? Was Ghezu less generous than he promised? Or was it fear that drove you to this godforsaken Outpost?"

"Not fear. I requested this post from Father Jyarti as a penance for my involvement in your failure at the Leadership Trials." He said it in a rush, not wanting to be interrupted a second time.

"You expect me to be impressed? Penance is for Vartra. The least you owe me is some justification for what you did." There was no trace of the drawl in Kaid's voice now.

"I have none, Tallinu. My actions that day were indefensible," said Tanjo, flattening his ears and tilting his jaw upward in the ritual gesture of surrender. He could hear his heart pounding. It was one thing to be intellectually prepared to face the male he'd wronged, another to actually do it. "I trusted the wrong people. It was my lack of judgment that lost you the Leadership of the Brotherhood and . . ."

"Trust? Lack of judgment? I never wanted to be Leader, Tanjo! You were the one who persuaded me to stand against Ghezu because of your reservations about him. I *trusted* you, then out of the blue, you betrayed me and conspired with him to put my son's life at risk so I'd fail!"

Shock flooded through Tanjo. "Dzaka's your son? Your natural son?"

"My legitimate son with Khemu Arrazo," said Kaid, his voice hardening. "It's because of Dzaka I'm here. Because you sent him on a mission which could only end in either his death or a kin-slaying!"

Tanjo let out a low moan of horror as he drew his arms free of his robe and clutched the chair beside him. Unsteadily, he sat down. "I had no idea. I swear by Vartra, I had no idea he was your son, or an Arrazo. Had I known, there's no way I'd have sent him after a member of his birth Clan." To be a kin-slayer was to be consigned forever to the eternal torment of L'Shoh, the Liege of Hell.

A shadow fell across him and he looked up to find Kaid towering over him.

"But you did, and at Ghezu's request, on the last day of the trials when you knew I'd have to go after him, even if he'd only been my foster-son," Kaid said, reaching out to take him by the throat.

Tanjo swallowed convulsively, feeling the pressure of the encircling hand. He could sense Tallinu's anger, controlled and deadly. Strangely, instead of fear, he felt an icy calm descend on him.

"You were the senior tutor, Tanjo, in charge of the Warriors till the new Leader was chosen. You knew exactly how green Dzaka was—barely more than a youngling, no age to be sent alone to kill a rogue telepath. You hadn't even briefed him properly about what he was up against!"

An underlying snarl of anger had deepened Kaid's voice, but the hand round Tanjo's throat didn't tighten.

"I didn't send him alone! He was one of three, sent to observe, nothing more!" said Tanjo, stung into defending himself by the accusation. "How could I know that the other two were Ghezu's creatures and had no intention of going with him? You heard them yourself at your hearing—they swore they'd accompanied him! I didn't even realize till afterward that matters between you and Ghezu were still so strained. Why wasn't Dzaka there to defend you, to tell the Tutors' Council the truth?"

"You're lying. Dzaka was alone when I found him prowling the margins of the Arrazo estate," said Kaid, his voice now deathly quiet. "He should never have been included in such a mission at his age. Did you never wonder how I found out what you'd done? That morning, before the final test began, Ghezu and his—creatures—told me what they, and you, had done, then held me at Stronghold until I swore to remain silent about the conspiracy. I couldn't save Dzaka without swearing, and once I'd given my oath, I couldn't defend myself without breaking it! I was prevented from even saying I'd sworn one! I had to kill the rogue telepath myself, then take Dzaka straight to Noni's. Did you really think I'd risk exposing him to you or Ghezu again so quickly, even to defend myself?"

"I didn't know, then," whispered Tanjo, closing his eyes. He should have known, it had been his job, his sacred trust to guard and guide all those at Stronghold until the appointment of the new Warrior Leader.

"But the repercussions didn't stop there, Tanjo. I watched Father Jyarti begin to die the day of my Hearing. His protege had chosen to go running off after a fosterling instead of facing the final test of leadership! No one dared mock me to his face, but he heard it!" His hand tightened around Tanjo's throat, claws just touching the flesh. "Why did you betray me?"

"As Vartra's my witness, Tallinu, I didn't knowingly betray you! Yes, Ghezu did suggest I send your son with Jebousa and Vikkul, but I knew nothing about the rest until two years later, after you were expelled! Ghezu told me the following day what he'd done—how he'd become Leader by changing Dzaka's orders, sending him on his own to terminate Faezou Arrazo. How he'd told you, binding you to silence with an oath you couldn't reveal: how he'd now driven a wedge between you and Dzaka by expelling you and preventing your fosterling from following. I went straight to Father Jyarti, told him everything. With you discredited for a second time, Ghezu had made himself untouchable. We could do nothing, and Ghezu knew it. We couldn't even risk telling Dzaka the truth for fear he'd try to kill Ghezu."

He stopped, putting his hand up to touch Kaid's wrist. "Take my life if you wish, Tallinu. I owe you it for all the reasons you've given, but as Vartra's my witness, I didn't knowingly betray you. I know you won't believe me, but my only defense is that I fell victim to Ghezu's Glamour."

A sharp pain stabbed through his temples and as he cried out in shock, he felt Kaid brutally push his mental shields aside, take hold of his mind, and examine it.

You're a telepath! I should have known! he thought before the contact was terminated.

Kaid let him go. "You were almost as much a victim as we were. Ghezu used you, played you like a fish on a line, then threw you away." He turned away and pulling up his hood, began to walk to the exit.

At the doorway, he stopped and looked back. "You can keep your life, Tanjo, on one condition. We never met here at Haven."

"We never met," Tanjo agreed quietly as he raised a shaking hand to massage his head. "Tallinu, for what it's worth, Father Jyarti never doubted you, even after your expulsion."

"I know."

Shola, Stronghold, the same day

Lijou was dream-walking in Vartra's realm. He'd found the cottage in the sunlit clearing, but of the Entity Himself, there was no sign. When knocking on the door had brought no answer, he decided to look round the lean-to forge.

It was summer and the sunlight shone down through the chinks in the roof, making a dappled pattern on the floor and workbenches. He went over to the hearth, but both it and the ashes were cold. It hadn't been used in several days.

He'd quickly learned the knack of ensuring which season it was when he visited the realm—he only had to fix in his mind the weather he preferred before opening the gateway—but as yet, he'd found no way to be sure of the month, let alone the day. As for whether or not Vartra would be present, that was a matter of sheer luck—or perhaps the will of the Entity.

Idly, he turned to the nearest bench, seeing the tools laid out ready for use. His eyes were drawn to a narrow metal cylinder about four inches high sitting near the far end. Curious, he picked it up. A seam ran round the middle, dividing it into an upper and lower section. Parting them, he saw the top section had a rod, about an inch in diameter, protruding from it. The lower piece had a corresponding hole—and there was something at the bottom of it.

Even more curious, he placed the top section down on the bench then tipped the contents of the bottom part into his hand. With a shock, he realized it was a Brotherhood coin, the token that each junior Brother or Sister was given when they had completed their training and were finally accepted into the Order. Only this wasn't made of bronze, it was silver, and like the original in Stronghold's safe, it had a tiny nung flower at the center of the triple spiral. He was holding Vartra's die and one of His coins.

From behind, he felt a hand clasp hold of his shoulder, making him jump in surprise. He dropped the die to the floor even as his other hand closed round the coin.

"You found it, then," said a quiet voice he recognized. "This one is yours to keep."

Lijou tried to turn around but the hand tightened, forcing him to remain where he was.

"You must leave now," said Vartra as gradually, the light in the forge began to dim. "Don't linger in the temple, return to your room with all speed. Your mate needs you."

"Kha'Qwa!" he exclaimed, breaking free of the Entity's grasp. "What's happened to her?" But there was no one there, only the darkness of the void lit by faint ribbons of colored light.

He spun back around, finding himself looking at the familiar wooden door with the carved triple spiral. Light sparkled off the crystal at the heart of the carving.

"Return in two weeks," said the voice softly from behind him. "I will be here."

Swiftly, he turned again, this time to a blinding glow of light. He put his hand up to shield his yes. "How? How can I be sure I arrive when You say?"

"Picture Me there, then think of the month and day," came the faint reply. He felt a hand touch the small of his back before he was pushed firmly into the light. "I will be there."

He was falling, and instinct made him cry out—seconds before he jolted himself back to consciousness.

The flames in the braziers flickered lazily, casting long shadows across the seated statue in front of him. He blinked several times, uncertain if he was really back in the temple. Then, as he put his hand up to rub his eyes, he dropped the coin and remembered Vartra's warning.

Snatching it up from the floor, he scrambled to his feet and ran for the doors at the far end of the main aisle. Using his wrist comm, he called Yaszho while mounting the stairs three at a time.

When he reached his office, through the open door, he could see Yaszho crouched behind the desk. The metallic scent of blood filled the air, so much so that he could taste it in his mouth. Heart pounding, he clutched at the doorpost, too afraid to enter.

Hearing him, Yaszho looked up, sympathy and compassion clear in his face and in the set of his ears. "Best you stay there, Father Lijou," he said gently. "I called Physician Muushoi. He'll be here any moment."

Lijou pushed himself away from the door and walked unsteadily over to the desk. "How bad?" he asked, surprised to hear how ragged his voice sounded as he tried not to look down at the still form of his life-mate.

Yaszho hesitated, obviously unsure how to answer him.

Lijou could sense his thoughts, knew his aide was wondering whether to treat him as he would a Brother, or an outsider. He looked, then gave a mewl of horror.

"Bad," said Yaszho, pressing a wad of cloth against Kha'Qwa's temple. "She's losing a lot of blood."

"Call Noni," Lijou said, crouching down beside her unconscious body. "What happened?" He reached out to push back the hair that had fallen over her face. *Kha'Qwa—my bright and beautiful love! How could this have happened to you?*

"She must have fallen and hit her head," he heard his aide say as he got up to use the desk comm. "I wouldn't move her, Father," Yaszho warned, grasping him by the shoulder to get his attention as he was about to move her head to a more comfortable position. "Leave her till Muushoi arrives. He should be here any minute now."

"She's bleeding," Lijou said as his fingers came away covered in blood. Then he saw the crystal chiddoe paperweight lying under his desk. He reached out and picked it up. A smear of red marred the smooth surface. "It was on my desk, on the pile of books," he said numbly, looking at the scattered papers and books that surrounded her.

He gave a soft moan as he saw the dark stain on the carpet beside her. Dropping the paperweight, he put his hand on her swollen belly, feeling it ripple beneath his fingers. He realized then that her black robe and the carpet beneath her were glistening, saturated with her blood.

Vartra, I beg you, don't take her from me! Great Goddess Ghyakulla, protect them! I couldn't bear to live without her!

"She's bleeding heavily and has gone into labor," Yaszho was saying to Noni over the comm.

"Get that physician to see to her till I arrive," he heard the elderly healer reply. "Maybe cluttering up my garden with your aircar and teaching Teusi to land it in that bird's nest of yours wasn't such a bad idea."

As they came out of the elevator, Noni saw Yaszho waiting for them outside the infirmary. She didn't need to see the set of his ears to know how serious the situation was. He hurried toward them, impatiently gesturing their escort away.

"Gods, am I glad to see you," he said quietly, but with heartfelt sincerity. "Father Lijou won't let the surgeon treat her properly. You have to talk to him, make him see sense before we lose both Kha'Qwa and the cub!"

"Stop babbling, lad," she said tartly. "Just take me in to them."

The sterile white room was silent save for the quiet rhythmic beep of the monitor. Kha'Qwa lay on her side, the bright titian of her pelt and hair matted and dulled by blood and pain. An infusion unit had been attached to one arm, the other was encased in a splint. The female nurse glanced briefly at Noni as she left carrying a container of blood-soaked dressings.

Lijou was standing still as a statue, looking out of the window. He turned as he heard the door close.

The white streaks at either side of his dark face highlighted the fact that the inner lids were beginning to show at the corners of his eyes. He was in shock himself.

"You look worse than her, Lijou," she said gruffly. "Good thing you left one of those mobile comm links with me. Had a feeling I'd be needing it about now." She turned to Teusi, passing him her walking stick. "Fetch us a drink of c'shar, lad. Plenty of sweetener, the Father looks like he could do with it."

Nodding briefly, Teusi put her bag and stick down on the nearest chair and left.

"What's this I hear about you not letting them treat her?" she asked softly, walking over to the bed to check on Kha'Qwa.

"He wants to cut her open," said Lijou, joining her at the bedside. "Remove our cub, and . . ." He stopped, obviously finding it difficult to continue. "She'd never be able to have any more, Noni. I can't make that decision for her! Muushoi knows nothing about birthing! He's scared, scared of losing them both! So am I! How could I let him operate on her?"

Noni could feel how terrified he was. She put a comforting hand on his arm, feeling him shivering despite the warmth of the room and the thickness of his wool robe.

"Your son needs to be born, Lijou," she said gently. "Or you will lose them both. She's bleeding too much, and in shock. That's why she's gone into labor. Her body is rejecting the cub, letting him die to save her."

"What?" he looked at her, eyes wide in disbelief.

"You want to hold that little son of yours, don't you?" she said, her voice a low, persuasive purr. "He's waited a long time to be with you. You wouldn't deny him that, would you?"

"A son?"

The door opened again but Lijou didn't notice it. As Teusi appeared at her elbow holding a mug of c'shar, Noni gently reached for Lijou's mind. Taking advantage of his distraction, slowly and carefully, she slipped past his mental shields.

Tightening her grip on his arm, Noni drew Lijou back a few steps from the bed. "You're tired," she said, taking the mug from

Teusi and holding it out to him. "A drink will make you feel better."

"It's a son?" asked Lijou, never taking his eyes from her face as automatically he took the mug from her and raised it to his lips.

"Oh, yes. A healthy boy," she said, keeping her voice low as she watched the priest drink. "He'll have your eyes and her coloring. You take your drink and go with Teusi now. We'll call you when the berran's arrived."

Lijou lowered the mug. "But Kha'Qwa . . ."

"Will be fine. You finish that drink and go with Teusi. Let me do what I must," she purred, letting him go with her hand and mind as she saw his eyes begin to take on a glassy look.

He nodded, raising the mug and draining it before handing it to Teusi. "You do what you must," he said slowly, letting the youth take him by the arm and lead him toward the door.

The drug Teusi had used, coupled with the suggestion she'd planted in his mind, would make him sleep for several hours. Dismissing him from her thoughts, she turned her attention to Kha'Qwa.

The door had no sooner shut than a voice from behind her demanded, "What did you do to him?"

She turned and glared at the physician. "None of your damned business," she snapped. "You got that operating theater of yours ready?"

"Yes, but . . ."

"I've been sent for to birth this cub, and by the Gods, that's what I'm going to do," she snarled. "You got a problem with that?"

"I can't operate without Father Lijou's permission . . ."

Noni stared at the physician. "You heard him say I was to do what I must, didn't you?" she demanded.

"Yes, but you've done something to him!"

With her free hand she reached out and grasped hold of him by the front of his blue medic's tunic, pulling him forward till they were almost nose to nose. "I'll be doing something to you in a minute! Now, will you give me the medical knowledge I need, or do I have to go into your mind and take it by force? We haven't got much time, Muushoi, so make the right decision now!"

"You can't operate on her!" he said, trying to remove her hand.

"Says who?" snarled Noni, flexing her claws till the physician yelped. "I want to try and stop that bleeding without butchering her! It can be done, but not by the likes of you! You're too damned scared of failing to try!"

"A skill transfer needs practice! You can't just take the knowledge from me and expect to be able to use it!"

"I've forgotten more about medicine than you'll ever know," she spat, reaching out mentally for him.

the *Couana*, Zhal-S'Asha, 19th day (October)

The cabin that had been assigned to him on the *Couana* was the one he'd used on the outward journey from Haven to Shola five months before. A private ship, belonging to the Touiban swarm led by Toueesut, it was normally captained by their Sumaan pilot, Shaayiyisis. There were two large adjoining rooms, one for the six Touiban males and the other for their six wives, with a third room large enough for Shaayiyisis and his crew of two. Since this swarm worked mainly on Shola, the remaining four cabins had been furnished to accommodate Sholans. It was one of these that had been set aside for him.

He had toyed with the thought of using the Sumaans' room instead, but balked at the thought of sleeping in an oval sand pit, even if it was heated. And the garish opulence of the Touiban suites was not something he could cope with right now. Sighing, he let the door slide shut behind him and approached the bed where his kit lay. Someone—probably Banner—had obviously thought he'd be more comfortable in the cabin he'd used before than in an unfamiliar one, forgetting the state of mind he'd been in during that trip.

Slinging the bag he was carrying on the bed, he sat down, reaching for the larger carryall. Opening it, he pushed aside the spare clothing then drew out a plain wooden box, checking it to make sure it was undamaged and hadn't been tampered with: the wax seal over the lock remained intact. Getting to his feet, he took it to the chest of drawers that stood against the far wall. Placing it inside one of the smaller drawers, he locked it then removed and pocketed the key. That done, he returned to his bed, and stripping off his jacket, swept both bags to the floor before lying down.

The bedding was faintly perfumed, a scent he wished he'd forgotten as more memories began to rise from his subconscious. Pushing them back, he rolled onto his side, letting his body relax into the curved dip in the center of the bed, and closed his eyes. He was tired, too tired to be troubled by any more memories.

He woke to the sound of a loud thump and an involuntary cry of pain. Still groggy, he sat up and peered across the room at the crumpled figure of Banner.

"Dammit, Kusac!" the other snarled. "What the hell did you do that for?"

"You know better than to touch me when I'm asleep," he said, his hand automatically going to his neck and finding it bare. Momentarily confused, he glanced at the night table, seeing his torc lying there. A vague recollection of it causing him discomfort while he slept came to him as he picked it up and put it on. "What did you want?"

"Time for third meal," said the older Sholan, picking himself up off the floor and checking his shoulder.

"Third meal?" He rubbed his eyes with his fists, wondering where the time had gone.

"You needed the rest," said the other. "I did check in on you, but you were deeply asleep. I thought it best to leave you since I know you came directly from Stronghold." He hesitated as Kusac swung his feet over the edge of the bed and got up. "Has Carrie had the cub?" he asked carefully.

"Yes," he said brusquely. Then belatedly, "A daughter. Born at sunrise."

"Vartra be praised."

He shot him a look, but there was only genuine pleasure on Banner's face—his Second had no idea what he was carrying. Tugging his tunic down, he headed for the door. "Next time you need to wake me, don't touch me if my torc's off. Use the buzzer on the door, or the comm unit. You know I can't control my responses when I'm asleep."

*   *   *

The evening meal was a quiet one. Since the *Couana* had been set on auto, and the main controls routed to the mess comm unit, they were all able to take a meal break together.

Conversation was sparse and sporadic because by convention, no business would be discussed until after the meal was over, and there was only one question on everyone's mind.

He picked at his food, delaying the inevitable for as long as he could before he had to eventually push his half-cleared plate aside and reach for the jug of c'shar and the remaining mug.

"Where are we going, and why did we steal the Touibans' ship?" asked Dzaou.

"I told you, you'll be briefed in three days, when we arrive at our destination," he said, reaching for the sweetener and powdered whitener to add to his drink.

"Why the secrecy? Who're we going to tell?" Dzaou demanded sarcastically. "I'm not convinced this is Brotherhood business. I think it's some mad scheme of your own."

"We're on Brotherhood business, that's all you need to know for now."

"But stealing a private ship, especially the one belonging to the only complete Touiban swarm on Shola—that's begging for an inter-species incident! You were brought up as a Clan heir, you should be putting Shola's good before anything else. You're a Brother, now, dammit!"

"There won't be an incident, and the *Couana* will be returned unharmed within three weeks," he said, rising. "I find your concern for the Touibans somewhat hypocritical, Dazou, given your past history."

There was a stillness. "What do you know of my past?" asked Dzaou quietly.

"Everything," he snapped, tail swaying in anger. "Don't presume to question me. Just obey your orders." He looked past the tan-colored Sholan to the black-pelted Banner. "I'll be on the bridge, standing watch for the next three hours. Route my controls there. Arrange a roster, two on, four off, every three hours. You're in charge."

*   *   *

Banner watched him leave then rounded on Dzaou. "What the hell are you trying to do?" he demanded. "Goad him into a fight? He's fought a Death Challenge. You willing to stand up to him and risk this mission and your life?"

Dzaou glanced uncertainly at the others but the support he hoped for wasn't there. "How d'you know about the Challenge?" he demanded.

"Because I made it my business to find out about him," hissed Banner, ears laid back. "What's your problem? Did something go wrong back at the 'port?"

"No, but he's unstable, for Vartra's sake! He should be hospitalized, not leading this mission, if it is one!"

"It's a mission, and he's stable, just getting over the TeLaxaudin attempt to cure him, that's all," Banner snapped back before switching his glare to the other three round the table. "Any of you got similar reservations about our Captain?"

"Not me," said Chima, sitting back in her seat.

Jayza hesitated. "I don't know him well enough to have an informed opinion. If not for gossip, I'd have no doubts."

"Then don't listen to gossip," said Banner harshly, getting to his feet and circling the table. "Khadui?"

The comms operator shrugged. "He's the Captain. A taste for his own company is no crime, nor is a short temper."

"He's different, alien compared to the rest of us," said Dzaou forcefully. "Am I the only one who can see how unbalanced he is?"

"You can see what you want, just keep it to yourself and do your job," said Banner, coming to a stop behind him. He placed his hand on the older male's shoulder, clenching his fingers till his claws extended and penetrated through the jacket to the flesh below. "You jeopardize this mission, and it won't be Kusac you'll need to worry about. I'll take you down myself."

Dzaou pulled away. "You made your point," he snarled, rubbing his shoulder and getting to his feet. "But since you're Second, I expect you to act as quickly if *he* gets out of line."

"It won't happen," said Banner flatly, returning to his seat. "Did you get any briefing from Stronghold?" asked Chima when Dzaou and Khadui had left. "I was told to report to you, that's all."

Banner's ears flicked back then raised in a negative. "Nothing, except that Kusac would brief us as we approached the rendezvous."

"So we're meeting someone," said Chima thoughtfully, reaching for the jug of c'shar. "How well is he?" she asked, lowering her voice to almost a whisper as she leaned closer under the pretext of refilling her mug. "There was gossip, as you know, out at the Palace, but no one had any facts."

Banner shook his head, a gesture he'd picked up from Brynne and the other Humans on the estate. "He was physically fine when he left for Stronghold, no more—episodes— but we've seen little of him lately. His personality has changed, Garras says, but then whose wouldn't after what he went through, what he lost. I know he refused to leave before the cub was born."

"Maybe this mission is to get his self-esteem back. It would have helped the situation if he'd given us some information about what we're doing out here."

"He needs our support," emphasized Banner, locking eyes with her. "I'm aware that you're attached to Master Rhyaz' staff and your last posting was with Commander L'Seuli."

"He has it," she said softly, raising her mug. "For now."

Stronghold, Zhal-Zhalwae, 24th day (May)

An unfamiliar sound dragged Lijou from his drugged sleep. Groaning, he pushed himself up and looked in the direction of the noise. On a chair beside his bed sat Noni.

"You'll have to wake a deal quicker than that when this little fellow wants his feed," she said. "You and Kha'Qwa got a name for him?"

Lijou stared at her, unable to fully take in what she was saying. "You put something in my drink," he said accusingly, falling back on his last remembered thought.

"I did not," she said, folding back the wrappings round the bundle she was cradling. "What you calling your son?" she asked again, holding the cub out to him.

Automatically, he took it from her. A scent that was still mainly

Kha'Qwa's drifted up to him. "Chay'Dah," he said, unable to look down at the cub that he knew lay nestled in the blanket. His arms tightened protectively round the bundle, holding him close. This might be all that was left of his love. "Kha'Qwa— how is she?" he asked, afraid of the answer.

"Sleeping," said Noni. "You're lucky, Lijou. Had I been much later, we'd have lost them both. You shouldn't have waited for me."

"You let him operate." His voice sounded flat and ungrateful even to him. "I don't mean I'm not obliged to you," he began, but she cut him short.

"No, Muushoi and I did it together," she said, leaning back tiredly in the chair. "Least now I know all that he knows about modern surgery. So does Teusi. I should have done it years ago, but then, I don't have an operating theater or the instruments to use at my place." She turned her head to look at him. "I did what I could, Lijou. Only time will tell whether or not she can have more cubs, but at least she wasn't butchered by your damned physician. Muushoi might be good at stapling wounds and setting limbs, but he knows nothing about birthing."

He felt a movement against his chest and a tiny mewl broke the silence before he could speak.

"You going to look at your son or not?" Noni asked, sitting up again.

He looked down, lost for words as he watched the tiny face, eyes closed and ears tightly furled, turning blindly around. Balancing the cub in the crook of one arm, tentatively he touched a fingertip to the fine ginger down on the infant's face. Immediately the head turned toward him, and as the cub mewled again, he felt his son's mind reaching for his.

"Chay'Dah," he said softly as their minds touched. "You were right, Noni. He's got Kha'Qwa's coloring."

She sniffed. "I'm always right. Now, shall we go see that mate of yours? She should be waking about now."

He tore his gaze away from his son. "I thought she'd only just had surgery."

"That was several hours ago," Noni said, grasping her stick and using it to help lever herself to her feet. "Yesterday, in fact. That cub of yours needs to be fed, Lijou. He's refused everything but a sip of water so far."

"You did put something in my drink!"

"No, I didn't. Teusi did. You were in no fit state to make the decisions needing to be made. I'm sorry, but I had to do what was best for Kha'Qwa and that little mite there."

Lijou felt a gentle vibration against his chest and realized his son was purring. He began to smile, all thoughts of being angry with Noni vanishing at the wonder of this small scrap of new life that he held in his arms. Carefully, he slid himself toward the edge of the bed and lowered his legs to the floor.

"She looks a lot better now," said Noni as she waited for him to get up. "They cleaned her up a bit once she came round from the anesthetic."

"Is she all right?" he asked again as he followed her to the door.

"She'll be fine, but you'd best get one of the villagers up here to help her nurse him. She won't be doing much of anything for a few weeks if she's to heal properly. And she's got a broken arm."

"She's got me to help," he said, following her out into the corridor.

"And you got a guild to run, as well as your mate to look after, Lijou. I know a couple of females from the village that'd be just right for the job. You need someone who's a mother, not one of the Sisters from here."

He sighed, remembering what Dhaika had said about arguing with Noni. Losing was not a concept she knew anything about. "Would you arrange it for me, then, Noni?"

She glanced at him over her shoulder as she opened the door into Kha'Qwa's room. "You're learning some sense," she said approvingly.

Kha'Qwa was sitting propped up among a pile of pillows. She opened her eyes as she heard him enter. As he hurried over to her side, her mouth lowered in a faint smile.

"I feared I'd lost you," he said, barely able to speak through a throat tight with emotion. "How do you feel? Are you in pain? Is there anything I can do for you?"

"I'm fine," she said, her voice slightly slurred from the analgesics as she reached up to touch him. "Teusi says we have a son."

The cub had suddenly begun to mewl again, a high-pitched, insistent sound this time. Bending, Lijou passed his bundle carefully to her.

"See for yourself," he said softly as he helped her settle the cub in the crook of her uninjured arm.

About an hour later, a low chime announced a presence outside the door of Noni's and Teusi's suite.

Noni cracked an eyelid at her apprentice. He was a typical young Highlander, tan-pelted, with rounded low-set ears. Shoulder length hair of the same color framed his oval face. He looked younger than his twenty years. "That'll be Father Lijou, lad. Let him in, if you will."

He got to his feet, then hesitated. "There's no village to visit, Noni. What do you want me to do while you talk to the Father?"

She gave a low chuckle. "You stay with me, lad. About time you were present when I talk to some of the most powerful leaders on Shola. It'll be part of your job, one day."

"Don't talk like that, Noni," he said, his voice suddenly intense, green eyes troubled. "You know I hate it."

The chime sounded again as Noni waved her hand at him. "Don't you fret, Teusi, I got no plans to leave you alone for some time yet. Now answer the door before the good Father breaks it down in impatience!"

Lijou swept in past Teusi, stopping only when he stood in front of Noni. "I just found out who's responsible for Kha'Qwa's accident," he said, voice deep with barely suppressed anger. "Raiban. She called while I was in the temple, demanding to speak to me. When Kha'Qwa said I couldn't be disturbed, she threatened to send her people to arrest me!"

"For what?" Noni demanded, sitting up.

Lijou opened his mouth to tell her, then closed it with a snap, suddenly looking at her uncertainly.

"So she's found out just how large a presence the Brotherhood has. You must have wakened some of the Sleepers," she said thoughtfully, reaching for the mug that sat on the low table beside her.

The Head priest emitted a small, strangled sound, eyes widening. "I don't know what you're talking about, Noni," he managed to say, glancing anxiously toward Teusi.

Noni laughed gently. "You think I didn't know about them, Lijou? They're in Kuushoi's Realm, touched by Winter Herself in their cold sleep. A few dream, like Carrie, but none remember it when they wake." She watched, amused, as Lijou stumbled the few feet to the nearest chair, and groping behind him for reassurance it was there, sat down.

"What do you think I do on the Guardians' Council, Lijou?"

"Same as the rest of us," he said, caught with no ready answer. "Look out for our planet's and species' best interests, irrespective of guild, clan, or politics."

She sighed. "Well, you're still fairly new, I suppose. Guardians are only appointed when one dies or retires, or another is felt to be needed by a majority of us. With one exception." She gave him a long look. "The one chosen by the Entities Themselves. They chose me, just as through me, They chose Teusi as my successor."

He stared at her. "You. Not from either the clans or the guilds . . ."

She flicked both ears in assent. "The bridge between us and Them. When I need to, I go to Their realms, bargain with Them for help. And when They need me, They call me, like over the matter of Keeza Lassah. As for how I know about the Sleepers, as I said, cryo puts them in Kuushoi's realm, doesn't it?"

"The Sleepers," he whispered, ears becoming invisible against his head in shock as he glanced again at Teusi.

"Aye, the Sleepers. I know about them, have done for a long time, as have those before me. The Entities have limits, you know. Only Kuushoi can travel beyond the bounds of our world, and then only through those Sleepers with enough mind-Talent for her to contact. Carrie, now, she's aware in cryo. Her mind still functioned on some level Kuushoi could reach."

"You knew this and kept it from me?" The shock of her duplicity added to the others he'd experienced this day.

"I knew only that Kuushoi had reached her, warned her about the threat to her cub here on Shola, no more, for that was all She knew. Once Carrie was awakened, the contact was gone. You have to realize, the Entities aren't much concerned with us, Vartra being the exception. By the time I knew, I had bigger things to worry about."

"What could be bigger than them and the U'Churians going missing?" he demanded.

"The Pledge's been broken."

"Pledge? What Pledge?" She'd lost him now.

"The agreement between Them and us. The threat to Shola's just begun, Lijou. The Entities are retreating from us so They can be sure of surviving. They want no more contact with us. If Shola falls, then so do They."

"No more contact?"

"Stop echoing me!" she snapped testily. "You heard me well enough! The gates to the realms are closing!"

"Vartra save us!" he whispered, ears flattening to his skull once more. "I thought this treaty with the Primes . . ."

"Aye, pray to Him, Lijou. Even His door has been closed lately." Her voice was grim.

"But He came to me in the temple!" exclaimed the priest. "Warned me to leave because of Kha'Qwa!"

"He did, did He?" she murmured thoughtfully, looking past him to where Teusi sat silently. "That's to the good. I was afraid He'd leave us too. What d'you think happened to Them the last time the Valtegans came here? You won't find it in *your* past, but it's in ours, the legends of the Highlanders."

"I thought you'd given all that information to us when we were collecting what clan and guild records existed for our new historians."

She shrugged, a Human gesture she knew he'd understand. "This isn't for the likes of them. They'd discount it out of hand. When the Valtegans came, they tried to sever us from everything we believed in. Apart from the obvious, which you already know, they tried to change our language, religions, the way we measured the seasons and time—everything that gave us an identity of our own."

"Calendars?" he asked, remembering what Vartra had said. "They changed the calendars?"

She shot him an irritated look. "You're still interrupting me! Yes, calendars! During that time, we were made to worship their Emperor. Temples were taken over, statues smashed. Like the one up at the ruins on Kusac's land."

"Varza," he said absently, his mind still on calendars. Vartra had said he must know *when* to visit him. "I thought the Cataclysm was what broke it."

"It was the Valtegans. That's how many of the lesser Gods and Goddesses were lost to us. By the time the floods and storms stopped, there were few people who remembered any but the Entities. But one new God rose from those times."

"Vartra." She had his attention again.

"The Valtegan idea of their Emperor being a living god was

transferred to Him. The Entities can survive without us, but we need Them. They'll only be forgotten if Shola falls again. But if any Valtegan visits Their realms, They could be destroyed."

"What of Brynne Stevens? He's been to Ghyakulla's realm."

"Through Vartra. She's not dealt with him in Her realm. With the gateways shut, our only contact with the Entities is through Vartra—if He decides to remain with us."

"Is there anything we can do? The Brotherhood has been recognized as a guild of Priests as well as Warriors—I'm Master of the Telepath priests too now. Our devotions to Vartra have never been mere lip service as in some religions. If the power of prayer keeps the Gods and Entities strong, then Vartra is surely in no danger!"

"Two things occur to me," she said. "One is that we have living relatives of Vartra in our time."

"Who?" he demanded.

"The Aldatan family. Didn't Kaid say Vartra bonded to the sister of his father's Leska? And took her name when she inherited the Clan?"

"Zylisha Aldatan. You're right. Kusac is His direct descendant. Is that why Vartra's interest in Kaid?"

"Could be. When you swear, what d'you say, Lijou?"

Startled, he sat back in his seat. "What do you mean?"

"Something wrong with your hearing?" she asked tartly. "What do you say when you swear at something?"

"It depends," he said evasively. "What relevance has that to anything?"

"Dammit, Lijou! What's one of the worst curses we use?"

"Vartra's bones!" he snapped, annoyed by her attitude. "What of it? It means nothing!"

"Oh, yes?" she asked archly. "Considering we burn our dead, why d'you think we say that, eh?"

"How should I know!"

"Take a minute to think, Lijou," she said quietly. "You have Vartra, a living God. Your people look up to Him, follow Him, do what He says. And when the inevitable happens and He dies, what do you do then? Have a public funeral and burn Him, so proving He isn't divine?"

"Vartra's bones!" he swore, appalled. "You mean they *buried* Him secretly?"

Noni nodded. "Not my idea, Teusi's. He was chattering away

as he does," she said, nodding toward the young male who sat patiently a few feet away. "And came out with this idea. Maybe, just maybe, what ties Vartra to Shola is His bones—the fact He wasn't burned."

"We need to find His burial place," said Lijou, getting to his feet and starting to pace. "If we can, perhaps we can persuade Him not to close His gateway." He stopped in front of her. "What exactly do you see as the nature of this continuing threat to Shola?" he demanded.

"Sit down," she ordered him. "Think I'm going to crick my neck looking up at you? The threat is the same—the Valtegans. And our answer is Vartra's bones and the Aldatan Triad—Vartra's descendants."

"But how? What can they do—and against what? We have a treaty with the Primes . . ."

"There're more Valtegans than Primes," she reminded him. "I can't tell yet whether letting them come to Shola will help or hinder our survival, but heed me well, Lijou. The darkness out there—" she waved her hand toward the window "—is thickening!"

"Have you anything in your legends that might suggest where they buried Him?"

"Nothing I know of," she said. "But considering He spent most of his life around these parts, chances are pretty good it's in the mountains."

"Vartra's Retreat! It could be there! Maybe even in the tomb of the sword-brothers! What better place to hide His body than in full view?"

She snorted in disgust. "What you going to do? Open the tomb to find out what's inside and outrage everyone by telling them what you're looking for? Don't be a fool, Lijou! You got to check out your records here. Teusi and I are doing what we can with our stuff, at least we know what kind of reference we're looking for, but another couple of folk to help us would be useful."

"You've got them," he said. "The answer's got to be here or at the Retreat." Lijou's wrist comm buzzed discreetly. He excused himself and answered it.

"General Raiban again, Father Lijou," said the elderly Brother regretfully.

"I'll take it in my office, Chaddo," he replied.

"Any news on Mistress Kha'Qwa, Father? Many of the Brothers and Sisters have been standing vigil in the temple through the night for her and the cub."

"She's fine," said Lijou, his features relaxing. The thought of so many concerned for their safety humbled him. "So is our son. And yes, you may release the news to Stronghold."

"Vartra be praised!" said Chaddo, his ears standing more erect in relief as he cut the connection.

"You're better loved than you know, Lijou. I'll come with you," said Noni, beginning to lever herself out of her seat. Teusi was at her side instantly to help.

"No," he said firmly, waving them back as he got up. "I'll go alone."

She stopped, eyeing him. "Take it easy with Raiban, Lijou. There's trouble enough brewing from her quarter."

"Neither I nor Stronghold will be threatened by the likes of Raiban, Noni, nor will Kha'Qwa. Dammit, she knew Kha'Qwa was pregnant!" he said, heading for the door as the temple bells began to ring out.

"That's a new tune," she said, raising an eye ridge.

"It's what they used to ring when a birth took place here," said Teusi, breaking his silence. "Last time I was here, Yaszho asked me if we knew of one. I'd come across it some time ago when we started looking through our histories."

"I didn't know they planned to do that," murmured Lijou, embarrassed, as he opened the door.

Noni looked at Teusi in respect. "Well remembered, lad." Her eyes seemed to unfocus slightly and she heard herself saying, "Likely we'll be hearing them more often in the years to come."

"We're not accountable to you, Raiban. I'll remind you that the Governor himself gave us a mandate, with the agreement of the High Command, to deal with the threat of the Primes in our own way. We have. Our resources are not common Forces property. We get no funds from central government. For generations all we've been able to afford is your outmoded ships, and it's cost us dearly to recondition them. Until now, you, like everyone else, have been content to ignore us. You had no right to demand my presence on the comm and threaten my mate when she told you I was unavailable!"

"When a member of the High Command leaves Shola without warning in a time of global crisis . . ." she began.

"What crisis?" interrupted Lijou, cutting across her. "We have a treaty with the Primes now, due entirely to the Brotherhood. We escorted Captain Tirak back to Jalnian space as a gesture of goodwill on behalf of Shola, and as thanks for aiding our people when they needed it. Your threats of reprisals against me were directly responsible for my mate's fall. You nearly killed both her and our son, Raiban!"

"You can't blame that on me," she countered, equally angrily.

"I can, and I do," he snarled. "I'll pass your message to Commander Rhyaz when I get the opportunity." He cut the connection, gratified by her final exclamation of anger. Then he called for Yaszho, telling him to contact the *Striker* as soon as possible.

"I took responsibility for sending Master Rhyaz a message as soon as Noni arrived, Father," Yaszho said, checking his comm unit for the time. "I also took the liberty of apprising him of the full situation. He should have received it by now."

Lijou looked at him a trifle uncertainly. "Was it necessary to worry him over Kha'Qwa?"

"He wouldn't have thanked me if I hadn't, Father," Yaszho assured him. "He will see to General Raiban."

Lijou nodded, privately glad that matters had been taken out of his hands while he'd been sleeping off the effects of Noni's potion. "I'm in your debt, Yaszho. I don't know how I'd manage without you. I'm going to the infirmary," he said. "If I'm not there, I'll be with Noni."

Lijou found a stranger in Kha'Qwa's room. She was a female of about the same age as his mate, dressed like one of the villagers. As he entered, she put down the comp pad she'd been reading and got to her feet.

"You must be Father Lijou," she said quietly, her Highland burr very noticeable. "I'm N'Gaya, here to look after your mate and the berran."

Noni has been quick, he thought, surveying her. There was nothing remarkable in her appearance, she looked like any of the villagers who lived in the Dzahai range. He realized he didn't know what he should say to her.

Her jaw dropped in a slight smile. "No need to say anything, Father. Been a day of shocks for you all, so it has. Best let them sleep for now. She needs to heal, and the berran will wake soon enough when he's hungry."

He found himself nodding agreement and backing toward the door before realizing what was being done to him.

"Are you Highlanders all so Talented?" he asked, keeping his voice as low as hers as he pushed her thoughts aside and advanced slowly toward the bed to see his mate. "I don't appreciate being manipulated, N'Gaya. My place is by the side of my life-mate and son. Neither you nor anyone else will keep me from them," he said warningly. Kha'Qwa lay on her side, Chay'Dah held close against her, both of them fast asleep.

"They said yours was a love-match," she said approvingly. "Like as not, we shall get on well, Father. I have no wish to work again for a home where the mate is just an acquisition."

He looked at her again, this time seeing the angle of her ears and the firm set of her jaw. "The Arrazo Clan?" he hazarded. "You raised Taynar, the youngest son?"

She frowned. "I did not. That was all his father's doing. The cubs I raise are not spoiled brats. I hear he has a Leska now. I pity her."

"Don't," he said, looking back at Kha'Qwa and reaching out to gently touch her cheek. "His Leska is Human. A resourceful young female, from what I've been told. They're due back in about a week." Satisfied that all was well, he moved away from the bed. "Have you been given quarters? Is there anything you need?"

"All is being taken care of by your aide," she said. "For now, I'll be staying in this room with Mistress Kha'Qwa. A bed will be set up for me so I can spend the nights here until she's well enough to return to your quarters."

"I'll see a junior is assigned to you in case you should need anything. Did Yaszho give you a wrist comm, show you how to use it?" When she nodded, he continued, "I'll be with Noni. Please send for me when my mate wakes."

She inclined her head in agreement, resuming her seat as he left.

"A telepath, Noni?" he asked as he relaxed back into his chair. "The Telepath Guild requires everyone with a trainable Talent to go to one of the Guildhouses for assessment and training."

Noni looked at him from under hooded lids. "Ah, well, it all

depends on your definition of trainable, doesn't it? We start them
at a much earlier age, but even so, most just couldn't handle the
life down there in the plains. Look at what you do up here in
this aerie of yours with those hunted down as rogue Talents. You
teach 'em, don't you? It's the same with us. I look after quite a
few villages around here, you know. Several years ago I trained
up those who'd do the teaching for me now so's I can concentrate on Teusi. Isn't that right, lad?"

Teusi stirred, and Lijou felt the touch of the youth's mind gently against his for the first time. Not probing, not listening mentally, just a gentle touch that was gone almost immediately. It
was enough for him to realize just how strong and disciplined
Teusi's mind was.

"I think Mistress Kha'Qwa and my mother will get on well,"
Teusi said, mouth opening in a grin.

"Your mother?" He looked from the lad back to Noni.

"You think I'd trust anyone less with your son?" she asked.
"Or place anyone else up here in Stronghold? Even Master Rhyaz
will be able to find no fault with her as your son's nurse."

"You keep your Talented out of the Telepath Guild, don't you?
Why?"

"Not all. I told you the truth. A few are chosen to go, mainly
those better suited to life in the towns and cities, and those whom
we don't want to be part of our community. And the Arrazos, of
course," she said. "As to why, look to the politics of it, Lijou.
The plainslanders do nothing but take from us here, be it minerals as in the past, or people, but they give damned little in resources back. We struggle to make a living from this harsh land.
They don't help us none, so why should we help them? You at
Stronghold get a goodly portion of our people, you know, but
then, you always have."

He could see her mouth opening slightly in a smile, and caught
a sense of gentle amusement from her.

"We see they're taught properly, one way or another, never
fear."

"Does Rhyaz know?"

"I don't tell the Masters," she said. "Don't need to. Usually
they work it out for themselves after a year or two. You know
the book you were given when you took over as co-Leader and
Head Priest here? Well, there's one for the Warrior Master, too.
They both cover the need to see the one in the position I hold

as an ally of Stronghold. Ghezu was the second Warrior Leader to try to keep me out. But the Brothers and Sisters still came to my door."

"Then you're going to take up the offer of running a surgery here?"

She sighed. "Once every two weeks, that's all. I have to, for the lad's sake. You'll be needing him more, and it's right the old ways should be reestablished now we got rid of Ghezu. Enough of that. I want something from you. News of Tallinu and his Triad."

"I had a Brother sent over with the news that he was safe as soon as we had it," he said. "And tried to ensure you were kept updated even when I was at Valsgarth Estate."

"I know, and I thank you for it. But I also know you're keeping something back from me. So spit it out, Lijou."

He hesitated, wondering again if it was better left to Kaid Tallinu to tell her.

"Tell me!" she said insistently.

He did, leaving nothing out, including the fact that Kaid was now Carrie's Leska.

As he did, the sparkle left her eyes and her ears dipped back till they were all but invisible against her white hair. "I wish for all their sakes that events had worked out otherwise. Tallinu worked hard at his Triad, Lijou. What's happened to Kusac will have hit him badly, though he'll try not to show it."

"The trust they built between them is what ultimately gave them the strength to survive, Noni," said Lijou. "Do you think you can do anything to help Kusac?"

"Clan Leader Rhyasha and Physician Vanna have both asked me to see him when they return, but I had no idea the situation was as bad as this. Alien technology worming its way through his brain." She shook her head sadly. "Doesn't sound hopeful. And he's killed using the power of his mind. Was hard enough for Tallinu to train him to kill in the first place. For a Clan Heir, brought up as he was to respect sentient life, he'll find it hard to justify having broken the rules bred into him. That I will probably be able to help him with, but as for the rest . . ." Again she shook her head. "It is possible that he's subconsciously repressing his Talent because he killed, maybe even because of Carrie's Link to Tallinu. He'll be well aware of the potential trouble it could cause them all if his Talent returns. I'll be staying here for the next few days. Get me copies of the tests they ran on him at this Haven place. Now I've gotten Physician Muushoi's experience, it'll help me to understand better what was done to him."

"I can have it for you within a couple of hours," he said.

Kz'adul, Zhal-Zhalwae, 25th day (May)

Kezule woke. He was not alone, the female was there with one of the soldiers. Dressed in black coveralls, the guard wore the gold insignia of the royal house on the left side of his chest. One of the Enlightened One's guards.

He sat up as she walked across the room toward his bedside. "Good morning, General Kezule. How do you feel today?"

"Well," he said, realizing that he did. He turned his neck, rotating his shoulders experimentally. All the small aches and pains that had plagued him since he'd been brought forward to this time had actually gone. He flung back the covers, then realized he was still naked and hastily covered himself up again. Even though he knew—somehow—that his lack of clothing in front of this female doctor wouldn't be construed by her as a threat, a lifetime of conditioning told him otherwise.

Glancing sideways at her, he saw a look of amusement, quickly suppressed, flit across her face.

"There are clothes for you in the drawers of the night table," she said, walking round to the chair beside his bed and picking up a robe. "But since you'll be remaining here until tomorrow, perhaps this would be more comfortable."

He took it from her, wishing she wasn't watching him. It was unnerving, and embarrassing. He slipped one arm into the appropriate sleeve and began fishing behind him for the other. Warring reactions fought briefly, then his temper broke.

"I'm not used to being watched!" he hissed, glaring at her, his crest rising in anger. Why the hell was it that these days, those in charge always seemed to be females?

She took a step back, and he smelled the faint scent of her fear as she turned aside. "I apologize, General. I forgot you aren't used to sentient females." Her voice was low and held a touch of uncertainty.

The guard shifted slightly, hefting his rifle, ready for trouble.

Kezule hissed again, showing his teeth, then continued fumbling his other arm into the sleeve. Wrapping the robe across his chest, he pulled the tie belt round and fastened it. Then he flung back the covers and, pulling the rest of the robe across his nakedness, eased himself out of the bed.

The floor was warm against his bare feet—obviously heated. He stood, finding himself still a little unsteady. He tried to clench his toes to get a grip on the floor with his claws but it was too smooth. As he clutched at the night table instead, her hand was there to steady him.

This time he didn't flinch away from her. Her touch was firm yet gentle, her claws as short as those of the males he'd known in the Court circles, and her scent was . . . different. Not the raw sensuality of the females in the breeding rooms, it was lighter, subtler, yet just as effective. He looked up at her face and as their eyes met, she let him go and again stepped away from him.

"Your strength will come back, General," she said. "As I said yesterday, you've been in a laalgo trance, healing. You need to take some gentle exercise." She gestured to a door opposite. "There's a dayroom through there where you can go to amuse yourself. You'll have access to our library, be able to familiarize yourself with our history since the Fall, or watch some entertainment if you prefer."

"I don't amuse myself." Having said that, he had to admit the library sounded worthwhile.

The rainbow-colored skin around her eyes creased. "Surely even in your day the benefits of leisure were known."

He grunted and pushed himself away from the night table, taking a cautious step toward the dayroom. He managed some four paces before he stumbled slightly, needing to grab the side of the bed for support. This time she didn't come to his aid. He began swearing, damning his weakness in front of her and the guard, wishing now that he hadn't placed himself in the position of having to ask her for help. He knew she was assessing him, and was acutely aware that the impression he was creating was not the one he wanted to make.

He heard her order the guard from the room, and as the door shut behind her, her hand closed on his arm, supporting him.

"Perhaps it's too soon for you to leave your bed."

"No!" he snapped, trying to ignore his automatic response to her scent. He'd been too long away from his own kind, was too vulnerable to her when she was this close. On Shola, he'd had his own female, one of the Emperor's many daughters as a wife. He'd gotten used to having her when he wanted, which hadn't been that often. "I will go to this dayroom. I must get my strength back," he said through clenched teeth as, leaning on her, he took another step.

"In our time, it's no weakness for a male to accept help from a female," she said quietly as they crossed the open floor to the door. "The Emperor's heir travels with us. His mistress accompanies him. Even the Captain has his wife."

"And you?" he asked as she opened the door. "Is your husband on the ship?"

"I don't have one," she replied as they made their way slowly to the easy chairs. "When you're fully recovered, the Commander will take you on a tour of the ship, then you'll be free to go where you wish."

His hand tightened round her arm briefly, then he forced himself to relax his grip. He was tempted, sorely tempted by her, but alien as the concept was to him, she was first and foremost a senior officer on this ship, and second an unclaimed female. And he had no idea how males went about claiming a female in this age.

Once he could hold onto the chair back, he pulled himself free of her and took the last few steps alone. With relief, he almost fell into the seat.

"I'll have Khiozh bring your breakfast to you," she said, coming round to stand in front of him. "She'll show you how to operate the entertainment unit."

He nodded, not fully aware of what she was saying because something else had claimed his attention. It was a scent, very faint, but unmistakable. Rubbing his palm across the arm of the chair, he lifted it to his nose and sniffed it. Pieces of a puzzle began to fall into place.

"You had a Sholan here," he said, hand snaking out to grasp her by the wrist and pull her closer.

"You're hurting me," she said, a pained expression on her face. "Let me go, General, or I shall call the guard back."

"Don't ignore me!" He twisted her wrist until she hissed in pain. "You had a Sholan here, didn't you?"

"Yes. He was a hostage for your return," she said, plucking at his encircling fingers with her free hand.

"His name!"

"General, release me this instant or I'll call the guard!"

He could hear the genuine note of panic in her voice. Common sense prevailed and he released her. He would get nowhere by antagonizing her. "I apologize," he said stiffly as she backed away. "This Kusac, he was one of those who brought me to your time." He had the satisfaction of seeing the shocked look on her face as she rubbed her wrist. "Was he traveling with others, a Human female and another male?"

"Yes," she said. "A female called Carrie and a male called Kaid. You know him?"

"It's not your concern. How did you come by them?"

"We saw their ship being attacked by the M'zullians we were following. We decided to take both ships."

Again the knowledge came to him. "The Empire fell, didn't it? The four worlds split, and now two of them are at war with each other—M'zull with J'kirtikk."

She nodded. "We think they suffered far greater damage than us during the Fall. When they finally regained their capacity for spaceflight, they started a war with each other that has gone on since. We've watched but not interfered. Now, though, it moves in our direction and we need to protect ourselves from both of them."

"What of Ch'almuth, the fourth world?"

"It's still at a low-tech level, no threat to us or anyone. Both the M'zullians and the J'kirtikkians leave it alone."

He grasped the arms of the chair with both hands as he leaned toward her. "How do I know all this? When did I acquire the knowledge?" he demanded. "What have you done to me?"

"Nothing," she said, backing off in earnest this time.

Behind them, he heard the door open and knew by the scent that the guard had entered.

"We use sleep tapes to update our knowledge and learn new skills. It's the most efficient way to do it. While you slept in the trance, we played tapes to you so you'd understand our world when you woke, that's all. They'd begun to use them even in your time."

Sleep tapes. He relaxed. She was right, he remembered hearing about them and deriding their use as laziness, no way for a real warrior to learn skills. Seemed he'd been wrong. The Sholan Dzaka and his mate hadn't been lying when they'd sworn their relatives were missing. The scent Kusac had left was interesting; it had been subtly altered by one of his people—no, by a Prime—to contain a marker. That intrigued him.

He remembered the guard. "You may leave," he ordered, turning to look at him. From the side of his eye he caught a slight movement from the doctor and swung his head back to look at her.

"He stays, General," she said, her voice colder now. "I need to know my staff will be safe in your company. I strongly suggest you make use of the library to fill in what blanks our tapes have left. We could only give you the most general view of the past millennium and a half. You'll find a section on our customs and socially acceptable behavior. Assaulting a female officer is not permissible."

Well, he'd certainly made an impression, he realized as he watched her stalk out, leaving the scent of her anger behind. Definitely not the impression he'd intended to make, though. He found himself noticing how slim she was, and how her hips swayed as she walked. It was hypnotic, exciting, something he'd never seen in the drugged females of his time. She was a potent combination of authority and femininity rolled into one, something he'd never experienced before. He wanted her, and one way or another, he intended to have her.

CHAPTER 4

Haven Belt, the *Hkariyash*, Zhal-Zhalwae, 24th day (May)

"CARRIE! You are being better!" the young Sumaan shouted, bounding over to them as they emerged from the *Venture*. "Captain Kishasayzar not letting me off ship to be seeing you!"

He skidded to a halt a few feet in front of them, his long neck snaking down till his face was on a level with hers. A large three-fingered hand descended heavily on her shoulder, making her stagger slightly as she was enveloped in a gust of his warm, sweet-smelling breath.

Kaid instantly steadied her. "Careful there, Ashay. You don't know your own strength."

The large head slewed round to glance at Kaid, muzzlelike mouth opening in a wide grin. "You joking with me! I like!" He turned back to Carrie, his long, pink tongue flicking out to press itself against her cheek. "Worrying about you, I was," he said, his brow creasing in concern. "Pleasing it is to see you well."

"It's good to see you again, too, Ashay. You've grown, haven't you?" she said, realizing his shoulders were now level with Kaid's head. Reaching up, she patted his arm in a friendly gesture. "I hear you've been showing off your piloting skills on the *Venture*."

"And shooting ones," he said, lips curling back in a wider grin to reveal even more of his teeth. "Was fun, but Jo said be careful, no shooting of *Hkariyash*."

"I can understand why," she murmured.

A guttural voice hissed out a command and Ashay let her go to turn and reply. His head snaked around to her again, an apologetic look on his face. "I have work to do making sure the *Venture* is latched down. I be seeing you later."

Watching him head off round the rear of their shuttle, Kaid shook his head. "I can see Dzaka in him when he was about twenty," he said as they moved off toward the cargo lift up to the main deck. "All legs and elbows. There's no real difference between them, you know. I wouldn't have believed it if I hadn't seen it for myself. T'Chebbi said Kisha had mentioned that he was very concerned for you."

Making sure none of the Sumaan in the landing bay could see her, Carrie surreptitiously wiped her sleeve across her damp cheek. "He reminds me more of a huge reptilian puppy," she said. "Complete with soggy tongue!"

Kaid laughed as he pressed the button and the lift began to ascend. "Puppy love, as you'd say. You should be flattered. I haven't heard of anyone who's been kissed by a Sumaan before. We always seem to see a side of our allies no one else has."

"Not surprising. We have intense relationships with them because we work closely with them in a way no Sholans have done before."

The elevator shuddered to a halt and they got off.

"I'll meet you in the mess in half an hour," said Kaid as they came to their cabins. "Unless you want me to come in with you?"

She shook her head. "I'll be fine. I could do with a shower and clean clothes."

He nodded. "You know where I am if . . ." he began, then stopped, remembering they had no need to tell each other where they were now that they were Linked.

She nodded again, and activated the door. "I'll see you later."

The room felt empty as she closed the door behind her. Twin beds, a night table between them; two drawer units with cupboards below, a large desk with a computer terminal and a door to the toilet and showering room were all it held. There were no personal touches—they'd stowed all their kit away before leaving the ship to join the Jalnian caravan. No one could have anticipated that the outcome of their mission would have been so drastic.

She had no baggage with her. When she'd been injured by Bradogan in the spaceport shoot-out, she'd been taken straight to Tirak's ship. Even when the *Venture* had ferried over medication for her, no personal possessions had been brought. All she had brought with her from Haven were the borrowed black coveralls she wore.

She went to her side of the drawers, unlatching and opening the top one, finding it as she'd left it—full of her toiletries, hair-brush, toothbrush, and the like. Had Kusac sent someone over to collect his things, she wondered, closing it again.

Fearful of the answer, she reached for Kusac's drawer then hesitated. It felt like prying, as if it were a stranger's drawer she was looking into rather than her life-mate's. A task that would have been so natural less than two months ago—dear God, was it so short a time?—now felt like an intrusion into his privacy.

She had to know and tugged it sharply open, sighing with re-lief when she found it full of his tunics. Laying her hand on them, she pressed, breathing deeply, but they smelled only of clean laundry. Slamming it shut, she opened the one below. An overwhelming need to find something that held his scent filled her. Tears she didn't know she was shedding rolled down her cheeks. Finally she found what she was searching for in one of the cupboards—his favorite olive-green tunic, tried on and soon discarded because it was too tight.

Burying her face in it, she began to sob.

In the mess, Kaid started to his feet, but Jo caught him by the arm.

"I'll go," she said, getting up. "I've been expecting this. She needs to grieve for him and what they've lost. She can't do it in front of you. The wonder is she's held it in this long."

"There's a damper in the room," he said quietly, aware that everyone could feel Carrie's grief. "It's by the door. You'll need to turn it on."

The *Couana* and the *Hkariyash* lay side by side just off the main Haven asteroid. Though both were disc shaped, they couldn't have been more different. It was the color he noticed first—the *Couana* was deep, electric blue, its serial number, name, and other iden-tifying details highlighted in gold.

"Can tell it's Touiban," said T'Chebbi from beside him.

He continued to watch through the pinnace window as it grew gradually larger in the view screen. The main accommodation and work areas were perched in the central area of the disk. The outer edges, where the fuel scoops were located, curved downward like the wings of some gigantic bird of prey. The illusion was heightened by the cockpit bridge with its twin laser turrets.

"Sure you don't want anything from *Hkariyash* for journey? Is last chance," she said quietly.

He shook his head. To do that would make him feel like he was abandoning her, never mind how bad it would make her feel. "I can manage," was all he said.

The pinnace came to a stop inside the tiny docking bay at the rear of the ship. As the hatch doors beneath it began to close, the lights outside came on. T'Chebbi dug him gently in the ribs, drawing his attention to the fact the others were getting to their feet.

He rose, following her into the narrow aisle between the seats, waiting till the air lock was opened. As they made their way through into the cargo area of the *Couana*, he felt the vibration and heard the clang as the landing bay doors beneath the pinnace closed.

Brynne and Keeza led them and Zhiko over to the elevator.

"What's this ship do?" asked T'Chebbi.

"It's purpose built," said Brynne. "The swarm we have on the estate works exclusively on Shola, so it's a small lab ship built to transport them from their homeworld to our solar system. They've got four cabins set up for Sholans and one specialist room for the Sumaan. The other two rooms are for them and their wives. On the lower deck are three labs with their own electronic equipment so they can work on board if they need to."

This roused his interest. "Wives? I thought the females stayed inside the hives on their own world."

"Not this bunch. Apparently we've had a complete swarm from the start, though none of us can tell the males from the females. Toueesut asked Mara if they could live on the estate and set up home there. Garras and your father said it was okay."

"Mara? How's Mara involved with this?"

The elevator came to a stop and Brynne was able to turn his attention to opening the safety gate. "I'll tell you about it later," he said. "Dzaou, you and Maikoi are in the room down the corridor ahead. Zhiko and Taeo, come with us. You're just beyond the lounge area. T'Chebbi, you're next to Dzaou. The galley is right next to you." He indicated the room on his left. "Your room is the first one, Kusac," he said, drawing him round the corner to his right.

"I see Kusac to his room first," said T'Chebbi, following them.

Brynne stopped almost immediately, activating the door for Kusac. "Keeza and I are next door if you need anything," he said.

He hesitated at the door, his hand going involuntarily to his neck to feel for the metal punishment collar. The trip in the pinnace had brought back memories of his flight from the *Kz'adul* to Haven.

T'Chebbi's hand closed on his arm, feeling the faint tremor. "You go," she said to Brynne and the two females from Dzaou's unit. "I see to Kusac now." She waited till they'd left before speaking. "Is safe," she said quietly. "We getting fighter escort home. Nothing can happen this time."

"We thought that when we left Jalna," he said, resisting her first gentle push as she encouraged him to enter the cabin.

The air smelled faintly of Touibans—a light, pleasant smell. The walls were brightly painted, an almost electric blue that matched the color of the ship's hull. A large Sholan bed stood against one of the walls with a night table beside it. At the foot was the usual locker, but there were also a recessed wall cupboard, drawer unit, and a desk with the obligatory comm. To one side, a door led to the bathing room and toilet.

"I can stay here with you if you want. No need to sleep alone if you want company."

He forced himself to look at her, ears lowering in embarrassment. "Thank you, no. Not after our conversation last night."

She put her head to one side in a Sholan shrug. "That was then. Was angry. You should have stayed with them, not come on *Couana* alone. Not good to be alone so soon after release."

"I have to get used to it," he said, walking over to the bed and sitting down. "You go and see to your own room. I'll be fine."

"You need me, use wrist comm, day or night. Is an order. We leave in about an hour. Meet me in mess fifteen minutes after takeoff," she said before leaving.

The faint hiss as the door closed seemed to fill the cabin, making him feel acutely alone. There was none of the subliminal faint white noise of other minds that he was so used to, now there was just silence. He lay back on the bed, staring up at the dark blue ceiling, smelling the faintly perfumed bedding beneath him, and thought of Carrie.

He remembered the first time he'd sensed her mind within his—it had felt as fragile and unsure as that of a cub—like their daughter's had done the day she was born. He'd never feel Kashini's mind again either. J'koshuk should have killed him, it was preferable to being half dead as he was now, cut off from those he loved. He was barely alive anyway. Carrie didn't need him now, Kaid could look after her, and Kashini since he was her Triad-father. Being born as she had been, in full possession of her Talent, she needed a father who was a telepath, not a mind-dead cripple like him. What good would he be to her? How could he help bring her up to respect the minds of others, to learn the necessary disciplines, if he was mentally deaf to her needs? His presence only complicated matters for Carrie and Kaid—dammit, he couldn't even make love to her safely! He was the past, not their future.

Slipping his hand into his robe pocket, he closed it round the tablets he'd taken from T'Chebbi's medikit. Anger filled him at what the Prime doctor and the priest had done to him, causing the familiar tingle at the base of his neck. It grew rapidly stronger till fire flickered throughout his body. Even from beyond death those two mocked and controlled him, he thought, trying to force his mind to calmness and failing. Whimpering softly, he curled into a fetal ball, managing to pull his arm up to his face and bite down on the sleeve of his robe to stifle the sound.

Haven, Zhal-Zhalwae, 26th day (May)

Their footsteps echoed round the central chamber that had been carved from the heart of the asteroid designated H173. On either side of them, serried rows of cryo units, connected by metal gangways, towered above them.

"I hadn't realized there were so many," said Commander Rhyaz, stopping to look at one of the control consoles. "Do you watch them alone, or have you a staff?"

"I watch them alone," replied the Instructor, automatically checking the readouts for that sector. "If I need help, as you know, Haven is only fifteen minutes away. I only have to transmit a security code to the current Captain or Commander, and he'll send the personnel I request. Again, they have the highest security clearance." He looked at the Commander. "Because of my gift, they remember only that they were working on one of the training asteroids."

"It must be lonely out here," observed L'Seuli as they moved off again, this time toward the tunnel that led to the exit.

"I am content," said Tanjo. "It has given me the time and peace for prayer and meditation. I'm not isolated. I'm kept abreast of our Brotherhood news, and that of the Alliance. I have the other Instructors to talk to. Every six months, I awaken thirty of our Sleepers and prepare them for their journey to the nearest training center, then welcome them back when they return. Occasionally, I'm chosen to host a training session here."

When Rhyaz stepped out of the cavern into the brightly lit sick bay, he had to screw his eyes up against the glare. He heard the gentle hiss of the concealed air lock closing. The silence that followed was overpowering after the constant hum of the cryo chamber.

"L'Seuli, I'll join you at the shuttle in a few minutes," he said as they walked through the resuscitation area and down to the initial briefing room. "I'd like a few words in private with the Instructor."

"Thank you for your hospitality and the tour, Instructor," murmured L'Seuli, inclining his head as he took his leave.

Rhyaz waited till he'd gone before speaking. "I acquainted myself with your files before I left Stronghold, Brother Tanjo, and discussed them with Father Lijou."

Tanjo clasped his hands within his sleeves and began to walk slowly toward the outer corridor. "How are the Father and his mate?" he asked. "I believe congratulations are due on the birth of their son."

"He was born three days ago," said Rhyaz. "From all accounts, he's a fine, healthy cub."

"The Good Goddess be praised. I'd heard of their accident. Please tell Father Lijou I will say prayers and burn some incense for Mistress Kha'Qwa's speedy recovery, and for a bright future for their son."

"I will, Brother, but wouldn't you rather tell them in person?"

Tanjo stopped dead, looking at the Warrior Master in confusion.

"You've been here for eleven years, Tanjo," said Rhyaz. "The

Father and I have been going through our records. We believe you have more than atoned for what little culpability could be leveled at you regarding Ghezu's assumption of Leadership. It's time you returned to Stronghold, and the world."

"Are you reassigning me?" he asked, unsure what to think.

"Not at the moment, Tanjo. But we think you should seriously consider it."

"I would prefer to remain, if I may, Master Rhyaz. As you said, if it hadn't been for me, Ghezu would never have become Leader. The misery and loss of life that he caused in the Desert War alone is something I can never forgive myself for. Then there's Brother Kaid and his son, and the distress I caused Father Jyarti in the last years of his life."

"You're taking on too much responsibility, Tanjo. You made one mistake, that's all. One that the majority of people have made with Ghezu at some time or another, namely that of falling under the influence of his gift."

"And look at all the evil that came from my mistake," he said quietly. He flicked his ears in a negative. "No, Master Rhyaz. I have nine years left to do. I wish to serve them out here. By guarding our Sleepers I feel as if I am going some way to paying my debt to our people."

"You know Kaid was here, don't you?"

"I knew," said Tanjo. "I woke Commander L'Seuli's team. I reassigned them to Brother Kaid only three days ago."

"You've no need to fear for your life at his hands. We intend to see he's apprised of the true facts regarding the Leadership Trials. He's a reasonable person. I'm sure once he knows the truth of the matter, he'll hold no grudge against you."

"I'm not afraid of Brother Kaid. There's no need for you to intervene on my behalf. I'm sure he and I can come to our own understanding of the matter, given time. Thank you for your concern, Master Rhyaz, but I prefer to remain," he said firmly, beginning to move on. "My penance is for Vartra. One doesn't negotiate with the Gods, even Father Lijou would agree with me on that."

"Hmm," said Rhyaz, thinking of the way in which Vartra had been dealing with the Brotherhood lately. "The choice is yours, of course, Tanjo. However, we are increasing the number of people here to three. Your two assistants will arrive sometime tomorrow. We're expecting trouble from General Raiban in the near future. This facility, and the others like it, must be kept secret at all costs."

"What kind of trouble?"

"It was inevitable that she and the High Command would discover that we have a fleet of our own and the personnel to crew it. The way I read it, she's going to try to compel us to become part of the combined Forces, which is something we want to avoid at all costs. Hopefully, we can keep the arguments to the Palace at Shanagi—Governor Nesul hasn't forgotten that it was Konis Aldatan who supported him against Raiban and the other members of the High Command as well as Esken when he needed a knowledge transfer to keep abreast of our inter-species politics. But, Vartra forbid, if she should come looking for us out here or at any of the other Outposts, things could get nasty. That's why we're increasing your level of security."

Tanjo flicked an ear in assent. "I understand, Master Rhyaz."

"The Brothers who are joining you are from the Warrior side of our Order. You can also expect new emergency plans drafted by the Chief Instructor to arrive shortly. From now on, you will have a minimum of thirty Sleepers awake here at any given time. They will be your frontline troops. In the event of a possible hostile takeover, you will have a procedure to follow regarding awakening more Brothers and moving the facility deeper into the asteroid belt. The safety of our Sleepers must not be compromised, Tanjo."

Tanjo looked shocked. "I would defend them with my own life!"

Rhyaz smiled gently. "I know you would. Let's pray it never comes to that. As I said, it's hoped we can keep our arguments with General Raiban to the council chamber."

By now, they had reached the small docking bay where L'Seuli waited.

"If you should change your mind about staying here, don't hesitate to contact Father Lijou, Brother Tanjo. Your island of calm is about to become very busy."

"Perhaps the Father is right and I have been alone here for long enough," the Instructor murmured, removing his hands from his sleeves to fold his clenched fists across his chest and bow his head in a salute. "Safe journey, Master Rhyaz and Commander L'Seuli, and thank you for your visit."

*   *   *

"I've spoken to Raiban," said Rhyaz to Lijou. "She wanted an inventory of all our ships and other resources. I refused, and reminded her as you did, that we are independent of the Forces, not under her command. She's not going to leave it at that, Lijou. We're going to have serious trouble from that quarter."

"If my actions have added to our problems, so be it. I will not have that female threatening us like that," Lijou said, a trace of anger in his voice. "What do you plan to do about her?"

"I have no fault to find with your response, Lijou. I agree completely. I plan to return to Shola with all speed. We've a meeting scheduled at the Palace in four days. I've already spoken to Governor Nesul on the comm; we have his continued support, and that of Konis Aldatan as head of AlRel, but I'd prefer to discuss it in person with them both. I need you along to keep a mental ear on the proceedings. An Alliance fleet is being formed, based at Touiba and their colony world, Teesul, also at Shola and our last surviving colony, Khoma. The area is to be constantly patrolled. Raiban was demanding we hand over the *Va'Khoi,* but when I said it was already patrolling near Prime space and could easily take in the M'zullian section, Nesul and the other Ambassadors decided there was no need to put it or us under Raiban's control because of the way we'd handled the Prime crisis. I actually intend to deploy the *Va'Khoi* to Anchorage, and increase our presence there and at Haven since those are the outposts closest to all three Valtegan worlds. To that end, we need to keep many of our Sleepers awake and redirect some of our undercover Forces personnel to those outposts."

"Nesul contacted me yesterday," said Lijou. "He wants ten of our undercover people as staff for the new Ambassador to the Prime world. Doesn't want anyone the wiser as to who they are."

Rhyaz raised an eye ridge. "So much faith in us. I wonder why."

"Simple. Konis Aldatan. Nesul is an honorable male, Rhyaz. He pays his debts."

"Kusac is still a pivotal force in our world," he said thoughtfully.

"And a thorn in Raiban's side. When do we get the first of the technological upgrades that the Primes promised?"

"They left behind a small shuttle outfitted with their stealth technology and the plans for constructing it for ourselves. Our engineers here are on it already," said Rhyaz.

"What about that beam they used to pull in M'ezozakk's and Tirak's ships?"

"We're going to pursue that one, but they have given us an environmental controller that looks suspiciously like the one the Chemerians use—it lets us have individual rooms at different gravities. It occurs to me that those tree climbing so-called allies of ours must have gotten their claws on ancient Valtegan technology too and are keeping it to themselves. Oh, they also left us plans for stasis units. That's going to be useful. They use far less power than cryo units."

"We can't afford to replace every cryo unit with a stasis one," objected Lijou.

"Gradually, we can. But we can ensure all our ships have them. They want our help to train their younglings, so that's the payment I've demanded. It's in our own treaty with them."

"So it is, I forgot. I'm afraid my mind's not been on business lately, Rhyaz."

"That's understandable," said Rhyaz gently. "How are Kha'Qwa, and your son?"

"Both doing well now, thank Vartra," said Lijou, mouth opening in a slow smile. "N'Gaya and Noni agree that if she's doing as well tomorrow, she can leave the infirmary."

"That's wonderful news. I'll be home in time for your son's Validation, then."

"We wouldn't have it without you here."

Rhyaz inclined his head to one side in recognition of the honor. "I'll see you in three days, Lijou. Until then," he said, then signed off.

Shola, Aldatan Estate, Zhal-Zhalwae, 30th day (May)

"Hello, kitling," said Taizia, looking up from her comm unit as Kitra opened the door. "What brings you here so early? I thought you and Dzaka would be shopping for your bonding ceremony."

"We haven't set a date yet. Anyway, Dzaka didn't want me with him when he picked up the torc for me," she said, walking over to the chair on the other side of the desk from Taizia. Looking at her sister, she wondered again how they could be so different—Taizia taking after her father and Kusac with their mid-night black pelts, and herself taking after their mother with a pelt the color of the estate corn in summer just before harvest. She strengthened her mental shields, anxious now the moment had come.

"He wants to surprise you, that's lovely," Taizia grinned up at her. "Give me a few minutes then I'll be through."

"What you doing?"

"I'm helping Mother by copying all the births of the mid-winter festival cubs from the estate books into the database. Thirty-two so far, with another fifteen still to come. Apparently we're also in for a bumper harvest in crops and livestock. Father Ghyan was right, it was a good midwinter dance!"

"The clan flourishes," Kitra agreed, surprised that she hadn't needed to lead the conversation to this subject. "I suppose a lot of the cubs are second births."

"Not many. More are firstborns, actually. That's why I'm help-ing out—all new entries."

"Must be a lot of work, suddenly having a cub."

"Not really, kitling," she said, mouth dropping open in a broad smile as she looked briefly up at her younger sister. "I should know, after all. We're lucky, we have a nurse just as Kashini does and the large nursery here. That's why the estate has a commu-nal nursery, to allow bonded parents to continue working or to give them some leisure time with other adults."

"Dzaka was brought up in a nursery and it was dreadful," she said, toying with the small comp pad on the desk. "He hated it."

"Our nursery is a far cry from the Arrazos', Kitra, I assure you. Why the interest?" She stopped dead, looking up at her. "You aren't! You can't be! Vanna gave you an implant the same day, even though you didn't show up as fully compatible!" She frowned, eye ridges meeting, nose wrinkling. "You didn't remove it, did you?"

"I didn't touch it," said Kitra, irritated, her hand involuntar-ily going to scratch her forearm where the implant was. "Why would you think I did?"

Taizia flicked her ears back, holding them there for a second or two in apology. "I'm sorry, it was unworthy of me to suggest that. I forget how adult you've become. You obviously think you might be pregnant, though, don't you?"

Kitra looked down at the desk and the comp pad, unable to

hold her sister's penetrating gaze. "I don't know, that's why I came to you." She looked up, trying not to tremble. "This must be between us, Taizia. I haven't said anything to Dzaka, or anyone."

"But how could you be pregnant? Surely Vanna checked you before inserting the contraceptive?"

"The genetic test, yes, but that was all. And, as you said, it showed I wasn't yet compatible."

"If your genetic change was rapid, faster than Vanna anticipated . . ." said Taizia slowly. "Hours rather than days, then you could be. Usually the couples are genetically compatible before they Link, but you and Dzaka—it was so sudden."

"And ordained by Vartra," Kitra said quietly. "Dzaka wasn't a telepath, only an empath till then. Remember, Father heard Vartra's voice, too."

"Oh, kitling," she said, getting to her feet and coming round to hug her. "What're you going to do if you are?"

"I don't know," said Kitra, relieved that she'd finally told someone her fears. She clutched her sister tightly as she rested her head against her chest. "But I won't see Vanna about it."

"You must know for sure. You can't just wait. By then it'll be too late to terminate if that's what you decide."

"It's already too late," she whispered, feeling her eyes filling with tears. "It's been nearly two weeks, but I didn't know. It's just a feeling I have. It could be my imagination."

"Too late for you to do anything," Taizia agreed, "but not Vanna. And you must have the implant removed as soon as possible if you are pregnant. You're just so young to be having a cub!"

"Mother was my age when she had Kusac," she said defensively, lifting her head to wipe a forearm across her prickling eyes.

"Mother was fifteen, kitling," Taizia said absently, stroking her sister's head.

"I'll be fifteen by the time it is due!" She stopped, realizing what she'd said and fresh tears began to well up.

"Hush!" Taizia said, giving her a little shake. "We can go see Father Ghyan. He's good at this sort of thing, and you're one of his charges now you're an adult."

*   *   *

The Shrine of Vartra on the Valsgarth estate had originally been a derelict schoolhouse from the days when the clan had been more numerous. A plague, several generations before, had wiped out almost half of the people on both estates. The clan had had no option but to abandon the Valsgarth estate and concentrate on the main Aldatan one—until Kusac and Carrie had Linked and returned to Shola. It would be several years before the En'Shalla Clan needed the services of a separate school building, so in the meantime, it had been converted to a Shrine.

Ghyan looked up as Taizia and Kitra were shown in by one of the acolytes. His curiosity had been aroused when he'd been told that the sisters wanted to see him, and it only took one look at the set of their ears to know this was a matter of some seriousness.

"Taizia, Kitra, always a pleasure to see you," he said, rising to greet them. "Please, take a seat." He indicated the informal chairs by the empty fireplace as he came round to join them. "I thought I wasn't due to see you and Dzaka till tomorrow, Kitra."

Because of troubled relations with the Telepath Guild, Ghyan had taken on the job of instructing the new Leska pairs on the estate. Now that Master Sorli had become Guild Master, that burden was gradually being lifted. Next to Father Lijou, he held the second most senior position within the Order of Vartra, and was known to be being groomed as his successor, both in the Order and the Brotherhood.

"I think I know why you're here," he said quietly, taking the seat beside Kitra.

Taizia surveyed the brown-pelted priest thoughtfully. He was an old friend of her brother's from his days as a student at the Guild. Kusac had gone to him when he'd needed help, that was why she'd brought Kitra.

"Why do you think we've come, Father?" she asked.

Ghyan glanced at her and smiled gently. "That's for Kitra to say, my dear." He turned back to the younger female. "You can speak to me in private if you wish."

Kitra shook her head mutely, sliding closer to her sister on the sofa.

"She came to me, Father. She's afraid she might be pregnant and she won't go to Physician Kyjishi. I heard that you can tell just by looking, even on the same day."

Ghyan regarded the sisters thoughtfully. He could feel nothing on a surface level; both their minds were tightly shielded, even from casual thoughts. "Why won't you go to Vanna? Surely you can't be scared of her?"

Kitra shook her head. "I don't want anyone to know yet. Not even Dzaka. They'll both start making decisions for me, and I don't know what I want to do."

"You're young, Kitra, but not that young," he said, leaning toward her and holding out his hand. Hesitantly she took it. "You have the right to make your own decisions now. You're En'Shalla under the direct protection of the Brotherhood of Vartra, no longer subject to Clan or Guild, only to Father Lijou."

"I am pregnant, aren't I?" she said with a sinking feeling.

Ghyan nodded, gripping her hand more tightly for a moment in reassurance. "I don't think you know yet how much you and Dzaka have been blessed," he said. "Dzaka was only an empath until you and he were forced by Kezule to try and take him back to his own time. You would have succeeded, too, if Vartra Himself hadn't intervened. It took Carrie, Kusac, and Kaid—three grade one telepaths—to bring him forward to our time, yet you and Dzaka would have done it alone."

He watched her face as he let that knowledge sink in for a moment or two. "Did you know that you're descended from Vartra Himself? It isn't common knowledge yet, but Vartra life-bonded to Zylisha Aldatan, sister to Zashou who's traveling back to Shola with Kusac's people. And Kaid is from Noni's kin, a Dzaedoh. So is Dzaka. You and Dzaka represent a bonding of those two families. I believe this was what Vartra intended."

"But I don't know what I want to do yet!" she said, pulling her hand free. "My Father resigned from the Clan Council to avoid a marriage that meant me having a cub immediately, and now this!"

"But you love Dzaka," said Ghyan. "Talk to him, see what he thinks. At the end of the day, it's your decision that matters, but you should tell him. There's time enough for more cubs if that's what you wish."

"He'll persuade me to keep it," she said, tail flicking jerkily on the seat beside her. "Once I tell him, it won't be my choice."

"I think you wrong him," said Ghyan gently. "But you must go to Physician Kyjishi today and have that implant removed. The drugs could well cause harm to your child if you intend to keep it. She won't feel she has to tell anyone if you remind her you are an adult and En'Shalla now."

"I'll see Vanna, but I'm not ready to tell Dzaka yet," she said.

"You may find this could be a good thing for everyone, Kitra," suggested Taizia. "Kusac's due home in a week and you know how worried they are about him. It could give all of us something to look forward to if you decide to keep the cub."

"No one would want me to keep it because of that," she said morosely. "More likely having it'll be another worry to add to the ones they already have."

"A cub that is wanted for its own sake is a blessing from Ghyakulla for us all, Kitra," said Ghyan, sitting back. "It has to be your choice, child."

the *Couana,* the same day

He had tried to integrate with the others on the ship, but each day just brought him fresh reminders of how much he'd relied on his Talent for everything. Conversations were fraught with episodes of him reading the body language of those around him wrongly, especially Dzaou. He wasn't sure if it was paranoia on his part, but it seemed that male was determined to find fault with everything he said and did. It was as if his presence was a Challenge to him. His thoughts kept returning to Carrie and Kaid, wishing that he'd traveled on the *Hkariyash,* then he remembered their Link days and was glad he was on the *Couana.* On top of all this, he could feel T'Chebbi's eyes on him all the time.

He took to staying in his room and sleeping during the day periods, venturing out into the common lounge only at night when he thought the others were sleeping.

He was sitting at one of the entertainment units when he heard the door opening. Since his captivity, his hearing had grown more acute, and he recognized T'Chebbi's footfall even on the carpeted floor before he smelled her scent.

"Is bad for you to isolate yourself like this," she said, coming round to sit at the unit beside his.

"Are you a counselor now, T'Chebbi?" he asked, continuing to read the latest news sheet from Shola.

"I helped Kaid when he went to Stronghold after his time as

Ghezu's captive," she said quietly. "No need for you to go through this alone. He didn't. Had me, then you to help him."

"I'm not Kaid. I don't want company or help. I want to be left alone," he said, voice deepening with the beginnings of anger that he tried to suppress.

"Know that. But are similarities. You both bone-headed about it."

Surprised, he glanced at her.

"Look, you lost your Link to Carrie, but you not lost her. You're the one pushed her away."

"You know why I did," he said, turning back to his monitor screen. "I told you, I don't want to talk about it."

"Need to. Carrie loves you, so does Kaid. He's your sword-brother and she's your life-mate! You're a Triad. Can't turn your back on them."

"You know nothing about it," he said, feeling the warning tingle at the base of his neck as his temper started to flare. "Nothing about how I feel."

"How do you feel then?" she asked after a moment's silence.

"Irritated by your persistent questions," he growled, trying to remember the litanies, anything to push back the anger before it took hold of him. "Just leave me alone, T'Chebbi."

"Are you jealous of Kaid? He had no option. If they hadn't paired, they'd both have died—so would you."

"I know that, dammit!" His hands clenched on the table, claws cutting into his palms. "I'm glad he did, glad he was there, was able to do it, but it should have been me! I'm her Leska, the one who should have protected her, stopped J'koshuk from raping her! It was my fault!" Pain began to flicker up and down his spine as he fought for self-control.

"You couldn't have stopped him," she said gently, reaching out to touch his arm.

He turned to look at her, eyes blazing with anger. "I told J'koshuk about Carrie," he said slowly, trying to push back the burning pain, prevent it from crippling him, and her from seeing it. "Kaid didn't. He kept the codes of the estate from Ghezu. I failed. He didn't."

"You rescued him. If you hadn't arrived . . ."

"He'd have succeeded in making Ghezu kill him!" he snarled, pushing himself up from his chair. "I see my failure every time I look at her! I remember her fear! I *felt* it, for Vartra's sake,

T'Chebbi!" *And later paired with one of them,* he thought with despair. "I can't forgive myself for that, even if she can."

"You can, if you let yourself. If not, then telepath medics can erase it."

He looked at her contemptuously. "You think I want that?"

"You'd forget it happened. If don't want that, then come to terms with it," she countered. "You think they're happy with what happened? That Kaid wanted to step into your place and share a cub with her because he had no option? That causes troubles between them! You cutting yourself off makes it worse for all of you!"

"I can't help that! It would be worse if I were there! They have Link days—I'll never have them again! They have each other—they *love* each other! I saw them, T'Chebbi! Saw them together when they Linked! J'koshuk made me watch!"

Agony coursed through him now. He lashed out at the monitor, hoping to dissipate his anger with a different pain. His fist contacted, smashing the screen which promptly imploded with a loud bang, showering him with shards. Pain lanced through his hand as he staggered back. But it had worked, the anger was gone leaving only the agony in his hand.

"You're bleeding," said T'Chebbi calmly, getting up. "Come with me, I'll dress it."

"I'm all right. Leave me alone," he said shakily, cradling his hand against his chest. He backed off, then turned and headed for the door, shocked by the violence of what he'd done.

His head was throbbing as badly as his hand when he tried to examine it. He was still bleeding copiously, and dabbing futilely at the gash with his towel did nothing except make him wince in pain. Giving up, he wrapped the towel tightly round it. T'Chebbi was right. His continued presence was only causing Carrie and Kaid problems. It would have been better for all concerned had he not survived.

Returning to the main room from the bathing room, he pulled out a small bottle of spirits from the cupboard in his night table. Brynne had given it to him. It was one of several the Human had brought back from the bar at Haven and he'd passed them out their first night on the *Couana* in an effort to lighten the mood. He'd drunk some to be sociable, but there was still plenty left. Sitting down, he fished in his pocket, pulling out the tablets he kept there. The medikits on the *Couana* were kept locked in the sickbay, so he was glad he'd had the foresight to take analgesics and sleeping tablets from the one in their room at Haven when he'd had the chance. Ten still remained. He couldn't sleep without them; his dreams were full of replays of his time on the *Kz'adul* with J'koshuk.

He washed them down one at a time with the alcohol, knowing that he was doing the right thing. With him dead by his own hand, there'd be no guilt for them. He couldn't go on like this anyway, living with the constant pain caused by the implant whenever he felt anger, living without Carrie and their Link. It was a shadow, a travesty of the life they'd shared.

J'koshuk had won in the end, he thought, cradling his hand as he lay back on his bed and stared up at the ceiling, waiting for the welcoming warmth and drowsiness the pills would bring.

Shola, Valsgarth Estate, the same day

"Well, Ghyan's not usually wrong, cub, so let's see what those blood tests show, shall we?"

Kitra nodded, clutching her sister's hand tightly as she watched Vanna go over to the sampling unit.

Vanna sighed inwardly. She should be used to it by now. Granted none of the mixed Leskas were as young as Kitra, and only one or two of the gene-altered Sholan pairs were, but usually they found out in time that they were about to Link and were able to give them the contraceptive implant first. She'd been so sure she'd caught it for Kitra. It was a lesson for the future— never take fertility for granted.

The screen confirmed what Kitra had guessed. "Looks like once again Ghyan—and you—were right," she said, keeping her tone light as she turned back to them. "It's been about two weeks, hasn't it? Then there's no rush to make up your mind. You have at least a month before we need to worry."

"Would it be like Kashini?" Kitra asked. "Part Human as well?"

"We think so, since you both carry part Human genes yourself. That's what being gene-altered is about. Don't let that put you off, though, Kitra. Your cub will look like you and Dzaka. It would take a good eye to tell the difference between our cubs and the pure Sholan ones," Vanna said kindly, touching her cheek in an affectionate gesture. "But then, you know that already, don't you, looking after Kashini the way you do."

The comm buzzed and she excused herself.

the *Couana*, the same day

T'Chebbi surveyed the damage in the rec area and cursed. She'd thought to jolt him out of his self-pity by highlighting the fact that Carrie and Kaid felt bad enough about what had happened, and that his refusal to see or speak to them, or anyone else, made matters worse for them all. Only he hadn't taken it that way. Not that he didn't have good reason to feel the way he did—the revelation that he'd been forced to watch them pairing had shocked her.

Sighing, she went over to the shattered monitor, seeing the amount of blood splattered across the table and remains of the screen surround. He definitely needed medical attention and couldn't give it to himself because she'd prohibited his access to medikits. She'd clean this up then go check on him, give him time to cool down and decide he needed her help in dressing the wound. She could apologize then for being so hard on him. No point forcing herself on him again too soon, he wouldn't bleed to death in the interim.

An hour passed before she pressed the door chime on his room. After several tries, she began to worry and placed her hand on the hand scanner, only to find it locked. At that point, she called Banner on the bridge.

Minutes later, he and Jurrel were dismantling the access plate. T'Chebbi heard a door in the corridor behind them opening and cursed quietly. "Hoped to keep this among our own," she muttered. "Don't trust Dzaou's lot." Right now, it was an effort to maintain her cool exterior.

"It's Zhiko," said Jurrel, glancing over his shoulder as the female came through the iris door toward them. "She's okay."

"Can I help?" Zhiko asked quietly when she saw what they were doing.

"No," said T'Chebbi shortly as the door finally began to slide slowly open. "Go back to bed. Door's jammed, is all." She squeezed in, leaving the other two to prevent Zhiko from entering.

"Nothing to worry about," said Banner, standing in front of the gap. "Everything's under control. Go back to bed, Zhiko."

"You should have been watching him," she said, refusing to move. "He's suicidal."

"You've been listening to Dzaou too much," said Banner.

She snorted. "You think I don't know what I'm talking about? I've seen too many telepaths returned like this after the war. We had a name for it back then, and he's exhibiting all the symptoms."

Banner's face creased in surprise. "I thought only a handful of telepaths were taken during the Desert Clans' war."

Realizing her mistake, Zhiko turned away. "There were, but their symptoms were identical to those suffered during the wars with the Chemerians. There's a sick bay down in the forward lab area. I'm going to get it ready." She turned to leave as T'Chebbi emerged, ears flattened to her skull.

"Get a floater," she ordered. "He's unconscious—taken something with alcohol."

"Told you," said Zhiko, pushing past them then heading down the corridor at a run for the floor hatch down to the lab level.

"There's a floater in the mess," said Jurrel. "I'll fetch it."

"Who's on the bridge?" demanded T'Chebbi, holding Banner back as he made to follow his sword-brother.

"Brynne and Taeo. They can cope."

She nodded and disappeared back into Kusac's room.

"I should have known he'd do something like this," muttered T'Chebbi, pacing the floor of the sick bay. "Shouldn't have goaded him like I did. Only made it worse."

Banner caught hold of her arm, pulling her to a stop. "Sit down, T'Chebbi, you're only wearing yourself out. Better he did it now when you were going to check up on him, than in the dead of night when no one knew. You only brought it to a head, you didn't cause it."

"Still my fault!"

"No. He intended to do it anyway," Banner insisted. "He wouldn't have stolen the pills otherwise. Thing is, what do we do with him now? Jurrel says he's stable, but we all know he'll try again. This was a serious attempt, he'd disabled the door ac-

cess plate on his side. He didn't intend us to find him until too
late."

"Nearly was," she said with a shudder, looking over at the
bed where he lay unconscious, hooked up to life-support systems,
trying not to think of how close he'd come to succeeding. They'd
had to make him vomit, then inject him with a series of drugs
to counteract the ones he'd taken. Even now, he was on a ven-
tilator to compensate for his depressed autonomic functions.
"Wish we had a Sholan autodoc, then we could keep him in it!"

"There's a Sholan cryo unit," said Jurrel quietly, coming over.
"We could put him in that."

T'Chebbi shot him an angry look.

"At least there he's safe," argued Banner. "We wouldn't need
to watch him twenty-six hours a day."

T'Chebbi hesitated. "I call Kaid," she said at last. "Can't keep
it from them anyway. Can I use this unit?" she asked, pointing
to the one on the dispensing counter.

"Should be able to," said Banner, going over to it. "I'll see if
Taeo can route a channel to the *Hkariyash* down here from the
bridge."

Kaid listened to her in silence. "You did what you thought
best," he said quietly. "Is the cryo unit a standard Sholan one?
Can it be removed from the *Couana*?"

She nodded. "Can keep him in it till we get to the med center on the estate and revive him there," she confirmed. "Then return unit to *Couana* afterward."

"Do it. We can't afford to take any more risks with him."

"One more thing, Kaid," she said, slipping into Jalnian so no
one else could understand her. "Are you alone?"

"Yes. Thank Vartra, Carrie's still asleep. What is it?" he replied
in the same language.

"J'koshuk made Kusac watch you and Carrie pairing."

"What?"

"He saw you and Carrie when you paired the first time on
Kz'adul."

A scene flashed before his eyes.

Hands bound behind him, he was being dragged
toward a large window that gave onto the room next
door. The hand holding his scruff pulled his head

painfully back, claws gouging his flesh as he was
hauled to a stop.

"Look, even now they betray you in this act of reproduction!"

He looked, seeing enough to know that one of the
two figures in the bed was Carrie. The other—was
Sholan, that was all he could tell. He turned his head
aside, saying nothing.

A hiss of anger from his captor and he was flung
against the transparent screen, his face pressed
painfully against the cool surface.

"You'll watch till I say otherwise! That is your mate,
linked mentally to you! Would you die for them now?
You're a bigger fool than I thought!"

It had all been there had he realized it—all the clues of their
captivity. The non-retractile clawed hands, the two-way wall, the
sterile, medical feel to the whole scene, the Sholan in bed with
Carrie. Only, in the vision, the captive hadn't been him as he'd
thought, it had been Kusac. He'd seen it through Kusac's eyes.
"Dammit! I'd forgotten that one!" he said, shocked.

"Vision?"

"I saw it happen, only I didn't realize it till now. It was all
there—our captivity, the Primes being Valtegans—only I failed
to recognize it! Even the fact it couldn't have been me seeing it!
Vartra's bones," he whispered. "Put him in cryo immediately,
T'Chebbi. He needs a telepath mind medic as soon as possible."

"You call Vanna or shall I?"

"I'll call her." He glanced at his wrist comm and did a quick
mental calculation. "It's day there. I'll do it now."

"Sorry, Kaid," she said. "Didn't do a good enough job. Got
it badly wrong. It worked with you, thought it would work with
him."

"No, you did what you thought was right," he said again. "You
couldn't know what was in his mind. He did this before, on the
Khalossa, when he thought Carrie was too scared to accept the
Leska Link. I should have remembered that too! Has he gained
consciousness at all?"

She shook her head. "Not what you'd call conscious. Too
drugged-up to say anything sensible. Cursed us a bit."

"You go now. Don't leave him alone for a minute, even when

he's in cryo. Watch that unit carefully. I don't want him conscious in cryo like Carrie was. Get him right under."

She nodded before cutting the connection.

Kaid leaned his chin on his hand and stared at the blank screen, wondering how the hell he was going to tell Carrie.

"Call from the *Hkariyash* for you, Physician Kyjishi," said Ni'Zulhu, head of the estate security.

"What?" she said disbelievingly, glancing round at Kitra and Taizia, hoping they hadn't heard. "I'll take it in my office," she began.

"Don't," said Taizia, coming over. "Take it here. If it's about my brother, I've a right to know."

"You shouldn't assume it's about Kusac," said Vanna.

"Sorry, Physician, didn't realize you were busy. Kaid said you were to take the call alone," prompted Ni'Zulhu.

"I'll take it here," said Vanna, turning back to the screen. Taizia was right: they were entitled to know.

Kaid frowned when he saw Kusac's sister. "This is private, Vanna."

"I've a right to hear," repeated Taizia.

"Vanna," he appealed. "I'm exhausted. It's the middle of the night for us. I don't think this is appropriate."

"It would be more cruel to keep it from them now, Kaid."

"Them?"

"Kitra's here too."

He shut his eyes briefly. "Very well. We'll be at Chagda Station in seven days, Vanna. We'll be transferring to the shuttle *Venture* for the journey planetside. Get yourself set up to receive a cryo unit, and I want a medical telepath standing by."

Vanna's mouth fell open in shock. "But what . . . ? Why . . . ?"

"Remember the *Khalossa*," he said tiredly. "And the files I sent you."

"Stop talking in riddles, Kaid," snapped Taizia. "What's happened to my brother? Why's he in a cryo unit?"

"Taizia . . ." he began, but she cut him short.

"Someone's going to have to tell our parents. It might as well be me. What's happened to Kusac?"

"He's tried to commit suicide," said Vanna, finding her voice.

Kaid had to give Taizia her due: she didn't flinch, though her ears disappeared from sight.

"How?" was all she said, her voice very quiet.

"Drugs and alcohol. He got the drugs from a medikit, probably on Haven. He's stable, but on a respirator until he's strong enough to place in cryo. We can't risk him trying again."

"I'm not equipped for cryo resus," said Vanna. "You'd do better taking him to the Telepath medical center at the Guild."

"No. I want this kept as quiet as possible, and he'll do better coming round in familiar surroundings. The unit's self-sustaining anyway, it has its own resus system. We'll land at the edge of the village. You have a grav sled waiting for us to transport the unit to your medical center, and a room to put it in. We'll revive him there, then you can transfer him up to a ward. I need that telepath medic there to scan him when he comes round. He's gotten himself behind so many mental shields that none of us can get through without forcing a contact."

"Even now?" asked Kitra. "When he's . . ."

"Why didn't you sense what he was doing?" demanded Taizia.

"He's on the *Couana,* not with us," said Kaid quietly. "Most of the telepaths are with me on the *Hkariyash.*"

"He traveled separately from you and Carrie?" asked Vanna incredulously. "That's not like him."

"He hasn't been himself since we got him back, Vanna. I have to go. Carrie doesn't know yet. One last thing," he said. "Tell Noni. Ask her to come to the estate—as a kin-favor."

"Send me what medical files you have on him," she said hurriedly, pushing aside her shock and curiosity over his last request.

"Sending them now," he said before the screen went black.

He didn't have to tell Carrie when she woke. It was there, in the front of his mind, inescapable. She listened anyway, gradually letting her grief surround her like a blanket, making her retreat that little bit more from him and the world around her.

TeLaxaudin ship above Jalna, the same day

He'd waited till his ship was empty before calling the cruiser hovering high above Jalna's surface.

"Skepp Lord," he said, lifting his face briefly upward.

"Your message most timely," said the other, acknowledging him with a gesture showing equal deference. "Able we were to send *Kz'adul* to help. Confirmed was your report. To find them together was not anticipated."

"Was inevitable," said the first. "As you intended, your children roam far. What of their request? Phratry Leaders say new circumstances alter matter. Intervention now of benefit to both."

"More data Camarilla needs before further intervention can be considered. Involvement costly for us both. Must be worth price we pay."

"It can be done? Beyond Naacha's skills alone."

"Matter is of small difficulty only. Repercussions larger. Not forget, we both wish to remain in background. Observe, not do. Intervention likely traceable to us both."

"Have responsibility . . ." the first began.

"To branch, not tree," interrupted the other firmly. "Situation becomes complex, too many variables now they meet. Too much at stake. Discovering past not desired."

"We know better than you what at stake." The first made an impatient gesture. "Phratry Leaders say remind you your children already cost us much in people and resources. Again this your error."

The other regarded him with still eyes. "Matter compiler went missing in jump space. Ship was untraceable, no action could we take. No potentialities flowed from its loss then. Each intervention must be researched, planned, all future potentialities examined. All know this from past experience. No more room for errors say Skepp Lords. Already action needed with sand-dweller returned to *Kz'adul*. Is enough. We wait for now, discuss further at Camarilla. If Phratry Leaders want further intervention, provide proof is necessary; then I support you. You alone of Camarilla in a position to observe and record potentialities for future."

"Not so. I on another mission . . ."

"Abandon it. Manipulate new circumstances." The reply was short, clipped in both sounds and words. "If Phratry Leaders want to aid them, must convince Skepp Lords."

**above Shola, Chagda Station, Zhal-Ghyakulla,
6th day, Ghyakulla's month (June)**

When the *Couana* and the *Hkariyash* reached Chagda Station,
they found two adjacent berths had been cleared for them as requested. Their arrival caused a stir, with both ships' comms constantly barraged by newscast journalists and minor station officials
hungry for news and interviews. In desperation, Captain
Kishasayzar switched off, leaving open only a direct line to the
Station Controller for essential communications. On the *Couana,*
Captain Shaayiyisis did the same. The Sumaan were baffled by
the attention their arrival had generated. As far as they were concerned, their passengers were only Warriors who had done their
jobs. They deserved the respect of others, but not this.

In light of the unwanted attention, Kaid decided they'd transfer personnel between the ships off-station, using the *Couana*'s
pinnace as they'd done at Haven.

Kusac's cryo unit, sealed for spaceworthiness, was loaded into
the *Venture,* then securely lashed down. Seating for six, plus pilot
and copilot, meant Kaid could take all their rescued personnel
down to Shola with him, leaving Banner and Jurrel in charge of
transporting Dzaou and the others on the *Couana.* They would
land in the goods park outside Valsgarth Town and be ferried
home by estate vehicles.

"I don't want a fuss," said Carrie tersely as the *Venture* sped
toward the Valsgarth peninsula. "You told them that, didn't you?"
she asked Kaid as she scanned the land ahead through the shuttle's windshield. The sight of the forests and plains she loved so
much failed to bring her peace—even the thought of seeing her
daughter again was not the comfort it should have been.

Kaid made a minor adjustment before glancing at her. "That's
why we're using the *Venture.* We can land right in the heart of
the estate, at the far end of the village main street."

She nodded, forcing a smile to her face. "They'll be there,
though, won't they? His parents and sisters."

He put a comforting hand on her arm. "Going through all the
reasons why neither of us should feel guilty is pointless, Dzinae," he said quietly. "It's out of our hands now, beyond anything we who love him can do, even his birth family. It's up to
the telepath mind physicians and Vanna."

"I want Jack involved," she said suddenly, seeing in her mind's eye the tall, slightly portly, middle-aged Human doctor.

"Jack?"

She could feel and hear his surprise. "Kusac's part Human, Tallinu. I'm not having him at the mercy of only the Telepath Guild medics."

"There's Vanna."

"She's also Sholan, and it's not her field of expertise," she replied, her face taking on a determined look. "Master Esken may no longer run the Guild, but his attitudes were shared by many of his staff at the medical center. They don't just go away because Sorli's the new Guild Master! I'm not having them encourage Kusac to give up on us!"

"As you wish. As female Clan Leader and his life-mate, your wishes will carry more weight than anyone's."

She sensed his reserve. "Do you disagree with me?"

Kaid began cutting back their speed as in the distance, the hill on the Valsgarth estate began to emerge from the skyline. All commercial air traffic had been cleared for their approach, allowing them to use speeds normally prohibited on their world.

I think you're being overly cautious, he sent. *You forget he's a Clan Leader in his own right as well as the only son of the Clan Lord. Finding medics with the courage to treat him is more likely to be our problem than subverting his will.*

I think not. Between them, Konis, Rhyasha, Father Lijou, and Master Sorli will make sure he has top specialists, regardless of their personal opinions in this matter.

And they will have taken all the necessary precautions to see they support our Triad, replied Kaid. *Trust them, Carrie.*

The village was approaching rapidly now and the whine of the engines increased as Kaid began slowing down to an appropriate landing speed. As they passed over the half dozen or so streets that made up their home, Carrie could see that the village was deserted.

They must all be at the landing site, she thought, tensing as it came into view, but only a handful of folk stood looking up at their approaching craft.

She relaxed a little, but kept her mind closed, fearful of any contact with those below.

Ruth's there, sent Kaid as he gradually lowered the craft to the ground. *She sends that she wants to get Kate and Taynar settled in at her place as soon as possible.*

Carrie twisted in her seat to look back at the passenger area, trying not to let her eyes be drawn to the dark cylindrical shape of the cryo unit behind them. "Ruth's waiting for you," she said to the two teenagers. "You'll like her and her Companion, Rulla. She'll tell you all you need to know for now, help you settle in and make friends on the estate. We'll get together in a day or two."

Kate nodded. "It'll be good to be on firm ground. I thought I'd never see the sky or feel the earth beneath my feet again."

"Neither did I," she said, then turned back as Kaid finished the power-down procedure and switched the engines off.

After the weeks of living with the constant subliminal hum of engines and recycling plants, the silence was almost deafening.

Kaid unfastened his safety restraints and stood up, turning to face the others. "We're home, but we've still got work to do before this mission is finally over," he said quietly. "I want the cryo unit unloaded first. Rezac, I'd appreciate it if you would help T'Chebbi get it ready to move out. Keep the shielding closed. Carrie, you help me with the main hatch. We're going to have to bring the grav sled into the *Venture* to load it. The rest of you, stay in your seats for now, please."

Outside, Taizia clutched her mate's arm. "What if they can't wake him?" she asked. "What if he's gotten worse in cryo?" Her tail began to sway in distress.

"There's no danger of that," said Meral, patting her hand reassuringly. "Vanna knows all about cryo resus, and he can't have gotten worse. Everything slows down almost to a stop in cryo."

"You shouldn't have come, Clan Leader," she heard Vanna say quietly from behind her. "There's nothing any of us can do until he's resuscitated and that will take several hours."

"He's my son, Vanna. Did you think I wouldn't be here?" she heard her mother reply.

Taizia was about to turn round when the cargo hatch swung open and the ramp began to extend. Moments later, Carrie and Kaid appeared in the opening, blinking in the strong sunlight.

*   *   *

It was like walking into an oven after the controlled environments they'd been used to. The heat surrounded her and as Carrie put her hand up to shield her eyes, she heard the sound of clawed footsteps coming rapidly toward her on the ramp.

Her heart sank as she recognized the scent. "Rhyasha," she said as her bond-mother stopped beside her.

The hug was warm, but even through her mental shields, Carrie was aware of Rhyasha's fears for Kusac.

"Vartra be praised you're home with us at last," said Rhyasha, trying to peer past her into the dim interior of the shuttle. Then she was released as her bond-mother laid a tentative hand on Kaid's arm. "Thank you for bringing everyone home safe," she said. Then almost faster than the eye could follow, she darted past them into the *Venture*.

"Is he in there?" she asked, slowing as she advanced on the dark cylinder. Almost reverently, she touched the smooth metal surface with her outstretched fingertips.

From behind her, Kaid gestured to Rezac and T'Chebbi, signaling them to let her be.

"Why is it sealed?" she asked, the tremor in her voice audible. "Why can't I see him?"

Kaid decided the truth was best. "After what happened on the *Profit*, it was safer to have the unit prepared for vacuum. Then if anything had happened to us, at least he'd stand a chance of survival."

Carrie watched Rhyasha's eyes widen in fear as her bond-mother put her hand to her mouth. A sudden movement to her left made Carrie look at the passengers. Zashou had stood up and was staring slack-jawed in shock at Rhyasha. They could have been mother and daughter so close was the resemblance between them. Both had pelts as pale as summer grain, with hair a shade lighter and worn woven into a myriad of tiny braids adorned with beads.

Carrie glanced at Rezac who'd also stood up. Even he was looking from one to the other, bemusement written large in the set of his ears and tail. Seeing an opportunity, she stepped forward, taking Rhyasha by the arm and turning her to face the couple from their far past.

"We have to let them take Kusac to Vanna's medical unit," she said. "We have guests, Rhyasha. This is Zashou Aldatan and her Leska, Rezac Dzaedoh. They're from the time of the Cataclysm. Zashou is kin to us, and Rezac is brother to Kaid."

"Well come," said Rhyasha automatically, barely taking in their presence as she tried to turn back to the cryo unit.

Behind them, Carrie could hear Vanna and the others coming up the ramp with the grav unit. She persevered. "The younglings are Taynar Arrazo and Kate Harvey. They're the Leska couple the Chemerian Ambassador kidnapped. And you've met Jo. She's become third to Rezac and Zashou."

She felt Taizia's mind touching hers, demanding contact, but she ignored it, retreating even further behind her mental barriers till she was no longer aware of her bond-sister. Never, in her worst nightmares, had she thought their homecoming would be like this. It was taking all she had to be strong for her bond-family.

Kaid's hand touched the small of her back, feeding her some of his energy, reminding her she wasn't alone.

Social ritual finally took over and Rhyasha gave some of her attention to the newcomers. "You're all well come to our estates. Taynar, your family will be relieved to know you're safe. Kate, you are most well come. My daughter, Kitra, will be pleased to meet you. There are few Leska pairs of your ages on my son's estate."

Aware of the quiet voices behind her, Carrie knew they were now ready to move the cryo unit. Unable to look, she kept her back to them. Kaid sent to her, telling her to evacuate their passengers now.

Carrie gestured to the civilians, indicating that they could now leave their seats. As they made their way toward the exit, she forced a smile on her face and greeted her bond-sister.

"Taizia," she said, putting her hand lightly on the other's shoulder. Gods, she'd forgotten how like Kusac she was! She had the same almost blue-black pelt, the high-set ears and dark-skinned nose. Thank Vartra Taizia's eyes were brown not amber, she thought, feeling her own start to sting with tears. Looking away, she blinked rapidly a couple of times. "Can you take Zashou and Jo to the villa, please?" she said, shocked at how husky her voice sounded.

Taizia's arms were suddenly around her. "Carrie," was all she said. It was enough: her bond-sister's emotions threatened to overwhelm her.

She pushed herself free, lowering her mental barriers for the first time in days. *Please. Taizia. I'm barely coping as it is . . . Later, please. There's nothing we can do but wait right now.*

Reluctantly, Taizia nodded. *Will you be waiting with him?* she asked, turning to lead the two females away.

We'll see Vanna start resus, then join you, interrupted Kaid firmly, glancing at Carrie as he supervised the guiding of the grav sled under the cryo unit supports. "Carrie, will you introduce the younglings to Ruth?"

Five minutes later, flanked by Kaid and T'Chebbi on one side, and Meral and Rezac on the other, the grav sled emerged, the cryo unit resting securely on top. Carrie and Rhyasha fell in beside Vanna and the two medics she'd brought with her.

Carrie felt strangely disembodied. Events had taken on an almost surreal quality. The heat of early summer beat down on her head and shoulders; a faint breeze blew round her, carrying with it the scent of blossoms. Childhood memories of watching state funerals on television came back to her, images of the family of the deceased walking behind the coffin sprang to her mind, making the dark cylinder of the cryo unit seem even more menacing. She shivered, feeling the emotions she'd tried hard to suppress beginning to well up, threatening to break free.

Cold and calm, Carrie, sent Kaid. *You can manage till we're alone.*

She took several slow, deep breaths, steadying her nerves as she pushed her emotions back deep into her subconscious then rebuilt the wall around them.

Kaid glanced back at her as she took Rhyasha's arm, right ear flicking in acknowledgment of the effort he knew it had taken.

Vanna had adapted a small IC ward on the second floor. Two of the three beds had been removed and replaced with a solid wooden table. While the males manhandled the cryo unit off the grav sled onto it, Carrie stood with Rhyasha at the nurses' station on the other side of the transparent wall, watching.

As soon as it was unloaded, Vanna and the medics set about initiating the resus program.

Kaid joined them outside, leaving the others to remove the grav sled. "It'll be three hours before he wakes," he said. "I suggest we go home, get some food and some rest while we can."

I want to be here when he wakes, sent Carrie.

You will be. Vanna will call us in time for that.

"I want to see him," said Rhyasha, moving away from them toward the doorway into the ward. "I'm not leaving until I've seen him."

"Vanna's lowering the protective shields now," said Kaid, following her.

Kusac lay still, his black pelt dull and lackluster against the bright white of the mattress below him. The dark flesh around his nose and eyes was gray, blanched of color, as was the new scar tissue where the implant had been. His right hand was swathed in a faintly bloodstained bandage.

Carrie swallowed convulsively but the lump in her throat refused to move. This was the first time she'd seen him and she hadn't expected him to look this bad.

Rhyasha let out a low, keening wail and flung herself across the transparent cover.

Kaid looked at Vanna, who gave a brief nod before turning to the treatment trolley beside her.

Anger flared briefly through Carrie. How could Kusac do this to them all? Did he have no thought for how they'd feel? She'd tried, the Gods knew, she'd tried to get him to talk to her, but he'd refused. Then this!

Anger won't help any more than grief will, sent Kaid, looking decidedly ill at ease.

Carrie suppressed her feelings and moved forward to wrap her arm around Rhyasha, making soothing noises as Vanna approached her from behind and applied a hypodermic to her neck.

Rhyasha jumped, turning on them in fury. "I don't need your drugs! I just need my son healed!" she managed to say before her eyes took on a glazed look and she began to sway.

Kaid leaped forward to catch her, lifting her up bodily in his arms.

"Why did you do that?" she asked in a faint voice as she struggled to stay conscious.

"You need to rest, Clan Leader," said Vanna. "You've been living on your nerves since Taizia told you what happened. You've hardly slept or eaten in five days. It's only for an hour or two, no longer. You'll be awake before he is, I promise you."

As Rhyasha's eyes closed and she went limp in Kaid's arms,

Vanna sighed with relief. "Take her to the room next door," she said. "I got it made ready for you to use."

Kaid nodded and disappeared with Rhyasha, leaving Carrie alone with Vanna and the two medics.

"You can go now," the physician said to them. "I'll page you in the common room if I need you."

"I'm so sorry this happened, Carrie," she said, once they'd left. "How are you coping?"

"How do you think?" asked Carrie tightly, turning her back on the cryo unit with an effort. "I'm coping because I have to, because I have a daughter to look after, and Kaid depends on me holding myself together. I don't have the luxury of choice with all those responsibilities—and a cub on the way."

Vanna closed her eyes briefly, ears folding flat in shock. "A cub? But you had an implant!"

"Which the Primes removed, knowing I would conceive," she said quietly.

"Vartra's bones! Were they trying to *breed* you?" Her eyes widened in shock.

"We have our suspicions," said Kaid, returning. "None of this must go beyond us, Vanna. I need you to examine Kate, find out if she was pregnant a few weeks ago, without her knowing what you're doing."

"Doesn't she know?"

Kaid shook his head. "We don't think so. She wasn't pregnant when we left the *Kz'adul,* that's for sure. If she was, we can only pray she aborted naturally."

"But the treaty . . . The newscasts paint the Primes as nonviolent, victims of the same hatred that the Valtegans have for us!"

"They will be, when the Valtegans find them," said Carrie dourly.

"There are two factions on the Prime world, those who want this treaty and those who don't. It was the leader of the latter group on the Prime ship who had Kusac. He kept us apart, and may well have operated on Kate," said Kaid. He reached out to touch Carrie's arm. "We should go now before it gets any later. Kashini is waiting for you and we need to eat and rest for an hour or two before we return."

She nodded, letting him draw her out of the room. At the doorway, she stopped. "I want Jack brought in on this now, Vanna.

I'm not leaving him to some Guild mind medic. And I want to be here when Kusac wakes."

Vanna nodded. "Kaid told me—I wanted Jack involved anyway. And I'll be sure to call you before Kusac wakes."

CHAPTER 5

the *Kz'adul*, the same day

KEZULE was waiting for Doctor Zayshul. He'd arrived early in order to observe the physical recreation area below him. His official tour with Commander Q'ozoi had included a brief visit, but he'd not had the occasion to return to it until now.

Because the meeting was social rather than professional, he was feeling, unusually for him, a shade apprehensive. He'd invested a fair portion of the last ten days pursuing the doctor with little success. She'd meet with him, but only in the company of her friends. While it hadn't furthered his goal, it had afforded him a crash course in the reality of Prime social life on board the *Kz'adul*. Comparing it with all he'd read and watched in the library on the subject, he now knew that it was also representative of life at the Court, which was his eventual destination. This knowledge had been one of the main driving forces behind his pursuit of her: it was to his advantage to have contacts in high places, and she was well placed. Just as his frustration reached its height and his patience was running out, Doctor Zayshul had finally agreed to a private meeting with him and had suggested a visit to the swimming pool.

His vantage point on the observation balcony afforded him a good view inside the open-topped gymnasium. Three fitness trainers were working their way round the off-duty officers, checking that each was following his or her exercise regime. Behind this little enclave, the moisture-covered transparent walls and ceiling of the bathing pool rose almost level with him, giving him a tantalizing glimpse of the environment within.

A cry of pain drew his attention to the obstacle circuit that surrounded the pool and gym complex. Someone had taken a fall from one of the many treelike structures provided for the practicing of climbing skills. A small knot of people was already gathering round the hapless individual.

Two medics emerged from the aid station immediately below him, making their way swiftly to the injured person. He shook his head slowly in disgust. The response of the medics had been instantaneous. Were they so unsure of themselves and afraid of any injury that they needed the area constantly monitored? As soon as the medics reached them, the small crowd began to disperse. Losing interest, Kezule returned to gazing out across the rest of the recreation area.

He'd found the Prime culture baffling at first, totally unlike anything he could have expected of his kind. Then he'd considered all the genetic modifications they'd had to make in order to breed successfully, like using the drones. Now they were, quite simply, alien to him. Once he'd grasped that concept, plus a few other basic facts, he'd begun to understand what motivated them as a species.

Drive and ambition were still there, but right across what he'd seen of the *Kz'adul*'s cultural mix, it had been sublimated and redirected by the need to excel in one's chosen profession. The strongest drive among the civilian officer class—the doctors and scientists who made up most of the nearly seven thousand inhabitants—was in academic excellence.

The Primes were like the intellectuals he'd met at the Emperor's Court in the City of Light on the occasions when either his family, or the Emperor himself, had demanded his presence. They advanced in status through bloodless conquests of mental excellence: matters were discussed endlessly with arguments that never went anywhere or got heated enough for an exchange of blows. It would be interesting to see if the Primes also resorted to assassination as the way to get rid of an intractable superior. If the attempt on Prince Zsurtul was anything to go by, some at least did.

Commander Q'ozoi had spoken no less than the truth when he'd said the lack of the Warrior caste meant their species was now incapable of breeding a body of people with the will to fight. Aggression was completely missing. It was there on the odd, individual level, but not in the species as a whole. Only by implanting volunteers were they able to have any kind of security force, and then it was unreliable. He found it unbelievable that on this heavily armed spaceship there was not one true Warrior. Even those taken from the M'zullian ship, the *M'ijikk,* had had their Warrior capability neutralized in the interests of safety.

He'd seen the remnants of that crew, all thirty-seven of them. There had been eighty-four, but the Primes had culled them, ensuring that only the most aggressive survived. Zayshul had told him their seed had been harvested, and they were in the process of cleansing the racial memories prior to using it to impregnate suitable females. The M'zullians themselves now worked in the docking and cargo areas, instantly identifiable not only by their colored coveralls, but by the small, black implants on their skulls which not only controlled them, but neutered them, turning them effectively into sterile male drones—if such a thing were possible.

He'd hidden his distaste when Zayshul had told him the fate of the M'zullians, keeping his true feelings to himself, aware that his presence and apparent freedom was dependent on the goodwill of his hosts. His rescue from the Sholans had come at a price, but the Primes didn't yet realize that he knew what it was and he wasn't prepared to pay.

He'd lived most of his life among the military, it was what he knew and trusted, his touchstone. For those in the lower echelons, hatched without his advantages of birth, it was a seething hotbed of diverse factions and loyalties. They constantly watched their immediate superiors for the first scent of indecision or bad judgment. Then they'd turn on the hapless officer, rending him apart before turning on each other to fight for which faction's leader replaced him. For higher-caste Warriors like him, related by blood to the Emperor's family, the violence had still been there, but it had been more subtle, ruled by logic and intellect. Self-confidence and force of personality counted for everything if one was to survive the early years, because those qualities attracted followers.

The City of Light, once the capital of their vast Empire, had been carved out of a hostile landscape by the blood and toil of the Valtegan people. From all he'd heard about it now, it had shrunk to a pale, anemic ember of its past glory.

His lips curled in contempt as he looked back to the medics treating their patient in the sanitized obstacle course. In his time, officers and enlisted Warriors both would have been honing their natural skills in far more challenging conditions. Their "obstacle course" wasn't fit for a one-week-old hatchling!

But the Primes' innovative freeing of their female population did have advantages of which he approved. His pursuit of the doctor had forced him to spend time watching the interplay between the two sexes, and he'd come to the realization that though much Valtegan heritage had been sacrificed, there was one Warrior pastime the Prime males had kept—the thrill of the hunt.

He'd been shocked at first to find the females were truly as free and independent as the males: owned only by themselves, they were at liberty to mate out of season and across their own shipboard rank with whomever they wished. They could have as many or few partners as they wished, and he'd seen none that were breeding. It intrigued him, at first against his better judgment, until he'd realized for himself how little mental satisfaction there had actually been for him in the harems of his own time. Similarly, the three females the Commander had sent to him as his personal "guides" to the Prime culture had initially been—absorbing. The memories made him smile. They'd not even waited to see what his inclination was before falling into his bed, but he'd learned much about pleasure from them while the novelty had lasted. In his time, there had only been the dubious thrill that his wife might recover from the sedatives before he was done. Or the drones used by the common soldiers and some officers.

These modern females had to be pursued gently, and with stealth, persuaded by a show of obvious interest and attention to them that one was the ideal companion and mate. The thrill of such a hunt, with the desired goal a prolonged mating with the female of his choice, was what interested him right now. Especially when his quarry was the doctor, and his careful pursuit of her was finally beginning to show some hope of success. It was also the cause for his disquiet. The concept of sentient free females was still very alien to him.

A footfall from behind made him relax his features before turning to acknowledge Doctor Zayshul's arrival. As he eyed her neat figure in its formfitting gray coveralls, he knew that winning her would afford him more personal satisfaction than any campaign he'd planned in a long time.

"Good afternoon, General Kezule," she said, joining him on the balcony. "Are you ready for our visit to the swimming pool?"

"I'm looking forward to it," he lied as they began to stroll along the balcony toward the walkway for the elevator. "I'm curious, though, why you should have one. In my day, our surroundings were far more austere, unless one was on the Emperor's own flagship."

"This is a civilian ship, General, its mission one of science and exploration. We spend many months at a time away from home. We need a few luxuries."

Kezule said nothing, merely stood back and waited for her to precede him onto the walkway.

"Besides," she said with a sideways look, "we have the Enlightened One with us."

"Ah, yes. The Emperor's only heir," he said, keeping his tone light. He'd met the youth the day they'd released him from the sick bay and moved him into his own quarters. A pleasant enough young male, but like all the Primes he'd met so far, lacking the steel that was needed to be an effective ruler. But then, the current royal family had drone genes in their past. It showed in the fact the Emperor had only one son.

"Emperor Cheu'ko'h has refused to take another wife," Zayshul said, in a tone that rebuked him. "I think it's extremely loyal of him."

The elevator door opened as they approached and Kezule followed her in. "His loyalty is, indeed, commendable," he heard himself murmur as they began to descend to the exercise area. He knew the right things to say to impress her—he'd always learned quickly—but sometimes, like now, they stuck in his craw. He preferred a straightforward approach to life, but that wasn't the way these hunts were played.

Zayshul looked sharply at him, opened her mouth as if to speak, then changed her mind.

The temperature in the pool area was hot, with just enough humidity to make it pleasant. A tiled path, meandering its way through beds of various small trees and shrubs native to K'oish'ik, led from the stripping area toward the actual poolside. A genuine effort had been made to re-create one of the lush hot springs from their homeworld. It was a custom followed, not usually so successfully, by every planetary governor, no matter how small the outpost world. Racial memory of these pools was embedded deep in the Valtegan psyche and it was a balm, not only to his

eyes, but to his body and soul. He could already feel himself relaxing as his pores opened and began to absorb the nutrients from
the airborne moisture.

Faint wisps of steam drifted up from the heated mineral water.
Islets and landing stages had been cunningly constructed among
the greenery, breaking up the geometry of the pool, making it
appear more natural and larger than it was.

The sound of voices drew his attention to the fact there were
others present. Pulling his toweling robe more tightly round himself, he frowned and glanced back to see where the doctor had
gotten to. As they'd arrived, she'd recognized a friend about to
leave and knowing his capacity to be embarrassed, had suggested
he go on ahead of her. He should have realized they wouldn't
be alone here either.

That the females would use the same stripping area had never
occurred to him, accustomed as he was to a single sex society.
Thankfully, he'd found a locker and somewhere to undress out
of their line of sight.

Wrapped in a bright blue robe and carrying a couple of large
towels, she emerged to join him. With a sinking feeling, he remembered that there was a larger hurdle still to cross.

"Impressive, isn't it?" she said, mouth widening in a grin.
"There's a separate aerated pool behind the main island, if you'd
prefer to try that."

He shook his head slowly. "Perhaps later," he said, hearing
for himself how strained his voice sounded.

Zayshul took him by the arm, drawing him toward a pile of
soft cushions lying near the edge of the pool. "We'll leave our
towels and robes here while we swim."

Before he could answer, she'd tossed the towels down and
unfastened her robe. Letting it drop to the floor, stark naked she
walked to the edge of the pool and dived in.

The brief glimpse he got of the rainbow-hued markings across
her lower belly and upper thighs, and the bright speckling across
her lower back, etched themselves instantly and indelibly on his
mind. He blinked in disbelief, then saw her looking up at him
from the water, her nakedness now partially concealed.

"Do you intend to stand there all afternoon, General?" she
asked, putting her head to one side and looking up at him as she
treaded water to keep afloat. "You really should come in. It'll do
you good."

All hope of making a quick, dignified entrance into the water vanished. He clenched his jaw in annoyance. If this was what it took to catch her, then he could be equally brazen. It wasn't as if he was unused to communal nude bathing, they'd done it in his time—only there had been no females present then. After all, she'd seen him naked before, he remembered with an embarrassed wince.

Deliberately, he walked toward her, untying his robe. Pulling it off, he threw it on top of the towels. As he dived into the water, he reminded himself that at least his body could stand up to her scrutiny after his weeks spent walking across the Sholan plains to reach the Aldatans' home.

The water was warm, enveloping and supporting him as he rose back to the surface. He emerged only a few feet from Zayshul. She let herself float to the surface and, once again, he had a tantalizing glimpse of the markings on her back before she began to swim slowly toward the island in the center.

Irritation flickered through him as he struck out after her. As he gained on her, she caught sight of him and began to increase her pace. Why wasn't she waiting for him? By now, she had to be aware of his interest in her. Why else invite him to the pool when its whole atmosphere was one of sexual provocation? He'd played her game long enough, allowed himself to be wrong-footed by her past behavior, embarrassed by the communal stripping room, and having to enter the pool naked in front of her. He'd had enough: time to close in for the kill.

Increasing his adrenaline level slightly, he used his powerful leg muscles to kick himself forward under the surface as he dived for her. Moments later, his hands closed round her waist. Before he could get a firm grasp, however, she'd twisted free and was gone, her body lost to him amid those of several other swimmers.

He surfaced, wiping the water from his eyes, his ears ringing with laughter and greetings. A large ball landed beside him with a flat thwack, splashing more water into his face. He gave a hiss of annoyance, both at the ball and the interruption of his plans.

"Zayshul! We haven't seen you in weeks. I thought you'd given up our swimming sessions," said a cheery female voice. "Who's your friend?" The tone had changed, now sounding sly as if the owner was probing for information.

"He's just a friend," said Zayshul. "His name's Kezule."

*   *   *

For half an hour, they played a lighthearted game of water tag with the ball. He had no option but to join in or look churlish. By the time her friends were ready to leave, Kezule had gone beyond irritation into anger tinged with frustration. This was no different from the other meetings.

Zayshul would have followed them had he not grasped her arm. Pulling her toward him, he anchored himself to the railing on the island's submerged steps.

"No," he said. "I wish to be alone with you."

"It's time we left, General," she said quietly, not resisting him. "We've been in the water long enough for today."

"I agree," he said, shifting his arm to her waist and lifting her bodily out of the water as he began to pull himself up the two shallow steps. "Definitely time for dry land." He ignored her protests and held her more tightly as she tried to squirm free.

Her struggles only served to fuel his interest. He set her down, still holding her close. Now that they were on dry land, the ambient warmth of the pool room and her body heat had begun to evaporate the odor-masking chemicals from the water. He breathed deeply, savoring her natural scent. He'd never been this close to her before.

"Let me go, General," she said, becoming still in his grasp. "I thought you knew by now what was and wasn't acceptable behavior toward a female officer."

"I've watched how you free females play this game, Doctor," he said, pulling her with him toward the interior of the small bush-covered island. "And I've done everything I've seen the other successful males do. You can't be ignorant of my interest, so why are you refusing me?"

He reached up to touch her face, tracing the iridescent markings around her eyes with a careful fingertip. She was altogether different from the females of his own time—even excluding her sentience and lack of ferocity. Smaller, lighter in build, she was pleasing to all his senses.

She stiffened, jerking her face away from him, eyes narrowing to angry slits. "You can't just follow a formula of behavior and expect me to be interested in you!" she exclaimed. "You've got to *feel* it!"

Confusion was dampening the remains of his anger. "Feel what?"

She gave a low hiss of exasperation. "Being attentive, saying the right things, wanting me even, isn't enough. You have to want *me,* the whole person, not just my body!"

As she tried again to pull away from him, he tightened his grip, taking care to prevent his claws from hurting her. "I just said I wanted you! What more can I say?" he demanded, frustrated at the need to gain her approval before mating with her.

This close, her scent was sending his heart rate soaring. The extra adrenaline in his system wasn't helping either. He could take her, it was what he'd have done back in his time, but he knew if he did, it would be the last time he'd have her. In his time, though, he'd never have been having this conversation.

Realizing it was futile, she stopped struggling. "I won't be like the three females the Commander sent you," she said coldly. "You have them for sex, why should you have me as well?"

"Those females?" he said, relieved it was nothing more serious. "They're nothing to me. They were merely a means to understanding your mating practices so I made no mistakes with you. Besides, the Commander only sent them to me so I'd impregnate them. He wants my genetic material for Warriors. He won't get it, though."

"What?" Her eyes widened in surprise.

"I can control the fertility of my seed," he said, aware by the changes in her muscle tension that she was beginning to relax. Blood was pounding in his ears as instinct took over and he felt his body responding to hers. Over the last two weeks he'd learned to trust those newly awakened instincts as fully as he did his Warrior skills.

Carefully, with his free hand, he began to draw his claws tips across the markings on her lower back. At least that much about these modern females was still the same.

"Not that, the other part," she said as, unwittingly, she began to respond to his touch.

"They were merely a means to understanding your mating practices so I made no mistakes with you," he repeated, lowering his voice as he switched his attention to gently stroking the curve of her spine. Where their bodies touched at belly and thighs, he could feel the heat radiating from her.

"You noticed me that quickly?"

He let his glance drop lower, seeing the darker colorations of skin on her flank. "From the first. I enjoy the combination of your independence, authority and femaleness."

Growing bolder, his hand traveled slowly across her side till it was resting on her hip. Stretching out his fingers, he let his claws move gently against the curve of her belly.

"You're the only female I've seen fit for me to mate with." He leaned closer, touching his lips to her neck just below her ear. He could feel the pulse throbbing in her vein, see her flesh tone darken. Flicking his bifurcated tongue against her skin, he tasted her for the first time. She couldn't deny her interest any longer: her color and the sudden change in her scent betrayed her. "I've no desire to breed yet, but if I had, I'd choose you," he said softly before closing his teeth on her shoulder.

Suddenly, he had an armful of supine and willing female. He grabbed hold of her before she could fall, looking around hastily for some suitable surface on which they could lie. A few steps away, hidden among the island's bushes, he found several of the ubiquitous soft cushions. Laying her down among them, he knelt at her side.

Instantly, his eyes were drawn to the markings that he'd glimpsed earlier. Where her belly curved down to meet hip and groin, the skin darkened, taking on a rainbow-hued iridescence that continued a short way down the insides of her thighs. It outlined and defined her femininity—and he'd never seen its like before. The visual stimulation, coupled with the scent she was now releasing, made her irresistible.

He clenched his hand on her hip and leaned over her, forcing himself to remember she was no harem female, and his life did not depend on how quick their mating was. He wanted to enjoy her—she was his trophy of a successful hunt. Crest raised to its fullest, his victory roar was muted as her hand closed suddenly over his erection. Shuddering, he grasped her hand, forcing it away.

Always thorough in everything he did, he roused her to a frenzy before they finally joined. He discovered that giving her pleasure pleased him as much as the frenzied coupling that followed. Experience had prepared him for some ferocity from her, otherwise he'd have thought she was turning as feral as the females from his own time. Even so, for a few anxious seconds, he'd feared the worst—and enjoyed it.

In the brief, quiet aftermath that followed, she admitted that she'd also wanted him from the first, when the Sholans had handed him over to her at the hostage exchange.

Kezule laughed quietly as he stroked the iridescent markings on her belly. "Perhaps we've found our match in each other," he said, wincing slightly as the bites she'd inflicted on him at the height of her passion pulled when he leaned over her again.

Valsgarth Estate on Shola, the same day

Taizia ushered T'Chebbi, Zashou and Jo into the den, leading them down the steps from the work area to the lounging level where her younger sister sat.

Kitra got up as they entered. "I always thought Kusac and you took more after Father's family," she said to her sister, surveying Zashou's pale beauty. "In the names of my brother and bond-sister, well come to Valsgarth estate. So you're my bond-grandmother."

Startled, Zashou looked from T'Chebbi to Taizia.

"You got it, kitling," said T'Chebbi, going over to the hot plate to help herself to a mug of c'shar. "Except Zashou's not Kaid's mother. Keep their real relationship to yourself, though. They're calling themselves brothers, so that makes her your bond-aunt. Anyone else want a drink?" she asked as she stirred hers. "I've waited a long time for fresh c'shar!"

"Are all the females in your family like us?" asked Zashou faintly as she took the nearest seat.

"Taizia's not," said Kitra, pointing to her dark-pelted sister. "There's always at least one of us this color, but not necessarily a female. Our grandfather was the last one, but he and Grandmother live on the Western Isles now. He's a tutor at the Telepath guildhouse there, and she's a priestess at the Shrine of Ghyakulla."

T'Chebbi took a quick swig of her drink before helping Taizia pour mugs for their guests.

"They've taken Kusac to the med unit, haven't they?" Kitra asked. "How is he?"

"Physically, he'll be fine," reassured T'Chebbi, passing a cup of coffee to Jo.

"But he tried to commit suicide, didn't he?"

T'Chebbi frowned and glanced at Taizia as she took the seat

next to Kitra. "You shouldn't know that," she said. "Who told you?"

"I was with Taizia and Vanna when Kaid called. Besides, I'm Dzaka's Leska, T'Chebbi," she said quietly. "I know what he knows."

T'Chebbi shook her head as she sat down in the nearest chair. "I forgot, kitling. My congratulations. The Gods have smiled on you. He'll make you a good life-mate, that one."

"I know," she said with a gentle smile. "Zhala's got a meal ready for you in the dining room, or you can eat in the kitchen if you prefer."

"In a few minutes, Kitra," said Taizia. "They'll want to feel the earth solid beneath their feet for a while first."

"Tell me why he tried to kill himself," requested Kitra. "I don't understand."

T'Chebbi sighed and pushed herself up from her chair. "C'mon, kitling. You and I'll go see to this food and I'll tell you."

"T'Chebbi," began Taizia warningly. "I don't think . . ."

"She's adult, got a Leska, and it's going to be discussed by everyone on both estates. Better she knows the truth than rumors," interrupted T'Chebbi, taking her mug with her as she shepherded Kitra out of the den.

Carrie pushed open her front door and stepped into the entrance hall. The familiar scent of polish brought back a flood of memories. As if in a dream, she headed for the stairs.

"Do you want me to come with you?" asked Kaid.

"Not just yet," she said, putting her foot on the first step. "I need to be alone with my daughter for a few minutes. I won't be long."

She went straight to the nursery, hesitating briefly in front of the closed door. Kashini was six months old now. She remembered the data cube Dzaka and Kitra had sent to Haven for them. Would Kashini remember her? Resolutely, she pushed the door open. As soon as she smelled her daughter's scent, all the maternal feelings that she'd had to push deep inside during their mission returned in a rush. As she ran to the high-sided cot, the nurse stood up, murmuring a greeting, but Carrie barely noticed her.

Kashini lay sprawled on her stomach, fast asleep. Her tiny

blonde-furred hands lay half-furled on the mattress, and beneath the hem of her small tunic, her tail tip twitched gently.

Unlatching the cot side, Carrie lowered it, reaching out to stroke the mass of blonde curls that covered her cub's head. The infant stirred, eyes flicking open, nose wrinkling at the new scent. Carrie felt her mind seized and held firmly for a moment or two, then with a mewl of pure delight, Kashini was scrambling to her feet and flinging herself at her mother.

Arms that could barely reach around Carrie's neck hugged her tightly. A small pink tongue began to lick her face as the cub continued to make small frantic noises of pleasure.

"Mamma's home," Carrie said, cradling her cub close and gently starting to sway from side to side. "I'm home, little one," she whispered. It wasn't until Kashini looked at her with Kusac's amber eyes that Carrie's tears began to fall.

It was fifteen minutes before she'd composed herself enough to come downstairs to the den, still carrying Kashini. As soon as she sat down, the cub squirmed free and clambered to the ground, toddling round unsteadily on two legs, inspecting the new arrivals.

"I hadn't thought she'd be walking upright so soon," said Carrie, gratefully accepting the coffee from Kaid.

"It's because their legs are too straight for running on fours like us," said Kitra. "So Vanna says. Her son, Marak, is everywhere now!"

"Has she been a handful?" asked Carrie ruefully, watching as her daughter headed over to Jo and held out her arms to be lifted up.

"I had Dzaka to help me," said Kitra.

"That one's a born father," observed T'Chebbi, catching Kitra's sharp look in her direction as she spoke.

Cautiously, Jo picked her up, surprised when the cub curled up against her belly, patting the just noticeable bulge. She looked up at Jo and began to purr and chitter in a way that sounded like speech.

"She knows I'm pregnant," exclaimed Jo, shocked. "I felt it in her mind!"

"Kashini was born with an awakened Talent," said Carrie, taking a sip from her mug.

Satisfied, with more little noises, Kashini clambered down and headed for Kaid, clutching hold of his leg and looking up at him, wide-eyed and curious.

Tentatively, he reached out and patted her on the head. "Good little cub," he muttered, withdrawing his hand. Kashini had other ideas and latched her fingers round his, extending her claws to make sure he couldn't get away.

At that moment, the door opened and Dzaka and Rezac came in.

Kaid winced, allowing Kashini to draw his hand back down to her level. "What does she want?" he asked, looking at Carrie, obviously at a loss to know what to do. He jumped slightly as a small tongue rasped its way across his palm. "What do I do?"

"Get used to it," said T'Chebbi with a laugh. "You'll be a father soon, too."

"You've got a cub on the way?" asked Taizia incredulously, looking toward T'Chebbi.

She shook her head. "Not me."

Carrie steeled herself for everyone's reaction. "Me. I thought your parents would have told you. They did tell you Kaid and I are Leska Linked now, didn't they?"

"Yes, but not about the cub," said Taizia, studiously keeping her eyes on Kashini, who'd turned away from Kaid and was now heading for Kitra. "I expect they thought that was private, yours to tell us when you were ready."

"The Primes saved my life," said Carrie quietly. "But at a cost."

"They had to remove her contraceptive implant," said Kaid smoothly, recovering his composure now that the cub had lost interest in him. "They said it interfered with their treatment. We think it's only because she's pregnant that any of us are alive."

"I wondered about that," said Taizia. "When Zhyaf died, Mara Linked to Josh, her third."

"Zhyaf's dead?" exclaimed Kaid and Carrie together.

"Kezule took him hostage when he escaped. Mara nearly died. It took Ghyan's help to stop her following Zhyaf into death."

"Kusac was still alive, but his talent was suppressed by drugs and the alien implant," said Kaid, glancing at Carrie. "So the third is potentially a Leska partner. That explains a lot."

Carrie's attention was on Kashini while the others were talking. She watched as Kitra tried to prevent the cub climbing up onto her lap, suddenly sensing from her daughter why. She looked up, catching Kitra's eyes, seeing the stricken look on the young female's face change to one of helplessness as she realized Kashini was in mental contact with her mother.

"Not you too!" Carrie whispered.

"What?" asked Dzaka as he came down the steps toward Kaid.

"Nothing," said Carrie, getting up to retrieve her daughter.

Kaid stood up and went to meet him.

"It's good to have you home, Father," Dzaka said as they held each other close.

"Good to be home," said Kaid, running his hand over his son's cheek as he released him. "I hear you and Kitra are to be life-bonded soon. Congratulations to you both. When is the ceremony?" he asked, glancing toward his son's Leska.

Dzaka's mouth opened in a slow smile as he looked across at Kitra. "As soon as Kusac and you are well enough to attend the service at Stronghold."

"Stronghold, eh?"

"Father Lijou wants to perform the ceremony himself," Dzaka said, moving over to Kitra. "You won't have heard yet, but he and Mistress Kha'Qwa have a son."

"A son?" Kaid shook his head as he returned to his seat. "Stronghold will never be the same."

"There used to be families there," said Rezac. "Back in our time."

"And up until two generations ago," said Kitra as Dzaka perched on the arm of her chair. "I've been looking into the history of the place. It was the last two Warrior Masters, particularly Ghezu, who prevented any bonded Brothers and Sisters from living there together. They were sent to one of the colony worlds until their cubs were old enough for them to return and be fostered in Dzahai village."

"No cubs of ours will be fostered, though," said Dzaka, his hand closing on Kitra's shoulder. *We need to talk,* he sent. *Why didn't you tell me you were expecting our cub?*

The stricken look returned to Kitra's face. *Who told you?*

You and Carrie—when I came in just now. Smile, Kitra. We'll talk later. They have enough troubles without us adding to them.

Dzaka looked over to Carrie. "Garras is organizing transport and accommodation for the new Brothers when they arrive," he said.

"Would you ask Ghyan to organize his usual Reception talk

for them," said Carrie tiredly, bending down to pick Kashini up. "Tell him the one called Dzaou needs watching. He's got a problem with both telepaths and any non-Sholans. Why Rhyaz wants him here, I can't fathom."

"He's here because until he changes his attitude, he's a time bomb waiting to go off," said Kaid.

"I'll see to it, Liegena," nodded Dzaka.

"We should eat now," said Kitra, forcing her mouth open in a smile. "The meal will spoil otherwise and Zhala will be angry."

Kaid's wrist comm buzzed, waking him from his light doze. It was Vanna.

"He'll be ready for us to move from the cryo unit in a few minutes," she said. "It'll be another half hour before he wakes, though."

"Thank you," he said. Uncurling himself, he got to his feet, stretching all five limbs to ease the kinks out of them. Sleeping on sofas was for the young, he decided ruefully, rubbing his stiff back as he went over to the bed where Carrie lay asleep, Kashini cradled in her arms.

Looking down at them, one part of him warmed at the sight, imagining how she'd look holding their cub. The other part shrank from the thought, afraid not only of the responsibilities of impending fatherhood, but the physical changes Carrie would have to endure while carrying their cub. He'd been afraid for her life when he'd helped Kusac birth Kashini. The pain he'd experienced—her pain, shared by both himself and Kusac through their Link with her, had been terrible. He hadn't wanted to put her through that again. And there was Kusac. He sighed, then reached down to caress the small head resting against Carrie's arm.

The scene blurred, and he saw Carrie lying in his bed at his home up in the Dzahai mountains, a tiny brown-furred newborn held close against her breast.

He blinked, and the vision was gone.

Carrie's eyes flickered open and she yawned. Still shaken by the vision, Kaid squatted down at the side of the bed, cupping his hand round her face.

"Don't pull away from me," he said gently as she began to move. "Ever since Kusac tried to kill himself, you've kept your distance from me, even on our Link days."

"I feel responsible," she said. "I know it doesn't make sense but I can't help it."

"You aren't," he said forcefully, letting his hand slip down to rest intimately against her neck. "Don't let Kashini feel this misplaced guilt of yours. We're a Triad, you're carrying our cub. If you go on like this, you'll harm not only our relationship, but Kashini's toward me and her unborn sister."

She lay still, looking up at him, then nodded slowly. "I'll try, Tallinu. It isn't that I love you less, it's that I feel guilty for loving you when Kusac . . ."

He leaned forward, silencing her with a kiss. *You have a right to be happy even while you grieve for your lost Link to Kusac,* he sent. *Vartra knows, I feel the same, but I won't let it affect us, Carrie.*

Between them, Kashini woke and began to squirm, reaching out to catch hold of a lock of Kaid's hair. As she tugged on it, he yelped, pulling back wryly as he tried to undo her strong grip. Next moment, she was crawling over his chest, mewling happily, still clinging onto his hair.

"What do I do?" he appealed to Carrie, clutching at the cub to stop her from falling. "I know nothing about infants!"

Carrie sat up, watching them, wishing that she could forget the guilt she felt. "You get used to it," she said, echoing T'Chebbi's earlier words. "I expect both my life-mates to help rear our cubs."

"Dzaka was four, a much more civilized age, when he came to me," he muttered, catching hold of her hand as she reached tentatively for his cheek.

He remembered his stomach hurt, so did his throat, and he was confused. He hadn't expected to wake at all. Familiar scents teased his nostrils: Vanna's, Carrie, and Kaid's. Then a mind touched his and agony surged through him. It robbed him of breath at first as his body arched upward before slamming back down on the bed.

"Stop it, Chiuduu! Stop it now!" yelled Carrie, rushing in from the other room to stop the telepath.

Kaid grasped her by the arm, pulling her close. "Finish it, Chiuduu," he ordered.

"Kaid! In Vartra's name, that's enough!" Vanna exclaimed.

The telepath physician glanced at Kaid.

"Tallinu! For God's sake, tell him to stop! Kusac's in agony! How can you do this to him?" demanded Carrie, struggling against him. "Stop blocking my mind, damn you!"

Kaid locked his arms around Carrie. "Get on with it, Chiuduu," he said harshly. "You can see how much pain he's in. Get what we need and get out."

The pain came in waves, each one worse until he felt the stranger's mind retreat, leaving him alone. A hypo spray stung his neck twice.

As the pain began to lessen, gradually he became aware of Carrie's presence beside him, and the gentle touch of her hand on his cheek.

"I'm sorry, Kusac," he heard Kaid say. "It had to be done. If not by us, then the Brotherhood and the Telepath Guild would have demanded it. We need to know what you're keeping behind that shield, what's causing the pain when your mind's touched."

"You planned this all along, didn't you?" said Carrie's angry voice from beside him. "How could you do this to him? How could you not tell me?"

"Why was I not informed that a mental scan would have this effect on Kusac?" demanded Vanna. "There was no mention of this in the data you sent me!"

"Kaid's right, lass," said Jack. "He had to be mind-scanned as much for his own protection as anything. It's like setting a broken limb, only we can't yet anesthetize the conscious mind."

The Human's voice came closer till he felt a hand grasp his shoulder briefly. "He's done, laddie. There'll be no more for now, you have our word. We've given you a psi-suppressant to make sure."

"You knew about this, too?" asked Carrie incredulously. "And you agreed?"

"We had to know if the suicide attempt had been programmed into his subconscious by Chy'qui," said Kaid.

"And was it?" demanded Carrie.

There was a short silence before the stranger spoke. "No. That was Kusac's own decision."

The voice sounded strained, and through the last vestiges of his pain and the worry that they'd discovered what he kept locked deep in his subconscious, Kusac felt some satisfaction that like Vriuzu, this telepath had felt the same agony he'd experienced.

Carrie's hands withdrew from his face and neck. "I think you should all leave," she said, her voice suddenly cold. "You've gotten what you wanted. Now I want to speak to my life-mate privately."

"Carrie," began Kaid.

"Leave us alone!"

He listened to the footsteps retreating.

"Carrie, don't be too . . ."

"I said privately, Jack."

Uneasiness filled him as he remembered just how uncompromising and angry she could be. He continued to lie still, eyes shut, waiting to see what she'd do next. He felt the bed move as she got up.

"You can sit up now, Kusac. I know you're not as bad as you're letting on."

He uncurled cautiously. Nothing hurt this time. He managed to push himself unsteadily up into a sitting position. "How?" he asked, keeping his eyes away from her face while watching her pace the room.

"I know you better than anyone, Kusac. Dammit, we were Linked for over a year!"

"You're angry," he began.

She came to an abrupt halt beside him. "Damned right I am! You told me how afraid you were of losing me yet what do you do? You try to kill yourself!"

"I thought it for the best," he said quietly, wishing this was over, that he'd succeeded.

"Thought? You didn't *think* at all! You didn't care about anyone but yourself! You intended to leave me and Kashini alone!"

He didn't see the slap coming and when it landed on the side of his face, he automatically grabbed her by the arm and looked up at her in shock.

Tears were rolling down her face as she began to cry.

"There's Kaid . . ." he began.

"Kaid isn't you! I need you both—I love you both! You don't have the right to decide alone what's best for the three of us! Why did you give up? Why leave us? We've faced so much together, why did you push us away?" She collapsed on the bed, leaning against him, sobbing.

He released her wrist, tentatively reaching out to stroke her head. "I didn't mean to hurt you, Carrie. I thought it would be easier for you and Kaid if I wasn't there." He felt a vague remorse at upsetting her.

"When did we ever choose the easy way? We've always faced things together, head on. Why did you shut us out?" Her voice was muffled, distressed.

"It's not that simple," he said. "You don't know what it's like living without my Talent—not being able to feel you or your love."

"It's no less real!" she said, lifting her head. "I can't sense you, but that doesn't affect my love for you!"

He remained silent for a moment, knowing the reply she wanted, but unable to give it. "I don't know what I feel right now, Carrie," he said quietly. "Everything still seems distant, as if it isn't happening to me. If it'll help, I'll give you my word I'll not do it again."

She sat up, rubbing her hand across her eyes. "You'll fight this? Let us help you and not try to shut us out?"

He nodded slowly. "I'll try."

A commotion in the distance made them look toward the door.

"Sounds like your mother's awake," said Carrie, scrubbing at her face again and getting up.

Rhyasha came flying through the door, closely pursued by Kaid. She stopped just inside the room, tail swaying anxiously beneath the hem of her short summer tabard.

"Kusac," she said, and her tone spoke volumes.

"Hello, Mother," he said tiredly, trying to force his mouth open in a smile. "You don't need to scold me, Carrie's already done it."

the *Couana*, Zhal-S'Asha, 19th day (October)

Roused from his semi-doze, he heard the door behind him open. Rubbing his eyes to dispel the dream, he turned to see Banner entering the bridge carrying two sealed mugs.

"Thought you could do with a drink," Banner said, coming over to the command console and handing him a mug. "It's nearly time for shift change."

Nodding his thanks, he accepted it, popping the lid free and pressing it onto the retainer on the bottom of the mug. He turned his attention back to his console as Banner took the comms seat in front of him.

"What's up, Kusac?" Banner asked, taking a sip of his own drink. "You aren't usually so stressed out. More memories? I thought you'd gotten over them weeks ago."

He took a drink before replying. He supposed he owed his Second an explanation. "So did I. They started when I went back to Stronghold," he said, cradling the mug in both hands. "It's as if I'm reliving everything again."

Banner shifted in his seat. "Is it anything to do with what Toueesut, Annuur, and whatzzis name did?"

He looked up. Now was not the time to tell him. Later, perhaps, when he had a better understanding of what they'd done, and his suspicions were proved one way or the other. "Kzizysus. No more than usual," he said with forced lightness. "I'm tired of being pushed in front of every medical expert who thinks they've found a cure." He took another mouthful, finding the drink suddenly bland and tasteless.

"Can't be easy," Banner said sympathetically. "Is it helping any? Reliving the memories, I mean."

"Some."

"Understanding includes realizing that choices are limited by one's mental and physical circumstances," said Banner, choosing his words carefully. "Realizing that sometimes our biological programming overrides our intellect. Until you met Carrie, your life was very predictable, very controlled, either by you or your family. Captivity took that freedom you'd found with her, and the luxury of choice, away from you."

He raised an eye ridge. "You've been researching me." There was a hard note in his voice.

The other shrugged. "Only talking to those who know you."

Suddenly he was aware of his heart beating a counterpoint to the rhythmic throbbing of the *Couana*'s engines. "I knew Rhyaz would send a Special Operative with me," he said softly. "I didn't think it would be you."

"I'm one," admitted Banner.

"One?"

"Rhyaz didn't send me."

"Lijou, then."

Banner said nothing, merely took another drink.

"Why two?" he asked.

"Because Rhyaz has been unsure of you since your return from Haven. I'm here to help you."

He digested this for a minute as he forced himself to relax. There was no reason for Banner to lie to him. "Why tell me?" he asked abruptly.

"So you know there's one person on board on your side. Considering some of the crew members, I figured it was necessary to tell you."

He gave a snort of amusement. "You mean Dzaou. Rhyaz picked the crew himself."

"You didn't think he'd make this easy, did you? I'm here to see his testing is fair."

"What did Lijou tell you about this mission?"

"There was little he could tell. Only that it related to a message sent to Haven to be delivered to you."

He'd told no one what the message meant. Rhyaz had his own interpretation, but it was wrong. "Rhyaz thinks the message is from General Kezule. It isn't." As he spoke, the odors contained on the message seemed to surround him once more. The real message was in the scents, yet it seemed no one but he could read them.

"Kezule? I thought he was safe on the Prime world."

"Apparently not." He put the mug down on the side of his console and reached inside his jacket.

"So who's it from?"

Taking the message out, he handed it over to Banner. "I'm not sure," he lied, "but Kezule is involved."

Banner unfolded and read it, unaware of Kusac's intense gaze. He handed it back to him. "It says very little, only that he must meet with you. Why you? Why not Kaid or Carrie?"

"Because he knows they're telepaths."

"And he knows you're not now, therefore he sees you as no threat," nodded the other. "I suppose it makes sense. What has he got that could be of interest to you?"

"We'll find out in three days," he said, folding it up carefully and returning it to his pocket.

"Do you need to keep it secret from the crew? Dzaou's having a real paranoia session over this."

"I expect he is, but he'll have to wait like the rest. It was Rhyaz who told me not to brief you until we were almost at the rendezvous. He's the one putting pressure on the crew, not me. Thank Vartra, Father Lijou is more perceptive than Rhyaz gives him credit for."

"Master Rhyaz is the Warrior Leader," murmured Banner. "A coin must always have two sides."

Shola, Zhal-Ghyakulla, 6th day (June)

When Kaid and Carrie had left for the medical center, Dzaka and Kitra retired to their suite, leaving T'Chebbi in charge. As he closed the door, Dzaka turned on the psi damper.

"Don't be mad at me, Dzaka," said Kitra, backing away and eyeing him warily. "It isn't my fault."

"Mad? Why should I be mad at you?" he asked, surprised. "I admit it came as something of a shock, but I couldn't be more delighted." He shook his head, mouth opening in a pleased smile as he came toward her. "I've loved looking after Kashini, but to have a cub of our own! I just hadn't thought we'd start our family so soon."

The moment he touched her, Kitra felt the magic of their Leska Link flow through her. Her resolve began to falter as his arms folded round her.

"I don't know that it's what I want," she murmured, returning his embrace. "Father and Mother won't be too happy. A cub was what the Chazouns wanted from me, and you know how hard they fought that."

"Forget the Chazouns. Even if they didn't accept your father's cancellation of your betrothal, the moment you became my En'Shalla Leska, they had no claim over you," he murmured, burying his face in her cloud of soft, blonde hair.

"Vanna's not sure how it happened."

He laughed, picking her slight form up in his arms and carrying her over to the sofa. "Maybe you need reminding," he whispered, catching hold of her ear gently with his teeth as he set her down then crouched beside her.

"That's not what I mean," she said, shivering with pleasure

as he began to caress her neck. "I wasn't compatible with you till two days after we Linked."

"I'm told I'm very potent," he purred teasingly, reaching for the seals on her tabard. "Perhaps that's what Vanna meant." Pushing her garment aside, he ran his hands lovingly down her sides then leaned forward to cover her face with tiny bites.

"I don't know that I want a cub right now," repeated Kitra, her voice becoming quieter as she reached out to pull him close.

"You have me, we'd be sharing the cub, what's to worry about?" he whispered, breathing in her scent as he began to nibble his way toward her neck. He put a hand protectively on her belly. "My little mother!"

Her concerns were being swept aside by his obvious pleasure. Perhaps it—their cub—wouldn't be the problem she'd feared.

How can our cub be a problem? he sent. *It was meant to be, Kitra. What were the odds on us becoming Leskas when I was only an empath? I've never heard of it happening. This is a joyful time for us both. There's our bonding ceremony still to come at Stronghold, your brother and bond-sister are back safe, as is my father. And now our child. He'll be company for Kashini while you finish your studies at the Guild. Think of the jealousy of your classmates—those who thought I wasn't even your lover!—when you return not only with one of the Brotherhood as your Leska and life-mate, but sharing a cub with him?*

You're right, sent Kitra. *They will be furious with envy! It isn't a very good reason to have a cub, though.*

Our love is the reason, Dzaka purred, sitting back to unbuckle his belt and pull off his gray tunic. *I don't expect you to give up the life you'd planned for yourself. You know what I'd like, but the decision's got to be yours.*

She watched him through half-closed eyelids, seeing the almost luminous glow in his eyes as he bent down toward her again. Reaching up, she ran her fingers through his brindled pelt, letting him feel the tips of her unsheathed claws. He shuddered as her hands came to rest on his hips and their minds began to merge.

"Having you was the life I planned," she whispered. "We'll keep our cub."

You're a dzinae, Kitra, sent by Vartra Himself! How can one so young be so captivating! You complete me, kitling.

"She's *what*?" exclaimed Rhyasha when Vanna told her at Kitra's request. "She's far too young! She'll have to terminate!"

"She's physically mature enough, Clan Leader," murmured Vanna. "And emotionally, in my opinion."

"Now who's interfering, Rhyasha?" asked her husband quietly. "Let them decide for themselves. Don't forget it was by Vartra's will that they became Leskas in the first place."

"But you resigned as Clan Lord rather than let the Chazouns force her into having a cub!" she exclaimed, passing a hand over her forehead. "With Kusac in the state he's in, I don't need this worry right now!"

"Then stop worrying. She's an adult by every definition of the word and circumstances," said Konis, taking her hand in his. "Our cubs are grown up, my dear. It's time to let them all run their own lives, even our youngest."

Rhyasha made an exasperated noise.

Besides, soon you'll have our new cubs to worry over, he sent, lovingly touching her face. *Twins should be enough of a handful even for you.*

Enough! I should never have let you persuade me to start another family, she grumbled, but her mental tone was slightly mollified.

"Don't spoil their joy," said Carrie from the doorway. "We could all do with some." She smiled wanly. "After all, 'Cubs are Ghyakulla's gift to us all,'" she quoted.

Konis gave her an approving glance while mentally reassuring his life-mate that no one was yet aware of her pregnancy. "Carrie's right. Our children are our salvation. Were it not for the cub she and Kaid are sharing, we'd have lost them all. And were it not for Dzaka's and Kitra's Link, Kezule would have succeeded. Our kitling couldn't have found a better mate. Let them make their own decision, Rhyasha. Just share in their joy."

Rhyasha leaned against him. "You're right. I'm sorry, I forgot myself. I'm just so worried for Kusac."

"Physician Chiuduu's ready to give his report," said Carrie. "That's what I came to tell you."

Leaving a medic on duty to watch Kusac, Vanna led them to

the common room where the physician sat waiting with Kaid and Jack. He was older than either the Human or Kaid, with flecks of white and gray dusting his pelt and streaking his once dark hair.

"What did you find?" demanded Rhyasha, perching on the edge of the sofa, still clutching Konis' hand tightly.

As Carrie moved past Kaid toward a seat at the other side of the room, he got up and caught her by the arm. Reluctantly she took his seat while he stood beside her.

Chiuduu waited for them to settle before beginning. He looked tired and worn. "It wasn't pleasant," he said. "I experienced much of his pain myself."

"We had no option," said Kaid, glancing down at Carrie. "I'm sorry we had to put both of you through that, but it was necessary."

"Yes, it was," agreed the physician. "There is a residual level of Talent there, but these—tendrils—are everywhere. And they're still active, after a fashion."

"Active?" whispered Carrie, turning ashen. "What do you mean active?"

He turned to look at her. "When the area of his mind that deals with psi talents is activated in any way, then the tendrils immediately respond by stimulating the central nervous system and causing pain. That's why he reacted so violently to being scanned."

"That bears out what you said happened on Haven when Vriuzu tried to read him," Kaid said to Carrie.

"There's more," continued Chiuduu. "Apparently, they also activate when he experiences strong emotions. Anger, for instance. I didn't feel any anger while I was scanning him, but I did find his memories of it."

Rhyasha moaned softly.

"We both saw it happen at Haven. Is that what he was hiding from us?" asked Kaid.

"Perhaps. I could see nothing else except a mixture of memories and nightmares of his experiences on the Prime ship." He shook his head, obviously trying to dispel the images. "Make no mistake, Physician Kyjishi, this Valtegan, J'koshuk, made a thorough job of breaking Kusac's spirit. Apart from that, there's not much more to tell you. My full report will be with you tomorrow for you to send to the Brotherhood as well as Master Sorli. As Master of the Telepath Guild, Sorli must be informed."

"Master Sorli has no authority over us," reminded Kaid. "But we'll send him a copy ourselves, out of courtesy. What can you do to help Kusac?"

"Medication and therapy, perhaps mental readjustment, is all we can offer, I'm afraid. It might be better in the long run if all memory of his experiences was erased, as well as the fact he'd once been a telepath."

"No!" said Konis, a split second after Carrie and Kaid. "As Clan Lord, I absolutely forbid it!"

"So do I," said Carrie, reaching for Kaid's hand and clutching it tightly. "There has to be something else we can do—some way of neutralizing the tendrils! Can't we use our psi abilities to destroy them?"

"How, without causing both yourselves and him such agony that you'd be unable to work?" asked Chiuduu.

"What about surgery?" asked Jack. "Can't we use lasers to burn out the dratted things?"

"And risk damaging other areas of his brain? I think not. If there is a cure, then it lies with those who implanted the device in the first place," said Chiuduu, getting slowly to his feet. "Those are avenues which you are more able to explore. If you'll excuse me, I would like to return to the Guild now. Despite your kind treatment, Physician Kyjishi, I still have a dreadful headache. I've given you the main points of my report, the rest you'll have by tomorrow morning."

"I'll arrange for a flitter to take you back," said Jack, getting to his feet.

When they'd gone, Kaid turned to Vanna. "What about Noni?"

"Noni! Yes, maybe Noni can help!" exclaimed Rhyasha, sitting forward in her seat.

"Noni said she'd come after we'd done all the preliminary tests," said Vanna. "That won't be for at least a week. In the meantime, I'm going to keep Kusac sedated. He's going to have to endure a lot of examinations and scans at the Telepath Guild medical center over the next few days. I'd prefer him to be subjected to as little stress as possible."

"T'Chebbi and I'll take him," said Kaid.

Vanna nodded. "He'll have to stay here, I'm afraid, under constant surveillance. I don't want him attempting suicide again before his medication takes effect. I've already implanted a bio-monitor in him, just to be on the safe side."

"Why can't he come home?" Carrie asked. "He promised me he wouldn't try again and I believe him. He's been distancing himself from us, Vanna. If you keep him here, it'll only get worse."

"I know, cub, but what option do I have?" she asked. "You heard Chiuduu. J'koshuk broke his will. It isn't as if this is the first time he's tried to kill himself."

"You can't count the time on the *Khalossa*!" Carrie exclaimed. "That was different! He didn't do anything, just . . ."

"It's not about what he did, Carrie, it's about his state of mind," said Konis heavily. "Twice now, he's been prepared to die."

"You've got a good understanding of the situation," said Kaid.

"I've had to deal with several people in similar situations in my time, Kaid. Being Clan Lord isn't just choosing mates and sitting at meetings, you know. They frequently call me in when there are problems with potential Leskas."

"There's nothing more you can do here today," said Vanna, getting up. "Kusac's resting for now. He's still recovering from the effects of the drug poisoning. I suggest you go home and get some rest yourselves. I'll sort out visiting times and let you know later when you can come."

"I want to stay here with him," said Carrie.

"Not this time, I'm afraid, Carrie," said Vanna with finality. "There's no need for you to remain now, and he really does need to rest. He's got a slight fever that I want to keep an eye on."

"You do understand why I had to have Kusac scanned, don't you?" Kaid asked Carrie, breaking the awkward silence that had come between them as they walked back to the villa.

"You should have told me what you were going to do."

"You'd have tried to prevent me."

"You're damned right I would!"

"And you'd have been wrong. Think of what we've found out."

"It wasn't worth it in my opinion," she said stubbornly. "I don't care if Jack did agree with you."

"Would you rather it was Vriuzu again?"

"You know I wouldn't! We already knew Kusac couldn't be

scanned without pain, and he even said something about the strong emotions, only we didn't pay enough attention to him."

"We know more than that. He still has a residual Talent."

"You took unnecessary risks. What if Chiuduu had found out about Kusac using his psi Talent to kill J'koshuk? What then, Kaid? Would he now be facing losing even that—residual talent—for breaking the Telepath Guild laws?"

"We aren't subject to those laws," said Kaid. "Lijou's the only one with authority over us, you know that."

She stopped dead and rounded on him. "The Telepath Guild—or at least Chiuduu—is afraid of him! You must have sensed that! They could send a Special Operative after him because he's become a rogue, with what Talent he has left unpredictable! Did you think of that?"

"Yes, I did," he said quietly. "That's partly why Chiuduu suggested erasing Kusac's memory of being a telepath. But if Chiuduu had discovered he'd killed using it, Konis would have helped me permanently erase the memory from Chiuduu's mind. Kusac was never in any danger of that being discovered, Carrie. Konis and I were monitoring the physician the whole time. If he saw J'koshuk's death at all, Chiuduu thought it was a nightmare, nothing more. Didn't you wonder why your bond-father looked so drawn?"

"All right. I grant you didn't overlook it," she said, starting to move off again. "What about the Guild's fear of him?"

"It's not fear, merely wariness. We needed this report to reassure not only the Guild, but General Raiban and Lijou and Rhyaz. As I said earlier, if we hadn't had it done—in circumstances that we could control—then they would have demanded it. Vriuzu's scan wasn't enough. This is. They now know Kusac isn't hiding anything, that he hasn't been programmed to suddenly turn kzu-shu and murder us all in our beds."

She said nothing, walking on in silence until they were within the villa grounds.

"I admit it. You were right and I was wrong," she said in a small voice. "It needed to be done."

above K'oish'ik, the Prime Homeworld,
Zhal-Ghyakulla, 10th day (June)

K'hedduk stood in the main landing bay, watching the loading of the transport shuttles bound for the research center at the City of Light on K'oish'ik, far below them. Gesturing to the brown-clad head of the cargo loaders, he called him over.

"K'hedduk! Thought it was about time you crawled out from under your stone!" he said, stopping to yell curses and threats as a small sealed container shifted dangerously on its grav sled. Finished, he turned back to the steward. "I've got work stacked up here, K'hedduk, this better be important. Everyone wants their pet project downloaded yesterday."

"You're handling Doctor Zayshul's embryonic growth tanks."

The chief loader glanced behind him to where three large triangular sealed units were being carefully stacked. Each one bore a painted code on the side.

"So?"

"They contain viable embryos and must be handled with the utmost care or abnormalities could occur. The doctor has sent me to oversee transportation to the surface."

The chief stared belligerently at him, eyes closing once in a slow blink. "You accusing me of incompetence?" he demanded. "I've worked this ship the last twenty years, handled cargoes like this more times than I care to remember! On my shift, there's never been . . ."

"Let's just get on with the job, shall we?" said K'hedduk coldly, looking at his comp reader. "I have sixteen units on my manifest. I counted only fifteen. Where's the other one?"

"Don't you come in here and talk to me like that, K'hedduk! I got every one of those units either on the shuttle, or sitting right there ready to be put on the minute you get your butt out of my cargo area!"

"You're one short."

"I'll be damned if I am!" he hissed, turning on his heel and stalking over to where his crew were now locking the seven foot tall units onto a loading sled. As the chief snatched the comp reader from his foreman, K'hedduk waited patiently.

Voices were raised, then the chief came storming past him

into the transport shuttle. Minutes passed then he heard more angry voices as the chief emerged again.

"I got fifteen units on my list," he hissed at K'hedduk. "And all fifteen are accounted for! What's this about another one?"

K'hedduk handed his comp reader over to him. "Sixteen."

The chief swore roundly. "Where is it then? It can't go down on this shuttle! I've allocated my load now, there's no weight allowance to spare. It'll have to wait till the next shift."

"It has to go now," said K'hedduk. "They need to be connected to the main computer tonight. Some change of nutrients or something that can't wait."

"Burn those damned scientists!" the chief muttered, thrusting the reader back at him. "Think they're damned gods the way they mess us about! Follow me," he snapped, heading across the landing bay for the dispatch office by the main elevator.

Half an hour later, K'hedduk was sitting in a small automated shuttle heading down to the City of Light, the sixteenth unit locked into position in the small cargo area to the rear. As the craft began to angle itself for its landing approach, he smiled to himself and reached out to override the controls. He had no intention of landing in the courtyard at the rear of the Palace where the research labs were situated. He and his cargo of hybrid Sholan/Human embryos were headed for an entirely different location.

Shola, Zhal-Ghyakulla, 12th day (June)

It had been a hectic week, with Kusac being taken on two consecutive days to the Guild medical center for scans. Then he'd come down with a sudden fever which had lasted for two days. During that time, Vanna had ordered them all to report to her med lab for checkups.

Kusac was on his feet now and fretting quietly at his continued incarceration in the small estate hospital, but Vanna had been adamant. Finally, she had called Carrie and Kaid, telling them to come over for the results of the tests and to take Kusac home with them.

"You'll be pleased to know you're all pretty fit," she said, as she ushered them into her office. "I can't tell you if your suspicions about Kate were right, Kaid, because she's pregnant now, by about four weeks—the same as you, Carrie."

"Will you be able to tell once she's had her cub?" asked Kaid.

"Not categorically. I'm afraid we've nothing more to base your suspicions on than her scent on the night she was taken by Chy'qui. That's not enough for me."

Kaid grunted, keeping his thoughts to himself as the memory of Kate's abduction made him aware of Carrie's scent.

Vanna reached for the three containers of pills on her desk and held them out to Carrie. "Your supplements. You know the drill, Carrie," she said with a gentle smile.

Carrie sighed, and juggling the squirming Kashini, took them from her.

"The third one's for Kusac. You shouldn't have any problem getting him to take them."

Carrie stuffed the bottles into her tabard pocket. "What about Jo? And Zashou?" she asked. "Are they both all right?"

"Fine, and so's Jo's cub. No traces of anything foreign in their systems at all. Same with Rezac. Whatever the Primes did, they didn't cause her or the cub any damage. And no long-term effects that I can see from the laalquoi in their diet on Jalna, either. Kris and Davies checked out healthy, too." She looked at Kaid shrewdly. "Your *brother* Rezac is very like you." She emphasized the word.

"Told you," said Carrie, glancing at Kaid. "You owe me."

"A bet?" murmured Vanna. "Your family relationships have to be the most complex I've ever come across, Kaid."

Kaid smiled faintly. "I try to keep you Challenged, Vanna."

"You can tell me the truth. Who is he? Your father? The blood tests suggest he is. Must be very strange having a father half your age."

Kaid frowned. "I'm not that old, Vanna."

"Rezac's only twenty-three."

"He'll have his fill of fatherhood soon," said Kaid. "Enough to age him! I wish him joy of it. It isn't as easy as he thinks."

"You'll feel differently about your own cub," said Vanna confidently, her hand going instinctively to her own belly. "Only seven weeks left for Garras!" she laughed. "You males are as broody as us, though you try to pretend you aren't! He can't wait."

She leaned forward to scratch Carrie's cub affectionately under the chin. "And don't think you know it all because you've lived in the same house as Kashini," she said. "When it's your own newborn, it's another matter entirely."

"I'll take your word for it, Vanna," he murmured, feeling even more unsure about the forthcoming major upheaval in his life.

Carrie stood up, hefting Kashini onto one hip. "Can we get Kusac now? I don't know why you wouldn't let me bring Kashini to see him before now, Vanna. She knows he's back and has been really distressed at not being able to see him. She's been touching his belongings and whimpering."

"She's too powerful a telepath, Carrie. Kusac might have his own residual psi ability suppressed, but we can still pick up his mental state. Until now, he's not been settled enough to be in her company."

"Any news about Kusac's test results at the Guild?"

Vanna shook her head, ears dipping back. "Nothing we didn't already know. The general consensus is to let his mind heal and hope that the tendrils die off or weaken of their own accord."

"Hurry up and wait," Carrie murmured as her friend got to her feet.

"I hear your father's due here in a few days," said Vanna, changing the subject. "Are you looking forward to seeing him? It'll be the first official visit by a Keissian, or Terran, Leader."

"I don't know, to be honest. He was never fully reconciled to my marriage to Kusac, or Kashini's birth. Thankfully, Konis and Father Lijou kept the worst of the news from him until we reached Haven. It's only a flying visit at least."

"He hasn't seen your daughter yet, has he?" asked Vanna shrewdly.

"Not yet. But he will."

For Kusac, the days in Vanna's ward had passed in a slow, repetitive haze. He found he hadn't either the interest or energy to do much beyond lie on his bed watching whichever entertainment channel the nurse switched on for him each morning. A small part of him was aware that this was due to the medication he was given twice a day, but he knew the futility of arguing over it so he endured. It wasn't till Carrie and Kaid came for him that he roused himself, and then it was only because of his cub.

With a delighted squeal, his daughter launched herself at him, landing on the bed then scrambling onto his chest where she fixed her claws deep into his pelt, pulling herself up to reach his face. Anchoring herself with hind legs and one hand, she began to lick furiously at his face, purring loudly. Something inside him began to stir as he held her close.

They'd brought a choice of clothes for him: the Brotherhood robe or one of his civilian tunics. He looked up at them blankly, incapable of making a decision.

Kaid picked up the tunic and handed it to him. "Wear this. It's hot outside. The robe will likely be too warm."

He accepted it from him but continued to sit there holding Kashini.

Carrie reached out and took the cub from him amid loud protests from her. "I'll hold her while you dress," she said quietly.

He was halfway through obediently putting his tunic on when the first spark of resentment woke. He quashed it and finished dressing, anxious to hold his daughter again.

In an awkward silence they walked down the village main street till they reached the villa. Kusac was barely aware of the furtive stares thrown in his direction by the odd passersby as he concentrated on holding Kashini close, feeling her tiny heart beating against his chest.

A hand touched his arm, bringing him to a stop as they entered the grounds leading up to the front of the house. Carrie: he'd forgotten she was there.

"You can put her down now," she said. "She likes walking and the ground here's safe for her feet."

Again, he found himself obediently about to disentangle his daughter's hands from his tunic, and stopped abruptly.

"No," he said, shocked by his own boldness. "She wants to be with me. Why didn't you bring her to see me sooner?"

"I couldn't, Kusac. Vanna wouldn't let me till today."

Kaid put a hand on his shoulder, making him look around sharply at him.

"She said you needed to rest, Kusac. You were very ill with a brain fever for two days."

He looked at Kaid, narrowing his eyes against the glare of the sun. Vague memories of being pushed down a long corridor on a floater came to mind, then they were gone, lost in the haze.

"Let's get you in out of the sun," said Kaid. "It's too hot for any of us after the time we've spent on air-conditioned ships."

He nodded slowly, letting the other male urge him on toward the house. Once inside, he followed Kaid to the den, pausing on the threshold and looking past him down to the lower level.

T'Chebbi looked up from the small comm unit she'd been using. "Look lot better than last time I saw you," she said, mouth dropping in a smile. "How you feeling?"

"Better," he agreed, trying to hide the surprise he felt at finding her in the private inner sanctuary of his home. He looked around the den.

Sunlight filtered in through the fine muslinlike drapes that hung over the clear doors leading out onto the garden beyond. The dark paneled wooden floor and walls were broken up by the brightly colored rugs and tapestries that he remembered so well. All was as it had been—before—but it no longer felt like *his* place of refuge.

Kashini touched the still tender scar on his neck, painfully drawing his attention back to her. Flinching, he reached up and took her tiny hand in his. "I'll take Kashini upstairs," he said, turning away from the room.

"I'll come with you," said Carrie.

"No!" he said sharply. "I want some time alone with my daughter."

Let him be alone, sent Kaid. *We both have bio-monitor alerts and Vanna said we didn't need to keep a close watch on him provided we know he's taken his medication. He needs time to adjust to being home again.*

The door shut behind him with a finality that made Carrie shiver. "It's like he's shutting us all out," she murmured, walking down the steps into the lower level.

"He kept to himself even on the *Couana,*" said T'Chebbi. "Last time he saw me I was yelling at him and making him throw up. Maybe I should leave, go back to Brotherhood house in village."

"No, I want you to stay," said Carrie, touching her friend on the head gently as she passed her. "You have every right to be here, you're Kaid's Companion, and family."

T'Chebbi closed the comp down. "Can come visit me nights you want to, can't you Kaid?" She grinned at him as he came down into the room. "Like old times, eh?"

"Carrie's right, there's no reason for you to leave," said Kaid, going over to the hot plate. "Kusac has to get used to being among people again. Better he does it here with those he knows and trusts."

CHAPTER 6

Shola, Zhal-Ghyakulla 17th day (June)

"HE does nothing but stay in the nursery," said Carrie in exasperation. "Dzaka and Kitra have had to move out and go live at the main villa. I can't get him to show a spark of interest in anything but Kashini!"

"What about the estate?" asked T'Chebbi, wiping a piece of bread round her plate to mop up the last of her egg yolk.

"Tried that. Says Garras is doing a better job than he could."

"Training?"

"Too tired, yet he sleeps when Kashini sleeps, which is most of the day and all night!"

"The Touibans?"

"Says it needs a telepath to work with them and Mara's coping, plus his father wants her to train up in AlRel. I've tried everything I can think of!"

"The digging in the hill?" persisted T'Chebbi.

"Again, too tired! This lethargy isn't right, T'Chebbi. Vanna's drugs are too strong. They need to be reduced." She thumped her mug down on the table.

"Then speak to Vanna about it," said Kaid calmly. "I think the dose is right, for now at least. You're just getting wound up over the arrival of your father."

"I won't have him see Kusac in this state," she said. "That is, if I can pry him out of the nursery in the first place!"

"Speak to Vanna," he repeated. "You've a couple of days before your father arrives. That should be time enough."

"I'm doing this for Kusac's sake," she said. "It isn't fair my father should see him so brought down by medication. Not just that, he needs to get an interest in life here again. He needs a reason other than Kashini to live."

Kaid reached across the table and placed his hand over hers. "I understand," he said quietly. "And you're right. In the long term, he does need to take up what he can of his old life. But he also needs time for his mind to heal, without pressure from us. I'll come with you to see Vanna."

"Thanks," she said. "I'd appreciate that."

Kaid gave her hand a gentle squeeze before letting it go and looking over at T'Chebbi. "You should feed yourself better," he said, knowing her tendency to skip meals when she was staying in the Brotherhood house. "Or move back here. How are Rezac, Jo, and Zashou settling in at Ruth's?"

T'Chebbi's mouth dropped open in a slight smile as she pushed her plate aside. "Well, Jo needs Humans around her even more because of the cub," she said. "Ruth's so practical, she's just what all three of them need. As for Rezac, he's taken to training with Garras like one born to it. Can see where you get it from," she grinned at Kaid. "We got Zashou up at the diggings with Touibans. Great help her knowing where everything was, what used for. Bodies and vehicles confuse her, though. As she says, they left monastery for Stronghold. Remains are nothing to do with them, so whose are they?"

"I've been thinking about that," said Carrie. "There were members of Zashou's family who refused to leave, non-telepath members. Perhaps it involved them."

"Perhaps, but remember, the floods came within two or three days of us leaving here for Stronghold. Whatever it was happened almost immediately after we left," said Kaid.

Carrie nodded. "Vartra's people left partly because of our warning that the remains of a firefight had been found. There were Valtegans posted nearby, in a city called Khalmer. Zashou said the small peninsula it was on was destroyed in the Cataclysm, washed away by the tidal waves. The Valtegans knew what was coming. What if some of them who couldn't be evacuated headed here as the nearest high ground? And the Aldatans would head there. That gives you the reason for the fight."

"You could be right. We may never know unless Zashou recognizes something among the belongings we found with the Sholan remains. Has she been shown them?"

"Not yet, but Jack said he'd show her today. Any news yet

on what's happening with Ambassador Taira's attempted abduction of Kate and Taynar?"

"Falma helped them write out affidavits which they then swore with Konis as the local Judge. They've been sent to the Chief Protector at Shanagi. He's preparing a special warrant ordering the ambassador to attend a hearing the day after the new ambassadors arrive. Shola's hosting the Allied Worlds Council for the next two years."

"I thought Taira had diplomatic immunity."

"He has, but I don't think any of the other Alliance Worlds will support him when he complains. Abducting minors of any species is a serious crime on every world. My gut feeling is that the others will see the possibility of it happening to them and will uphold the warrant. Especially as they'll all know about the Chemerians withholding knowledge of the Free Traders from the Alliance and passing off Trader imports as their own goods. The Chemerians can't deny that charge when members of the U'Churian and Cabbaran worlds are sitting opposite them."

"What about the Primes and the TeLaxaudin?" asked T'Chebbi.

"The Primes are a special case. We can only grant them Associate membership in the Alliance at this time, though if all goes well, I'm told their status will be reviewed at the end of a year," replied Kaid. "They'll join Earth and Jalna round the table at a lower level of discussions on Alliance policy and trade. We can't afford to take chances with them. The TeLaxaudin are due later this month."

"Glad they're being so cautious," said T'Chebbi. "Was afraid Primes'd be granted full status and be privy to defense plans against Valtegans."

"The Primes are Valtegans," said Carrie, her voice hard. "Am I the only one to remember that?"

Kaid sighed. "No, but we need them, Carrie. It was only one faction that was responsible for what happened to us, not all of them."

"I want to find out exactly who else was involved and if they've taken samples from us for a breeding program." She looked from Kaid to T'Chebbi. "You do realize what we're talking about here, don't you? The possibility that they may use those samples to create hybrid cubs. They'd be our cubs—yours, Kaid, and mine and Kusac's, as well as Rezac, Kate and Taynar's!"

"They need a female Human or Sholan to implant any fertilized eggs into, Carrie. We've been through this," said Kaid. "Without a host, they can do nothing beyond observe early cell division. No embryo has been successfully grown in an artificial womb."

"Not on Shola," she corrected.

"Not on any Alliance world—the old Alliance at least, but I doubt that the other species have managed it either. And even if they had, they'd have to duplicate our hybrid womb environment, not use a Valtegan one, or a TeLaxaudin." Kaid pushed his chair back. "Father Lijou and Master Rhyaz are dealing with it, Carrie. If there's anything to find out, they'll find it, believe me. You're getting yourself worked up about nothing. Why don't we head over to Vanna's now and talk her into coming to see Kusac?"

It was the third time in the last week that Kaid had called Noni. As the comm screen cleared, once more he found himself facing Teusi.

"May the sun shine on you today, Tallinu," Noni's apprentice said.

"And you," said Kaid automatically, trying not to let his impatience sound in his voice. "Where's Noni?"

"Unavailable, I'm afraid. I have passed your messages on to her."

"And what did she say?" he asked, ignoring the slight note of reproach in the other's voice.

"She'll get back to you when she can. She's very busy right now, setting up the new surgery at Stronghold."

He frowned, eye ridges meeting above his nose. "She's avoiding me, isn't she?" he said, angry now that he was having this conversation with Teusi. It wasn't Noni's way to let Teusi deal with callers, and certainly never him.

"I'm afraid that isn't for me to say," replied Teusi, keeping his voice and expression carefully neutral.

"Dammit, Teusi! Stop giving me the runaround!" he snapped. "I know her well enough to recognize when she's avoiding me! What I don't know is why!"

"I'm afraid I . . ."

"Teusi," said Kaid warningly, clenching the edge of the desk out of the other's line of sight. "I need to know. One way or another, she's refused to speak to me since I got back from Haven. What's up?"

"You invoked kin on her." This time the unspoken reproof was noticeable in the set of his ears as well as his voice.

"That's why I want to talk to her." He hadn't missed the slight movement of Teusi's head to one side.

"You had no right to . . ."

"I have every right," he interrupted. "This is none of your concern. I know she's there. Tell her I brought kin of hers, and mine, back with me from Jalna."

"She has none."

"Not from this time," said Kaid. "But then neither am I."

"Who you brought back with you, boy?" Noni's voice demanded harshly from off-screen.

"Rezac Dzaedoh."

Teusi disappeared to be replaced by Noni. She stared out of the screen at him, brown eyes almost black with anger.

"I'm listening."

This was a Noni he'd never met before. He'd seen her as angry with others, but never him. "He's my father, Noni. He's the one we went to Jalna to rescue, whose mind touched Carrie's here on Shola as Jo's team released him and his Leska from the stasis cube. He's from the time of Vartra and the Cataclysm."

"I remember," she interrupted. "You said nothing about him being my kin."

"I didn't know myself till we rescued them."

"How do I know you're not lying?"

His ears flattened to his skull in a mixture of anger and disbelief that she could accuse him of such a thing. "I've never lied to you, Noni," he said. "Taynar Arrazo asked him his clan name, in front of all my people."

She snorted contemptuously. "Then he's lying."

"Why are you trying so hard to deny the relationship?" he asked, realizing she was attempting to manipulate him through anger. "I think it's time you gave me some answers, Noni. Why did you take an interest in a cub found abandoned near Vartra's Retreat when you were known to dislike all younglings? Why let him come plaguing you every day with his questions till you started teaching him your craft, taking him on walks to learn the plants for healing, showing him how to make up the potions and salves? You kept that interest in him over the next twelve years to the point where you even made him your apprentice." He dropped his voice. "Why did you help him escape the Protectors when he killed his foster father? Why go to the Brotherhood and persuade them to find him, pull him from the heart of the Claw Pack in Ranz, make him one of theirs and have the Protectorate wipe his slate clean? Why did you do all that for someone who meant nothing to you—unless you felt the pull of blood, Noni?"

"You still ask too many questions, boy! Always causing me trouble, you were." She scowled at him, eye ridges meeting in an annoyed frown. "Haven't changed, have you?"

"Neither have you. You never gave me any answers, that's why I keep asking," he replied. "I won't be put off this time, Noni."

Her gaze looked straight through him. "Why should I tell you anything?" she asked crossly. "I owe you nothing, boy."

He looked away from the screen for a moment, wondering what she wanted him to say—what he could say that would make her talk. "Carrie's pregnant by me," he said at last, looking back at her. "You were right. We're sharing a cub—a daughter."

Noni raised a quizzical eye ridge at him. "Oh?" she said, her tone suddenly neutral.

"I know you've been told Carrie and I Leska Linked while on the Prime ship," he said, letting her hold his gaze this time. "The Primes healed her, but they removed her implant."

"I want to hear those three words again," she demanded.

"You were right," he sighed. "I was wrong, Noni. There will be a cub."

"Cubs," she corrected him, but her voice was gentler. "There will be cubs, I said. I remember it well. You called me an old fool, you did."

"Cub. One," he said firmly.

"There was T'Chebbi's," she reminded him.

"All right!" he snarled, irritation getting the better of him as his ears flicked angrily. "How much groveling do you want me to do, dammit? I had the right to invoke kin on you, and you know it!"

"That remains to be seen, when I've met this Rezac and his Leska."

"You still haven't answered me! Why did you always look out for me?" he demanded. "You must have felt something, suspected there was a blood tie between us!"

"Why should I tell you? Seems to me you're still more trouble than you're worth!"

He bit back another angry retort, knowing it was what she wanted—to divert him. Then he remembered what had worked well in the past. Lowering his ears to half height, he tilted his head to one side and looked up at her, widening his eyes slightly. "Because I'm asking nicely?" he said, softening his tone.

Noni began to laugh, a deep, belly rumble that lit her face all the way to her eyes. Eventually she subsided into chuckles and wiped her streaming eyes on her sleeve. "You always knew how to reach me, you did. You got your own measure of Glamour when you put your mind to it, Tallinu. Vartra warned me, you know. Said I'd get more than I bargained for when I got you back. He was right. You trying to charm me, your cub on the way, and your father!"

"You went to Vartra about me?" He righted his ears, the revelation astonishing him.

"You were missing," she snapped acerbically. "What was I supposed to do when I knew the Valtegans had you? Wring my hands and weep?"

"You bargained for my return?"

"He gave me no choice. I was owed a favor. He gave me you."

"The price?" he asked quietly, dreading her answer. "What did it cost you, Noni?"

"Just told you! I lost my favor! A favor from an Entity isn't to be chosen lightly, and I had to go waste it on you," she grumbled, scratching herself vigorously behind one ear.

He knew he'd won now and pushed the point home. "Why do that for me unless you suspected we were kin?"

Her face softened and she reached out to touch the comm screen with her hand. "Vartra said it, Tallinu. You were the cub I never had. Yes, I suspected something when they brought you to me the day they found you. It frightened me, that's why I didn't dare keep you. Vartra knows, it was the biggest mistake I ever made. I've been paying for it every day since you came to me saying you'd killed Nuddoh M'Zushi."

As she closed her eyes, Kaid could see how much the confession was costing her. For a brief moment, he felt her mind touch his. Instinctively, his hand went out to his own screen.

"I chose to live alone because my work as a Guardian meant everything to me—more than a mate or cubs. I wanted no distractions. Then you came along, so small and hurt—too terrified to even speak for that first month. You smelled and felt like kin, and you Challenged the life I'd chosen. I had to give you up."

"But you didn't." He let his hand drop back down to the desk. "You watched over me, gave me hope, an escape from Nuddoh."

"Not well enough, or I'd have known what Nuddoh was doing to you! I should have seen what was happening!" She took her hand away from the screen, ears laid back and a look of distress on her face.

"We're only mortal, Noni," he said quietly. "I couldn't stop the Valtegan priest raping Carrie, nor did I believe her when she said Kusac was still alive. You couldn't have known what Nuddoh was doing till it was too late. We both need to accept what we cannot change, what we had no control over, and let the guilt go."

She nodded slowly. "It isn't easy, though. What's this father of yours like?" she asked, her voice becoming crisper. "Too like you for comfort, I'll be bound. Arrogant, self-opinionated, takes a personal responsibility for everyone! Am I right?"

"Well, I know where *you* got it from," he grinned.

"Cheek of you! Just remember one thing, Tallinu. No matter what time you come from, you're still young enough to have faint cradle marks on your arse! I'm still Noni to you!" Her eyes twinkled at him. "More so since you're going to make a grandmother of me again."

He raised his eye ridges in mock defeat. "Yes, Noni," he said. "Rezac's formed a Triad with Jo, a Keissian friend of Carrie's. They're expecting a cub shortly. His Leska, Zashou, wasn't my mother, though. It was a female called T'Chya, someone from Ranz that he knew before the Claws claimed him."

"The same Pack you ran with. History repeats itself. You claiming to be brothers, I suppose."

"The blood-tie is there, Noni, neither of us can ignore it. As brothers, we can cope. But it's really about Kusac that I contacted you."

"I got the medical reports. They don't look good, Tallinu. I doubt there's much I can do," she sighed. "I wish there was."

"You'll come, though? Rezac wants to meet you and I know Carrie would like to see you again."

"Nice to be so popular. I'll come, but not till next week. Maybe at least I can give him something better than the drugs that Vanna of yours is giving him."

"She's just cut them down. He was so sedated, there was no life left in him."

"And your Telepath Guild medics can do nothing for him, I'll be bound. Well, maybe I can, we'll see. In a week then, Tallinu."

Kaid touched his fingers to the screen in thanks. "Thank you, Noni," he said, aware that now her nickname of Grandmother meant more to him.

Zhal-Ghyakulla, 19th day (June)

He opened the den door, stalked past Kaid at the work console, down the stairs into the lower leisure area and over to the large entertainment comm. Ignoring Carrie, he switched it on, then turned to look at them.

"Why didn't someone tell me the Valtegans had landed on Shola?" he demanded.

Kaid stopped working and turned to look at him. "I didn't think you'd be interested."

"I've been watching reports of their arrival yesterday. The newsvids all paint them as white as our honored dead! Sorli's really got his Guild working overtime with subliminals!" His rumble of anger was getting deeper.

"Yes, the government is using subliminals, within the allowed parameters," said Kaid placidly as the large screen came to life showing the Governor's Palace at Shanagi. "All the new ambassadors arrived yesterday. And they aren't Valtegans, they're Primes, not the ones who . . ."

"There's no difference," he snarled, hand going to his neck to massage it as he began to pace in front of the screen. "Has everyone but me forgotten what they did to us?"

"Of course not," said Carrie, getting to her feet and going over to him. "How could I? But it was only one Prime who separated us. Remember the doctor who helped you?"

"You can't have seen the vids," he said, stopping to point at the newscast. "Look at that! A state reception for them, with a full Warrior honor guard! I refuse to believe that Chy'qui and J'koshuk could torture us without their Commander being aware of what was going on!"

"Relax, Kusac," said Kaid, getting up and coming down to join them. "They have no military, their command structure is very different from ours. I scanned the Commander during the treaty talks. He had no idea of what was happening, believe me. Besides, all this happened yesterday."

He stared at Kaid for a moment then looked away. Kaid, who'd not known he was a telepath until a short time ago, was now doing what he should be doing. He rubbed his neck harder, kneading it in an effort to stop the tingling sensation. He knew he was letting his anger get out of control but could do little about it.

"They're manipulating the public to make them accept the Primes as allies," he said slowly. "They didn't do that when Carrie arrived on Shola. We had to defend ourselves against prejudiced dissidents."

"We had Kaid and the Brotherhood to protect us," reminded Carrie.

"The estate was fortified—it still is," said Kaid. "Both Chy'qui and J'koshuk are dead, Kusac. We have to accept the Primes as allies now. We need their help against the real Valtegan enemy."

He turned away from them to stare at the screen, forcing himself to breathe more slowly, to recite the Litany for Relaxation. He was damned if on top of this insult, the sight of those Valtegans was going to get him in such a rage that it triggered the neural pain. It was humiliating to suddenly find himself lying on the floor unable to stop whimpering.

On the screen, the autovids had homed in on the Sholans standing waiting to greet the Prime Ambassador and his party as they walked toward the Palace entrance. Standing among the Sholan High Command and representatives of the World Council, were Master Rhyaz and his father.

"I don't believe it!" he began, the hair on his neck starting to rise as the tingling became a definite pain. "It's my father and . . ."

He got no further as Kaid grasped him firmly by the shoulder and pressed a hypodermic to his neck. The sting barely had time to register before the drugs hit him and he began to sway.

"Easy there," said Kaid as he and Carrie supported him over to the nearest seat. "As Head of Alien Relations and one of the signatories to the treaty, your father had no option but to be there, Kusac. If it's any comfort, Father Lijou refused to go and Rhyaz was only there because he'd other business to attend to."

Carrie knelt in front of him, taking his hands in hers. "I'm sorry we had to drug you, Kusac. It's fast acting but won't last long. It's better than suffering all that pain."

"Your father," he said, forcing the words out. He could barely keep his eyes open. "That's why he's here."

She nodded, glancing up at Kaid. "The trade treaties were signed yesterday by all the Alliance and Associate members. Like Rhyaz, he didn't stay for the banquet. He said he wasn't associating with the Primes any more than he had to because of what happened to us. He stayed with Rhyaz in his apartment at the Palace last night. We didn't tell you about the Primes because we didn't want this to happen."

"Worse not knowing," he said, blinking to keep his eyes open.

"I promise we'll tell you next time," she said, letting him go and moving aside.

"Lie down, Kusac. You'll sleep for about an hour, then you'll be fine," Kaid said.

The comm on the upper level buzzed and while Kaid went to answer it, Carrie spread a rug over Kusac then settled down on a floor cushion, watching him. Reaching out, she took hold of his hand, feeling his fingers curl around hers as he drifted off to sleep. It was the first time since they'd returned from Haven that he'd made any affectionate gesture toward her or allowed her this close. She leaned forward, resting her head against his side, content for now.

A few minutes later, Kaid rejoined her, a strange look on his face. "Remember I told you that Raiban's been getting petty with the Brotherhood by refusing to issue Forces ammunition to our people when they're working for her? That she's making them buy their own? Well, we've just had a very strange request from Rhyaz. He's asked if we'd allow Captain Kishasayzar and two of his crew to stay on the estate for several weeks while we train them in appropriate Brotherhood skills. Seems that our Sumaan friend went back home and told his superiors what happened at Haven. Now he's free to take contracts where he wants, the Sumaan decided that it's time they improved their fighting skills. In return, they've offered to gather information for us. Not just Kisha, but all his people. I'm sure the two are connected. I wonder what Rhyaz is up to."

"You're joking," said Carrie, sitting up. "The Sumaan actually said they want to spy for the Brotherhood?"

Kaid nodded. "They'll only pass on what they consider we should know, but they get to places we can't, like the Chemerian worlds. Who'd suspect the Sumaan of being agents for us? I'd say they were harboring a pretty deep resentment of their tree-climbing employers, wouldn't you?"

"But alien Brothers?"

"We have gene-altered Humans," he reminded her gently.

"I don't consider myself Human now," she said after a moment's thought. "What did you tell Rhyaz?"

"That the decision is yours and Kusac's, not mine. Dzaou's unit settled in fine, apart from Dzaou himself, but I don't know if Kusac wants your home estate to become a training camp for alien Brothers."

"You've got a say in it too," she reminded him. "It's also your home."

"I know you both gave me that right, but I think I should take a back seat for the foreseeable future. I don't want Kusac to feel Challenged by me in every area of his life with you."

"What life with me?" she asked, getting to her feet. "We have none. He sleeps in the nursery, and when it's our Link day, you know he takes Kashini up to his parents' home. I don't know where I am with him, Tallinu. It's as if all the love was burned out of him by J'koshuk and Chy'qui."

"I didn't realize it was that bad," he said, touching her arm briefly.

"Oh, it's that bad. You're not helping me any, either," she said pointedly, looking at him. "When we arrived home, you asked me not to back away from you. Now it's you who seems afraid of any real closeness. I feel as if I've lost you both."

"I've only been thinking of Kusac," he said awkwardly, not meeting her gaze. "Everyone comes to me now they realize Kusac won't get involved with estate life. Even Garras asks me about major decisions he handled himself while we were away. I feel like I'm stepping into Kusac's tracks, taking over his life, and I don't like it." He looked up at her. "I don't want Kusac's life, Carrie. I want my own."

His thoughts surrounded her as he removed the privacy barrier between them. *I love you, Carrie, I always have, but I never wanted us to be Leskas. It's too much for me.* His hands cupped her face as he rested his brow on hers.

I know, but it happened and we have to cope as best we can, she replied, wrapping her arms around him and holding him close, locking deep within her the hurt for him, for Kusac, and for herself. She felt imprisoned within the dark vault that was her own mind, as if she was running around hammering on the walls, desperate to escape, only there was no way out.

Since we're being so honest with each other, do you believe there's any hope that Kusac will be cured? she asked.

His hands moved to rest on her shoulders. *There's always hope. Noni will be here in five days, and we've yet to hear from Kzizysus, the TeLaxaudin. It shouldn't be long before their Ambassador arrives and when he does, we'll have an official channel through which to reach them. Go and get yourself ready to meet your father, Dzinae. I'll stay with Kusac.*

What about you? You need time to change, too.

I'll be there, but with Dzaka and Kitra. Better your father doesn't learn too much about our Triad. If he found it difficult to accept one Sholan husband, the thought of you having two will not comfort him.

They sat waiting in the family garden at the rear of the main house. Kashini, brushed till her pelt shone like new cut corn, toddled around the edges of the flower beds, examining each blossom with her nose, then fingers and mouth. Rhyasha was telling her stories of Kusac at just the same age but she couldn't really concentrate on them because Konis was in the lounge talking privately to Kusac.

"Carrie, stop fretting," admonished her bond-mother in a low voice as she leaned toward her. "All will be fine. Your father has had plenty of time to get used to our people on his own world, never mind the day he spent at the Palace."

"I'm not worried about him, it's Kusac," she said. "He's been so different since the Primes had him. I want my father to see Kusac's true self, not what he's become."

Rhyasha took Carrie's hand in hers, squeezing it gently. "I know something of what's been happening lately," she said. "That's why Konis is having a word with him now."

Carrie looked up sharply. "What do you mean?"

"I know my son well, cub. I can tell, even without being able to sense his mind, when things are wrong between the two of you. And I know you. I can only imagine what it's been like with both of them carrying around their guilt for what happened." She reached up to caress her cheek. "And you with a cub on the way." Abruptly, she changed the subject. "I invited T'Chebbi. As

Kaid's Companion, she should be here. Involve her more in your life, cub. Don't always be worrying you'll put Kusac's nose out. He has to learn to cope with the changing relationships between the four of you. Don't let your friendship with her, or her relationship with Kaid, suffer because of worrying that my son will feel you're filling his home with people. It's your home, too, and they were living with you before you went to Jalna."

Carrie gave a wan smile. "You're far too perceptive for my good," she murmured.

"I can't run the Aldatan Clan and estate without knowing something about Sholan nature, cub," she smiled. "No need for you to live like a widow because your life-mates are practicing self-denial. Encourage them! I hear T'Chebbi has an interesting range of perfumes," she whispered, eyes twinkling with mischief.

Carrie choked, trying to suppress her laughter. "You heard about that too?" she grinned.

Rhyasha flattened her ears in embarrassment. "Not only that, I had it used on me by Konis."

"Konis?"

"Shush!" hissed Rhyasha, looking round to see if anyone had heard. She leaned conspiratorially closer. "He was so worried about me just after we had the news of Kusac from the *Hkariyash* that he went to Vanna for advice rather than to our usual physician. She'd heard the story of T'Chebbi and Kaid from Garras—apparently Kaid told him—and she suggested Konis use this perfume she'd heard of."

"But how did he get hold of it with T'Chebbi away?"

"Konis is too embarrassed to tell me, but I gather Vanna got Dzaka and Kitra involved in finding it, then she went to her sister, Sashti, to make up something for him based on that perfume."

"And it worked, I take it."

"Too well," murmured Rhyasha. "I haven't told anyone else in the clan yet, but he persuaded me it was time to have another family, so now we're expecting twins in four months."

Carrie hesitated, unsure whether or not to congratulate her bond-mother.

"Oh, yes, now I'm used to the idea, I'm very happy, and so is Konis. But twins!" She shook her head and smiled wryly. "So much work. It provided the distraction I needed, and has given me the ability to sit back from my son's problem and be a little more objective."

They heard the sound of an approaching aircar. "Time for us to get Kusac, don't you think?" said Rhyasha, getting up and smoothing down the skirt of her more formal long purple robe.

"I have every sympathy with you, Kusac. There's little worse that a telepath can suffer than the loss of his Talent, but life has to go on. You cannot continue neglecting your duties toward the clan you fought so hard to found. Nor can you let your Triad fall apart."

"Garras manages the estate far better than I can right now, Father. He did well while we were away."

"How do you know? Have you checked through his reports? Gone to inspect the crops in the fields, examined the herds? We both know you haven't. And before you assume I'm spying on you, or someone has been coming to me complaining, they haven't. I can see the evidence for myself in the way those closest to you are behaving. I may not be able to feel your moods any more, Kusac, but I can feel theirs. You let yourself down, and the trust these people put in you."

Kusac sat silently, trying to deny the truth in what he said. How could his father expect him to just pick up the pieces of his old life and fix it as if it were a broken toy?

Konis reached out to touch him on the knee. "It's only because I love you that I'm telling you this," he said quietly. "You're pushing those closest to you away, like Carrie. She says nothing, but I can feel her unhappiness. She carries it everywhere with her. Only you can lift it. Not Kaid, not anyone else but you. She suffered badly too, and like you, she's living with the result of her captivity. And I don't just mean the cub she's expecting, I mean you. Every time you turn aside from her, you make it worse."

"Why do you think I tried to kill myself?" he asked, feeling the beginnings of anger stirring again. Why did everyone feel they had a right to lecture him about his life?

"To avoid dealing with the situation," said Konis, his tone becoming colder as he withdrew his hand. "Just as you're using anger now to avoid talking about it. Go ahead, lose your temper, Kusac. Let Carrie down in front of her father. Neither your mother nor I are prepared to avoid saying what we think for fear you'll lose your temper. That's your decision, not ours. You were brought up to have more self-control. It's time you exercised it."

Shocked, Kusac could only look at him in disbelief.

"You have responsibilities, Kusac," Konis said more gently. "You've a mate and a cub. Time you remembered that and got on with your life instead of giving in to self-pity. Carrie's father is Governor of the Human world of Keiss. He alone of the Humans has a place on the Allied Worlds Council. Will you humiliate your life-mate and all Shola in front of him by treating Carrie as if she were a stranger? You do realize she now has the right to go back to Keiss, taking her daughter with her, don't you? She can dissolve the marriage to you if she wishes, now she's no longer tied to you by a Leska Link. Are you going to continue to give her reasons to want to leave?"

"What?" It had never occurred to him that she'd be free to leave and take Kashini with her. "But she can't! We'd never get our Link back if that happened!"

Konis' expression softened. "You do still love her."

"Of course," said Kusac automatically. "Has she spoken to you or Mother?" he asked, suddenly afraid. "Is this why her father's visiting us, to take her home?"

"No, Kusac. He's on Shola in an official capacity. It's the first opportunity he's had to visit, that's all." Konis sat back, watching him carefully. "I knew that you were missing weeks before your mother did. I had to keep silent, carry it around inside me without her finding out because of the security involved. My behavior during that time nearly lost me not only Kitra but your mother. Don't make the same mistake I did. For Vartra's sake, Kusac, show her you care, now, before you do alienate her."

His head had started to ache and he put his hand up to rub it. "How can I, Father? I failed her. It's my duty, as you said, to protect her. If I hadn't told the Valtegan priest about her sister, he wouldn't have been interested in her at all. It was my fault she was . . ."

"Kusac, stop this," Konis interrupted him firmly, leaning forward and shaking him by the shoulders. "The priest was asking questions about her from the first. I know, I've read a transcript of your debriefing. He recognized her before he even saw you! There was no way you could possibly have stopped him. He wanted Carrie because her sister had died without giving him any information about the Keissian guerillas."

"I should have been able to keep quiet too!" he said, dropping his head to his hands, distraught at the memory. "If a Human female could do it, why couldn't I? Kaid trained me in what to do if we were caught and interrogated. He succeeded in keeping information from Ghezu! Only *I* failed, Father!"

He felt his father's hand on his head, then a glass was held in front of him. He smelled the sharp scent of arrise.

"You didn't fail, Kusac," said his father gently. "Kaid has told you, Carrie has told you, and now I'm telling you. Will you finally believe us all and stop surrounding yourself with guilt? Drink this. You need it. Even with the psi suppressants, you're still managing to broadcast. Is your wrist damper turned up to full?"

He released his head, sitting up to take the glass. "Yes," he muttered before downing the drink in one swallow and handing the empty glass back. It tasted as bitter as it smelled. "My Talent's gone. I don't see how you can possibly be picking up anything from me."

"You know I can pick up a newly emerged latent telepath from just about anywhere on this continent, Kusac," said Konis, putting the glass on the table behind him. "It's not surprising I should sense you. The arrise will help the headache by damping all the residual psi activity. Your Talent isn't completely gone, there is something left."

"Just not enough to use, and when I do use it without realizing, I suffer for it," said Kusac morosely.

"Be grateful there is something left," said Konis, sitting beside him. "There's still hope. We've only just begun to find out what can be done to help you. The TeLaxaudin are still working on it. The Prime Ambassador M'szudoe assured me word would be sent directly here when they have news of any kind. In the meantime, you have to adapt, live your life as normally as possible. And that includes making an effort with those who are your closest friends."

They heard footsteps and looked round to see Rhyasha and Carrie coming in from the garden.

"We heard the aircar," said Rhyasha. "Time for them to go and greet Mr. Hamilton."

"You're not coming with us?" asked Kusac, looking over at his mother.

"No, that's for you and Carrie," said Rhyasha, pushing Carrie forward. "On you go, don't keep him waiting. We'll be in here.

The others will stay in the garden till the time is right to introduce them."

Carrie, holding Kashini, accompanied Kusac along the colonnaded corridor that flanked the interior ornamental garden. The air was fresh here, cooled by the fountain in the center. She was nervous about meeting her father for the first time in over a year. Her thoughts were a jumble of memories from her childhood and worries about how he'd react to Kashini. For the life of her, she couldn't remember if her daughter's Validation had been broadcast to Keiss. If it hadn't, then her father would be seeing his half-Sholan granddaughter for the first time.

"Carrie," said Kusac, suddenly coming to a halt.

"What is it?" she asked, stopping.

"You looked preoccupied. Is Kaid—sending to you, or can we talk for a minute?"

"No, no one's sending to me," she said, trying to stop Kashini from wriggling free. "What is it? Do you want to go back to the lounge? Would you rather not come with us?"

"No. I wouldn't let you greet your father alone," he said. "I have to know something first. Are you planning to leave me? Go back to Keiss with your father?"

She looked at him in disbelief. "Excuse me?"

"Is your father coming to take you home?" he asked. "Because, if he is, don't go. I need you here." He reached out to touch her face.

"Kusac! What's gotten into you? Of course I'm not leaving you," she said, battling with the determined Kashini. "What maggot's gotten into your mind to make you think that?"

"Give her to me." Kusac took the squirming cub from her and holding Kashini firmly on one hip, he reached out again for Carrie, resting his hand on the back of her neck. "I know things have been difficult between us, Carrie, but I do love you." Hesitantly, he leaned closer till their lips touched.

It was all Carrie needed to hear. She moved closer, closing her eyes as she rested her hands against his chest. It was like their first kiss, when they were still unsure of each other. She let him lead, enjoying the moment as his kiss gradually grew bolder.

Footsteps and a cough sounded from the far end. Guiltily, they stopped, but Carrie remained where she was for a moment longer.

"I will never leave you," she whispered. "Without you, part of me would die, Kusac."

As they parted, Kusac lost his grip on Kashini. She tumbled to the ground, landing on all fours. Like a flash, she stood up and headed straight for the newcomer who stood just behind Che'Quul, the head attendant.

"Mr. Hamilton is here, Clan Leaders," said Che'Quul, trying not to smile as he attempted to catch the runaway.

Kashini, sensing what Che'Quul planned to do, had already dropped back onto all fours and was making a mad dash at him.

"Kashini, no!" exclaimed Carrie, starting to run after her errant daughter.

With the determination of youth, Kashini darted between Che'Quul's legs and, without missing a pace, leaped up to land smack in the center of her grandfather's chest, arms and legs splayed, claws extended.

Carrie's father staggered back slightly under the unexpected weight, grabbing for the bundle of fur and dusty tunic. A bedraggled flower head was thrust into his face as the cub began to trill and purr happily.

"Oh, Gods," muttered Carrie, skidding to a halt as Kusac stopped just behind her.

"I see you've met Kashini," said Kusac, realizing there was nothing they could do to salvage the moment.

"Hello, Dad," said Carrie, watching as her father adjusted his grip on the youngster before accepting the battered flower.

"Thank you, Kashini," Peter Hamilton said. He looked past Che'Quul—who excused himself and beat a hasty retreat—to Carrie and Kusac. "I hadn't expected quite so enthusiastic a greeting."

Carrie held out her arms. "I'll take her, Dad."

"No, thank you. I think I'd like to get to know this young lady better since she so obviously wants to meet me."

Rhyasha went back out to the garden and headed over toward where Kaid sat with his son and Kitra.

"She's got a sense of purpose about her," said Kitra in an undervoice. "I wonder which of us she wants."

"I hope it's not me," muttered Dzaka.

Rhyasha stopped in front of Kaid. "I'd like you to stay behind, if you don't mind, Kaid. I need to have a word with you about Carrie and Kusac."

Kaid nodded, watching Rhyasha sweep off back to the house in a billow of purple robes.

"I've seen that look in her eyes before," said Dzaka with a shudder. "I sympathize with you, Father."

"You don't know what it's about," said Kaid, flicking his ear as a buzzing insect got too close.

"Did I tell you about the time Rhyasha gave me a lecture on what was acceptable behavior toward a young female whose first lover you're about to become?"

"I think you mentioned it," said Kaid as Kitra began to laugh quietly.

"Well, like I said, I sympathize with you."

Kaid grunted and wondered how he could escape the forthcoming conversation.

Shanagi, Governor's Palace, the same day

At roughly the same time, in the Governor's Palace, Ambassador Taira Khebo was called before a disciplinary council made up of Alliance Ambassadors and a representative from Sholan Alien Relations. The meeting was chaired by Toueesut and his swarm of five male Touibans as they were deemed the most neutral.

"No right have you to call me here," said Taira belligerently in pidgin Sholan as he stopped his powered chair opposite the semicircle of people facing him. "Ambassador, I am. Have diplomatic immunity like yourselves. Why you not allow my guards to be with me?"

Toueesut's translator began to speak, drowning out the quieter sounds of his trilling. "Personal guards not needed at Hearing. Diplomatic immunity not prevent prosecution for kidnapping of young Sholan Leska couple which is a crime against all Alliance. The young of us all are our future and their safety when traveling in Alliance space should be assured. This matter the concern of every species."

"Not kidnapping them. Young Sholan misunderstand. I take them to Chemer homeworld for safety. Hospitality of our people extended while contacting their kin. Always Sholans misunderstand our motives," said Taira angrily, his large ears beginning to curl and uncurl at the outer edges.

"The complaint was made by Kate Harvey, actually, Ambassador Taira," said Peter Jordan, the representative from Keiss. "We have her statement here." He held it up for Taira to see. "I believe you were sent a copy."

"I see it. Female Human not trustworthy. Hysterical, you call," said Taira with a wave of his long-fingered hand. "She watched as Valtegan killed her family on Keiss. Still shocked when we find her. Trust her you cannot."

"Complaint made weeks later," pointed out Mrocca's translator as she raised herself on her forelimbs to give him a long stare. "Why she say this if not true?"

Taira turned his large brown eyes on the Cabbarran and regarded her thoughtfully for a moment. "Humans and Sholans become very close allies. Can even breed together. New Alliance members like yourselves not know of bad blood between us and Sholans in past. I say this is fabricated by both to bring dishonor on my species."

Jordan glanced at Falma. The Sholan stirred. "Are you accusing us of collaborating to invent these accusations, Taira?" His voice held a low rumble of anger. "That's a very serious allegation to make."

"So is kidnapping!" snapped the Chemerian, glaring at him.

"And accusing us of working with the Sholans against you isn't?" demanded Jordan. "If anyone is being divisive, it's you, Taira, by suggesting we're trying to undermine the Alliance!"

Taira glanced at Jordan, blinking rapidly. "I not say that!" he protested. "I say that young ones invent story!"

"Did we also invent it, Taira?" asked Shaqee, the U'Churian, quietly. "Because we put in our own complaint. Not only about the kidnapping, but about the fact you withheld information about the existence of the Alliance from us."

"What complaint?" asked Taira, glancing nervously in her direction. "I not been sent that."

"You were sent it at the same time as the ones concerning Taynar Arrazo and Kate Harvey," said Falma, lifting a sheaf of papers.

Taira's blinking increased and he looked up at the lights overhead, holding a hand up to shield his eyes. "Too bright in here," he muttered, his long fingers whitening as he gripped the arms of his chair more tightly. "Gives bad head. Cannot think straight."

"Lowering of lights please for all our comforts," said Toueesut to the Sholan Recorder who sat at the end of the table taking notes. "Thinking straight not the issue here, Ambassador Taira. What we meet to find out is truth of matter of kidnapping and withholding of information vital to Alliance and Free Traders. Waiting for the answers we are."

"U'Churian allies taken in by young ones. Not their fault. I did no harm to them. Were free to do as wished. Not prisoners, honored guests." He looked at the Sumaan representative. "Ask Hteiwossay. His people my guards."

The Sumaan lifted his neck to its full height, staring down at everyone there. "Those working for you are not being allowed involvement in legal matters. Disagreeing with you, Taira, is not permitted. Is in their contract. It is why we could not be telling the Alliance of Jalna and the Free Traders. Reprisals against us were promised."

"Let me get this straight," said Jordan, leaning forward slightly to get a better view of Hteiwossay. "All Sumaan have to sign a contract preventing them from being called as witnesses? They're prevented from discussing anything their employers do? Surely that's illegal?"

"Not illegal," said Hteiwossay dryly. "Normal Chemerian business policy. I saying this only because I as Ambassador not contracted to Chemerians like many of my people. Reprisals cannot be taken against me or my family."

"I do nothing illegal! My guards go everywhere," said Taira stiffly. "Hear much that's confidential. I cannot have them telling anyone else what they hear. Am Ambassador. Would breach security for all of us! Would affect trade contracts!"

"Damned convenient," said Jordan in disgust, sitting back.

Toueesut turned to his swarm companions and began conversing with them in a chorus of high pitched trills and riffs of sound. Faint perfumes permeated the air.

After a few minutes, he turned back to the council. "Ambassador Taira is denying the accusations; therefore be bringing in those involved in the incident for the telling of their side of events."

"No need!" exclaimed Taira, leaning forward anxiously in his chair. "I tell you truth! Young ones misinterpret my actions! I take them to Chemer only for hospitality, not as prisoners!"

Toueesut frowned, the bushy brows almost hiding his eyes. "You are changing your version to say the young ones now made mistake, they did not lie on purpose about your intentions?"

Taira's head bobbed on its spindly neck several times. "Yes! I say they made mistake, not say they lie. I make mistake in doubting them. No need to bring them in."

Toueesut signaled the Sholan guards at the door. "We bring them in anyway," he said shortly. "Concerned I am that you are changing your side of this incident many times. Needing to hear the truth direct from them we are."

Taira slumped back in his chair, ears curling up till they were barely visible.

Kate and Taynar, accompanied by Ruth, were ushered in.

"Who she?" demanded Taira, rousing himself as the three were shown to seats at one end of the semicircle of tables. "This Human was not there!"

"Ambassador Taira, I presume," said Ruth, staring at him as she sat down and settled the folds of her long skirt. "I'm here because Taynar and Kate are minors. I won't allow them to be intimidated by having to appear before this council of Ambassadors and Alliance officials. They're entitled to have a representative with them, and I'm it!"

Taira subsided again, muttering darkly.

"You will tell us, if you please, what happened to you after your ship was found by Ambassador Taira," said Toueesut.

Nervously, Kate began to speak, recounting how Taira had at first been friendly, treating them well, feeding them and showing them to comfortable quarters on his ship. Then the next day, they'd been taken to the ship's doctor to be checked out. That's when they'd told him they were Leskas. From then on, everything had changed. Taira had questioned them closely about their abilities, getting angry when they couldn't give him the answers he wanted because they knew so little about it themselves.

Taynar added his bits in here and there, expanding on what Kate was saying, adding that it was only when they landed at Tuushu Station in the Chemerian sector that they'd realized they were prisoners.

"Kate had been trying unsuccessfully to read the Ambassador's mind, then she tried the doctor. She didn't get much, just enough to know that they were planning to experiment on us, find out what caused our Link. They wanted to keep us, force us to work for them. Taira had the Sumaan on his ship guarding us," he said, looking nervously at Hteiwossay. "When we got off, we were trying to find a way to escape when we saw Captain Tirak and his crew."

"We thought they were Sholans," said Kate. "We yelled but they didn't hear us, so we refused to move. Taira got mad and ordered the Sumaan to carry us if necessary. That's when I reached out for Captain Tirak and made him come to rescue us."

"Not true!" exclaimed Taira, glowering at Kate and Taynar. "Guards did not touch them! U'Churian captain suddenly came running at us. He took the female and ran off carrying her! His crew followed and took young male! He kidnap them, not I!"

Kate looked uncertainly at Ruth. "He didn't. I made him take us off the station. I controlled his mind."

"She lies," hissed Taira, ears furling and unfurling rapidly again in agitation.

"*He's* lying," said Taynar, getting to his feet, tail swaying angrily. "I asked for a comm link to call my parents on Shola and he refused. He got so angry with Kate that he grabbed hold of her and his claws punctured her arm!" He began to advance on the Chemerian but Ruth brought him up short with a few warning words.

"I want him prosecuted," said the outraged youngling, looking at Toueesut. "No one harms my Leska and gets away with it!"

Jordan developed a cough at about the same time Falma found he needed a drink of water.

"I have heard enough to convince me that whoever is lying, it isn't Kate or Taynar," said Shaqee with a faint smile.

Toueesut nodded. "Has anyone got any questions to ask of the young people?" He looked round the other members of the council as Taira continued to protest his innocence. "You excused are from this hearing and grateful are we for your coming here to answer our questions," he said to Kate and Taynar.

"This is conspiracy to keep valuable resource from rest of us!" blustered Taira as Ruth shepherded her charges out. "Why only Shola have Leska telepaths? Why they not work for rest of us?"

"Our telepaths have worked for other Alliance members, Ambassador Taira," said Falma. "I don't, however, remember your people requesting such a service from us. Perhaps because of the bad blood you mention?"

"Not want Sholan Leskas! Want hybrids," hissed Taira. "More powerful. No argument with Humans from us. Less likely turn on Chemerian employers!"

"You've certainly given us grounds to be cautious of further involvement with you now," said Jordan sharply.

"The mixed Leskas are very few in number, Taira, and most are still in training. They aren't old enough or ready to accept private contracts yet."

"Not true! You prevent them from doing this! Are prisoners on Shola!"

Shaqee looked at the Sholan. "Are the mixed Leskas free to take contracts from other Alliance species?"

"Ambassador Shaqee, your people on Jalna aided a mixed Leska pair when one of them was seriously injured in a local insurrection," said Falma. "You know we don't keep them chained to Shola."

She nodded. "This is true. It's hard to believe that given the chance to escape they would stay loyal to you if they were treated as prisoners. Or indeed, what such prisoners of Shola were doing on Jalna in the first place," she added, looking back at Taira.

"In fact," said Falma pointedly, "they were on Jalna at the specific request of the Chemerian government."

Toueesut's translator began to talk again. "Captain Tirak and his crew also are waiting outside, Ambassador Taira. Is there a need for them to be coming in here one at a time to tell us what happened at Tuushu Station?"

"No," muttered Taira, shifting restlessly in his chair. "I only asked questions of young ones. Not breaking the law, not kidnapping! Guards only escort us off ship, nothing more. Is dangerous place, Tuushu Station. Free Traders come there."

"Now we want to know why you hiding Free Traders from us," said Toueesut. "And why you allow them alone to visit Tuushu Station when none of Allied worlds but Sumaan allowed there!"

"I not make Chemerian policy," hissed Taira. "Not up to me who goes to Tuushu Station!"

"As Ambassador to the Allied Worlds Council, it is up to you to keep us informed of any new species you meet," said Falma. "You knew we were searching for the species responsible for killing millions of our people, yet even when we found them on Keiss you said nothing about the Free Traders. Instead you came and demanded we find 'our enemies' as you call them. Jalna held the key we needed! If we'd known about it earlier, we'd have found out about the Primes!"

"And maybe caused us a war with them," countered Taira. "We knew nothing of them either! Not been trading there long enough for Prime visit!"

"Asking the questions is for me," Toueesut rebuked Falma. "We finding out you trade at Jalna with Free Traders for twenty years, Ambassador Taira. Why your government not telling us about them? This second way you breach Alliance policy and is not acceptable to any member of council, be they Free Trader or Alliance."

"Not my decision," repeated Taira, blinking rapidly as he looked at all the council members. "I not Ambassador twenty years ago. I not admit to kidnapping young ones either. Told you they misinterpret my intentions."

"You have responsibilities as Chemerian representative to Allied Worlds Council," said Toueesut, frowning. "When you heard of tragedy of Sholan colonies, your responsibility was to advise your government to tell us all about the Free Traders. Quick in coming to the Council asking for protection from the Valtegans you were. Not so quick in sharing information."

"Obvious why they kept silent about us," said Mrocca, her prehensile snout wrinkling with distaste. "Greed. Want to keep Trader market for themselves. We find many goods from our worlds they sell, claimed to be of Chemerian origin."

Shaqee nodded, her black mane of hair rising slightly in anger. "Home is not pleased either. Some items of ours were also sold as Chemerian goods. Action must be taken against you and your people, Taira, from all of us. On our world, to do this would result in imprisonment for a long time."

Toueesut looked at Jordan.

"I agree," the Human said. "What's the point in having treaties if they're broken without fear of reprisals? Your people have been exposed as kidnappers, liars, and frauds, Taira, and my government wants to see you held personally responsible for your attempt to kidnap Kate Harvey and her Leska."

Hteiwossay lowered his neck, looking around his fellow councillors before speaking. "Warriors are we, Chemerian. Pride ourselves on our honor. There is no honor in anything you have done. My government owes you much but is prepared to cancel all contracts with your people unless you swear this will not happen again."

"You can't do that!" exclaimed Taira, his voice rising in pitch. "Your government owes us much for the ships we have leased to you!"

"Paying off the debt we have been doing for many years," said Hteiwossay with a deep hiss of anger. "Vast sums you have charged for the ships which take us into space. Knowing now we are that you hid the existence of Alliance until we had signed many contracts with you. Even if we have only those few ships we have paid for, finding work elsewhere with more honorable people should not be difficult."

As Taira began an angry reply, Toueesut gave a high-pitched trill that made everyone clap their hands to their ears in distress. While they recovered, he consulted again with his swarm companions.

"Arguing is not what we came here for," he said sternly, looking at Taira, who was still rubbing his ears and moaning. "Is it being agreed by us all that you did try to kidnap the young ones?" He looked around the semicircle, receiving nods and gestures of agreement.

"Obvious it is that you purposely hid the existence of the Free Traders and the Alliance from us all, so a punishment must be set for these crimes you and your species have committed. I have decided you will be sent back to your world under escort and not allowed to return for two months. Your world will hand over to the Alliance Council the papers dealing with all the ships you have supplied to the Sumaan, the amounts you are charging and the amounts they have paid. They will be looked into by our auditors and fair prices determined. Long enough have you held the Sumaan to ransom over these ships and long enough have they been tied to only you as their suppliers and employers. The Chemerian homeworld and its colonies will also be made accessible to all Alliance members, not just the Free Traders. This is the price you will pay to the Alliance and the Free Traders for your duplicity."

He stood up as Taira began to protest loudly. "You can choose to leave the Alliance if that is more to your liking. This is my judgment. Does any member of the council disagree with it?"

Again there was a quiet chorus of agreement from all present.

Toueesut looked over to the two Sholan guards at the door. "See the Ambassador is taken to Lygoh Spaceport and boards his ship. Arrange for him to have an escort back to his homeworld." With that, Toueesut, surrounded by his swarm, left in a cloud of scented air.

Falma and Hteiwossay were the last to leave the council room. As the Sholan gathered his papers and looked over at the large Sumaan Ambassador, he said quietly, "That was unexpected. Hit the damned Chemerians where it'll really hurt. In their banks. And it frees your people from them."

Hteiwossay shrugged, lips curling back from his teeth in a small grin as he got to his feet. "It is being to everyone's benefit that we are no longer tied to the Chemerians. Fighting for them not appealing to Warriors such as us. They have little honor." He lowered his neck until his head was close to Falma's ear, then in what was for him a whisper, he said, "Our people let U'Churians take the Sholan hatchlings. Waiting for word still we are from Kusac, the son of your employer. Closer links with Sholan Warriors there will soon be."

Startled, Falma took a step backward. "Excuse me?"

"Ah, knowing about this you aren't," he said, tilting his head from one side to the other. "No matter, soon you will. Toueesut's judgment making this easier." With that, he ambled off, leaving behind a very puzzled Falma.

Elsewhere in the Palace, Rhyaz was meeting with Raiban.

"Cutbacks?" said Rhyaz. "I've heard nothing about cutbacks for the military. If anything, your budget was increased because of the Prime crisis."

"Call it economies, then," said Raiban, sitting back in her chair. "You wanted independence, Rhyaz, I'm giving it to you. Your people will have to pay for their own arms and munitions if they're working for the Forces."

"Then put their wages up, dammit!" said Rhyaz angrily. "Your budget includes cash to employ the Brotherhood as specialists and tutors to the Forces."

"Does it? I haven't got that in writing. Have you?" she asked urbanely.

"What is it you're really after, Raiban?" he asked quietly,

keeping a tight rein on his temper. "What is all this aggravation of my people in aid of?"

"I'm letting you experience a few of life's realities, Rhyaz. You're more ambitious than Ghezu, I'll give you that, but you're still new at your post in the Brotherhood. Ambition without substance will get you nowhere, and you have no financial backing. You need the Forces. We're your main employer. Trying to sustain that fleet and outpost of yours without the money your people get from us is impossible. All you have to do is become part of us and your problems will melt away."

He stared at her for a long moment. "I see," he said quietly, then got to his feet. "You know, Lijou was right about you."

She frowned. "I don't know what you mean."

"He said the threat you made to Kha'Qwa wasn't an empty one. I told him you wouldn't be foolish enough to send troops to Stronghold to have him arrested."

"Look, that business with Kha'Qwa was unfortunate," she said, sitting up, her indolent pose dropped. "I forgot she was pregnant. No one's more glad than me that their cub was born safely."

"She nearly bled to death, Raiban. I don't think you realize how ill she was. She'll never have any more cubs," he said coldly. "And all because you couldn't speak to Father Lijou the instant you wanted."

"She only fell over, for Vartra's sake!"

"She had a medical condition that wasn't discovered till then."

"That's hardly my fault! Why has it suddenly become an issue, Rhyaz? This happened nearly a month ago!"

"Kha'Qwa had to have further surgery yesterday, that's why Lijou didn't come to the ceremonies."

"Why didn't you say so instead of giving us some other half-broiled excuse?" she demanded. "Your people are always trying to create an air of secrecy around you. It's time you joined the real world, Rhyaz. You can't survive without us."

"My friends' private lives are just that. Private. And Hell will freeze over before the Brotherhood joins the Forces, Raiban. You don't give a damn for my people. They do all the dirty jobs your Forces haven't the training or the stomach for, and still you despise us. You haven't even offered an apology to Kha'Qwa and Lijou!"

"It wasn't my fault, dammit!" she snarled, her short hair rising till it stood out like stiff bristles on a brush. "If you hadn't been so damned secretive about what you were doing, none of this would have happened. You want to blame someone for Kha'Qwa's fall, then blame yourself for running off to Haven!"

"The Forces need us, Raiban; we don't need you, as you're about to find out," he said quietly before turning to leave.

"You pull any stunts, Rhyaz, and you'll find your contract with us torn up!" she yelled out after him.

"You can't do it," he said, opening the door and looking back over his shoulder at her. "Just as you haven't the right to arrest the Father, only Kha'Qwa didn't know that. Governor Nesul agrees with the contract, not you. Just make sure you're prepared for the consequences if you carry on this war against us, Raiban."

He was fuming as he headed down the corridor to the vehicle park, L'Seuli following silently in his wake. Lijou had come to him yesterday after Noni had broken the bad news. He wouldn't soon forget their distress. At least they had their son. But Raiban's attitude incensed him. Had she shown any remorse over the incident, it would have been another matter. Let her assimilate the Brotherhood, make it part of the Forces? Never! If she wanted a fight, by Vartra, she'd get it!

He barely noticed the group of U'Churians ahead until one blocked his path. Startled, he looked up, aware that his Second was now by his side, hand resting warningly on his arm.

"You are Commander Rhyaz of the Brotherhood? I recognize the uniform."

The Sholan was good and well accented, as if the speaker had learned it from a native.

"Captain Tirak?" asked L'Seuli, stepping forward.

The black-pelted male nodded, mouth widening in a smile. "I'd not expected to see you here, Commander. Can we talk privately? I have a matter of importance I must discuss with your Guild Master." He handed Rhyaz a sealed letter. "From Ambassador Shaqee. It will explain much."

"The aircar, Commander," suggested L'Seuli in a low voice. "Raiban's . . ."

"Come with us," interrupted Rhyaz, taking Tirak by the arm. "There are ears everywhere at present."

Valsgarth Estate, later the same day

Her father decided to accept Rhyasha's and Konis' invitation to extend his visit.

"I'll have time to call in on Jack," he said. "See more of my granddaughter." He scratched Kashini behind the ears but the cub was tired and did no more than yawn before snuggling down in Carrie's arms, purring gently.

Kaid excused himself, saying Rhyasha wanted him to remain behind, probably something to do with Kitra's and Dzaka's wedding, he reassured her. T'Chebbi decided she wanted to walk back, so Carrie was left to return alone with Kusac in the aircar.

"I thought the visit went well," she said, attempting to break the silence as they skimmed along the roadway between the two estates.

"Kashini certainly captivated your father."

"Who wouldn't be captivated by her?" she murmured, resting her head against her daughter's. "You were good company tonight, Kusac. Thank you for making the effort."

Kusac raised the vehicle's nose, taking it over the wall into the villa grounds. "I'm glad it went well," he said, slowing down as he took them round to the side of the house to park. "I thought I'd go to Vanna's tonight," he said awkwardly. "Tomorrow's your Link day with Kaid. I can't stay with my parents as usual with your father there, and I have an open invitation from Vanna and Garras."

"There's no need," she began.

"*I* need to go," he interrupted, turning to look at her. In the moonlight, his eyes were almost luminous. "I've got a session with her therapist tomorrow anyway."

"I thought things were better between us." His decision had taken her by surprise.

He leaned forward to stroke her hair. "It's a start," he said gently. "I can't go too fast, Carrie. You take Kashini in tonight. Yashui can bring her over to me tomorrow morning."

Her heart sank as she nodded mutely and began to get up, but Kusac stopped her.

"I do love you," he said, resting his palm against her neck in an intimate gesture that startled her. "I wish we could turn the clock back, but we can't. I have to start again. I can't pick up from where we were before."

"I understand," she said, voice husky with tears she didn't want to shed in front of him. "I'd better go. I don't want Kashini to get chilled."

Once inside, Carrie gave the sleeping cub to Yashui to put to bed. In her current state of mind, her distress would only wake her daughter. She headed for the den, waiting for Kaid, only to have him send to tell her he was spending the night at the Shrine with Ghyan.

Zhala bustled in moments later to put a fresh pot of coffee on the hot plate and the next thing she knew, T'Chebbi was there. She found Carrie hugging a crumpled, tearstained cushion.

"What happened now?" T'Chebbi asked, sitting down beside her. "I thought everything went well."

"Oh, don't mind me," she sniffed. "Yes, everything was fine. Dad's staying another couple of days and Rhyasha's got him organized. He's meeting Jack tomorrow for a tour round the main estate. He's coming here the day after."

"Uh huh. So where're the males?" she asked shrewdly, taking the cushion away from her.

"Kusac's gone over to Vanna's and Garras', and Kaid's spending the night at the Shrine."

"What? Both of them away? I thought Kusac at least would be with you. Seemed much better tonight."

"He is, but he's saying we have to start again."

She frowned. "Again what?" Then she figured it out. "Ah. Has he spent a night with you since Haven?"

Carrie shook her head miserably.

"Me neither," she said thoughtfully as she put an arm round Carrie's shoulders. "Kaid told me Kusac hurt you accidentally that night. Figure he's afraid it happens again."

"Kaid told me he went up to the observation deck with you. What did you talk about?"

She shrugged. "This and that," she said vaguely.

"I need to know, T'Chebbi. It might help," she said, sitting up.

T'Chebbi sighed, taking hold of her hands. "Kusac realized he'd relied on his Talent with you. Never learned his own strength. You have to realize he was still growing till then, physically working out with Kaid before we went to Jalna. His whole life had changed in a year—from Telepath to Brother. Takes time to know your own strength in every situation, Carrie. We're much stronger than you to start with. And he got it wrong with you. Happens to us all at least once, especially the first time. Probably what he means about starting again. No need for you to be afraid of him."

"I understand, I think. But he's the one keeping his distance, not me." She gave a small grin. "Rhyasha suggested your perfume."

T'Chebbi raised her eye ridges and grinned. "She told you about that? Story's got around some. Not a good idea with Kusac. Let him take time with you. If he gets it wrong again, do more harm than good. However," she said with a grin, "no reason why you can't use it on Kaid. He'd enjoy it."

"I can't make him stay with me if he . . ."

"Not *make,* just encourage. Maybe time I taught you a few Consortia tricks. Two males like them not easy to handle. You need advantages."

"I don't think . . ."

"Don't think. Trust me." T'Chebbi patted her hand before pulling her to her feet. "Too many nights alone not good for any of us. Time we females fought back."

CHAPTER 7

RHYASHA'S talk had brought to light several issues that Kaid needed to consider seriously. With his Link day due to start in a few hours, he knew the only place he could do that was the Shrine.

Ghyan was not surprised to see him. "It's good to see you again, Kaid," he said, getting up from behind his desk to greet him.

Kaid glanced around the book lined office that was the priest's personal sanctuary. "Good to see you, too, Ghyan." Strangely, it was. They hadn't always seen eye to eye, but whatever his faults, Ghyan was first and foremost Kusac's friend. "I see nothing's changed here. I've come to pay my respects to Vartra, and spend the night meditating."

"You're always welcome here, Kaid," the priest said, holding his hand out in the telepath's greeting. "Actually, I've acquired a few more books. Human ones, courtesy of Brynne. Can I offer you a drink?"

"No, thank you," said Kaid, returning the gesture. "I've just come from the Aldatans."

"I heard Carrie's father was due today. Did the visit go well?" he asked, ushering Kaid to an easy chair.

"Very. He's staying on another two days. He spent most of the time with Kashini."

"Carrie will be relieved. Her father had problems accepting her relationship with Kusac, so she was particularly concerned about how he'd see their daughter. How is Kusac by the way? He hasn't yet come to see me."

"Give it time, Ghyan," said Kaid, sitting down. "He's not been doing much of anything, but I think he's finally beginning to improve."

Ghyan's mouth dropped open in a smile. "You don't know how relieved I am to hear that. Perhaps I should go and see him."

"You should. That Valtegan priest took him to the edge and he's only just beginning to back away from it. It's going to be a slow journey. He needs all the friends he has."

"I heard he'd had a particularly bad time. Brynne has been keeping me up to date."

"Brynne surprised me. Your work?"

Ghyan flicked his ears in a negative. "Not mine. Father Lijou's, mainly. And Vartra, of course. He's another visionary, Kaid. You two should get together. He's finding it difficult to cope with at times. The visions have stopped since you all returned."

"I sympathize with him," murmured Kaid. "Being singled out by Vartra is not the easiest of paths. I see he also found a life-mate."

"Keeza?" Ghyan settled back in his chair. "Now there's an interesting female."

"I seem to know her face," said Kaid cautiously.

"Perhaps you do, but take my word for it, she's an asset to your clan, Kaid. Such determination and loyalty is refreshing."

"I must be missing part of the story." Dzaka had updated him concerning her past and her involvement in the Shanagi Project, but loyalty?

"It only came to light when Father Lijou spoke to L'Seuli about her. When he went to the correction facility, he realized she was a latent telepath. Her mind was still undeveloped enough then for him to pick up why she'd killed the Pack Lord."

"I thought L'Seuli was only able to receive, not initiate a mental contact."

"It was at the forefront of her mind, Kaid. Not surprising since he went only hours before she was due to be executed."

Kaid looked quizzically at Ghyan. "Well, out with it," he said. "Why did she do it?"

"Her father. The Pack Lord had him framed for embezzlement. His case didn't go to trial because her father committed suicide rather than put his family through the public humiliation. The Court telepath had only given Keeza a cursory scan—she was caught with the murder weapon on her during a shoot-out

with the Pack, after all—so she'd been able to hide her latent
Talent, and her motive, from him. Brynne knew, but she refused
to let him tell anyone. Had it not been for L'Seuli, she'd still
have that hanging over her head. Lijou had Sorli instigate a further investigation and her story was confirmed only today."

"I see what you mean by determination and loyalty," he said.
"How does it help her clear her name publicly, though? Officially
she was executed."

Ghyan smiled. "She doesn't need that, Kaid. We know she
was collecting a blood debt, that's what matters to her, and their
cub."

"Our clan increases," said Kaid dryly. "Soon you won't be
able to walk the main street without being deafened by the mewling of berrans!"

"Yours among them," said Ghyan quietly. "How are you coping with your new role? And Carrie. This can't be easy for either of you."

"We manage," he said, getting abruptly to his feet. He wasn't
prepared to talk about himself and Carrie. Those nerves were too
raw after his conversation with Rhyasha. "Carrie's helping Kitra
prepare for her wedding to my son."

Ghyan nodded as he rose. "A busy time. Has a date been set
yet?"

"Not yet. As you know, Kha'Qwa's not recovering as well as
was hoped. Father Lijou obviously has her on his mind at this
time."

"Very true. I won't delay you any longer, Kaid. The Shrine is
empty now, and your room is as you left it."

"Thank you, Ghyan," he said, inclining his head to the priest
as he made for the door.

The click of his clawed feet on the stone floor seemed to echo
around him as he walked down the corridor that led to the Shrine
room. It made him feel vaguely claustrophobic. Reaching the
door, he put his hand on the knob and was about to open it when
his surroundings seemed to fade and he was returned to an earlier visit.

He shivered, feeling the air cold against his un-
clothed pelt and the half-healed wounds on his back.

*   *   *

It lasted only a moment, then the world righted itself and he was back in his own time once more.

He hesitated, afraid now to open the door, unsure what waited for him on the other side. He could turn and walk away right now, go back to the villa and no one would be the wiser, save for himself. Resolutely, he turned the handle, pushed the door open, and stepped inside. He had a purpose in coming here and it wouldn't be served by turning back.

Flanked by braziers, the small statue of Vartra sat on its dais facing him. There was a familiarity about everything that was slightly unnerving and he was once more reminded of that visit.

In the flickering shadows at the base of the dais he could almost see a seated figure, the cowl of her hood concealing her face.

He inhaled sharply in fear. The scent of nung flower incense filled the air, bringing back even more memories of the night he'd suddenly found himself here while still a captive of Ghezu's at Stronghold. He rubbed his eyes, looking again, but there was nothing, only shadows. Cautiously, he moved farther into the room, eyes still fixed on Vartra's statue. Whatever—or whoever— he thought he'd seen, it was gone now.

He stopped to pick up a piece of incense from the bowl near the left-hand brazier, holding it above the glowing coals and crumbling it into the heart of the flames. Scented smoke billowed up, spreading out a few feet above his head before drifting toward the ceiling. He closed his eyes, letting it surround him, finding in it the comfort and familiarity that was lacking in his present life.

A chill draft carrying the scents of night ruffled the guard hairs on his arms, making him shiver again. He froze, knowing instantly that it was no draft. Mentally, he reached out, searching for the presence he knew was there. He found it behind him, about five feet away, a null zone where there should be a person. The faint sound of laughter filled the Shrine. Opening his eyes, he spun around.

"You're always so surprised," said Vartra. "You should be used to it by now. I expected you sooner."

It was only Vartra. Kaid relaxed, feeling the dampness of the earth seeping up around his toes. "Why dusk?" he asked, looking around at the shadowy shapes of the trees, following their trunks upward toward the darkening sky. Faintly, in the distance, he could hear a night hunter calling to the rest of its pack.

"Because night is coming to Shola."

He looked back at the Entity. "Why? Because there are Valtegans on Shola again?" he asked, afraid once more. "We had no option but to make peace."

"You've merely bought time, Tallinu. The darkness still gathers around our world, and the Entities are retreating from it."

He moved closer, trying to see Vartra's face through the deepening shadows. "Why are the Entities retreating? What does it mean to us?"

"The pledge has been broken, Tallinu. The Entities have set it aside so they may be sure of surviving if Shola falls."

"What pledge? You're not making sense, Vartra."

"The pledge is an agreement between the Entities and the Guardians of Shola to restrict access to our realms. Once, most Sholans could, and did, dream-walk, but the less scrupulous used this to advance themselves, wreaking havoc on the world and for the Entities. So the realms were created, places where each Entity could watch over his or her aspect of life, where those faithful to them might enter if permission was sought. Guardians were needed to watch the entrances, to guide those who were suitable and keep out those who were not. Like the Derwents of the Human world, or the Fyaks of ours."

He'd heard the word Guardian before, but in what context? "Noni!"

Vartra nodded. "She's one, one chosen by the Entities themselves. The others are chosen by their suitability to lead their faithful. They represent law and order. Noni represents chaos, the old wild magic of the time before the Guardians were needed. It is with her kind the pledge is renewed in each generation. Noni acts among you for the Entities."

Stunned, he sucked in a breath. "She said You owed her a favor, that You brought us home safe."

"Whoever breaks the pledge—be it Noni or Entity—must pay the forfeit. She chose to have you returned safely."

"I thought Your influence was restricted to Shola."

"It is. Only Kuushoi can travel beyond the bounds of Shola, and then only with those who sleep and dream in cryo."

"Like Carrie," he said, a shiver running down his spine as he remembered the whisper both of them had heard on the Prime ship. *Remember Winter's kiss.*

"Like Carrie," Vartra agreed. "I made it possible for Brynne to dream-walk so he could reach Kusac on the Prime ship and warn you of the danger he saw."

With difficulty, he pulled his thoughts back to the reasons he'd come to the Shrine. "I had a vision, Vartra. In it I was a prisoner, taken to watch Carrie when she paired to form a Leska Link with a Sholan."

Vartra's eyes glowed in the darkness at about waist height. "You're her Leska now. I warned you what the cost of this mission would be."

"I know," he said, peering through the shadows. He still couldn't see Vartra properly, even though he knew now that He was sitting down. "You once gave me Your oath that You'd not call me back in time. I'm asking You to revoke it and take me back to make the vision come true," he said, taking yet another step. "It should have been me, not Kusac, who was the watcher. Take me back, Vartra. Make it happen the way I saw it."

Vartra stirred. "No. Don't ask it of Me. It's impossible."

"I could cope without my Talent. I didn't even know I was a telepath until a few months ago. Kusac can't. This is tearing him—us—apart!"

The eyes glowed brighter, and His voice this time held the trace of a growl. "Had it been you, events would not have worked out the way they did. To change what is would cause untold damage, even if it were possible. You must rebuild your Triad."

"How, dammit?" he demanded. "Tell me how when he's no longer a telepath! It isn't a Triad any longer!"

"That's for you to discover, Tallinu. You built it between you. If you forged the links between you properly, your Triad will survive."

"I never wanted her as a Leska! Only as my lover!" he said angrily. "This closeness, the dependence, *I* can't cope with it!"

"Then learn, and rebuild what you seem bent on destroying by neglect!"

"I can't! It isn't up to me alone, dammit!"

Vartra rose to His feet in one fluid movement, startling Kaid, making him stumble backward. Moonlight illuminated Him clearly now, letting Kaid see His ears folded sideways in anger amid the halo of bushed out hair.

"Look up there, Tallinu," thundered Vartra, pointing to the sky above them. "See the darkness? That's what you must fight! If the Entities withdraw, Shola herself will suffer. The land will wither and dry, there will be droughts and famines! I have told them this but they will not listen to me, the youngest among them! And you waste what little time I have left in arguing with me over something that you know in your heart is impossible!"

His hand snaked out, grasping hold of Kaid by the front of his tunic. "You forget *I* called you here! You three are Shola's best hope! Alone of the Entities, I could remain, had I the means! I have the will and the power to fight, they have not! Find Me a way to remain, to stop the Entities retreating, to fight the darkness! Now get you back to the Shrine and pray that you can before I, too, am beyond reaching by any Sholan!"

Kaid found himself flying backward till he crashed against something solid. Shaking, he painfully pushed himself into a sitting position only to find he was back in the Shrine. He got to his feet as around him clouds of incense swirled and dark shadows, cast by the violent flickering of the braziers, danced on the walls. Keeping his face to them, he limped toward the door. Never before had he faced such anger from Vartra.

Stopping only long enough to tell the night porter he was leaving, he made his way hurriedly back to the villa. Like Kusac, he'd tried to do what he thought right and faced the God's wrath. Now he had to think again about what Rhyasha had said. Right now, all he wanted was to be somewhere bright, where there were no shadows.

The front of the villa was in darkness by the time he reached it. He checked his wrist comm, discovering he'd been gone longer than he thought.

As he passed Carrie's room, he saw a chink of light and stopped. The prospect of spending the night alone with the possibility that Vartra would return, did not appeal to him at all. He needed someone to talk to.

He knocked on the door and, getting no answer, reached mentally for her.

I thought you were spending the night at the Shrine, she replied.

Preoccupied, he didn't pay much attention to the note of panic in her mental voice. *I changed my mind. Can I come in? I need someone to talk to.*

Wait a minute.

He leaned against the wall, wondering what she was doing. The door was suddenly flung open and he found himself almost nose to nose with T'Chebbi. A smiling T'Chebbi.

"G'night," she said over her shoulder before stepping past him. "Night, Kaid."

He watched her saunter down the corridor, tail held up at a jaunty angle, the tip swaying slightly. Her long plait was damp and bobbed gently against the small of her back as she walked.

Curious now, he went in. Carrie, swathed in her large toweling robe, was in the lounge closing her bedroom door. He could feel her nervousness from where he stood. Like T'Chebbi, her hair was still damp.

"What happened to you?" she asked, coming into the room. "You look like you went hunting!"

He looked down at himself, seeing the dirt and pieces of twigs and dead leaves stuck to his jacket and feet, and felt a tingle of fear. He'd almost convinced himself that the experience had been in his mind. He realized then he couldn't tell her all that had happened.

"Sort of," he said lamely, looking back at her.

"You need a shower," she said, bustling over to him. "I'll come with you and get it ready."

He caught hold of her arm as she went past him. He didn't want to use his room tonight. "No need. I'll shower here if I may."

"Um. Yes. Right. I'll go get you a towel, then," she said, taking a couple of steps back from him before turning and fleeing from the rom.

Puzzled, he followed her, thankful for something to divert his mind. In the bathroom, he found her picking up several towels from the floor.

"These are wet," she said, dumping them in the bath. "T'Chebbi and I shared a shower." She opened the small closet where the towels were kept and hauled one out for him, thrusting it against his chest. "There. I'll leave you to it," she said, then vanished, leaving him to grab for the towel before it fell.

All this fuss just because she and T'Chebbi had shared a shower? He shook his head wonderingly as he slung the towel over the side of the bath and began to strip.

He was about to step into the shower when the noises from the other room got the better of his curiosity.

Opening the bathroom door, he peered into the bedroom. Carrie was digging frantically in the chest at the end of the bed. Around the room, all the other chests and cupboards were lying open, their contents rumpled and sticking out untidily. It looked like the room had been hit by a whirlwind.

"Carrie, what's going on?" he asked, pushing the door open and surveying the mess.

She spun around, backing up against the chest till she lost her footing and began to fall.

He didn't make it in time to stop her from banging the back of her head, but he did catch her before she hit the ground. Picking her up, he carried her around the bed and laid her down. She moaned, putting her hand to her head as he began to check to make sure she was all right.

"You need to be more careful," he said, sitting back. "That could have been a nasty fall. Whatever it is you're after can surely wait till tomorrow when you've got one of the house attendants to help you." He reached out to pat her leg.

Her eyes opened and she looked up at him, taking in where she was and where he was sitting before closing them again with another moan.

"What's wrong?" he asked, face creasing in concern. "You didn't hurt yourself anywhere else, did you?" He slid his hand higher, trying to check her ribs through the robe.

"No, I'm fine," she said, her voice faint. "I didn't hurt myself anywhere else."

He reached for her tie belt. "I should check you properly."

Her hand was there first, covering the knot as she sat up. "I'm fine, really. You go and have your shower," she said.

"In a minute. What were you looking for?"

"Nothing. It isn't important," she said, giving him a gentle push. "Go get your shower."

The shower was becoming less appealing than the prospect of remaining with her. "I'm in no rush," he said, reaching out to flick her hair back from her face. "Did you enjoy your shower with T'Chebbi?" he asked, letting his fingers linger on her cheek.

"Yes, I always do. We used to do it a lot when Kusac was at Stronghold with you."

"That's good. Your skin's incredibly soft tonight." It was soft, softer than he remembered. His subconscious began to prickle, warning him that all was not as it seemed.

"I know," she said, taking hold of his hand and putting it firmly on his lap. "Sashti's oils, remember? I really think you should have that shower, Tallinu."

He could smell the oil now, enhancing her own gentle musk. The warning grew louder but he chose to ignore it. Lifting her hand, he held the inside of her wrist to his lips, running the tip of his tongue across the sensitive skin, watching her reaction. She tasted as good as she smelled.

"I'll have the shower later," he said, his voice deepening as he started to purr. "You don't really want me to go now, do you?" It had been a long time since he'd felt like this about her outside their Link days.

His brown eyes were wide and soft in a way she'd never seen before. His tongue flicked across her wrist again, first the gentle tip then the rougher midsection. It sent tingles through her whole body, making her close her eyes in pleasure. She tried to remember what T'Chebbi had said the perfume spray did, but Kaid's other hand was touching her face, his fingertips drawing patterns across her cheek, evaporating all serious thoughts. Shuddering, she turned her face till her mouth touched his hand.

As her tongue touched his sensitive palm, he spread his hand wide for her, his purr briefly rising in pitch till it seemed to vibrate right through her.

Releasing her wrist, he leaned closer, teeth gently closing on her throat. She could smell his scent changing, strengthening as he became more aroused. There was a depth to it she hadn't noticed before, something that woke a matching response in her. Suddenly light-headed with desire, she had no will to stop him when he eased her robe off her shoulders, his tongue moving lower.

As his fingers touched her breast, she moaned gently, almost dropping his hand.

He lifted his head, lips brushing hers. "What is it?" he whispered. "One of T'Chebbi's perfumes?"

"A spray. She put it on the bed," she said, clenching her hand round his. "I told her not to."

He laughed gently, twisting his hand free and placing both of hers against his chest, pushing her fingers through his long fur until they touched his nipples. "It's sensitizing us, enhancing what we feel." He sucked his breath in sharply as her fingers teased him to hardness.

"Slowly, Dzinae," he whispered, kissing her while his free hand unfastened the tie belt and pushed it aside. T'Chebbi's potion was more powerful than he'd anticipated. Making sure he stayed on her robe, he urged her to lie down on the covers. "We should take our time."

And take his time he did, stroking her, licking her, teasing her with every trick he'd learned from T'Chebbi, into shuddering paroxysms of pleasure while denying her what she wanted most.

At length he let her catch her breath. Making sure her robe was still under him, he lay on his side, watching her. Her responses combined with the contact aphrodisiac he'd absorbed from her skin had aroused him to the point where he could delay his own pleasure only a little longer.

Carrie reached out for him, running her fingers across his chest and belly. This time, he didn't stop her.

"My turn," she whispered, her voice husky with desire. She pulled him closer, her hand sliding firmly over the smoothness of his groin till he felt the familiar tightening of his muscles.

He held his breath, tensing as her fingers moved lower, pushing through the long fur that concealed his genital cavity. She stopped just short, daring him to lose his control before she went farther.

Against his chest, their crystal grew warm, pulsing in time with his heart. He arched his body toward her hand, losing his balance and collapsing onto the bedcovers but now he didn't care. "Don't stop," he groaned, clutching her wrist, trying to urge her hand lower, shuddering with the effort of holding himself back. She'd never been this bold before, but then, he'd always been ready for her till now.

Her fingers moved, touching his sensitive flesh, sending his groin and belly muscles into spasms. He moaned, a mixture of pleasure and relief as finally his genitals descended. Then her hand closed round his nakedness, holding him tightly as he began to swell. He gasped, reaching for her, but she batted his hand away with a warning sound not unlike a growl.

She teased him just as he'd teased her, almost shocking him with her knowledge of how far she could take him without triggering his secondary erection. Twice she did this, leaving him so highly strung the second time that he did lose his self-control and grabbed her, flipping her onto her back and pinning her to the bed by her hands.

"No more! By all the Gods, you really are a Dzinae," he growled, taking his weight on his forearms and matching his body to hers. As her warmth surrounded him, he shuddered, so sensitized now that every slight movement sent waves of pleasure rippling through him. As he swelled inside her, it was almost enough to finish him. The crystal flared hot, its pulse changing pace, beating faster, vibrating through him till his heartbeat matched hers.

Slowly, he began to withdraw, his mouth searching frantically for hers, their fingers lacing, his clenching as he stopped then pushed forward again. Their minds reached for each other, becoming as entwined as their bodies.

Kaid woke with a start, aware of the weight of her head on his shoulder and the warmth of her body tucked against his. More, he felt the magic of their Link flowing gently between them. Soon it would grow stronger, but not for an hour or two yet. That pleased him because a part of him had grown to dread that pull. What they'd shared a few hours ago had been triggered by T'Chebbi's spray, but it had been worth it to forget their guilt over Kusac and rediscover their love. He'd done his best to hide, even from himself, his desire to have her carry his cub—a desire forged as a three-year-old when she'd held him on her lap during the long journey from this estate to Stronghold fifteen hundred years ago. He had never wanted a Leska Link with her, but even Vartra couldn't undo the past. The God had been right. It was up to them to make what they could of the future.

Carrie stirred, her hand moving across his belly to curl round his side, the still gentle flow of Link energy following her touch. He yawned and closed his eyes again, looking forward to their day together as he drifted back into a contented sleep.

K'oish'ik, Prime homeworld, Zhal-Ghyakulla, 22nd day (June)

Zayshul followed Medical Director Zsoyshuu down the ranks of growth tubes. His visit was routine, the hatchlings were well past any danger. At the equivalent of just over two years old, all they had to do now was mature.

Zsoyshuu stopped by the unit nearest the exit, surveying the inhabitant. Floating in its tank of nutrient fluid, the small, pale green body bobbed gently, tethered by the fine cables that attached it to the control panel placed on the tube's exterior.

He reached out and tapped his scriber against the tube, studying the reaction of the Prime child within.

"One of the females, I see," he said. Slowly, it began to uncurl itself. Its head came up, closed eyes looking blindly at him, tiny legs straightening as its arms reached out toward the direction of the sound.

Zayshul tried not to look away, wishing she'd not gotten involved with Kezule. Because of him, she'd lost her objectivity, and it was impossible for her to see them as anything but his hatchlings. At least their eyes were still closed.

The Director turned away, a satisfied smile on his face as he made notations with his scriber on the pad. "Response time is good, Doctor. Well done. Looks like you've done an excellent job. As you said, time to hand them over to the developmental team. I want their education program initiated as soon as possible."

She nodded, glad her involvement was almost over. Now she could face Kezule with a clearer conscience.

As they left the growth chamber and reentered the lab, Zsoyshuu glanced at her. "You're still seeing General Kezule socially, aren't you?"

"Yes, Medical Director."

"I'm told he's settling in well at the Court. His test results certainly show no elevated levels of stress, but tests don't necessarily reveal everything. How is he really adapting?"

What should she tell him? That Kezule was impatient with the rigid protocol of the Court? That his patience with the fawning courtiers who plagued him with requests for details of the old days of the Empire was wearing thin? "Why do you ask?"

"None of the three females from the *Kz'adul* were impregnated by him," he said. "And despite having quite a following of our eligible young females here, again no pregnancies. I confess I'm curious as to why not. Which is why I'm wondering about his stress levels."

"He needs a purpose, sir," she said carefully as she opened

the door for the Director, letting him pass out into the corridor before her. "He was a line officer, leading his troops into battle, planning campaigns from the bridges of starships. Now he's nothing but a curiosity."

"He's more than that, Doctor Zayshul. He's the future for us, the progenitor of our Warrior class. I'd prefer him to be doing what comes naturally, but I'm afraid that if I don't see some sign of his natural potency, I'll have to authorize his sedation so more samples can be taken from him. Unless you think he'd be prepared to donate them voluntarily?"

"I wouldn't even suggest it to him, sir," she said as they stopped outside his office. "He's proud, and the thought of being used like that would enrage him."

"I presume then that you've said nothing to him about our breeding program. Keep it that way, Doctor. Well, let's hope at least one of his females falls pregnant within the next month."

Zayshul watched the door close behind him before she moved off. Deep in thought, she headed for her quarters.

The City of Light was one vast, rambling building constructed originally on an East/West axis around a small inner courtyard. Now, visible even from space, it covered many square miles, dominating the surrounding countryside. Each successive Emperor had added to the Palace, building outward until even the fields had been enclosed, turning it into the walled city it was today.

Zayshul's apartment was near the science block in the northwest quadrant, a fairly affluent area, reserved for those who held senior positions in the employment of the Emperor.

At this time of night, the corridors were quiet, and her walk back was undisturbed. Pulling her key tag out of her pocket, she pointed it at the door, waiting impatiently for it to open.

She stepped inside, about to command the lights when she was grasped firmly from behind and a hand clapped over her mouth. For the space of five terrified heartbeats, she was held like this, then she was released.

"I wasn't expecting you for another hour," said Kezule's voice from the darkness.

"Lights," she said, trying to keep the tremor out of her voice. "I don't remember giving you my access code."

"You didn't," he said, bending to pick up the door tag and

reader she'd been carrying and handing them back to her. "I needed to get away from the Court and the damned guard who's following me around." He returned to the chair he'd been sitting on.

Still shaking, she went over to the table, putting the reader and key down on the polished wood surface. "Don't do that again. You scared me," she said, sitting down in the other chair. She noticed his drink. "I see you've been making yourself at home."

"I was thirsty. You don't have a nourishment dispenser."

"I don't live in the Court apartments," she retorted. "If you wanted food, why didn't you go back to your own apartment?"

"I'd only have been followed and told to return to the audience hall. How much longer will your Emperor keep me waiting until he gives me some kind of commission?" he asked, leaning forward in the chair. "There must be something I can do. He certainly doesn't need any more useless courtiers."

"I don't know, Kezule," she said, getting up and going over to the drinks unit to fetch herself an herbal tea. "I'm not part of the inner Court." She selected her drink, waiting for it to be dispensed. As she picked up the widemouthed cup, she realized she was still shaking. "There's gossip that the Emperor might choose you as his third adviser." She returned to her seat and sat down.

Kezule hissed his derision. "Your Emperor Cheu'ko'h needs to command, not listen to so many advisers!"

Zayshul eyed him as she took a sip of her drink. "Your Emperor, too."

"Not mine, yours. Q'emgo'h was a leader with fire in his veins. Yours has only ice water!"

"Times have changed," she murmured. There was something different about him tonight, but she couldn't put her finger on it.

"Not for the better," he scowled. "What of the young Warriors you have? They need training and there's no one fit to train them here. Or the implanted guards? The right training techniques could remove the need to control them. Can't you ask for me?"

"I'm a doctor, Kezule. I don't have the contacts. You need to mix with the Inner Court and make your own relationships. Your uniform," she said triumphantly, realizing what was different. "You're not wearing your uniform. Where is it?"

"Concealed in a rest room in the Outer Court. I told you I was trying to evade my shadow." Irritated, he got to his feet and began to pace round the small lounge. "I need to do something, Zayshul! This place, it hasn't changed!" His expansive gesture took in more than the whole room. "It's what it always was, a home for sycophants, for those who want to appear important but do nothing! I shall go mad if I remain here much longer!"

She watched him, well aware that he wasn't exaggerating. "I might be able to help. My superior, the Medical Director, was concerned you were suffering from stress. I could speak to him again about finding you something. Perhaps, as you suggested, training the young Warriors," she said slowly.

"Speak to him," said Kezule, stopping and resting his hands on the back of the chair and staring intently at her.

"There will be a price, though. I don't know if you'd be prepared to pay it in light of what you've said before."

He stiffened. "What price?"

She looked away. "He wants you to breed."

He was silent for so long that she looked up, afraid something had happened to him. There was a curious expression on his face, a mixture of shock and—almost pleasure.

"I had thought to wait a while longer, but if you are so anxious to have hatchlings . . ."

"Not me," she said hurriedly. "My work is vital. The Medical Director wouldn't allow me to take the time off. There are many young females interested in you. Already you've got quite a following."

He gave a derisory laugh. "They are nothings, as empty-headed as drones and those on the *Kz'adul*. I told you, I will breed with you. You alone have the intellect I wish my young to inherit."

"You don't understand. You haven't got a choice, Kezule. If you don't breed, they'll drug you and take what they want."

The look on his face made her regret her decision to warn him.

"Have you told them I can control my fertility?" he asked, his voice deathly quiet.

"No, of course not," she said, offended that he thought she'd betray his confidence.

"I was unconscious for three days before I woke on the *Kz'adul*. What was done to me during that time?" His grip on the chair back tightened, claws puncturing the fabric.

"Tests and scans to see if you needed any medication to help you heal, nothing more," she said, breaking eye contact, unable to stop the fear scent she was emitting.

Time slowed: she saw the chair thrown to one side, watched as it hit the far wall and smashed against it. Almost simultaneously, she felt his hand grasp her throat as she was plucked out of her own.

She grasped his arm with both hands, utterly terrified, her scream choked off before it was made.

"You're lying," he hissed, tongue flicking out, crest raised to its full height. "Was I harvested like those from the M'zullian ship?"

Barely able to breathe, she was unable to do more than make gargling sounds. He shook her violently, making her head reel. When he stopped, he set her feet down on the ground, releasing the pressure just enough so she could speak. Head spinning, stomach heaving, she continued to clutch at his arm for support.

"Was I harvested? Are there hatchlings of mine in some laboratory?" he demanded, his face inches from hers.

"Yes!" she wept, tears running down her face. "It wasn't my decision! It was the Director's!"

"How many? What kind of doctor are you?"

"Med research, I work in med research." Her legs buckled, refusing to keep her upright any longer and she began to choke again.

With a hiss of rage, he flung her back in the chair and stood towering over her.

"Tell me how many and where they are!"

"One hundred. In the growth lab," she whimpered, reaching for her throat with a trembling hand. It felt damp and sticky and she could smell blood.

"Take me there now!" he commanded, grasping her by the shoulder and hauling her to her feet again.

Almost incoherent with terror, she shook her head.

"You *will* take me," he hissed, tightening his grip till his claws bit into her again.

"I can't! They'll see us!" she shrieked in pain. "I'm bleeding!"

He hesitated, then shifted his grip to her upper arm, dragging her toward the sanitary facilities. Pushing the door open, he hauled her toward the washbasin then released her. "Clean yourself up," he ordered. "You will take me there."

Pulling the towel off the rail, with trembling hands she wet it under the tap and began dabbing at the blood.

"They'll see us, recognize us both," she said, in a hoarse voice.

"Without my uniform? I doubt it. You'd better pray they don't!"

"They'll think you're a doctor if you wear one of my jackets."

"Fetch me one."

Half an hour later, she activated the palm lock on the entrance to her lab. Not knowing whether to be relieved or not when she saw it was deserted, she led him to the far end, placing her hand on the lock panel.

He stood in the doorway, looking beyond her into the dimly lit room. Ten deep they stood, each bathed by the faint blue glow of the accelerated growth field. Within them, the tiny occupants twitched their limbs gently, obeying the commands of the neural stimulators.

Pushing her aside, Kezule entered, taking several steps into the room before stopping.

"They aren't in any pain, they're only being exercised so their muscles don't atrophy," she said.

Snarling, he approached the nearest tank, raising his clenched hand as if to hit it.

"Please don't!" she exclaimed, reaching out automatically to stop him as she took a step forward. "The tanks are alarmed and you could kill her!"

"If it costs me my life, I'll destroy them all before I'll let this abomination continue!" he hissed, his crest rising to its full height.

"They're yours, Kezule, your sons and daughters!" She was distraught herself now at the thought of the innocent lives he was prepared to sacrifice.

"They're nothing to me," he snarled, turning on her. "You brought them to life, not me!"

She held her ground, knowing that to back away would enrage him further. "Then why kill them? You'd only destroy a few before the guards came. The authorities wouldn't kill you, they'd keep you alive and unconscious, use you to replace them! They'd never allow you to be free again! Is that what you want? To be kept alive only for breeding purposes?"

"It's what they're doing to me now!"

"No, they're not," she said. He was listening to her at last. "These are only the foundation of the new Warrior caste. The Emperor and his advisers are afraid of suddenly having too many Warriors all at once. They want to study them, educate them so they can be sure they'll fit into our society, become our protectors."

"What of me? Where do I fit in this godlike scheme of theirs?" he demanded.

"If you do what they want, breed with some of our females, they'll do what they can to keep you content. You have a weapon they know nothing about, after all. You can control your fertility."

"And them?" He indicated the hatchlings behind him. "How much of the Warrior remains in them? I saw what you've done to the M'zullians. Have you emasculated them, too?"

"Of course not! I told you, they want them to breed true. Very little has been altered in their genetic makeup, only your personal racial memories have been edited."

He came closer, his crest beginning to sink down out of sight again. "Will they know me, or have you deprived them of that?"

Startled, she didn't know how to reply. "I don't know. Our young don't rely on instincts like those. They're brought up with both parents, not by drones as in your time."

He pushed her aside and stormed off through the lab toward the door.

"Kezule! Wait!" she called after him, hurriedly sealing the door behind her.

the *Couana*, Zhal-S'Asha, 20th day (October)

Tired, but unable to sleep, he'd gone to the lounge, taking a mug of coffee with him. The first thing he noticed was the replacement entertainment unit. Going over to the table, he sat down on the chair where he'd sat the night he'd attempted suicide. He'd been serious when he'd told Banner that this journey was forcing him to relive the past. Whichever way he turned, there was no escaping the memories.

Running his hand across the surface in front of the console, he felt the faint scars the Sholan craftsmen had been unable to remove, and remembered the anger and hopelessness he'd felt that night. Toueesut had been more understanding about the damage than he'd had any right to expect. The Touiban's main concern had been him from the first, but Toueesut had held his species' natural enthusiasm and curiosity in check until he'd finally ventured outside the villa on foot for the first time.

Involuntarily, his hand went to the torc he wore round his neck. He owed Toueesut a lot, there was no doubt about that.

Yawning again, he put his mug down and resting his elbow on the table, propped his chin up on his hand.

It had been just after Carrie's father had left for Keiss. Rhyaz had contacted the villa, asking that Captain Tirak and his crew be allowed to join the Sumaan as students of the Brotherhood. Kaid had called him to the comm, refusing point-blank to deal with the matter, even to the extent of leaving the villa so he was forced to make a decision.

Shola, Zhal-Ghyakulla, 22nd (June)

"Good to see you taking control again, Kusac," Rhyaz said. "I want to thank you for allowing the Sumaan to train on your estate."

"We got on well with them during the Jalna mission, Commander," he said.

"I assume Kaid has briefed you?"

He nodded.

"I've had Captain Tirak and his crew here as guests for the last two days. They came to me with an interesting request from their government."

That caught his interest. "Tirak's at Stronghold?"

"Times are changing, Kusac. I've told Kaid to expect your military support at the estate to be suddenly withdrawn."

"He told me. He and Ni'Zulhu have already implemented alternative arrangements." Belatedly, he asked, "What's going on?"

"Raiban's making life damned difficult for our people working for the Forces. Petty things like demanding we be responsible for our own munitions and laundry bills."

"But they've been employed by the Forces, it's their responsibility."

"Not according to her. She's claiming her budget doesn't include cash for looking after Brotherhood personnel. It's making life tight, Kusac, damned tight. So we're having to look elsewhere for contracts. Like Captain Tirak's. His government want his people trained up to our standard of operational excellence, and they're prepared to pay well for it. Naturally, you'll also benefit financially if you'll allow them to come to your estate. We just don't have the facilities here and, to be honest, I'd prefer not to have outside influences around our juniors."

"Tirak's welcome, of course, Commander. He and his crew helped us when we needed it."

"I realize they aren't telepaths . . ."

"Alien minds aren't a problem, Master Rhyaz," he interrupted, aware of the tension in his own voice. "It takes years of training, or a rare Talent, to even be aware of their surface thoughts."

Rhyaz nodded. "There are seven U'Churians, four Cabbarrans, and a Sholan, Jeran Khesrey. Essentially, those who were aboard the *Profit*."

"I'll see to arranging accommodation for them today. When will they be arriving?"

"Today, if possible. The Cabbarrans request permission to park their shuttle inside the estate to serve as their living quarters. Their quadrupedal bodies make it the most sensible option."

"I'll tell Ni'Zulhu to expect them."

"Thank you. By the way, the Prime Ambassador is sending a package to you. Seems you and Carrie's torcs turned up on the *Kz'adul*. They were found among Chy'qui's personal effects."

He sat looking at the blank screen for several minutes before rousing himself. Someone had to go down to the estate office and see the foreman to arrange suitable accommodation.

Carrie was up at the main house involved in preparations for Kitra's wedding a few days hence. And Kaid had gone out, but T'Chebbi was somewhere around the house.

"I'll go with you," she said when he tracked her down to her room on the ground floor. "Not for you."

"T'Chebbi, I'm not ready to go outside, and there's Kashini . . ."

"You're not her nursemaid, you're a Clan Leader. Want to go alone?" she asked.

He could tell from her tone she meant it. "All right," he snapped. "I'll go!"

He didn't like being outside the safety of the villa. Already the muscles on his scalp ached with the effort of constantly turning his ears this way and that to hear every little noise. The unexpected sound of voices in a back garden had him pivoting round in a crouch, ready for a Challenge.

"Calm down," said T'Chebbi, putting her hand on his arm. "Is your home estate, you're safe. And I'm here."

"I can take care of myself," he said, straightening up.

Her clear gray eyes looked back at him calmly. "I know you can, Kusac. I'm here to keep you company, nothing more."

He stopped dead and stared at her. "You're speaking normally," he said. "I didn't think you could."

"You were wrong. How do you think I became a Consortia?"

"What happened?" he asked, his customary indifference giving way to real curiosity about her past. They'd been occasional lovers before—the Primes—but she'd said little about her life before the Brotherhood.

"I lost my voice for several months when the Fleet took me."

"And the Claws."

"Them too," she agreed. "Toueesut's up ahead. Looks like he wants to talk."

He looked around for an escape but her grip on his arm tightened.

"I had to live again, so must you."

"I can't cope with them right now," he muttered, looking at the six garishly dressed bewhiskered aliens coming toward them. In the midst of the dancing and gyrating group, one figure stood out because of his stillness. Toueesut.

"You always got on with them better than anyone else did."

"I *read* them, T'Chebbi! And I had a translator. I've got neither now. Mara's the one they relate to," he said, trying to back away surreptitiously.

"Translators not needed now," she said, refusing either to let go or be dragged away. "Nor is Talent. They spoke better Sholan than they let on. You should have read the report from your father. Was all there."

There was no time to say more as the group came to a halt a few feet from them.

"Clan Leader Kusac! May the sun shine on you! Welcome it is to be seeing you about the village at last! Now we be knowing for ourselves you are indeed getting better."

Though Toueesut stood relatively still, his swarm companions did not. Like waves on a restless sea, trilling and chirping, they wove around their speaker and each other in an intricate dance that was almost too fast for the eye to follow.

"May the sun shine on you, Toueesut," murmured Kusac, trying not to look directly at them. Already their gyrations were beginning to make him feel nauseous.

Immediately Toueesut turned to his swarm, gesturing them to move back. As he emitted a high-pitched riff of sound, they began to slow down until they were almost stationary.

"Apologies we make for crowding you when you are not yet used to the company of so many people. Not long will we be staying. If the matter was not of great importance to you I would not be bothering you at this time."

Kusac's nausea was already lifting as he focused his attention on the being before him. When standing at rest, they lost much of their almost balletic grace, their long arms and forward leaning posture making them look as if they were shambling.

Toueesut stood barely four feet tall, and was dressed in the usual sartorial elegance of his kind. Beneath the elaborate multicolored swirling embroidery, it was just possible to tell that his jacket was red, as were the trousers with their broad decorated panel down the outside of each leg. A shirt of deep blue, its pleated neckline almost concealed beneath the numerous gold pendants and chains that hung round his neck, completed his outfit.

Toueesut's eyes gleamed out at him from under heavily ridged brows. His mouth, barely visible beneath his bristling mustache, was open in a smile. It was sometimes hard to remember that these Neanderthals, to use a Human word, were the communications experts of the Alliance.

"What is it, Toueesut? How can we help you?" he asked.

"This we are bringing for you from Palace," the Touiban said, handing him a box. "Ambassador M'szudoe of the Primes is sending this to you and saying to me it is your torcs."

He accepted it, holding it close against his chest, trying to concentrate on what Toueesut was saying.

"Better understanding there has been between our peoples these last few months so now you are knowing that we have another way of communicating between ourselves. We hear the music of the minds of those around us, including yourself. Knowing as we do of your misfortune at the hands of an evil member of the Primes, we are thinking that maybe we can help you."

He stiffened, displeased that his condition was a matter for open discussion, then common sense took over as well as curiosity. Mind-music? T'Chebbi was right, he should have read his father's report about the Touibans.

"I'm sorry, Toueesut, but I don't see how you can help. I know you're the comm tech specialists, but . . ."

"You say the most important word, friend Kusac," Toueesut interrupted, wagging a gold be-ringed finger at him. "Communications. Mind-music is not unlike telepathy, both of which are being means of communications, are they not? Devices we can make. Before now you have not been asking us for any help in this field, but Garras came to us for advice with the wrist psi damper units he was making as gifts for your midwinter festival last year. We helped him so perhaps is possible we can help you. Nothing is lost in the trying, is it?"

He hesitated, not wishing to offend them. It was such a long shot it wasn't worth the effort in his opinion.

"He can't use his Talent, Toueesut," interrupted T'Chebbi. "Device was implanted in his brain making new connections. It's gone, but left connections. They cause pain if he tries to use what's left of his Talent."

Toueesut's head bobbed in an affirmative as his swarm began to trill gently. "Hearing of this we are. All I am asking for now is to see information about implant and what it did, then maybe, just maybe, we can help. To even be without the pain would be good, would it not, friend Kusac?"

For the first time hope surged through him. He looked at T'Chebbi who shrugged and smiled. "Nothing to lose by trying, as Toueesut says."

"Vanna has the information. Tell her I said you could have a copy of what you need."

Toueesut's gnarled hand reached out to take Kusac's, his fingers gently dancing over his palm. "Sad we are to see this happening to you, friend Kusac. Like family we are to each other now. Anything we can try to help you we will do."

"You're very kind," he murmured. "We're pleased to have your swarm in our village."

"Not swarm, hive," corrected Toueesut. "We are a breeding family. We have our mates with us. Sometime soon you must visit."

That shocked him. Though Sholans, and the Alliance, worked on the Touiban homeworld and the colony of Teesul in their towns and cities, access to the hives was strictly forbidden.

Toueesut cocked his head to one side, mustache and whiskered chin bristling as his smile grew wider. "Not knowing you were all along that we had our mates with us. Long time now we have been interested in Sholan Talent and more so now you have Human mind-mates. In the Alliance you are most like us so time now to make stronger bonds between our kinds. Time to exchange much information we neither of us tell other species. Already we are practicing your custom of exchanging visitor between our *home* and theirs. When our mates bear their young, we will become the first hive on Shola."

He didn't know what to say and found himself wondering if Touibans dressed their cubs in as garish clothing as they wore themselves.

"We got more visitors coming, Toueesut," said T'Chebbi, filling his silence. "We're going to sort out accommodation for them. Is the U'Churians who helped us at Jalna. Captain Tirak and his crew, plus Annuur the Cabbaran and his sept."

"Ah, this is good news. Much we have heard of Cabbarrans, and U'Churians. Met Ambassadors Shaqee and Mrocca at the hearing for Chemerian Taira who kidnap your young ones." He frowned, bushy eyebrows almost concealing his eyes. "Going now we are to diggings. So useful it is to have the new female Zashou and sometimes Rezac. They know the workings of devices we excavate. Perhaps you come there later and bring your little one with the sweet mind-music. Missed her have our ladies. Soon I think they will be wanting young of their own." He gave a deep sigh but his eyes twinkled.

With that, he turned and was engulfed by his companions as they swarmed toward the vehicle landing pad on the outskirts of the village.

As the nausea hit him again, T'Chebbi pulled him around to face her.

"Careful, Kusac. You forgot the knack of how to watch them."

He nodded, then remembered the box in his hands. Opening it, he saw two bronze torcs nestling on a bed of gossamer-fine white cloth.

"Heard the Primes found them," said T'Chebbi. "And they wrapped them in white for honor!"

"I don't think they know that custom," he said, touching them with a disbelieving finger. Carrie had given him his the day their first cub had been conceived—the cub that had died when Carrie had fought the Death Challenge with Ralla Vailkoi, the bride chosen for him by his father. The other was his original one, given to him by his parents, and in turn given by him to Carrie as his chosen life-mate.

"They know. Look at material. Makes even jotha seem coarse. They know importance of what they returned to you. Put yours on, Kusac."

Taking his out, he handed her the box. As the familiar weight settled in its usual place round his neck, he found himself beginning to shake uncontrollably. T'Chebbi's arm went instantly around his shoulders, pulling him close against her chest. "Is all right," she said gently. "Been too much at once. First time walking outside villa, Toueesut's offer to give you back some Talent, now this. When we seen Naeso, we go see your mother, give Carrie her torc."

He nodded his head against her shoulder, unable for now to trust his voice.

the *Couana*, Zhal-S'Asha, 20th day (October)

A hand touched his and he became aware of his name being called.

"Kusac. Wake up. You should be in your bed, not here."

He opened his eyes and found himself looking into Banner's face. Surprised, he blinked, then realized he'd fallen asleep at the table, head sprawled across his forearms.

Groggy with exhaustion, he let Banner help him to his feet and out of the lounge to his room. Once there, he collapsed on his bed, vaguely aware of being undressed before the covers were thrown over him.

"I'll wake you for first meal," said Banner, getting up. "Just do me a favor and keep that damned torc of yours on tonight. I don't fancy going flying across the room again."

Prime world, Zhal-Ghyakulla, 25th day (June)

For two days Zayshul, worried about what Kezule would do, had to put up with odd little asides from her colleagues who'd heard about the broken chair in her quarters. She was stopped in the corridors by the very people she despised, the cognoscenti who reflected the moods of the Court, asking how she was, obviously soliciting her acquaintanceship for some obscure reason of their own. But of Kezule there was no sign, until the morning the Medical Director called her to his office.

Her heart leaped when she saw the General was with him, then fell as she feared he'd told her superior he knew about the growth tanks.

"Doctor Zayshul! How good of you to join us," Zsoyshuu said, getting to his feet. "I believe congratulations are due. The General tells me the Emperor himself has agreed to your marriage."

Stunned, she looked from one to the other of the two males.

Kezule moved smoothly to her side, gasping her arm and holding it firmly. "Don't look so surprised, Zayshul," he said gently, his tone belied by the strength of his grip. "I know we agreed to keep it quiet for now, but Emperor Cheu'ko'h, *may his memory be revered for all time,* was so delighted that he insisted on bringing forward the date of the ceremony to tomorrow."

She made a tiny, strangled noise.

"In fact, he was so pleased, his wife, Empress Zsh'eungee has offered to see to all the arrangements. We've to meet her now in the Royal apartments."

Director Zsoyshuu beamed happily at them. "Go, go. You've a lot to do before tomorrow! Don't let me detain you. It isn't every day one of my staff marries into the Royal House. I hope your duties training our young Warriors won't prevent you having the customary nuptial holiday, General?"

"I wouldn't miss it." He smiled broadly.

She managed to speak then. "My work . . . I can't leave it now!"

"Nonsense! It will only be a week. I can see to it myself," Zsoyshuu said, coming out from behind his desk to usher them out. "By the time you'll need leave, Zayshul, you'll be ready for reassignment anyway. I'll see you both tomorrow at the temple."

She found herself standing in the corridor with a grim-faced Kezule and two Royal guards.

"What the hell do you think . . ." she began in a low voice.

"Come along, Zayshul," he interrupted. "We can't keep the Empress waiting, can we?"

As they headed toward the Inner Court, flanked by their escort, she tried to gather her wits.

"What do you think you're doing? This joke has gone far enough," she hissed.

"Oh, it's no joke," he said grimly. "We are getting married tomorrow. You owe it to me."

"I owe it to you? For what?"

"For what I saw in your lab. I told you I'd breed with you, and I will."

"I refuse!"

"Then regretfully, I shall have to inform the Medical Director you showed me the growth tanks."

"You shell-breaking son of a burrower!" she swore, trying to pull away, making the guard in front turn to look at her.

"I wouldn't," Kezule warned, dragging her inexorably onward. "The guards are all implants, they recognize me as being of royal blood. Until you're my wife, they'll see you as a threat to me, and you know better than I how unstable they are."

"You're despicable! You're using them to make me go through with this!"

"Yes," was all he said.

Shola, Valsgarth Estate, Zhal-Ghyakulla, 25th day (June)

The last three days had been intolerable for him. As if his emergence from the villa had been the sign that Vanna and his father had been waiting for, suddenly he found himself at the mercy of various experts.

His father had brought the top neurosurgeon over from Shanagi to see him, and he'd been compelled to go to the Guild medical center and sit through a day of interminable tests. He hadn't needed any Talent to know the specialist's words of encouragement were empty.

The following day, Vanna's therapist decided it was time to talk about his experiences on the Prime ship in more than general details, which he'd flatly refused to do. He couldn't even talk about them to his family, let alone anyone else. When she'd pushed the issue, accusing him of refusing to face his emotions, he'd only just managed to control his temper and walk out.

T'Chebbi got up from her seat in the small waiting area as he came out. She followed him as he flung the outer door open and leaped down the steps to the dirt roadway outside.

"Don't say anything," he growled, ears rotating sideways and flat, tail lashing from side to side as he waited for her to join him.

She took him by the arm and pointed down the street to the training center. "We go there," she said. "Not home. You need to get rid of anger."

A moment's hesitation then he nodded once, his ears righting themselves as he followed her to the low stone building just beyond the end of the village.

The training center was by far the largest building on the estate. Though the interior was complete, the exterior facing was still being finished. Like all the buildings on the Kaeshala continent, it was built to take advantage of the hot climate. Rectangular in shape, it was surrounded by a colonnaded walkway. Plain open doorways were spaced evenly down each side to let in the cooling breezes from the ocean. Wooden screens and energy fields could be activated to provide protection in inclement weather.

It was his first visit to the center as the foundation stones had only just been laid when they'd left for Jalna. T'Chebbi led the way up the three steps into the main entrance.

"Group of the Humans and our people have designed murals," she said, gesturing to the plain white walls of the small entrance hall. "Athletes. They look good on paper. Plans were sent up to the villa for your approval two weeks ago." She pointed to the door on her left. "Gym is there. Ahead is bathing and showering area, and to the right is massage room and first aid, and a small mess."

"They've done a good job," he said, impressed despite his disgruntled mood.

"Are classes on now, but is area for workouts," she said, pushing the door into the gym open before he could stop her.

To refuse to go in now would draw the kind of attention that he suddenly wanted to avoid. He was left with no option but to follow her.

With the help of Kaid, Banner, and Jurrel, Garras was drilling a class made up of U'Churians, Humans, and Sholans. A couple of heads turned their way as they entered only to snap back as Garras let forth a string of invectives at them.

Feeling acutely uncomfortable, he followed T'Chebbi round the edge of the room to a door on the right near the far end.

This was the workout area. Like the main room, it was naturally lit, the transparent ceiling overhead filtering out the sun's glare. Beneath his feet, the wooden floor was smooth enough to ensure those with claws would learn to grip with their feet. There the similarity ended. Several different exercise machines were provided as well as upright padded posts and bags suspended from wall brackets. On their left, a single doorway, flanked by lockers, opened out onto the colonnade.

Only one other person was there, Meral. He was working on a bench press. As they entered, he looked up.

"Liege! It's good to see you," he said, mouth dropping open in a pleased smile.

"Out, youngling," T'Chebbi said amiably, jerking her thumb toward the door. "See no one comes in while we're here."

"Was just leaving," he said, getting up and grabbing his towel.

As the door closed behind him, T'Chebbi strolled over to the hanging kick bag and grasped hold of it. "You plan to work out in your tunic?" she asked.

"I'm not in the mood for . . ." He stopped in mid-sentence,

diving hastily to one side as the long bag came scything through the air toward him.

"What's mood got to do with it?" she demanded, catching it deftly on its return. "You were mad as hell five minutes ago! Know you can't lose your temper, but you sure as hell can kick this damned thing!" She sent it swinging toward him again. He stood his ground, sure it would miss him, shocked when it sent him reeling. Snarling, he picked himself up off the floor.

"Hit it, Kusac. Hit back at what's hurting you," she said, her voice low and intense. "Focus that anger."

He did.

When he'd worked himself into exhaustion, she sent him off to the showers and told Meral they were done.

She surprised him by joining him under the stream of warm water. "Turn around," she ordered him, taking the soap container from his slack grasp.

Too tired to object, he did. Vigorously, she rubbed the soap into his pelt, kneading his aching muscles back to an acceptable level of discomfort.

When she'd done, he returned the favor. As he made to undo her long braid, she stopped him. "No need," she said. "You were one working out, not me."

He began to feel some pleasure as he massaged her, his hands remembering the feel of her body. He needed the familiar around him, Sholan benchmarks to remind him who he was. Though smaller than the average female, she was well proportioned, her muscles firm yet not too large. As he worked his way down her flanks, he could feel her body vibrating as she began to purr. Startled, he stood up only to have her lean her weight against him, reaching her hands up to rest on his shoulders.

"Been a long time since we spent a night together," she said, folding her ears back to keep the water out of them. "You know where I am if you feel like coming to me." She touched him intimately on the neck, then stepped past him out of the shower, leaving him speechless.

"We go to mess now," she said, picking up her towel and beginning to rub herself vigorously with it.

The mess was on the western side, a small room with tables spilling out onto the colonnaded walk. T'Chebbi led the way over to the self-service snack and drink dispensers, digging into one of her belt pouches for change.

"Coffee?" she asked. "Or you still drinking c'shar?"

"Neither," he said, going to look for himself. He chose a fruit juice and accompanied her outside to where the U'Churians sat.

Conversation died out as they saw them approaching, making him cringe inwardly.

It was Rezac who stood up and offered him a seat. "There's room here, Clan Leader."

T'Chebbi's hand in the small of his back gave him a gentle shove. Propelled forward, he had no option but to take the offered seat.

"Are you liking it here, Tirak?" asked T'Chebbi, taking a seat opposite.

"Very different from Home," said the U'Churian. "So much space, and so clean."

"We did it that way after the Cataclysm," said T'Chebbi.

"It's a great improvement," said Rezac. "Zashou and I couldn't believe the difference." He shook his head as he picked up his drink. "Take the forests, they'd almost disappeared in our time."

"You getting used to female equality?" T'Chebbi asked.

Rezac grinned. "Sure. I like the way they tell you if they're interested. They're more likely to approach the males than wait. Mind you, coping with two females is more than enough."

Jeran gave a snort of laughter, glancing at Giyesh. "Sometimes one is more than enough!"

"How you getting on with training?" she asked, returning to Tirak.

He nodded. "Well, I think. The way you mix prayer with military disciplines is intriguing. Of course, we say our prayers to the Prophet Kathan. The medical knowledge makes sense—each Warrior can treat not only himself but his companions. There's much for me to consider, and learn."

"Each one of us is capable of commanding a Pack comprising ninety to a hundred Brothers," said Kaid. "In any given situation, we all have to be able to make command decisions and justify them afterward. Once qualified, we are an army of equals led by the one with the most appropriate skills for the job. This is what we're teaching you to become."

He heard the sound of a chair being put down, then the creak as Kaid sat. He glanced sideways, seeing him now sitting on the other side of Rezac.

"That's why we're here, Kaid," said Tirak. "And to learn the undercover skills."

"That's another matter entirely. We'll deal with it when your other skills have acquired the extra polish our training will give. You did well enough on Jalna and with the Chemerians, until you got involved with us."

"Not good enough. We were lucky that it was you we were dealing with. Next time might not go so well."

"Apart from information gathering on the illicit drugs trade and keeping an eye on our good friends the Chemerians," said Kaid, "what other functions do you perform for Home?"

"Our Matriarch is currently discussing our role with your Guild Masters. I can tell you we also protect our shipping en route to the other Trader markets."

"From what?" asked Rezac.

"There are four other species in the Free Traders, but two of them are banned from Jalna because they're untrustworthy. They didn't regulate their shipping the way we did and more than a few of them became raiders, preying on cargo ships. Their worlds contain great contrasts. A few noble families or large mercantile groups own nearly all the ships, controlling the flow and prices of off-world goods. These raiders belong to neither category and feel justified in preying on the rest of us."

"What species?" asked Rezac, ears widening in interest.

"The Mryans and the Vieshen," said Sheeowl.

Rezac leaned forward intently. "The Vieshen, are they bird-like, tall and thin almost to the point of being emaciated?"

"Superficially, yes," said Tirak, obviously surprised. "You know them?"

"They're one of the slave races who helped us in the revolt against the Valtegans. What about the Mryans?"

"Heavyset, gray leathery skin, face that'd give you night-mares," said Manesh. "And strong. They're argumentative, too."

"That's them," said Rezac. "I wondered what had happened to the other slave races. Not surprised those two are working to-gether considering their worlds are relatively near each other."

"The raiders are past masters at the sudden attack," said Tirak. "In and out jobs. They disable the ships, kill the crews and strip the craft bare of anything useful, leaving only the hulks. Occasionally they'll take the ships as well." He shook his head. "The area's too big for us and the Cabbarrans to police alone. That's why we've concentrated on trading at Jalna."

"The Mryans and Vieshen will have no love for the Primes, I'll be bound," murmured Kaid. "I wouldn't be surprised if the Primes were at the back of the ban to avoid being recognized."

"It was the Cabbarrans, actually," said Manesh.

"The raids are getting more frequent, despite us changing our shipping schedules. It's as if they had inside information," said Tirak.

"Do Chemerian ships get hit as often?"

"We don't have the figures with us," replied Tirak. "But I don't think they do, now that you mention it."

"The Chemerians can't possibly be selling that information," said Manesh. "Can they?"

"With the Chemerians, it's best not to trust them at all, then you don't get disappointed," said Kaid thoughtfully.

"What did the Chemerians do to rub your people the wrong way?" asked Giyesh.

"We were involved in a series of major conflicts with them some two hundred and fifty years ago," said Kaid. "They never actually declared war on us, instead they attacked our colonies and the industrial bases on our moons. Quick in and out hits," he said slowly, looking at Tirak.

"Why? What happened?" asked Sheeowl.

Kusac had been quietly sipping his drink, glad to have the focus of attention anywhere but on him, but now he began to listen. He knew something about the wars, he'd needed to working for AlRel, but though he knew the Brotherhood had been heavily involved in them, he'd never heard exactly in what capacity.

"It started when one of the Forces survey ships landed on the Chemerian homeworld. Chemer is heavily forested and where the forests end, the dust and sand deserts begin. The Captain couldn't see any settlements from the air as Chemerian cities are set deep under the tree canopy, so he assumed it was uninhabited. That was the second mistake. The first had been to send out a bunch of eighteen- to twenty-year-old raw recruits with only one experienced crew member, the Captain, who'd been demoted to flying surveys for incompetence. But that's the Forces for you."

"I hadn't heard that bit about the Captain," Kusac said.

Kaid glanced at him. "You wouldn't," he said. "The Forces

tried to cover it up. Anyway, they'd been in space for about a month by then and the younglings wanted to get out and stretch their legs, so the Captain let them. It was midmorning, the landscape was flat, and the tree line a good several hundred yards away. He thought it would be safe. It would have been if some small jumping creatures hadn't suddenly appeared out of holes, taken one whiff of their scents and bolted for the trees."

"With the younglings in pursuit, I assume," said Rezac.

"Three of them, and on fours," said Kaid. "Next thing they knew, two of the younglings had been shot dead and the third was down, badly injured. The other two alerted the Captain and started off after their comrades as the Chemerians emerged from the trees. A firefight followed which resulted in several Chemerian deaths and the Captain escaping off-world with only two of his crew, both of whom were injured. That started the wars. The Chemerians claimed they thought the younglings were large predators, but there are no predators that size on their world, and their explanation ignores the presence of the scout ship."

"How did the Brotherhood stop the wars?" he asked.

"You have to remember this really was First Contact, our first meeting with another species. The Sholan Forces were led by a General Ryjik, the most xenophobic member of the High Command. He refused to even consider anything but total surrender by the Chemerians and his terms were so draconian there was no way they could have agreed to them. He was no worse than the Chemerians, though. Their terms of surrender were equally unrealistic. Then there were the prisoners taken in the skirmishes—ours and the Chemerians. Tales of our people being tortured were common. The Brotherhood was on the front line. We'd flown raids against the Chemerian colonies from which the attacks were being launched, but no attacks had been made against their homeworld. Talks had broken down because of the unrealistic surrender demands on both sides. Something had to be done to break the stalemate. The Brotherhood did it by taking out General Ryjik, and by bombing the Chemerian homeworld's capital city, then issuing an ultimatum to both sides."

"What was ultimatum?" asked T'Chebbi.

"Unless they both started negotiating for a lasting peace treaty, further punitive actions would be taken against both sides. Luckily they both listened."

"A harsh solution," said Tirak quietly.

"There was no other way to break the deadlock," said Kaid, sipping his drink.

"I can see why the Forces are wary of us," he said.

"They always were because we train every one of our people to take the initiative in battle if the need arises. After that incident, the Forces ensured the Brotherhood presence on Shola was kept to a minimum by posting us near the Chemerian border flying regular patrols. Which is how we found Haven and the *Va'Khoi* and started building our own presence in space."

"That's why when the Chemerians met the Sumaan, they brought them into the Alliance, provided ships, and hired them as mercenaries," added T'Chebbi. "A buffer between us and them."

"What exactly is the Brotherhood's role?" asked Manesh.

"It's many things. Back at the time of the Cataclysm, we were the only military Shola had after overthrowing the Valtegans. We protected the first generation of enhanced telepaths, like Rezac and Zashou, because they'd lost their ability to fight. We were also among the first to be chosen by Leska pairs as Triad partners because of our own gifts."

"Gifts?" asked Giyesh.

"Psi talents that exclude telepathy," said Kaid. "Sixth senses that tell you of danger, whether a person is lying, or lets you feel the mood of individual people or a crowd."

"What's your role now?" asked Tirak.

"Same as then," said T'Chebbi. "We protect our species above all other considerations. The Forces may protect Shola, we do more. We ensure enough of our kind will survive to start again if Shola should fall."

"We protect Sholans from themselves," said Kaid. "Like assassinating Ryjik, and we still guard our boundaries in deep space. But until now, Shola was unaware of our involvement in space. We also provide specialist protection as we do on this estate, and we train the Forces in certain advanced combat skills."

Manesh looked round the table grinning. "I know I'm going to enjoy my time here," she said. "It's what I like doing."

"Well, you have the advantage that you come to this with a reasonable skill level," said Kaid. "We may be running you through routines you think are too basic at first, but it lets us gauge your skills accurately. The real work will start next week." He got to his feet and looked at Kusac. "Time we headed home," he said. "Third meal isn't far off and I at least need to get cleaned up."

"What do you think of the training facility?" Kaid asked him as they walked back up to the villa.

"Impressive," he said. "They did a good job, followed the plans exactly."

"I'm pleased with it. It's got the flexibility we need, and the mess forms a natural meeting place. I think it will promote a sense of community among our clan members." Kaid glanced sideways at him. "It's good to see you out and about at last."

"Mm," he said noncommittally.

"Getting back in training is wise."

"Yes," he said. He supposed it was. It was something to do to keep busy, and he could always go there in the morning or late at night when no one was around.

"Lijou and Rhyaz would like you to get involved with us in training the U'Churians. You're certainly good enough."

"Occupational therapy?" He kept his tone light, but the request, and the praise, surprised him.

"I won't lie to you, yes, it is, but we also could do with your help. You're a qualified member of Alien Relations, and Brotherhood trained. Your help in both fields would be invaluable."

A few months ago, he'd have jumped at the chance, found it an exciting Challenge. Strange what a difference a few months made. "I'll think about it," he said finally.

the City of Light, the Inner Court, Zhal-Ghyakulla, 25th day (June)

Resplendent in the black uniform of the newly formed Warrior Caste and flanked by four of his similarly clad young M'zullian warriors, Kezule waited for Zayshul beside the altar at the God King's temple in the heart of the Inner Court. The ceremony was civil, with a blessing from the Emperor as the personification of Diety.

"She's late." Impatiently he shifted his weight. "There was none of this in my time. Papers were signed, yes, then my wife, heavily sedated, was delivered to the new seraglio. None of this fuss or bother, no waiting around for her to turn up. I knew where she was."

"She'll be here," reassured Prince Zsurtul. "Our way is far better. I can't imagine what a world with only males was like. I must admit I'm surprised that she agreed to marry you."

Kezule looked at him and Zsurtul realized what he'd said.

"I only meant that it was very sudden," the Prince said hastily. "No offense intended."

"None taken," he said dryly. He glanced over his shoulder in time to catch her entrance. The blue gown she wore was slashed to the waist in a deep V and held in place by a broad leather belt of a darker color. Accompanying her was her superior, Medical Director Zsoyshuu. As she came closer, he could see that her head and hands had been painted with the same swirling blue patterns as the dress.

"Burn it, my Mother's made a courtier out of her!" said Zsurtul quietly to him. "Who'd have guessed the doctor could look so fine? The dress is traditional, you know, made of finest TeLax-audin spider silk."

The fabric, Kezule had just realized, was gossamer thin. He could smell her scent now, artificially enhanced by some perfume. Dressed like this, she did indeed put many of the court beauties in the shade.

"Why's she painted?" he asked abruptly.

"Again, part of our traditions. They are the symbols of the demi-Goddess of fertility, La'shol. I wish she'd walk more slowly," the prince added candidly. "She's got to stop striding now that she's your wife and part of the Inner Court. The other females will only torment her about it. They can be rather cruel, you know."

More talk was impossible as she strode the final few feet to his side.

"You can still do the decent thing and call this charade off," she hissed in a low voice as they bowed formally to each other.

"I think not," he replied, enjoying the expanse of pale green skin her dress revealed. He found himself looking lower, hoping to catch a glimpse of the iridescent markings on her hips through the almost transparent material. It was an effort to force his eyes back to her face. "I had not realized I'd chosen so well."

She gave a short hiss of anger. "I will refuse the drink!"

Kezule smiled. He was prepared to remain calm about her intransigence. He knew when the time came, she'd have no option but to accept the drink that would permit her to breed because the Empress herself would hand it to her at the start of the banquet.

CHAPTER 8

Shola, Zhal-Ghyakulla, 27th day (June)

NONI arrived the next day. Rezac, Jo, and Kaid met her out at the front of the villa.

"So this is your father, Tallinu," said Noni, looking the dark-pelted young male up and down. "Brotherhood like you, I see," she added, taking in his purple-edged black tunic. "Darker than you, but the family resemblance is there, right enough."

"You must be from my sister's line," said Rezac, holding his palm out in the telepath's greeting.

"Likely," she said, touching his fingertips with hers. "Seeing as how the only cub you sired before the Valtegans took you was Tallinu!"

Rezac's ears disappeared in his black hair in embarrassment. "I didn't know about him, Noni," he said, glancing at Kaid. "Believe me, if I had, I would have . . ."

"What, lad?" she asked kindly. "You had work to do then, a destiny to fulfill. So had he." She turned to Jo. "And you'll be Jo, his Third. Yes, definitely related," she chuckled. "Both of you with a liking for Human females!" She reached out and patted Jo's obvious bump. "Well come, child. It takes a strong female to live with a Dzaedoh male, believe me! Strong-minded, proud, and self-willed the lot of them!"

Jo laughed, linking her arm through Rezac's. "What about the rest, Noni? The gentleness, the love, the loyalty?" She smiled at her mate, then looked back to the elderly Sholan.

Noni didn't miss the way Rezac's hand closed round Jo's, nor the soft look that came into his eyes. "Besotted, both of you!" she snorted good-humoredly. "You'll do well with each other,

I've no doubt, and provide me with many grandchildren all wanting to clutter up my tiny kitchen! Now, who's going to birth that cub of yours, Jo?"

"You, I hope, Noni," she said. "Only . . ."

"Only you want to have it here, in Vanna's hospital," she said. "I understand. I'll come here, don't you fret." She turned to Kaid, leaning on her stick and looking up at him. "You two go on ahead of us," she said over her shoulder to Rezac and Jo, her voice suddenly gruff. "I got things I need to say privately to Tallinu."

She waited till they'd gone, then, as Kaid opened his mouth to speak, she held up her hand. "No, you listen to me first," she said firmly, wanting to say her piece before she lost the nerve to do it.

"I'm always listening to you, Noni," he murmured.

"Then listen now," she admonished. "You were right to call kin on me, Tallinu. I should have known you better, known you wouldn't do it without proof. I had my own plans for you, and you being my kin didn't fit in with them. In the end, they meant nothing, only kin matters. You were right, Tallinu. I was wrong."

He raised an eye ridge in surprise. "An apology, Noni?"

"Don't rub it in! I thought I'd outlived all my family. Lost my parents in that landslide back in eighty-seven, my brother a year later on a mission for Stronghold. Been alone a long time, Tallinu. Now I find I have living kin." Taking a deep breath, she looked away, shaking her head and resting both hands on the handle of her stick. "Hasn't been easy for me, readjusting my thinking to take that in, especially since you both come from another, older time."

"You said it yourself, Noni. You're still older than us. Still Noni."

"It's not that, lad," she said, looking up at him again. "I've looked at myself, what I've lost over the years by having no family, by ignoring the pull I felt to you."

"I thought we agreed to forget our guilt," he began.

"I thought you agreed to listen!" she said with a touch of the old acerbity.

Kaid grinned, a sideways, Human grin. "Same old Noni."

Quick as a flash, her hand reached out and grasped him by the hair that grew at the side of his neck, yanking him close. He winced but said nothing, even though she knew it must have hurt. "I swear Vartra Himself sent you forward to annoy me! Why are you making this so difficult? I'm trying to say I want my family! I want you, Tallinu, to be for me the son I never had."

She almost jumped when his hand curled gently around her neck.

"You can let me go, Noni," he said quietly. "I'd be honored to have you replace the mother I lost." Then his cheek was touching hers. "Doubtless we'll both find it difficult to adjust, but I want a family of my own, too."

She sighed, resting against him for a moment as his other arm held her close, enjoying the feel of his strength. It had been a long time since they'd exchanged hugs. The last time had been before he ran from the Protectors to Ranz. For the first time, she let him sense the love she'd always felt for him, pleased beyond measure when she felt it returned.

"That'll do," she said gruffly, blinking rapidly and pushing him away. "No need to get maudlin over it. Now, where's that sword-brother of yours?"

Kaid sighed. "In the garden with Carrie and the others. He says he's happy to see you but he's had enough of being examined."

"Oh he does, does he?" said Noni grimly, walking toward the entrance to the villa. "We'll see about that."

"Remember he's still on psi suppressants. Wait, Noni," he said, holding her back. "Vartra called me. He told me about your role as their Guardian and said the Pledge had been broken."

Noni stared at him. "Go on," she said.

"He says the realms have been closed because of the darkness threatening Shola. The Entities are retreating so They can survive if Shola falls, but They're putting Shola at risk by doing this. He's willing to remain and help us if we can find a way to keep Him here. He didn't say how . . ."

"Lijou and I know how," she said. "But to retreat from our world! That could be a bigger threat to us than the Valtegans. The news we wanted to hear is that Vartra is willing to stay!"

"How can we make Him stay?"

"By finding His grave, Tallinu," she said, taking him by the arm. "They buried Him secretly when He died. Why d'you think we curse by saying 'Vartra's bones'? We'll talk to Lijou tomorrow at Stronghold."

*   *   *

Just outside the main lounge, under an awning, a table ringed with comfortable chairs had been set up for them. Carrie and Kusac stood up to greet her, but Noni wasn't fooled by their appearance of closeness; she noticed the distance between them. Nearby, Kashini played under the watchful eye of her nurse.

"Well come, Noni," said Carrie, coming forward to hug her.

Slightly taken aback by the display of affection, but pleased nonetheless, Noni patted her back with her free hand.

"So we're all family," she said, heading for the nearest chair when Carrie let her go. "Don't you go thinking you can take advantage of old Noni now, you hear me?"

"Wouldn't dream of it," murmured Kusac, instinctively holding out his hand to her in a telepath's greeting.

Noni was quick to reach out and return the gesture. She knew instantly that Tallinu was right, she'd get nothing in the way of information from Kusac's mind unaided, unless she was prepared to cause him pain.

"Good day to you, Clan Leader," she said, smiling so he'd know there was no sting in her words.

Kusac gave her a look that spoke volumes, then retreated to his seat on the far side of the table.

"Zhala's bringing out some coffee and pastries," said Carrie, taking a seat beside Noni. "How was your trip?"

"Shorter than usual, thanks to Teusi borrowing one of those fast aircars," she said, leaning her stick against the side of her chair. "He's gone inside to annoy Zhala, so don't you be worrying about him." She looked critically at Kusac. "I see your pelt's grown back nicely over that scar. How you feeling these days?"

"I'm fine," he said, a slightly bored look crossing his face. "Apart from meeting Rezac, Jo and Zashou, I'm afraid your trip's going to be wasted, Noni."

"I should let me be the judge of that, Kusac," she said as Zhala, followed by Teusi, came out carrying trays of drinks and small cakes and pastries.

"Why should you find anything different from the others?" he asked. "You haven't any equipment with you and you can't read my mind because of the psi suppressants. And tomorrow we leave for Stronghold and Kitra's wedding."

"I know, I've got an invitation," she said, slipping her hand into the copious pocket of her green and black robe. "I'm surprised at your attitude, boy. Here's me coming all this way to see you. I never thought you a quitter."

"I'm a realist," he said, reaching out to take hold of the jug of c'shar and pull two mugs toward him. "You should have left it till tomorrow when we get to Stronghold."

"I'm not interfering in your time, Kusac. You got things to do, setting up the temple for the following day, and you're one of Kitra's witnesses, aren't you? You'll need to be there for the practice. No, today suits me better. Where've Rezac and Jo gone?" she asked as Carrie poured out coffee for them.

"They're in the kitchen with Zhala and Teusi," said Carrie. "They'll join us later."

Noni nodded, keeping an eye on Kusac as he pushed a mug of c'shar over to Kaid. "Here, catch," she said, suddenly throwing something at him.

Startled, his hand nevertheless went up to catch it. "A crystal," he said, a puzzled frown on his face as he looked at it.

"Hold it up to the light," she said, aware of Kaid's and Carrie's sudden concern. "It's one of the new ones from the mines near Dzahai village. Thought you'd like to see it. Looks like there's a creature trapped inside, don't you think?"

Suspiciously, Kusac held it up, peering through it, turning it round one way then another. "I'm sorry, I can't see anything like that," he said, leaning forward to return it.

She took it from him, putting it in her pocket with a small, satisfied smile. By handling the crystal, Kusac had allowed her to take an imprint of his mind. She might not be able to scan him, but she could scan the crystal. It wouldn't be as good because it merely held an echo of him, but it should be enough.

Later that evening, Kaid came to her guest suite. Teusi let him in, taking him through to Noni's bedroom where she was sitting up in bed, the crystal on her lap.

"What did you find?" he asked, picking up a chair and bringing it over to sit beside her as Teusi left.

"Not much," she said. "He's got his mind shut tight behind barriers the like of which he shouldn't be able to use. He's afraid of something, Tallinu. He knows what it is and he's hiding it even from himself."

"Is he refusing to face the loss of his Talent?"

"No, not that. Something more," she said, picking the crystal up and placing it in a small, leather bag.

"You know he killed the Valtegan priest with his mind," said Kaid. "Is it that?"

She shook her head slowly. "I don't think it's that either, though there is the conflict between guilt at using his Talent like that and his training that says it must never be done. He knows there will be no reprisals. He believes he's got no usable Talent, so he's not afraid of killing again."

"As he woke from cryo, I had his mind scanned by a medical telepath," said Kaid. "I was hoping he'd be caught unaware with those barriers down. He was. His father and I monitored both him and the medic to make sure nothing about the killing was discovered, but we sensed nothing out of the ordinary."

Again she shook her head. "No, this is something more, something I feel may have happened to him on the Prime ship."

"We've got to try and find out what it is."

"No!" she said sharply, looking up from tying the bag. "You'll leave him to come to terms with it himself, Tallinu. We can't interfere, not without causing his mind more trauma than it's already suffered. It could push him into another suicide attempt."

"There must be something we can do, Noni."

"Tallinu, there's nothing I can do," she said, reaching out to touch his hand. "Vanna's drugs seem to be working, no need for me to interfere. As for the tendrils from that implant, and whatever it is that's frightening him so, unless I can link to his mind, I can't help. And for now at least, that's impossible. He's having problems with his emotions because of what the tendrils have done. Try if you can to help him with those."

She hesitated. "There's one chance I can think of, but it's a long shot. I've been thinking of what happened to Mara and Josh when Zhyaf died, and has happened to Rezac and Zashou. Carrie will lose her Link to you around the fifteenth week, as Jo will to Rezac any time now. Watch what happens to Rezac and Zashou. Their link will probably reestablish itself, if not then, as soon as Jo's had the cub. The same may happen for Kusac. His Link may reassert itself as soon as Carrie has your cub. If that should happen, then I can work to heal him."

"How can it when he's lost his Talent?"

"He may well have, but something is enabling him to put up those barriers, Tallinu. Maybe he'll only have a minor link to her, like you had at first. It's at least better than nothing, isn't it? It lets us into his mind to try to remove or readjust those tendrils. He needs to be awake for that." She took hold of his chin and tipped his face up to hers, studying him. "Are you that keen to lose your Link to Carrie? Be honest with yourself if not with me."

"I don't know," he said, moving her hand away. "I don't know, Noni."

"For the God's sake, don't let her know that, Tallinu!" she said anxiously. "She's going through enough without carrying the burden of that."

"I already told her I didn't want the Link," he said. "I have to be honest with her, Noni. She knows what's in my mind without me telling her."

"You keep things back, don't tell me you don't, even with your Link! Remedy it by telling her it isn't so any more."

"I won't lie to her, Noni. She knows I love her, even if I don't want the Link."

"And the cub?"

"We don't talk about it," he said, looking away.

"It! What d'you mean it!" she said, outraged.

"Her, then!" he said, looking back at her. "We don't talk about our daughter."

"Why not? Don't you want her either?"

"Yes, when we conceived her, of course I did," he said quietly, not rising to her bait. "But the responsibility, Noni—and I don't know how to behave with Carrie! I can't act like she's my mate with Kusac around!"

"You've got to work it out, Tallinu, and soon. An unhappy pregnancy makes an unhappy cub, you know. At least treat her as your mate when Kusac isn't there. And talk to her about the cub! Make plans with Carrie for the berran's arrival, otherwise she'll go on feeling like it's a burden of guilt she's carrying, not a child to be loved. You could even do worse than talk to Kusac about it, too."

"I don't want him to feel threatened by . . ."

"He's not," she reassured him. "Right now he's trying to cling to what's familiar, what's Sholan. That's part of why he feels distanced from Carrie and life here right now, and why he was clinging to his daughter at first. And don't you forget T'Chebbi at this time. She's getting broody now. It didn't come easy to her to terminate that cub of yours."

"What?" He looked startled.

"You heard. Watch her with Kashini sometime."

He groaned and put his head down on the bed. "I'm not cut out for this domestic life, Noni. I'm a Warrior!"

She stroked his head gently. "There's a time for everything, Tallinu. Where do the next generation of Warriors and Brothers come from if not from those like you? How many times in the ten years you spent outside the Brotherhood would you have given everything for a Companion like either of those two females? You have to be home with Carrie now. Why not let T'Chebbi have the cub she wants, too, get it over with at the same time? You never know, it might ease the situation."

He lifted his head and looked up at her. "You're joking, Noni. Both of them pregnant by me? I don't think so. Kusac and T'Chebbi are occasional lovers, he used to go to her when Carrie and I were together."

"He's not going to either of them, or anyone else right now. Might give him the impetus to do so, or to find an amiable Companion from the estate. There's plenty would be willing, I've no doubt," she said robustly.

"I'll think about it," he sighed, getting up.

"You do," she said, putting the crystal in its pouch on her nightstand. "Nothing upsets one's home life like a broody female—or male, come to that! By the by, I got something for you. Over there on the dresser, in the small wooden box," she said, pointing to the drawer unit opposite the end of her bed.

Curious, he got up and fetched it. Measuring around nine inches square, it wasn't what he'd call small. He handed it to her as he sat down again.

"It's for you," she said, passing it back.

"It's lovely," he said, admiring the different inlaid woods that made up the mountain landscape on the lid. "But it isn't my birthday, Noni."

"Not the box, what's in it, fool of a boy!" she said tartly. "Open it!"

He did. Inside on a bed of plush fabric lay a bronze torc, a dagger, and a buckle. Startled, he looked up at her. "I can't take these."

"You shouldn't have called kin on me if you weren't prepared to *be* my kin," she said. "It's yours, Tallinu. Were my brother's, but he's dead as I told you earlier. You're the oldest Dzaedoh male now. They're yours. Put the torc on. I'd like to see you wearing it."

Placing the box on her bed, he lifted the torc out. The round terminals at either end were embossed with the sigil of the Dzaedoh Clan. "I never thought I'd wear a torc of my own," he said, putting it slowly round his neck.

Noni regarded him critically. "It looks good on you, boy. Why shouldn't you have your own torc? You belong to a family of your own now. You have your father, a son, a grandchild on the way as well as a new daughter for you. And you're also Clan Leader within the En'Shalla Clan. Come a long way from your days as a foundling, eh, Tallinu?"

"A long way," he agreed quietly, closing the box.

Tucking his torc inside the neck of his tunic, Kaid went back down to the den. It was all too new for him to want to draw attention to it yet. What Noni had said about T'Chebbi concerned him; he'd never have thought her interested in having cubs of her own. It was yet one more worry to add to his suddenly burgeoning family life. When he opened the door, he found Kitra lying on the sofa curled up against Carrie while Dzaka was filling mugs from the hot plate.

"I almost wish we'd decided to have a civil ceremony," the young female was sighing. "It's utter chaos at home right now. Choa, the cook, is busy packing all the food she's prepared, and Mother and Taizia are packing clothes for us. I'm not even getting to choose what I take with me!"

"Everything you'll need will be there," said Dzaka imperturbably as he came over to them with mugs of coffee.

"So you say. You won't even tell me where we're going for the next two weeks!"

He grinned at her as he put them down on the table. "A surprise from your father, I told you."

"I'm sure you don't mean it, Kitra. I'm just hoping that Choa hasn't made any fish pastries," teased Carrie, stroking the young female's head gently.

Kitra groaned. "Gods, I hope not! I haven't forgotten the time Mother was away on the *Khalossa*! We lived on fish for weeks!"

"I thought you were staying at the main house tonight," said Kaid, joining his son at the hot plates.

"Master Konis could see Kitra had had enough and sent us to spend the night here," said Dzaka quietly, pouring out a c'shar for his father. "Kitra's pregnancy sickness has just started and it hits her pretty badly in the evenings."

"You should speak to Noni about it. There's a simple remedy for it, as I remember."

"Mother and Vanna have both suggested things she could take, but she refuses. Doesn't want to risk our cub." His mouth opened in a gentle smile. "I can't fault her for that. How's Carrie coping?"

He hesitated. "Fine," he said, aware that he really had no idea. He turned to look round the room. "Where're Kusac and T'Chebbi?" he asked, keeping his voice low.

"We passed them heading for the gym," said Dzaka. "I get the feeling he isn't handling the forthcoming wedding well."

"He keeps to himself, Dzaka. I know he'd wanted a full temple wedding for himself and Carrie. The reality was a little different." He remembered it well, the terse summons from Kusac in the middle of the night, trying to land an aircar at the Valsgarth temple by flickering torchlight, and the simple ceremony Ghyan had carried out. "He'd just found out she was pregnant for the first time, and that they were both gene-altered. Then we came here, to tell his parents." He grasped his son's shoulder briefly. "I do know that he doesn't begrudge you your wedding. He loves Kitra very dearly."

"I just hope it isn't distressing him. I was worried when Kitra insisted on choosing him and Carrie as our witnesses. Was there any good news from Noni?"

Kaid shook his head. "Enough of that. We're going to Stronghold tomorrow to make ready for your wedding! Tell me, where are you taking her?"

Dzaka laughed, moving off to join his bride-to-be. "No, I'm not even telling you! She'll enjoy herself, so long as the nausea isn't too bad."

"Neggu," said Kaid, suddenly remembering the name of the remedy. "That's the name of it. Give her ground neggu in warm milk at first meal and again before bed. They make crystallized sweets of it she can take during the day." He went over to Carrie. "I'll get some for you tomorrow from the village store be-

fore we leave," he said to her, sitting down in the chair next to
her. "I don't want the next few days spoiled for you either."

"Mmm?" she asked lazily, reaching for her mug.

"Anti-nauseant," he said, taking a sip of his c'shar. "For morning or evening sickness. I remember it from my time with Noni.
She used to take me out collecting it. Even had me crystallizing
pieces of the root for her patients!"

"I told you, I'm not taking drugs," began Kitra.

"It isn't a drug, kitling," said Zashou. "It's a spice. The ground
root is used in cooking. We used it in our time. It really is perfectly safe, so safe that you can eat them as sweets as Kaid says.
Try them. No point in feeling miserable for your wedding."

"If Carrie uses it, will you give it a try?" asked Dzaka, moving Kitra's feet so he could sit down.

"It's not that bad," she said. "Honestly."

Dzaka rubbed his fingers gently across the pads of her toes.
"I can feel exactly how bad it is," he said quietly. "Will you try
it?"

"If it's really one of Noni's remedies, and it stops you nag-
ging me, all right," she sighed.

T'Chebbi called a halt to their sparring at the nineteenth hour.
"We stop now," she said. "We're leaving for Stronghold in the
morning. I need to pack and rest."

"I'm packed," he said, remaining in a fighting crouch.

"I'm not. Unless you can spar with yourself, we go now," she
said firmly, walking over to her locker at the other side of the
exercise hall.

"I don't want to go back yet," he said, following her.

"Then walk back alone," she said, pulling on her tunic.

"What about a shower?"

"Will shower at house." She glanced at him as she picked up
her belt and began to fasten it round her waist. "You going to
be all right the next two days?"

Kusac reached for his own locker door, opening it and pulling
his tunic and belt out. "I'll cope," he said offhandedly, not looking at her. "I'm happy for Kitra and Dzaka."

"Why not partner me at Stronghold," she said. "Let Kaid be with Carrie. Might make it easier for you—less memories."

"I can cope, I said."

"Can you? Will all be couples apart from Rezac, Jo, and Za-shou—and us. Am only giving you another option."

He looked up. "I know you are," he said, his tone less sharp. "And I thank you. I have to try to cope. We'll all stay together, then there's no need to be seen as couples."

"Sounds fine," she said, grabbing her towel and beginning to head for the exit.

Though they walked back in silence, it was companionable, and T'Chebbi was content. The workout sessions were having the effect she'd planned. Kusac was beginning to relax a little at last. As they entered the villa's central courtyard, she stopped. "I'm going to the main bathing room. Want to join me?"

He hesitated, then nodded, following her down the colonnaded walk. When they came to the door for the grooming and mas-sage room, she held it open for him. "Bath or shower?" she asked as they walked past the single couch into the bathing room.

"Bath. Do you have soap? Mine is upstairs."

"My room's across the courtyard. I'll get it," she said. "You run the water."

The bath had a raised step where he could stand while she soaped him. His pelt was still longer than usual due to the drugs they'd taken for the Jalna mission and because she was tired, it was hard work working up a lather and rubbing the soap deep down to his skin. She was used to it, though, having a naturally long pelt herself. She worked on his muscles at the same time, using it as an excuse to slowly turn the experience into a more sensual one.

He had a good body, she thought as she ran her hands firmly over his buttocks and the inside of his thighs, forcing the suds out of his fur. Well muscled, yet still lithe enough for her taste. Muscles, in her opinion, should be built up to better perform their function, not for show as some Brothers—and Sisters—believed.

He jumped, moving away from her as her hand accidentally touched him too intimately. "I can manage now," he said, back-ing into the water to rinse himself.

She sighed and began to unfasten her hair. He was still too skittish. She'd hoped that by now he'd have been relaxed enough in her company to enjoy some intimacy again, perhaps enough to give him the confidence to want to spend the night with her. Never mind, there would be other times. Then she felt his hand on her waist.

"Let me help you," he said as she turned round.

Kaid's wrist comm buzzed gently. Cursing under his breath, he sat up and answered it.

"You alone?" asked T'Chebbi quietly.

"Yes, what is it?" he asked, passing his free hand over the light sensor. Something about her didn't look right.

"Need you in my room with Kusac's medikit," she said. "Surprised your bio-monitor didn't alert you."

"On my way," he said tersely.

"What happened?" he asked, taking in her state before scanning the room for Kusac. "Where is he?"

She nodded toward the other side of her bed. "On the floor. See to him first. He's had another pain episode. He's in shock, needs his drugs."

He took hold of her arm, steering her to the bed, making her sit down. "You stay there," he said. He looked across at Kusac. Limbs shaking uncontrollably, he lay curled in an almost fetal position, eyes staring blankly ahead. "I need help. I'm sending for Rezac."

Unhappily, she nodded.

Rezac was there in minutes, by which time, Kaid had managed to make Kusac comfortable. Between them, they got his now unconscious body up to his room without waking anyone else.

"Rezac's spending the night with him," said Kaid when he returned. "Tell me what happened," he asked, sitting beside her.

She leaned drowsily against him, fumbling at the belt of her robe. "My back. I can't reach it, Kaid. Need you to treat it."

"Have you taken anything?" he demanded, taking hold of her hands, suddenly worried about her. Despite them being slick with sweat, she felt cold and the skin around her eyes and nose was gray.

She nodded. "Analgesic. But I hadn't gone into shock when I took it."

Almost roughly, he turned her around, pulling her robe down to her waist. He hissed in shock as he saw the blood welling sluggishly from several deep cuts on her sides.

"I know," she said as he pulled the robe up around her shoulders again and got to his feet. "I'm a fool. I should have left him be, but he asked, Kaid. First time since we got back. And it wasn't his fault."

"Later," he said grimly, picking her up in his arms. "Those wounds need closing. I'm taking you to Jack."

Jack lived with his Sholan Companion, Jiszoe, in an apartment within the estate's small hospital. Leaving T'Chebbi lying facedown on a bed in one of the two treatment rooms, Kaid went to rouse the Human doctor.

By the time Jack had swabbed her wounds, cut back her pelt and stapled them closed, T'Chebbi was beginning to come round.

"He must have reached for me mentally, Kaid," she said, twisting her head to see him. "Then the pain hit him. That's when I got hurt."

"He can't have. He's on psi suppressants," said Kaid from his seat beside her head as Jack sprayed antibiotic sealant over the wounds. "Anyway, why would he do that?"

"It's obvious," said Jack, placing a gauze dressing over each set of wounds. "He's using the pain to achieve pleasure. We know he's lacking some physical sensitivity because of the neural damage, couple that with what that Valtegan priest did to him, and it's not to be wondered at that his responses have got cross-wired, so to speak." He looked over the top of his glasses at Kaid. "Thing is, how do we uncross them again? T'Chebbi's wounds are bad enough, but her pelt gave her some protection. On Carrie, they'd be down to the bone."

"How did he respond to you?" Kaid asked her. "Did you use one of your perfumes on him? Was he forceful at all?"

Her ears flattened in embarrassment as Jack began to chuckle.

"I've been hearing quite a bit about those perfumes of yours, young lady," he said. "You and I will have to have a talk about them some day. They could be quite useful to people back home with certain medical conditions."

"Why'd you have to tell Garras," she grumbled, pulling her hand free of Kaid's and batting weakly at him.

"He asked me what I'd done to seduce you," he said with a faint smile. "Didn't think I was going to take the blame for that, did you?"

"Huh! Not mine to give, Jack. Is Consortia product, sold only to us. Kusac didn't force me, Kaid. Some things I did he hardly noticed, yet with others, he was oversensitive," she said, carefully lifting her stomach off the bed so Jack could wrap the bandage round her.

Kaid got up instantly, supporting her till Jack had finished.

"All done," Jack said. "You can sit up now."

"If he did it on purpose, then he got it wrong," T'Chebbi continued as Kaid helped her up. "He was in agony. Couldn't be any pleasure in it for him."

"Could it be part of what Chy'qui did? Conditioned him to like his response to pain?" asked Kaid, helping her into the fresh robe he'd fetched from the hospital's store.

"Perhaps," said Jack. "If it was, they'd have needed some form of sexual stimulus, be it even as little as those sleep tapes with images of Sholan and perhaps Human females. And I'd have expected Carrie to have suffered injuries from him, too."

"She did, but nowhere near as severe as these. Scratches and a couple of shallow puncture wounds, that's all. He's not been with her since."

"Nor with anyone else, until tonight," said T'Chebbi, tying the robe belt. "He knows he was overly rough with Carrie, maybe that's why."

"He needs to be asked," said Kaid grimly. "As Jack said, your wounds are bad enough, next time it could be worse. I'd rather you didn't pair with him until we find out what's happening, T'Chebbi." He was angry at what had happened to T'Chebbi, not with Kusac, but for him, too.

"I don't intend to," she said with a shudder. "Jack's right. Was taught about the darker sides of pairing at the Consortia House, but tonight scared me. He was so out of control."

Kaid sighed and reached out to pick her up. "We have to get back."

"I can walk," she objected as he took her up in his arms.

"No, and you're staying with me tonight. I want to keep an

eye on you," he said, making sure he kept his arm clear of her injuries. "Thanks, Jack. Sorry we had to wake you."

"No problem," said Jack, walking them to the door. "I take it you've no objections to me discussing this with Vanna."

"You'd better. The God knows, we can't leave him like this." He stopped at the door, looking back at the pyjama-clad Human. "I don't want Carrie hearing about this yet. I'll find my own way to tell her."

the *Couana*, Zhal-S'Asha, 20th day (October)

He stirred in his sleep, his dreams going back to his last night on the *Kz'adul*. A faint noise had woken him from his light doze, drawing his attention to the door. Still groggy from his medication, he watched as it opened a crack, letting in a sliver of light from the corridor outside. A feeling of unreality gripped him as he watched the gap grow wider, then darken as someone entered.

The scent reached him before any sound; dry and slightly musky, like the smell of leather. Valtegan, certainly, but more. He knew it held species specific overtones he couldn't identify. Raising himself on one elbow, he peered through the dim light, trying to identify the figure as it closed the door. Few people came into his room, even the guard was gone now.

"Doctor Zayshul?" he asked.

"Hush," she whispered, switching off the light. Apart from the faint-colored glow from the monitors, the room was in darkness. "You leave tomorrow. I thought I'd come say good-bye to you tonight."

Puzzled, he listened to her footsteps come up to his bed then stop. Her hand touched his face, the palm brushing across his lips then stroking his cheek gently before it was gone. As he sat up, straining to see or hear her, a sudden dizziness overcame him and he fell back to the bed again.

Her scent grew stronger, then cool air hit his body as the cover was lifted. He felt the bed move, its strange, almost living fabric pulling away from him as she eased herself in beside him.

He tried to speak, but found it difficult to even gather his thoughts as she pressed herself against him.

"Hush," she repeated, her hand passing gently over his face again. "Relax, nothing can harm you. This is only a dream of home and the one you love," she said, running her hand down his back and gently pulling him onto his side. Behind him, the bed flowed against his body, forming a warm, supporting wedge.

A hand closed round his, lifting it and placing it against her smooth, naked skin. "See? This is just a dream of your Carrie."

Was it Carrie? He knew she'd been on the ship but he thought she'd escaped with Kaid and the others. His senses befuddled, he gave up trying to figure it out and lay there, passive, as she began to stroke his side. She was warm and soft, his first pleasurable physical contact with anyone since he'd been wakened from cryo. Her hand moved lower, grasping his thigh, pulling it across her hip while her knee gently eased itself forward between his legs, pressing gently upward against him.

He responded instantly, blood rushing to his head and groin as he felt the familiar tension begin to build. As her teeth closed gently on his shoulder, he shuddered, clenching his hand round her hip. Whoever she was, what she was doing to him felt unbelievably good.

She grew bolder, the nips becoming more like bites, letting him feel the tips of her claws against the sensitive flesh on the underside of his thighs. The tension built until it was imperative he move her leg. He tried, but she prevented him.

He began to growl his distress, using his strength against her for the first time, hauling her leg aside so his genitals could drop, moaning gently in relief mingled with pleasure when they did.

She began to laugh then, a sound he recognized instantly. She wasn't Human, she was Valtegan! He froze, then tried frantically to push her away.

"No, no," she said, running her hands across his face, lowering hers till he could feel her breath on his cheek. "It's only a dream. Relax, this is good, Kusac. This is good."

He felt her tongue against his cheek, flicking across his

lips and nose. Almost instantly, his senses began to blur again. Powerless to resist, he could do nothing as she pushed him gently onto his back. Her scent surrounded him as she rose up from the bed, overpowering in its raw sensuality as it swept every consideration but the need to couple with her from his mind.

Time seemed to stretch endlessly as, obviously in no hurry, she played with him, exploring his body. If he'd learned the meaning of pain and fear from J'koshuk, from her he met only pleasure. He didn't care any longer what species she was, only that she didn't stop.

When she finally joined with him, instinctively he reached for her mind. Agony coursed through him, setting his body on fire. Crying out, he tried to stop her, to throw her off, unable to bear even her touch let alone her weight. As his unsheathed claws dug into her hips, he began to keen. Frantically, she used her greater strength to pin him to the bed, her mouth covering his in an effort to keep him silent. Every nerve aflame and hypersensitized, the effect was shattering.

He woke covered in sweat and tangled in his sheets, her scent as fresh in his nostrils as if she'd just left his bed. Shuddering, he pulled himself free of the covers and sat up. The dream had scared him, full as it was of dark and disturbing memories. He'd thought he'd buried it so deep in his subconscious that it would never surface, but he'd been wrong.

Swinging his legs over the side of his bed, he reached for the pack of stim twigs on his night table. As he pulled one out, he noticed that his hands were shaking badly.

Sticking the twig in his mouth, he bit down on it, the slightly bitter taste flooding into his mouth, bringing with it a brief light-headedness. He cursed himself for not anticipating the nightmare. But had it been a nightmare? Though he might try to deny he'd felt any pleasure, he knew the truth was otherwise. He knew now she'd drugged him. But why? Perhaps to keep him quiet. But why had she wanted him in the first place? Until then, she'd not shown in any way he could understand that she'd been interested in him. Had it been no more than curiosity?

From the moment Rhyaz had given him the message, he'd been afraid of meeting her again. The words might have been written by Kezule, but the General knew that what would draw him to the rendezvous was the scents; Zayshul's, and that of a Sholan. His deepest fear was that somehow, during that insane night, he'd sired a cub on her. How else could there be a Sholan cub's scent on a message from the Prime world? Neither their Ambassador nor his staff had taken their families with them to K'oish'ik. She'd done something to him that night, something that had changed him. Even the memory of her scent acted like a drug, with him the addict.

He had to see her again and find out the truth.

His teeth clenched involuntarily on the twig again, the natural stimulant this time clearing the last of the sleep from his brain. He lay back on the bed, staring up at the ceiling as he had the night he'd waited for death. The dream had reminded him of something else he'd tried to forget: he wanted her again, and hated himself for it. How, in Vartra's name, could he have paired with one of them, and want to do it again? She and J'koshuk had twisted his nature out of true, leaving him stranded between extremes; they were the reason he'd been rough with Carrie—and worse with T'Chebbi.

Angrily, he pulled the twig from his mouth, remembering his earlier dream of her, snarling as he threw it as far as he could. Round his neck, the torc began to vibrate gently, warning him his anger was reaching a dangerous level. His subconscious was making him face the past, relive each awful memory so he'd realize what had happened to him. He'd been told that the procedure they'd used would help him come to terms with the past but he'd never anticipated this! Lijou had taught him mental exercises to help him cope but his first attempts had left him afraid to try them alone. He was no longer afraid. If the message was genuine, which he feared it was, he knew he'd need all his wits about him in the days to come.

Kezule was no one's fool. He'd studied the main transcripts of Rhyaz's interrogations of the General, and read Dzaka's report on his and Kitra's captivity in the ruins. He knew just how dangerous Kezule was. With sleep beyond him, now might be as good a time as any to go through those exercises.

He took off the torc, setting it on the night table. Closing his eyes, he slowed his breathing and began to murmur the litanies.

Shola, Zhal-Ghyakulla, 29th day (June)

Kusac had awakened two hours later. His first thought had been for T'Chebbi. He sat bolt upright, looking around wildly only to see Rezac sitting calmly beside his bed.

"T'Chebbi's fine," the young male said. "Kaid told me to tell you they know you're not to blame." He picked up a mug of c'shar and handed it to him. "Here. I felt you waking."

He took the mug, not knowing what else to do. "How is she?" he asked.

"Sore. She's got three deep gouges about waist high on either side. Her long pelt kept them from being worse."

Kusac's ears flattened to his skull as he looked away. Putting the drink back on his nightstand, he moved toward the other side of the bed to get up.

"I wouldn't bother," said Rezac, a hard undertone to his voice. "You're not leaving here tonight. You can't undo it, nor can you run away from it, so you might as well stay where you are."

"I wasn't going to . . ."

"Don't give me that crap! We both know you were. Of all the mindless, stupid, insane things to do, that really takes the prize, Kusac. You risked her life!"

"You've no right to talk to me like that!" he snarled, sitting up on his haunches.

"I've every right, because no one else will," Rezac snapped, his dark hair beginning to rise. "Thanks to your stupidity, I'm spending the night doing nursery duty with you rather than being in a comfortable bed with Jo! I don't appreciate it."

"Then leave! I'm not asking you to stay!"

"And let you spoil Dzaka's and Kitra's bonding ceremony by disappearing overnight? Forget it!"

"I can't face them!"

"You're damned well going to! Just because you went through

hell on the *Kz'adul* doesn't give you the right to behave irresponsibly for the rest of your life."

With a snarl of rage, Kusac launched himself at Rezac.

Rezac was ready for him and dived to the side, allowing him to go crashing into the chair.

Lying there stunned, he felt Rezac grasp him by the scruff and start hauling him to his feet. Training took over, and fighting the natural response to freeze, he forced himself to reach for Rezac's hand while trying to bend his neck forward to take up the slack.

"Enough, Kusac," he heard Rezac say. "I'm not going to fight you. You want to know what I really think now you've heard the response you expected?"

"What?" Sheer surprise made him relax and he'd have stumbled to the ground had Rezac not slipped his other arm round his chest to support him.

"I think you're being used," Rezac said, turning him around so they were face to face. "I know the Valtegans. Zashou and I spent two years living on their world as nothing more than slaves. They've conditioned you, turned you into an unexploded bomb, programmed to feel nothing but fear, trust nothing but violence. J'koshuk was no different from the Inquisitor priests we knew and that's what they did to those they took prisoner. Early on we managed to get a few of our telepaths back, but they were like you, emotions burned out, incapable of living without the constant fear and pain. The first two or three just disappeared into the night, gave themselves back up to the Valtegans rather than try to fight it. Is that what you're going to do? Just let them control you even now?"

He pulled away from Rezac. "I don't know what you're talking about," he snapped, moving back to the bed.

"Sure you do," drawled Rezac, picking up the chair. "Your world was predictable. People meant pain. You learned to tolerate it, prided yourself when you could withstand more because you kidded yourself he wasn't getting to you." He sat down on the chair again. "Only that's not what was really happening. Every time the priest used the collar on you, he was causing damage to your central nervous system. They're keeping that information from you, Kusac, but I think you've got a right to know. I'm afraid you got a fair bit of neural damage and they can't do anything about it."

He stared at Rezac, shocked by what the younger male was saying. "How did you know?" he asked, sitting down. "I told no one."

Rezac reached out for the mug of c'shar and passed it to him. "Because when they took Zashou and me, they tried the same with us," he said quietly. "Telepaths had to be broken, made into amenable pets who would obey commands instantly. When they found out we were a Leska pair, we were taken to the planetary governor. It's all that saved us. So I know what you were put through, and why. As I said, they had torturer priests then. Even the Valtegans feared them because they were bred to love their work. And J'koshuk had special reasons to hate you."

Kusac took a drink, turning over in his mind what Rezac was saying. "What about the others, the ones who didn't give themselves up to the Valtegans?"

"I won't lie to you," he said. "Most of them eventually suicided one way or another, be it an overdose of drugs like you tried, or a suicide mission. Some even lasted for four or five months, not long enough for us to know how permanent the damage was. But we were at war, we were the only resistance Shola had. The stress and pressure on us was unimaginable. That's not the case for you. Are you going to risk killing Carrie and Kaid by giving in to this, or are you going to try to fight it? Until you do, you're still J'koshuk's captive."

"I know. I'd worked that much out for myself," he growled.

"Tonight's incident is private. Neither Kaid nor T'Chebbi want Carrie to know about it, so you're going to have to get up in a few hours and behave in public as if nothing happened. If they can, so can you," Rezac said, his voice hardening. "If you can't feel any emotions other than fear and anger, pretend! You still have the moral values you grew up with, you know when you should be feeling remorse or sadness. Say the words, try to sound like you mean them, even if now you don't, because in time you will. One thing we learned after Vartra enhanced our psi abilities was that the mind has an infinite capacity to change itself if you persist."

"You're still a youngling," Kusac said, his voice strained. "At least seven years my junior. Where did you learn all this?"

Rezac shrugged. "By living. On the streets of Ranz with the Packs, and here, fighting the Valtegans. You grow up quickly when you're constantly on a razor's edge. When the telepath program recruited me for the university at Khalma, I had to learn to fit in. Education was expensive. The other students didn't know my background, but they knew I didn't belong to their world." Rezac glanced at his wrist comm. "Look, we've got to get up in about four hours. How about we get some rest even if we can't sleep? We've got a long day ahead of us helping decorate the temple for Father Lijou."

"Aren't you afraid I'll leave when you're asleep?" Kusac asked with a touch of sarcasm.

Rezac leaned forward to touch his hand briefly. "No. I haven't had the chance to get to know you yet, but the measure of a person is his friends. I know Kaid and Carrie. You're a Warrior, Kusac. You'll fight this; you won't let them win now. And all your friends are willing to help you."

Stronghold, Zhal-Ghyakulla, 29th day (June)

The temple was beautiful, Kitra had to admit as she looked up at the pillars wreathed in summer flowers and vines. The air would be heavy with their scent, but she could smell little of them as they were overwhelmed by the perfume from the circlet of sacred nung flowers she wore.

She was getting restless. She hadn't realized the life-bonding ceremony would take so long. Carrie's had been short, she'd said, but then they'd gotten bonded in secret in the middle of the night. Sighing, she thought it must have been much more romantic than this, even though she'd have missed all the lovely flowers.

The Brotherhood choir was singing, the voice music strange to her ears because of its Highland influence. Smaller in height than the group of adult females who stood between her and Dzaka's family, she could see very little except their backs. She shifted her feet, stiff from standing still for so long, and glanced sideways, catching Mistress Kha'Qwa's eye. Still convalescing, Father Lijou's life-mate was seated in a chair on their side of the main aisle, not far from Father Lijou and the statue of Vartra.

Kha'Qwa smiled, then moved her hands in a couple of small gestures which Kitra recognized. *Not long.* Kitra grinned in relief and tried to remember what Dzaka had shown her for the Brotherhood sign to acknowledging a message. She gave up and just flicked an ear in affirmative.

An elbow dug her in the ribs, making her jump.

"Pay attention," hissed Taizia, glancing over her shoulder. "And for goodness sake, remember what you're supposed to do!"

Her mind went blank instantly as Taizia and her mother moved to one side allowing her to see Dzaka standing opposite her for the first time that day. Her heart leaped when she saw him, sword hanging on his left hip, looking so smart in his formal Brotherhood tunic and jacket. He was hers, her Leska, and very soon to be her life-mate. Nervously, she ran her hands down the skirts of her long green dress, smoothing out the imagined creases. Across from her, Dzaka's mouth opened in an encouraging smile.

Then Carrie was at her side, taking her gently by the elbow and urging her forward.

"It's time," Carrie whispered. "Didn't you hear Father Lijou?"

Panicking, she looked back at Dzaka, seeing him moving toward the center of the aisle with Kusac, waiting for her.

"No need to run!" said Carrie, trying to keep up with her as she hurried over to him. "He isn't going anywhere!"

"I'm not," she protested, coming to a stop beside him and taking hold of his outstretched hand.

"Not what?" he whispered, grinning.

"Running," she said as they began to walk toward where Father Lijou stood in front of the statue of Vartra.

"Of course not," he agreed, his hand gently squeezing hers. "You knew I'd wait for you."

They stopped in front of the Father, Carrie standing to one side, Kusac to the other.

"Do you have the bracelets?" Lijou asked Kusac.

He nodded and handed them to him.

Taking them from him, Lijou placed them on the small table beside him.

"We're gathered here today because Kitra Aldatan and Dzaka Dzaedoh wish to become life-mates. Is there anyone here who would deny them that right?" Lijou asked, looking around the congregation. He waited a moment then smiled at Kitra.

"Do you both wish to be made one, to share your life together from this day on?" he asked, looking from her to Dzaka.

"Yes," said Dzaka, gripping Kitra's hand more tightly.

Kitra nodded. "Yes."

"Blood is life, linking families and clans, bringing peace to our people," continued Lijou. "To be made one, you must share your blood. Are you both prepared to do this?"

"I am," said Dzaka, glancing at Kitra.

"Yes," said Kitra, eyeing the knife dubiously.

Lijou picked up the knife and held his hand out to Kitra.

"It won't hurt, Kitra," Dzaka whispered reassuringly, letting her hand go.

Nervously, Kitra put her right hand, palm uppermost, in Lijou's. Before she had time to think, the priest had flicked the tip of the blade across her hand and blood was welling up from a tiny cut. She bit back an exclamation of pain, but Lijou had already released her and had done the same to Dzaka.

Passing the knife to Kusac, Lijou reached for Kitra's hand again, pressing her palm to Dzaka's, holding them both over the bowl of incense.

"Blood is life," said Lijou. "It binds these two young people together, making them kin. You, Kitra and Dzaka, are now one, kin to each other."

Fascinated, Kitra watched as blood gathered on the edges of their hands, dripping onto the cubes of incense below.

Lijou released them, waiting for Carrie to come forward and wipe the blood from their palms before pressing a small, sterile dressing over the cuts.

Kitra dabbed at the dressing, pressing it down more firmly, watching as Dzaka took a piece of incense from the bowl. She did the same, then accompanied him to the statue of Vartra where they threw the incense into the brazier held between the God's hands.

Let it blaze up, Kitra thought frantically when nothing happened for a moment or two. Then, with a hissing and spitting, the flames flared up briefly as clouds of incense began to rise toward the ceiling.

"A good omen," murmured Father Lijou, picking up the silver bracelets as a collective sigh came from the congregation.

"As an outward sign of your bonding," he continued, passing a bracelet to each of them, "here are your bracelets. Wear them with Vartra's blessing on your union."

Dzaka took Kitra's right hand and carefully pushed the bracelet onto her wrist, tightening it before holding out his hand for her to do the same.

In her nervousness, she almost dropped it and Dzaka had to help her.

"May Vartra and the Green Goddess grant you long life and happiness," Father Lijou said, embracing first Kitra then Dzaka. "Now there's only the temple register to sign. It's waiting for us in the Goddess' Shrine." He gestured to his right, between the pillars of the main aisle where a brightly lit doorway stood.

Leaning on her mate's arm, Kha'Qwa and Lijou followed Kitra and Dzaka into the Shrine where on another small table, twin to the one in the main temple, an ancient book lay open.

"I remember our wedding," Kusac said quietly to Carrie. "It was much quieter than this. Not at all what I'd wanted it to be."

Carrie looked up at him. "I've never regretted that night," she said.

His hand tightened round hers. "Neither have I."

"It's your turn to sign," said Kitra, turning round to them.

When Kusac put the stylus down, Kha'Qwa let go of Lijou's arm to embrace the young couple. "May the Goddess and her Consort bless you! I know you'll be as happy as we are," she said.

"It was a pleasure to have the ceremony here," said Lijou. "It's been too long since we celebrated the brighter side of life at Stronghold for our Brothers and Sisters."

"Not that long," said his mate gently, taking hold of his arm again. "Our marriage was only at midwinter."

"Apart from ours," he said, mouth opening in a smile as they heard the temple bells begin to ring.

"That wasn't too bad, was it?" Dzaka whispered, putting his arm round her shoulders as they left Ghyakulla's Shrine.

Kitra shook her head, taking a deep breath. "Not too bad, but my hand stings."

"You won't notice it in half an hour," he promised.

A roar greeted their return as family and friends crowded around to hug the newly bonded couple.

The wedding had been small, with only family and very close friends invited as Lijou and Rhyaz had only been prepared to open up Stronghold so far. A buffet had been provided in the ju-niors' common room, which had been specially decorated for the occasion. By midafternoon, people were beginning to head home, Kitra and Dzaka having left several hours before.

While Kaid had accompanied Noni and Lijou to Rhyaz's office for a private discussion, Kusac remained with his family in the Father's quarters.

"I'm not going back with you," he said, taking advantage of a lull in conversation. "Father Lijou said I can stay on to continue my training."

His mother, who'd been sitting holding Chay'Dah, looked up at him in disbelief. "You're staying here?"

Kusac flicked his ears in assent.

"You can't. You've got medical appointments to attend at the Guild hospital."

"I've canceled them. The therapy sessions were worse than useless, and we know there's nothing the neurosurgeon can do. There's no point in seeing him again. I need to face reality, Mother. There's not going to be a cure for me, we all know that."

"I never thought I'd see the day you'd give up without a fight," began his father.

"I'm not," he interrupted. "I'm fighting this my way. I've had enough of being paraded in front of medics and specialists! I can't just pick up the pieces of my life and rearrange them, Father. I need to start again, and I can't do that when I'm being constantly reminded of the past."

"What about our discussion regarding your responsibilities to the estate?" Konis said.

"Garras is handling them far better than I did. There's nothing for me to do there, Father. I prefer to be here. I'm hoping the exercise and meditation will help me," he said, getting up and walking over to the window. The objections they were making were the ones he'd expected. "I also have religious responsibilities to my clan and my training with Kaid didn't give me much time for them." He turned around, leaning against the wall. "Delegation. Didn't you teach me that's the key to running an estate and a clan successfully, Mother? Not trying to do everything yourself, but picking the right person for the job and letting them get on with it? That's what I'm doing." He looked over to where Carrie sat. "Carrie, you can run things on a day-to-day basis with Kaid's help, can't you? I'll be here if you need me."

"You're being ridiculous, Kusac," said Rhyasha. "What about

your daughter? You can't delegate fatherhood like you're trying to do with the rest of your life!"

"I don't intend to walk away from my family and friends, Mother. I plan to come home every few weeks."

"He has to make his own decisions, Rhyasha. I believe that deciding to stay here is a responsible one," said Kha'Qwa gently. "We aren't without good medics here, you know, if he should need one. There's Physician Muushoi, and Noni holds a surgery here twice a week." She looked over at him. "Father Lijou has already asked me to take you on as my personal student, Kusac. I'm sure the peace of Stronghold is just what you need for now."

"You can't give up, Kusac!" said his mother, handing Chay'-Dah back to Kha'Qwa. "There are other specialists still to see— brain surgeons . . ."

"No!" he said forcefully. "I wouldn't let them operate anyway. I'm not prepared to take any risks with what's left of my health."

"Carrie, you try and persuade him," said Rhyasha, exasperated. "He's not facing reality, he's running away from it!"

"I assure you, neither Lijou nor Rhyaz allow any Brother or Sister to use Stronghold as an escape," said Kha'Qwa.

"What about the TeLaxaudin, Kzizysus, Kusac?" asked Carrie quietly. "He's looking for a way to undo the damage. If he comes up with something, will you at least speak to him? They did design the implant for the Primes, it's not as if they don't know anything about them."

"I'll listen to what he has to say," he said tiredly. "Why can't you all understand that I can't keep living in false hope, seeing physician after physician? It'll drive me mad eventually! You're making it worse for me. I've made my mind up, I'm staying here."

"I wasn't trying to change your mind," said Carrie. "Just asking you not to turn your back on our one, real hope."

Surprised and relieved, he looked back at her. "Thank you," he said. "I will return, and I will listen to Kzizysus. Believe me, I'm not running away from you, Carrie."

K'oish'ik, Prime homeworld, the same day

The Summer Palace was farther south than the City of Light, nestling on the shores of the hot springs that had been duplicated on the *Kz'adul*. High walls surrounded it, enclosing not only a lake but also parkland and a small wood.

The Court wasn't due to arrive for another three weeks, so when the Emperor's Chamberlain suggested they go there for their nuptial week, he'd accepted. Isolation from the rest of the City suited him as he knew Zayshul would need time to accept the inevitability of her situation. More importantly, he needed to know more about her role in creating the abominations he'd seen in the tank room and he wanted no outside interference when he questioned her.

For now, he was content to play a waiting game. Her behavior had been impeccable during the day-long wedding festivities, and if he'd found her cold toward him that night, he hadn't been unduly worried. He'd told her from the first he intended her to be his wife. Considering that she'd told him the Medical Director wanted him to breed now, he was only doing what they both expected of him.

However, in the three days since they'd arrived, her anger had been gradually building. She concealed it well, he had to admit, not giving him cause for concern in front of the various servants who looked after them.

Sitting on his lounging chair in the small outdoor recreation area, Kezule watched her now with amusement through half-closed eyes. She was trying to work her anger off by hitting a ball against an electronic scoring board. Her score was high: she had both speed and accuracy, not to mention aggression in plenty.

Her anger now was because he'd left her to sleep alone since their wedding night. Her passiveness had been too reminiscent of his previous wife, making him realize he preferred a willing bed companion. He'd made it clear to her that in future, she'd have to come to him. She'd sworn she wouldn't, but he knew it was just a matter of time. He knew enough about Valtegan nature to know that despite her anger, she was highly flattered at the lengths he'd gone to to ensure she'd become his wife. For him to now ignore her was not something she, with all her pride, could tolerate for long, and he found that amusing.

While she'd attempted to work her rage off with various sports, he'd been more gainfully employed in the library, searching through the archives for old maps and charts of the Empire, looking for the locations of the various worlds and outposts, and surreptitiously copying them. He had no intention of staying on this decadent world of the Primes. They'd become a sick parody of a once proud people—they were all intellect, cold and hard, with none of the fire or moral responsibility of the people of his day. It was one thing to make use of slave races, quite another to use one's own species the way he and the M'Zullians were being used. When he left, she and their offspring were coming with him, voluntarily if at all possible. To that end, he realized he needed to improve their relationship.

Lost in his thoughts, he heard the ball coming toward him rather than saw it. Automatically, he caught it, then sat up and waited for her to retrieve it.

She snatched it from his open palm and turned to go, then changed her mind.

"I want to know why," she said.

He didn't pretend not to understand her. "Because I wanted you for my wife," he said. "You're the only one worthy of bearing my sons. And daughters," he added as an afterthought. "I want a wife who is a companion."

She stared at him. "You've got an inflated opinion of your importance."

"I think not," he said, showing his many sharp teeth in a smile. "I am the last true Valtegan Warrior. I need a wife capable of bearing fighters, not intellectual drones."

"That's sedition. And what about the M'zullians? You're not the only one with Warrior genes!"

"It's the truth," he countered. "Look around you when we return to the City. There's no fire, no life in them! No challenging of accepted ways, no ambition for change. They're content to sit and wait for the inevitable attack. They should be planning ways to subdue the M'zullians and J'kirtikkians! The key to overpowering them is their racial fear of the Sholans, it weakens them. No true Warrior lets fear or hatred dominate him."

She hissed angrily, looking around to see if he'd been overheard. "Don't ever repeat that! I won't have my career threatened by the Enforcers because of your arrogance!"

He shrugged. "I've no wish to be seen as a dissident. Knowledge of one's superiority isn't arrogance. I'm at least of royal blood—even your Emperor is disposed to consider me as a member of his family. I assumed I could speak the truth to you, no more." He waited for her answer. It would give him a clue as to whether she would eventually work with him, or be a liability. In the end, whether she wished it or not, she would accompany him when he left.

"I care about my work," she said coldly. "Nothing else. I don't get involved in politics."

"You like working with those abominations?"

"They're not abominations! They're people! You're as bad as . . ." She stopped, biting back the rest of what she'd been about to say. "You're going to be training the first group of twenty, produced the same way. How can you do that and not accept the ones I showed you as individuals, people in their own right?"

"They're not mine! The seed to make them was stolen from my body while I lay helpless in your care!" he hissed angrily, trying to keep his voice low.

Again she turned to walk away but this time he grasped her wrist, preventing her.

"Who did the harvesting?" he demanded. "Was it you?"

"Let me go, Kezule. It was the late Doctor Chy'qui's orders. My work was with the injured Humans and Sholans. I was studying their physiology, developing treatments for them."

"Chy'qui?" he asked, ignoring her attempts to twist her wrist free. "Wasn't he also the Emperor's counselor? The one they just replaced? The one who attempted to kill the prince?"

"Yes, now let me go!"

"Why would he work against his Emperor?"

"I told you about the dissidents when we woke you. That's why you were guarded until you'd recovered, remember?"

He nodded. "But why kill the prince?"

"With no heir, and the Emperor refusing to remarry, it would create a constitutional crisis of which he hoped to take advantage."

"How?"

"A new heir would have to be elected and he intended it to be him."

"Are there no other close relatives?"

She shook her head. "The Emperor's family is not as prolific as in your day because we honor single wives."

"There is me now," he said thoughtfully. "Killing the prince at the hostage exchange, and instigating a war with the Sholans would mean I would have remained with them, and he would have pushed to rule immediately because of the war." It seemed there were those with ambition after all. No wonder they'd had him guarded.

"I've told you what you wanted to know, now let me go," she said, tugging against him again.

He returned his attention to her, pulling her closer. "So you didn't do the harvesting. How did they make those—things—in the tanks? Did you give them life?"

"It's automated, Kezule. I did no more than follow my superior's instructions and key in a sequence of events."

"How do you automate the act of reproduction?" he demanded. "Who are the mothers?"

"Does it matter?" she asked, trying to pry his fingers off her wrist with her claws. "You said they were abominations! You were going to destroy them!"

"Tell me," he ordered, taking hold of her other hand to prevent her.

"You wouldn't understand."

He waited.

"Volunteers who donate eggs," she said angrily. "Your seed is injected into the eggs then, when they're mature enough, they're transferred to growth tanks. Now let me go, you've had your answer, and your revenge on me!"

"It wasn't revenge," he said, surprised she should think it was. "Is it that bad being the wife of a royal General?"

"You don't know what you've done to me, do you?"

"I've chosen you, honored you as my wife," he said, surprised at her continuing outburst.

"You've made me pregnant!" she hissed.

"You're my wife, of course I have. I didn't force you to my bed on our wedding night."

"What choice had I? You blackmailed me into it! You could have bred naturally with any number of the court females, but no, you had to choose me!"

"Bred naturally? What do you mean?"

"We don't bear our eggs like animals, we use the birth tanks! We're all born like that! Only the Royal Family have to bear their own young!"

Shock made him loosen his grasp just enough for her to pull one hand free and start hitting him.

"You've made an object of ridicule of me! I can't see my developing child on the viewing screen like the other mothers, it'll be inside me in a shell! I'll have the agony of birthing the egg and still the hatchling will be hidden from me for another three months!" Her words were almost drowned within her hisses of rage.

He needed all his Warrior reflexes to dodge her slashing blows while attempting to capture her free arm. Pain lanced down his cheek and neck as he grappled with her, spinning her round till he had her contained from behind in an armlock.

Triggering the release of endorphins to dull the ache, he increased the pressure on her arm and shoulder till she cried out in pain and stopped struggling.

"Enough!" he hissed angrily in her ear. "Are you telling me all your young are grown in tanks? That you were grown this way?"

"Yes! How else could we have bred after the Fall? Even you must have realized we're smaller! Many females died because they were too small to bear their eggs!"

He had noticed, and now that she'd mentioned it, he remembered he hadn't seen any pregnant females. Used as he was to the breeding chambers of his day, he'd thought nothing of it till now. He relaxed his pressure, letting her arm drop lower.

"If that's so, how can the Royal Family bear their own young and survive?"

"They don't always. Empress Zsh'eungee only just managed to carry her son long enough. She lost three others because the eggs were born too soon. If she were allowed to use the breeding tanks, she could have more, but the law prevents her. That's why the Emperor won't choose another wife."

She twisted her head around to look at him, and he could see the tears streaking her face. "You've put my life at risk, Kezule, that's what you've done."

"I didn't intend to do that," he said, mind spinning as he let her go. "What about the other females sent to me, on the *Kz'adul* and here? Are they similarly affected? Why do they want me to breed if the risk is so high, and why those in the tanks if my young have to be born naturally?"

"Their eggs would be removed after the first month and put

in a breeding tank. And those in the tank are considered illegitimate because of who you are. You decided to marry me, that makes it different. Our child will be in line to the throne, just as you are," she said, taking a few steps back from him and rubbing her arm.

One fact stayed with him in the face of all this outpouring of information. She, Zayshul, had been grown in one of the tanks. Suddenly they weren't as vile as he'd thought. "What if I demand that you be treated no differently? That the egg be removed and put in a tank?"

She shook her head. "Not even if my life is in danger. And once it goes past the first month, it can't be grown in a tank because of the shell."

This didn't suit him at all. He needed Zayshul, had come to appreciate—maybe even care for her if he was being honest.

"Burn it!" he swore, lashing out at the nearby table, sending it crashing to the ground. "Why didn't you tell me?"

"I saw how you reacted when I told you about the M'zullians," she said quietly. "I didn't want you seeing us all as abominations, non-people, like the slave races of your time."

"I never treated my slaves badly," he said absently. "You want the Warrior genes because Warrior females were always larger than those of the other castes. It would give you females back what you've lost." This cast a huge shadow over his plans to escape. If he did, without proper medical attention, or drugs to stop future conceptions, she'd be even more at risk than she was now.

"I didn't intend you any harm," he said awkwardly again. "You should have refused me on our wedding night. You were the one who went to the bed first!"

She held his eyes with hers. "You have a temper, Kezule," she said quietly. "I wasn't going to be hurt by you forcing me."

"I have never harmed you, and had no intention of forcing you!" He was surprised to find that her accusation hurt.

"You nearly killed me the night I told you about the growth tanks."

"How would you feel if you'd found out that while you'd been unconscious your body had been harvested?" he countered, feeling suddenly unsteady on his feet. He felt behind him for the lounger and sat down. His neck was itchy. He put his hand up to it, bringing it away covered in blood and remembered she'd injured him. Frowning, he reached for his shirt while mentally adjusting the clotting agents in his blood.

"Here," said Zayshul, bending down to pick up a napkin from the table. "I didn't meant to cut you."

He took it from her and wiped his cheek and neck. "Yes, you did," he said, looking up at her with a faint smile. "You're a fighter, unlike those docile herd-beasts at the Court. I told you that you were the only one fit to breed with. If you weren't, I wouldn't have wanted you as a wife." He threw the soiled napkin on the ground. "I want you to give up your work and join me while I turn these hatchlings into Warriors. I want to be there for you if anything goes wrong. I'll do without children before I'll risk your life, Zayshul."

"There's no need for that. At least not till the end of the second month," she said, coming forward to touch his cheek. "It's stopped bleeding already. What did you do?"

He could hear the surprise in her voice. "It's a Warrior skill," he said. "I'm accelerating the healing process. You must know that from your records. The Royal family always had Warrior caste wives—most of the main families had some Warrior blood mixed with their Intellectual blood. It gave them the aggression needed to lead or to challenge the leaders."

"Not much was documented about the Warriors. Could the Intellectuals of your time control their bodies the way you can?"

"Some," he said, aware that in her desire for information, she'd forgotten her anger. This might be the common ground he needed to win her friendship. Friendship with a female? The concept would have been utterly impossible in his day, but without it, he'd get nowhere in this time. "Perhaps you have the glands and the ability to use them. I can teach you if you have."

Shola, Valsgarth Estate, evening

As soon as they got home, Carrie went up to see Kashini. Kaid and T'Chebbi exchanged glances before heading to the small kitchen for hot drinks and a snack.

"Kusac staying on at Stronghold was a surprise," said T'Chebbi when Zhala had left them with jugs of c'shar and coffee. "Did you know he was planning that?"

"He told me before we left for Stronghold," said Kaid. "Said

Rezac had spoken to him, said that what's happening to Kusac happened in their time when they rescued telepaths who'd been tortured by the Valtegans."

"Could they help them?"

"They knew very little about telepathy then, and all their efforts were redirected into the war and turning them into a weapon against the Valtegans. Of those they saved, several returned to their captors. The rest either committed suicide or lived on the edge in an effort to feel some emotions. None lived for more than five months."

T'Chebbi sighed. "Stronghold is definitely best place for him, then." She lifted her mug, taking a drink.

"Kusac actually came to me to apologize for what happened to you."

She dipped her ears. "He spoke to me, too. Said he'd lost control, didn't intend me any harm. I said I was fine, not to worry." She looked up at him. "You didn't tell him different, did you?"

Kaid shook his head. "He knew. Rezac must have told him to drive the point home. It did," he sighed. "He was expecting me to take it out of his hide." He caught her look of concern and hastily reassured her. "I didn't say or do anything, T'Chebbi. There's no point in being angry with him. I told him Stronghold was a good idea, that's all."

She banged her mug on the table. "Damn, why'd it happen to him?" she asked angrily. "It's a wonder we didn't get him back insane! Bad enough for one of us, let alone a Guild-trained telepath!"

"We did get him back partly insane, T'Chebbi. You know I trained him properly," he said, taking a sip of his drink. "At the time, you said I was too hard on him. I wasn't, I should have been harder, spent more time doing interrogation survival techniques, taught both of them what to expect if we were captured. I didn't because of Kashini. But I never expected us to be in a situation where we could be captured! I've been over it again and again in my mind. I should never have let them send us to Jalna so soon."

T'Chebbi raised her eye ridges in a frankly disbelieving look. "I can really see you having their hides beaten raw to learn that! If we hadn't gone when we did, Rezac and the others would have been dead, you know that. Choice of when to go wasn't ours."

"No one I train will get caught short again. We incorporate

our Special Op training for everyone, T'Chebbi, from now on. Starting tomorrow."

Again she raised an eye ridge. "Everyone? The U'Churians, and Carrie?"

"Everyone, especially her, especially now," he said, his voice taking on a hard edge. "I'll have her and any other pregnant Sister monitored carefully. No one could have anticipated what happened to us, but if it happens again, I want everyone prepared for it. On a mission, the enemy isn't going to respect her condition."

"The Sumaan?"

He let himself smile. "Not the Sumaan. Kisha is preparing data on their training methods for me. They have their own ways of questioning their people. But we need to be prepared for questioning by them."

"How do you practice dying as flat as a pan-fried cake?" she asked with a grin of her own. "Are you serious about Carrie? Who you going to get to do this?"

"Rulla, Dzaou, me, and you," he said.

"Is it necessary to put Carrie through this? What about you? You'll feel everything she does."

He locked eyes with her. "I'm only as strong as the weaker of us now, T'Chebbi," he said quietly. "We have to know our limits."

She nodded. "How's she coping with Kusac staying at Stronghold?" she asked, changing the topic. "Can't be easy for her."

A strange expression crossed Kaid's face, then he got hurriedly to his feet. "Badly, though she's trying to hide it. I just got called by Kashini. At least this training will keep Carrie's mind off him. I'll catch you later." He stopped briefly at the door. "Forgot. It's our Link day. Start the intensive training tomorrow anyway for the U'Churians and those who're up to it. Usual drill, make sure we've got enough Brothers acting as medics. Garras has the training records, go through those with him. Only those designated nonactive personnel, or unfit for health reasons, are exempted."

"Aye," she said. "I'll take Kashini with me tomorrow."

He nodded, heading along the colonnade toward the stairs. It was unusual for T'Chebbi to volunteer for anything that involved cubs, then he remembered what Noni had said about her being broody and sighed.

CHAPTER 9

Valsgarth Estate, evening, the same day

AS Kaid came into the nursery, Carrie looked up from where she'd been playing on the floor with Kashini.

"Thought I'd come see how you two were doing," he said awkwardly, standing just inside the door.

"We're fine," said Carrie as Kashini dropped down onto her fours and loped toward him. "Someone's pleased to see you."

Kashini stopped in front of him, rearing upright to walk the last few feet.

She had grown again, he realized, almost coming up to his knees, standing straighter than he did because of the slightly different shape of her legs. He knelt on one knee, resting on his haunches till he was nearer her height. "Hello there," he said, reaching out a hand to her.

Her small hand grasped his fingers firmly as she stared up into his face and began to chatter.

Surprised, he looked over her head to Carrie. "It sounds like she's talking."

"Won't be long now," agreed Carrie. "Kashini's pleased to see you. She says you don't come into the nursery often enough."

"She's sending you all that?" Focused on Carrie, when the cub began to climb carefully up onto his knee, he barely noticed her, but his hands were there automatically to support her.

Well aware of her daughter's ability to go unnoticed when she chose, Carrie sat back to watch.

"She's been sending for some time, but over the last few days, she's been managing to put her message across more clearly."

A tug at the torc round his neck drew Kaid's attention to the cub. "Not to pull it," he said gently, detaching her hand and holding onto it for a moment. "You're getting heavy, you know. Too heavy to sit on my knee like that."

She clutched at his neck hair as he got up, making him wince slightly until he'd settled her firmly on his forearm with his other hand gently supporting her, making her feel more secure.

Watching him, Carrie remembered that he'd had some experience of cubs before, albeit older ones. Dzaka had been four when he'd been left by his mother at the gates of Stronghold.

"It's late, Kashini. Mamma's tired and hungry. I came to take her for something to eat," he said, unable to look away from the large amber eyes that were regarding him so seriously. "I expect you're hungry too, aren't you?"

She began to make a sound halfway between a trill and a purr, her hand reaching up to touch Kaid's cheek, her small face alight with joy.

"Then let's get you both fed," he said, turning to Carrie. Kashini leaned against him, wrapping her arms around his neck and laying her head against his shoulder. "Why don't you take a break yourself, Yashui?" he said to the nurse. "Get yourself a snack from Zhala. Come to my room for Kashini in half an hour."

"Thank you, Liege, I will," murmured the nurse, slipping out past him.

Linked as she was to both of them, Carrie was still surprised at the expression that flitted across Kaid's face. The softness she'd glimpsed once before was there, and in his mind, astonishment. Then she felt for herself her daughter's unconditional outpouring of love. It was so familiar to her that it had never occurred to her that Kaid might never have felt it. As she watched, he began to stroke the shock of dense blonde fur that still covered her cub's head.

She scrambled to her feet, surprised to find his hand held out to help her. He was being unusually attentive for him.

"I wish I'd shared this with Dzaka," he said quietly as they walked toward the door together.

"You will, with your grandchild," she said, smiling at the thought. He was too young to be a grandfather. "And you're Kashini's Triad-father. She's giving you that love now. All you have to do is visit us more often."

"I intend to," he said, opening the door for them.

Valsgarth Estate, Zhal-Ghyakulla, 30th day (June)

Kris had arrived at the estate that morning and had checked in with Naeso in the estate office. Naeso was the manager, running the day-to-day minutiae of business, third in the chain of authority after Garras and any one of the Triad Clan Leaders. He was around fifty, with a pelt of dark brown, lighter brown hair that stopped just above his shoulders, and a pair of humor-filled green eyes. Originally from the Aldatan estate, he was known for his sense of humor and youthful outlook. Being a level four telepath helped him keep his finger on the pulse of his community.

The office was a small building, located at the east end of the main street on the edge of the landing pad and vehicle paring lot. Built several generations ago, large sections of the side walls and entrance were set with louvered panels which could be adjusted to allow the passage of air and sunlight yet provide shade when necessary.

As Kris entered, Naeso had come in from his back office, mouth open in a friendly smile. He'd been surprised to find himself in an oasis of cool air until Naeso indicated the concealed environmental units.

"Ingenious," he'd murmured, dumping his kit bag on the ancient scarred wooden counter.

Kris had declined the offer of accommodation in the Human only building in the smaller western estate village, saying he preferred a couple of rooms in one of the mixed species houses in the main village.

"The choice is yours, of course, Djani," said Naeso. "Granted only a few of our Humans prefer to live among their own kind, but it is best to offer. Besides," he said, raising one eye ridge and opening his mouth in a sideways smile that conveyed all the nuances a human smirk could, "the main village is closer to Djanas Zashou and Jo."

"You're on the wrong trail, Naeso. Just because I . . ."

"Then you'll not be wanting the key that Djana Zashou left for you," said Naeso, reaching under his counter for the accommodation book for the main village.

"What? She left me a key? And you've been stringing me along all this time!"

Naeso opened his ledger before looking up at him, his green eyes echoing the smile on his face. "Ah, you young ones are so earnest," he said, pulling open a drawer and taking a key card out of it. "And you Humans, so anxious to hide what is natural and so obvious."

"Less of your assumptions, man! I'll have you know that you're still on the wrong trail! There's nothing going on between us . . ." he began, making a grab for the card.

"Soon, soon," said Naeso, waving the card a few inches from his reaching fingers. "Mark my words, she does not leave a key lightly, that one. Too proud for that, she is."

Scamp solved Kris' problem by leaping off his shoulder and grabbing the card as he sailed down to the desk.

"Thank you, Scamp," grinned Kris as his jegget scampered back to him with the offending card before clambering up his arm to perch on his shoulder again. Pocketing it, he picked his bag up. "Are you sure it was Zashou, not Jo, Naeso? When did she leave it?"

"Yesterday, I believe," said Naeso, entering Kris' arrival and destination into the book. "You think I don't recognize an Al-datan, Djani? With so many braids in her corn-white hair that it chimes as she walks?" He turned his eyes up to the ceiling and sighed. "A male doesn't easily mistake such a female!" He returned his attention to the book. "How long will you be with us? Is this a summer flirtation or something more?" Again the raised eye ridge and smirk.

"Depends on the lady herself," grinned Kris as he turned to leave the office. "I'm on leave right now. My time's my own for a few weeks. I'll check in again with you when I know."

He'd reached for her mentally, only a light touch to find out where she was, and located her in the mess at the training center. Stopping to drop his bag at the house she shared with Rezac and Jo, he made his way there, thinking about the key and what Naeso had said. He hadn't been expecting to stay with them when he'd contacted Jo to take her up on her offer of a break on the estate, so it was doubly a surprise.

*   *   *

The small mess at the training center was a convenient leisure meeting place for all the inhabitants of the Valsgarth estate. It wasn't uncommon to find even the odd individual from the main Aldatan estate there.

"Here's Kris," said Jo.

Zashou looked up to see the Human approaching. He wore the T-shirt and jeans favored by many of his kind, and his long fair hair was now held back by a plain suede headband. As he drew closer, she could see his bare feet through the open leather sandals.

He waved, mouth widening in a smile and she realized his skin had darkened considerably since they'd been with him on Jalna.

"Our skin does darken in the sun," said Jo quietly with a grin.

Zashou looked at her.

Jo shrugged. "You're broadcasting quite loudly. Even I can pick you up."

Hurriedly strengthening her mental barriers, Zashou turned away to watch Kris.

"Hi there," he said, taking a seat opposite them. "Thanks for leaving the key, Zashou." He held it out to her. "Better take it back. I don't want you to be stuck without it. It's very quiet around here, isn't it? Hardly saw a soul in the village."

"Keep the key for now," said Zashou. "I've got another."

"They've started some new training routine down on the west coast of the estate," said Jo. "They're camping there for at least the next week. We've been designated noncombatants."

"Sounds interesting," said Kris. "What does it entail?"

Jo shrugged. "Survival stuff, that's all I could get out of T'Chebbi."

"Maybe I should find out more about it."

"I wouldn't," said Zashou. "It's Brotherhood training, not Forces. Rezac made sure we couldn't pick up anything mentally from him before he left." She held out her wrist, showing him the slightly larger than usual comm unit. "It has a psi damper in it."

Jo leaned forward to look then pressed a small stud on the side of her unit. "Try turning it on," she grinned then sat back.

Flustered, Zashou examined the unit more closely.

"Maybe not, then," said Kris, filling the small silence. "I

planned to enjoy my leave, not work through it. Can I get either of you a drink?"

"I'll come with you," said Jo, pushing her chair back. "You'll need help carrying them."

She waited until they were standing in front of the dispensing machines before speaking. "I wanted the opportunity to talk to you," she said. "And apologize for what happened on Jalna over Rezac and you."

"There's nothing to apologize for," he said, smiling as he looked up from counting out his change. "How's it going, by the way? You look happy, and well."

Jo smiled, putting a hand up to brush her shoulder length dark hair off her face. "We are happy," she said. "We've got our own place now, as you know. Rezac's really getting into the fatherhood thing, wanting to set a room aside as a nursery and decorate it for our cub. I would never have believed it if you'd told me. None of the men of the same age on Keiss would want to be so involved."

"Family is everything to Sholans," said Kris, feeding coins into the machine for a coffee. "Especially the young males. Their biological urge is geared toward finding a mate and siring cubs." He grinned up at her again. "I did tell you that they were a very sensual and sensitive people. How long is it now?" He eyed the obvious bump beneath her short tabard.

"Six weeks," she said, leaning against the wall. "I'll have a mixed fruit drink, please, and Zashou'll have the same."

"Apart from training, what's Rezac doing?" he asked, handing Jo his drink and inserting more coins.

"We're compiling our knowledge of the Valtegans for AlRel right now. Now, what brings you out here? Zashou?" she asked with an arch smile.

He handed her the second drink. "Not entirely. I wanted to see you for myself and know you and Rezac were doing well."

"That was sweet of you," she said. A slow smile lit her face. "I take it you picked up Zashou's thoughts."

He picked up the final drink, taking back one of the ones that Jo held. "Kind of difficult not to," he said with a grin. "Is leaving the key for me some kind of subtle message?"

"That surprised me," she admitted. "It's more obvious than I'd have expected from her, but then, Zashou's changed in the month we've been here. I can see what attracted Rezac to her in the first place."

"How are things between the three of you?"

She began to walk back to their table. "We've found our own solution," she said carefully, "as have some of the other Triads." She looked up at him again with a smile. "Just enjoy your visit, see how things go with Zashou. She could do with having a lover of her own."

On the west coast of the estate, in a clearing opposite a small uninhabited island, one of the larger tents had been designated as a mess hall and lecture room. It was in this that the group of trainees were gathered listening to Garras.

"This is the advanced phase of Brotherhood training," he said. "For Special Operatives. Not everyone is suitable for it, not everyone can handle it. If you find you can't cope, there's no disgrace in admitting it. You are still valuable to the Brotherhood—and your own world. You've all passed the basic fitness tests and had wilderness training, both field and theory. Now you're going to put it to practice. You'll remain in your original teams, group leaders will be the same as before. Orienteering maps with a destination marked on them will be given to you when you're dropped on the island. Your objective is to reach that destination unseen, set up camp with perimeter defenses and wait for further instructions. You'll be given water but that's all. If you want to eat, you find food. Weapons are a new type of electronic tagger which interacts with your body armor. If you're hit, you'll feel it as painfully as if it was live ammunition and the effects will last several hours. Teamwork is what counts here, people. You got ten minutes to be outside here with full kit. Dismissed."

"But . . ." began Manesh.

"I said dismissed!" roared Garras, getting up.

Rulla watched as the forty-seven Sholans, Humans and U'Churians surged to their feet and headed for the door. "Are you sure about including Dillan and Nikuu?" he asked. "With her having lost the ability to sense anyone but her Leska, is she fit enough for this?"

"She asked to be included and Kaid approved it," said Garras. "They've done well so far. Keeping them together is essential, though. They may never make it into the field as operatives, but Ruth says they need the sense of achievement this will give them."

"So long as they don't fail," said T'Chebbi, handing Kashini a feeder mug of water.

"I've issued orders to pull Dillan and Nikuu out long before they look like failing," said Garras. "We've tailored this course carefully so that as each group successfully completes a section, they can advance to the next. Those who don't will be praised for their achievement so far. That way, we increase the overall level of capability, they have a sense of achievement, and we gain a varied range of operatives. Hell, we're trying to do in a year or two what we spent between five and seven years learning, and we were handpicked! We got a job lot here. Though we can keep accelerating the training of the best, many will drop behind. In time, most will catch up. Meanwhile, we still need people here to do their turn of guard duty and help run the estate alongside those unsuited to the Brotherhood way."

"What's with bringing the cub?" asked Rulla suddenly. "I wouldn't have thought this was a suitable environment for her."

"Our little Liegena will get used to it," said T'Chebbi placidly, as, one arm around Kashini, she scribbled on her comp pad with the other. "It's what her parents are, what she'll be in time."

Rulla made a noise of disagreement.

"They know she's here. The desert tribes start the cubs young. She's already been kidnapped by Kezule and held hostage with Dzaka and Kitra. She saw them being tortured. Kaid thinks like me that sooner she realizes her clan trains to protect its own, more secure she'll feel."

"She's only—what?—coming on for seven months, T'Chebbi!" exclaimed Rulla. "You're not being realistic about this, neither is Kaid."

"Leave it, Rulla. T'Chebbi knows what she's doing," said Garras, picking up a bottle of water.

"Kashini's sending thoughts almost as clear as words now," said T'Chebbi. "She knows what goes on, don't you, Kashini? Not like I'm taking her out into the field with us."

Kashini leaned toward the table, putting her mug down with studied carefulness, then, looking at them all, began to chatter animatedly in cub-talk.

Garras laughed as he wiped the back of his hand across his mouth. "There you are, Rulla! You got your answer!"

He growled good-humoredly. "You might be able to make sense of it, Garras, but I'll be damned if I can! What about Keeza and Brynne? I thought they'd be involved."

"Vanna's too near her time to risk Brynne or Keeza out here. Besides, neither Vanna nor Brynne are field op types. They're better on the home front, or at most, in the rear of any action we take," said Garras. He checked his wrist comm. "About time you got out there with the transports, isn't it?" he said pointedly. "I've got to get back to the ruins and check out how our Sumaan undercover agents are managing. Carrie will be joining you tomorrow when her Link day is over. She's in Rezac's group. When are your people planning to attack them?"

"Twenty-third hour, when the watch will be nice and drowsy," Rulla said, heading for the door. "Tomorrow night they attack each other, see if they are capable of dealing with friends who become the enemy."

Kris woke with a start, wondering what had roused him until he sensed Zashou's presence in the darkened room. Maintaining slow, even breaths, he lay there, waiting to see what she'd do. Despite the faint breeze that came in through the open window, the room was hot, hot enough that he could smell her scent, and her apprehension.

She'd been watching him for several minutes, he realized, as he peered through half-closed eyes trying to see where she was. He found the thought highly erotic. Then he remembered he was lying naked on top of the bed and there was no hiding his interest.

Even as he heard her quick intake of breath and the sound of her feet turning on the wooden floor, he leaped from the bed and dived for the door, blocking her exit.

"Don't go," he said as his jegget, roused by the noise, sat up and began to chitter. "I was hoping you'd come to me."

"It was a mistake," she said, trying not to let her nervousness sound in her voice. "The idea was Jo's. I thought if she could have the courage to . . . I was wrong, I don't have that kind of courage."

"That's not true. It took a lot of courage to come here," he said, touching her face gently with his fingertips. Jo's idea? Why should Jo suggest Zashou take a lover?

She pulled away, setting the beads in her hair chiming as she backed off from him. "I can't," she said, a note of panic creeping into her voice. "Let me go, Kris. I'm sorry to have—wakened—you."

He almost smiled but stopped himself in time. "I wouldn't keep you against your will," he said. "But you owe me something for raising my—expectations. A kiss," he added hastily, feeling her panic and distress. He was sure one kiss was all he'd need to convince her to stay.

"I can't," she began but he reached out to grasp hold of her hand, gently urging her closer.

"You have my word I won't stop you leaving," he said, putting her hand on his shoulder and placing his arm round her back. He leaned toward her, feeling her trembling increase. "I promise," he whispered, his mouth gently covering hers. His tongue teased her lips apart, flicking against her teeth before he began to nip her gently. She opened her mouth slightly in surprise and he took advantage of it, parting her teeth, tongue darting into the softness of her mouth.

She began to relax and he pulled her closer, gently pressing her belly against his erection.

See what you've done to me? he sent, nibbling at her bottom lip as he let his hand move down to caress her thigh. Her breathing was more rapid now, her scent changing as, despite herself, she became aroused. He lifted his head, reaching for the hand that was clutching his shoulder.

"Don't stop," she whispered, closing her eyes.

"I won't," he said.

Stronghold, Zhal-Ghyakulla, 31st day (June)

"Have you seen the latest reports from our Forces personnel?" demanded Rhyaz, sliding the comp pad across the table to Lijou. "It's the same everywhere, on the ships, and on Shola and Khoma. Damned female's trying to starve us into submission!"

Lijou picked it up and scanned the report. "Raiban's not far off succeeding," he murmured. "With so many Sleepers awake, our resources are stretched to the limit. We need to look for commissions from other sources."

"I expected her to be angry when we took the ships without her crews, but not this!"

"I wondered why you didn't keep some of her people. It might have defused the situation," said L'Seuli.

"Couldn't afford to compromise Haven's security," said Rhyaz, glancing at his Second. "Also I didn't want her seeing just how many Brothers and Sisters we have. It's one thing to have our Sumaan friends there, they aren't involved in Sholan politics, but Raiban's agents are another matter. Besides, she had no right to try and force personnel on us. Our mandate from Nesul and the World Council was clear—we were in charge of our own operation."

"You know my opinion of Raiban," said Lijou with a low rumble of anger. "Since she got formally promoted to Head of High Command, she's become as bad as Chuz!"

"Not quite as bad," temporized L'Seuli. "She does admit we have our uses and are independent of her—that's what's at the heart of this problem."

"We've the U'Churian contract," said Lijou. "Captain Tirak and his people are on the Valsgarth estate. We have an income from that."

"So has the estate, and rightly so," said Rhyaz. "We need more and larger contracts."

"There's also the twenty young Primes we're going to train at the Nezule Warrior Clan estate," said L'Seuli.

Rhyaz' mouth dropped open in a huge smile. "That was one exchange I enjoyed with Raiban," he purred, eyes glinting. "She thought the Forces had that contract, then Ambassador M'szudoe tells Governor Nesul he wants us! You should have heard her when she found out!"

"There's a trend starting," said Lijou thoughtfully, putting the pad back on the table. "Since we were forced to show our strength at Haven and Jalna, the Alliance species have become aware of us. I believe our main market now may be off-world."

"Our primary concern is to protect Shola and our remaining colony, Khoma, as well as our species," objected L'Seuli. "How can we do that if we take alien commissions? There could be a conflict of interest."

"We'd hear of trouble before anyone else," replied Rhyaz almost automatically. "And the danger threatening Shola is from space."

"We forge stronger links with the Alliance in working with them on their worlds, L'Seuli," said Lijou. "We already have alien Brothers because of our Links with Humans. I don't think we have an option, if we wish to remain free of Raiban."

"What about appealing directly to the Governor for funding?" suggested Yaszho. "He asked us to provide ten undercover Brothers and Sisters for our embassy on the Prime world, and to keep it from Sholan High Command. If Raiban refuses to use money allocated by our World Council for our employment with her, then the Governor and the Council should be made aware of it. We may even find the funds reallocated directly to us."

Rhyaz made an impatient gesture. "We can't afford to draw that kind of political attention to ourselves right now."

"We can't," said Lijou thoughtfully. "But the Clan Lord can, and I've no doubt he would. Since that business on the Clan Council when certain Leaders tried to blackmail him, he's been particularly intolerant of any form of coercion. I could speak to him, informally, of course, and acquaint him with our situation."

Rhyaz narrowed his eyes. "You're too devious for a priest and a telepath, Lijou," he said, an amused purr underlying his voice. "We've corrupted you."

"I'll take that as a compliment," murmured Lijou, aware that his personal wish to break free of Raiban's attempts at control had much to do with what had happened to his life-mate. Lost in his own thoughts, he was startled when Rhyaz' hand touched his, initiating a low-level link to the Brotherhood's Warrior Master.

"It isn't revenge when Raiban's in the wrong, Lijou. The Brotherhood stands behind you and Kha'Qwa to a person in our contempt for Raiban," Rhyaz said quietly. "Will you speak to Konis Aldatan?"

Lijou nodded, forcing himself to leave his hand where it was, aware of the deep anger his co-ruler felt. "I didn't realize you felt as strongly as I did about Kha'Qwa."

"You were chosen for the Brotherhood, just as we all are, Lijou. It makes you one of us. I remember how hard you worked to learn our ways and fit in when you arrived here. I know it wasn't easy for you, brought up to respect only the Telepath Guild, but you've always been as loyal to us as anyone could have asked. Not an easy task with Ghezu as co-Leader and Master Esken running the Telepath Guild, yet you managed."

Lijou gave an embarrassed smile. "Well, there was always the fear you might have me—replaced."

Rhyaz threw back his head and laughed. "I'll say it again, we're lucky to have you, Lijou!"

"Getting back to the matter of contracts," said Lijou hastily. "Even leaving Raiban's antics aside, ordinary Sholan contracts have been falling off. The Telepath Guild under Sorli is trying to identify those with unstable Talents early enough to train them in such a way that they never go rogue. While this is good news, it means we'll be called upon less often to track any rogues down."

"Private contracts are less frequent too," said Yaszho.

Lijou nodded. "We still have sensitive government ones, like Nesul's, but it isn't enough. Even if Nesul gives us the funding that Raiban currently has for us, the next governor may rescind it, and Nesul's up for reelection in three years. We need to be completely free of all political factions on our world."

"There's the raiders Tirak spoke of," said Rhyaz. "I now know where the four other Trader species live, all of whom are ex-slave races of the Primes." He leaned forward and activated the holo-projector on his desk comm.

Between the four males, a cube formed. Floating within it were many tiny colored points of light. Reaching into a desk drawer, Rhyaz pulled out a pointer.

"It's color coded," he said, aiming the fine red beam at a point of blue light within the holo-cube. "This is Shola, in blue, about a third of the way into the cube from your side." He moved his point of light upward and toward himself. "Here's the Prime world in red—about a third in from my side and almost level with Jalna." He pointed to a smaller red light on the same axis but slightly lower and closer to himself. "This is M'zull, their first colony, and lower to the left are the J'kirtikkians. You can see that our two colony worlds and Keiss were in a direct line with M'zull. Now we know where they are and that they're at war with each other, it's obvious our colonies were destroyed because we were in the wrong place—and because of their inbred hatred of us. We were seen as a potential future threat."

Lijou leaned forward to see the holo image better. "Where's the fourth Valtegan world?"

"They won't give us its location," said Rhyaz. "This green light is the TeLaxaudin homeworld and just beyond it, the other four Trader worlds."

"Why doesn't the holo show the slave worlds?" asked Lijou.

"It has a finite size," said Rhyaz, adjusting his comm so the images in the cube moved forward, some of them gradually disappearing from view. "Now you can see the four slave worlds. These two, the Delmoi and the Hrana, are nearer the Cabbarrans. Currently they lack the jump capability to travel as far as Jalna, so the Cabbarrans call there regularly to collect and deliver trade goods from them for the Jalnian market. With their ability to halve jump time, it's a viable trade option."

"And the other two are the raiders," said Lijou.

"Not quite," said L'Seuli. "The Mryans and the Vieshen are recent members of the Traders' Council. Being near neighbors, so to speak, they trade extensively with each other. Because of this long-term familiarity, they don't regulate their shipping the way the rest of us do. Both worlds are run by somewhat xenophobic autocratic regimes. Given their mutual history of enslavement by the old Valtegans, it's understandable that they prefer to meet the Traders at a U'Churian space station rather than allow them into their sector of space. Several factions, dissatisfied with their homeworld regimes, have broken away from their worlds to raid not only their own shipping, but some Cabbarran and TeLaxaudin ships as well."

"Tirak says neither the Mryans nor the Vieshen will police the area and go after them," said Rhyaz. "They claim they haven't the resources to fight raiders, and rely on escorting their shipping to the U'Churian station instead. Their occasional losses are cheaper than outfitting a navy, they say. Tirak said the raiders were growing bolder, stealing ships as well as cargoes, so five years ago the Council refused to allow either species to dock at the U'Churian station until they'd dealt with the problem."

"Haven't they recognized the Primes?" asked Yaszho.

"They haven't met them. Remember, the Primes only go to Jalna every fifty years. What little trade they have is carried out through the TeLaxaudin."

"Luckily for them," murmured Lijou. "I take it the Traders need to resume trading with the Mryan and Vieshen again."

Rhyaz nodded. "Key items like minerals and ores are running low."

"Where's Haven and the other Outposts?"

"Haven's not visible just now but it's just above the Jalnian and U'Churian worlds. Anchorage is here between the TeLaxaudin and the Prime worlds, Safehold here between the two Valtegan worlds, and Refuge, again not visible now, is above Keiss on a level with Jalna."

"And these two points here are the Mryans and Vieshen. I wonder if the TeLaxaudin ever met the Primes before," said Lijou. "Maybe they were even allies as they are now."

"The Primes remain very closemouthed about their past, Lijou. We've pieced this together with what little data they have given us, and Tirak's help while he was here," replied Rhyaz. "Like me, he thinks they didn't turn their attention to either the U'Churian or TeLaxaudin sectors of space. The remaining two ex-slave species are down here by M'zull and J'kirtikk."

"What does Allied High Command intend to do now that we do know where the M'zullians come from?" asked Lijou, sitting back thoughtfully.

"As you know, we and the Touibans are closest to the Valtegans. Alliance fleets are in place at Touiba, Teesul, Shola, and Khoma. They're flying regular patrols and monitoring the area constantly for any unusual activity. Events have cooled down between M'zull and J'kirtikk for now, with both of them sending out irregular recon missions and engaging in confrontations only when they encounter each other. We know they had several major engagements before M'zull lost Keiss. It's my bet they're both licking their wounds. Meanwhile, I've reduced the crew at Safehold and set it up as a listening post. Luckily we had very few Sleepers there. They're still being awakened and shipped out when it's quiet. It's in a high risk location—too much activity from us and we'll draw attention to ourselves. I've increased our fleet presence at Anchorage and, of course, Haven, where we have the largest numbers of Sleepers still in cryo, and sent security forces to protect both Outposts against any incursions by Raiban and her troops. Call me paranoid, but I'd rather we were able to defend ourselves if her snoopers find us." He stopped and looked at each one of them in turn. "Refuge is being prepared as our fallback position in case there is a conflict between us and the Valtegans. Unused cryo units are being shipped there ready to hold our families and certain key individuals to ensure the survival of our species."

A small silence followed his remark as they all absorbed what he'd said.

"It's come to a fine pass when we're having to take measures to defend ourselves against the likes of Raiban as well as our own ancient enemy," murmured Lijou, taking the topic back to less troubling ground.

"Raiban's ambitious and still can't accept that we also work for the good of our species," said L'Seuli. "She helped us against Chuz because it suited her purposes, no more."

"The point is, Lijou, we need the income Raiban is denying us. I didn't bring up the matter of funding the other day because you're the better diplomat."

Lijou smiled absently as he studied the projection. "Since we're planning to patrol the area adjacent to Trader shipping routes anyway, could we approach them and offer our services policing this area? With the Valtegan threat, none of us need raiders in our backyard as well. A contract like that could give us more than the income we need."

Rhyaz nodded. "I've considered it, but we'd be stretching ourselves too thin."

"How about a combined force made up not just of us, but of the Traders as well? At the moment, neither Shola nor the Alliance can really ask them to commit either ships or people against the M'zullians and J'kirtikkians when the threat is so far from them. However, they will see the logic of dealing with the raider problem now. And the Primes—what about them?" Lijou asked, warming to his theme. "They surely can't want their ex-slave species finding them without us to intercede on their behalf. They have higher technology than we do, ships capable of Vartra knows what! Surely they can be persuaded to give us some smaller craft capable of doing fast recon missions."

Rhyaz sat back, a satisfied look on his face. "You've come to the same conclusions L'Seuli and I did," he said. "If the Traders are prepared to put people and cash where their shipping wants to go, it could indeed meet our financial needs. I had Shaqee, the U'Churian Ambassador, corner me after the meeting, asking for Brothers and Sisters to work on Home and the Rryuk Family ships training their Warriors. She's offering us a very generous sum."

"We have to accept non-Sholan contracts," said Lijou. "It will give us our independence once and for all, yet still allow us to fulfill our duty to Shola."

"Then we're in agreement. We'll accept alien contracts. In that case, we need commanders permanently on Haven and Anchorage since our primary fields of operations will be there from now on."

Lijou's ears flicked back to half height in consternation. "Are you considering moving Stronghold completely off Shola?" he asked quietly. The thought was almost unthinkable—or was it? To protect their world from space where they were closer to the enemy, and therefore further from Shola, made a lot of sense. Beside him, he could feel Yaszho's shock, but not L'Seuli's. Rhyaz' next disclosure therefore came as no surprise to him.

"It's been a difficult decision to make, Lijou. I'm afraid I see Shola itself playing a smaller part in our lives. Our future lies in space where we can continue to fulfill our charter and be Shola's front line. I don't want to move permanently off-world myself, so I've decided to divide my time between here and Haven and have the Haven Commander do the same. I'd like to choose L'Seuli to lead our Warrior Brothers and Sisters with me."

Little bits of the puzzle began to drop into place. "That's why you sent him out to oversee the Prime situation," he said. "You've had this in your mind for some time, haven't you, Rhyaz? I can't say I'm comfortable with it, but I can see there is a need to move some of our operations off Shola. Congratulations, L'Seuli. You'll do well, I know."

"Thank you, Father Lijou," murmured the young male, dipping his ears in embarrassment.

"We'll need someone from the priesthood out there, unless you and Kha'Qwa wish to move to Haven."

"I can't, Rhyaz. I have commitments to Shola that prevent me from leaving. Kha'Qwa and I will remain here," said Lijou, shaking his head. "We've a son to bring up and space is not what we'd wish for him. I'll appoint someone for you within the next few days."

"As you wish. Meanwhile, if you could see Konis Aldatan about funding, I'll pursue negotiations with Ambassador Shaqee and through her, the Free Traders' Council, for suggesting the setting up of a combined force to police their trade routes."

"Before we finish, I'd like to bring to your attention something of a religious nature that has great significance for us all," said Lijou as Rhyaz turned off the holo-projection. "Have you been watching the weather forecasts over the last couple of weeks? It's been unseasonably hot and dry over most of the Kaeshala continent."

"I'd noticed. But we've had hot summers before, Lijou."

"This isn't due to normal weather conditions, Rhyaz. When do you remember it being so hot up here? I've been informed by Kaid that the realms have been closed and the Gods are retreating because of the threat to Shola."

"There isn't actually a threat yet," said Rhyaz. "Reports from Safehold show all is quiet out there. We have a treaty with the Primes and even our people in the Sholan embassy on the Prime world are feeling positive about the future."

"The potential threat, then," said Lijou.

"I swear we're taking every precaution, Lijou. Both the Forces and we have got people flying patrols in those areas, ready to alert us if the Valtegans start gathering forces, never mind begin moving in our direction. And what does the closing of the Gods' realms have to do with the weather anyway?"

"They are the essence of Shola. They govern every aspect of our world—its weather, its fertility, everything. If they retreat, then life on Shola will be threatened at every level. We won't need the Valtegans to destroy us, Rhyaz, the Gods will do it themselves!"

"I think you're getting overanxious . . ." Rhyaz began.

"No, I'm not. You've heard of slash and burn, haven't you? I learned about it here. It's when you make a territory unlivable so the enemy can't use it. That's what the Gods are in the process of doing to Shola unless we stop them!"

Rhyaz hesitated. "But why? If they destroy us, what's left for Them?"

"Shola's left, and life will eventually start up again, but not for us. We'll be long gone. We lost two or three billion people on Khyaal and Szurtha, so vast a number that ordinary people can scarce comprehend more than the loss of their own relatives. We can't afford to lose our homeworld as well. The threat is real, Rhyaz. I don't tell you how to organize the Warrior side of the

Brotherhood," said Lijou more quietly. "Please allow me the same insight into my area of expertise."

"What is it you want from me?" Rhyaz asked. "How can I help?"

"We need to stop the Gods retreating from us as soon as possible. Even Vartra's realm is closing. I can reach it, but not Him. There's nothing but darkness, Rhyaz. When He called Kaid, He told him we have to find a way to keep Him here so He can help us. Noni and I have been searching through what records both of us have and we know how to make Him stay here. We need to find His tomb."

"His tomb!" exclaimed L'Seuli.

Lijou turned to look at the younger male. "We know He was alive in the time of the Cataclysm, therefore, like any mortal, He must have died. They couldn't admit that in those days so they must have buried Him secretly. As Noni says, why curse by saying 'Varta's bones' if He was cremated?"

"How will finding His remains help?" asked Rhyaz.

"There's a belief among telepaths that you can call your forefathers to our time and ask them for help. That's why we keep the ashes of our families in shrines. If we can find His tomb, we can ask Him to stay."

"I'll take your word for it, but I can't see why just asking Him isn't as good."

"I can reach His realm, Rhyaz, but not Him! I've been trying for weeks now with no result and He's expecting me!" All his frustration came out in his voice.

"Why don't you just go back to a slightly earlier time? I've heard you say before that you can do that."

"I would," he said, "but I can't figure the when properly. The calendar was different in His day and we have no records of what it was—even the month names were different."

"Why? What made them change the calendar?"

"The damage to our moon," sighed Lijou, dropping his chin against his chest and staring morosely at his comp pad.

"Why not ask Rezac and Zashou, Father," said L'Seuli. "They lived then."

"Of course! Why didn't I think of that? Too damned close to the forest to see the trees, that's my problem," he exclaimed, lifting his head. "Thank you, L'Seuli."

"Do you know where to look for this tomb?" asked Rhyaz.

"No, but logic tells us it may well be within Stronghold it-self. Why risk smuggling a body out of here unless you have to, and the lower levels of Stronghold are carved from the natural chambers in the living rock of the mountains. I need help to ex-plore those levels that date back to the earliest times, the ones that we don't use any more."

"The lower levels aren't used for a reason, Lijou. They're un-safe. Be careful where you go," warned Rhyaz.

"I have maps, but I need some of your people with a knowl-edge of rock climbing."

"More like potholing and caving! Take them, but take every precaution, Lijou. I don't want to lose anyone, especially not you."

"I'd like to help, Master Rhyaz," said L'Seuli. "Until you need me, that is. I've had some experience with caving and climbing. Our tribal land backed onto the Rozoa mountain region where I grew up."

"Very well. You can keep an eye on Father Lijou. I don't want him—or you—taking risks. Check through our records and find anyone with similar experience to help you."

Rhyaz waited until L'Seuli and Yaszho had left the room be-fore calling to Lijou to wait.

"Shut the door a moment, Lijou. Did you request that Jebousa and Vikkul be reposted to guard duties at the Telepath Guild?"

"Not that I remember. Why?"

"I've just received confirmation from both of them that they're on their way here to take up those new duties."

Lijou stared at him. "When were the orders sent?"

"Yesterday, from here."

"They were friends of Ghezu, weren't they? I thought they were stationed out at Anchorage by him years ago."

"They were, until yesterday."

"Ah." Lijou leaned thoughtfully against the wooden doorpost. "Their names came up recently, didn't they? Linked to Tutor Tanjo. Or I should say, Instructor Tanjo."

Rhyaz nodded. "Part of the conspiracy Ghezu put together to ensure he became the next Warrior Leader here. You know Kaid went to see him before he left Haven, don't you?"

"No. How did you find this out?"

"All traffic to the Sleeper asteroids there is carefully moni-tored. I was notified immediately."

"You let him go? How did he know about the Sleepers and Tanjo in the first place?"

"Kaid has been privy to much sensitive data at one time or another. Likely Father Jyarti told him before he died. As to the rest, the matter has needed resolution since Ghezu was killed, Lijou. Until then, none of us could do anything. I'd rather have Kaid deal with it than open the whole matter to the light of day myself."

"You went to see Tanjo when you were there, didn't you? Did he mention it?"

Rhyaz flicked his ears in a negative.

"What of Jebousa and Vikkul? Will you let them take up their posts?"

"I don't intend to interfere. They broke the Brotherhood code, Lijou, turned Brother against Brother. It's as well to let Kaid deal with it as a warning to all who'd follow in Ghezu's tracks. Kaid wasn't exactly subtle in either visiting Tanjo or in tracing them. He wanted us to know what he was doing. Damn, but I wish he hadn't turned us down yesterday when we asked him to head Haven!"

"You know Kaid has never wanted to lead. It was Tanjo and Jyarti between them who pushed him into standing against Ghezu, otherwise he'd never have done it. The Brotherhood put him back in Ghezu's sights by doing that, so I suppose it's fitting he be allowed to deal with those who set him and Dzaka up."

Valsgarth estate, the same day

"No," said Carrie, unequivocally.

"What d'you mean, no?" asked Kaid.

"I mean no. And if there are any other pregnant females on your course, pull them out immediately. We need those cubs."

"It's safe enough, Carrie. Sisters go to three months before dropping out of training," he said, trying to keep his voice reasonable.

"Have you ever been pregnant? I think not. Maybe some Sisters are well enough to keep going, but the choice is theirs. Mine is no. As it is for my clan members." Flinging back the thin sheet, she got up and headed for the shower.

He lay there, staring at her retreating figure, completely taken aback by her attitude. Grumbling he'd expected, but not an out-and-out refusal. He felt nothing from her mind, either. When she'd said no, she'd closed off their Link. After the intensity of their mental contact over the last twenty-six hours, that had cut him like a knife.

Well enough? What did she mean she was well *enough*? Out of bed in an instant, he followed her, standing at the door to his bathing room, watching as she let the water stream over her.

What do you mean by well enough? he sent, hoping she'd pick up on it. *Is something wrong?*

Nothing's wrong, she replied, expanding their Link again to allow him to feel her normal day-to-day physical condition which she usually kept to herself. *Unless you count the evening sickness that lasts from sixteenth hour till I fall asleep, then the broken sleep, the sore back, the increasing pressure on my . . .*

Stop! he sent, coming further into the room. *I get your point. You'd no problems last time. Why now? What's causing them?*

Your cub, she replied, turning to face him. *And I was exactly the same last time, only you weren't aware of it because we weren't Linked then. It's worse for Human mothers, they have to make more physical changes to carry a hybrid cub.*

I'd no idea . . .

I know. You thought life goes on as usual until we grow too big for comfort. It's all right. I don't expect the same attention from you that I got from Kusac—he was still young enough to be focused on wanting to raise a family. She turned off the shower and wrung the water out of her hair.

He winced at the implied indifference. *That's unfair. I want this cub, Carrie. I've wanted it since I first met you.*

Then prove it by being with me, by sharing my pregnancy rather than setting up courses to find out how you'd react if I was taken hostage again! She pushed past him and reached for a towel, wrapping it around herself. "Stop practicing for life and start living it, Tallinu!"

"I don't know how to," he said quietly. "I've lived alone . . ."

"No one does," she interrupted, picking up a smaller towel to dry her hair. "We just try, that's all. Stop being so afraid of your gentler side. I know it's there, you showed it with Kashini the other night." She peered out at him from under the towel. "And last night."

Suddenly, embarrassingly, he wanted her again.

She laughed, reaching out to cup her hand round his neck. "You are worth loving, you know. You have to trust me on this. Both T'Chebbi and I can't be wrong."

"You make it sound easy," he growled, pulling her close and hiding his face against her neck.

"It is," she said, feeling his arms holding her tight. "Just call Garras, say you've reconsidered and he's to pull out any pregnant females. If he wants you, he can reach you here this afternoon, but not before," she whispered, stroking his long brown hair. "Say you're spending time with your mate."

"I shouldn't."

Her hand unerringly found him. "This says otherwise."

"You win, Dzinae," he purred, lifting his head to kiss her. "I'll call Garras."

Shola, Zhal-Vartra (month of the Consort), 3rd day (July)

Dzaka followed Kitra down the stairs from Master Sorli's office. They'd spent a pleasant hour chatting with him and his wife Mayoi before being shown their quarters at the Telepath Guild for the next month. Now they were on their way to the refectory for second meal.

"Well, look who's back," he heard a young female voice say. "I'm surprised you've the nerve to show your nose here after getting expelled in the spring! And I hear the Chazouns dumped you too!"

"I wasn't expelled, Ghaysa," said Kitra quietly. "And it was my father who canceled the betrothal, not the Chazouns."

Dzaka stayed where he was, just out of sight. As she'd be the first to tell him, Kitra had to fight her own battles.

"That's not what everyone here was saying."

"Everyone was wrong."

Almost as if he was seeing through her eyes, Dzaka saw the other female shrug. "No matter. You missed the exams, by the way. They'll be keeping you back a year."

"No, they won't. Don't be so spiteful, Ghaysa," said a new voice. "Kitra's been through a lot recently, what with her brother and bond-sister going missing like that. 'Lo, Kitra. Heard you'd arrived with one of the Brothers. Are you back with Dzaka?"

T'Chya gave a tiny yowl of shock as Dzaka suddenly materialized beside them.

"Good day," he said, draping an arm around Kitra's shoulder and handing her his key card. "You'd better have your key, Kitra. You might need access to our quarters when I'm not around."

It was his key, and Kitra knew it as she accepted it from him, but it was a neat way of letting them know he was there to stay.

"Thank you," she said, taking it from him and pocketing it.

"A bonding bracelet!" exclaimed T'Chya. "You're not married, are you? To a Brother?"

"Of course she isn't!" said Ghaysa. "He's just playing a part for her!"

"Yes, kitling," said Dzaka, reaching out to flick her nose as one would a cub's, "We're life-bonded. Now if you'll excuse us, we have to eat before attending Master Sorli's first class in an hour."

"Master Sorli only takes the Leska pairs," began T'Chya, then she noticed the small bronze stud Dzaka wore on the neck of his Brotherhood jacket. She looked at Kitra, then reached out to touch a twin stud on her black tunic. "You *are* Leskas," she said, a gentle purr of humor audible in her voice. "And those aren't your family colors, are they, Kitra? You're Brotherhood now! Congratulations!"

"They can't be life-bonded," said Ghaysa. "There have been no weddings at the temple. We'd have known if there had been."

"As a priest of Vartra, I'm entitled to be life-bonded in the temple at Stronghold," said Dzaka. "Which is what we did."

"Stronghold!" said T'Chya, her voice almost a whisper of awe. "You have to tell me about it! Can I sit with you during second meal? Please?"

"You're not falling for . . ."

"Shut up, Ghaysa! Please say I can come with you!"

"Of course you can," said Kitra as Dzaka began to urge her gently away from the stairs toward the refectory. "Dzaka's still got his comp pad with the holos of our wedding. We were showing them to Master Sorli and his wife. We've just come back from a cruise round the Western Isles."

*   *   *

Dzaka's wrist comm buzzed discreetly, rousing him from sleep: it was a Brotherhood signal. Beside him, Kitra stirred briefly. He answered it, reading the coded message on the screen then turning it off. No reply was necessary. As he carefully untangled himself from the sheet and Kitra, she began to stir again. Leaning over her, he gently stroked her forehead and nose, following the lie of her pelt. It worked with Kashini, it just might with Kitra. "Go back to sleep, kitling," he whispered. "I have to go out for a little while. I'll be back soon."

She mumbled a few half words, then soothed by the rhythmic strokes, drifted off again.

Getting up, Dzaka went to the drawer unit, pulling out a civilian tunic. Picking up his belt from the top, he took his gun and knife and slipped from the bedroom into the small lounge. He dressed hastily, stowing both knife and pistol into holsters on the back of his belt. Grabbing a jacket from a peg by the door, he quietly let himself out.

The club was one that had adapted to suit a mainly Human clientele, but was equally popular among some of the younger Sholans. Music with a heavy drumbeat could be heard from the street as he approached the door. Pushing it open, he stepped in and was instantly engulfed by the sound.

As he looked around, he felt a gentle touch at the edges of his mind, drawing his attention to a booth at the back of the inn. Pushing through the mixed crowd of revelers, he made his way across the room. There, in a tiny booth, sat his father, though he had to look twice to recognize him physically.

Kaid pushed a large drink toward him as Dzaka sat down beside him. "Try this," he said quietly. "Terran drink. Pleasant and mildly intoxicating for us."

Dzaka picked the glass up, eyeing the dark liquid with the creamy froth on top before tasting it. "Why the meeting?" he asked, taking a larger drink.

"Some time ago you asked why I refused to let you leave the Brotherhood when I was expelled. I couldn't tell you then because I was oath-bound, but with Ghezu's death, that's no longer the case."

Dzaka glanced at him. "I've been waiting for you to tell me."

"I know, and your patience hasn't gone unnoticed," said Kaid, canines gleaming white against the darkened pelt of his face as he smiled. "I needed to be sure of the facts myself before telling you, and taking further action."

Dzaka waited, aware of his increased heart rate. He'd waited so long to hear his father's explanation for what at the time had seemed a betrayal of all the trust there had been between them. Now, finally, that moment had come.

"It began two years earlier," said Kaid, sitting back against the padded booth seat. "During the Leadership trials. I was able to shield you from most of what happened by leaving you with Noni, but you never quite forgave me for coming after you on your first mission."

"I couldn't understand why you did," said Dzaka.

"No missions should have been authorized that last day of the trials," said Kaid. "But there was a rogue telepath who needed to be dealt with. Ghezu used his gift of Glamour to persuade Senior Tutor Tanjo to send you along as an observer with Jebousa and Vikkul."

"An observer? But Ghezu said to deal with him alone," Dzaka said slowly.

"I know. It gets worse," he said, leaning forward and resting his elbows on the table. "The telepath was Faezou Arrazo, blood-kin of yours. If you'd succeeded in killing him, you'd have been branded as a kin-slayer and been driven from the Brotherhood, outcast by all Guilds and Clans. And if you hadn't, you'd be dead. Rogue telepaths aren't dealt with by Brothers as young as you were, Dzaka; they're dealt with by a special operative team. Even now you wouldn't be aware of that as special ops are kept very quiet. Ghezu had set us both up very nicely."

"How did you find out?" Dzaka asked, unable to keep the suppressed anger from his voice.

"Ghezu made no secret of it with me, he told me himself. He, Jebousa, and Vikkul came to my room that day just after dawn. They gave me a simple choice," said Kaid, catching his son's eyes. "Save you and lose the Leadership trials, or let you die and win." He looked back at his own drink, picking it up. "It was an easy choice—I never wanted to be Leader anyway."

"Why did you leave me at Noni's? I would have stood with you, told them what had happened!" When he'd returned to Stronghold four weeks later to take up his new post with Father Jyarti, it had all been over—the hearing, his father's humiliation—but not the comments from others in his year. His anger now wasn't directed at the father who wouldn't tell him why he'd thrown away the Leadership to be with him, it was for Ghezu, Jebousa, and Vikkul.

"I couldn't," said Kaid simply. "I had to swear to not even admit I was oath-bound or they wouldn't release me. When Faezou had been dealt with, I took you to Noni for safety. I assumed Acting Leader Tanjo had been in on it. He knew there was no love lost between me and Ghezu yet he'd put you in danger by sending you on that mission. You're my son, Dzaka. I had to protect you at all costs. Ghezu was going to be the new Leader, and he'd just tried to kill you. I could no longer protect you. Noni used her influence to contact Father Jyarti and have you transferred to his protection before Ghezu was inducted as Leader. At my request, she kept you with her until it was all over because if the full story had come out, make no mistake, Ghezu would have had you killed."

"Noni knew about this?"

He shook his head. "No, but she knew me," he said quietly. "And she knew you. I had only to ask for her help and tell her your life was in danger from Ghezu for her to do what she did."

"All this because Ghezu wanted my mother," he said, trying to suppress the surge of anger. When Kaid put a hand on his arm, he jumped in shock.

"Let it go, Dzakayini," he said, using his son's cub-name with a lopsided Human grin. "Ghezu paid, and paid dearly, I made sure of that," he said, his voice now grim. "In our Challenge, I broke his neck, left him paralyzed and choking on his own blood."

"The Liege of Hell has him now," murmured Dzaka with satisfaction.

"Yes. And He'll soon have the others," said Kaid, lifting his drink again. "The next two years under Ghezu weren't easy. Father Jyarti never believed I'd willingly lost the trials but there was no way for him to ask me what had happened. He tried to protect me in the the priesthood, too, but Ghezu refused. Ghezu made life a misery for me, sending me on the most dangerous missions he could find, then giving me mind-numbingly repetitive tasks. I tried to force the issue, to have him Challenge me or throw me out. Either would have relieved the situation for you. At least it did focus his attention on me rather than you because he didn't know what I'd do next." Kaid smiled. "I found creative ways to do every task he gave me, ways that showed as openly as I dared my contempt for him. I was a permanent thorn in his foot. With me dead or gone, there'd be no need to turn his hate on you."

"That's why he expelled you," said Dzaka, reaching into his pocket for a pack of stim twigs. All along, his father had been protecting him, not betraying him, and his own resentment and anger during that time had only added to the burden.

Kaid nodded, setting his glass down on the table. "He did something I hadn't anticipated, though. He told me that you had to remain in the Brotherhood as good faith for my behavior. Relations between you and me hadn't been good," he said, looking at Dzaka. "It never occurred to me that you'd want to leave with me."

"Kaid, I'd spent two years defending you," said Dzaka, taking a twig from the pack then handing it to his father to cover his feelings. "You don't know what it was like for me. I'd been the foster son of one of the most respected Brothers, then suddenly that was all destroyed, apparently by your own actions. I stood by you against them, even when you were publicly humiliated for the second time and thrown out!" He stopped abruptly, aware his voice had cracked as he'd relived that dark time at Stronghold.

"Surely you could have given me some explanation," Dzaka said more quietly.

"I know you did," said Kaid softly, putting a twig in the corner of his mouth. "Ghezu knew it too. It was the price I had to pay to take the heat off you. That day, he drove a wedge between us that lasted ten years. And it hastened the death of Father Jyarti." Kaid sat silently for a moment, then smiled gently. "But that's behind us now. Even after the worst Ghezu could do, I got my son back." He handed the pack back to Dzaka.

As he took it from him, Dzaka held onto his father's hand for a moment longer than was necessary, letting his feelings flow to him, surprised when his father echoed them. Embarrassed, he said, "You said soon L'Shoh will have the others in Hell."

"Yes. Vikkul is here with Jebousa. Ghezu sent them to Anchorage just after he was invested. He wanted to be sure no one found out what he'd done. I thought you and I should settle this matter together, decide what to do about them."

Dzaka nodded. "What have you in mind?"

"A two-part poison, colored so they know they've been given it."

"With no rush to give them the second part," murmured Dzaka. "I remember those lessons. They'll live in total fear that everything they touch, eat, or drink, could contain the second part. It could even be put safely on their lover's pelt."

"More, they'll come to the point where they'll go mad or take their own lives. I've seen it happen."

"Do it," he said abruptly, lifting his drink to take a sip. "What about Tanjo?"

"Tanjo was used, Dzaka. He honestly thought you were going along only to observe," said Kaid. "I've seen him, and read him. After Ghezu expelled me, he told Tanjo the truth, and he's been paying a penance ever since."

"I hope it's a good one," growled Dzaka.

"That's a matter for him and Vartra," said Kaid, passing him a small tablet no bigger than the tip of his smallest claw. "It's activated by alcohol." He smiled, showing all his teeth. "It'll turn their piss red so they'll know what's been done."

"Where are they?"

Kaid flicked an ear toward a group of two Sholans sitting in a booth with two Human females. The four were talking animatedly.

"They haven't taken long to get in with our Humans," murmured Dzaka. "I know them. They're attending the Telepath Guild."

"Do they know you?" asked Kaid.

He shook his head. "No. Won't Jebousa and Vikkul recognize me?"

"You've changed a lot in twelve years, Dzaka. Are you up for a fight?" Kaid asked, raising an eye ridge.

"Sure, but . . ."

"You object to their familiarity with the telepaths. And they're out after curfew."

"Ah. Right." Dzaka pushed the tiny pill beneath his claw tip and finger pad, took a deep breath, and got to his feet. Around his face, his hair began to rise slightly, and as he walked across to the table, his whole demeanor changed. The quiet Brother was gone, now he was a belligerent youth.

Remember to use your gift to change their mood.

"What d'you think you're doing here with them?" demanded Dzaka, stopping beside the nearest of the Humans, a plumpish brown-haired female with a pleasant round face. "You should be back at the Guild by this time of night!"

"We've got a late pass," she began but one of the Sholan males interrupted.

"What business is it of yours? You heard her," said Vikkul. "She's got a late pass. Now leave us alone."

"You keep out of this," said Dzaka, pointing at him. "Late passes run out at twentieth hour, Djana, you know that. And you want to stick to your own kind, telepaths, not lowlifes like these. Best you head back to the Guild now."

"Who you calling lowlifes?" demanded Jebousa. "We're not causing any harm. The Djanas chose to sit with us. Why don't you just keep your nose out of what doesn't concern you?"

Heads were beginning to turn in their direction.

"We better go, Pat," said the other female, getting to her feet. "He's right, we don't want trouble from the Guild."

"You just stay put," said Vikkul, reaching out to pull her back down to her seat. "He's got no right to come over here like that and order you around."

Dzaka's hand lashed out across Vikkul's arm, swiping it aside as the female let out a small shriek of shock. "You know the law for laying hands on a telepath," growled Dzaka. "Want me to call a Protector?"

"Leave it, youngling," said Kaid's voice from behind him. "The Djanas are old enough to look out for themselves."

Dzaka swung round belligerently on him. "I don't like the way those males are treating them," he said loudly. "Telepaths shouldn't be handled like they were goods in a store, they're protected by law whether they're Human or Sholan!"

"They chose to be here with these two," Kaid pointed out reasonably. "Their business if they get taken advantage of, or lose their passes for the next month by being back late."

"We should watch out for them. They're guests on our world. I won't have them thinking all Sholan males are only after one thing," said Dzaka, turning back to the table so suddenly he collided with it, making the drinks slop over the tops of the glasses.

Jebousa and Vikkul leaped to their feet with exclamations of annoyance, brushing ale off their damp tunics and pelts.

"Come *on*, Pat," urged the dark-haired Human, tugging at her friend as they got up. "Let's leave now."

Kaid grabbed hold of Dzaka as his son clutched wildly at the table. "Apologies," he said. "He's had a little too much to drink. I'll take care of my friend."

I'm done, sent Dzaka as Vikkul took a step toward him, raising his hand threateningly. "It was an accident," he said. "You want to make more of it, fine."

Jebousa swore roundly as the tables beside them began to empty. "Leave it, Vikkul," he growled. "It isn't worth getting the Protectors involved. These Human Telepaths aren't worth it. There's plenty more females where they came from."

Dzaka let out a snarl and surged forward, wrenching himself free of Kaid so his father went sprawling against the nearest chair, once more jarring the table. Hearing his yowl of pain and seemingly diverted, Dzaka turned back to him.

Kaid righted himself, grabbing hold of Dzaka again as one of the large male bar staff loomed over them all.

"Is there a problem?" the male asked.

"No," said Kaid hurriedly. "My friend just got overprotective of the two Human Telepaths, that's all. They're out after hours. We're going back to our seats now."

The male turned to Vikkul and Jebousa, looking them up and down. "You're new in Valsgarth. We look after Guild Humans here," he said heavily. "Especially the females. Don't like to see them kept out after their curfew. This isn't a place to make those kind of contacts, you get my meaning?"

"We were only talking," began Vikkul but his friend dug him in the ribs.

"We're just back from a tour in space," said Jebousa. "First time we've met Humans. Had no idea the Djanas had curfews. They've gone now, so no harm done."

"Just a friendly warning, this time," he said, checking to see that Kaid and Dzaka were heading back to their seats before lumbering back to the bar.

"It's good to know the staff here are watching out for them," muttered Dzaka.

"It's a good place to come," Kaid said. "Quite a few of our clan come here once or twice a week to relax." He grinned. "And there's always at least one Brotherhood member on duty."

Dzaka looked startled and reached out to pick up his drink, then hesitated, remembering what they'd just done. "Want another drink?" he asked.

Kaid grinned again. "Wise move. They're on their way, along

with our Sister on duty tonight." He nodded toward Zhiko who was making her way over to them.

"What was that all about?" she asked, setting the glasses down in front of them before lifting a chair and putting it next to Kaid so she could see the room.

"Just making sure two young Humans get back to their Guild safely."

"Right," she said, giving Kaid a long look as she took a sip of her own drink.

Shola, Zhal-Vartra, 4th day (July)

"Remember that discussion we had about Jebousa and Vikkul?" said Rhyaz, letting himself into Lijou's office.

Lijou looked up from his desk comm. "Yes. What's happened?"

"They're here, clamoring for Physician Muushoi to give them an antidote for roelda poisoning."

"Excuse me?" Lijou looked baffled.

Rhyaz came and sat down on the chair opposite the priest. "Strictly speaking, they thought it was something else but the blood tests showed it's roelda. It's a two-part poison," he explained. "One of the ones they're taught to use here. Harmless until the second part is administered either through skin contact or ingestion."

"How do they know they've been given it?"

"Normally they wouldn't, but this one had a dye with it. They thought they were pissing blood." He tried not to smile.

"Surely knowing they'd been given one part of a poison rather defeats the purpose. Ah," said Lijou, realization dawning as he spoke. "The point is not knowing when or how the second part will be administered. Won't it wear off in time?"

Rhyaz nodded. "Or if. And no, not roelda."

"That kind of knowledge could drive a person insane. Do they know who's responsible? I presume it is Kaid."

"What do you think? If they do, they aren't saying, but they are panicking for all to see. And everyone is making the connection with Ghezu."

"Is there an antidote?"

"None," said Rhyaz, getting up. "Have you chosen someone yet to head the priesthood on Haven?"

"Yes. Sister Jiosha."

"She's a good choice. She performed admirably on her assignment to the *Rhijissoh* when they liaised with the U'Churians at Jalna."

"She arrived here yesterday. I start work with her today to bring her priesthood training up to the level needed to run a major shrine on Haven."

"I think L'Seuli will be pleased with your choice," Rhyaz said as he made his way out. "They were in the same intake. L'Seuli's been on too many missions lately to form any relationships. It's time he did."

"Talking of which, what about yourself?" asked Lijou with a smile. "Isn't it time you found someone?"

"When I have time, my friend," said Rhyaz, closing the door firmly behind him.

Prime world, the same day

In the far southwest quadrant of the grounds of the City of Light, remote among the crop fields that served the inhabitants, was a small complex of buildings that had long ago been the animal breeding center. Like all the outbuildings, it was connected via a labyrinth of underground passages to the main City. It was along one of these that K'hedduk, lately a steward on the *Kz'adul*, was headed.

He picked his way distastefully around the debris caused by the many small earthquakes over the centuries, wishing it weren't necessary to leave the rubble there. Still, it gave the place the look of abandonment needed to continue their work. Turning a sharp corner, the blast-proof door came into view. His ancestors had built to last in those days, he thought with pride as he approached it.

Pulling the tiny transmitter from his pocket, he keyed in his access code and waited for the door to open. Flashing his ID at the guards on duty, he passed between them to the next set of doors. This time, he placed his palm over the lock, waiting for the scanner to recognize him.

More guards waited, rifles coming to bear on him as he stepped into the second room. Again he held his ID up, biting back his hiss of annoyance. These people were almost as bad as the implants. Restructured by gene therapy, they at least retained the ability to think for themselves, but the trade-off was almost as high because they had been recruited from the dregs of the cities outside.

Faded trousers, scuffed boots, thick animal-hide jackets worn over pull-on shirts was the uniform they affected, resisting any attempts to persuade them to wear something more formal. They were a far cry from the affluence that typified the City inhabitants. But it was the tattoos on their faces and heads that he disliked most. The imagery was bright and brutal, done to shock, worn as a badge of arrogance by them, displaying what they perceived as their status among the inhabitants of the nearest city to where they now lived.

"Damned psychopaths," K'hedduk muttered, striding past them to the elevator, but he said it very quietly.

Pressing the third level recess as the door slid shut and the elevator began to go down, he began to relax. These trips stressed him as there was always the danger of being discovered. At least this time he could stay for the next five days.

When the door opened onto the reception area for the Directorate's own Medical Research Facility, the scene that greeted him was far more to his taste. Architectural plants draped the walls, breaking up the smooth rock face. On the floor, a deep pile carpet of green added to the restful atmosphere.

He turned to his left where the nurse on duty looked up to greet him. "Good afternoon, Doctor K'hedduk," she said. "We've been expecting you. Your colleagues are already waiting in the lounge for you. Here are your patient records." She passed him a reader.

"And how have our patients been?" he asked, taking it from her and scanning the contents.

"368 went into labor last night, Doctor. Medical assistant Zhengu is with her because we think she's delaying the birth somehow. As you can see from the notes, we've had to restrain her from trying to do herself and the unborn child damage."

K'hedduk nodded, reading the notes. "And her mate?" he asked, looking up at her.

She pulled a face. "We eventually had to sedate him because the punishment collar was having little effect. He kept howling and throwing himself against the cage bars in his efforts to escape and join her. The noise was annoying our resident staff. I hadn't realized these Sholans were capable of such depth of feelings."

"Most advanced animals want to be with their mates when they're giving birth," said K'hedduk absently, flicking through the records. "Make no mistake, they are just animals, even if they strut the halls of the City dressed as ambassadors. Tell Zhengu to remove the child surgically. The female will kill it before she'll let us have it, I've seen it happen before. See there's a stasis unit ready and waiting for it to be put in immediately."

She nodded. "And the mother?"

He hesitated. The female was young and healthy, had only been revived to be impregnated by the male and her pregnancy accelerated to give them the information they'd needed to provide a growth environment for the hybrids. They had another five Sholans left, four of them females. Still, discarding her would be wasteful. "Treat her. I'll decide when she's recovered whether she's being returned to stasis or not, but keep her from the male. He must learn that such self-destructive behavior will not be rewarded with her return."

"Yes, Doctor," she said as he headed down the corridor toward the lounge.

"Directors," he said, nodding to the other four males as he took the seat left vacant for him in the small medical staff lounge. Placing his reader on the elbow-level table at his side, he looked round the group. Politically, they represented several powerful but as yet small factions in both the City and the Palace. Alone among them, he had medical knowledge: they depended on his expertise and leadership.

"You've had three weeks to observe our General. What do you think?" he asked.

"Three weeks isn't exactly long enough to see the quality of the male," said Ghoddoh, Director of Education, glancing at his neighbor. "I can, however, confirm his relationship to Emperor Q'emgo'h, but it was a distant one. It was the Emperor's cousin who sired him."

"He's a damned sight closer to royal than what sits on the throne now!" snapped Zsiyuk, the Director of Shipping. "Hell, my own ancestry is purer! No drones in *our* family. I say be done with it, K'hedduk. Have him approached. I've seen him curl his mouth in contempt at the Court and its airs and graces. He's as impatient with it as we are."

"Impatient isn't enough," said K'hedduk. "We need him to be capable of leading a coup, of overthrowing Cheu'ko'h. He's had loyalty to the Emperor bred into him. We need to be sure he won't turn against us because of that."

"We risk everything if we move too soon," said Schoudu of the Treasury. "We've made an enormous investment of money and time in this. We need to be sure."

"Have him sounded out now," said Zsiyuk. "He's begun building a life here. Don't want him getting too comfortable to turn the tide our way. And he's started training the first of those M'zullian hatchlings. Do it now then he can train 'em to overthrow that egg-licking drone who calls himself Emperor! Be damned if I want to keep bumping into those Sholan animals in the Court every five minutes!"

K'hedduk turned to the fourth member, head of sciences in the City. "Zhayan, you've said nothing so far."

Zhayan stirred. "Half of our total number of Warriors have been sent to the Sholan world for training, the other twenty are now working with General Kezule. In return, Shola has sent an ambassador and staff here. Our people mix daily with them, seeing for themselves that they can think and communicate as well as we can, and fight better than us. They see our Emperor trusting them with our future. As you say, K'hedduk, Kezule was bred for loyalty, but *his* Emperor is long gone. I don't see how we can afford to let this insidious attitude of allying ourselves with inferior species continue. We must speak to Kezule soon or let him indoctrinate those young Warriors into serving our current Emperor. Kezule is in a unique position to safely train an army loyal only to himself and us. Zsiyuk has the right of it," he said, looking at the older male.

Zsiyuk leaned forward, wide mouth splitting into a grin as he hissed with amusement. "Good for you, Zhayan! Got more sense than the rest of 'em put together!" He patted him robustly on the shoulder.

"I didn't say we shouldn't approach him," objected Schoudu. "Just that we needed to be cautious about it."

"Kezule's building a future for himself," repeated Ghoddoh. "He's taken a wife, and consolidated his position with the royal family. It may be that our offer isn't going to be attractive to him."

"Nonsense! He's old-fashioned like us," said Zsiyuk. "There's half a dozen Court females following him around and he's bedded most of them. We won't find him wanting to stick to one female, even if she survives dropping that egg she'll be carrying by now! It's obvious he dislikes Court protocol and the Emperor's policies as much as the rest of us, including this single wife nonsense! He'll have the good old days back quick enough!"

"If he's so tired of Court protocol, what makes you think he'll want to be Emperor?" asked Schoudu.

K'hedduk sat back and let them argue. They were doing exactly what he wanted—convincing themselves to approach Kezule now rather than later.

"He won't, till it's pointed out to him we want the old Empire back!" said Zsiyuk. "K'hedduk's got guards here that we can use, and more where they came from, eh, K'hedduk? From the back streets of the cities. Then there's Kezule's hatchlings in the vats, a hundred of 'em, plus the forty we already got and the implants. Give General Kezule a ship and an army and point him toward M'zull and Jkirtikk and he'll be off, won't he, Ghoddoh?"

"It's a strong possibility," agreed Ghoddoh. "He was a front-line General who preferred to actually lead his troops in the field. Reuniting the Empire might be the inducement he needs."

K'hedduk frowned briefly at the mention of his guards. An army of psychopathic killers was not what they needed roaming his City during a coup. For ground troops taking back M'zull and J'kirtikk, they were ideal, but not loose in his City.

"This will take time," he warned. "They're keeping Kezule's twenty daughters in the tanks until they're sexually mature so they can start breeding them immediately with the forty Warriors we already have. If Kezule is willing, we'll need another couple of hundred of his accelerated offspring."

"And if he isn't?" asked Ghoddoh.

"Take 'em!" said Zsiyuk. "You got contacts in Med Research, K'hedduk, use 'em! Why you didn't do it when he was on the *Kz'adul*, I don't know!"

"I couldn't get near him, or his samples," said K'hedduk. "Thanks to Chy'qui's little informal assassination attempt, Kezule was well guarded."

"What about those Sholans you took from the M'zullian ship

back a year ago? Found a way to make them work for us yet?" demanded Zsiyuk. "You've had 'em long enough."

"The ones we have aren't telepaths," said K'hedduk, "but they could be implanted and controlled as a diversion during a coup— dress them up like the ambassadors and no one will suspect who or what they are. The punishment collars alone aren't enough, we can't trust them to do what we want, or even to tell us the truth. In their way, they are almost as ferocious as the M'zullians and J'kirtikkians."

"What about those telepathy experiments Chy'qui ran on the priest J'koshuk?" asked Schoudu. "Are you planning to continue them? Controlling the minds of people in key positions in the Court would be useful. Maybe even avoid the need for a coup."

"Chy'qui's research was wrong. Our tests here have established that we don't have the capacity for telepathy. The gene therapies we used on volunteers to stimulate those areas of the brain that would govern that ability have proved futile so far. As for Chy'qui's experiments on the priest, we're duplicating them at present but with no success so far."

"What about your guards? Can't they be turned into Warriors?" demanded Zsiyuk.

"They're only altered Workers. The Warriors were more than aggressive Intellectuals, Zsiyuk," said Zhayan patiently. "They were genetically different from us in many ways. They were a caste on their own. You cannot make a drone into an Intellectual, they don't have the brain capacity for it. We don't have the internal organs of the Warriors. No one does, except Kezule and two of our lost colonies."

"What's so special about them apart from that they can fight?" asked Zsiyuk.

Zhayan glanced at him, irritated. "They have extra organs that release certain hormones and pseudo hormones into their systems at will. They have total control over their bodies."

"We have some families where the females still carry those organs—we think they were once Warrior caste, but none of their males have them," said K'hedduk. "And they breed few male children. It will be interesting to see what Kezule's child with the good Doctor Zayshul will be like since she is one of those whose families we've been watching for several generations."

"Females aren't much use," hissed Zsiyuk. "Only any good as breeders."

"That's what he's doing," said K'hedduk patiently. "It's possible they may breed true Warriors. Same with the females we sent to him on the *Kz'adul* and those at the Court. All have the hallmark of Warrior genes in their ancestry."

"Does Med Research know this?" asked Zhayan.

"I've done my best to make sure they don't," lied K'hedduk with a toothy smile that didn't reach his eyes. "So we're decided. We need to make the first approach to Kezule as soon as possible."

"How do you intend to do it?" asked Schoudu. "Not through one of us, I hope."

"I've several young males planted near to Kezule. At present, they're gathering at the old parade ground watching him teach. All that's needed is for one of them to say the odd word in Kezule's ear, then we'll see which way the wind blows," said K'hedduk.

Zsiyuk grunted as he got to his feet. "Good. You get on with that, then. Meanwhile, I have to go. Got a meeting I have to attend with a firm wanting to build us two new commercial trading ships. The Emperor and his TeLaxaudin allies want us to start trading openly. And there's the small matter of military ships the Sholans say we'll need." He laughed as he walked over to the door. "Ironic them helping us design the fleet that'll destroy 'em, isn't it?"

CHAPTER 10

Shola, Zhal-Vartra, 7th day (July)

"PHRATRY Leader," said the caller, hands moving in a gesture of respect. "Before the Camarilla your report was put."

He surveyed the Skepp Lord in the comm monitor. To be called so often by his counterpart was unusual, but then the situation he found himself in was far from ordinary.

"With your findings, the Camarilla agrees," the Skepp Lord continued. "Transcripts of hunter captive show what you were dispatched to locate has indeed been found. In this and the other matter, consequences are graver than anticipated. Further ranging. Greatest fears we all have for outcome."

"No less than mine, Skepp Lord," he murmured. "Projections of future potentialities show we must intervene at this juncture, must give requested aid. No less than us they wish what has become a weapon of terror located. What was decision of Camarilla?"

"Report was accepted. Darkness is outcome if matter compiler is not recovered or destroyed. Danger they may use it again. Balance it continues to upset greatly. Many species at risk, including ourselves."

He watched the Skepp Lord's hands move restlessly, eyes shifting their focus from him to beyond, then back: he was scared, and with good reason.

"What is decided? What to be done?" he asked. "Sand-dwellers obviously run out of necessary consumables. When discover how to replace, will use again."

"A weapon is needed . . ."

"Another?" His exclamation of shock was made before he could stop it. "For who?"

"Matter compiler not weapon. On dead worlds it creates potential for life. You know this. Sand-dwellers find and misuse to kill organic life on hunters' worlds." The Skepp Lord stilled his hands and stared straight at him. "A weapon is needed," he repeated. "We combine with aid, make hunter the weapon. Interference only justified on that condition. Balance *must* be returned. Your projections show this is only way."

"Surely that draws unwanted attention to us?" he asked, confused by the Camarilla's conclusions. "How we make a being into weapon?"

"Decision has been made. Have done once before to hunter. Already word to children has been sent saying granted their request is. An envoy shortly will you join to implement decision. Your sept's cooperation and skills needed now. Regulator must be made, given to hunter. Details as we talk transmitted are being."

"Why regulator needed? This not our field," he objected. "Living matter is what we manipulate, not devices. Energy your skill, not ours."

"Hunter will take time to learn use regulator. Until then, danger there is as with all weapons. Controls needed. Regulator does this. Access you have to aid you; builders of such devices live where you are. Biological components you will know when to add. Regulator must be used on hunter before aid can be given."

"To work so closely, they will see what we do," he objected. "They will wonder who and what we are."

"Risks must we take." Again, the hands began to move. "We feel it too, the movement of matters, the potentialities flowing, those that could be, those that must not. Vital guiding of the future is to keep balance or succumb to darkness will we all. This hunter is the nucleus, from it grows what will be. You it was that said we must intervene. Doubt yourself now do not, Phratry Leader."

He sighed. "No, Skepp Lord. No doubts have I. I will do as the Camarilla bids."

"Take all precautions," said the Skepp Lord anxiously before ending the transmission.

Shola, Zhal-Vartra, 8th day (July)

It was Midsummer's Day, one of the principal festivals of the year. Preparations at the main Aldatan estate had gone on till late the night before. Carrie had left early, tired out by the blistering heat, accompanied by Dzaka and Kitra who were home for the holiday. T'Chebbi and Kaid had stayed longer, helping secure the huge prefabricated hall where the feast would be held. When they'd finally returned to the villa, they'd remained together.

Too tired to do anything but sleep, they'd awakened early, early enough to enjoy each other while the air was still cool. Now, after their shower, T'Chebbi lay on her stomach, enjoying the feel of the brush against her skin as Kaid groomed her, ridding her naturally long pelt of the loose, dense fur that could make the hot summers so uncomfortable for her.

He stopped, and she felt him checking her injured sides properly.

"They're healing well," he said.

"I've been using Noni's ointment on them," T'Chebbi said lazily, letting her tail search for him then curl round his ankle.

He lifted her hair in one hand then began to brush through its length. "When we were on the *Kz'adul,* I made you a promise," he said quietly, drawing the brush down first one side of her head then the other. "Do you remember?"

"I remember," she said cautiously, her whole body suddenly tensing. Where was he going with this? "What of it?"

"I think it's time we discussed it."

She felt him lean to one side and put the brush down then start to divide her hair. Moving her hand over his, she stopped him. "I want to wear it loose today. What's to talk about?" she asked lightly. "I won't hold you to . . ."

"Did I say I wanted to change my mind?" he asked, sliding down beside her so they were face to face.

"No, but I assumed . . ."

"Don't assume," he interrupted, taking hold of her hand. "I asked Vanna for this." He placed something into her palm. "It gives you back your fertility."

Heart pounding against her ribs, she clutched it tightly, searching his face, gauging the set of his ears for clues as to what he really felt. "What're you saying?" she asked. "I don't want a cub because of a promise."

He stroked her cheek. "It's not only to keep a promise," he said. "You're my Companion and I love you. I've seen and felt you with Kashini these last few days. I know you'd like a cub and I want it to be ours."

"Are you feverish?" she asked, trying to cover her confusion. "Something fall on your head yesterday? Carrie know what you're suggesting?"

He let his hand rest on her neck. "Carrie thought it a good idea, if it's what you want," he said. "And no, I'm not feverish, nor did anything fall on my head yesterday." He grinned self-consciously, trying not to look away. "I find myself rather liking the thought of being a father. Ridiculous, isn't it, at my age?"

She gave a derisory snort. "You really asked Vanna for this?" She opened her hand to look at the plain capsule. It wasn't like him to be so open with others about such a private matter.

"It was easier than having had to listen to Rhyasha's lecture on family responsibilities to you and Carrie," he murmured. "You'd be surprised how many people have taken you to their hearts, including me." He leaned forward to flick his tongue across the top of her nose. "If you take the pill and I remove the implant, you'll conceive within the next day and a half. A cub conceived over midsummer is considered specially blessed as it's born in midwinter."

"Gods," she said, pushing him back and sitting up. "You're trying to persuade me!"

"Yes," he said simply, looking up at her. "I know deciding to terminate our last cub was difficult for you, especially since neither of us expected it to happen. It can't be easy for you now with everyone around you pregnant."

It wasn't easy, and fight it as she might, there was still enough of the young female educated as a Consortia by a doting foster father within the hard Brotherhood shell she'd erected around herself to desperately want a cub of her own. Torn two ways, she didn't know what to say.

"Besides," said Kaid, half-closing his eyes and stretching languidly against her. "With you and Carrie both pregnant, I'll get some peace."

She laughed, taking a swipe at his uppermost ear. "You think so?"

He pulled her down beside him, kissing her fiercely. Then,

knowing what was in her mind, he took hold of her left forearm, pushing her pelt aside and nipped the tiny bulge just below
the surface of her skin.

The unexpected pain was sharp, almost making her jerk free
before he released her. She watched as a tiny amount of blood
welled from the bite, and with it, a needle-thin rod about an inch
long. He took hold of it, gently pulling it free, then placed it on
her night table. Picking up the glass of water she kept there, he
held it out to her.

"It's time we all lived our own lives, T'Chebbi. There's more
to us than just the Brotherhood. We're safe here, and we have
the time. Share a cub with me now. I know it's what you want."

She took the glass, and the pill. "Damned telepaths, can't keep
anything private from you," she muttered before swallowing it,
but there was no rancor in her voice.

the *Couana,* Zhal-S'Asha, 20th day (October)

As he completed the last mental exercise, he felt the final
barrier between himself and the memories go down.

Let it play out like images on the entertainment vids,
he'd been told by someone—he couldn't remember who.
Try to be a watcher, not experience it.

He thought of midsummer, how he'd tried to back out of
his promise to return home, but Tutor Kha'Qwa had been
more determined that he should go. She'd reminded him
Stronghold was no place to hide from the world, his responsibilities must be honored or he'd not be allowed to
remain. So he'd gone home.

Waiting for the images to form, he pushed the happenings of the last few days deep into his subconscious so
they wouldn't intrude and focused totally on the midsummer festival. He realized he'd already faced some of the
worst memories and survived them. It began with the music,
then as the drumbeats grew louder in his mind's eye, he
smelled the scents. It all seemed brighter, clearer than he
remembered it as he watched himself weave his way
through the crowds of dancing people till he reached the
shade of the hall. Everyone had been there, even the
U'Churians, and Annuur, the Cabbarran with his sept.

His family were sitting in the usual place, Carrie chatting to Ghyan, their daughter on her knee; Kaid with T'Chebbi. They looked up as he approached. With his new objectivity, he could pick up the signs he'd missed then. Carrie, pleased but wary of him; T'Chebbi's air of distraction as, through Kaid, she felt the changes beginning within her as the tiny cell that was her cub began to grow and divide. And Kaid, alert to his every movement, no matter how slight, as he read him like an open book. He'd looked away, unable to accept the depth of feeling in his sword-brother's eyes. This time he didn't flinch, accepting and acknowledging what had been between them then. He saw his parents, concerned and afraid for the black-robed stranger their son had become.

Then he studied himself, seeing how he resembled a coiled spring waiting to explode. Hindsight clarified one's vision wonderfully, but at the time he'd seen none of this, felt nothing beyond his own wish to be elsewhere.

Ghyan had spent some time chatting to him, but even his old friend hadn't been able to reach through the indifference. Only his daughter had that gift as, unusually for her, she lay curled quietly against his chest, chewing contentedly on her piece of rag, her small fingers twined round his thumb. She brought him a measure of peace he could get nowhere else.

Once more he watched the people he knew come up to greet him, then move away as it grew obvious he had nothing to say. Zashou with Kris, Rezac with Jo, Kitra with Dzaka, Taizia with Meral and their daughter, Khayla. And Davies, sitting with Carrie. He'd wondered if perhaps she might take him as a lover until Vanna's sister Sashti came to take the Human off to dance and they didn't return.

Carrie had neither asked nor assumed anything of him. Now he could see the strain on her face, tell by her scent how difficult that day had been for her. Yet through it all he'd sat isolated, alone within the heart of his birth family and his bond family.

With the remembrance came the beginnings of understanding. Surrounded by his own kind, he'd felt alone for yet another reason. Everything and everyone around him smelled different, not quite right. Alien. Scent had been the key, and until Kezule's message arrived, he'd not realized why he'd felt so isolated, so at war with himself.

The shock jolted him out of the memories, left him sweating and swearing as he reached for his torc. With fumbling hands, he put it on again.

Tears filled his eyes and he rolled over to bury his face in the bedding, wanting Carrie there, wanting to smell her scent so it drove the memory of the other alien one from his mind forever. She was his first love, the one he'd been prepared to give up everything for—even his life.

A chime sounded at his door. He barely heard it, nor was he aware of the door opening until Banner's hand touched his shoulder.

"Captain," he said softly. "A message from Stronghold."

He sat up, keeping his back to Banner as he scrubbed the tears from his face then held out his hand for the message.

As it was given to him, Banner asked quietly, "Can I help, Kusac? Seven weeks isn't that long . . ."

"I'm fine," he said tiredly, reading the message. "Our own transport will be waiting for us in a few days." He crumpled the message and handed it back to him. "Destroy this, please."

"It's still night," said Banner. "Khadui can cover for me on the bridge. Why don't you let me deal with this stress of yours?"

He felt the bed move as Banner knelt behind him, felt the other's hands on his shoulders and flinched away from them. Banner persisted.

"Your shoulders and neck are rock hard," he said, moving Kusac's hair aside to probe the juncture of neck and shoulder with his fingers. "You're on duty again in another six hours and from the look of you, you haven't had any rest. You need to sleep, Kusac."

Even the little Banner was doing felt good, he had to admit. And his touch didn't disturb him with flesh-to-flesh messages as once it would have done.

"Lie down," Banner said quietly, sitting back. "Then you can relax fully. I guarantee you'll sleep."

He did, resting his head on his forearms, flicking his tail

down to lie between his legs, watching Banner as he spoke to Khadui on his wrist comm.

"Don't you miss Jurrel?" he asked as Banner stripped off his jacket and flung it on the nearby chair.

"Sure, but we've worked on separate missions before," he said. "And he's got Brynne," he added. "They're still occasional lovers."

"That doesn't bother you?" he asked, acutely aware of the hard muscles of Banner's thighs pressing against his hips as the other knelt astride him and began to work on his neck.

"No. We know when we need to be there for each other," Banner replied, a gentle purr of amusement underlying his voice. "That's part of our gift of empathy, and the fact we've been Companions for three years. Stop holding yourself so tightly," he admonished. "This will only hurt if you don't make some effort to relax."

He forced himself to relax his body, finding when he did that he enjoyed the physical contact. It disturbed him, awakening as it did more memories he didn't want to face right then.

"Were you and Jurrel lovers before you became sword-brothers?" he asked abruptly.

"I don't remember," said Banner, working his way across the top of one shoulder. "We worked together, we trusted each other, and one day the need for more was there. It grew with us, Kusac. You have a sword-brother, you should know."

"It was different," he said, hearing the defensiveness in his voice.

"It's different for everyone," said Banner gently, moving his hands to the complex shoulder joints. "Each brings what he's prepared to give to his sword-brother when they take the oath. Maybe they're lovers, maybe not. But if the need is there . . ." He left the sentence unfinished.

If the need is there . . . Kaid had said that too. Memories tried again to rise but were firmly suppressed.

"Stop talking," said Banner. "Use the Litanies and relax your mind as well. Your body is only half of you."

Gradually, he did relax, slipping into a trancelike state where memories could no longer be suppressed.

Stronghold, Zhal-Vartra, 12th day (July)

They were clearing out the lower levels of Stronghold, why, no one was prepared to say officially, but each had his or her own guesses. Kusac found himself working with Dzaou, Maikoi, and Taeo who'd all recently been reassigned to Stronghold.

Black tunics stained with sweat and covered in dust, they approached yet another boarded up doorway, the last in the corridor. Taeo grasped hold of the uppermost plank, placing her foot against the flat of the door, and heaved. Nothing happened. He stepped forward and lent her a hand. The board came off suddenly, catapulting them backward into Dzaou, then Maikoi.

"Watch it," snarled Dzaou, pushing him aside.

"Leave it alone, Dzaou," said Maikoi tiredly, righting himself. "The fault is yours. You shouldn't have been standing right behind them."

Hefting the plank, Kusac looked at Dzaou, eyes glinting in the artificial lights. "Touch me again and you'll regret it," he said quietly before throwing the plank into the trolley cart on the opposite side of the narrow corridor.

"You, too, Kusac," said Maikoi sharply. "This is our last room. After this, we can go upstairs and shower this grime off us."

"It'll be like all the others," grumbled Dzaou. "Empty of everything but dust and crumbling sticks of furniture."

"Get to it, moaner," said Taeo, picking bits of wood out of the fur on her hands. "We did the first plank."

Standing back, he leaned against the wall, grinning and watching.

Angrily, Dzaou grabbed the next plank and wrenched it free, tossing it backward to Maikoi to catch before grasping hold of the door handle. When it failed to move, he began to curse.

"Let me see," said Maikoi, bending down to check the hinges. They were rusted solid. Picking up the lubricant gun, he sprayed both them and the opening mechanism liberally before trying to open it for himself.

The metal screeched, protesting loudly, making them all fold their ears down in distress, but it did open.

Picking up his large flashlight, he stepped forward to shine it in through the open door. This room was different. It was full of ancient pieces of furniture stacked in haphazard piles, not in ordered ranks. The torch glinted off the odd reflective surface, breaking up the beam of light and sending it scattering round the rest of the room.

"Another furniture dump," said Dzaou in disgust from behind him. "It's not worth the effort."

"We're to check every room," said Maikoi, stepping over the threshold.

"We'll find nothing of use in there!"

Following Maikoi inside, he picked his way between a stack of chairs and a table piled with various pieces of bric-a-brac. Spiderwebs, covered in thick dust, were festooned everywhere—between upturned chair legs, across the empty shelves of old bookcases, and when he flicked the beam up to the ceiling, he saw they hung down in long festival-like streamers.

Left briefly in the dark, Maikoi let out an exclamation of disgust and staggered backward into the table, sending a pile of junk crashing noisily to the floor. With a yelp of shock and pain, Maikoi fell over too.

Shining the torch down, he saw him lying amid a cloud of dust and a pile of disintegrating pieces of wood. Leaning forward, he held out his free hand to help Maikoi up. The other grasped it, there was a moment's resistance, then Maikoi came staggering to his feet. Something hit the floor with a small, metallic clatter and began to roll away from them.

"What was that?" he asked, flicking the light in the direction of the noise. He got a glimpse of something bright disappearing under the piles of furniture.

"My sigil," swore Maikoi. "I knew I should have replaced the chain today! Where'd it go?"

"Toward the back of the room," he said.

Maikoi swore again. "We've got to move everything now, not just check it!"

He turned to Taeo, standing silhouetted against the doorway by the light in the corridor outside. "Another flashlight would be useful."

She nodded and disappeared.

Finding a high and stable enough surface on which to put the flashlight took him several minutes, but by the time Taeo returned, he and Maikoi had lifted the table and placed it hard against the opposite wall. The remaining junk on top of it had disintegrated into piles of dust and pieces of wood as soon as they'd tried to lift them. They were discussing what to do with a group of several chests and nightstands when she came in.

"Where's Dzaou?" asked Maikoi as Taeo placed the flashlight with the other one and came to help them.

"Taking the cart back to empty it," Taeo said. "Says the room's too small for more than three of us to work in at the same time. I doubt he'll be back."

Maikoi straightened up and looked at her. "That one's heading for a fall," he said. "He should never have been relocated from Haven. He's not going to adapt to this . . ."

"I know," said Taeo loudly, drowning out his last words. "He's getting to be a real liability."

Intrigued, he pretended not to be listening in the hope of hearing more, but after exchanging a long look, they bent to their task again.

"Be careful, Taeo," warned Maikoi as she leaned forward to lift a small chest, "most of this stuff is disintegrating the minute we touch it."

For about fifteen minutes, they toiled on, shifting all manner of ancient furnishings. As he and Maikoi hefted a badly corroded metal headboard, Taeo stopped.

"Has it occurred to you that these are the contents of just one office and bedroom?"

As they wedged the frame behind a couple of nightstands, Maikoi looked over at her. "They could be," he conceded. "But why pile them all in here?"

She lifted one shoulder in a shrug. "They wanted to free up the other rooms? But why not relocate the furniture, or destroy it? Why keep it?"

"It's not been properly stored," said Kusac, leaning against the large table to take a breather. "No dust sheets or packing wrapped round it to protect the surfaces from scratches like they did in the other rooms. It's just been piled in here in any order. And it was left here permanently."

"What exactly are we looking for?" she asked. "I know we were told anything strange or useful, but what's that mean?"

"No idea," said Maikoi, kneeling down to peer along the floor under what was left of the furniture. "Maybe they put it all in here because this is the last room in the corridor. It's solid rock after this. Hand me down a flashlight, please. I think I can see my sigil."

He fetched one, passing it down to him.

"This is what I call unusual," Taeo continued. "The furniture here is ancient, far older than anything I saw the others had found when I went upstairs for the flashlight. And why the sudden interest in searching the old tunnels?"

Maikoi sneezed violently several times and pushed himself back up to his feet. "Not my sigil," he said, eyes watering as he tried to find a part of his arm that wasn't coated with the fine, cloying dust. "You know why," he said, giving up and blinking furiously instead. "Most of us are being deployed up to Haven or Anchorage. Father Lijou wants to make sure nothing of importance is overlooked before we start moving."

"That's rumor talking," said Taeo.

Bored, he'd moved past them to drag away the last few remaining items. A large chest blocked his way and as he knelt to grasp hold of the metal looped handle on the end, he stopped, reaching out a disbelieving hand to touch the carving on the flat top.

This chest remained quite solid under his fingers as he traced the double sunburst symbols. "Maikoi," he said, his voice strained even to his ears. "Call Father Lijou. We've found something odd."

"What?" demanded Taeo, running to his side, followed by Maikoi. She made a sound of disappointment. "It's only a carved chest."

"The symbol," he said, looking up at them, ears flattening in shock. "It's ours, the Aldatans'."

"What's it doing here?" asked Maikoi. "You're a Telepath Clan, not Brotherhood types at all. Pardon me saying," he added.

"One of my ancestors life-bonded with Vartra." He searched his memory for a name. "Zylisha Aldatan. Call Father Lijou." He reached for the hasp.

Taeo reached out to stop him. "You shouldn't. Leave it for the Father."

"Why not?" he countered. "Vartra was my kin. I have more right than anyone to open it." He flicked the rusty hasp back and opened the lid.

Faded purple cloth, now almost brown with age, formed the top layer. With a cautious claw tip, he touched it. When it didn't disintegrate, he reached in with both hands, lifting it out, aware of Maikoi's voice in the background talking to Father Lijou.

Setting it aside, he pulled out the second layer, which had

been tightly wedged in around the contents, revealing an object he recognized instantly from his time digging at the ruins on his estate. It was an ancient computing unit, but it was in far better condition than any he'd seen in the lab under the monastery.

More cloth filled the space beside it. Lifting it out, he found a small utilitarian gray box made of an artificial substance used commonly in the time of Vartra. Picking it up, he opened it. Inside lay half a dozen shaped crystals. On the inside of the lid, something had been inscribed.

"What are they?" asked Maikoi, finished now with his call. "Look like data crystals."

"They are," said Kusac, closing the lid and handing him the box. "The first of their kind. Crystal technology wasn't being used before the actual Cataclysm, but we told them we used it."

"*You* told them?" repeated Maikoi incredulously, opening the box for himself.

"He and Kaid went back to Vartra's time, remember?" said Taeo, leaning round Maikoi to watch Kusac. "He found out about the Humans from you, didn't He? That's why you're able to Leska bond with them now."

"Carrie came with us," he said, turning his attention to the computing unit once he'd discovered there was nothing else in the chest but more material for packaging. "She was pregnant, I had to tell him the cub was mine. He took a blood sample from her." He found a small panel on the side of the unit and managed to flip it open. The space inside was the right shape and size to take one of the crystals. Satisfied, he closed it.

"We tried not to tell him about the future, that he'd become a God in our time, but Goran, his chief of security, was suspicious of us, didn't believe what we said about the impact damage the chunk of moon debris would cause. Getting them to leave the estate and come here was more important than any other consideration because we'd found the remains of a firefight between the Valtegans and some of our people at the ruins. We couldn't let it be him. Shola's future depended on Him surviving."

A noise in the corridor outside drew their attention to the door. Dressed in short tunics no less filthy than their own, they saw Father Lijou, Yaszho, and L'Seuli.

"What have you found?" the head priest demanded, coming over.

"An ancient computer and six data crystals," he said, getting up.

"This room, Father," said Taeo. "All the furniture, it's ancient. Could it have been His?"

"Perhaps it was," said L'Seuli, taking her by the elbow and gently steering her out of the room. "You and Maikoi should go freshen up. We'll take over here. Say nothing of this to anyone, you understand?"

"Yes, Commander," she said reluctantly, waiting for Maikoi.

Lijou took the box from him, opening it up to inspect the crystals for himself.

"This must be one of their first crystal data recorders," he said as the Father knelt beside him. Despite himself, he was curious. "What are you looking for, Father? Evidence of Vartra in Stronghold?"

"You should go, too, Kusac," said L'Seuli. "You've done well."

"He stays," said Lijou abruptly, placing the box back in the chest and closing the lid. He ran his fingers over the double sunburst. "He's Vartra's kin. He has a right to know what we intend."

He began to think this through. The furniture, the chest, and the secrecy could only add up to one thing. "You're looking for His tomb," he said quietly. "They buried the important people back then, like the Warriors in the tomb at Vartra's Retreat."

"Yes," said Lijou, getting up. He looked over to Yaszho. "Clear this room," he ordered. "Watch for anything of value, but clear it quickly."

Pushing himself upright again, Kusac touched the Father's arm to get his attention. "We should wait outside," he said. "A lot of the furniture turns to dust when touched."

Lijou nodded, following him into the corridor.

"His remains will have to stay here, you realize that, don't you?" said the priest, running a hand through his white-streaked hair, a worried look on his face. "I know you have kin-rights, but He's more than just kin to you, He's our God."

"My mother will have to know, as will Zashou. Her sister life-bonded to Vartra. She has the greatest claim on His remains."

"If we find Him, it can't be made public knowledge, even here at Stronghold."

He nodded, understanding why. From the room came the

sounds of heavy objects being dragged across the stone floor, and from the doorway, faint clouds of dust drifted out.

Lijou's mouth opened in a faint smile. "You were right about the dust."

L'Seuli suddenly appeared. "We found a section of hollow brickwork," he said, barely able to conceal his excitement.

Security was intense, even for Stronghold. Lijou had ordered that all the psi dampers Ghezu had installed be switched on, and all entrances to the lower levels were guarded by a handpicked team of senior Brothers and Sisters. Artificial lighting had been strung up from iron pegs hammered into the walls, illuminating both rooms and allowing them to see everything clearly. All they waited for now was the arrival of Kaid and Noni.

"Why Kaid?" Rhyaz had asked impatiently as he looked down on the stone sarcophagus that stood in the center of the small room that had been concealed beyond the brick wall. "What has he to do with opening this? Noni I can understand, but Kaid? Why can't we open it now?"

"Have a sandwich," offered Lijou from the other room, holding out the plate to him. "Some food'll calm you."

Rhyaz glared balefully at him as he left the tiny crypt. "It's the middle of the bloody night, Lijou! I don't want a damned sandwich, I want to see what's in this thing!"

Lijou put the plate back on the table they'd commandeered. "We need Kaid because Vartra ordered him to find a way to keep Him here. He'll expect Kaid, and may even talk to him."

"All right, I concede that," Rhyaz said, sitting down on the carved wooden chest. "How do you manage to keep so calm? Here you are, face to face with the physical reality of our God, and all you can do is eat!"

Lijou indicated the sarcophagus. "That isn't my God," he said mildly. "At most, that's His mortal remains. I've seen and spoken to the living Vartra."

Kusac smiled, helping himself to a sandwich as Rhyaz muttered darkly under his breath. It gave him some amusement to see the Father so calm and the Warrior Master so rattled.

L'Seuli came out, checking his vid unit and ejecting a full cartridge. "It feels sacrilegious taking images of it."

"We can't leave it here," said Lijou, picking up his mug of c'shar. "We need a record of where we found it for posterity.

One day we may be able to let the world know, but not yet. It isn't as if Vartra didn't tell us to find a way to keep Him here, and I know of no better way than placing His remains in the temple."

Yaszho, looking weary, came in. "I've finished preparing the floor to the right of Vartra's statue," he said. "I don't think anyone's going to be fooled into believing that we found a new sculpture with all the activity that's been going on down here since third meal."

"They'll believe it," said Lijou confidently. "That's another reason why I need Noni and Kaid. We're going to plant false memories in the minds of everyone here, except ourselves."

"What?" Rhyaz was stunned. "You can't do that! Can you?" He looked from Lijou to Kusac.

"It can be done," he said uncomfortably. "It's like crowd control on a much more complex level. The sarcophagus itself has enough crystal set into it to store the false memories. If they do it right, it'll be self-perpetuating. No one will think to see more than a sculpture. You should have asked Carrie to come, too, Father Lijou. She knows more about the crystals than Kaid—or me. Not that I can do anything to help." He tried to keep the tinge of bitterness from his voice.

"Damn me, but I'm glad you're on our side," Rhyaz said, scrubbing his eyes with his hands. "It scares me to hear you telepaths have so much power over people."

"That much energy costs us dearly, young Rhyaz," said Noni's tart voice from the doorway.

He looked round to see Kaid standing there, Noni held in his arms.

"You can put me down now," she said, tapping Kaid on the chest with a bony finger. "Undignified is what it is, arriving like this!"

Kaid lowered the elderly Sholan carefully to her feet as Lijou and Rhyaz stood up to greet her. "You know it was too far for you to walk," he said. "Since you wouldn't use their chair, you left me no option but to carry you."

"Taking liberties with old Noni, you are," she grumbled, leaning on her stick as she made her way over to the two Guild Masters, but her tone was one of affection. "Keeping your own mind on one thought for long enough to do the work is difficult enough, Rhyaz. I got to not only do it myself, but link in to Kaid and

Lijou and use their minds to create the falsehood. Thank the Gods it's at least night! With nearly all of them asleep upstairs, it'll make it easier!"

"I didn't mean to imply it was easy, Noni," Rhyaz said awkwardly.

"I know you didn't," she said, moving past him to Lijou. "Think of it like driving two riding beasts who want to go in opposite directions from each other and where you want to go, then you see why group work is rarely done." She held out her palm to Lijou in greeting. "You've done well, Lijou. Good work."

Lijou touched her fingers briefly with his own. "It wasn't me, Noni. It was Kusac."

Noni turned to look at him. "Makes sense. An Aldatan finding an Aldatan. Then you have my congratulations, Kusac."

"It was luck, nothing more," he said as she reached down to touch his cheek with her hand.

"I don't believe in luck," she said. "You found the chest and recognized the carving. Now where's this stone tomb?"

Lijou pointed. "Through the hole in the wall," he said. "We think these may have been Vartra's own rooms here at Stronghold. Kusac says you never saw His quarters," he said to Kaid.

"Apart from the temple and the rooms we stayed in, we only saw His lab," said Kaid.

"I'm not going in there!" said Noni, eyeing the ragged hole in the wall with horror. "What d'you think I am? A lizard to go climbing over rocks? You bring the damned thing out here for me!"

"I wasn't suggesting you go in there," said Lijou hastily. "While we waited for you, we had a grav cradle bolted round the sides. We didn't want to move it out of there without you seeing it first."

"I've seen it, now bring it out," she ordered, sitting down on the chest beside Kusac.

It took half an hour and all six males before the huge sarcophagus was finally sitting in the center of the room. Unbolting the padded grav cradle, they stood back, leaving room for Noni to come forward and examine it for herself.

Carved from one block of flawless pale gray stone, the painted carvings round the sides and on the lid glowed with vibrant colors. Leaving her cane lying on the floor, Noni hobbled over to it. Almost reverently, she placed her hands on the sides, running her fingers over the carvings and inset crystals.

Too small to see the top of the lid clearly, she was just the right height to examine the sides without bending down like the males.

"This one, He's Vartra," she said, fingers stopping on a tan-pelted figure in the center of a group of gray- and purple-clad warriors. "See the sword at His side? It has a crystal pommel. Those are the first Triads with the Brothers and Sisters around Him. And there," she said, her fingers moving on. "He's with the first Guild Masters." She moved round to the bottom panel. "Here, the Highlanders again," she said, looking up at Kaid. "See, behind them the Retreat with more Brothers. And this side is the Cataclysm. Look, He's at Stronghold with the Brothers and their families. They lived here with their cubs, Rhyaz," she said, looking at him. "I told you there had been berrans here in the past. They were a community then, not just Warrior Priests."

"I didn't disbelieve you, Noni," he said soberly.

"And this last panel," she said, now at the top end of the sarcophagus. "Have you looked at this?"

"We can't make sense of it," said Lijou. "It's just crystals set randomly into the black background."

She laughed, looking at Kaid as he slowly stretched out his hand to touch the dark panel. "He knows what it is, don't you, Tallinu?"

"Haven," he said softly. "It's Haven and the stars of the Alliance. The new Alliance."

"It can't be," said Rhyaz sharply, coming round to see. He frowned, moving one way then the other. "Well I'll be damned! You're right! The crystals are the stars! And that painted one is Haven. How did they know about that in those days? We hadn't even gotten beyond our own moons then."

"Some of our telepaths had. They'd been out to the Prime worlds," Kusac said. "We know Rezac could send as far as Shola before he became gene-altered. They must have sent images of the Valtegan Empire back home."

"There's more to it than that," said Noni, standing back. "I'll wager this panel is where His head is, isn't it?"

"Judging by the carving of Vartra on the lid, yes," said Lijou.

"You're going to have to send a part of Him to Haven," she

said. "He can't retreat from Shola then! And in space, He can help us even more."

"Break up His body?" said Rhyaz, his voice almost inaudible.

"You can't do that!" exclaimed L'Seuli, horrified. "That's desecration!"

"We don't know for sure He's in there," said Lijou calmly. "It could be just what we're saying, a sculpture to honor Him."

"He's in there," said Kaid, reaching up to push the lid aside. "Help me, Kusac."

While Rhyaz and the others looked on in shocked silence, Kusac put his weight against the lid. Then Lijou joined them.

Held by a decorative metal spike at the bottom end, as the three of them pushed it, the lid began to pivot. The scent of nung blossoms filled the air as, with a grating sound, the lid slowly slid aside, exposing the interior.

"Don't just stand there, lad," Noni admonished Rhyaz. "Get me something firm to stand on!"

Kaid stopped, hands on the edges as he looked down onto the cloth-wrapped body lying on its bed of long dead nung flowers. This was the body of the Male who'd shaped not only his life, but that of his friends; the Male who'd spoken to him—appeared to him—from beyond the grave. A wave of light-headedness passed through him. Beside him, he heard Noni grumbling and the chair creaking as Rhyaz helped her up.

"It looks like any body ready for cremation," said Kusac, breaking the silence.

"Cut the wrappings," ordered Noni. "L'Seuli! Get your ass over here with that vid recorder of yours!"

"Cut it?" asked Lijou, looking across the coffin at her.

Kusac pulled his knife from his belt and handed it to Kaid.

"Cut it," she confirmed. "See that lump there on His chest? It's a crystal. We want it."

"How d'you know that?" asked Lijou, peering into the coffin.

"Found references to it in some of those records we been looking through," she said, looking up at him. "Back then, when their leaders were dying, they gave them a special crystal, one of the kind I use for mind workings. They did it so what they wanted folk to remember of them after they were gone could be recorded. Then when they died, they buried it with them. That's

why to this day we still put a crystal in with the ashes up here
in the Highlands."

Taking the knife, almost in a daze, Kaid leaned forward and
carefully slit the thick shroud. It parted easily, revealing the desiccated remains of a male Sholan. Between both hands lay a large
faceted crystal.

With a muffled cry of shock, Lijou stepped back.

Noni looked over at him, grinning evilly as Rhyaz averted his
face. "What's the matter, Father? Not afraid of a dead body, are
you?"

Lijou, ears invisible against his head, said nothing.

Hands shaking, Kaid stood up and returned the knife to Kusac.
His sword-brother was right: it looked like any other corpse ready
for cremation. Somehow, he'd expected something more. He
looked over at Noni. "Don't ask me to pick it up."

She nodded, stepping down from the chair with Rhyaz' help
and coming round to stand beside him.

He didn't want to do this. To actually touch Vartra's corpse,
move those desiccated hands and take His crystal from Him was
not at all what he wanted to do.

Kusac bent over the edge of the sarcophagus and, carefully
unfastening the mummified fingers from the crystal, picked it up.
As he overbalanced at the unexpected weight, Kaid had the presence of mind to grab him by the belt and haul him upright again.

Kusac turned and held it out to him. "Here."

He eyed it warily, not quite sure what it could do to him. Cautiously, he closed his hands round it, his fingers touching Kusac's
as he did so.

Light flared, blinding him with its intensity. Kaid's presence
exploded in his mind as a power greater than the gestalt flooded
through them, forcing down both their mental barriers, paralyz-
ing their bodies.

Alone for so long, his mind, suddenly bonded to Kaid's, was
filled with a voice they both knew well.

Blood to blood, Kusac. I hear your call and answer it, whispered Vartra.

Suddenly released, pain flared briefly down his arms making
his hands spasm and break the contact with Kaid. At the same
moment he let go of the crystal, so did Kaid. Frozen, they watched

in horror as it slowly began to fall. As it hit the ground, a single, clear note rang out and it split down the exact center.

The air between the halves seemed to shimmer, moving, swirling, coalescing into the shape of a crouching male. As it solidified, the male rose sinuously to his feet. Tall and slim, the short dark gray tunic he wore did little to conceal the muscles that rippled beneath the surface of his tan pelt. As he looked from Kaid to Kusac, his hand automatically went to rest on the pommel of the sword that sat on his left hip.

The narrow ears flared wider as he spoke. "You called kin-right on me, Kusac Aldatan," he said, his voice low, the accent holding more than a touch of the Highland in it. "You've found my tomb. What is it you wish of me?"

He took a step backward, feeling the hard surface of the sarcophagus behind him. His mind, still reeling from the shock of contact with Kaid, refused to take in what was happening.

"We called you," said Lijou, his voice trembling as he stepped forward. "We need your help, Vartra."

The faint blue glow surrounding Him shimmered as Vartra lifted His right hand, gesturing to the priest. "Be silent. Only one of my blood has the right to call me."

"We need you to stay with us, Vartra," said Kaid. "Don't follow the other Gods into . . ."

"By what right do you presume to ask anything of me?" demanded Vartra, eyes flashing as He turned to look briefly at Kaid. "You're no kin of mine!"

"He's my kin," said Kusac, pushing himself away from the tomb and taking a step forward. He forced himself to remember that what stood before him right now, no matter how strangely He'd arrived, was the flesh and blood Male he'd met before. "Our Third, bonded to me and my life-mate."

"Bonded by blood to your mate, but not yet to you," said Vartra, eyes still glowing, voice still harsh. "For the third time I ask, why did you call me? What is you wish of me?"

"Shola needs You. You fought the Valtegans before and won. We need Your help again. I ask it as my kin-right."

"My war is done," He said. "I brought Shola peace. Valtegans no longer walk on our world."

"You formed the Brotherhood," said Noni from behind him. "Led them down into the plains as Warriors with the Telepaths to reunite the people after the Cataclysm. I know what You are, Vartra, and what You did."

"You! I should have known you'd be here," He said with a low rumble of anger as He turned toward her voice. "The pledge is gone, Noni. You have no power in this, Guardian or no."

"I'm Kusac's negotiator," she said. "You owe them it, Vartra. You used Tallinu, shaped him to form the future, and he did what You asked. He forged their Triad strong enough to withstand what the Primes did to Kusac, strong enough to bring them here, together, before You. It's time You repaid them for their loyalty."

"Repaid?" Vartra roared, making Lijou and the others in the room retreat hurriedly. "Repaid, Noni?" He took a step toward her, the blue nimbus darkening briefly. "I repaid you! I gave you back Tallinu and his Triad! They have their lives because of me!"

She stood her ground, staring belligerently up into the face of the enraged Entity. "What good are their lives on a dead world, Vartra? Because if You follow the other Entities into hiding, that's what Shola will become! The Pledge has another part to it, one I discovered a few days ago. You alone of the Entities have a geas placed on you . . ."

"Enough!" roared Vartra. "You try my patience, Old One! I have not yet refused!"

"You told me you wanted Shola free of the Valtegans," said Kaid. "You told me to find a way for You to stay with us when the other realms closed. I've done what You asked. What more do You want?"

"I asked nothing of you for Myself!" he said, pointing at Kaid. "All I did was to ensure you were where you could best help Shola. I'll stay, not because of the geas, but because My kin demanded it of me! You and I will have words later, Tallinu!"

The blue glow intensified, then vanished, taking Vartra with it.

For several minutes, no one moved, no one spoke. Then Rhyaz broke the silence.

"Why did you anger Him, Noni? There was no need. We almost . . ."

"Shut up, Rhyaz," said Lijou. "You've never dealt with Vartra before. Noni knew what she was doing."

"You noticed it too?" she said, sitting down suddenly on the chest. "He needed to be forced to stay. What He said went cross-grain to what He told Tallinu earlier. Put the crystal pieces in the tomb, lad, then close it," she said to Kaid. "I reckon we should start our work now, then we can get that thing," she waved a hand at the sarcophagus, "upstairs to its new home. I'd like to get back to my bed before dawn!"

"I can still go to Noni's for tonight," said Kaid, following him into the suite.

"I've told you it's all right," he said tiredly, unbuckling his belt as he headed through the lounge for the bedroom. "It was your suite. They only put me in here because we're sword-brothers."

Throwing his belt on the bed in passing, he began hauling off his tunic as he made for the bathing room.

"Want a hand?" he heard Kaid call out. "That dust will have settled deep into your pelt."

"If you like." Turning on the shower, he flung the filthy tunic into the bath, aware he was actually glad of Kaid's company. The encounter with Vartra had left him as exhausted mentally as he was physically. He remembered trying to get the dust and plaster out of his pelt when he'd been helping rebuild the villa. He hadn't been looking forward to trying to get clean on his own, and he couldn't face the communal bathing room.

Stepping into the cubicle, he leaned his forehead against the back wall, letting the hot water cascade down his back while he waited for Kaid, remembering how good it had been, for even a brief moment, to not be alone in his own mind. Then he felt Kaid's hands on his shoulders.

"You all right?"

"Exhausted, that's all," he said, bracing his hands against the wall as Kaid began to rub the liquid soap deep into his back.

"It took some courage to talk to Vartra like that."

"You and Noni did most of the talking. I just remembered the person we met in the Margins."

"That wasn't a person," said Kaid, soaping his hair. "That was the Entity."

He said nothing, too tired for a discussion on deities. Kaid's hands moved lower, one tapping his inner thigh to tell him to spread his legs.

"You know we were Linked, don't you?" Kaid said, hands running across his hips and lower back.

"Yes, I've—missed that contact," he said hesitantly. It hurt to talk about it, but he and Kaid hadn't talked for so long.

"So have I. To have thought you dead, then to find you like we did . . ." He let the sentence tail off and concentrated on scrubbing. "Did you feel any pain during our Link?"

"I dropped the crystal because of it." Obviously he had.

"I hoped you hadn't," said Kaid.

"What did Vartra mean we haven't shared blood?" he asked at length as Kaid indicated he should turn round.

Kaid's ears tipped backward briefly as he poured more soap into his hand before putting the bottle back on the shelf. "When you and Carrie married, you shared blood, just like Kitra and Dzaka did."

"I know that," he said as Kaid began to soap his chest. "And I know you and Carrie shared blood on the *Kz'adul*."

Kaid stopped and looked at him. "Yes." He reached up and touched Kusac's jaw fleetingly, a strange expression on his face. "I didn't know you were there, that you were forced to watch us," he said, the pain evident in his voice as he let his hands fall to his sides. "I'd had a vision about it, I knew it would happen, but I was the captive. I never for a moment dreamed it would be you! If I could go back and change the past, have been the Primes' captive instead of you, I swear I would, Kusac."

"It can't be changed, Kaid," he said awkwardly. "We've each got our own destiny. I know the situation we're in isn't easy for you either. How's Carrie managing? I don't like to ask her."

"It's difficult for us all, but she's coping. And forget what Vartra said about us sharing blood. I'm sure it isn't necessary."

He nodded, sensing Kaid's sudden uneasiness by the set of his ears. "I can finish myself off," he said, aware of a similar feeling. This conversation was getting way too intense. He reached for the bottle, noticing the other's torc for the first time. "I didn't know you wore a torc," he said. "From Noni?"

Kaid nodded. "It was her brother's."

He handed him the bottle. "Some things have worked out well, for you at least. Start on yourself, I'll do your back when you're ready."

Sleep hadn't come easily as he lay in bed listening to Kaid's quiet breathing. His upbringing as a telepath had isolated him physically from all but close family members and lovers. Nothing had prepared him for the intense mental Link he'd had with Carrie and Kaid. Part of him craved the company and the physical contact it brought, the other part rejected it because of the fear of the pain and of harming those he loved. He wished it was Carrie in his bed, wished he could just hold her, feel her warmth against him. Sighing, he turned his back on Kaid and began to mentally recite the litany for relaxation.

Stronghold, the next day, month of Zhal-Vartra, 13th day (July)

When he woke, he found himself curled round Kaid's back, Shocked, he moved instantly away and lay there, heart pounding, praying he'd been first to wake. When Kaid didn't stir, he slid carefully out from under the sheet and padded silently across to a drawer to get a clean tunic before going into the bathing room to dress. When he emerged, Kaid was up and, apart from washing, ready to leave for first meal.

A message was waiting for them on the desk comm in the lounge. They were to report to Rhyaz and Lijou in the Warrior Master's office after first meal to discuss the training of the Prime younglings.

Rhyaz had decided to relocate his office to the west wing of the building, near Lijou's. Apart from any other consideration, the western rooms faced down onto the Kysubi Plains while Ghezu's old office had been above the reinforced munitions and weapons store set into the mountainside itself. He'd wanted a clean start for them all after Ghezu's traitorous leadership.

The meeting was formal, with Rhyaz sitting behind his heavy wooden desk and Lijou seated to one side.

"The Prime younglings are being housed on the Warrior Guild estate at Nazule. Kusac, I think you should accompany Kaid and help train them," Lijou said.

"I don't want to work with them," he said flatly.

"The matter's been decided," said Rhyaz. "The Primes are part of the Alliance now, albeit junior members. It was J'koshuk who was responsible for what actually happened to you, Kusac, not the Primes, though Chy'qui authorized it. The Primes are almost a different species from the M'zullians. Even Vartra said last night there were no Valtegans on Shola now. It's time you made an effort to differentiate between them."

He felt his hair beginning to stir and fought to keep it from rising. Kaid's tail tip touched his leg briefly, warningly.

"It might be too soon, Lijou," said Kaid. "If it doesn't work out, can he return here?"

Lijou hesitated, looking from one to the other, then to Rhyaz who'd remained silent.

"Kusac is Brotherhood," reminded Kaid quietly. "He asked to come here to train on the religious side. You accepted him. He has a right to remain here at the Temple until his training is complete."

"If it doesn't work, he can return," agreed Lijou. "But Kusac, try it. Please."

Again the warning flick from Kaid. "I'll try," he said reluctantly.

"You can choose your own team, Kaid," said Rhyaz, leaning forward and handing him a comp pad. "Here's the schedule we worked out. If you need to make any changes to it, call me. They're expecting you sometime tomorrow."

"Not tomorrow, Rhyaz. Link day. I'll send my team tomorrow, though, and we'll join them on the fifteenth. I'm working with our own people right now. I'll set the training program up, but I'll have to return to the estate a couple of days later."

"So long as you keep close tabs on them," said Rhyaz. "I want them confined to the Nezule estate, I don't want them roaming the city. We can't afford any incidents."

"Then you'll have trouble," warned Kaid. "Remember what happened with the Forces people on our estate. That's how Kezule got in. I suggest they be allowed out, but in controlled situations. Social skills are important too. They can be taken to places like a storytelling theater if it's booked for our exclusive use first. The Nezules will want to go too, I'm sure. There should be no problem selling the extra tickets."

Rhyaz considered the matter. "You have a point," he said. "Very well, but clear it with me first. Going on to other matters, Father Lijou and I have looked over the request you brought from the Touibans. You can tell Toueesut we'll be in touch with him shortly with a draft contract for him to consider." He looked briefly at Lijou, then handed Kaid a data crystal. "I'd like you to look this over in the next few days, Kaid. It concerns some proposals you made to us just after returning from Haven. Let me know what you think of them. I'm sure I don't have to tell you how confidential it is. Father Lijou disagrees with me on this matter, but I feel we've no option but to pursue it. You may need to consult with Kusac."

Kaid nodded, reaching out to take the crystal from him.

"What about the ancient comp and crystals I found?" Kusac asked abruptly.

"They've been in our tech workshop from the moment we got them upstairs," said Lijou. "Finding a power source is the first problem."

"Get the Touibans on our estate onto it," he said. "No point in duplicating what they're doing."

"We may have to," said Rhyaz. "We're considering having them look at it when they come here to sign the contract."

Kaid got to his feet. "Is that all?"

"For now. I'll be expecting weekly progress reports from you and your people."

Once outside, Kusac turned on Kaid. "Why did you allow him to send me there?" he demanded.

"Because he's right. Listen to me a minute," said Kaid, holding him back as he turned away with a sound of disgust. "You'll be helping shape these young Primes, Kusac. If you want to be sure they don't turn on us, what better way than to help form the attitudes they'll take back with them to their own world?"

"You know how I feel about the Valtegans—and don't tell me these are Primes because there's no difference as far as I'm concerned!"

"Give it a try," Kaid said. "You heard Rhyaz. If it isn't working out, you can leave. You don't have to stay there, you can travel daily from the estate."

"I'll stay there," he said shortly. "What did the Touibans want?"

"To hire the Brotherhood as bodyguards, both on a personal and a governmental level. Even inside their Hives."

He glanced at him, aware of the importance of the request, and its unique nature. "So that's why all this interest in finding Vartra's remains," he said quietly. "And taking alien contracts. We really are cutting free from Shola."

Kaid nodded. "It isn't common knowledge yet, but as you know, the scent's been picked up by most Brothers and Sisters.

There'll always be a presence here, though—Father Lijou is re-maining, but Rhyaz and L'Seuli will share the running of Haven between them. It's being renamed Haven Stronghold."

"I'm sure it's too soon, Rhyaz," said Lijou, getting to his feet. "So is Kha'Qwa. It's barely three weeks since he came here."

"You said he was doing well and beginning to settle in, even using the common areas for eating and relaxing."

Lijou found his feet taking him to the window. The view of the plains and the Ferraki hills opposite had always helped clar-ify his thoughts. "Yes, he's doing well with his religious studies. He's got the patience for the meditation, and the attention to de-tail for the rituals and the services. But he's still not being what you could call sociable. He may be in the common areas, but he's not interacting more than's necessary. And when he's in class sparring, I'm told he's not holding back as much as he should." He stared down into the valley below and sighed.

"He's been scanned and tested more than anyone I know, Lijou. He should be capable of handling this mission. He has to be given some responsibility, otherwise he'll think we don't trust him," said Rhyaz reasonably. "And we have to know he can take that responsibility."

"I know, but he needs to get his self-confidence back."

"How can he do that if we don't trust him?"

"Perhaps you're right."

Valsgarth Estate, later that day

They'd just finished third meal when Dziosh, the main house at-tendant, came into the family kitchen to tell them that Toueesut was waiting in the lounge to speak to them.

"He'll be wanting to know about the contract," said Carrie, refilling her coffee mug.

"Could be," said Kaid, looking across at Kusac. "Mind if I handle it?"

He dipped his ears in a Sholan shrug. "It was you he spoke to."

A few minutes later, Kaid returned. "It's you they want," he said.

He looked up, catching Kaid's glance at Carrie. Irritation flared but was quickly suppressed: he knew how difficult it was not to communicate mentally rather than verbally with one's Leska. He got to his feet and followed Kaid out.

A smell resembling that of freshly baked bread met his nostrils as he entered the lounge. He remembered the scent; it was one that signified a sense of purpose. Alone of the six Touibans, Toueesut was standing.

"Clan Leader!" the Speaker trilled, hands outstretched, approaching him in his inimitable dancing gait. "Glad we are that you will see us. A proposition we have to be putting to you from ourselves and the Cabbarran, Annuur." He stopped a foot away from Kusac and held out his hand, palm up in fair imitation of the telepath's greeting.

Automatically, he touched the Speaker's fingertips with his own. "Well come to my home, Toueesut," he said. "What nature of proposition?"

"Permission you kindly gave us to be looking at your medical records to see if any help we could be to you. Annuur sees what we are doing and some suggestions he was making to improve on our design. We have crafted something to be helping you for now until we have done more research on your regrettable medical situation."

He succeeded in keeping his ears upright and his eyes from closing, but inwardly he sighed. Why couldn't everyone leave him alone and stop trying to force false hope on him? There was nothing they or anyone else could do and that should be an end to it!

Toueesut began to shake his head, making small, negative noises. "Ah, wrong you are being, friend Kusac. Hope one should never give up. Always advances there are being made. Understanding we are of your sad perspective on your state but some hope we are offering." As he spoke, his swarm companions began to trill gently and stir on the sofa.

Startled, he blurted out, "You heard me!"

"Hearing is not the right word. An awareness there is of your mind-music, but it is dulled, grayed with pain and twisted from its customary harmoniousness. What we sense is not like your telepathy."

Suddenly interested, he gestured Toueesut to a chair. "Please, sit down. What does this device do?"

Toueesut danced over to the chair and settled on its edge, waiting till Kusac and Kaid had taken seats nearby.

"Testing it we need to do with you to see if it performs as we hope. A warning it is for you of when you are getting overly angry. Against your neck it will vibrate, giving you more time to calm yourself and be avoiding the terrible pain that such anger causes."

Disappointment surged through him. A warning that he was angry? Was that all?

"Do not be so negative, my friend and Clan Leader," said Toueesut gently, reaching out to touch him on the knee with his gnarled hand. "More we are hoping it will do. Against your skin it will be and constantly monitoring your life rhythms. We have also devised a way to put into it a harmonic receptor and transmitter that if you have patience you can learn to hear. If it works, then it is our hope that you will get something back of your natural ability to know the moods of those around you."

Empathy? They had empathy using harmonics? "How does it work? I won't have anything implanted into me," he said flatly.

"No implanting is necessary," said Toueesut. "That solution was not one we considered, knowing the nature of your mind damage. We believe if you are willing to give us your torc our device can be set into it, then as you are wearing it, it will pick up the harmonics from those around you and translate them into a form you are more fitted to understand." He stopped, an anxious look crossing his face. "You must be understanding no testing of this except on ourselves were we able to do until now when you return from Stronghold. It may be that only the warning will work. Never before have we tried to construct something of this complexity."

"I'll try anything," he said, his hand clenching on the arm of his chair. To have something back of his abilities, even if it was through electronic means, was more than he'd hoped for. It wouldn't ease the mental loneliness, but he would feel less excluded from his own kind, more aware of the constant subliminal messages normal in telepath company.

Toueesut's smile stretched across his face, making his deepset eyes twinkle. "Then your torc we are needing. A hole or two will have to be made and a groove to carry the electronics. If this is unacceptable then perhaps you have a plain torc that we could be using instead of your Clan one."

Reaching up, he removed his torc, hesitating before handing it to the Touiban. It was the one Carrie had bought for him.

"It's my betrothal torc," he said quietly, passing it over to Toueesut. "And very precious to me."

"Great care indeed will be taken with it," said Toueesut earnestly, accepting it. "A love of beautiful things have we, it will not be damaged you have my assurance. Only an hour or two will be required to fit it," said Toueesut, getting up. "Annuur has been generous enough to let us house some of our large equipment in his ship on the village landing pad. There it is that we have been working on this. On your wrist comm we will call you when for testing it is ready."

He nodded, getting to his feet as the rest of Toueesut's swarm surged to theirs. "I'll see you shortly," he said, showing the bright tide of Touibans to the door.

When they'd arrived at the estate, the U'Churians had flown in on the Cabbarrans' own shuttle, carried on the *Profit*. Being quadrupedal, Sholan accommodation would have been uncomfortable for them at best, therefore their craft was permanently parked at the edge of the village landing pad.

Followed by Kaid, he made his way up the floodlit ramp to where Toueesut's swarm brothers were waiting to welcome them.

"We go Speaker. You follow, yes? Come. Come," said one, slightly smaller than the other five.

He glanced at Kaid, surprised by the speech. "Etishu?" he hazarded, looking back to the Touiban. It was rare for anyone but the swarm's Speaker to talk to other species.

Etishu grinned, bushy eyebrows lifting upward, mustache quivering in pleasure. "You remember. Good! Now follow," he said, gesturing into the interior.

They followed them inside the shuttle, turning into the open doorway on their right.

The lab, obviously for Cabbarran use, was lined with workbenches covered with Touiban electronics equipment. Four couches with access steps, as well as several ordinary stools, stood close to the benches. Annuur, on his sloping couch, was working closely with Toueesut who stood beside him. As they entered, Annuur's long head swiveled round to look at them.

"You have arrived, Clan Leader!" said Toueesut. "A moment, then Annuur will have finished."

Annuur's mobile top lip began to twitch as he uttered chittering sounds, then the flat mechanical voice of his translator drowned him out. "Greetings, Kusac Aldatan and Kaid Tallinu. Welcome to our ship you are. Please, sit." Then he turned back to the bench to finish what he was doing before picking the torc up in his mouth.

Executing a graceful turn, the Cabbarran leaped down to the ground and trotted over to him, rising up on his haunches. The broad-clawed, four-fingered hand closed delicately round the torc, taking it from his mouth and offering it to Kusac.

He'd not met the Cabbarran before and the intricacy of the colored tattoos on cheeks and left shoulder almost mesmerized him.

A sudden high-pitched gurgle of sound made him jump and transfer his attention to Annuur's face. Along the narrow jaw, the top lip was curled upward revealing yellow rodentlike teeth.

"Heard much of you I have, Clan Leader," said Annuur's translator. "I forget we not yet met. Tattoos are my rank and sept. Identify us to our U'Churian brothers and each other."

The Cabbarran had been laughing, he realized with surprise as their eyes met. "I meant no insult," he murmured automatically, the habits of his training in AlRel taking over. "I was admiring them."

Annuur glanced down at his shoulder before looking back at him. "They please me," he said. "Not everyone commands this artist." He gestured toward Kusac. "Please bend down. Your tallness makes fitting of this difficult."

He lowered his head, bending forward so the Cabbarran could twist his torc into place. He flinched as something nicked the back of his neck.

"Apologies," said Annuur, settling the torc. "My claw has sharpness from working the metal. Sit up now you can."

He sat up, rubbing his neck under the excuse of rearranging the torc. Whatever it was that had nicked him, it had stung.

"How feels it friend Kusac?" asked Toueesut, joining them. "No discomfort should you be feeling from the inside because of the work we have done."

"It feels fine," he said, stretching and twisting his neck to be sure. "Do I need to take it off when bathing?"

"Is waterproof," said Annuur, looking up at him. "You keep on all time now."

"How does it work?" he asked. "I don't feel any difference." He felt disappointment that he didn't. Not that he'd had any preconceived ideas as to how it would feel.

"Works automatically," said Annuur. "Toueesut, test harmonics now."

Toueesut looked toward the door and began to utter trilling sounds in his own language. Moments later, his swarm companions came dancing in to join him, each one of them whistling and chirping in a tune that wove its way harmoniously between those of the others.

Puzzled, he sat there, unfocusing his eyes to prevent the nausea as he watched the Touibans encircling their Speaker.

He shook his head. "Nothing."

The sound increased in pitch slightly till suddenly he could *feel* it penetrating his flesh and traveling into the bones of his skull. He yelped with the shock and the intensity of it, clapping his hands to his temples and pressing them hard in an effort to stop the vibration.

Immediately the Touibans fell silent until he took his hands away, then they began again, at a lower pitch.

"Stop!" he said, putting his hands back. "It's too much!"

A single sharp note from Toueesut then the sounds stopped raggedly, creating a dissonance he'd never heard from the Touibans before. All but Toueesut fled the room.

"A multitude of apologies, Clan Leader," said Toueesut, face creased in concern as he skittered over to him, wringing his hands. "Higher than we thought had the harmonies to be created for you to hear them the first time. Are you all right?"

"I'm fine," he said, ignoring the faint throbbing in his temples as he rubbed his eyes and dropped his jaw a few times to equalize the pressure in his ears and nose. He felt a nudging against his leg and looked down to find Annuur holding up a sealed cup with a drinking spout.

"Drink," the Cabbarran said, offering it to him.

He took it, taking a long sip of the water before handing it back. "Thank you."

"Headache will go in few minutes. Drug is quick. Works well for us, should be safe for you."

He stared at Annuur. "You gave me a drug?" Then he felt a faint warning tingle where the torc touched his neck. Shocked, he immediately put his hand to it, feeling the torc's faint vibration stop as he broke its contact with his neck. He looked sharply from Toueesut to Annuur, suddenly aware of their amusement and realized that he'd been set up.

"You did that on purpose," he accused them, but the anger had gone.

With the same gurgling sound of laughter, Annuur stretched up to put the drink back on the workbench.

Toueesut let out a veritable song of pleasure and began to flit between his Cabbarran colleague and Kusac, hands caressing them both fleetingly.

"It is working! By all that is holy it is working, friend Kusac!" He stopped dead in front of Kaid, forcibly taking hold of both his hands. "Is it not great what we have done today?"

"Wonderful," said Kaid, grinning at Kusac.

"Was analgesic in drink," said Annuur, "but from your medic, not ours. Not risking interfering with your medication are we. Headache was expected. Now you know what torc does."

"It is vibrating at the first sign of elevated emotions to give you early warning," said Toueesut, letting Kaid go to come and stand in front of him. Standing on tiptoe, he reached out to touch Kusac's forehead. "Harmonics of mental activity it picks up and transmits direct to your head. You will have to work out yourself how you hear and feel the different emotions. Not all species will sound the same so is learning process that may take some time."

"It doesn't work like the Prime punishment collars, does it?" he asked, putting his hand up to grasp his torc again as he looked from Annuur to Toueesut.

"It does nothing but warn," said Annuur, dipping toward him the crest of stiff hair that grew from between his ears to his shoulders. "Wear it or take it off as you wish. Ignore it also. It does nothing to you but inform."

He nodded, reassured by the serious looks on their faces. As he released it, he became aware of a faint sound and turned his head trying to locate the source.

"Is harmonics," said Toueesut quietly. "The sound you are hearing is our concern. Knowing we both are of the punishment collars and what they did to you. Soon you will recognize a different sound for each emotion around you, and each species."

"I don't know that I'm going to be comfortable with this," he said, folding his ears down instinctively even though he knew it wouldn't stop the sound.

"Removed can be that function if you wish," said Annuur. "Try for a week first. Is new, takes getting used to."

"Is like the mind-music we hear all the time," added Toueesut.

"Does every species have this mind-music?" he asked.

"Every one but not all are harmonious, just as not all individuals are. Some are dark and you wish them far from you so you need not be listening to their dissonance."

Annuur dropped down onto all fours, crouching low to the ground, his crest of hair now lying flat. "Go now you must. Tiring this was. Time to rest."

He felt Kaid's hand close round his arm.

"We need to be off, too," Kaid said. "Thank you for your help."

He slid off the stool. "Thank you both. I appreciate what you've done for me."

CHAPTER 11

Shola, Nezule Estate, Zhal-Vartra, 15th day (July)

THEY were directed to the landing area outside the Warrior Clan's large training center. Waiting to greet them was Rhayfso, Guild Master of the Warriors and Clan Leader Naraan.

"Well come to our estate, Clan Leaders Kusac and Kaid," said Naraan, holding his hand out in greeting. "Your people arrived here yesterday. They're out on the exercise field with our charges." He gestured to two attendants to pick up their luggage. "Your belongings will be taken to your quarters."

He accepted, finding his forearm grasped just beyond his bonding bracelet: he returned the gesture, repeating it with Master Rhayfso.

"Good to see you again," said Rhayfso as they began to walk toward the entrance. "Sensible decision of yours to get involved with our guests, Kusac. If you don't pick yourself up and get back into the saddle immediately after falling off a riding beast, you lose your confidence. Though I heard that you did meet with some decent Primes on their ship as soon as they discovered what was happening."

"The Valtegan physician was pleasant enough," he said, trying not to focus on the change in the sound he heard in his head.

"I thought you only met the one Valtegan—that priest." Rhayfso glanced sideways at him.

"It's not as easy for us to see them as two distinct species, Master Rhayfso," said Kaid. "You have to appreciate that our experience of the Primes were as beings in armored encounter suits who kept us confined as if we were captives."

"Well, we got a Prime or two here with their Valtegan hatchlings," grunted the Master. "There's no confusing the two, take my word for it!"

They passed through the high double doors into an entry hall dominated by a wide staircase. The shade and coolness was welcome after the heat outside.

"Oh? Who's here?" asked Kaid as they followed Naraan toward the archway leading out to an open courtyard.

"Prince Zsurtul and his Companion as well as some Court Adviser."

"The prince is here?" asked Kaid, surprised.

"Seems he and his father want him to be given the same training as the hatchlings," said Naraan. "They've been here a couple of days now, and we've been keeping them busy learning team games till your people arrived." He looked at Kaid as they stepped out into the large grassy training area. "I don't know where they've kept these younglings till now, but they've no idea of how to mix with other people, let alone each other."

"They're a competitive species," murmured Kaid, looking over at the group of thirty or so youths running after a large ball that was being passed from person to person. The three paler-skinned Primes stood out starkly even amid their own kind. "Has there been any trouble between them and our people?" he asked as they stopped to watch.

"None. Observing them today has reminded me of my own sons when they were no more than kitlings. They were damned curious about everything!"

"The fact we were furred caused them great interest," said Naraan. "They kept wanting to touch and stroke the students assigned to look after them."

"Probably measuring us up for floor coverings," muttered Kusac, watching to see how the others would react to his comment. At this distance, leaving aside the green skin, they resembled Humans too closely for his peace of mind.

Naraan looked shocked while Rhaysfo laughed and slapped him jovially on the back. "Good to see you've not lost your sense of humor," he said. "You'll be wanting to join your people. I'll let you get on with it."

They walked over the earth track that circled the exercise field and headed across the sun-bleached grass to the group of Primes.

"Prince Zsurtul was responsible for freeing us," said Kaid quietly. "Remember that when you meet him."

He looked sideways at Kaid. "You escaped, he didn't free you."

"He had persuaded the Commander to release us that day and was coming to escort us to the *Profit* when we escaped," replied Kaid, coming to a halt. "He was also responsible for Carrie being returned to us, and you being discovered. We owe him a lot, Kusac. Try to be open-minded when you meet him."

"You don't ask a lot, do you?" he murmured.

A command rang out and the game suddenly stopped. Confusion ensued for several minutes, with more raised voices as the hatchlings ran about every which way before finally assembling in a ragged line in front of four black-clad Sholans. Off to one side they could now see a lone Prime standing watching.

Kaid sighed. "Well, it's a start I suppose."

"Brother Kaid, Brother Kusac," said Khy, leaving the lineup to step forward and salute them.

"At ease," said Kaid, touching his clenched right fist to his left shoulder in return.

Kusac did the same.

"Initial assessment?" Kaid asked.

"They're like nothing I've ever come across before," said Khy, standing easy. "We reckon they've been kept segregated from the rest of their society. They're like playful kitlings exploring the world for the first time. Friendly, curious, willing to cooperate. I can't believe this is their specialized Warrior caste."

"What are you feeding them?" asked Kusac. "Raw meat?"

"No. We were told they'd be easier to handle on a cooked diet. Can it really make all that difference to them?"

"It can," said Kusac, stepping past him to look at the line of twenty-one young alien males dressed like Humans in summer shirts and shorts, and wearing soft protective footwear. He shuddered and turned back to look at Kaid and Khy. "They ate raw meat on Keiss."

Kaid nodded. "Anything else?"

"They're fast, unbelievably fast," Khy said. "Both at learning and moving. And almost as strong as us, though they're not fully grown yet."

"Have they had their medicals yet?" asked Kaid.

Khy jerked an ear in the direction of the lone adult Prime.

"That one, Seniormost Aide J'kuqui, won't allow it," he said quietly. "Says they're here to be trained, not medically examined, even when we told him why we needed medical data on them."

"Then I suggest we talk to Prince Zsurtul about it," said Kaid, strolling over to where the other three Brothers stood in front of the young Primes.

Kusac stood his ground, watching. Being in their presence, smelling their scents, made his skin crawl. With their pallid green skins they reminded him of the Valtegans he and Carrie had met on Keiss. Against his neck, his torc began to vibrate gently. His anger peaked briefly, making the warning vibration rise to the level of discomfort before it died down. Why was he behaving like the Valtegans, letting hate and fear dominate his rational mind? Was he no better than them?

He took a minute or two to calm his thoughts, then slowly walked over to join Kaid.

His sword-brother was talking to one of the young ones—one with a skin the color of the sand—and an adult male of the same coloring.

"You forget that you're my aide, J'kuqui," the sand-colored one was saying calmly. "I've told you what to do."

"Enlightened One," began the other, but Kaid cut him short.

"You've been given your orders, J'kuqui," he said crisply. "Don't presume to question your Prince in front of these trainees. You weaken his authority. Get those medicals set up for this afternoon."

Stiffly inclining his head, the aide left.

"Thank you, Kaid," said Zsurtul, casting a curious look at him. "I wasn't aware of the problem."

"Still treating you like a kitling," said Kaid.

Zsurtul grinned. "Hatchling," he said. "And yes."

Kaid gestured to the others. "Back in line, Zsurtul. The hard work starts now."

Zsurtul opened his mouth, then hesitated before saying, "Yes, sir."

"That's the Emperor's son?" Kusac asked Kaid. "He's not like any Valtegan I've seen before."

"He's a Prime," said Kaid. "Rezac and Zashou were responsible for making many of the next generation of Valtegans sterile. They had to use what breeding stock they had to survive. Many of them have drones in their ancestry."

"I thought the drones were infertile by definition."

"They were hatched that way by adjusting the temperature of their eggs," said Kaid. "The others, they're from M'zullian stock like those you met on Keiss."

"Paler," he said. "And nothing like the temperament of those on Keiss."

"Now you're beginning to see for yourself the differences I spoke about."

He grunted noncommittally as they strolled over to stand in front of their new recruits.

Stronghold, Zhal-Vartra, 17th day (July)

Sighing, Lijou began to stir on his meditation mat. This was the fifth night in a row he'd come here hoping to find Vartra in His realm, but each time, he'd found the door with its carved triple spiral closed. The braziers flickered, casting giant shadows across the pillars and ceiling high above him. A faint sound, accompanied by the scent of nung blossom, drew his attention and he froze, looking round the temple. He could sense no one, but that meant nothing these days. As for the scent, five days ago, nung blossoms had been placed in vases on the floor at each corner of Vartra's tomb.

Looking around, he saw nothing but the flickering of his own shadow and the flames from the braziers. He thought he caught sight of a slight movement by the statue of the God and looked there again, holding his breath, afraid he'd been right. He stared at it for perhaps two minutes before allowing himself to relax. Then he saw the reflected light from the crystal eyes of the God blink out and reappear.

Anger rose in him, lifting his hair, and beneath the long black robe, the pelt across his shoulders and back began to rise. Why should he allow himself to be intimidated like this every time the God decided to call on him?

"Don't play with me, Vartra," he said quietly. "I know you're there. I tried to reach you again, but I didn't know the date in your time I was there."

A mist seemed to form around the statue, blurring its outlines. Then it was as if the statue stood up and stepped off the dais to walk toward him, shrinking in size as it advanced until it was the height of a normal male.

"I wondered how long it would take for you to lose your fear, Lijou," Vartra said, stopping in front of him. "Fear can paralyze the mind, make thinking impossible."

Lijou, heart beating wildly, looked up at Him. He was dressed as was the statue, in a tunic of gray, the sword harness crossing His chest, held in by the broad leather belt that circled His waist.

"Why did you tell me to come to you when you knew I couldn't possibly do it?"

Vartra's mouth widened slightly in an almost Human smile. "To make you indignant," He said softly as He reached down and took hold of Lijou's arm. "Come, show me this tomb of mine. I want to see if they carried out my wishes."

Lijou stumbled as he was drawn to his feet, but the Entity's hand was there, supporting him.

He was left holding onto a pillar as Vartra slowly paced around the sarcophagus before coming to a stop in front of the panel showing the first Triads and Guilds. He ran his hand across the carvings, stopping just below where His image stood amid the first Triads.

A faint click echoed round the temple and, curious, Lijou stepped forward just in time to see a small drawer slide slowly out of the side of the sarcophagus.

"Ah, they did well." There was a purr of pleasure underlying His voice as he picked up the book that had been concealed within. A touch on the drawer, and it slid slowly back into the sarcophagus.

Lijou reached out to run his own fingers across the carving, trying to find the outline of the concealed compartment but he could feel nothing.

"You need to know what to look for," said Vartra. "In this light you can clearly see the crystals, They're arranged in groups of three."

"I see them," said Lijou.

"Look closer. Find the Brotherhood sigil."

Lijou bent down, running his fingers slowly around the area circumscribed by the three crystals until at last he found the symbol concealed among the grass and rocks beneath the feet of the figures. He pressed it and once more heard the click as the drawer began to open.

"There are several of them," said Vartra as the drawer slid shut again. "Each one contains something that may be of use to you. Look for them only when you have a need."

Lijou nodded. "The book. What's in it?"

"This contains our knowledge of the Valtegans, their weaknesses and strengths. Before the Cataclysm, several were taken prisoner and brought here for study—and experimentation. We had to find out how to read their minds, how our telepaths could influence them from a distance without exposing themselves to the risk of capture. We were fighting for our survival, we couldn't afford to be ethical."

"La'quo. Did You know about its effect on them?" demanded Lijou.

Vartra held out the book. "What we discovered is in there," He said. "Don't view us too harshly for what we did, we've already been judged. Instead, give it to those it can help in your fight against the Valtegans."

Lijou took the slim volume from Him, clutching it tightly against his chest as the Entity turned away from him and reached out to touch His tomb again.

Silently the heavy lid began to pivot to one side, exposing the body lying within. Vartra remained motionless until Lijou, easing the stiffness in his limbs, drew His attention back to the here and now. He turned away, looking again at the priest. "The Brotherhood needs to take part of Me with it to Haven," He said. "Then I can walk realms that no Entity of Shola has ever traveled."

Lijou shut his eyes briefly, shuddering at the thought.

"You, and only you, must remove My head and have it concealed within the Shrine on Haven."

Lijou moaned softly. "I knew you were going to say that."

When there was no reply, he opened his eyes. He was alone with the body and the open tomb.

Valsgarth Estate, Zhal-Vartra, 18th day (July)

Kaid was in the den reviewing the latest training reports on the gene-altered telepaths when Vanna's call came through.

"We've got a problem," she said. "I need you here at the hospital."

"I thought you were on leave now," he said. "Your cub's due any time."

"I am," she said. "I still need you here now, please."

"It's not Kusac, is it?" he asked, suddenly afraid.

"Nothing to do with him," she replied. "We need to talk and I don't know how secure this line is."

"On my way," he said, getting up.

He passed Jeran and Giyesh sitting outside her office. Nodding to them, he rapped on Vanna's door then went in.

"Now maybe I'll get some answers," said Tirak.

"What's wrong?" asked Kaid, taking the seat by her desk. "I thought you were still out on the island training," he said to the U'Churian.

"We were, until Giyesh told me she was pregnant," Tirak said grimly. "And by Jeran."

"What? That's not . . ." he stopped, well aware that the same had been said about his people's Links with the Humans.

"She is," said Vanna. "But that's not the best bit. I ran some other tests. Turns out that although we're not genetically compatible with the U'Churians, we come from the same stock, Kaid."

"How? How can our species possibly be related?"

"More than related, we share some of the same DNA, way back in the early history of our species."

"How far back?" Kaid asked, trying to take in the enormity of her findings.

"Several thousand years."

Kaid focused on the more immediate problem. "I see, but we're not capable of mating and bearing each other's cubs?"

"No. This isn't a natural conception."

"Have you asked them how it happened?" He looked back at Tirak.

"Repeatedly," growled Tirak. "They won't tell us."

"Could anyone here have helped them?"

"Only me and I didn't do it," said Vanna.

"What about your medics?" he said to Tirak. "Could they do it? Could Mrowbay?"

"No. Your medical science is more advanced than ours. Learning from you is part of our trade deals."

He thought furiously. Who could have helped them? Abruptly, he got to his feet. "Give me half an hour," he said. "I think I might know how it was done. Meanwhile, get in touch with Master Konis and tell him what you've found out. If you're right, the implications of this are going to hit both our species at the very foundations."

He went back outside to Jeran and Giyesh. "Come with me," he said. "We're going to see someone about a cub."

As he headed out into the street, he reached mentally for Zashou, tying to locate her. He found her at the training center mess.

"I don't see what the fuss is about," said Jeran. "This is no one's business but ours."

"As far as I'm concerned, it is. You can face the consequences on your own. However, there's the small matter of who helped you, and how she did it."

"They'd recalled me Home to take a mate, Kaid," said Giyesh, trying to keep pace with him. "What Jeran and I wanted didn't matter to our Matriarch."

He glanced at her. "I don't think you'll need to worry about it for much longer," he said. "I think your Matriarch is going to have larger concerns on her mind soon."

"What concerns?" asked Jeran.

"Patience," he said. "I want to find out what Zashou did."

"We never said it was Zashou," said Giyesh, grinding to a halt.

"Didn't have to," said Kaid, turning back to look at her. "Only she and Rezac have the ability to do this, since you didn't get help from Vanna."

Stronghold, the same day

"Governor Nesul says when the new allocations come around in two months' time, he'll make sure you get your own funds," said Konis, speaking from his office in the Palace. "To ask Raiban to return a portion even of the last half-year's allocation would only inflame the situation between the two of you to no purpose."

"Meanwhile, we're being starved of funds," said Lijou. "I don't mean to sound ungrateful, Konis, but our situation is desperate."

"Is this line secure?" asked the Clan Lord, eye ridges meeting briefly.

Lijou smiled briefly. "Your office comm is, Konis. We make sure of that on a regular basis. You can speak freely."

Konis raised a sardonic eye ridge before continuing. "Raiban has been asked to submit accounts and an explanation of where the funds are going. Given the current situation, it's sensible to do a review to see if extra funds are needed. Confidentially, Nesul says he'll put what contracts he can your way in the meantime. At least you have the Rryuk contract to tide you over as well."

"Thank him for us, Konis. His gesture is greatly appreciated."

"How're Kha'Qwa and Chay'Dah? Doing well, I hope."

"They're doing well, Konis," he said, mouth opening in a slow smile. "Chay'Dah is more hard work than I imagined, but the joy he's already brought us . . ." He laughed gently. "I must sound like a fool to you."

"Not in the least," said Konis with a matching smile. "I know exactly how you feel. I'll tell you now since we plan to announce it to our family tonight. Rhyasha and I are expecting twins."

"Twins? Many congratulations, Konis!" said Lijou. "And we thought one was hard work!"

Konis laughed. "You have a nurse, surely."

"Noni wouldn't let us be without one. It's her assistant Teusi's mother. But we like to do as much as we can ourselves."

"So did we, but when you have the responsibilities we have, it's necessary to have the help. Give Kha'Qwa and your son our warm thoughts, Lijou."

"I will, and thank you again for interceding for us, Konis. We've no wish to make an issue out of this unless Raiban does."

The call over, Lijou switched his comm link off and sat back in his chair, his eyes going automatically to the wooden box that sat on the shelf at the opposite side of the room. He shuddered at the memory of what he still considered a desecration despite the fact he was following Vartra's orders. When he'd returned to the temple with Yaszho, his aide had offered to do the deed for him but he'd refused. He couldn't ask others to do what he balked at.

Even now, a Shrine was being constructed on Haven to house the relic, but it would be some time before it was ready. Until then, Vartra's head and he would continue to share his office. His wrist comm buzzed gently, reminding him he had an appointment with Sister Jiosha, who would lead the Shrine. It was with relief that he got to his feet and left.

Aldatan Estate, later the same day

Konis' office was in the main Aldatan house on the first floor. It was in his capacity as head of Alien Relations that they'd come to see him.

He listened in silence to what they had to say, then read the comp pad Kaid handed him.

"Just let me get this straight," he said, looking at each of them again from his side of the desk. "Giyesh is pregnant and you're responsible, Zashou?"

Zashou confirmed with a brief nod of her head. "They asked for my help, and I couldn't refuse them," she said. "They so obviously cared for each other."

"How, in Vartra's name? I still don't understand how you did it!"

"How do you decide to speak mentally on a private level to your mate?" she countered. "If you had the Talent to do what we did, I could show you, but tell you?" She shook her head.

Konis sighed. "Point taken."

"I'm glad you understand, because by Kathan's beard, I still don't," said Tirak with a rumble of anger.

"Cell manipulation," said Kaid. "Zashou and Rezac used this Talent of hers to make the eggs of the Valtegan females in the City of Light sterile. That's why the Primes are so different from the Valtegans. She used a reverse technique on Giyesh and Jeran."

"I can't tell that to the elders expecting me to send Giyesh Home for her first mating!"

"There is a way out," said Kaid. "You're carrying a cub, too, aren't you, Zashou? It's Kris', isn't it? You did the same for yourself."

Braids chiming as her pelt started to rise, Zashou turned her cool amber gaze on him. "You had no right to read me," she said, ears folding in anger.

"I didn't," he said. "I can tell. It's one of my gifts." He looked back to the Clan Lord, "Master Konis, everyone knows Sholan females are far from rational when carrying cubs," he said quietly. "We offer our sincere apologies to the Rryuk Matriarch, offer whatever bride price they demand—within reason—and explain that this is a Talent Zashou didn't know she possessed, one of the strange ones that sometimes emerge briefly when our female telepaths are carrying a hybrid cub."

Konis regarded him thoughtfully. "It might work at that," he said. "There's a lot at stake here, Kaid. We can't afford to have this become an inter-species incident."

"I take it Father Lijou hasn't mentioned that we have our own contracts with the Rryuk family. The Brotherhood can't afford this to escalate either."

"I'm aware of them, Kaid," said Konis uncomfortably. "Sometimes I feel as if I'm an undercover Brother because of the amount of information I'm privy to."

"You joined our hunt, Master Konis," Kaid said quietly. "If you give the Matriarch the information proving our common ancestry at the same time, then it may divert her from Giyesh's news."

"It'll certainly do that," said Konis dryly. "Captain Tirak, given you can see why we can't be candid about what really happened, are you willing to present this reason to your elders?"

"Don't see I have much option," he muttered. "But as her uncle, I insist on a marriage between them! Her honor's been compromised enough. If they don't accept the explanation, she could be disowned, cast out of the Family."

"I've offered," interrupted Jeran, speaking for the first time. "You see if you can make her accept me, I can't."

"She'll do it if she wishes to remain here," said Kaid sternly, looking over at Giyesh. "In asking Zashou to help you, you knew you were abusing our Clan's hospitality, risking our reputation to get what you wanted. Now it's time for you to repay the debt. If you and Jeran don't take out a bonding contract, you could jeopardize our contracts with your people."

"I think a three-year contract should be sufficient," said Konis. "Have we your agreement on this, Giyesh?"

The young U'Churian female scowled angrily before slumping down in her chair. "Agreed," she muttered.

Kaid checked the time on his wrist comm. "If we leave now, we can catch the registrar in Valsgarth before the office closes. Unless you still need us, Master Konis?"

Konis shook his head, sighing inwardly with relief. "Go. I'll see Vanna's findings are passed to Councillor Rhuha with copies for our Ambassador on Home to present to their ruling council. When you contact your elders, Captain Tirak, you can mention that we'll be sending them in the next day or two. And, Zashou, this must never happen again. I'll have to report it to the Telepath Guild for . . ."

"No," interrupted Kaid as they got to their feet. "We're En'Shalla, Master Konis, not subject to anyone but Father Lijou. If this becomes common knowledge, then everyone will know they're from the past. You know we can't afford that to come out. She won't do it again without official sanction, will you, Zashou?"

Yet another principle bent out of true, Konis thought, while admitting to himself Kaid was right.

"I don't know if I could do it again," she said frankly. "It took more energy than I thought. If it hadn't been for . . ."

Don't complicate matters, sent Kaid. *I know you can only do it when you're pairing. Do you want everyone knowing your domestic arrangements? No need for them to know it took your Triad and Kris pairing together to do it.*

Embarrassed, she looked away from Konis. "I couldn't do it again," she said. "Since we were woken, our abilities have lessened considerably. I'm told it has to do with us becoming gene-altered."

Nezule Estate, Zhal-Vartra, 24th day (July)

For the last week, every time he'd turned round, Zsurtul had been there, following him around like some lost cub. He was finding it difficult enough to cope with being in close proximity to the young Prime as it was without this. He'd spoken to Khy about it, and taken a break from training to work with the Warriors for a couple of days, but even then his shadow was there at every opportunity.

He'd been sparring with one of the seniors when Naraan, the Clan Leader called a halt to the bout. Disgruntled, he'd left the gym for the showers only to be called back by Naraan.

"In my office, if you please," said Naraan, gesturing to the door opposite.

Wiping the sweat from his body, Kusac followed him through the main office into the room beyond. A desk stood in one corner, but it was to the less formal seating Naraan directed him.

"If you don't ease off, Kusac, I won't let you work with my people," he said, sitting down. "I rarely have to stop a sparring session because of excessive force, but you were using Myar as a punching bag."

"I was fighting fairly," he said, surprised by the accusation.

"That's my point. You're not sparring, you're fighting, and it has to stop now. There have been too many injuries. Our training techniques aren't as advanced as the Brotherhood's. Not even our seniors are able to stand up effectively against you. Just what's your problem?"

"I don't know what you're talking about," he said stiffly. "I'm pulling my punches and kicks. Myar was hitting me hard enough."

"Myar's a senior. He can't afford to lose face by appearing outclassed in front of the others, none of the seniors can. These are supposed to be practice sessions, nothing more. You know your skills are superior. What can you possibly gain by beating him into the ground?"

"It was only a friendly match," he said, aware of the torc beginning to vibrate gently. "I wasn't aware I was using undue force. I kept pace with Myar, using more advanced moves only when he did."

"You aren't even aware of what you're doing, are you?" Naraan said, getting up. "I'm sorry, Kusac, but until you can learn some self-control, I don't want you working out with my people again. Stay with your own."

Realizing he'd been dismissed, he got to his feet. He could feel the vibration increasing and was aware his pelt was beginning to rise. "If that's what you wish," he said, turning on his heel and heading for the door as he tried to damp his anger.

In the corridor, he collided with Zsurtul. Grabbing the young Prime by the front of his tunic, he pushed him aside. "Stop following me around," he snarled. "Haven't you got something better to do? And in future, stay out of the gym when I'm sparring!"

Pain flickered briefly down his spine, making him stagger as the strength left his legs. Sucking in air, he leaned against the wall, pushing the anger back, frantically reciting the first litany that came to mind in an effort to calm himself. He refused to collapse here in the middle of the corridor in front of a Valtegan!

"Is something wrong? Can I get help?" asked Zsurtul quietly.

"No," he snarled, pushing himself away from the wall and staggering down the corridor. "Just stay out of my way!"

Valsgarth Estate, the same day

"I'm sorry I had to disturb you on your Link day, Kaid, but you did say to contact you immediately if we had problems with Kusac," said Khy.

"That's all right," said Kaid. "You did the right thing by calling me. It's my brother's Triad bonding tomorrow, he'll be over here for that. I'll have a talk with Kusac then."

"As Jayza said, it would be so much easier if he could read him," murmured Khy.

Kaid didn't bother answering. "How's he been with our M'zullians?"

"He's coping, but then he only takes one session a day and Jayza's there to help. I don't feel comfortable leaving him alone with them. He's only doing pattern exercises, no combat."

"How's our princeling doing? Have you sent his mistress packing back to the embassy yet? And what about that aide?"

"Zsurtul reluctantly agreed that the Warrior Clan estate wasn't an appropriate place for a female of such nice sensibilities as she has," Khy grinned. "As for the aide, he sent him packing himself, with his mistress. He's as game as any of them, but he lacks their potential depth of aggression. You've been getting my reports, haven't you? I hope we never have to fight them, Kaid. They're almost faster than the eye can follow, and have the ability to consciously trigger whatever extra hormones or pseudo-hormones they need. Total bio feedback. One of them managed to break his leg yesterday. Believe it or not, he was climbing a tree of all things! Came crashing down through the branches. It wasn't a clean break, and he was in a great deal of pain when we got to him, but then his eyes just glazed over and he became very calm. When they tested him in the infirmary, he had levels of natural endorphins that were almost off the scale. I hope we're doing the right thing by training them."

"The idea is that by exposing them to us, hopefully they'll see us as friendly, not a threat. Are they enjoying themselves? You're implementing the entertainment program as well, aren't you? It's important they see the other side of us."

"I'd say they're enjoying themselves. They've got an insatiable capacity for learning and training—can't get enough of it. They watch the entertainment channels each evening—they like the factual programs about other species and some of the Terran ones about wildlife on their world. Storytelling hour is one of their favorites too. In fact it was Zsurtul who asked if we could visit a theater. I'm hoping to arrange it for next week if you've no objections."

"None. It sounds like they're doing well," he said, relieved that his carefully worked out choice of programs was proving popular with the younglings.

"We're also keeping up the team games, and individual sporting activities to build an appreciation of both teamwork and individual attainment."

"But," encouraged Kaid.

Khy grinned, ears flicking in recognition of being caught. "Our prince has a bad case of hero worship."

"Kusac."

"You guessed. That's causing problems. I've spoken to Zsurtul about it but he says he's not following him around, only doing what was agreed—observing life outside their training camp. He says he respects Kusac as a Warrior who suffered much and survived it with dignity."

"Zsurtul's got too much of the Intellectual in him," muttered Kaid. "The Primes are right, they need the leavening of the Warriors, and Warriors need the intelligence of the Intellectuals to prevent them becoming like the M'zullians. I'll come back with Kusac," he said, deciding he needed to see for himself what was happening. "Until the day after tomorrow, Khy."

"Until then, Kaid."

Kaid switched off his comm and rejoined Carrie on the sofa. She held out a plate of cut meats to him as he sat down beside her.

"You better have some more before I finish them all," she said. "What do we do about Kusac?"

"There's nothing you can do, Dzinae," he said, spearing a couple of chunks with his claw tips and popping them in his mouth. He climbed back to his place beside her, lying down with his head on her lap. As soon as they touched, the magic of their Link flowed through him again, sensitizing his body to hers, making it difficult for him to focus on anything but her.

"When I started training Kusac, T'Chebbi accused me of working him too hard, of trying to prove I hadn't lost my edge because of what Fyak and Ghezu did to me," he said quietly. "I didn't think I was, then. But Kusac's doing exactly that now, only it's himself he's driving too hard."

"What changed you?" she asked, putting the plate down so she could stroke between his ears.

He turned his head and looked up at her. "Two things. Deciding to make Kusac my sword-brother was the first. I didn't want to do it but he left me no choice."

"Why didn't you?"

He took hold of her hand, turning it so he could run his tongue across her palm. "You know the answer, Carrie. Because I love him, just as I love you."

"I don't understand why that was a problem."

"It wouldn't have been, if he hadn't been brought up a telepath. I knew I couldn't hide what I feel if we took the oath. You've no idea how hard I tried to put him off the idea."

"I have. Don't forget I shared his experiences, particularly the execution detail you took him on," she said dryly.

"It was necessary," he said, remembering how T'Chebbi, who'd been with Carrie at the time, had torn a strip off him for taking Kusac on that duty. "He needed to be able to kill our own people, or the U'Churians, if it came to it, and that was the only way I knew how to harden him. Anyway," he said, letting his thumb rub gently across her palm, "he stuck with the training, and anything else I could throw at him. In the end, I realized I wanted him as a sword-brother, regardless of the risks. By that time, I'd made sure he knew what it entailed, and when we did take the oath, I asked only for his loyalty. I gave him what you already had, myself. I opened my mind to him, expecting only a brief mental contact as is common when two empathic Brothers take the oath, only it didn't quite work like that."

"That's why you had T'Chebbi bring me to the Retreat. You were afraid we'd make a full three-way Link."

"Of that, and that a Link compulsion like we have now would be generated between us. And I was right." He looked away from her, aware of the complex emotions he was experiencing as he remembered that day. He wasn't sure even he understood exactly what he felt for Kusac.

She nodded. "I remember. Before I passed out, I was drawn to T'Chebbi as if we were lovers. Kusac said the same happened between you and him, but he said you didn't love him, that it was me you loved."

"He meant I'm in love with you, not him. Which is true," he murmured.

"Why are you telling me all this now?" she asked after a moment.

"Becoming sword-brothers is a time of training and testing for yourself, and your partner, to find out what you can each bring to the relationship, what you're prepared to give," said Kaid, his hand tightening round hers as he looked up at her again. "Garras and I had been sword-brothers. He was the senior partner, he asked me. We shared a minor Link because of the Talent I didn't know I had. We were close—closer than lovers, because our lives depended on each other—but we never actually became lovers. The need to ask for more never came for either of us. I love Kusac as my sword-brother, as a Triad mate, and because I love you."

She regarded him steadily, refusing to read him, waiting for him to tell her what was in his mind.

"I think he's losing his grip, Carrie, like the telepaths in Rezac's time. He can't and won't turn to you for help, nor to T'Chebbi, because of what happened when he was with you on Haven, and with T'Chebbi here. As his sword-brother, it's my place to be there for him, at Nezule."

"I wouldn't expect less of you," she said quietly, taking her hand from his and stroking his head again. "You should have told me sooner what happened to T'Chebbi. I'd have understood better what was happening to him. I wish there was something I could do to help him."

He pushed himself up on his elbow, drawing her one-handedly down beside him. "I love you," he said, leaning forward to kiss her, his hand pushing her robe aside so he could touch her belly. Beneath his fingers, he felt a gentle fluttering as their cub moved.

Slowly he broke the kiss, moving down until he could lay his cheek against her, waiting to feel the movement again. When it had passed, eyes shining, he lifted his head, beginning to lick and caress her, his worries for Kusac submerged for now while they were Linked by the magic of this shared time.

the *Couana*, Zhal-S'Asha, 20th day (October)

Kusac muttered, moving fretfully in his uneasy sleep. In the chair by the side of the bed, Banner stirred, getting to his feet and looking toward the door, ears wide, muscles tensed.

With a faint hiss of compressed air, the door slid back, silhouetting Chima. She waited for Banner to join her.

"You'd been gone for so long, I came to check that everything was all right," she said quietly.

Banner grunted disbelievingly. He'd seen her hand on the butt of her pistol. "I'm seeing he sleeps," was all he said.

"What's the message say?" she asked.

"I haven't been cleared to tell you," he said, turning back into the room. "You'll be told at the briefing."

She caught him by the arm. "He told you what was in it?"

He looked at her and when she let him go, he joined her outside in the corridor, closing the door behind him.

"What's important here, Chima? That this mission—whatever it is—succeeds, or that you prove Master Rhyaz right?"

"I'm not out to prove anything, Banner, only to observe and, if necessary, act to prevent a disaster."

"Then like me, you'll know we're on course to the rendezvous and all is going as planned," he said coldly, turning back to the door.

"If he needs you to spend the night with him, he's not coping, Banner. He should step down now as Captain and have you head the mission," she said, her tone equally harsh. "The fact he can't see that proves Master Rhyaz's view."

Banner raised an eye ridge, glad he'd left his uniform off, and reached out to run his fingertips gently across her cheek. "Do you always sleep alone when off duty, Chima?" he asked. "Captain or no, he has the same rights and needs as you and I."

Flattening her ears, she snarled soundlessly at him before stalking off down the corridor to her room, tail swaying in angry arcs.

Grinning, Banner slipped back into the darkened room, locking the door this time with a small device he had in his bag. As Kusac's shadow for the last seven weeks, he knew better than Chima or Master Rhyaz what was happening to him now, and why he needed to be watched. All was going as Master Lijou had said it would.

Valsgarth Estate, Zhal-Vartra, 25th day (July)

The Triad ceremony had gone well, Rezac taking Jo as his life-mate and Zahsou agreeing to become their Third. Their choice had surprised many, not least Jo herself when Rezac had proposed to her several weeks previously. Because they were already a Triad, the three of them had shared the blood-rites, becoming kin to each other.

Though he'd stood with Carrie and Kaid during the ceremony, he'd not felt he was with them or even part of the proceedings. Life was moving on for everyone, except himself. He felt out of place at the festivities in the garden afterward and would have slipped inside the villa for peace if Kaid and Toueesut hadn't found him.

The harmonics from the torc were working overtime, and he found it impossible not to concentrate on the sounds and attempt to understand them in terms of the Touibans' emotions. It was like knowing just enough of an alien language to have an inkling of what they were saying, and it was exhausting.

After half an hour, Kaid took him by the arm and, making their excuses, drew him off to one side where an elderly tree offered shade from the afternoon sun.

"Will you talk to Carrie?" Kaid asked without preamble. "She's hurt that you're keeping your distance."

"I've spoken to her, Kaid," he said, sitting down and leaning back against the trunk of the tree. "And I spent time with Kashini before the nurse took her in out of the sun."

"Carrie's your life-mate, Kusac, the female you fought for the right to marry. Or has all that changed?" Kaid asked, sitting down on the grass beside him.

"She's carrying your cub," he said quietly. "Seeing her pregnant brings back too many memories of what I've lost right now."

Kaid reached for a pack of stim twigs in his belt pocket. Opening the pack, he offered one to Kusac. He accepted it, putting one end in his mouth and biting down on it.

"Do you intend to go on like this, Kusac?" Kaid asked, taking one himself and putting the pack away. "Being a stranger to us?"

"Kaid's right, Kusac," said Kitra, coming round from the other side of the tree. She stopped in front of him, making him squint up against the sun to see her. Crouching down beside him, she wrapped her arms around his chest, hugging him. "I want my brother back," she said. "Nothing seems to touch you but anger these days. You won't let anyone close, not even me."

Startled, his arm automatically went around her, holding her as he used to when she'd been a cub.

"That's not so, kitling," he said, taking the stim twig out of his mouth and letting his chin rest on the top of her head. "You know I care for you, and always will." His eyes caught Kaid's and he saw the sardonic look in them. He held Kitra more tightly, aware he needed this contact with her. He brushed her ear tip with his tongue, making her look up at him, her eyes bright with unshed tears.

"No, don't cry," he said forcefully. "I really am all right, Kitra. I've not stopped loving you. It's just—difficult—for me now to express it. It's like I have to learn to use emotions all over again, but it's beginning to pass. A few weeks more, then I'm sure I'll be through the worst."

A sudden commotion near the house drew their attention. Kitra sat up, her serious expression lightening with a smile. "Vanna's having her cub," she said. "Jack and Garras are taking her to the hospital."

"Exciting times," he murmured, helping his sister get to her feet.

She hesitated, torn between her wish to stay with him and her desire to join in the adult excitement.

He hugged her, his first spontaneous loving gesture in a long time. "Go on, kitling," he said, genuine warmth in his voice. "It'll be your turn soon enough. You should be with them."

She bounced up to kiss him then sped off to the knot of females crowded near the door into the lounge.

"She's a remarkable young female," said Kaid, standing beside him, watching her. "My son is very lucky. If not for her, he would have wasted his life in bitter regret for the family he lost in the massacre at Szurtha. We owe her a great deal."

"Sunlight and midnight," he murmured, forgetting for a moment Kaid was even there. "My sisters are so different, yet they both light up our lives so very much."

Kaid touched his cheek in a familiar gesture, letting his hand fall to his shoulder. "It's sometimes easy for you to forget just how loved *you* are, Kusac," he said quietly. "When you push us away, we can't show you and in turn, you feel isolated. Maybe you've begun to heal at last."

"Maybe," he said, putting the twig back in his mouth, listening to the new tune that had started to vibrate inside his head, wondering what it meant.

Vanna's and Garras' daughter was born three hours later.

"Jikkoh, we're calling her Jikkoh," said Garras when he returned. "Brynne and Keeza are with them now."

"Who's she like?" asked Kitra. "You or Vanna?"

"She's beautiful," said Garras, looking bewildered and elated as he accepted the glass that Dzaka put into his hand. "Small, but then so is Vanna. And she's dark like me."

There was laughter, and congratulations

"Soon be your turn," said Garras quietly, looking to Kaid, but Kusac heard it and moved back to the edge of the group, remembering the circumstances of Kashini's birth. Not in comfort, but on an aircar floor, with only himself and Kaid as inexpert birthers.

He'd heard more. T'Chebbi, the hard, unflappable, ever-vigilant T'Chebbi, was pregnant by Kaid, and neither of them had thought to tell him. That had hurt.

"It's kind of nice to feel a superiority over all these new and soon-to-be fathers," said a voice at his elbow. "No broken nights walking the floor or dirty diapers to change for us."

He looked round to find Banner and Jurrel standing beside him.

"Clan Leader," murmured Jurrel as Banner flicked an ear in greeting.

He looked from one to the other, recognizing them but slightly confused by the sounds he was receiving from the torc.

"Banner's my Companion and sword-brother," said Jurrel.

"Ah. I thought you were with Brynne."

Jurrel grinned. "Now and then, when we need each other."

"You have no cubs?" he asked.

"Nor plans to as yet," confirmed Banner, glancing at Jurrel. "Though Jurrel might, being younger."

"A cub might be nice one day," Jurrel conceded, "but my experiences haven't made the proposition of a three-year bonding contract to any female attractive enough."

"We're heading into town for a drink. Want to come with us?" Banner asked.

"I leave early in the morning for the Nezule estate."

"We don't intend to be late either," said Jurrel. "We've got classes to take tomorrow, and we've an appointment with Master Sorli in the afternoon to discuss training schedules for a new batch of Terran telepaths due in at Chagda Station in a couple of weeks."

"More Terrans?"

"Yes, this time more females, and younger ones. Forty altogether."

"I heard we'd sent teachers to Keiss and Earth to work in the Humans' own centers. Train them there," he said.

"We have. These ones are the last of those agreed on in our original treaty with Earth. I have a feeling they won't voluntarily send any more."

"Are you coming with us?" asked Jurrel.

He'd gone with them, glad to escape from the surfeit of pregnant females in his Clan—even his own mother was expecting cubs, twins no less!—that only served to make him more afraid that the implant had done one last destructive act in making him sterile. It took a great many drinks that night before the edges of his world blurred enough to make them less painful.

Shanagi Space Port, Zhal-Vartra, 26th day (July)

In the early morning heat, the dark surface of the landing field seemed to shimmer as they waited for the door of the alien shuttle to open. Without a joint or seam, the bronze-colored vehicle had an organic look, as if it had grown naturally or were some strange sleeping creature. Ovoid in shape, the outer surface undulated upward from the blunt bow, sweeping back toward the stubby rear end. The sides flared upward, almost to the midsection, revealing the undercarriage before flowing down again toward the stern. Whatever method of propulsion they used, nothing was visible.

"A ray fish," Nesul murmured to himself. "It looks like a ray fish. I hope the heat doesn't distress them."

Surrounded by an honor guard of the Brotherhood and Warriors, the Governor waited on the white carpet beside Ambassador Mrocca of the Cabbarrans for the TeLaxaudin Ambassadorial party to emergence.

Mrocca lowered her haunches to the ground, looking up at the Sholan leader with an expression of amusement on her long, narrow face.

She began to speak, the translator taking over almost immediately. "You think? I think flying creature. Sits on flowers on your world. Not to be worrying, Governor," she said. "Heat will please Ambassador Zeashimis."

"So I'm told," said Nesul, looking down at the smaller being. "But this is excessive heat, even for us." He squinted briefly up at the blazing orb of the sun. "Is Zeashimis a male or a female?" he asked, suddenly realizing he didn't know the gender of the person he was about to greet.

"Neither. They are both."

Nesul shut his eyes briefly. If the holo images were to be believed, this was the strangest of the Alliance species to date. Now he discovered at the last moment they were genderless! Why hadn't his aides picked up on this matter before now?

Mrocca made the sound of laughter. "This information not public. Think of them as male if you prefer. They not travel in female phase."

Relieved that he hadn't been let down after all, he glanced back at the shuttle. A doorway was beginning to appear in the fuselage as the fabric of the craft seemed to part and shrink back. A short gangway emerged and moments later, two bronze spindly-limbed beings, clad only in breechclouts under skirts of thin floating panels of dark blue cloth, emerged holding staffs almost as tall as themselves. Lifting their feet high, with a swaying, rocking gait, they made their way down to the gangway until they stood on the white carpet. They stopped, obviously waiting for the rest of their party.

"Honor guard," said Mrocca. "Staffs are potent energy

weapons. Very nasty." She shook her head, the stiff crest over her shoulders briefly bushing out then settling again.

The Ambassadorial party emerged then, six of them, dressed in different shades of gauzy cloth strips held in at the waist and floating from a band round their necks. Behind them came two more of the strange warriors.

The morning breeze blew their scent toward Nesul. It was strange, alien, unlike anything he'd ever smelled before. He noted the distinctive way they held their arms tucked close to their bodies, elbows bent, the hands drooping forward. Their heads moved constantly, looking not just from one to the other, but around them at the various shuttles and cargo tenders lying in their bays.

As the TeLaxaudin party drew close, the two guards at the front stepped to either side to allow their Ambassadors to meet the Sholan and Cabbaran leaders.

They stopped, forming a small wedge with one standing alone in front of him. Nesul was struck by how small they were, reaching only to mid-chest height. They were almost as small as the Chemerians.

Pulling his thoughts back to the moment, Nesul bowed. "Ambassador Zeashimis. Welcome to Shola. I trust your trip was a pleasant one."

Zeashimis, eyes swirling as he adjusted them to close vision, dipped his smooth oval head to one side, his tiny mandibles clicking softly, hands moving in small, graceful gestures.

Nesul heard a gentle humming that seemed to vibrate the very air around them, then Zeashimis' translator began to speak.

"Arriving better. Grateful voyaging done. Sholans from invitation pleasing be."

Nesul tried not to glance at Mrocca for a better interpretation. "You honor us with your presence," he said, thinking that at least couldn't be misinterpreted. This close, he realized the TeLaxaudin scents were more like perfumes. His nose could pick up at least four distinct ones. "If you would accompany us into the building, we have transport vehicles waiting to escort you to the Governor's Palace."

"Pleasing to us." Then there was a burst of humming that the translator couldn't render into speech.

At a loss, Nesul glanced at Mrocca, only to see the Cabbarran nodding her head. Obviously the speech was directed at her.

Moments later, Mrocca was replying in her own high-pitched chittering language, her translator also remaining silent.

Nesul waited patiently. Here was proof that the Cabbarrans were the only ones capable of fully understanding the TeLaxaudin.

After a minute or two, Mrocca turned to him. "Ambassador wishes to thank you for kind greeting," she said. "With him is one named Kzizysus. Annuur of the Rryuk Family is meeting and transporting him to location on Shola. Telepath estate."

"Excuse me?" Nesul stepped back in sheer surprise, unable to believe what he was hearing.

The situation was resolved by the sound of raised voices and the clatter of hooves repeatedly hitting the hard surface of the landing field. Nesul turned to see a Cabbarran, chased by Sholan guards, galloping toward them.

"This be Annuur," said Mrocca calmly as around them the Brotherhood and the Warriors sprang into a defensive circle. "No need for protection," she said, looking round the circle of armed Sholans.

Nesul waved them back. "Stand down. It seems Annuur's expected," he said as a loud squeal of protest announced Annuur's capture.

As the Brothers and Warriors powered down their weapons and fell back to a wary defensive position, Annuur, held firmly by his belt harness, was escorted in front of Nesul.

"No patience have you," said Mrocca indignantly as Annuur was released. "Wait you should have. Coming in we were."

"Anxious I am to get working," said Annuur, dipping his head to his Ambassador, his crest flat in abject apology. Not for long, though. He raised his head, looking bright-eyed and anxiously toward the TeLaxaudin group. "Captain Tirak waiting for news. Waiting to tell Clan Leader Carrie help arrives."

Singling out the one he wanted, he trotted over to him, rising up onto his haunches.

"Physician Kzizysus. Craft waiting ready. We go now."

"Equipment needing. Unloading now." The TeLaxaudin pointed behind him to where the crew of their shuttle was already unloading a series of solid containers.

Annuur turned to look at Nesul. "Maybe Sholans helping speed up departure," he said hopefully. "Annuur and Kzizysus leave. You get on with official reception then."

Nesul turned to the nearest Sister, raising his eye ridges expressively.

"On it already, sir," she said, activating her throat comm.

"I don't suppose one of you would like to explain what's going on here?" Nesul asked, a rumble of anger in his voice.

Annuur led his TeLaxaudin over to him. "Kzizysus Physician on *Kz'adul*," said the Cabbaran, sitting up again. "He work on Kusac. Try to help after Chy'qui gone."

Kzizysus began to hum. "Experiments continue must here."

Things suddenly became clear as Nesul remembered Konis asking if he could petition the TeLaxaudin Ambassador for help from them for his son.

"Governor Nesul, the handling crew are on their way. If Annuur and Kzizysus would like to go to their vehicle, the luggage will join them in a few minutes," interrupted the Sister.

"We go," said Kzizysus, starting to walk through the reception committee toward the main buildings, Annuur trotting behind.

As they went, two of the Brotherhood followed them.

Nonplussed, Nesul looked back to Zeashimis and his party. "Ah, Ambassador, perhaps now would be a good time for us to leave too. We have a meal set out for you in the Palace. Mrocca was kind enough to advise us on suitable dishes for you."

"Following we will," said Zeashimis, starting to move toward him.

Valsgarth Estate, later the same day

Carrie heard the banging on the front door and looked up at Yashui.

"No one bangs on the door like that, Liegena," she said. "Perhaps it's one of our visitors. Dziosh will see to it."

She got up, handing Kashini over to the nurse. "I'll go anyway," she said. By the time she reached the top of the staircase, Dziosh had already let Tirak in. The U'Churian looked up at her.

"He's here, Carrie," said Tirak, tail swaying in excitement. "Annuur's just called me."

"Who's here?" she asked, coming down. She had never seen the U'Churian acting like this before. He was behaving for all the world like one of the Sholan younglings around the estate.

"We asked Annuur to speak to the TeLaxaudin and ask for help for Kusac. They agreed, and when the Ambassador arrived today, Kzizysus was with him. He thinks he can help."

"What?" She clutched the banister rail for support.

"Kzizysis thinks he can help Kusac."

"Wasn't he the TeLaxaudin on the *Kz'adul*? The one who helped when I shot Kusac's implant?"

Tirak nodded, a gesture he'd picked up from the estate dwellers. "The same. Annuur sent me to fetch you."

"Dziosh, tell T'Chebbi where I am," she said, strengthening the shields between her and Kaid for fear of giving him false hope.

The air was fresh and cool inside the Cabbaran craft, a welcome change after her hot walk through the village's main street. Boxes were still being transferred from the aircar that sat alongside it and she had to dodge around one being towed up the ramp on a grav sled by two of Annuur's sept brothers.

"Apologies," they intoned as Tirak shepherded her round to the right where the living quarters were.

Tirak gestured to the open door and Carrie stepped in, recoiling back instantly in shock.

Grunting in pain, Tirak held her firmly by the elbow. "Annuur, dammit! You could see us coming! Opaque those damned walls! I told you not to leave them on when you've got company! It's perfectly safe, Carrie, just a shock when you aren't expecting it," he said, urging her into the room as Annuur began to apologize.

Cautiously, she stepped back into the room, relieved to find the walls now a uniform neutral beige. Transparent bulkheads? What else had they? Beneath her thin sandals she could feel the woven texture of the vegetable fiber matting that covered the floor. Even as she was automatically assessing her surroundings, her eyes were drawn to Kzizysus, the Cabbarran's exotic companion.

The oval head turned to face her, eyes swirling, neck stretching out as the mandibles began to move.

"Sit," said Annuur, raising himself on his forelegs. Lifting one, he indicated a vacant couch and the deep cushions spread on the floor. "Welcome you are. Sit where you will. Our U'Churian family prefer the cushions."

"Thank you," said Carrie, stepping farther into the pleasantly scented room. She stopped at the cushion nearest the Cabbarran. Unasked, Tirak's hand was there to steady her as she sat down. Hauling over another cushion, he joined her.

A low buzzing that reminded her of the sound of grasshoppers filled the room as Kzizysus began to speak. "She reproduces."

Annuur answered in his own language, his translator remaining silent.

Tirak leaned toward her, his mane of black fur tickling her bare neck. "A visiting TeLaxaudin is rare," he said quietly. "But when they do come, they and the Cabbarrans can spend hours talking between themselves without the translators. They forget we're here."

"Do not, Tirak!" said Annuur, hurt. "Some concepts are not translating for you is all."

"Am I mistaken or is your translator rather more expressive?" asked Carrie, eyeing her host.

Annuur's mobile top lip curled up almost like a mini trunk in appreciation as he began to laugh. "This normal translator. Used inferior one for last mission. Lack of communication sometimes advantage."

"Definitely," Carrie smiled. "What about Kzizysus' translator? Is his the same?" She arched a questioning eyebrow at him.

"Tirak telling you truth. We have ancient dialect that closer to TeLaxaudin speech. Easier translate than any other species. Some words of yours he understands. We translate concepts for him. Now you seated, I will turn off walls. Do not like small spaces," he said firmly, reaching out to press a control on his couch's small console. "Too many there were on *Kz'adul*."

Carrie watched entranced as the walls of the ship gradually seemed to dissolve, revealing the view outside the shuttle. "How did you cope on the *Profit*?" she asked. "Or is that why we weren't allowed down to your avionics level?"

"Only navigation room like this," said Annuur. "I get drinks for you." He got abruptly to his feet, backing down off his sloping couch.

Carrie turned her attention to Kzizysus. "Physician. Tirak tells me you may be able to help my mate, Kusac."

The bronze head nodded once as Kzizysus reached for a morsel of food on the tray beside him. "Perhaps. Implants Primes re-

quested. Large device want, not small. Easy be seen. Small make
we usually." He held his finely boned hand up, indicating a barely
visible gap between two of his three fingers. "Controls for sick
bodies make we better."

"They're bio-engineers," said Tirak. "They make micro-
implants used in medicine to regulate hearts, prevent brain
seizures, that kind of thing."

"Then why were you on the *Kz'adul*?"

"Primes employ," said Kzizysus, picking up a small bowl with
both hands. "Long travel. Excuse. Need fluids."

She watched, fascinated, as the TeLaxaudin dipped his face
and mandibles into the bowl and began to make quiet slurping
noises. She caught a glimpse of a long, thin tubular tongue.

"Can you help my mate or not?"

Kzizysus put the bowl down. "Experiment have I on animals.
Results hopeful are. Study now need live Sholans."

Carrie stiffened, glancing in horror at Tirak who grasped her
arm warningly.

"Annuur, he isn't saying he needs to experiment on Sholans,
is he?" Tirak called out.

Annuur came back, guiding a small grav unit bearing cookies and glasses of cold drinks. He stopped it beside Tirak before
answering.

"You have hospital and Physicians Vanna and Jack. Kzizysus
need visit there, observe patients, learn about Sholans. Then try
computer simulations. Last test is on native animal responding
like Sholans. This he has done on animals on his world and it
worked. Please, take refreshments," he said, climbing back onto
his padded couch.

Once again, Kzizysus began to talk to Annuur in his vibrating hum. The conversation went back and forth for several minutes before Annuur spoke to them again.

"Kzizysus needs you to be understanding about Primes. Long
time past Primes request implant to be made. No Warrior caste,
need law forces for after their Fall for long ago civil war. TeLaxaudin help. Also help now M'Zullians spreading wider in war
with J'kirtikkians. Primes too vulnerable now. Help them take
M'zullians to breed new Warrior caste, better, not so violent. Implant essential to control them or they need to be terminated.
Kzizysus on *Kz'adul* to implant safely M'zullians. Implant not
for other species. Kzizysus told after Kusac implanted. Kzizysus

only TeLaxaudin on *Kz'adul*. Afraid of Chy'qui. Little could be done then. TeLaxaudin people not condone use of implant on your mate."

Carrie listened in silence. The TeLaxaudin had been helping the Primes that long? The ethics of the whole business were dubious as far as she could see, but her concern right now was Kusac.

"I understand what you're saying, Annuur, tell Kzizysus that. I appreciate his desire to help us, and the fact he's come here to Shola. I'm sure Jack and Vanna will be more than happy to show him around the hospital and give him what help they can." After having her hopes raised so high, to find out that what Kzizysus needed was more research, and more time, was a great disappointment.

"Work it did on simple-minded animals Kzizysus tested," said Annuur. "Do not be disappointed. Not wise to assume it work on complex sentient brain of another species. Wise to research a little, then test again and again."

She forced a smile to her lips and picked up one of the two glasses. "Your presence, Kzizysus, gives me hope again," she said, taking a sip of the fruit cordial.

Prime world, the same day

Shielding his eyes from the sudden tropical rainstorm, Kezule surveyed the assault course from his vantage point on top of the specially armored vehicle. The bulk of his remaining sixteen Warriors had reached the automated live range and were flinging themselves facedown in the mud. Markers on poles, now barely visible through the splashes of dirt, showed the level they needed to stay below in order to survive their crawl to the other end of the range.

Wriggling like snakes, they plowed through the thick mud, trying to keep their bodies low and their guns just high enough to stay clean and dry.

The stragglers were arriving now, two of them, staggering as they approached the start. He sighed, wondering which of them it would be. The rearmost one clutched the other, making him stumble, almost dragging him down. He was thrown aside, shrieking as the energy weapons caught him, their phased pulses buffeting him from one emplacement to the next. He took seven seconds to die.

Kezule roared his anger, looking briefly away. He hated waste, and this was waste on an unacceptable level. Five dead in as many weeks. When he looked back, the last youth had flung himself under the beams and was crawling frantically for the other side.

Lifting the trapdoor in the roof, he dropped down to the rear of the vehicle. "This isn't working," he hissed, turning to Zayshul who sat huddled in a rug in front of the mobile data unit. "It worked in my time! What's different about these hatchlings?" he demanded. "What haven't I been told about them?"

"I don't know what you were told, and nothing is different, except we erased their racial memories," she said.

"All of them? Or just those to do with the Fall?"

"We can't be that specific," she apologized. "We have to take all and use our own to replace them."

He slumped down in the canvas chair next to her. "The M'zullians lack the Intellectual caste, is that correct?"

"We think they were left with a very reduced Intellectual caste. The majority of those on M'zull were ordinary soldiers with a few harems belonging to the ruling families there. There were a great many female drones, of course, who were probably turned into breeding females, but they'd only produce workers. There wouldn't be upper caste drones on a colony world. J'kirtikk would be the same."

"What about the fourth world?"

"They have a homogenous society with all the castes mingling now. There is no real caste distinction," she said. "But these Warriors were bred from mothers from our caste."

"Then your genes are less dominant then the M'zullians. Looks like this lot have the aggression without the common sense to control it," he muttered. "I didn't expect officer-class Warriors, but I didn't anticipate them having an intelligence less than that of the common soldier!"

"Does that mean you can't turn them into Warriors?" she asked, shifting uncomfortably on the hard chair.

"I can turn them into Warriors, but they'll be grunts, nothing more, and you'll have trouble curbing their aggression. Your society isn't equipped to cope with soldiers like that. They'll get bored and walk all over you as soon as they've enough experience to see you lack the ability to defend yourselves against them."

"What do we do?"

"Get them off K'oish'ik, if you want to keep them," he said, getting up. "They'll start fighting for position within the group soon enough, then they'll look to the junior officers. Only you don't have any."

"What about your offspring?" she asked. "They'll all be officer class. Medical Director Zsoyshuu anticipated the need for officers, that's why he had yours bred."

Kezule looked balefully at her. "When are they due to be released from the growth tubes?" He was still not reconciled to what had been done to him.

"Ten days," she said quietly. "And there are another fifty M'zullians as well."

"You've had these awake for over a year," he said. "Mine will be too immature to lead, even though they'll possess all the right scents to signal their superiority. By the time they're ready to take control, these ones will have either staged their own coup and be in charge of the City, or dead, killed by each other or us in self-defense!"

"We can tell Zsoyshuu. He can accelerate the learning program and development of your male hatchlings so they're birthed at the same age as these."

Kezule hissed, tongue flicking out angrily as he walked over to the side window and looked out at his helpers who were monitoring the young Warriors. "You know my feelings on that."

"Then this experiment fails, or we end up being dominated by them out there and the other fifty due in ten days," she snapped. "Take your choice!"

Surprised at her outburst, he turned to look at her. She was sitting back in the chair now, the rug thrown aside so she could rub her distended belly.

"Are you all right?" he asked, suddenly concerned for her safety. He'd never seen a female after mating with her, and had no idea of how quickly the eggs they bore developed, but her rapid increase in size had him worried.

"I'm fine, just uncomfortable," she said, pulling the rug closely around herself again. "What are you going to do?"

"Tell your director," he said with a sigh. "These," he gestured to the window, "need to be controlled now and I can't do it alone. And have them taken off the raw meat diet. We don't need highly aggressive grunts. If you want to subdue the M'zullians and J'kirtikkians, we need intelligent troops capable of waging both space and ground war. Recreating the old Empire won't work, our task then was different. We went into worlds that didn't have spaceflight and subdued them on the ground after a sustained aerial bombardment. It was a glorified mop-up operation, nothing more."

Zayshul made a few notations on the keyboard, then looked back at him. "Now what?"

"I'm recalling them for the day," he said, heading up to the front of the vehicle. "I need to review their training schedules."

Back at their quarters in the City, he found a message waiting for him. It was from one of the young males who'd become part of the group that liked to gather round him when he had to attend Court functions every few days, and he was requesting a meeting with him.

Annoyed with himself for failing to predict the problems he was having with his young trainees, he wasn't disposed to go, then the name tweaked a memory. One or two of them had made the odd comment against the current administration under Emperor Cheu'ko'h. Nothing much in themselves, but added together, he'd detected a definite undercurrent of dissent among them. He'd said little either way in return, but had decided to keep an eye on them. For that reason he'd employed four of them to help him train the young Warriors, using them as spotters as he had today, to mark their progress through the various courses he'd devised. This Q'akuh hadn't turned up today, claiming he had pressing business in the Court.

He sat looking at the message, tapping his claws on the desktop, considering the matter. Q'akuh was older than the others in his little group, around thirty in age. He was an attaché with the newly formed Cultural Exchange that had been set up following their alliance with the Sholans to coordinate the training of the twenty Warriors currently on Shola. Now their brief was broader, encompassing the true exchange of culture such as music and performing arts. If the dissident movement hadn't died with Chy'qui on the *Kz'adul*, and he had every reason to suspect it hadn't, then who better than this young male to approach him with a view to recruiting him to their cause?

"What is it?" asked Zayshul, coming in from the bath room, a warm toweling robe wrapped around her.

"Nothing," he said, typing in a quick reply and sending it before deleting the message and closing his communications unit. He still wasn't sure enough of her loyalty to himself to take her into his confidence. "I have to go out. You'll go to your Medical Director about accelerating the other Warriors?"

"I said I would, but you know I'm supposed to be on leave right now," she said, making her way to the drinks dispenser.

He swung his chair round to look at her. In the robe, she looked even larger than before. "Call him," he said abruptly. "You will rest from now on. I told you I want you to take no risks with your health at this time. You only have three weeks to go. Has your physician said anything about the size of the egg yet? Will it be too big?"

Collecting her hot drink, she made her way to the sofa. "If it grows any larger, I'll have problems," she said, holding onto the arm of the sofa as she eased herself down.

"Why in the name of all the God-Kings didn't those TeLax-audin do something about reducing the size of the eggs when they were helping you breed yourselves out of extinction?" he demanded angrily, getting to his feet.

"They did. They helped us develop the growth tanks and the techniques for using them."

"That's no solution!" he hissed. They needed breeding stock, females who were larger and could carry the eggs without risking their lives. The genetic meddling of the last two thousand years hadn't bred a better race, it had destroyed them! They needed to turn the clock back, return to the time when they were one caste, before the Matriarchy had started selective breeding. Even as he thought this, his mind froze for an instant, leaving him wondering how he'd acquired this ancient knowledge. Then a small seed of an idea began to grow in his mind as he looked at her.

"Call Zsoyshuu," he said. "I told you I won't have you risk your life over this hatchling."

She looked up at him, a strange expression on her face. "Getting sentimental over your brood female?" she asked. "Not like you."

"Common sense," he said, trying to pass her comment off. Then he hesitated, aware that she needed more if he was ever to gain her trust. "I do have an affection for you," he admitted awkwardly. "You're like a colleague, someone I can talk to, not like a female at all."

"Thanks. I think," she said dryly. "And I thought I was just head of your unofficial hareem."

He made an impatient gesture, turning away from her. "They are bed companions, nothing more. They don't have the qualities I need in my offspring, I've told you that. They don't carry the scents that mark them as breeders."

"Excuse me?"

"They have too much drone in their ancestry. They can't breed true for me," he said. "That's why your hundred in the tanks will be a mixed blessing at best. My wife was a daughter of the Emperor, of good breeding stock, not chosen randomly the way you chose their mothers. Now I must go."

CHAPTER 12

AS he crossed the Great Courtyard, he glanced up at the sky, seeing the rain clouds dispersing now that the storm was over. No drop of water had fallen here though, the City of Light was protected from the elements by force fields.

The establishment where he was to meet Q'akuh was in the small commercial section at the far side of the courtyard. Not one of the more exclusive houses of refreshment, it still provided a reasonable degree of quiet and luxury for those who had business at the Court.

Great fans studded the high ceiling, turning slowly to freshen the air. At the four tall windows, employees were busily adjusting the blinds, partly closing them again to protect their customers as the sun came out. As he walked over to the table indicated by the steward, his senses lurched briefly as he experienced an attack of déjà vu. He knew the place, had used it during visits to the Court in his own time: little had changed, except the people.

"General Kezule," said Q'akuh, getting up as he approached. He indicated the other seat. "I received your message. I'm delighted you could come, and so early. Did the weather drive you in?"

Kezule ignored what was probably an unintended insult and pulled out the chair, turning it so he could see most of the room before sitting down. "A little rain never hurt anyone," he said. "There was another death. Bad for morale."

Q'akuh made sympathetic noises and glanced up at the waiter hovering at his elbow. "Can I get you a drink, General?"

"Kheffa," he said. "Large." He could do with a hot drink after his soaking, and the herbal drink was both refreshing and stimulating.

"Two large kheffas," Q'akuh said then looked back to him, waiting until the waiter had left before speaking. "Your escort," he said, nodding in the direction of the black-clad Palace guard hovering by the entrance. "Is he necessary?"

Kezule had grown so used to them following himself and Zayshul around, he often forgot they were there. "They have their advantages," he said, nodding to the already returning waiter. "Doesn't do any harm to advertise my royal connections. Besides, I had ours reprogrammed to suit my needs." He relaxed back in the chair, resting his elbow on the padded arm and surveyed the younger male. Q'akuh exuded a slightly anxious scent, no more. Obviously the presence of the guard didn't worry him overly and he wasn't concerned about being seen in public with him.

"General," murmured the waiter, serving him with his widemouthed cup first. "Complimentary sweet biscuits from the manager," he added, putting a plate of them in the center of the table before serving Q'akuh. Then, with a low bow, he was gone.

"I chose here because I thought a familiar place would put you at your ease, General."

He frowned, the skin around his eye ridges creasing. "I'm at ease anywhere in the City, Q'akuh. You forget, for me, very little time has passed since I was last here. All places have a familiarity."

"Of course," murmured Q'akuh, picking up his cup and sipping from it carefully. "I meant only that this place is pleasant enough as well as public enough not to bring attention to us meeting here."

"Is there a reason why you should want to avoid attention?" he asked, picking up his own cup. He took a moment to smell the drink first, enjoying the fresh scent of the herbs. It tasted as good as it smelled.

"I have been asked to approach you with an offer of help."

"Help?" He arched one eye ridge. That did surprise him. He put the cup down. "Why would I need help?"

"Not for you, but for your wife," said Q'akuh, leaning slightly closer. "I take it you're aware of the risks she takes now she's one of the royal family."

"I'm aware of them," he said shortly, his amusement at the

ineptitude of this would-be plotter vanishing. "What business is
it of yours?"

"None, General, but my contact wishes to be of help to her,
medical help, should either you or she wish it."

He had to fight the impulse to lean across the table and throt-
tle him where he sat.

Q'akuh pulled back instantly, aware he'd offended Kezule.
"Hear me out, General," he said hastily. "My friends deplore the
practice of making the royal family carry their own offspring. It
puts lives at risk, lives more precious than those tended in the
growth tanks every day! They're offering their help, should you
or your lady want it. Nothing more."

Expressionlessly he looked at the male before him, every sense
suddenly on the alert. Yes, dissidents, and those with powerful
resources and contacts if they would risk offering him this illegal help—help which they must know he wanted.

"How would they accomplish this, given its illegal nature?"
He forced the words out as calmly as he could.

Q'akuh leaned cautiously forward again. "A simple matter.
Our physician is above reproach. No scandal is attached to him,
no one is watching what he does. You bring your wife to us in
two weeks' time, sooner if she goes into premature labor, and
he'll safely remove the egg. Your wife pretends to be still carrying it, and on the appointed day, she calls in our physician who
will arrive with the egg already in the incubator and pretend to
deliver it naturally."

"How can it survive if you remove it early?" he demanded.

"There is a way to continue nurturing the egg and keep the
shell soft until it reaches birth maturity, but it isn't widely known."
He dipped his head to his shoulders in a shrug. "There's no call
for it to be known when only the royal family bear their eggs."

"And the penalty for doing this?"

"Ah," said Q'akuh, sitting up again. "The risks are high. Destruction of the egg, revocation of royal status for the parents,
and imprisonment for all concerned."

"And what do your—friends—want in return?"

"Not a great deal, General. Just your ear to some other proposals they want to put to you, ones advantageous to yourself
and your new family, and your word that you'll not reveal our
conversations to anyone."

Abruptly he got to his feet. "I'll consider your proposal," he said tightly before turning and leaving.

On autopilot, he began walking, his mind almost numbed. He remembered nothing until a hand touched his shoulder and he looked round to find himself sitting on the edge of a fountain in the ornamental gardens at the rear of the palace.

"I didn't expect to find you here, Kezule," said the gentle voice of Empress Zsh'eungee.

He rose rapidly, bowing low. The hand touched his shoulder again. "No need for that, Kezule, we're private here. What brings you into my garden with such a thoughtful look on your face?"

"Nothing, Empress," he murmured, trying to hide his confusion. "I hadn't realized this was your garden. I used to come here when . . ." He ground to a halt, keeping his gaze on the ground as was the custom in his time.

She laughed. "Me, too! The sound of the water is so soothing, isn't it?" She sat on the rim of the fountain, gesturing him to do the same. "Sit! Be comfortable. Come here when you wish, Kezule. After all, you are part of our family."

He looked up now that she'd reminded him he'd no need to avert his gaze. Wearing a simple dress suitable for the hot weather, she looked like any of the females he could see about the City.

"I'm sorry I intruded," he said hurriedly, beginning to back away. "This is your private garden, isn't it?"

"Don't go," she said. "There's no need. I get very little chance to be informal, and there are very few I wish to share that time with."

He hesitated. In his day, he'd not been welcomed into the inner royal family like this. There were many others with a greater familial claim. "I'd better go, Majesty," he said.

"Then I'll walk with you," she said, getting up. "I hear you're working with the new Warrior caste."

"Yes," he said, falling in step beside Zsh'eungee.

"I'm grateful to you for endorsing my son's request to go to Shola." She looked at him. "He was so anxious to go and take part in the Warriors' training so he could understand for himself what it's like to be one. We're very proud of him."

Kezule stopped dead. "The Enlightened One is still on Shola with the Warriors? I thought his visit would only be a short one."

She frowned, iridescent skin crinkling gently at the edges of her eyes. "Didn't I just say so?"

"Bring him back," he said urgently. "Recall him, Majesty. His life is at risk among them. These aren't officers, Majesty, they're common soldiers, M'zullians. They have no respect for anyone except for superiors of their own caste."

"Our advisers have assured us that they've been bred and educated to be loyal to the royal family. They wouldn't turn on their Crown Prince," she said firmly. "I appreciate your concern, Kezule, but my son will stay there. He's the first Prince to train as a Warrior since the Fall and he's gaining respect in the eyes of the Court and our people by doing it."

"It's a scent . . ." he began.

"Kezule, we will not speak again about this. When you come next, bring Zayshul, your wife, with you," she said, smiling too brightly at him. Inclining her head, she turned and left.

"Damn!" he muttered, watching her retreating figure. He'd spoken to the wrong person. What could she know about the technique they'd used to breed the Warriors? The only reason he knew they'd gotten it wrong was because he knew what motivated the ordinary soldier, what scent commands they obeyed—unless the Primes' tampering with their genetic memories had altered even that.

His communicator buzzed and he reached into his pocket for it. "Accept," he said, waiting for the image on the screen to resolve. It was Zayshul.

"Zsoyshuu wants us to meet him in his office," she said. "I had to tell him you knew about your hatchlings. He needs to discuss your theory with you."

"Coming," he said, heading for the exit out into the palace. "I'll meet you there. Get your guard to call a floater, don't walk. It's too far."

"You're saying that unless these twenty are controlled by an officer class more mature than themselves, they'll rebel against us within days?"

"Yes," said Kezule. "You have perhaps five days at most, that's all, unless you're prepared to keep them sedated. You couldn't know that there's a genetic scent that differentiates the two Warrior castes. It creates controls, prevents them from wiping each other out. They know who's superior to them, who is untouchable. You can't just re-create the Warriors and put them into your society, Zsoyshuu, it won't work. You Primes smell alien to

them—hell, you even smell alien to me!" he said candidly, leaning back in his chair and surveying the Medical Director. "In my
time, only the officers were allowed on K'oish'ik, never mind in
the City of Light. Every soldier in the City was an officer, no
matter how lowly his position, because we didn't look for weaknesses in our superiors and turn on them in their hour of weakness! You're basing your understanding of all Warriors on the
officer caste."

"We did tests, computer simulations, showing that the merging of M'zullian genes with those of Intellectual females would
lead to more intelligent Warriors," objected Zsoyshuu.

"Life doesn't work that way," said Kezule dryly. "I know nothing of medicine or genes but I know if you strip the M'zullians
of their genetic memory and give them yours, you'll get grunts
who know how unprepared the City is for any determined Warrior. These come from stock genetically modified thousands of
years ago to enjoy killing, Zsoyshuu, and they'll see a target ripe
for the taking."

"Why didn't you pick this up sooner?" Zsoyshuu demanded.
"You've been working with them for over a month!"

"They were still developing. Now that they're fulfilling their
purpose in life, learning to fight and kill, they're maturing and
their adult scents are kicking in."

Zsoyshuu looked at Zayshul. "You agree with his prognosis,
Doctor?"

She inclined her head in an affirmative. "I've watched them
alongside my husband, Director. They've definitely become more
aggressive among themselves. And the fifty M'zullians due to be
birthed in ten days were selected for aggressiveness by Chy'qui.
He had them culled specifically for that."

"What do you suggest we do, General?"

"I've told you. Accelerate the hundred from my line, so that
when you birth them, they're more mature than these. Then they'll
have a fighting chance. Literally," he added. "And my advice on
the other fifty is to do something if you can about their racial
memories. They need Warrior ones, not Primes. If you can't, then
terminate them, or leave them without any."

"Without?" The director sounded scandalized.

"Correct me if I'm wrong, but you no longer have drones, do
you?"

"No. No drones, only Workers and Intellectuals with drone ancestry."

"So how do you pass on racial memories these days? You're grown in tanks without shells, birthed at any age from hatchling to fully mature, so how do the racial memories get passed on from generation to generation?"

"Injected into the growth nutrient," said Zayshul. "We update the stock racial memory every two generations and use that for the next two. And only the Warriors we're trying to breed have been kept in the growth tanks until fully mature."

Zsoyshuu looked thoughtfully at Zayshul. "We could ask the TeLaxaudin if it's possible at this late stage," he said. "You could do that, Zayshul, while I start amending the growth and the sleep tapes for the General's offspring."

"You've another problem," said Kezule, even as he absorbed the fact there were TeLaxaudin in the City. "Prince Zsurtul. If you'll excuse me saying this, his scent is too like a drone's for his continued safety with them. He'll be recognized as a legitimate target. Prey, if you prefer."

"Our reports from the Sholans show them to be doing well," said Zsoyshuu. "There's no mention of the aggression you're seeing with the ones here."

"I met the Empress today and tried to explain to her the need for her son to be recalled, but she wouldn't listen."

Zsoyshuu looked horrified. "You spoke of this to Empress Zsh'eungee? You can't do that! There are proper channels to go . . ."

"I know all about proper channels," Kezule interrupted. "I didn't have time for them. I only found out about the Enlightened One being with them when she told me!"

"It's not her you need to convince," said Zayshul. "It's the Prince himself. He's determined to get out and find out about his people while he can, not stay shut up in the Palace like his father. What he wants, he has a way of getting." She smiled at the memory. "He's a nice young male."

"He could be a dead young male if he's mixing with the Warriors," said Kezule. "And it won't do your treaty any good when those twenty—you did say all twenty are still alive, didn't you?—go on the rampage against the Sholans. Take it from me, physically the Sholans are inferior. They haven't our speed, strength, or physical resources. At least the Warriors on Shola haven't been taught how to use bio-feedback yet."

"I thought it was a natural ability."

"Some, but training enhances it," he replied, trying not to look at Zayshul. He'd promised to train her. He prayed to all the God Kings that she'd stay silent about it. "I'd like to see the Sholan reports if I may, compare them to mine. You know I've had a high death rate, don't you?"

"I've read your reports," said Zsoyshuu. "And the fact that you've tried to amend your training regime to lessen them, but with little success."

"I told you at the start, Zsoyshuu, you can't create a Warrior race out of thin air and put it into your culture," he said impatiently. "You don't need to reproduce what we had fifteen hundred years ago, you need an army for today's conditions, today's Primes, not yesterday's Valtegans! Give me a ship and a competent crew and I can keep the ones I have usefully employed until mine are ready."

"We work with the schematics our Emperor and his advisers decided," said the Medical Director stiffly, standing up. "I'll see to warning the Sholans and getting their reports sent to your quarters, and changing the schedule for the hatchlings. You and your wife go and talk to Kouansishus and his colleagues."

Sighing inwardly, Kezule got to his feet and accompanied Zayshul to the door.

"General," Zsoyshuu called out after him.

He stopped and looked round.

"I doubt you'll get much thanks for this from the royal family yet, but you have mine for drawing this to our attention. It would have been easy to remain silent and let what you predict happen. As the last surviving member of the royal family, you must know you'd inherit."

Kezule smiled sardonically. "I've no wish to rule here, Zsoyshuu. I'm a military person, I prefer getting my hands dirty, not getting others to do it for me. I never did like watching a slaughter, and believe me, if we don't address this now, that's what will happen."

"I'll see what I can do about your ship."

"What are you hatching?" asked Zayshul as they walked slowly down the corridor to the TeLaxaudin labs.

"Me?" he asked, surprised. "I don't know what you mean."

"I can tell when you're turning something over in your mind," she said. "When are you going to start trusting me, Kezule? For good or ill, we're both involved in whatever you do. You weren't being totally altruistic back there."

"If those warriors get out of hand, Zayshul, even I couldn't stop them," he said seriously. "All our lives would be at risk. And I only told the truth in there about not wanting to rule. I don't."

"There's more," she said, glancing shrewdly at him.

"You're getting as bad as the Sholan mind-stealers," he grumbled, trying to hide his surprise. "We'll talk about it later."

Kezule had seen Kzizysus on the *Kz'adul*, so Kouansishus and his three companions came as no surprise to him.

Squatting on his cushioned seat, head to one side and eyes swirling, the TeLaxaudin heard him out. Mandibles clicking gently, hands clasped, the alien took several minutes to reply. A low buzzing hum filled the room as they began to talk among themselves. Finally, the translator began to speak.

"Difficult. We confer. Later give answer."

"We haven't got long, Doctor Kouansishus," said Zayshul. "Ten days are all that remain. We need to decrease that time for my husband's offspring and make them two years older or they'll not survive against the M'zullians we want to alter."

"Soon you told." Kouansishus pointed at her. "Why egg? Other way give. Why this?"

"Because I'm from the royal family," Kezule said suddenly, ignoring Zayshul's startled outburst. "They insist she do it this way. You can help her, can't you?" If anyone could, it had to be them.

Kouansishus looked at him then slowly unfolded himself and stepped down from his chair, picking up a small hand-sized device from his desk.

As he approached them, Kezule suddenly felt uncomfortable. In his time, the only alien species they'd known had been slaves, inferior beings not fit to be called people. Now, most days he rubbed shoulders with at least one of the Alliance species. Trusting them was another matter. He began to regret his hasty outburst.

As the ridiculously fragile being stopped by Zayshul and held the device in his hand out to touch her, a series of unexpected emotions swept through Kezule. Protection was foremost among

them, protection of his female. The TeLaxaudin had been helping the Primes alter themselves since the Fall. What if that help
wasn't as altruistic as it appeared? As part of his mind found the
thought ludicrous, the older, more primitive part wanted to rear
up and tear the TeLaxaudin limb from limb. Shuddering, he fought
hard to repress the urge: here was a chance of ensuring Zayshul
survived the birth of their egg with no dubious commitments attached to it. He couldn't afford not to take it.

Kouansishus stopped and glanced at him "Want, or not?" he
asked.

"Want," said Kezule through clenched teeth.

"Just a minute," began Zayshul, looking over at him, then
Kouansishus' device touched her neck and she hissed in surprise.

Kezule began to rise in his seat only to find it impossible to
move. Paralyzed, he watched in fear as the TeLaxaudin made
some adjustments to the device then activated it. Where Zayshul's
hands gripped the arms of the chair, he could see her knuckles
whiten, could smell her sheer terror. He fought the paralysis, then
suddenly the TeLaxaudin moved away from her and he was free,
The suddenness of his release catapulted him out of the chair to
land on the floor in a heap.

Kouansishus watched him scramble back to his feet, head on
one side, mandibles clicking gently. He could swear the tiny being
was amused.

"Done now. Egg every and this time be fine," the TeLaxaudin
said, shutting off his device.

"What did you do to her?" he demanded, taking a step forward angrily. The paralysis hit him again, rooting his feet to the
floor.

"Fixed she. Too untrusting you. Go. We try later tanked ones
fix."

From behind him, one of the others spoke. "Not tell fix her.
We unfix easily."

Shocked, he found himself free again. This time, common
sense took over and he forced himself to relax. "You fixed her?
How? Are you all right?" he asked, turning to Zayshul who, pale-
faced, was getting to her feet.

"I think so," she whispered, putting her hand up to her head
to wipe the sheen of sweat from it.

"Said fixed," confirmed Kouansishus, returning to his chair.
"Carry eggs she can. Birth safely."

"If you can do it for her, why the growth tanks?" he demanded.

"Easy correct genetic mistakes. Long time fix Prime breeding. Complicated."

"Prime not ask change," said one of the two sitting behind him.

He swung round. "You mean that because they haven't asked you to change it, you've left them using the breeding tanks?" He couldn't believe what they were saying.

"Not interfere unless asked," said Kouansishus.

"The Empress," murmured Zayshul. "She lost three eggs. The pain and suffering you could have prevented."

"Not ask."

"We've got to tell her," said Zayshul intensely.

"Not tell. Balance lost."

"What if we ignore you and tell her?" asked Kezule.

The device came sailing through the air toward him. Automatically he put his hand up to catch it.

"Take. Use it. Not tell. Keep, will need for your plan."

"What?" He looked from it to Kouansishus disbelievingly. How could the TeLaxaudin know what he was only just beginning to consider?

"Logical. Go now."

He looked at the device again. "How does it work? How do I use it?"

"Only for eggs. Press and works. She tell how long for," said Kouansishus. "Go. Got working to do." He waved a hand in the direction of the door.

Pocketing the device, Kezule took Zayshul by the arm and led her out into the corridor. There he stopped to check she was all right.

"What did he do to you?"

"I don't know," she said, her voice unsteady. "I was paralyzed, like you, then suddenly I felt everything moving inside me." She shook her head. "It was really strange, not exactly pleasant, but not unpleasant either." She looked up at him. "I'm not making sense, am I?"

"Not at all," he said, taking her by the elbow. "Can we trust them? Did he actually do what he said?"

"I think so. They're so far ahead of us in medical technology that there's no point in comparing us. We're lucky to have them as allies. We would have died out as a species after the Fall if not for them."

"Why keep this to themselves, though? What do they gain from it? And why give it to me?"

"They obviously think you'll need it. As for keeping it to themselves, he said why. They think it would affect the balance in our society. I can't see how, though. So what are you planning? A hareem of your own?"

He gave her a sour look. "I'm not, yet. It's only an idea right now. It needs thought, a lot of thought. And we mention this to no one." What was disturbing him was how the TeLaxaudin knew to have the device ready and waiting for him. He didn't believe in coincidences.

"I don't intend to. Even asking for help for me was risking your freedom and mine, Kezule. Thank the God-Kings you didn't ask Zsoyshuu! He'd have had to report us to the Enforcers!"

He grunted, well aware after his talk with Q'akuh what the penalties would have been. He wondered what Kouansishus had done to her. Made the egg smaller? More than that, surely; he'd said the cure was permanent.

"When you see your doctor tomorrow, let me know if she finds anything different," he said.

"I can give you an educated guess now," she said. "Either the egg will stay the size it is and any I bear in future will also be small, or somehow he's enlarged me internally."

"Let me know," he said, looking for a public floater as they entered the more populated corridors. Suddenly his idea had become possible again now she could safely bear his young. And if she could, so could others, and not just his young. He had in his hands the way to breed back into the Primes what had been lost so long ago, to return them to a casteless people. And within the next few days, he might even have a ship.

Stronghold, Zhal-Vartra, 28th day (July)

The weekly meeting was being held in Lijou's office this time. Rhyaz had just finished briefing them on the latest report from their labs at Anchorage.

"So the journals Vartra gave you were of immense help, Lijou," said Rhyaz. "All we need now is a live Valtegan on which to try out the la'quo spray."

Lijou shifted unhappily in his seat. "I don't like chemicals being used as weapons, Rhyaz. They're banned throughout the Alliance, you know that."

"It only reduces their aggression permanently, Lijou," said the Warrior Master. "It isn't like a nerve gas or a poison."

"It destroys several of their glands. That's tantamount to the Valtegans developing a gas or spray that destroys the area of our brains responsible for our psi talents. How would you feel about that?" he asked. "I know how I'd feel."

"It's a last resort, Lijou. It isn't as if we plan to go blanket spray their worlds with this, even though they did the equivalent of that to two of our colonies. I didn't say I was comfortable with it either. I've consulted with Kaid and Rezac on this because of their experience with Valtegans and Primes, and they reckon, regrettably like all of us, that we have no option but to continue this line of research."

"At least now we have a good working knowledge of the Valtegan Warrior anatomy, thanks to Vartra and his people," said Noni. "We can be ethical and dead, Lijou, if you prefer."

This was the first time she'd been called to Stronghold to take part in such a discussion and she was rather pleased. It was her medical knowledge they needed, and they'd called her in rather than their own physician because he owed his loyalty to the Medics guild. With Noni, they knew where they were.

"No, I don't prefer," he said. "But I don't have to like it."

"Are you saying we need a live subject?" asked L'Seuli.

"I'm afraid so," said Rhyaz. "It has to be tested."

"In what form?" asked Yaszho. "Are we talking chemical missiles from fighters, or up close and personal?"

"Up close," said Rhyaz. "We need to capture a ship and its crew, preferably a small craft, and take them to Anchorage where they'll conduct the experiments. A method of delivery has to be decided, be it a spray or a projectile pellet."

Lijou looked up. "We should be there, Rhyaz. If we're going to order these experiments, then we should be there to witness just what suffering we're causing. It makes a difference when you know what damage your weapons do. You aren't so ready to use them."

"He's right," said Noni unexpectedly. "You should go. We can't afford to be as careless of life as them."

Rhyaz nodded slowly. "Very well. Lijou, L'Seuli, and I will go when they're ready to start the experiments. I'll issue the appropriate orders after this meeting. I've got some more welcome news now. The Free Traders Council has agreed to us starting a unit made up of our people and theirs to patrol the shipping lines as discussed last meeting. Each member species will initially supply three craft built to specifications being agreed by the Touibans and the U'Churians. It will incorporate the Prime stealth technology. They will be six-to eight-person small scouters, capable of jumping in half the time it currently takes us thanks to the new hull and drive configurations. Initially we'll have fifteen such vessels because with our currently limited resources, it has been agreed that our contribution will be to provide the training and the base of operations. When we can, we'll provide the wherewithal to have our three craft built."

"I take it the Touibans make up the fifth species," said L'Seuli, examining the plans.

"They do. We aren't currently expecting that level of contribution from the Sumaan because they're still in the process of being released from the Chemerian contracts, but they are interested in helping crew them."

"What about Shola? When do we tell our own people?" asked Yaszho.

"Once we're installed in Haven Stronghold, and the unit has been activated," said Rhyaz. "Which it will be within the next few months."

"What's the unit going to be called?" asked L'Seuli.

"We decided on the name Watchers," said Rhyaz, with a glance at Lijou. "It encompasses all our functions of watching for any threat from the two Valtegan worlds, plus protecting the Traders."

"Watching has always been our traditional role," said Lijou. "We hope to have at least one telepath on each ship."

"Then I assume our core recruitment area will be from Valsgarth estate," said Yaszho.

"Not necessarily," said Rhyaz. "We have a few telepaths among our own members. Crews, where they exist, will be kept together. But our first Watchers will be taken from among those currently training with Kaid and Garras. Captain Tirak's people come to mind."

"We're a religious order, Master Rhyaz. What will hold other species together the way our beliefs hold us?" asked Yaszho.

"We've given it a lot of thought," said Lijou. "I've gathered what information I could on the religions of our allies and had my students working on collating common viewpoints." His mouth dropped open in a slight smile. "That's what all that work was in aid of, Yaszho. Deities, or concepts relating to them, vary from the sentience of planets that the Cabbarrans believe in, to the prophet Kathan of the U'Churians, to the belief we are all the stuff of Deity from the TeLaxaudin, to the personification of God in the form of their Divine Emperor."

"The Primes," murmured Rhyaz.

"Us and the Humans with our pantheons of Gods, the forests of the Chemerians . . ." he stopped for breath and spread his hands expressively. "You name it, someone has deified it."

"Could have said that at the start," grumbled Noni. "Rhyaz left it to us to decide and what we came up with was an oath of allegiance to their Brother Watchers sworn in the name of their own Deity."

"They do what we're doing—step outside their own small world and its individual politics to protect the greater good. Make no mistake, if war comes with the Valtegans, with that weapon they've got, they could wipe every last one of us out," said Rhyaz, looking around the small group.

"Are you basing the Watchers at Haven?" asked Yaszho.

"No, though there will be a presence there. We'll base them at Anchorage. Now we've lost the Strikers to Raiban, our first priority is for fast transport to Haven and between the Outposts. Toueesut's government is helping with that. Like us, their home-world and only colony are too close to the Valtegans for comfort."

"We need worst-case rendezvous plans for survivors, Master Rhyaz," said L'Seuli. "Somewhere safe for them to head. We have our own, but none for the people of Shola."

"It's being organized, L'Seuli," said Lijou. "We're expanding Refuge and using it for all refugees."

"What plans are Allied High Command making?"

"Our colony of Khoma will be used as an initial evacuation center for ourselves and the Touibans. Then, if necessary, the Alliance as a whole will make their combined stand there, evacuating all the people we can to Jalna and Home, the U'Churian world. They're gearing up for war, possibly even a preemptive strike if they can get enough intelligence about the situation."

"Then they'll be knocking on our door soon enough," said Lijou. "They always come to the Brotherhood for missions where lives are on the line."

"We'll have our own intelligence by then," said Rhyaz. "And without risking lives or drawing attention to our presence."

The patio style doors in the den had been thrown open and an awning erected so Carrie and T'Chebbi could work outdoors. They were reviewing the livestock and reading reports on the current state of the crops and their projected harvest.

Pushing her comp pad aside, Carrie groaned. "And I thought managing the inn on Keiss was boring! How're you doing?"

T'Chebbi looked up from her computations. "Well, the jotha we bought through Tirak sold well, very well in fact. So did some of those semiprecious stones. Suggest we double quantity of jotha and the price! Make it real luxury item."

Carrie stroked the pale lilac tunic she wore, lifting the edge of one panel to feel the almost suedelike texture of the fabric. The jotha clung to her fingers, the heat of the day making it behave as if it were alive. "It is beautiful," she said, looking over at her friend.

T'Chebbi grinned, looking down at her own brief tunic of flame red. "Is nice," she admitted. "Feels strange wearing what others pay fortune for."

"Look at what we had to go through to get it. If anyone deserves it, we do."

"Trouble," said T'Chebbi, nodding toward the far side of the garden, already on her feet, her hand reaching for the pistol at the back of her belt.

Carrie looked, reaching mentally as she watched the dark-furred person approaching at a run. "Giyash," she said, "with Jeran not far behind."

T'Chebbi relaxed, returning her pistol to its holster as she sat down again.

Jeran appeared from behind some ornamental bushes and seeing them seated outside, put on a spurt of speed to catch Giyesh.

"She's not happy," murmured T'Chebbi.

Carrie sent to Jeran, telling him they weren't disturbing her. His reply was faint, but as only a level seven, he'd done well to reply at all.

Jeran caught hold of Giyesh, causing her to turn on him angrily, but within moments, they were coming over at a more sedate pace.

She could see that Giyesh's eyes looked swollen and her face was definitely tear-streaked as they drew closer.

"Fruit juice, I think," murmured T'Chebbi, getting up. "I tell Zhala."

"What on Earth's the matter, Giyesh?" asked Carrie, gesturing to the empty chairs round the table. "Sit down, for goodness sake."

"I need a favor," she said, lowering herself into the chair, Jeran hovering at her side, looking apologetic. "They've expelled me from the Family. I'm an outcast, Carrie. I can't go Home." Her face creased briefly as she put a hand up to rub her eyes, her ears disappearing into her mane of hair. "I want to stay here. Can I join your Clan?" she asked, her voice on the verge of breaking.

"Who's expelled you, and why? What could you possibly have done to warrant that?" asked Carrie. "Not because of Jeran, surely?"

Giyesh nodded. "They say," she began then stopped, unable to go on as her eyes overflowed and she began to whimper.

Jeran gathered her close, looking helplessly at Carrie. "I told her she couldn't ask you, but she said we've nowhere else to go."

"I can't, Jeran," she said, leaning forward to stroke Giyesh's head. "We're an En'Shalla Clan. Membership can only be granted to gene-altered telepaths, and then only to those who can cope with the responsibilities membership entails."

"I can't be without a Family," Giyesh sobbed. "You don't understand! I'll cease to exist as a person!"

"Maybe Clan Leader Aldatan can help," Carrie said, thinking fast. "You were a latent telepath, weren't you, Jeran? You're training to be a level seven, aren't you?"

"It's not enough, I know," he said as Giyesh clutched him like a lifeline, sobbing quietly.

"It's enough to get you enrolled at the Telepath Guild, so it

should be enough for Rhyasha. It isn't as if you'll be living anywhere but here. All she'd have to do is enter you on her books
as being Clan members," she said thoughtfully. Hearing T'Chebbi
returning, she got up. "Give me a few minutes to call her. I'm
sure she'll say yes."

When she returned, Giyesh was sipping fruit flavored water
and smiling, despite herself, at T'Chebbi's acerbic sense of humor.

"Well," she said, sitting down. "Rhyasha's on her way over
now. She can't take you into her clan, Giyesh, but," she said,
raising her voice over the young female's exclamation of distress, "she can take Jeran and his wife. Since you're his wife,
the problem's solved."

It had been a little more difficult than that. What had swung
it had been reminding her bond-mother of the evolutionary link
between their two species and the fact that Giyesh was carrying
what would possibly be the only cub of such a union.

It isn't as if the U'Churians are really an alien species to us,
she'd said. *We're branches on the same tree.*

"If Clan Leader Rhyasha coming over, should freshen up,"
said T'Chebbi. "Jeran knows the way."

"What does your uncle say about all this?"

"He said it was my own fault and stormed off to call Home
from Annuur's ship."

"So he may have sorted this by now?"

"It won't be sorted," she said, shaking her head and setting
her mane flying in every direction. "And even if it were, I don't
care! So what if I have to join Jeran's Clan? He'd have had to
join mine if he'd been U'Churian."

"Being taken in by a Clan is a serious business, Giyesh," said
Carrie. "It means the Clan is willing to be responsible for not
only your welfare, but your cub's and so on forever. You have
to be sure it's what you want."

"I am," she said firmly.

Nezule Estate, Zhal-Oeshi, the month of Harvest, 1st day (August)

Kaid stood with Khy on the balcony overlooking the small practice hall, watching the class below. Nijou, Tyak, Jayza, and Kusac

were going around the pairs of Valtegans, checking each one's attacks and defenses as they were sparring.

"He's quieted down a lot since you came back with him a week ago," said Khy. "But I still feel it's got more to do with your presence than any intrinsic change in him."

Kaid rested his forearms on the safety rail. "I need to spend a couple of days with our U'Churian and Sumaan friends," he said. "And I need to do a final assessment on our mixed Leskas so they can be sent to Stronghold to take up regular duties there. I can't be constantly looking over Kusac's shoulder. You can call me if anything changes."

"I was thinking of . . ."

Kaid gestured him to silence as he saw Kusac separate two of the young Valtegans and launch a series of fast, hard blows at one of them.

Nijou called out to him, but Kusac ignored him, lashing out sideways at him when he attempted to put a hand on his shoulder.

"Halt!" Kaid called out loudly, pushing himself away from the rail and heading for the stairs down to the exercise level. "Take a break!"

It immediately became obvious Kusac still wasn't responding as everyone stopped and turned to watch. Cursing under his breath, Kaid grabbed the banister rail and vaulted over it, down to the floor. Angrily, he called out in Highland to Khy who was following him, "Get them out of here now!"

Grasping hold of Kusac by the arm, he swung him around. "Enough, Kusac," he said, but Kusac wasn't listening. He blocked the first punch but the next got through, winding him.

"Jayza, move that youngling," he snarled, realizing that for the good of the class, he had to put his friend down immediately and publicly.

Moments later, he had Kusac in an armlock and slammed him against the wall under the balcony. "Mind explaining what this is all about?" he asked, holding him there till he felt the tension leave the other's body.

Kusac swung around, glowering at him. "You'd no right to interfere!"

"I have every right. You're supposed to be correcting their moves, not engaging in combat with them!"

"I was correcting his blocks—the hard way. He'll learn more quickly if he gets a few knocks."

"Dammit, he's no match for you and you know it! He isn't even a Warrior, Kusac! That was Prince Zsurtul!"

"They all look the same to me," he snarled, hair rising not just around his head but across his bare shoulders as he remained in a fighting crouch.

"What the hell's gotten into you, Kusac?" he demanded. "Since we came back after Rezac's marriage, you've found any reason you can to Challenge my authority! It has to stop now!"

"Or what?" Kusac countered, letting his hair and pelt settle back down as he straightened up. "There's nothing left you can do to me. Everywhere I turn, you're either there or have been there, doing what I'm trying to do better than I ever could. You've effectively cut me out of not only my life, but yours!"

"That's unfair and unwarranted," said Kaid quietly. "I have never wanted your life, Kusac, only my own. I've purposely stayed out of all estate business for just that reason. Garras and Carrie handle it. I do what I've always done—train and protect. I didn't push you aside, you left."

"Then just when did you intend to tell me about T'Chebbi?" he asked coldly. "It was common gossip at Rezac's wedding. That's how I found out she's pregnant—by you. We're supposed to be bound as family by Triad and sword-brother oaths. Obviously they mean nothing to you."

Kaid regarded him steadily. "T'Chebbi's pregnancy is her news to tell, not mine. As far as I'm aware, she's told no one but Carrie. What you heard was just that, gossip. As for our Triad, I've never stopped believing in it. I take all my oaths seriously."

Kusac lunged forward, taking him by surprise as he grasped hold of his belt knife and wrenched it free. "Then prove it," he said, holding it up.

Kaid froze, resisting the impulse to take a step backward even as he cursed himself for not seeing it coming.

Kusac smiled sardonically, eyes glowing golden. "I'm not that mad, Kaid," he said, grasping the blade tightly with his free hand before pulling the knife sharply down. Keeping his hand clenched, he reversed the knife then held it out hilt first. "Prove you still believe in our Triad by finishing the blood ritual with me now."

He took it from him. "Is that what this is all about?" Kaid

asked. "Anger with me? You thought I'd betrayed you by not telling you about T'Chebbi?"

Placing the blade against his right palm, he heard the faint echoes of Vartra's voice—*Bonded by blood to your mate, but not yet to you*—then felt the steel burn as it sliced into his flesh. Returning the knife to its scabbard, he held his hand out to Kusac.

Kusac locked hands with him. "We're one blood, one kin, one Triad. Say it, Kaid."

It was the Triad oath his father had taken. Why? Why was it important they swear it? "We're one blood, one kin, one Triad," he said, watching the glow in Kusac's eyes begin to dim and sanity return.

When Kusac would have let go, Kaid held onto him. "I owed that cub to T'Chebbi," he said. "I was responsible for gene-altering her, and making her pregnant not long before we were due to leave for Jalna. She chose to abort."

He had the satisfaction of seeing Kusac look startled. "I told you, I have my own life. So has T'Chebbi." He increased the pressure on Kusac's hand, letting him feel the bite of his claws. "Don't ever question my loyalty to you again. Prince Zsurtul is at the First Aid room. We're going there now. You owe him an apology."

the *Couana*, Zhal-S'Asha, 20th day (October)

On the *Couana*, he drifted up to a kind of consciousness, still held by the memory from the past. How could he have doubted Kaid? No one except Carrie was more loyal. Fretfully, he tried to move and found his limbs restricted by an unfamiliar weight.

On the verge of panic, from the darkness a hand reached out, easing the slight pressure on his chest. He realized it was only the covers, and that there was a warm body beside him in the bed.

"It's only a dream," said Banner's tired voice. "Go back to sleep. I'm watching you."

A wave of exhaustion swept over him, dragging him back down into sleep.

Nezule Estate, Zhal-Oeshi, 1st day (August)

Jayza was dressing the cut on Zsurtul's face as they walked in. Sitting on the treatment bed, legs dangling over the side, the Prince glanced warily at them. He looked young and vulnerable, posed no threat to him. The reverse in fact; he'd been responsible for saving all their lives. He realized then the stupidity of allowing himself to lose control, and the possible political implications of his actions.

"Nothing serious," said Jayza, putting a couple of thin strips of tape over the cut. "Usual cuts and bruises you get when sparring." He turned to put away the swabs and antiseptic. "You can go now."

"I owe you an apology, Zsurtul," he said stiffly, staying by the door. "I shouldn't have attacked you the way I did. It wasn't my intention to hurt you."

"What you did was understandable," said Zsurtul, climbing down. "You suffered greatly at J'koshuk's hands and have had no chance to fight back. Scent is a powerful stimulus, we probably smell too alike for you. Besides, it was a valuable lesson. I learned what you intended me to learn," he said, with a slight smile. "I need to move faster and defend myself as if my life did depend on it."

"Your scent is different," he said. "Not like J'koshuk's. It's the others who smell like him, not you."

"Then their scents affected you," he said with a shrug. "I hadn't thought your sense of smell sensitive enough to pick up the difference." He touched his hand cautiously to the bruise on his cheek. "It's a small price for a lesson I won't forget. Yours looks to have been more painful."

He clenched his hand, lifting it up, aware it was still bleeding. "It was," he said quietly. "Again, you have my apology."

"Accepted. Kaid once said you were not our enemy. Perhaps we could meet, share a meal, so I can convince you I'm not the enemy either."

"A good idea, Prince Zsurtul," said Kaid, moving Kusac aside so the young Prime could leave. "I have to return to the estate tomorrow. Perhaps we could arrange it for the day after?"

Zsurtul nodded. "That will be fine. I've been here for some time, yet there's so little I know about your people and your world. There's a lot I'd like to ask, and tell you about us."

"Time to go," said Jayza, chivying him out past Kusac and Kaid. "If you keep talking, you'll lose the break time and be late for the next class."

"The sink first," said Kaid as the door closed behind them. "Your hand needs disinfecting before I can treat it."

He went over to the sink, leaning against it as he rested his forearm on the edge, holding his wrist and hand over the basin. Blood still welled from the two deep cuts, forming a small pool in the hollow of his hand before dropping down onto the stainless surface beneath. He heard Kaid taking a bottle off the shelf before coming over to him.

"I didn't know you could differentiate between Zsurtul's scent and our M'Zullians," Kaid said, taking hold of his forearm before pouring the antiseptic over his hand.

He yelped, trying to pull back. "Vartra's bones, Kaid! That hurt!" A wave of light-headedness swept through him and he clutched the sink one-handed for support.

Kaid released him and capped the bottle. "Don't expect sympathy from me, Kusac. You're damned lucky the Enlightened One didn't decide to make a diplomatic issue out of what you did. The only way to get rid of your anger is to let it go, as Lijou's been teaching you. Get up on the treatment bed." He passed him a wad of gauze dressings. "Hold them over your hand and keep it elevated unless you want to clean up the blood."

Clutching the wad in his cut hand, he took the place recently vacated by Zsurtul: it was still warm.

"So. Zsurtul smells different from the others," said Kaid, as he collected sterile clippers, stapler, and dressings.

"Yes. Don't you smell it?" he asked, adjusting the blood-soaked wad and holding both hands upright above his shoulder level. He was beginning to feel decidedly queasy and the sight and smell of the blood wasn't helping at all.

"No. No one but you seems to notice it. Has anything other than your sense of smell changed since you came back from Haven?" Kaid put the tray of utensils on the narrow bed beside him and dragged over a tall stool to sit on.

"Nothing's different. I can just smell them, that's all. What about your hand?" he said.

"I wasn't so enthusiastic with the knife," said Kaid, taking hold of his hand and removing the wad. "You made a good job of it. Almost down to the bone for both cuts," he said, putting a fresh pad of gauze on it. "It's still bleeding. Hold it up again. I'll see to the wound above your eye first."

Kaid stood up, dabbing the cut with an antiseptic soaked pad, making him flinch as he rested his upheld hands against his shoulder.

"You shouldn't have Challenged me in front of the class," Kaid continued unsympathetically, shielding Kusac's eye before spraying the small wound with sealant. "We can't afford to let those young Valtegans see us as less than their superior officers, secure in our rank even among ourselves."

"I know," he said as Kaid took hold of his aching arms and drew them down again. "I'm sorry. He was there, he was Valtegan—Prime," he corrected himself before Kaid could, "—and I was angry."

He felt dizzy and hot. Sweat began to form on his forehead and he could feel it running down his back. He heard the sound of the clippers, felt them on his wrist as Kaid snipped back the small amount of fur at the shallow end of the cuts. Inside his head, the sound the torc was sending seemed to vibrate through his skull.

"You're doing what I did when we were at Stronghold, before we left for Jalna," said Kaid quietly as he sprayed a local anesthetic over his head. "Overworking yourself. You need a break, Kusac. Time to relax."

He laughed, but it came out wrong. "Where, Kaid? Everywhere I go reminds me of my past. I need a future, and right now, I don't have much of one."

"When I come back the day after tomorrow, we could hire an aircar, go hunting in the Taykui game forest for a few days."

He felt the coldness of the stapler, heard it firing and felt a slight sting each time as Kaid closed the wounds.

"There's no point. I can't run away from it," he mumbled, clutching the edge of the bed with his other hand. "I'm tired, Kaid. Tired of feeling isolated, tired of fighting the fear and the anger." His head began to droop forward till his forehead rested on Kaid's shoulder,

"Then stop fighting it," said Kaid, glancing at him before putting a dressing over his palm and fastening a bandage round it. "Let it go and you'll be free of it."

"I can't. It's all I have left."

"It's destroying you. And it isn't all you have left. You have

Carrie and me. We're a Triad, remember? That's what this was all about."

He felt Kaid touch his neck, his thumb rubbing gently along his jawline. "Help me, Kaid," he mumbled, clutching at him as the room spun crazily around him.

the *Couana*, Zhal-S'Asha, 21st day (October)

He woke clearheaded, the worst of the exhaustion gone, but not the memories of his dreams. He lay in the darkness, remembering that he'd collapsed through loss of blood and shock, but much of what followed was still a blur. The injury had triggered a fever which had raged through his system for five days—something to do with the tendrils in his brain, the Cabbarran who'd accompanied the TeLax-audin physician had said. Banner had brought them and Carrie to the Nezule estate the following day. He'd stayed with him part of the next day and night because it had been Kaid and Carrie's Link day and they'd had to spend some time alone.

The fever dreams had been terrifying, full of armored Primes and J'koshuk and pain. Only Kaid's and Carrie's presence had kept him sane, holding him, talking to him, giving him water when he was burning up. He couldn't remember when she left and only Kaid remained. The need had been there then—his need, not Kaid's as he'd once feared. It had changed everything between them, bound them closer than ever. Until this message had come.

At the other side of the bed, he felt Banner stir. With a sigh, he let go of the memory. Regrets would do him no good now. If their relationship was strong enough, their Triad would survive. They'd see the truth of his actions, would know he'd not turned traitor. He reached out to trigger the light. As he sat up, a gentle glow filled the room.

Rubbing his eyes, Banner looked owlishly at him. "Sorry," he muttered, sitting up. "You fell asleep during my massage. I stayed with you for a while, then it got cold."

Experimentally, he lowered his mental barriers, tensing himself for the pain just in case. Slowly his awareness and sensitivity increased, and the torc remained quiet. "There was trouble last night," he said, relaxing slightly. "Who?"

"Who isn't important," Banner said, flinging back the covers and stumbling out of the bed. "I was hoping you hadn't noticed. Someone came to the door." He grinned as he stretched. "Afraid I shot your reputation. I implied we were spending the night together."

"Thanks," he said dryly, getting up. "Rhyaz' operative, I take it."

"It was necessary, Kusac," Banner said more seriously. "Father Lijou briefed me on what to expect. He knew the change in you was almost complete before we left Stronghold. Master Rhyaz' operative is looking for signs of instability in you, but I can see them for what they are."

"And what's that?" he asked, picking up his tunic and pulling it on.

"The dreams are disturbing, may even affect your waking hours, but they're cathartic. By the time you're done with them, you'll be able to leave the past behind and move on, whole again. It's what Father Lijou said the TeLaxaudin intended should happen."

"He probably told you I may show instances of psi abilities," he said, picking up his belt. "You shouldn't believe everything you hear. Only I know what's happening to me right now. There's a device in my torc that mimics Talents."

"Then why did I go flying across the room yesterday when I woke you? Your strength alone didn't do it."

He shrugged, looking up at Banner again. "I still have that much residual Talent left. You know it's not wise to touch a sleeping telepath."

Banner looked at him, then came round the bed to fetch his own tunic from the chair where he'd left it. "Keep your own counsel, Kusac. But remember, I'm on your side, and damned few here are."

"They'll all be on my side, as you put it, soon enough," he said quietly. Then he found the name he'd been looking for. "You'd better sleep here again tonight if you want to keep Chima on the same scent." He reached out to touch his Second's arm. "Thanks, Banner. I know you didn't do it lightly with your own reputation at stake, too."

Banner nodded slowly. "Like I said, Kusac, remember

I'm on your side. Don't leave me in the dark unnecessarily."

Shola, Zhal-Oeshi, 3rd day (August)

"Skepp Lord," he said, inclining his head and clasping his hands in front of his face. "Biological component has activated. Hunter receptive is to regulator."

In the communications screen, his superior signaled approval. "Compliments. Research progresses how?"

"None needed, Skepp Lord, as expected. Opportunity occur for use similar technique on others here. We operate long-term brain damage patients. Success limited. Basic and median cognitive function restored, regrettably higher functions destroyed. Same technique for hunter would repair . . ."

"Not authorized! Risks not you take! Attention not wished to us! Why do?"

He winced at the outburst. "Camarilla say be not suspicious. Situation developed here. Tree discovers branch. Need to dissemble unless our role exposed. Phratry Leader also of Camarilla. He decide sharing simple medical techniques diverts attention, makes result on chosen hunter less obvious."

There was a short silence from the Skepp Lord. "Accepted. How our children exposed?"

"Relationship develop between two from *Kz'adul*. Now produce offspring."

"Not compatible—made sure when species combined! How this possible?"

"Hunter telepaths here changed female of ours. Not reproducible, takes many of them and cost of energy too high. A fluke, no more, but questions and answers exposed. Inevitable both species will discover their past."

"But not our part."

"Not ours." He hesitated. "But will discover unavoidable later Phratry intervention. Not secret with children."

His superior went to the unusual length of making several noises of extreme annoyance. "Troublesome always have been the sand-dwellers! Much they cost us! If not for aiding them, solar flare not missed, Phratry intervention not needed for children!"

"Almost cost our children," he agreed softly. "Lucky Phratry Leaders saw danger. Second time nearly they be lost. A question, Skepp Lord. For balance and harmony, must be reciprocal plan for sand-dwellers."

"Deduction is correct."

He could hear a note of respect in his superior's voice and lifted his head in pleasure. It wasn't easy to impress the Lords of the Camarilla.

"What happens there?"

"One among them has been chosen. We continue directing his course toward fulfilling our goal. Successful your early work on him was. Remembers far past of his species now."

"How will recovery or destruction of matter compiler be achieved through hunter and sand-dweller, Skepp Lord? Possible resolutions I have tried to see but are many. One clear way eludes me."

"As it should. Agents do. Responsibility is of Camarilla to see changing potentialities and weave to keep balance."

"As you say, Skepp Lord."

"Talk again we will when next phase complete. Tell Phratry Leader all is as it should be." The screen went blank.

Beside him, out of range of the comm, the Phratry Leader stirred. "Explains why Watcher ships we make for Sholans," he said thoughtfully. "Doing is good, knowing is good. Not enough knowing for now. I think more on this, speak Phratry soon."

Nezule Estate, same day

Kaid looked up as the door opened.

"Call for you from Stronghold," Banner said. "They have a secure line in the office you can use."

"Stay with Kusac," he said, slipping out of his jacket and handing it to him before leaving.

The heat outside was welcome after the chill of the air-conditioning in Kusac's room. Although he was now on the mend, Kaid wasn't happy leaving him and he made his way hastily to the office. He was shown into the side room where the comm was already waiting for him. Slipping into the seat, he switched it on.

"I've just been speaking to Ambassador M'szudoe of the

Primes," said Rhyaz. "He had some disturbing news for us. General Kezule is training the other twenty of their Warriors and it appears the matter of their Warrior caste isn't as simple as they thought. There are two distinct types of Warriors. The ordinary, more aggressive ones we met on Keiss, and the officer class, like Kezule, who were interbred with the Intellectual caste. We have the more aggressive ones."

"How come?" Kaid asked, leaning his elbows on the desk and trying not to yawn.

"It's in their scents. Kezule can tell that the M'zullian stock they used for breeding had no Intellectual caste in it. Officers smell different, apparently."

"The implication being?"

"They are constantly seeking to improve their position within their own ranks by looking for weaknesses in their superiors. At the first scent of fear, they'll turn on that individual. Only the presence and scent of the officers keeps them under control."

He grunted. "Sounds somewhat implausible to me."

"I'm assured it's not. They've lost five of their Warriors already due to this. They want Prince Zsurtul pulled out immediately. With his drone ancestry, he's more at risk than any of them. And so are we."

"Then they're doing something we aren't because we've had no more problems with them than with any bunch of new Warriors," said Kaid, smothering a yawn with his hand.

"They want their Prince sent back to the Embassy, Kaid," said Rhyaz firmly.

Kaid roused himself. "I'll pull Zsurtul out, but I want him kept here, Rhyaz. He'll be their ruler one day. It's important that he continue working with us. As for the others, they respond well to our people and there have been no problems between them and the other students here, but I'll have them watched more closely, split into smaller units for training and accommodation. If the Primes are that worried, I'll even make sure we have people standing by armed with trank guns at all times."

Rhyaz hesitated.

"Zsurtul will want to stay, I can tell you that now. I can put him in with Khy and the others, have him train only with them and a small group of Naraan's students. I'll even twin him with one of ours so he's never alone. He couldn't be safer."

"I'll see what the ambassador says, Kaid. But take no chances with those Valtegan Warriors."

"I don't intend to. You know, I remember Kusac saying Zsurtul smelled different from the others. Maybe there's something about our scents that makes them respond to us as if we were their officers."

"Maybe. It could even be as simple as their diet. Weren't you told to feed them cooked food, not raw, to curb their aggressiveness?"

"Yes. It might be worth getting Annuur back here to check on the scents. This might help that research of yours, if you get my drift."

Rhyaz nodded. "Follow that up, Kaid. Obviously, get back to me immediately if there's any trouble from the young Valtegans. How's Kusac? You look like you're having a rough time of it."

"On the mend, but he's still feverish."

"Try and get some rest yourself. I'll let you know what the ambassador says."

As he left, he called Khy on his wrist comm, telling him to take Zsurtul immediately to the small common room that had been allocated to them.

"I'm staying," Zsurtul said before he'd finished explaining the situation to him. "My place is here with my people."

"You can't be with them," said Kaid. "If you want to stay, then you'll have to observe my safety instructions. I'm moving you into Khy's dorm, and twinning you with Tyak. He'll be your bodyguard and you'll go nowhere without him, understood? We can't afford to have you mauled or killed by your own people. Think of what that would do to our treaty."

Zsurtul nodded slowly. "You're right. I'll stay with Tyak, you have my word, Kaid."

"Good. Khy, call Tyak and brief him, then divide the rest into two groups of ten for all activities. I've sent for another eight of our folk from Valsgarth Estate. They should be here within the hour. I want two people armed with trank guns at every class from now on. Sort out their dorms, too. If the worst happens, we can handle them in groups of ten. And keep this as low key as possible. I don't want them smelling any fear from our folk. It might be all that's needed to push them over the edge."

"Not going to be easy," said Khy. "I'm going to have to explain why all the extra security."

"I don't want them looking like security. Those on guard can be lounging around watching, or training on their own at one end of the hall. Divide up the extra personnel any way you want—you'll need to replace Tyak anyway."

"Who will I train with?" asked the Prince.

"With us or some of the other Warriors," said Kaid, getting up. "Get him some target practice, Khy. Maybe he can even help with the trank guns. I need to get back and relieve Banner. You know where I am if you need me."

"Kaid, thank you for letting me stay," said Zsurtul. "You're going to a lot of bother for me. I appreciate it."

Kaid shrugged. "We have a dinner date with you when Kusac's well again," he said. "You don't think I'm going to let you leave before then, do you?"

The young Prime grinned. "My treat, then. I'll send for food from the Embassy. It will be a meal you won't forget, I promise!"

"Uh huh," said Kaid, wondering if he'd live to regret it.

CHAPTER 13

WARMTH and peace were all he'd known as he floated weight-lessly in the liquid of the growth tank. Awareness there was, of a distant voice, quieter than the ever-present heartbeat that sur-rounded him. It murmured constantly within his mind, whisper-ing to him of the might and glory of the Prime Empire and his place within it. He was a vassal, one of eight, who owed obedi-ence and loyalty to the compassionate and generous Overlords who looked after him. His life was theirs, his greatest pleasure was to serve them: he would gladly live, or die, for them. He felt contentment in the security of knowing his place in the universe.

A vibration set the fluid in motion, sending rippling waves washing against his body. Sensitivity intensified as he became aware of the movement of each individual hair swaying gently in the liquid that surrounded him. He felt himself begin to sink, become heavier. Unpleasant sensations he identified as pain ranged across his body as catheters and umbilicals were auto-matically detached. The steady heartbeat began to quicken, and beneath his toes, he felt a solid surface. As his head broke the surface and he gasped his first breath of air, he knew terror.

K'hedduk watched as the growth fluid was slowly drained from the last tank. Even through the toughened fabric of the tube, the child's shriek of terror was audible. His black pelt slick, he lay there gasping for breath as he coughed up the liquid that had nurtured him for the past eleven weeks.

As the cylinder began to slowly rise around him, he looked up, amber eyes meeting K'hedduk's with a steadiness at odds with his birth age of ten years. A nurse stepped forward and clasped a narrow metal collar round his neck before helping him to his feet. Wiping his face, she wrapped his shivering body in the large towel she carried.

K'hedduk grasped him by the shoulder as they passed. "Wait. Who are you?" he asked, as he'd asked the seven others before him.

"I am a vassal of the Prime Empire, Seniormost," the cub said quietly, a hint of a tremor in his voice as he kept his eyes averted from the doctor's face. "My purpose is to serve it."

K'hedduk nodded and released him, gesturing to the nurse to continue. When they'd left, he turned to Zhy'edd. "All eight successfully birthed," he said, taking the other's reader pad from him. "And only one exhibiting signs of brain damage. Not bad considering we only had the one dead hybrid fetus Chy'qui took, and the pregnant female." He turned to go.

"Not necessarily brain damaged," said Zhy'edd as they began to head for the exit. "Slow is more appropriate. It could be natural, an inherited trait from her parents."

"The tests will confirm it one way or another," said K'hedduk, unperturbed. "My main concern for now is that the programming has taken and they don't exhibit any independence of spirit. They must know their place. They're slaves, nothing more, and I want them compliant, not rebellious. Pity we couldn't have kept them in until they were more mature. It'll be four years before we can breed them. At least we were able to salvage the memory scan Chy'qui did of his captive Sholan. We don't have to worry about training their telepathic abilities."

"The toxin levels . . ."

"I know all about them," said K'hedduk, irritated. "I made the decision to birth them now, remember?"

"Yes, Seniormost."

"Go and help Doctor Zurok with the medicals, and remember, I want them treated gently for now. The collars are only to dampen their telepathic abilities, nothing more. And Zhy'edd, find out what Q'akuh is up to when you're done! He should have had some news for us by now on the General."

"I believe the General's off-planet for the next week, training the young Warriors on one of our ships."

"Get in touch with him anyway."

the *N'zishok,* Prime space, the same day

Kezule had his ship. The *N'zishok* was a medium-sized destroyer, used for patrolling the border of Prime space. Heavily armed for its size, it was capable of taking on a couple of raiding ships were they foolish enough to attack it, but like the *Kz'adul,* its strength lay in its stealth technology and its intimidating exterior and armaments.

Right now, Kezule had completed his rounds and was going off duty. The crew of fifty had been reduced to accommodate his fifteen Warriors. For this first cruise, he had them in nonessential positions with mature and experienced crew members. So far, they were doing well, but then he hadn't expected any problems. The young males were aggressive, not stupid. They knew they were here to learn. Trouble would come when they decided they were more competent than their teachers.

"The ship is yours, Captain," he said into his communicator, stopping outside his own quarters and opening the door.

His suite was the largest on the ship and boasted a small lounge, an even smaller office area, and a double bedroom with adjacent sanitary facilities. More comfortable than the standard military facilities he'd been used to in his time, it wasn't quite up to the standard of the *Kz'adul.*

Zayshul had made a nest of cushions on the sofa and was curled up there eating snacks. Her constant presence had irked him somewhat at first, but mindful she was there because he'd ordered it—asked her, he corrected himself—he'd curbed his impatience. Now he was not only getting used to her presence, but was grateful to have someone at his side, or to come back to in his quarters, someone who wasn't overawed by his rank and to whom he could talk intelligently.

"You have a message," she said, looking up as he entered. "One of the young males that you recruited to help you with the training."

"Q'akuh?" he asked, unbuttoning his uniform jacket as he came over.

"No idea," she said, picking up another morsel of spiced meat. "It was forwarded here by your aide."

He'd contacted Q'akuh before they'd left, turning down his offer by feigning indifference to his wife's fate. The incident had bothered him far more than their encounter with Kouansishus, the TeLaxaudin.

"I had a message from the Medical Director," said Zayshul as he threw his jacket over the back of the far end of the sofa. "They completed the tests on your officers," she said carefully. "Their classes started today."

"And the others?" he asked, going over to the desk in his office and turning on the communicator.

"The TeLaxaudin procedures were unsuccessful and resulted in the deaths of all fifty."

"Good," he said, keying up his message and decoding it. "They'd end up having to be killed at some point. Better now than later." He read it thoughtfully then deleted it, switching the unit off. Q'akuh was being persistent. Getting up, he joined Zayshul back in the lounge.

"You're very callous about those Warriors," she said.

He shrugged. "They're a danger to us all, and a threat to my officers. I wouldn't put it past those TeLaxaudin to have ensured they didn't survive. Enough of them. What do you know about Q'akuh?" he asked, sitting in one of the chairs. "And the other young males who've been helping me."

"I wondered when you were going to ask me," she said, pushing herself up against the cushions. "Most of them are all right— Zhafsul, Zolmoi, and Chiozo. But Q'akuh. I don't like him. They all want something from you, but whereas the first three are prepared to work to be seen as attached to your staff, Q'akuh wants more. He wants you."

He frowned. "Me? How can he have me?"

"I don't know, but be careful of him. Whatever you're planning, keep him out of it."

He surveyed her curiously, as if she were some strange creature he was meeting for the first time. "What do you know?" he asked slowly, wondering whether he'd been that transparent, or if she really had a mental ability like the Sholans.

"Nothing for sure, but you've been preoccupied by more than your concern for the young Warriors."

"That's so," he admitted, wondering how much he could safely say, how much she'd already worked out one way or another. "This world, this time, it isn't mine, Zayshul. I don't feel at ease in it. And going back to my own time isn't what I want either."

"I know," she said quietly, her attention on the plate of nibbles. "When are you leaving and where are you planning to go?"

"It's that obvious?" he demanded.

"Only to me."

"I want you to come with me," he said, sitting up. "I never had any intention of leaving you behind." That startled her, he saw with satisfaction.

Her face composed itself into a neutral mask. "Of course. You want me to breed your dynasty."

"Not just that. I can talk to you." He gestured toward the door. "In the past I had aides and those who assumed friendship with me, but there was always the politics behind them—the jostling for position, the plots. It's the same now. Nothing's changed at the City. There was no one I could trust."

"Why didn't you just let the Prince die? You'd have become heir in his place."

Now it was his turn to be startled, at her choice of topic as well as the abrupt change. "There was no need. You know I don't want to rule here. I want to get away! You Primes are no longer Valtegans—you've lost what it was that made us who we were. Even the way you breed is unnatural, it sickens me."

"I told you, without the TeLaxaudin and their growth tanks, we'd have died out after the Fall. And they did free us females," she said pointedly.

"All right, maybe there are a few things about your culture that are an improvement," he admitted, "but it's not for me, Zayshul. I want to get away from here, start again. Something better this time. What's left of our people, whether it be the M'zullians, the J'kirtikkians, or you Primes, they're wrong, unbalanced. Stagnant. Just as you can't graft my Warrior culture into yours, you can't graft Intellectuals into the other two."

"You're planning to start again with just you and me?" she asked, disbelievingly.

"Hardly," he said with a trace of acerbity. "What's needed is a different approach. We need to turn the clock back to what we once were. Not separate castes but one. Warriors, Intellectuals, drones, and Workers—combined, with the best qualities of each. The speed, bodily control, and healing abilities of the Warriors, the Intellect of your caste now combined with the drones, and whatever it is the Workers have."

"Strength and tenacity," she said dryly. "Where do you plan to get these people? Ch'almuth?"

"That's an option," he agreed. "While we were at the Summer Palace, I was busy in the library going through past records and copying what I thought I might need. I've got charts, a way for you females to breed safely without the growth tanks, a ship, and several possible destinations. All I need is a crew."

"Birthing this egg safely has yet to be proved," she said. "Getting a crew loyal to only you isn't going to be easy. Is that why you're asking me about Q'akuh?"

"Not him," he said, dismissing him with a gesture. "The others. Zolmoi, Chiozo, and Zhafsul. They were training with me and did well, considering their caste. I want a crew of useful people. Doctors, scientists, people like that, and maybe a few Warriors."

"Where did you get ideas like this?" she asked.

He sat back in his chair again. "My time with the Sholans made me think about a lot of things. They beat our Empire with only a handful of well-placed telepaths who couldn't even fight. Can you understand the enormity of what they did? They don't have castes, why do we need them?"

"But there have always been castes."

"Have there? I have memories of a time when we were all one species and females weren't feral," said Kezule quietly.

She looked at him dubiously. "You're talking of setting up a colony, Kezule. Fifty people is nowhere near enough. You'd need hundreds."

"It's a start. We can get more from Ch'almuth. You're young and the young here are restless, some are ripe for adventure. Draw up a list of professions we'll need, see who you know who would be interested in filling them. And make sure you have more females than males."

"We've only one ship, with no infrastructure to support us if we need repairs or to build more. With such finite resources, farmers and miners are likely to be of more use."

"I have a solution for that, too. The old Empire had a network of outposts that protected its borders as well as the heart. I know where they are. Given that our three colony worlds were reduced to low-tech levels, I assume our fleets were also destroyed. They're still out there, waiting for us to salvage them."

"What about the threat from the M'zullians and J'kirtikkians?" she asked.

"Not my fight. You Primes have what you wanted from me, breeding stock. I want my own life."

"You really do believe in this, don't you?"

"Yes. You compile your list and when you have, we can discuss a way to approach them," he said, getting up to go to the food dispenser. The more he thought about it, the more convinced he was that Q'akuh was part of the faction that Chy'qui, the Emperor's late counselor had belonged to.

"If you suspect Q'akuh is working against Emperor Cheu'ko'h, you must find out more."

"I'm not getting involved," he said automatically. "You were the one urging me to be careful of what I said because of the Enforcers."

She stirred, pushing herself to her feet. "Kezule, look at me."

He turned round. "What?" he asked.

"*Look* at me," she commanded him.

Anger rose in him at her tone, but reason reminded him she was just as used to commanding as he was.

"You've demanded a lot of me, Kezule. This hatchling of ours isn't all."

He looked, seeing her gravid belly as if for the first time. "I've said . . ."

"Listen to me for once!" she said. "You've demanded a lot of me. If you want my help and involvement in this plan of yours, then I expect something in return."

Her impertinence took his breath away. The words wouldn't come as he stared at her, mouth hanging open in shock.

"You'd give something in return to a male colleague," she challenged him, placing her fists against her hips. "Why not me? I'll help you recruit your crew, and come with you, if you find out what you can of any plot against the Emperor."

"You dare try to force me?" he demanded, outraged.

"You forced a marriage and a hatchling on me! Either I'm a colleague you can talk to and trust, or I'm worth no more than the slaves or pets you owned back in your own time! You make up your mind which I am, Kezule, because your plans for the future depend on your answer!"

Skin flushed dark with anger, eyes narrowed, she was ready to take him on if need be. The males might lack the Warrior genes and spirit, but she lacked nothing. Walking toward her, hand held out, he began to smile.

She swiped his hand away. "Don't mock me!" she hissed, baring her teeth, her tongue flicking out as she checked the air for his scent.

"I'm not," he said, stepping back, aware that her temper was up and remembering their early intimate encounters. "I'll do as you ask." He emphasized the last word. "Only so long as it doesn't jeopardize our plans."

She nodded slowly, beginning to relax her tense posture. "Leaving here is one thing, Kezule, being aware of a plot against the royal family and doing nothing is not acceptable to me."

"I'll do what I can," he said, holding his hand out to her again. "I'll reply to Q'akuh's message and we'll see what happens."

Satisfied, she accepted his hand and his help in walking to the food dispenser unit to choose a meal.

Chagda Station, above Shola, Zhal-Oeshi, 9th day (August)

Since they'd been discovered stowing away on board the *Odyssey,* they'd been closely guarded by the marines. Now they were being transferred from the merchant ship to a small military corsair to be returned to Earth.

As they left the gangway of the *Odyssey,* she hung back, desperate for any view of the station and the people who lived on the planet below. Shola had been their goal, specifically the Telepath Program. This was as close as they would ever get.

"Get a move on," said the guard holding her by the arm.

She tried to pull away but his grip tightened and he began to drag her along the dockside toward the berth where their transport back to Earth waited.

"C'mon," she said. "Let me have a look at least."

The soldier glanced at her. "Kids like you don't deserve a look," he said, yanking her onward. "Ship leaves in ten minutes. You're going to be locked up in the brig in three."

Ten minutes! She looked frantically over her shoulder at her companion.

I heard, he sent as he was hauled along behind her.

A group of five gray-clad Sholans stood ahead of them, isolated by the crowd in the middle of the busy concourse. They moved back, looking toward her and the guards and as they did, she saw two more wearing robes edged with purple.

Concentrating, she reached with her mind, desperate for a chance to plead their cause.

"You'll find Haven still full of construction teams, I'm afraid," said Rhyaz. "You particularly, Sister Jiosha. The Shrine won't be finished for several weeks yet, but I'm sure your presence as spiritual head will speed up the process."

Jiosha returned the Guild Master's smile. "I'm sure it will," she said. "So long as we can use the Shrine once a day, I'll be content for the next few weeks."

"Excuse me, Master Rhyaz," interrupted Lyand, "there's a group of Humans coming toward us. Soldiers."

The group parted, turning to look at the approaching soldiers and their prisoners.

"They're very young," observed Rhyaz. "I don't recognize them. Lyand?" he asked his new aide.

"Not from the Telepath Guild, and certainly not the En'Shalla estate."

L'Seuli stepped in front of Rhyaz. "I think they expect us to move, Master Rhyaz," he murmured as the approaching soldier indicated with his gun barrel that they should stand aside.

"Stop them," said Jiosha, a startled look on her face as she grabbed hold of the Brotherhood Guild Master. "The female, she's claiming sanctuary with us!"

"What?" L'Seuli glanced at her, seeing she was serious, then looked at Rhyaz for orders. There was a curious expression on his superior's face, one that made L'Seuli gesture to Lyand before stepping in front of the lead soldier.

"My apologies, Trooper," he said. "We need to talk with the officer in charge of this detail."

"Captain's on the *Seattle*," he said, indicating a location behind the Sholan. "Have to hurry if you want him. Liftoff's in nine minutes. Now if you'll excuse me, we gotta get these young criminals on board."

"What have they done?" asked L'Seuli.

"Not my business, Brother," said the soldier, moving forward. "Now stand aside. I got a job to do."

"So have I," said L'Seuli, halting him by placing a hand on his chest. "They come with us. Your Captain meets us on our ship in fifteen minutes."

The soldier looked at L'Seuli in amazement, then laughing, turned to glance back at his companions. The laughter died. Half a dozen more gray-clad Sholans had materialized from nowhere and the two prisoners were now in their custody. He felt his weapon grasped and with a sigh, released it.

"On the *Chazoi* in fifteen minutes," said L'Seuli quietly, gesturing to the Brothers and Sisters before turning to Rhyaz.

"What the hell's going on?" demanded Rhyaz as they followed the two young Humans up the ramp into the *Chazoi*. "Why did you interfere?"

"They asked Jiosha for sanctuary," he said, leading the way to his office. "Take them to the mess, Lyand," he said over his shoulder, "and release them from those restraints."

As soon as the door closed behind them, Rhyaz walked over to the nearest chair. "I think you should tell me why you felt it necessary to interfere in the Humans' lawful business, L'Seuli," he said quietly, sitting down.

L'Seuli looked at the telepath. "Jiosha, you'd explain it better than me," he said.

"The younglings were on the *Odyssey*, Commander," she said, taking one of the other chairs. "It brought in the last of the Human telepaths from Earth earlier today."

"I remember hearing it was due about now. That doesn't explain why you felt it necessary to kidnap those younglings. You know this could escalate into an incident with us at the core? We don't need that kind of attention right now."

"They sent to me, Commander," said Jiosha. "They're telepaths. If they're returned to Earth, they'll be sent to one of several military establishments to be trained against their will."

Rhyaz raised an eye ridge. "They're a sovereign world, Jiosha. If they choose to recruit their telepaths into the military, we can't interfere."

"Not recruit," she said. "Force. These are unregistered ones, hiding from their authorities. They were trying to reach us."

"We can't interfere," he repeated.

"We must. They asked for sanctuary."

"I heard you the first time," he said, irritated. "Naturally we can't grant it."

"We have to," said Jiosha. "They appealed to me. As a priestess and a leader of the Order of Vartra, I have to honor their request. And there's possibly another reason," she said, glancing over at L'Seuli.

"More compelling than asking for sanctuary? I'm all ears," Rhyaz said with heavy irony.

I'm not telling him. We might be wrong, she sent to L'Seuli.

He looked at the ceiling, closing his eyes briefly. If they were right, there was no way they could allow the female at least to leave this ship, and if they were wrong, this could be highly embarrassing for all concerned.

"If they're rounding up the telepaths and forcing them into training centers for military use, that's persecution," said L'Seuli. "And that is against Alliance laws, Commander. It's a matter for AlRel. Chagda is considered Alliance soil, so Alliance law takes precedence over Terran ones."

Very diplomatic! sent Jiosha, her mental tone highly sarcastic. He wished for the thousandth time he had the ability to send telepathically as well as receive.

"Contact the Clan Lord, Lyand," sighed Rhyaz. "And my ship. Tell them to stand down, we'll not be leaving for several hours. I'm surprised we haven't heard from the Captain of the—was it the *Seattle*?"

"Yes, Commander," said Lyand.

"I don't think we'll hear from him, Commander," said Jiosha. "If they're engaged in illegal acts, they won't want to argue the matter of those two telepaths with us."

"Call Port Control and have them hold the *Seattle* and its crew for questioning," he ordered. "I'll be damned if they head out of here leaving this mess in our den!"

"Three tugs have been diverted to see the *Seattle* stays in its berth," said L'Seuli. "We got them just in time, they were continuing to undock. I also called the Palace and spoke to Master Konis. He's putting an impound order on the *Odyssey* and sending troops to escort the Captain of the *Seattle* down to Shola for an explanation of his actions."

Rhyaz got to his feet. "Well done, both of you. All that remains is for us to have these two young people escorted to the Port Protectorate office until AlRel arrives."

"I'm afraid it isn't so simple, Commander," said L'Seuli. "Master Konis wants us to remain here as well."

"And the younglings will have to go to Father Lijou at Stronghold," added Jiosha. "They've been granted sanctuary. They're our responsibility, not AlRel's."

"Lyand, tell Captain Fyshar to present my apologies to the Rryuk Matriarch but I've been detained on sudden and unavoidable Alliance business. He's to proceed to Home without me," sighed Rhyaz, getting up.

Lyand nodded and slipped out.

"Let's go and see these two young people," he said, heading for the door.

Jiosha threw L'Seuli a frantic look but all he could do was raise his shoulders helplessly, trying to convey the question what did she expect him to do about it?

She stood up, moving swiftly to reach the door before him. "Commander, it might be better not to see them," she said.

"Excuse me?" he asked, obviously baffled by her behavior.

"I don't know what your gift is, Commander, but did you experience anything strange when we stopped the Human soldiers?"

"I'm sorry, you've lost me, Jiosha," he said as L'Seuli joined her between him and the door.

"No, we lost *you*. For a full minute. We don't think you should go near the younglings until we've had advice from Father Lijou. You might be forming a Leska Link with the female."

Rhyaz' mouth dropped open in shock as he stared disbelievingly at her.

"That's why I couldn't let the Humans take them away," said L'Seuli. "We could be wrong, Commander," he added hastily, "but we couldn't take that chance."

"I appreciate your concern, L'Seuli," he said quietly, moving them aside and opening the door. "But I will see the younglings."

"Commander," said L'Seuli, catching up with him outside the mess. "If we're right and you go in there . . ."

Rhyaz stopped. "When the Brotherhood recruited me, L'Seuli, I accepted because I believed you can either take life by the throat and fight it, or run and cower in your den. Do me one favor if you will."

"Anything."

"Get everyone but the female out of there," he said, reaching for his gun and his knife and passing them to him. "And ask Jiosha to be on hand."

He stood back and waited as L'Seuli ordered the two Brothers and the young male out. Then he went in, closing the door behind him.

She was seated at the first table, holding a mug.

"Djana," he said, walking round to the head of the table and pulling out a chair. "Do you speak Sholan?" he asked, sitting down.

She looked quizzically at him and shook her head. "Sorry, I don't understand," she said in Terran.

He recognized the accent and language. "You come from England?" he asked in her language.

A smile lit her face. "Yes. Thank you for rescuing us. You did rescue us, didn't you?" As she frowned, her eyebrows met under the fringe of almost white-blonde hair that framed her oval face. "The one in the long black robes is a priest, isn't she?"

"Yes, sanctuary has been granted," he confirmed. "And yes, Sister Jiosha is a telepath priest. You sent to her."

She looked puzzled. "No, I didn't. I knew by your gray robe you were in charge."

Icy shock ran through him and his ears began to flatten until common sense took hold. "You thought you did. It's easy to make a mistake when you're an untrained telepath."

She shrugged, lifting up her mug and taking a drink. "I don't make those kind of mistakes," she said. "Ask her, this Sister Jiosha. She knows it was you I spoke to. She's outside the door, isn't she?"

"Why did you want to come to Shola?" he asked abruptly.

"Got nothing to keep us on good old Earth," she said, putting the mug down. "Where have they taken Kai?"

"To another room. I wanted to speak to you on your own."

"What happens now? When do we go down to Shola?"

"I'm asking the questions, Djana," he said, allowing a faint growl to creep into his voice.

"Alex. My name's Alex," she said. "I told you everything that's important."

"You told Jiosha," he said firmly. "Now you'll tell me. Do you know who we are?"

"Some religious group," she said. "You're telepaths. You've got purple on your robes."

He frowned, wishing she wouldn't keep insisting he was a telepath. "We're the Brotherhood of Vartra, an Order of Warrior Priests," he said. "Ours is the main religion of Shola."

"So I'm impressed. Now will you tell me what happens next? And who are you? I've told you my name. You could be polite enough to tell me yours."

"Commander Rhyaz. I'm the leader of the Warriors in the Brotherhood," he said, annoyed by her attitude.

She smiled, and he knew she was following his surface thoughts. He was being purposely baited for her amusement. He got to his feet. "You'll remain here for the time being, Alex. Seems the Captain of the *Seattle* was prepared to leave you here with us. However, granting you sanctuary has put us in an awkward position with Earth. You'll have to wait till the head of our Alien Relations arrives."

He made it as far as the door before she called out after him. "You going to feed us or what? It's been a long time since we last ate."

"You'll be fed," he said shortly as he opened the door.

Once outside, he leaned against the wall, breathing more easily. "Nothing," he said to Jiosha. "I felt nothing."

"Nothing?"

"Oh, she gave me some tale about it being me she sent to, not you, but she was trying to manipulate me," he said. "Get a cabin set up for them and put them in there. Show them how to use the dispenser to get some food. We'll wait here till Konis arrives. Any idea how long he'll be?"

"Several hours, L'Seuli said. Commander," she replied, reaching out to touch his arm. "It was you she sent to. I received it, too, but it was directed at you."

"Come on, Jiosha, you didn't fall for that, did you?" he asked, heading back down the corridor to L'Seuli's office. "I'm not a telepath! And I knew nothing about her, you had to tell me."

"What is your gift then, Commander?" she asked, almost running to keep pace with him.

"Empathy," he said shortly, stopping dead and turning on her. "And don't say a damned thing about Dzaka and Kitra and how he was only an empath!"

When L'Seuli returned after escorting Konis down to the cabin where the two younglings were being kept, he threw a handful of cutlery onto the low table beside the sofa on which Rhyaz was lying.

"You starting a collection?" Rhyaz asked, sitting up and eyeing the assorted knives and spoons.

"They had the access panel hanging off the wall," said L'Seuli, sitting down in an easy chair.

"What?"

"They had . . ."

"I heard you! What the hell were they doing?"

"Trying to escape again."

"And Jiosha wants us to take them to Stronghold!"

"We can tag them. It's been done before. I believe there was a time Kaid was tagged. In his early days," he added hastily, seeing Rhyaz' expression. "He left to fetch T'Chebbi from one of the packs in Ranz. They tagged him when he returned, but only for a couple of months."

"They should go to Vartra's Retreat. Let Dhaika have 'em," Rhyaz grumbled, sitting up and swinging his legs to the floor. He'd spent most of the last three hours fielding official complaints from the *Odyssey* and the *Seattle* as well as the Human Ambassador on Shola.

"The Telepath Guild would be most appropriate," said L'Seuli. "Not the nicest thing to do to Master Sorli, though."

"What do these younglings want here?" he asked. "Is it just to escape from their authorities?"

"That's a pretty powerful motivation on its own," said L'Seuli. "Jiosha says they haven't thought that far ahead. They're orphans, ran away from the orphanage about four years ago when it was discovered they had psi talents. They've been living on their wits ever since."

"Well, they've chosen the wrong place to come if they think it's any easier here. If Konis grants them Residence permits, then they're not our problem any longer. He can pack them off to the Telepath Guild. Did she find out if they're a couple?"

"Just friends. They know each other too well for anything else. You know, it was pretty enterprising of them getting as far as they did with that access plate," said L'Seuli. "They knew nothing about our power sources or devices. They might just be Brotherhood material."

Rhyaz gave him a vitriolic glare. "Don't talk up trouble," he said, picking up his mug of cold c'shar. "I should be on my way to Home now. How's it going to look to the Rryuk Matriarch when she hears I canceled her personal invitation at the last minute?"

"At least she's getting our people to teach her specialist fighters," said L'Seuli. "You can visit her another time."

Rhyaz muttered darkly until Lyand put a fresh mug of c'shar beside him and L'Seuli.

"Would you like third meal now, Commander?" he asked.

"We'll wait for Master Konis," said Rhyaz. "I wouldn't mind a small snack in the meantime, though. Something to take the edge off my hunger. Thank you, Lyand."

As the door closed behind his new aide, Rhyaz leaned back on the sofa. "I'm going to miss you," he said. "Lyand is good, you trained him well, but he's not you."

L'Seuli folded his ears back in embarrassment. "I'm glad I was able to help," he murmured.

"Don't work too hard out there on Haven. Remember to take time off. And find yourself a Companion, for Vartra's sake!"

Again, L'Seuli's ears disappeared. "I won't have time to get to know any females, Master Rhyaz. There's far too much to do."

"You know Jiosha. I've seen the way you look at her when you think she isn't aware of you. Father Lijou tells me you and she were in the same intake year."

"I'm sure I don't know what you're talking about, Master Rhyaz," he said, his voice sounding distinctly strangled.

"Yes, you do. Do it now, L'Seuli, before you get too settled into a routine of nothing but work. Then you'll never do it. I've seen the difference Kha'Qwa's made to Lijou and have moments when I regret not following his advice. I'm too set in my ways now, though." He narrowed his eyes briefly. "And no, I'm not trying to convince myself!"

L'Seuli tried to cover his startlement by picking up his mug.

Jiosha caught sight of the distinctive red- and purple-edged overrobe of the Clan Lord outside the room the two young Humans were in and hurried over to talk to him.

"Clan Lord," she said, dipping her head in respect. "I must talk to you."

Konis excused himself from the crewmale he'd been talking to and, taking her gently by the shoulder, led her down the corridor to L'Seuli's office.

"Were we right?" she asked.

"Perhaps," he said. "I do know the Commander is now capable of receiving telepathically. He isn't one of the gene-altered Brothers, that I do know, so it would seem unlikely that he'd develop a Leska Link to a Human, but stranger things have happened, as we all know. I'm going to give him my psi damper bracelet. I can get another, but I feel it's imperative he wear one from now on. L'Seuli and you, too. I'll see we have some sent out to you at Haven."

"Thank you, Master Konis. What about you, though? Surely your need is just as great?"

Konis smiled. "No, I'm more than able to block any but the most determined attempt to read me against my will, Jiosha, and I'd notice any such attempt. The Touibans have miniaturized the device now to the point it can be inserted into any wrist comm. I've always meant to have mine done, just to be rid of the need to wear two, only I've never gotten around to it. This will be an incentive."

"If you're sure, Master Konis. And thank you, the personal dampers will be most useful, I'm sure. What do you plan to do with Alex and Kai?"

"I'm granting them Residence, but in view of your fears, I think it advisable that both they and he stay at Stronghold for the next few weeks. If nothing happens within that time, then likely it won't. Has he touched her, do you know? Touch seems to be the trigger."

"Not that I know of, but he was alone with her in the mess."

"The best thing we can do is let nature take its own course. I'll speak to Father Lijou about this personally so he can be alert for anything happening. You and L'Seuli just put your minds at rest that the matter is well in hand and head out to Haven to take up your new posts. You'll have problems enough of your own, I'm sure."

"Thank you, Master Konis. I'm sure you're right and there's nothing to worry about," she said, relieved.

Prime world, Zhal-Oeshi, 10th day (August)

"General. Nice to see you back from the dark reaches of space," said Q'akuh, opening the door to him. "Was it a good trip?"

Several answers sprang to his mind but he satisfied himself with saying, "Yes."

"I must admit I was surprised not to be taken with you," Q'akuh said, gesturing to him to enter.

"Well, it was you or one of my favorite young females, Q'akuh," he said lazily, looking round the small lounge as he entered. Two males, both vaguely familiar. "Hardly a difficult choice." Zayshul had suggested he take at least one of his camp followers with them and pay some attention to her to stave off suspicion. Now he recognized the wisdom of her advice, though at the time he'd balked at any action that suggested he had an unbridled sexual appetite.

Q'akuh laughed politely. "Then I can't in fairness complain. Sit down, General. A glass of wine perhaps? This is Zhayan, Director of Sciences in the City, and Director Zsiyuk, in charge of shipping contracts. They've been anxious to meet you for some time, but unfortunately your aide said your calendar was full. Under the circumstances, I hope you don't mind me inviting them here today."

The room was small, with three doors leading off it, one in each wall. Furnishings were basic, nowhere near the level of comfort he'd had even in his single quarters. Predictably, there were no windows. It was the apartment of a minor courtier, such as he'd stayed in when summoned to the Court by his Emperor.

He chose a seat with a view of the door, set to one side of where Q'akuh's guests were sitting.

"Of course he minds," said Zsiyuk in his gravelly voice. "If he's anything like me, he can't abide all the claw sharpening that goes on behind the scenes to get anything done around here! Well, we aren't here to ask you to get concessions for us at Court, Kezule."

"I'm sure you aren't, Director," said Kezule, accepting the glass Q'akuh held out to him.

"You're an old-fashioned type, like myself, aren't you, General?" continued the elderly male. "Things were simpler in your day. You needed ships, you ordered 'em. None of this bureaucracy with its advisory committees and budget priorities!"

"Quite so," murmured Kezule, tongue flicking out, apparently to test the wine before sipping it. He smelled nothing from Zsiyuk, a hint of apprehension from the scientist, and fear from Q'akuh, roughly what he'd expected. "However, we had the revenue from three colonies and at least four slave worlds to play with. A far cry from now."

"The golden age of our Empire," agreed Zsiyuk, taking a sip from his glass of spirits. "We should be working toward reestablishing that Empire, Kezule, don't you think?"

"We don't need the territory from what I've seen of your population, Director. Females were larger in our time, the higher castes capable of laying two, occasionally even three eggs a season. Yours manage only one in that time."

"Expansion is easy," said Zhayan. "We breed our own people the way we breed the M'zullians."

"I'm aware of that," said Kezule dryly.

"Disgraceful business, that," said Zsiyuk, shaking his head. "No way to treat a member of the royal family like yourself. One could almost call it a betrayal."

"I'm none too pleased," he admitted, taking another sip from his glass.

"I hear you'll be training the new officers along with the M'zullian batch. Where're they going to end up?"

"The Emperor's personal guard, of course, then the Palace guard and other posts as the need arises. They'll be a great improvement over the implant volunteers."

Zsiyuk sighed. "I said they'd be squandered, didn't I?" he said to Zhayan. "What I could do with a hundred Warriors all loyal to me!"

"Eighty," Kezule corrected. "Twenty are females for breeding. What would you do with the officers, Zsiyuk?"

"Use 'em to mount an offensive against M'zull and J'kirtikk," he said promptly. "You were on the *Kz'adul*. I presume you've seen its offensive capabilities. We should be launching a preemptive strike against them now, while they're quiet. We don't need ground troops, just blast 'em from space and the air!"

"The *Kz'adul*'s a science ship, Zsiyuk, not a warship," Kezule pointed out.

"A few weeks in my yards and we can convert her. They'd never even see us coming with our chameleon shields!"

"Your Emperor thinks otherwise," said Kezule quietly. "Emperor Q'emgo'h, *may his name be revered for all time,* valued his Warriors. Through us, he controlled his Empire with claws of steel. Your Emperor is content with his one world and making treaties to keep the others at bay."

Zsiyuk lifted his chin a fraction. "Do I detect a hint of criticism of—our Emperor?"

Kezule shrugged, sipping his drink. "Interpret it how you wish, Zsiyuk. It came as a shock to find I was a member of an extinct caste in this time, and that despite your authorities trying to breed more Warriors, they've no intention of utilizing their skills efficiently."

"What if you were given that chance, Kezule? Would you take it?"

"The likelihood of that happening is small."

"Would you take it?" insisted Zsiyuk.

Kezule leaned forward and put his glass back on the table. "You're asking me to commit treason, Zsiyuk," he said. "Why should I want to do that? Emperor Cheu'ko'h has been generous to me, welcoming me into his family, giving me a commission that at least utilizes some of my talents. For all I know you could be agents of the Enforcers, testing my loyalty."

"We take as many risks approaching you, General," said Zhayan quietly. "You could report us just as easily."

"I didn't invite this conversation, or this meeting. I've no wish to be associated with a small fanatical group of activists who have more ideas than resources."

"We're not without resources, General," said Zsiyuk. "You want ships, I can give them to you. Zhayan and another colleague of ours can provide medical support, including breeding any number of Warriors to your specifications—we have techniques not used by the City Medical authorities. Believe me, we have resources, including funding."

Kezule got to his feet. "I don't think so. You've not convinced me that the risks are worthwhile. There's still the matter of your Emperor. Even if an unauthorized campaign led by me against M'zull and J'kirtikk was successful, I'd still have gone against the wishes of the Emperor and would face treason charges."

"General, we're not suggesting an unauthorized campaign against our old colonies," said Zsiyuk. "We're asking you to head a coup against Emperor Cheu'ko'h. You are in a unique position, General: you're a blood relative of the last royal family, you have the Emperor's trust, and you're training a large number of Warriors who are your own offspring. You can train them to be utterly loyal to you."

"You expect me to stage a coup with only ninety-five Warriors? They may be adult in years, but they've little experience of the world!"

"Not just with them. I told you, we have other resources, Workers from outside the City, genetically enhanced to be aggressive. The current Palace guard and the Emperor's own security people are all implants—they can be disabled within seconds. You'd have no opposition worth considering."

"How can they be disabled?" he asked disbelievingly.

"By remotes," said Zhayan. "They control the level of various hormones in their systems. Send the right signal and the guards will drop where they stand and remain there till reactivated or until the designated period of unconsciousness has expired."

He'd known how the guards were controlled but this was the first he'd heard of how they could be disabled. What bothered him most about their plan was that it could succeed.

"You're hesitating, General," said Zsiyuk, putting down his now empty glass and getting to his feet. "Good. I wouldn't want you to make your decision in haste. Perhaps it would help if you visited the Directorate headquarters, saw for yourself what we're doing and the resources you will have at your command. Q'akuh, would you take the General's jacket, please? Bring him one which will attract less attention when you take him to our medical facility."

This was going too fast. Collecting information was one thing, getting into this even deeper was not at all what he had in mind.

"I don't think so, Director Zsiyuk," he said as Q'akuh went over to one of the three interior doors. "I've heard enough today to make me prefer to think this over before I get involved any further with you."

"Afraid you don't have a choice, Kezule. Unless you do, your young wife will have a tragic accident when she goes into premature labor in the next few minutes," said Zsiyuk, clasping his hands behind his back. "Perhaps you'd like to give her a call right now and assure her you'll be back in a couple of hours when you've seen to some urgent business."

Kezule stared unblinkingly at him for a moment, then slowly began to unbutton his uniform jacket, keeping his face expressionless. Inside, he was seething. These were not the amateurs he'd assumed them to be. He'd not make that mistake again.

While every instinct was telling him to destroy them here and now, he knew that wouldn't help Zayshul.

Shola, Nezule Estate, the same day

He stood beside Kaid on the edge of the parking area, watching Carrie's aircar landing. Prince Zsurtul had invited her to the meal he was planning for them and she'd surprised him by accepting. It had been at least three weeks since he'd last seen her—he barely remembered her visit when he was ill.

"Stop worrying," said Kaid, glancing at him. "She's only come because it's an excuse to see you."

The aircar door opened, relieving him of the need to find a reply. When Carrie appeared, he saw she was carrying Kashini. The cub let out an excited high-pitched mewl as she saw him and started struggling with her mother.

Automatically, he moved forward to help her but Carrie was already bending down to deposit their daughter on the ground. Stumbling a little, Kashini ran toward him, chattering loudly. Crouching down on one knee, he waited for the small cannon-ball to reach him.

"Da-Da!" she shrieked, throwing herself at him and trying to scramble up his leg to wrap her arms around him. "Da-Da! 'Shini miss you!"

He scooped her up and stood, holding her tightly as Carrie came over. "She's talking," he said lamely.

"Never stops," grinned Carrie, reaching out to touch his cheek. "I wanted you to hear her for yourself. I've missed you."

Kashini squirmed round in his arms and squeaked loudly with pleasure in his ear. "Mama and Da-da both!"

He winced, flattening that ear as he put an arm around Carrie's shoulder to draw her close, only to discover her belly got in the way.

Embarrassed, she would have pulled back but he leaned closer, resting his cheek briefly against hers. "It's good to see you," he said, letting his tongue gently flick over her cheek. "How long now?"

"Only ten weeks," she said, glancing behind him to Kaid as he let her go.

"Kaida-da!" Again Kashini started squirming and wriggling,

trying to get down. This time, Kusac grabbed her more firmly and turned to Kaid.

"I think she wants to see you now," he said, ruffling his daughter's curls before passing her over. The slight look of panic that crossed Kaid's face made him smile.

"Hello, Kashini," Kaid said. "We weren't expecting you tonight."

"'Shini come too," she said, giving him a cuddle which he dutifully returned. "Down now," she said imperiously.

"Only if you hold Mama's hand," he said, stroking her cheek.

"No, Da-da's hand."

Kaid bent down to set her on the ground beside her father.

She reached up, slipping her small hand into his and began tugging him toward the entrance.

"She knows what she wants," said Kaid, grinning at them as he greeted Carrie and took her bag.

"Why did you bring her?" Kusac asked as they walked into the building. "It isn't really a suitable occasion."

"She was missing you so much," said Carrie, "And, of course, she knew where I was coming. How could I say no?"

As he glanced down at her, Kashini looked up, amber eyes widening as she smiled happily. His apprehension vanished at his daughter's obvious pleasure to be with him.

"I see what you mean," he said, tightening his hand round Kashini's. He looked back at Carrie and smiled. "She'll break hearts one day, just like her mother."

Carrie laughed. "I never did anything of the sort!"

"You've two casualties right here," he said quietly.

"Flatterer."

"Are you sure you can cope with meeting Prince Zsurtul?" he asked as they headed down the corridor to the small common room they'd borrowed for the evening.

"I'm fine, Kusac. If you can work with him, then I can accept his dinner invitation. I met him on the *Profit,* it isn't as if I don't know him."

He let it rest, trying not to remember his own difficulties in learning to work with the Prime Prince. He still wasn't at ease with him.

One of the kitchen staff was helping Zsurtul finish setting the dishes out on the table. As soon as they entered, the young Prime shooed him out and came rushing over. He stopped as Kusac picked up Kashini.

"A hatchling!" he said incredulously.

"Cub," corrected Carrie. "Kusac's and my daughter."

Zsurtul looked from one to the other, obviously having great difficulty in reconciling what he saw with the reality of the cub.

Kashini sat back in his arms, leaning against his chest for security and put her fist into her mouth as she stared wide-eyed at the Prince. Over his arm, her short tail began to sway gently.

Zsurtul reached out a curious hand toward her then stopped, looking anxiously at Kusac. "Is it permitted for me to touch her?"

All his paternal instincts made him want to step back and say no but he knew he couldn't. The point of this meal was to build bridges between them. Unable to trust his voice, he forced himself to nod.

Zsurtul touched her cheek with his fingertips. "Such softness," he said, awed. As he continued to gently stroke her, Kashini removed her fist from her mouth and grabbed his hand.

"No, Kashini!" said all three of them as, quick as a flash, the hand went in her mouth.

Zsurtul's eyes widened and his own mouth opened soundlessly. Kashini abruptly let go of him. "Teef!" she pronounced, pointing.

"I'm sorry," said Carrie, moving forward to take Zsurtul's hand and examine it. "Did she bite you?"

Zsurtul shook his head. "No, but her tongue—it scratches!"

Kashini had lost interest in him now that she'd caught sight of the food on the table and was leaning over perilously to see it. "Hungwy!"

"I'm sorry," said Zsurtul, withdrawing his hand gently from Carrie's. "I forget my manners. Come and sit down. I hope you'll like the food, it's a mixture of our dishes and yours so I could be sure there was something you would be comfortable eating. I don't know that your—cub—will like it though," he said, forehead creasing in a concerned frown.

"Don't worry about that, Zsurtul. I've brought her own food with me, but she can try some if she likes. Kashini has her own ideas about everything," said Carrie wryly, taking her bag back from Kaid.

The ice broken by Kashini's presence, the evening went better than he thought it would. He even began to feel a little at ease with the young Prime. For the first time, he saw the person behind the Valtegan shape the Prince wore and realized Zsurtul wasn't that different from themselves or the other species that currently lived on his estate. However, there was still something about the young Prince that kept him on edge.

As they were leaving, Zsurtul called them back. "I meant to tell you, Kaid," he said, "I think I know why you have no problems from our Warriors while General Kezule does."

"Oh? Why's that?" asked Kaid, hesitating in the open doorway.

"Two reasons. One, you'll be training them differently from the General. We have no records on the Warrior caste, I'm afraid, but given their greater level of aggression in his time, I'm sure they'd not have been allowed the freedoms they have here, and certainly they wouldn't have had another species taking the training lessons."

"That goes without saying," said Kaid. "We didn't get any guidelines from your Embassy apart from not allowing them any raw meat."

Zsurtul looked a little crestfallen.

"You did well to work that out for yourself, though," said Kaid encouragingly. "What was your other reason?"

"Your scent. The teachers here aren't afraid of them. The Warriors respond to the fear scent from those of their own rank and above them in authority. You've no reason to fear them because you see them as just students. And they see you as knowing far more than you're teaching them so they don't feel impelled to try to take your places. The ones who died were all victims of training incidents caused by each other."

Kaid nodded thoughtfully. "You might be onto something there. Thank you, Zsurtul. And thanks for a pleasant evening."

"The food was lovely," said Carrie, tucking a small rug inside Kusac's arms and round the sleeping Kashini. "Thank you. Next time, you'll be our guest."

Zsurtul watched them leave, wondering if he should have disobeyed Doctor Zayshul and told them about the scent marker that Kusac carried. It would explain to the Sholan why he'd felt compelled to attack him in the gym, and why he continued to be uneasy in his company. The marker had changed the Sholan, was making him react to male Primes as if they were potential male rivals. He sighed. The Doctor was older, more experienced than him; if she said stay quiet for fear of damaging the fragile treaty, then he'd best do as she said. But it struck him as very unfair to Kusac when he was being blamed for an attitude he could do nothing to control.

Prime world, the same evening

"General Kezule, a pleasure to meet you properly," said K'hedduk, standing up. "Welcome to the Directorate Medical Facility. I'm Doctor K'hedduk,"

"I remember you from the *Kz'adul,*" said Kezule, staring at him. "You were a steward then."

"A steward has far more freedom on board a ship like the *Kz'adul* than a doctor. I believe you've had some of our aims explained to you already?"

"I don't appreciate being forced into meeting your people or visiting this facility," said Kezule coldly, allowing his crest to rise in anger. "Nor do I appreciate the threat to my wife."

"Come, General, don't overdramatize the situation. Please, sit down." He gestured to the seats around him in the conference room. "It was necessary to ensure you were given a clear picture of who we are. We've no wish to harm either Doctor Zayshul or your unborn and unhatched child. Your wife will be a valuable asset to our cause, and one at the heart of the City's own research establishment. Through her, we'll be able to access data and samples otherwise denied to us."

"I don't respond to force, K'hedduk," he hissed. And he didn't intend that his wife and child would be used as lab samples.

"But you're here," said K'hedduk, sitting down. "Stand if you wish, Kezule. I can call you Kezule, can't I? What we're trying to achieve is to restore to our civilization the glory it had at the height of the Empire—your time."

His time? In his time the Empire had been so arrogant and sure of itself that a handful of weak Sholan telepaths, unable to strike a blow without folding up retching, had toppled it not to its knees, but flat on its face. It had taken him much soul-searching to realize this, but now that he did, he saw things a lot more clearly.

"To do this, we need a strong Emperor on the Throne of

Light," continued K'hedduk. "And that isn't our revered Emperor Cheu'ko'h."

"I don't want the throne," he said. "Zsiyuk spoke only of me leading a campaign against M'zull and J'kirtikk."

"I'm sure he would have mentioned that you are a direct descendant of the last true Emperor," murmured K'hedduk. "Never mind. If you prefer to lead the campaign to reunite our Empire again, then your son can rule instead, with a regent appointed until he reaches his majority. Or you can do both—rule and lead the battle."

"I have no son," snarled Kezule, crest beginning to rise.

"Not yet," said K'hedduk complacently. "But your wife is due to lay within the week. Her egg will survive even if she doesn't. And if the hatchling should be a daughter, you can take another wife—or more—once we've toppled Cheu'ko'h. We're offering you the chance to start your own dynasty, to put the blood of your Emperor Q'emgo'h back on the Throne of Light, and lead a military campaign to take back all our old territory. All this with our backing."

"All our old territory?" he asked, surprised.

"Ah, that's got you interested," smiled K'hedduk. "I thought it would. The Sholans ripped you from your own time, held you prisoner and no doubt tortured you. We offer you the chance for revenge, to take Shola again and return them to the slavery which is their natural place in the order of the universe."

"And just how do you propose to do that when it was their telepaths that toppled our Empire in the first place?"

"We have our own telepaths," said K'hedduk. "Hybrid Sholans, birthed from the growth tanks a week ago. And others, adults we captured from a M'zullian vessel a year ago."

"Sholan hybrids? The children of a Human and a Sholan? Where did you get them?" He sat down, stunned.

"We had an agent on the *Kz'adul* who took samples from them when they were in captivity there. The telepaths are loyal to us, Kezule, and they can already use their psi powers. You'll have them at your side, ready and willing to follow your orders, even against their own species."

"Not at my side," he said automatically. Knowing their past, he wanted them as far away from him as possible.

"They are loyal," insisted K'hedduk. "I'll take you to meet them shortly. We've been doing noninvasive experiments to try to find out what makes them telepathic but with no success as yet. The late Doctor Chy'qui had a theory he was trying out on a M'zullian, but although it initially looked promising, his results haven't proved reproducible here."

"You're experimenting on our own people?"

"Of course. How else can we find out if Chy'qui's research was valid? Believe me, we'd all be a lot happier if we had our own telepaths, but it doesn't look possible."

Kezule sat silently, appalled by the depths to which these people were prepared to go to restore what they saw as the glory of their Empire.

"I can see you're concerned over experimenting on our own. Don't be," said K'hedduk, standing. "They were convicts, due for execution. At least here they are fulfilling a purpose, repaying our society for the harm they've done. Come with me and I'll show you around our facility."

Kezule followed him back along the corridor toward the elevator.

"We keep our young Sholans in here," said K'hedduk, stopping outside a guarded room.

While the doctor went about unlocking the door, Kezule stared at the large tattooed male holding an energy rifle. The guard stared back at him, his jaw clenching slightly as a belligerent look came into his eyes. This had to be one of the altered Workers Zsiyuk had spoken about. That they were even considering letting people like this loose on the City, with or without weapons, was insane! Even he felt somewhat intimidated by the male's sheer bulk.

The door swung open and K'hedduk invited Kezule to enter. Immediately his eyes were drawn to the eight young Sholans. Even taking into account that they were seated at a table, they were small. The youngsters got to their feet as soon as they entered, standing by their chairs, faces tilted toward the ground. One, slower than the rest, earned a sharp rebuke. The adult Prime with them also rose.

"Good evening, Doctor K'hedduk," she said.

"Good evening, Seniormost Doctor," chanted the youngsters.

K'hedduk nodded. "This is General Kezule. He's come to inspect you."

Kezule moved closer, fascinated despite himself. The Human

female, one of the three who'd brought him to this time, had been carrying a hybrid child. Hers would look like this.

"How old are they?" he asked.

"Ten years old. They mature later than us. Around thirty for the males to attain full growth, but both sexes are capable of breeding from fourteen."

Kezule looked at the array of body colors. They ranged from gray through several shades of brown to one black-coated child. He looked again at the black one, going closer to inspect it, remembering who'd been on board the *Kz'adul*. The pelt had a blue sheen to it, and his scent held a familiarity. He took hold of the child's jaw and gently lifted up the face. Amber eyes stared steadily, almost challengingly, back at him, then blinked, and the look was gone, replaced by that of a nervous child. Letting him go, Kezule exhaled slowly. This one belonged to Kusac. He had within his grasp a greater chance for revenge than K'hedduk could ever guess. By all the God-Kings, the Directorate wouldn't keep this one, he would!

A slight sound from one of the other children drew his attention to it. He saw a dampness on its cheeks and recognized it as the one who'd been rebuked. He put his hand on its head, gently ruffling the long gray hair.

"She's easily upset," said the teacher by way of explanation. "Not as bright as the others."

"Is it a problem?" asked K'hedduk, a note of concern in his voice. "There's no point in our efforts being wasted if she's incapable of learning."

"Her usefulness will be limited, Doctor, but her gender makes her valuable," said the teacher.

"That's hardly a concern. Keep me briefed on her progress, or lack of it. We'll review her viability in a week. I'm not prepared to waste any more time than that."

Rage boiled up inside Kezule. He let his hand slip to the child's shoulder, giving her a gentle and reassuring squeeze before turning away.

"I've seen enough," he said, going back to the door.

Outside, K'hedduk spoke about the research on telepathy being conducted on Primes but it went over Kezule's head. He could hardly believe that they were callously discussing whether or not to keep the young Sholan alive in front of her. For one thing, it would be unlikely to engender trust for their keepers in the others. He'd never debased his pet telepath like that.

"They're being treated carefully, General, and wear psychic inhibitors unless they're actually being trained in using their abilities. I want willing, compliant slaves, not rebellious untrustworthy ones," said K'hedduk, catching sight of his face. He stopped in front of another door. "This is where we run our telepathy tests on the criminals."

He came back to reality with a jolt. "I don't need to see them," he said tightly.

K'hedduk lifted his head slightly. "Squeamish, General? I'm surprised. I would have thought you'd be used to the dirty side of war."

He bit back his reply. He was, but this wasn't war; and this went against all that was natural or reasonable in the treatment of even slaves.

"Very well, I'll show you our other Sholan subjects."

The scent of antiseptics drifted out into the corridor when K'hedduk opened the next door. He entered, finding himself in laboratory with two large cages at the far end. K'hedduk led the way past a workbench down to them. One looked to be empty, and in the other, on a straw-covered floor, he could see the hunched figure of an adult Sholan female.

"We have another three females but we're keeping them in stasis for the moment," K'hedduk said. "She was of great help to us. We bred her to enable us to work out the conditions necessary for growing our hybrids in the tanks." He snapped out an order, telling her to look up. When she did, her eyes were as dull and lifeless as her brown pelt.

"Her child died, I take it," Kezule said, feeling some comment was expected from him.

"No, it's in stasis. We don't need it at the moment. When we do, we can accelerate its growth. An infant is no use to us at present. Unfortunately, we couldn't be sure of sustaining our hybrids in the tanks beyond the age they are now or we'd have grown them to adulthood, too." K'hedduk turned and pointed to the cage opposite.

"That was her mate. We've been running experiments on him to find out which portions of his brain to stimulate in the hopes of generating psi abilities. He was even implanted with the device Chy'qui used on the M'zullian. But it failed on him as well."

Kezule took a couple of steps toward the cage, realizing that what he'd mistaken for a pile of straw bedding was in fact another Sholan. He could see the white of bandages showing against the dull tan pelt. "His arms. What happened to him?"

"Oh, that's self-inflicted," said K'hedduk as he headed back toward the workbench. "He kept trying to escape from the cage to rejoin his mate. Some of them have very little common sense, as you probably know. This one was convinced he could get through the bars by the sheer effort of throwing himself repeatedly at them. His wounds keep going septic because he keeps worrying at them and getting dirt from the cage floor in them."

He stepped closer, seeing the small implant on the back of the male's neck where the hair had been cut and shorn back. Other areas on his head had been shorn at some time and through the new growth, he could see the bright pink of older surgical scars.

Hearing his footsteps, the Sholan male lifted his head from the floor and looked out at him. His eyes carried the same dead look of hopelessness as his mate's.

Impelled by some force he couldn't resist, Kezule stepped closer until he was touching the bars. He saw the male's mouth moving and realized he was trying to talk. Glancing over his shoulder, he saw K'hedduk was engrossed at the lab bench, checking a display on one of the monitors. He turned back, bending down and moving slightly so his own body shielded him from being seen.

"What?" he asked quietly in the other's language. "What do you want?"

"Soldier," the male whispered, sliding his arm painfully toward him. "You're a soldier." He clenched his hand on the bar, fingers still swollen and cut from his efforts to escape, knuckles showing white through the tan pelt. There was a feverish spark of life in his eyes now.

"Yes." How had he known that? Unless . . .

"Stop this. No way for a soldier to die."

"I can't."

Without realizing what he was doing, Kezule's hand reached between the bars and gently closed around the Sholan's throat. The male laid his head back down on the floor and shut his eyes.

By all the God-Kings, what am I doing? he asked himself as his hand suddenly clenched in a stranglehold. Appalled, he let go only to hear a last gentle sigh from the male before his body went limp.

Snatching his hand back, he stumbled to his feet with an exclamation of shock.

K'hedduk looked round questioningly.

"I think he's dead," he said, unable to take his eyes off the Sholan.

"What?" He heard footsteps as K'hedduk ran over to see for himself. When poking and prodding him got no response, K'hedduk began to swear.

"Burn it! We only have two adult males! We hadn't finished with him!"

"It happens," said Kezule, trying to affect an unconcern he didn't feel. There wasn't a shred of doubt in his mind that he'd been mentally manipulated by the male. K'hedduk had succeeded in turning the Sholan into a telepath—unless somehow he'd been able to conceal his ability all along.

"I'll have to get someone in to clear up," said K'hedduk, getting to his feet. "I need to have an autopsy done. I hope you won't mind if we curtail the tour here."

"Not at all," said Kezule, glancing back at the female as he followed K'hedduk. She'd moved and was now sitting by the bars staring at her dead mate. Her eyes caught his and he could tell she knew what he'd done and was grateful. He shivered and looked away, hurriedly following K'hedduk out into the corridor. Every time he came up against Sholans, they challenged his beliefs about them. He wondered how many of his caste in the same situation could have achieved what that male had.

"Q'akuh will take you back to the City, General. I hope you've seen enough to know we're serious. Will you join us?" asked K'hedduk, locking the door behind them.

"I'll join you," he said, trying to keep his true feelings from sounding in his voice. "The thought of vengeance against the Sholans is appealing. I always preferred an active life to the sedentary one of the Court. But there's something I want in return."

"I think you'll be more than recompensed," said K'hedduk. "But tell me anyway."

"I used to have a pet, a Sholan telepath. All the leading people of my time had one. I want the gray-pelted child. You said she's slow and of little use to you. She'll amuse my wife and be a symbol of my status."

Kezule stopped and looked at him curiously. "I hadn't thought your taste for revenge would go quite that far. I can't give her to you now, General. To take her out of here would be inviting discovery. It wouldn't be possible for you to keep her existence secret. Once the coup is over, she's yours, will that do?"

"If I can trust you to keep your word."

"I'll keep mine for as long as you do," said K'hedduk quietly. "If you don't, then not only will she die, but so will your family. As we've shown today with your wife, we have long arms, General."

Kezule stopped dead and turned on him, hands itching to wrap themselves around his throat. "If you harm her or my wife, K'hedduk, I will find you and squeeze every drop of blood from your body. Do you understand?" he hissed. "That Sholan child is mine!"

"I think we understand each other perfectly, General. This is a mutually advantageous business arrangement, nothing more." K'hedduk gestured to the far end of the corridor where Q'akuh waited by the elevator. "We'll be in touch, General Kezule. So nice to have met you at last."

Kezule inclined his head briefly before stalking off toward the waiting male.

CHAPTER 14

ZAYSHUL was alone again when he got back to their apartment, unaware of the danger she'd been in. Before he did anything else, he went through every room, searching it thoroughly for any listening or recording devices. He found none. By the time he'd finished telling her what he'd seen and heard, she was gray with fear.

"We're leaving as soon as possible," he said grimly. "As long as I'm here, we're a focus for them and our lives are in danger."

"I can't believe Chy'qui actually took samples and bred hybrids," she moaned. "And K'hedduk! He was a doctor all along!"

"Forget that. We've more important things to worry about."

"We can't leave those cubs there, Kezule! We have to tell the Enforcers what they're doing!"

"I don't intend to leave them, and you'll say nothing to anyone. I don't want the Prime authorities knowing K'hedduk has tame captive Sholan telepaths. I'll deal with this my way. I don't like being threatened, Zayshul. K'hedduk forgets that I can also use my Warriors against him. Have you compiled that list I asked you to make?"

"I did it this afternoon, after that person left." She reached for the reader on the table beside her. "I've thought of forty-two people, but that's stretching it. I can't vouch for them all."

"Good. We'll go through it and I'll make up the shortfall from my Warriors. Are they high profile people? Likely to draw attention to us if we suddenly start keeping company with them?" He began scanning through her list. The bulk were in the medical sciences but that was her profession. The rest were in communications and other related fields—skills found on ships such as the *Kz'adul*.

"No. Most are either already my friends or are friends of theirs."

"How many have skills that would allow me to legitimately recruit them to help handle the eighty new officers? Weapons, tactics, maintenance, defensive skills, that type of thing."

"About fifteen have some training in weapons and weapons maintenance. We had to double up our skills as part of our courses. The rest could come to watch the training on their days off, maybe even take part on the pretext of seeing their friends."

"We start recruiting them tomorrow, Zayshul," he said, handing the list back to her. "Get in touch with those you trust most first."

"I can invite most of them over here for a small party in a week if all goes well," she said quietly.

"What do you mean if all goes well? And why in a week, why not now?" he demanded.

"The egg," she said.

"Oh, that," he said, sitting down and looking at her. "Are the TeLaxaudin ever wrong?"

"Not that I've known of," she said, examining her claw tips carefully.

"Then everything will be fine," he said, keeping his worries to himself while wishing he could sound more convincing. He'd grown used to her company. Without her, he'd be without a confidante, a friend. The threat to her from K'hedduk's people had brought home to him just how much he relied on her, and how important a figure she now was in his life. He'd never let anyone this close to him before.

"I'm going to have one of the officers guard you, and the egg when it's laid, at all times until we leave here. I'm not risking your safety again."

Once more the color left her face. "Don't say that, you're scaring me."

Shola, the Governor's Palace, Zhal-Oeshi, 15th day (August)

"The wages you're paying them now, Raiban, are barely enough for them to continue working for you!" said Rhyaz angrily to the Head of the High Command.

"Don't blame me, Rhyaz," she said, tapping her stylus against the tabletop. "Our budget's almost used up for this half year. We're only deducting standard costs for munitions and laundry, nothing more."

"You're making them pay for their meals. They're included for the Forces, and were for our people until now."

"We're spread thinner now that we're monitoring around the M'zullian and J'kirtikkian sectors, Rhyaz. I'm sorry, but there have to be cuts from nonessential areas."

"Since when were training and deep reconnaissance missions considered nonessential?"

"I'm using more of our Forces people. It's time they got involved in those missions."

Konis Aldatan stirred. "Rhyaz has a valid argument, Raiban," he said. "Your budget included funding to hire the Brotherhood for certain regular services, which you've now either drastically reduced or cut completely. You're surely saving enough money in those areas without going to the lengths of charging them for meals and ammunition used when training Forces personnel."

"I'm ruled by my treasury department, Konis, just as you are by yours. It's not my choice."

Rhyaz hissed in disbelief, but as a gesture from Konis, he fell silent.

"That's not the issue. President Nesul wants a compromise from both of you."

"My hands are tied, Konis," said Raiban, laying her stylus down and leaning her chair back on its rear legs. "I can do nothing until new funds are released next month. If the Brotherhood were an integrated part of our Forces, then what we'd save on processing various wage and equipment claims might well pick up the shortfall we need."

"That's a load of crap and you know it," snarled Rhyaz, getting to his feet. "I've had enough, Konis. As far as I'm concerned, this meeting is over." He turned and stalked out, tail swaying angrily.

Raiban waited until the door of Konis' office had slammed before speaking. "Is it my imagination, or is our Guild Master a little more short-tempered than usual?"

"Raiban, don't treat me like a fool," said Konis. "No one has any illusions about what you're doing, we just can't prove it. Mark me well, you're being extremely foolish in making enemies of them."

"The Brotherhood doesn't frighten me, Konis," said Raiban. "Vindictiveness isn't their style. Revenge, yes, but not over this footling little business."

"You minimize the importance of freedom to the Brotherhood at your own peril," said Konis. "And there's the small matter of Kha'Qwa. If I were you, I'd not be pushing Rhyaz and Lijou so hard."

Raiban's chair sat upright with a crash. "Hold on a minute, Konis! There's no way I can be held responsible for what happened to Kha'Qwa!"

"Legally, no, but morally, yes. You intended to frighten her, played on her emotional state knowing she was pregnant. You've never even offered an apology for what happened."

"Dammit, Konis, you've no right to moralize over this! And what the hell has it to do with Rhyaz?"

"Raiban, take a lesson from what happened to Chuz," said Konis, getting to his feet. "You're in danger of becoming him." He turned and began to walk out.

"What do you mean by that?" demanded Raiban, jumping up and following him.

"Perhaps it's the position that changes the incumbent," mused Konis, opening the door and heading out into the corridor. "Ambition is a terrible master, Raiban, a terrible master, as Esken discovered." He stopped and turned to look at her. "He lives quietly now, you know. Doesn't attend any of the functions Master Sorli has held at the Telepath Guild since he took over. Nice to see him injecting some life and youth into the Guild, don't you think?" Then the vague look on his face left as he spotted his aide coming toward him.

"Falma! Just who I wanted," he said, heading purposefully over to him. As he did, he mentally touched Raiban's mind, listening in to her surface thoughts. They were exactly what he wanted. Troubled. She was going to look more deeply into the matter of Esken's stroke, see if the Brotherhood had indeed had anything to do with it and his sudden departure from his Guild on the grounds of ill health.

Konis smiled. She'd find nothing to link the Brotherhood to that, but it might just make her think more clearly about her attitude toward them. Fear could be a great teacher: Raiban should know, she used it as a matter of course. It was about time the tables were turned on her. He must, however, warn Rhyaz and Lijou of what he'd done.

He found Lijou in his office beside the Palace's Shrine to Vartra. The Head Priest looked up as Konis entered.

"Well met, Konis," he said. "You're lucky to catch me. I was just about to leave. Rhyaz is already waiting for me in our vehicle. What can I do for you?"

As Konis told him of his session with Raiban and Rhyaz, the priest's brow began to crease, his ears folding to the side in anger.

"It's only because of Kha'Qwa and Rhyaz that I haven't ordered some action to be taken against her," Lijou said. "What she did was unforgivable." The stylus he held in his hand snapped. He looked at it in surprise before putting the pieces down carefully on his desk.

Shocked at his normally mild friend's outburst, Konis had nothing to say.

"What would you do if it had happened to Rhyasha, Konis?" said Lijou, seeing the look on his face. "You'd want to tear her limb from limb, wouldn't you?" He sighed and forced himself to relax. "That's why Rhyaz encourages me to turn my energies in other directions."

"Like the alien contracts?" he asked quietly.

Lijou looked at him sharply, then smiled. "Of course, you were called up to Chagda Station that day, weren't you?"

"Is what you're doing wise, Lijou?"

"Very wise. We can see more clearly where the danger to Shola lies, and we don't have the interminable infrastructure of the Forces to slow down our decision making. We can act the minute we identify a problem."

"Not very democratic, though," said Konis.

"Neither is the threat we face," he countered. "For too long we've been used as the Forces' cannon fodder, sent to hold hopeless positions, scouting deep within enemy lines, all missions with little chance of survival for our people. Our original purpose has been debased, Konis. You know that, you've read the ancient records. It's long past time we broke free and defended our world and species the way Vartra intended. You admit that to yourself, even if to no one else, otherwise you wouldn't support us when you can. I'll pass on your message to Rhyaz and I can't say I'm sorry you've managed to shake her arrogance. It's about time someone did."

"Thank you. How are things at Stronghold? Rhyaz was definitely not himself today."

"He's tired," said Lijou, beginning to gather his papers and comp pad into a pile. "The two new Humans have kept us on our guard this past week. They've been into everything, even trying to break the security codes on our comm system. Thankfully, they aren't fluent enough in our written language to be too great a danger yet. Once we managed to identify their areas of expertise, we arranged classes for them and intensified our security. Our cryptology department considers them an entertaining Challenge. They're beginning to settle down now they know we're not trying to make them conform. I've got Tamghi and Kora training them to use their psi abilities."

"That's not quite what I meant, though I'm glad to hear they're settling in."

"Nothing," said Lijou, getting up. His hand hesitated over the broken stylus then swept it resolutely into the bin. "Nothing has resolved itself. Yes, he's gene-altered, tests confirm that, but they aren't. Alex has figured out enough to know we're keeping them at Stronghold because Rhyaz seems drawn to her in some way, and she's running him ragged. Whenever they're in the same area, she finds excuses to talk to him, blowing first pleasant then arrogant, tying him in mental knots because he doesn't know how to respond. Lately he's been staying in his office as much as possible. Lyand has taken over his classes for the time being."

"I don't blame him. Younglings of that age can be very trying."

"We only have to remember Zhyaf and Mara to know that," said Lijou, picking up his belongings and stuffing them in his briefcase. "I hope we're wrong, Konis, and this is nothing. Are you sure it wouldn't be better to send them to the Telepath Guild so there's no chance of any Link forming?"

"It wouldn't do any good. If it's meant to happen, the Link will form even if we try to separate them. All we can do is wait."

Lijou sighed. "I forget my manners. How are things with you?"

"Fine," said Konis, getting up. "You know the TeLaxaudin from the *Kz'adul* is staying on my son's estate, don't you?"

"Yes. And I heard the good news about Shi and Raza," said Lijou as they walked to the door.

"I saw them just before they were due to be released from the hospital. The change was unbelievable, Lijou. They'll never function as telepaths again, but they went from a vegetative state to being capable of doing quite complex tasks and sustaining a conversation. They'll be able to lead relatively normal lives now."

"Their clans must be delighted. How did he do it? All I heard was that it was a new surgical procedure."

"It was. He used a series of microscopic implants—processors or something, Annuur said there isn't a word for them in our language—inside their brains. They take over the functions of the damaged areas. The TeLaxaudin has promised to teach our surgeons the technique, and provide us with the implants. It opens a whole new era in restorative brain surgery."

"And ultimately, hope for Kusac," said Lijou, opening the door. "Has Kzizysus said anything about that yet?"

"He's still researching it, though he learned a lot from working with Shi and Raza. I live in hope, Lijou," said Konis. "We all do."

"You know Kha'Qwa's and my thoughts and prayers are with him," said Lijou as he locked the door behind them.

"Thank you," said Konis. "It's appreciated, believe me. Let me know if anything changes for Rhyaz."

"I will," said Lijou as they separated, each to go his own way.

Stronghold, Zhal-Oeshi, 16th day (August)

It took Lijou a moment or two to recognize the gray-robed figure leaning against the banister rail at the top of the staircase as Rhyaz.

"Unusual to see you dressed like this," he said quietly, stopping beside him.

"It's a stronger reminder of my rank than our uniform jackets," Rhyaz said shortly. "I need to distance myself from them for a while."

Lijou followed his gaze down to the ground level where the students were milling around as they changed classes. Sure enough, he saw Alex, clearly visible with her friend Kai, both wearing their brightly colored Terran clothing.

"Watching her again?"

"I can't help it. She's like a drug, Lijou," he said, forcing himself to turn away from the view and looking bleakly at him. "Only there's no cure I can see for this addiction. Dammit, I'm a Guild Master! I can't afford be held to emotional ransom by an adolescent female!"

"She's a child, Rhyaz. She doesn't know what she's doing," he said soothingly, laying a hand on his friend's arm.

"She knows," he growled. "She's flexing her powers as a female for the first time, Lijou. I can feel her doing it. She flatters our juniors, flirts with them, holding out the promise of much while delivering nothing but smiles and gentle touches!"

"Let her. They'll soon realize she doesn't give what she tempts them with. It's just part of growing older."

"I can't! Get her moved, Lijou. Have them both taken to the Telepath Guild. Now. I won't end up like Zhyaf."

Lijou could feel him trembling, see the effort it cost him to keep his back turned to her. "You're not Zhyaf. She must stay here till we know one way or the other," he said quietly. "You can force the issue, Rhyaz. See her on her own and confront her. It won't take more than a touch to know if you're Linked."

"No! I don't want a Link with her or anyone!"

"The choice is no longer yours, I'm afraid. It's already been made by the Gods."

Rhyaz pulled away from him. "Then I'll appeal to Vartra!" he snarled, turning and heading down the stairs in a swirl of gray.

Lijou moved closer to the rail, watching him, but his eyes were drawn to the Human female. He felt the touch of her mind, then her head turned to glance briefly at Rhyaz before looking up at him. She grinned. He felt her amusement that she'd managed to discomfit both of them and knew then that Rhyaz was right.

As she passed out of sight under the balcony, he sighed and turned to go back into his office, his heart heavy for his friend.

Stronghold, later the same day

Kai looked over at Alex as he heard a knock on the door. *Who is it?* he sent. *I can't sense anyone outside. Can you?*

No. Go answer it.

Scrambling off the sofa, Kai crossed their small lounge and opened the door. He stepped back hurriedly as one of the Brotherhood juniors and a Human woman came in.

"Over there will do fine," she said as the junior struggled with her two large bags. "Thank you." She walked over to the sofa and sat down, waiting until the young male had left before speaking. "Hi there. I'm Ruth, and you're Alex and Kai, unless I'm in the wrong suite."

Kai blinked, taken aback by the way she'd made herself at home. Her presence seemed to fill the room with warmth and a sense of well-being he hadn't realized it had lacked till then. She wasn't a small woman, being a little taller than himself, and she was certainly heavier, but in an attractive way. Long ginger hair rippled across her shoulders, disappearing out of sight down her back.

"Yes, I've come to stay with you for a few weeks," she said, her smile lighting up her green eyes.

"Why?" demanded Alex, getting up from the small desk where she'd been working and coming over to stand in front of her. "We don't need anyone, we're fine on our own."

"Father Lijou felt it was appropriate, considering your age."

"We've managed on our own for years," said Kai, finding his voice.

"All the young people on our estate live at my house for at least a month," said Ruth complacently. "Since you can't come to me, I've come to you."

"Why?" asked Kai, moving over to the nearest chair. "Why do they stay with you?"

"It doesn't matter why, we don't need her," said Alex. "These are our quarters, we don't want you here."

"I'm afraid it's all been arranged now. As to why, well, you stowed away to get here so I assume that like everyone else who comes to Shola, you want to stay. So you need to learn about the culture of this world, how to behave, what to expect. Be a good lad and get me a mug of coffee, would you, Kai? I'm parched after the journey."

Automatically Kai got up and began to go over to the small dispenser set in the wall. Alex grabbed his arm as he went past.

"Let her get it for herself," she said. "We're not her servants. Look, I don't know how many ways you need it said, but we don't want you here."

"It isn't up to you, Alex," Ruth said quietly. "I've been asked to stay with you for the time being and help you fit in here."

"We don't want to fit in," said Kai, shaking Alex's hand off. "We want to leave here and get a place of our own in the capital. You know, do our own thing. Only they won't let us leave."

"How are you going to earn a living?" Ruth asked. "Unless you belong to a Guild, no one will hire you."

"That's what they tell everyone," said Alex contemptuously. "The truth's different. There's always someone needing something done on the cheap. It's what we did back home."

"That would be after you ran away from the state orphanage. You were thirteen then, weren't you? And you've been living rough since. With a background like that, it's easy to see why you know nothing of the Sholan culture. No Guild, no work, and once they find out you're telepaths, they'll call in either the Protectorate or the Guild to come and get you. Not very different from back home, is it? Except here, telepaths are respected— once they're fully trained, of course. No matter where you go, there are always rules to be followed. Wouldn't it be easier to learn them now and save yourself all the problems you had on Earth?"

"We'll manage, once we get away from here," said Alex.

Ruth got up and went over to the dispenser, setting it for coffee. "There are two ways to do everything, Alex. The hard way and the easy way," she said, waiting for her drink. "If you cause too much trouble, they have an easy solution. They'll deport you as illegal immigrants. And don't say they'll have to find you first," she said, turning round. "There are people here with the ability to track you right down to the room in the house you're hiding in from clear across the other side of the Kaeshala continent! So why don't we save a lot of time and do it the easy way?"

Kai sensed Alex link with him and start to reach mentally for Ruth. As she did, he felt a sudden brief flare of energy coupled with a slight stinging sensation between the eyes. Startled, he glared first at Alex, then at Ruth.

"Sholans learn not to do that one at around the age of eight," said Ruth, sitting down again and taking a sip of her drink. "You've got a lot to learn, kids, and the people outside these doors won't be so forgiving if you go messing with their minds. I expect people stayed out of your way on Earth, left you alone because of your Talent. Believe me, it's not like that here. Every telepath is identified when they start using their Talent and has to go to the Telepath Guild to be educated. You wanted a new life or you wouldn't have stowed away on the *Odyssey* to get here. At the moment, you're on sufferance under the old laws of Sanctuary. It's Stronghold that will have to apply for work permits for you, so why antagonize them?"

She's got a point, sent Kai grudgingly.

You want her living here, ordering us around, organizing our lives like one of those damned Welfare workers? Alex demanded.

No, but what's the alternative?

"Stay if you want," said Alex abruptly, heading back to the desk and the comm unit. "I don't give a damn."

"That's the spirit," said Ruth cheerfully. "I'm sure we'll get on fine. Kai, they're bringing a folding bed for you to use in here, and a chest for your clothes. I'm afraid you're going to have to move out of the bedroom. If we shift the furniture around a bit and put up some privacy screens, you'll still have your own area."

Alex gave a derisory laugh. "And she's only been here five minutes!"

Kai sighed. He hated it when Alex got into a difficult mood. Lately, though, she'd been more like her old self. Playing her mind-games on the Guild Master had kept her amused and actually made her pleasant to be around again. There were advantages to sleeping in the lounge. The comm unit for one, and the small kitchen. He headed off into their room to pack the few belongings that he'd brought with him from Earth.

Stronghold, Zhal-Oeshi, 17th day (August)

"You'll wear a uniform like everyone else here," said Ruth placidly as she poured coffee for the two teenagers.

"I want my own clothes back!" fumed Alex, clutching her toweling robe closer about her.

"They're in storage with Kai's," she said. "Hurry up and get dressed or you'll be late for prayers."

"I'm not wearing this!" she said, throwing the gray one-piece down on the floor. "And I'm not going to prayers!"

"Suit yourself," said Ruth, putting down the coffeepot. "But you'll go to prayers. The Brotherhood made it possible for you to stay on Shola. Without them, you'd be on Earth right now, in a military telepath training center. You owe it to them to respect their religious services. You'll only make a fool of yourself if you turn up in that bathrobe. Kai's wearing his uniform."

She rounded on him. "How *could* you wear it! Don't you see what she's doing? Turning us into exactly what we ran away from!"

"I wasn't going out in my underwear," said Kai, stuffing a forkful of bacon into his mouth. "You can if you want. Where'd you get food like this from, Ruth?" he asked. "They've never served anything like this in the mess since we got here."

"I brought it with me. Food from Earth is one of the perks of having me stay with you," she said. "You've got ten minutes to eat your breakfast and get to prayers, Alex, and ready or not, you go out that door at eight on the dot!"

Alex made a strangled noise of anger before flouncing off back to the bedroom.

"Will you really throw her out in her bathrobe?" Kai asked curiously as he shoveled more bacon and eggs into his mouth.

"If I have to," said Ruth, picking up her own knife and fork. "Discipline isn't a bad thing, Kai, it's just a matter of who administers it. You, or them. Since you decided to come to Shola, it makes sense to follow their rules. Then it's your decision to wear the uniform and so on. You're imposing it on yourself, not the other way round."

He looked at her dubiously.

She laughed "Look, you're only here for a few weeks, then they'll move you to the Telepath Guild, or maybe even our estate. Things are less formal there, but there are still rules. Play it straight with the Brotherhood. You never know, you might even be asked to join them one day."

"Asked?"

"They choose you if you have the right type of psi skills and other abilities. This is the Warrior elite of Shola, you know. Now come on, you don't want to be late."

Stronghold, Zhal-Oeshi, 18th day (August)

"In some ways, she's just a typical teenager with all the usual mood swings, angst, and attitude problems," said Ruth, cuddling Chay'Dah. "He is so cute! And his coloring!" She smiled up at Kha'Qwa. "The best people have titian hair," she said.

Kha'Qwa laughed.

"What about Alex?" demanded Rhyaz. "Can you do anything with her?"

"One thing at a time, Master Rhyaz," she said, glancing over at the brown-pelted Highlander. "From what Kai told me last night while she was having a bath, they've lived off their wits and skills since they were twelve or thirteen. They got what they needed by fraud and outright theft, using their computer skills with a bit of mental manipulation thrown in. Society was their enemy, trying to force them to conform and lose their individuality. They need to be able to fit into our Human community before we can expect them to adjust to Sholan culture."

"What about the way she's behaving toward me?"

"Part of the same problem. I'll warrant she stayed away from other male company for fear of being attacked or raped. Now she's in a place where she knows she's physically safe, and suddenly, a great many young males are paying her a great deal of flattering attention. She's doing what any Human, and probably Sholan teenager would do, lapping it up and seeing just how much power she has over them. You have to admit that it's no mean feat being able to count the Guild Master as one of her conquests."

He began to growl. "I'm not! The interest is involuntary, believe me! Can't you speak to her about it? She's undermining my authority by making a laughingstock of me."

"Not a laughingstock, Master Rhyaz," said Ruth, letting the cub grab hold of her finger and play with it. "I'm afraid there is some amusement, but even that's died down today because you kept to your office."

"She has to realize she can't treat either Rhyaz or our students like this," said Lijou. "Everyone here was chosen, hand-picked for their abilities. They're serious about their studies, and their commitment to the Brotherhood."

"Excuse me speaking frankly, Master Rhyaz, but if you'd had a Companion, then there wouldn't be this problem," said Ruth, looking over at him. "The fact you're not currently in a relationship with anyone hasn't helped matters. Almost as soon as she found out you were the reason they'd been brought to Stronghold, she also found out you're considered unattainable. That's a Challenge to any red-blooded female, let alone a teenager just discovering she's capable of attracting males."

The growl deepened and his hair began to rise around his shoulders. "Are you saying that it's my fault this has happened?"

"Of course she isn't," said Kha'Qwa soothingly, reaching out to touch him. "She's saying the fact you're single is attracting her."

"What do you want me to do? Go out and flirt with some of our Sisters?" he asked caustically, ears flattening as he slumped back in his chair. "I can't believe we're talking like this. I can't even believe this is happening to me! I should be with the U'Churians on Home right now, not stuck at Stronghold being plagued by this youngling!"

"Have you seen her today?" Ruth asked. "Felt her touch your mind at all?"

"No, nothing since yesterday," he sighed, passing his hand across his face and ears in defeat.

"This isn't the way Leska Links usually happen on the estate. In fact, only Vanna and Kusac actually Linked to their Leskas before they were gene-altered. Nothing about this is what we've come to consider standard. You're having symptoms and she's apparently having none. I think the only thing you can do is what Father Lijou suggested. Confront her. One way or another, the waiting will be over."

"Easy for you to say. At least like this I can hope nothing

happens," he muttered, sitting up. "Has anyone considered what I do with her if we do Link? She's undisciplined, untrained, and a sociopath! I don't want to be another Zhyaf!"

"She'd have access to your experience, Rhyaz," said Lijou. "That will surely make a difference."

"Master Rhyaz, you're nothing like Zhyaf. He was staid, old well before his time, and Mara was—Mara," Ruth smiled. "You're young and energetic. For Alex, life here would be far from boring. In fact, it would almost be like a legitimate continuation of what she and Kai were doing on their own."

"Nice to know you see us as a group of thieves and frauds, Ruth," he said sarcastically. "Alex would have access to all the information of the Brotherhood if she was Linked to me, have you considered that? With her past, she's a security risk we can't afford."

"I don't think she would be once you were Linked," said Ruth, breaking the silence that followed. "Anything that harmed you or the Brotherhood would harm her, too."

"Not if anger overtook reason. The need for revenge can be powerful enough to face self-destruction as an acceptable cost."

"You'd be aware of what she was thinking and saying, Rhyaz. She could do nothing without you knowing. What strikes me most is that Alex hasn't told anyone why they're here," said Kha'Qwa thoughtfully. "Yes, there's speculation and rumors, but she's not adding to them. What she's doing is playing off an older male against several younger ones. If she wanted to cause you real embarrassment, she'd have made a point of telling everyone that you're waiting to see if a Link will form between you."

"Maybe there's some hope for me yet,' said Rhyaz.

"What has Alex said about the possibility of a Link?" asked Ruth. "I haven't broached the subject with her yet."

"Nothing," said Kha'Qwa. "Kora says she's adept at mentally sliding the conversation away from issues she doesn't want to consider. She and Tamghi have at least made the data on Leska Links available to her, but whether or not she's read it is another matter."

"Oh, well," sighed Ruth. "Which of us would be doing what we are if we didn't enjoy a Challenge?"

"Some Challenges are lost causes," Rhyaz muttered.

*   *   *

It was past the twenty-third hour before Rhyaz dared venture out of his quarters and go downstairs to the temple. He wasn't as religious as Lijou, but he still sought the solace of the temple when there were difficult decisions to be made, and Brothers and Sisters lives hung in the balance, or had been lost. As he closed the great door behind him, he felt as if for a while at least, he was shutting out the world.

He crumbled the incense into the brazier on the God's right-hand side, murmuring the ritual prayer of supplication. He remembered how Varta had last appeared to Lijou and shuddered slightly before bowing to the statue and moving away from it toward the sarcophagus.

Leaning against it, he rested his arms and head on the lid and sighed. He was tired but couldn't sleep, and the headache that had plagued him all day wouldn't lift. He heard a footfall and wondered vaguely who it was. He'd checked that the temple was empty before coming in and he hadn't heard the door opening. As he lifted his head to look, a shadow fell across him.

"You were alone, but no door built can keep Me out," said Vartra, looking at him from beyond the other side of His tomb. "You'll need a Companion in the days to come. Don't be so quick to wish this one away. You know nothing about her."

Fear rushed through him. "I know all I need to know," he said, hearing the tremor in his own voice.

"One conversation and her very short life history? That's not knowing, Master Rhyaz." The tone was gently mocking.

"Why couldn't You leave me alone? I was content as I was! How can I do Your work, protect our world, with a youngling like her compromising me and our Order?"

"The Brotherhood is changing, Rhyaz. What better way to show it than through leading it with a Human Leska at your side? She's not the person you fear she is. Would you rather have a quiet, predictable female?"

"I don't want any female!"

Vartra began to back away from the tomb, merging into the flickering shadow His statue cast on the crimson velvet curtain behind Him. "You don't yet know what you want." He laughed gently. "You'll find out soon enough."

"Wait!" he called out. "Nothing's happened between us yet! You can stop this going any further!"

The laughter grew fainter until it echoed only inside his mind.

He groaned, leaning his head against the cool stone again, forcing himself not to be rattled by the visitation. How long he stood like this, lost to everything around him, he had no idea, but the voice when he heard it, startled him.

"Master Rhyaz, are you all right? Should I call the porter?"

He spun around, taking a step toward her. "What are you doing here?" he demanded. Shock at seeing Alex standing there fought with his inability to look anywhere but at the long expanse of bare muscular legs below her short sleeping tunic.

"I couldn't sleep and thought I'd visit the temple," she said. "Wasn't aware it was a crime."

"You should be in bed. It's after hours for juniors."

She shrugged. "Too hot and humid. Feels like a storm's coming."

He remembered she was quartered in one of the empty tutor suites above the workshops. "You came across the courtyard dressed like that? Didn't anyone send you back?" he demanded, then realized the futility of what he'd said.

"Yeah, like I'd be here now if they had," she grinned, looking at the sarcophagus behind him. "I came to see that. I haven't had the chance to look at it yet. We only get to come in here for morning and evening prayers. What is it? His tomb?" She nodded toward the statue of Varta.

"An altar," he said shortly. Her presence had destroyed the fragile peace he'd almost achieved. "Go back to your quarters, Alex. A visit can be arranged tomorrow if you ask your tutor."

"I'm here now," she pointed out reasonably, moving a few steps closer to him. "What's the matter, Master Rhyaz? I'm not disturbing you, am I?" she asked quietly, raising an eyebrow as she put her head on one side.

The gesture was so Sholan, he could almost see her ears flicking coquettishly. He blinked and it was gone; only a small blonde Human dressed in a short white tunic remained. He felt the touch of her mind at the edges of his and backed away from her.

"It's my tunic, isn't it? You think it's too short," she laughed. "I didn't have you down as being so old-fashioned! All the females here show their legs, Master Rhyaz, what's so different about me?"

"Go back to your quarters now, Alex," he said firmly, stopping only as his heel struck the edge of the sarcophagus. A torrent of emotions were running through him, each one warring with the others. He tried unsuccessfully to remember what Lijou had taught him about shielding his mind.

"I know you don't mean that," she said, dropping her voice until it was so quiet he had to strain his ears forward to hear her. "I've seen you watching me when you think I'm not looking. I know you find me attractive." She moved closer. "That's why you had me brought here, isn't it? This stuff about a Link, it's all an excuse."

Almost hypnotized, he could only stand and watch her. As she stepped past him to lay her hands on the stone carvings, he smelled her scent strongly for the first time.

"You needn't worry, Master Rhyaz. Your reputation's safe with me. I'm not interested in you," she said disdainfully. "This tomb really is beautiful. Why did you lie about it being an altar?"

The spell broke, leaving him able to think clearly. "Why are you doing this to me?" he demanded. "I helped you, gave you and your friend sanctuary when you asked for it. Is this any way to repay me, by mocking and teasing me in front of my students and colleagues?"

"I think I'd better go," she said, turning away. "You're taking this too seriously."

His mind suddenly made up, Rhyaz lunged for her, catching her by the arm. As she tried to pull away, she stumbled, her bare feet slipping on the flagstones. He caught hold of her with his other hand, making sure she stayed on her feet. He had to know what was going on.

"You don't realize what could be happening to us, do you? Hasn't anyone told you?" he asked, his face inches from hers. The night *was* hot and humid; he could see the faint sheen of sweat on her face, feel it on her arms, and smell her scent more strongly now.

"Let me go, Master Rhyaz," she said, trying to pull away from him. "I don't know what you're talking about."

"Don't lie to me! Until your mind touched mine at Chagda Station, I couldn't hear thoughts. You know damned well everyone's waiting to see if we form a Leska Link!" He smelled her fear and saw it leap into her eyes.

"They're lying! That kind of thing can't happen!" There was a note of panic in her voice as she struggled more frantically to pull free of him.

Annoyed, he swung her around till she fetched up against the side of the sarcophagus. "That's what I intend to find out," he said. Pinning her against the tomb, he took hold of her jaw.

"You wouldn't," she said, dropping into her own language in sheer terror. "I'm only a kid! I'll scream!"

He ignored her and leaned forward, his mouth closing over hers, sure that such an intimate touch would trigger any Link that existed between them.

Suddenly, with a pain as intense as any physical blow, his mind was assaulted by hers. Images of her past, flickering so rapidly he could make no sense of them, began to surge through him. Even as it began, part of him was aware of the same happening to her.

Transfixed like insects in amber, they could only endure until gradually the flow of memories slowed, finally stopping, leaving their minds Linked, and their bodies aching to join.

Where his hand held her face, he was acutely aware of the texture and feel of her smooth skin. Where their lips touched, it was as if electricity flowed between them like a two-way tide, letting them each experience what the other felt.

He accepted the inevitable, knowing that if their Link wasn't sealed physically, they'd die, their minds unable to sustain the intensity of such a complete mental bonding as they now had. The decision wasn't as hard to make as he'd thought now that the Link compulsion had begun. Every fiber of his being wanted her.

Reluctantly, he lifted his face from hers. Here, on the cold flagstones of the temple floor, was not where he wanted that pairing to take place. It would have to be Ghyakulla's Shrine. A least it had grass and bushes: there they could be more private. He sent a mute appeal to Lijou, praying he'd be awake and receive him.

"No way!" she said, trying to fight him off as he pulled her toward the dim glow that marked the entrance to the Shrine. "I told you, I'll scream!"

"Then do it," he said grimly, stopping to pick her up and throw her over his shoulder. As his hand clasped her bare thighs and her scent enveloped him, he felt the muscles in his belly and groin start to clench.

I don't want this! I didn't intend this to happen! she sent, squirming in his grasp and battering her fists against his back as she tried to sit up.

He felt the familiar faint tingle as he stepped through the weak force field. "Believe me, neither did I," he said, stopping and setting her down. "You wanted to tease an adult male, get him aroused. Well, congratulations, Alex, you've succeeded beyond your wildest hopes. Remember this for the future. Never start something with me that you're not prepared to finish. We pair now, or we die. That's the only choice we have." He began to pull her close but she held him off.

"Wait," she said, looking round the dimly lit cavern. "Ghyakulla. She's your earth Goddess, isn't she?"

"Yes," he said impatiently, then realized he was seeing the Shrine as if for the first time through her eyes.

It was dusk here, and the grass beneath their bare feet was still warm. They stood in a small hollow beyond a clump of bushes that partially screened them from the entrance. Insects chirred, and the gentle sound of running water filled the cavern. A movement of air brought with it the scent of nung flowers from the tree nearby. It was easy to forget one was in the heart of the mountain.

"Lights in the ceiling simulate the rhythm of day and night," he said.

"It's beautiful."

He touched her shoulder, making her jump and turn back to face him. "We have to pair," he reminded her. "I don't want to force you, but I will if I have to."

"No one could ever accuse you of being romantic," she said tartly.

"You put me through a week of hell and you expect romance?" He was taken aback by her insolence.

She shrugged and reached for the hem of her tunic, beginning to lift it up.

"No!" Shocked, he reached out to stop her. "That's not what I meant," he said lamely.

Giving him a curious look, she let her tunic go. "You don't know what you want, do you?"

He remembered Vartra saying exactly the same and shivered slightly as he pulled her into his arms. Where they touched, once again he felt the flow of energy between them. Suddenly, he felt more alive than he'd ever felt before.

"I want you," he said, aware that for all her bravado she'd never paired before. "There's no need to be afraid. I'm no striped youngling with his first female, Alex. I am experienced. Many of your people have chosen Sholan males as lovers."

She touched his face, stroking the soft pelt there before moving her hand down his neck to the longer hair that grew there. "It's soft," she said. "I thought it would be coarser, like an animal's."

For the first time, he felt her look at him as a desirable male, and like what she saw. "You said you weren't interested."

She grinned and shrugged, moving her hand to where his robe overlapped across his chest, slipping her fingers beneath the edges. "So I lied."

He reached for his belt, unfastening it and letting his robe fall loose. Wrapping his arms around her, he buried his head against her neck, content for the moment to smell her scent and taste her skin. He could feel that she lagged behind him, not yet caught up by their Link's compulsion to pair. The fire in his belly burned so fiercely that it took all his self-control to wait for her. Then he felt his robe move as her cool fingertips tentatively touched his sides.

"I can feel how much you want me," she whispered, resting her hands on his hips. "You like me touching you." She pushed her hands up through the longer pelt of his chest, her fingers searching through his fur till they found his nipples. "You like this, don't you?" she said, rubbing her palms across them.

He began to purr, impressed that she'd learned so quickly how to access his memories. With one hand, he clasped the bare thighs that had been maddening him since she'd appeared in the temple, letting his fingers explore their shape, touch the soft inner surfaces. His licks turned to nips which he tried to keep gentle. He sensed an echoing fire begin in her, starting low in her belly and flooding suddenly outward till it touched him.

He slid his hand under her tunic, pushing it upward, shocked when he realized she was naked beneath it. She helped him, eyes as heavy-lidded as his own. As she discarded her tunic, he slipped out of his robe and dropped it to the ground, never taking his eyes off her.

"You're certainly enthusiastic," she observed as he pulled her into his arms again, covering her face with tiny licks until she took hold of his head and held it still. "No. Like this," she said, kissing him deeply.

He'd heard of Human kisses, but wasn't prepared for their

reality. "Self-control be damned," he muttered against her lips as he hoisted her off the ground, wrapping her legs round him before carefully lowering them both onto his robe.

He couldn't touch her enough, the sight and feel and smell of her was intoxicating him just as the touch of his pelt on her bare skin drove her wild. Every sensation was doubled, experienced by the giver as well as the receiver. The intensity of the sensations they were sharing was so great that within minutes, unable to wait any longer, they'd joined. As bodies became one, so did their minds, Linking them irrevocably together for life.

"You knew I was in the temple," he said lazily, his hand stroking one breast, his head pillowed on the other as they lay there still entwined. "You came here to torment me."

She ruffled the hair between his ears. "Only a little."

"That was foolish, and dangerous. If it hadn't been me . . ."

"I knew it was you," she interrupted. "Was it worth the teasing?"

He lifted his head, pushing himself up on one arm and fastened his mouth over her breast, nipping her, making her shriek in mock pain.

"All right! All right! I won't do it again!" she said, squirming and trying to cover her breasts with her hands to protect herself.

"Only for me," he said, then froze. Groaning, he let his head fall down on his arm. "Hello, Lijou."

"*You* called me," said the priest, coming into the Shrine. "I switched the dampers on and set a guard on the temple doors for you, but it took me a couple of minutes. Only you would bring her here, Rhyaz." He stopped just inside the entrance.

"You might have taken the poor child somewhere comfortable, Rhyaz," said Kha'Qwa. "And you might have given her something to cover herself up with!"

As Rhyaz raised his head to look up at them, Alex began to laugh. A blanket, thrown by Lijou, came sailing through the air to land beside him, closely followed by a second.

"Take her up to your room, Rhyaz," said Lijou. "I really don't recommend a night on the grass." There was a rueful tone to his voice that suggested he'd tried and regretted it.

He reached for the blanket, trying vainly to open and spread it over them as Kha'Qwa came closer. With his new sensitivity, he could feel Lijou's amusement at his acute embarrassment. He thanked Vartra that the artificial day was over and it was almost dark.

Bastard, he sent. Lijou laughed.

"You'll need these," Kha'Qwa said, crouching down to pass him a pair of wrist comms. "Ruth brought them over from the estate for you. They've got psi dampers set into them. Put them on now, they're already set to full. Your room isn't damped but we can get it done once this first Link day of yours is over."

He saw her mouth open in a slight smile as her eyes traveled the length of his exposed body. She reached out and ran a fingertip down his spine, stopping at the root of his tail, making him squirm, and Alex laugh even louder.

"Kha'Qwa," he said warningly. "Lijou, make her stop!"

"You know Kha'Qwa has a mind that's very much her own," said the priest.

"I'd forgotten just how trim a body you have," she purred, patting his rear before getting up. "Goodnight, Alex. Ruth knows where you are so don't worry about her. I'd say sleep well, but knowing Rhyaz, I don't expect he'll let you get any!"

"Stop laughing," Rhyaz said to her as he watched his friends leave. "You should be dying of embarrassment like any decent person."

"Like you?" Alex sniggered as he struggled some more with the blanket then gave up and collapsed against her with a sigh. "They're all right, you know. Not at all what I expected them to be."

"You've ruined my reputation. This is going to be all round Stronghold tomorrow."

"How? They're not going to tell anyone," she said, stroking his chest.

"We were broadcasting raw sex until Lijou put the dampers on. It's strong enough to affect anyone with any sensitivity, which is anyone who was awake."

"Never mind," she said, trying to reach down to kiss him.

"No," he said firmly, shifting her leg and easing himself off her before passing her the other blanket. "We're going up to my room. Lijou's right, this grass is too damned damp." He groaned again. "There's a guard on the door, dammit! We'll be seen leaving!"

Alex sat up, fumbling for her tunic, trying to stop laughing.

"Maybe they'll have gossiped it out by the day after tomorrow," he said, handing her a wrist comm before taking off his own and exchanging it for the new one. Getting to his feet, he wrapped the blanket round himself. "You might have brought us robes instead of blankets, Lijou!" he muttered, picking his damp and crumpled robe up from the grass.

Let them have their day of gossip, sent Lijou privately, making him start with shock at the contact. *Upstairs with Alex, you'll be oblivious to it. It'll be old news by the time you join us again.*

Bastard, he sent again as he helped his Leska with her blanket. *I want her sworn in now, Lijou.*

At this time of night? I know you've got better things to do!

He grinned, pleased to be getting his revenge so quickly. *The Creed won't wait. Brotherhood business first.*

Prime world, training barracks, Zhal-Oeshi, 20th day (August)

Kezule looked up as the young officer entered and saluted. "At ease, M'kou," he said.

"All units have reported in, General. Units One and Two identified their targets at their workplaces and proceeded to follow them to their domiciles."

"And units Three to Eight?"

"All twenty targets were located either at the given domicile or at their workplace. Those units then familiarized themselves with the locations as ordered."

He nodded. "Tell them to stand down and prepare their reports. I want all problem areas identified so alternative measures can be explored. Have the reports on my desk by 08.00. Remind the group leaders we have a meeting at 09.00." He got to his feet, picking up his reader. "Who's Officer of the Watch?"

"Kho'ikk, sir."

"Tell him I'm going home now. He's not to bother me till 06.00."

"Yes, sir," said M'kou, saluting as Kezule passed him on his way out.

As D'haalmu steered the small grav flitter back to his apartment on the edge of the Palace, Kezule's thoughts were elsewhere. Despite his rage over his tank-grown offspring, he had to admit that events had turned out far better than he'd expected.

He'd first seen them eight days ago, after they'd been examined and processed by the medical department. It was with relief that he discovered they had all inherited a knowledge of their family relationship to each other, and to him.

His first task had been to explain the Prime situation, and the reason for their genesis. His next had been to lay down his basic rules. He was their Commanding Officer and they would follow his orders before any other consideration. Their primary objective was to protect the Emperor, God-King of the Primes, and his family, with their lives if necessary. Their secondary objective was to protect the people of the City of Light. He'd told them that during the next few days, he would choose leaders from among their number on the basis of merit and ability. Then he'd started training them.

The changes induced by the TeLaxaudin at his request had worked, and his offspring had all his memories and experience as well as the extra two years of maturity he'd asked for. Training was merely a matter of reminding them, not teaching them from scratch. And the aggressiveness of the fifteen M'zullians was more than contained by the presence of so many of their obvious superiors.

Each of his eighty sons was different, an individual in his own right, as were his twenty daughters. More importantly, he discovered their loyalty to him was total. After two days, he'd identified the twenty most able. Dividing the remainder into eight groups, he placed two of his chosen ones in command of each unit and set the remaining four to act in rotation as bodyguards to himself and Zayshul, who was now too near her time to leave their apartment.

He'd also forced the issue with Medical Director Zsoyshuu over meeting his twenty daughters. With them, too, there had been the instant recognition of family. Playing a hunch, he'd asked that they be allowed to live at the barracks and train with his sons.

"We want them for breeding, Kezule," the Medical Director had said. "Not fighting."

"You want them all for breeding eventually, Zsoyshuu. Unless you want my sons facing the same problems I faced when I woke in this time, they need to get used to company of the opposite gender. What better way than by living next to their sisters?"

Later that day, his daughters had arrived at the newly refurbished barracks and had been installed in quarters next to their brothers. Slowly, piece by piece, his plan was coming together.

Kezule roused himself as the flitter came to a stop. He'd taken to using the vehicle for several reasons, one of them being a means of getting his wife quickly to medical attention if necessary. As he was getting out, his communicator buzzed.

"Q'almo here, sir," said the young officer. "It's your wife, sir. She's . . . I think you should get here as soon as possible, sir," he said, a note of panic in his voice.

"Make your report, soldier!" he snapped, gesturing D'haalmu to follow him as he leaped out of the flitter and began running for the building entrance, communicator held to his ear. The two doormen flanking the entrance sprang to life, opening the heavy ornamental doors for him.

The youth's gulp was audible. "Your wife's in great pain, sir. Says it's the egg and you should get back now."

"I'm downstairs." He stuffed the communicator into his pocket, slowing down just enough to call to his bodyguard. "D'haalmu, fetch those TeLaxaudin doctors I told you about!"

"Already on their way up, General," interrupted the doorman. "May the God-Kings smile on your wife," he added.

"General?" asked D'haalmu as he caught up with him.

"Never mind," Kezule said, speeding up as he ran across the wide marble reception area to the elevators.

Chaos reigned in his apartment. A heated argument was in progress between the Prime doctor who had been attending Zayshul, his female assistant, and one of the TeLaxaudins. Q'almo stood beside the TeLaxaudin, the two of them blocking any entry into the bedroom beyond. The spectacle of the young officer and the small stick-thin alien with his staff holding off the two officials would have been ludicrous had he not been so concerned for Zayshul. Unaware of his arrival, they continued arguing loudly.

"Enough!" he roared, crest rising as he gave vent to his rage. "What the hell is going on here?"

The doctor turned on him. "We must have access to your wife immediately," he said. "This birth is a royal one and we must ensure there is no medical interference! I must attend her, not one of these TeLaxaudin! And my colleague, as the recorder of Royal births, must witness it! You jeopardize your child's rank in the succession if we're kept out!"

"You only need to see there's no interference, is that right?" he demanded, looking from one to the other.

"I must deliver . . ."

"Answer my question! Observing is the important thing, yes?"

"Yes," said the female, hastily stepping behind the doctor for protection.

Kezule grabbed hold of her arm. "You come with me," he said, hauling her with him past Q'almo and the TeLaxaudin. "Q'almo, D'haalmu, keep everyone else out." He opened the door and thrust her inside first.

The bedroom smelled of blood and fear and other scents he didn't want to identify. Zayshul was crouching on the floor at the far side of the bed. All he could see of her was her face and arms as she clutched the bedding. Her skin was chalk-white with pain, the rainbow markings looking obscenely bright against her pallor. At the foot of the bed, another TeLaxaudin sat folded up in a compact arrangement of limbs, watching her calmly.

"Get out!" she hissed, seeing him. "Get *out* of here!"

Letting the female recorder go, he backed off a few steps. "Are you all right? Can I do anything?"

"You've done enough! Just get out of here, right now!"

Kouansishus stirred, turning his oval face toward Kezule, eyes swirling as he adjusted his sight for longer range. "Leave. With me she safe."

"General, you must remove this alien," the recorder began.

His hand snaked out, grasping her round the neck, then he stopped, remembering who she was. Slowly, he released her.

She backed off, rubbing her throat, making a small whimpering noise of fear.

"Leave," repeated Kouansishus.

"I don't want to leave you alone with this recorder. She might try to interfere," he said.

"He's the one interfering," the recorder said, retreating to the far side of the bed.

Kezule hissed his anger, crest rising and darkening with rage. The female moved, skittering across beside Kouansishus.

"I do nothing," said Kouansishus as Zayshul gave a long drawn out shriek. "I watch."

Kezule fumbled for the doorknob behind him. "She's the important one," he said forcefully. "I don't give a damn about eggs or succession, see she's safe!"

"I hear."

The door opened, catapulting him back into the lounge.

"This interference by another species is not acceptable," began the doctor until he caught sight of Kezule's face.

"If she dies, so will you," he said quietly, pointing a finger at him as he advanced into the room. "Inch by inch, as I flay the hide from your living body to make a grave covering for her! Do you understand me? Your pointless rules are what placed her life at risk!"

He thrust the doctor aside and headed for the cabinet where they kept their strong liquor. Taking a bottle and a glass from it, he sat down in a chair facing the bedroom and poured himself a drink.

"D'haalmu, guard him. Q'almo, cover the outer door," he ordered, taking a small sip.

He'd drunk half the bottle before the door opened and the recorder came out.

"She's fine, and so is the egg," the female said, glancing nervously at the gun D'haalmu was holding on the doctor.

Kezule put his glass down, and, as sober as when he'd begun, got to his feet. "Hold onto her too, Q'almo," he said. "I want to see for myself."

Zayshul lay motionless in the bed but now there was a healthy green tint to her skin, rather than the deathly pallor he'd seen earlier. At the far side of the bed stood an incubator. In it sat an ovoid leathery egg not much bigger than the size of his clenched fist.

As Kouansishus unfolded himself, Kezule noticed the smell. The scents from earlier had gone, replaced by an odor he could almost taste. It was pleasant, reminding him vaguely of warm grass. He could smell none of the perfumes that had filled the TeLaxaudins' own quarters, only this.

"Is fine. Sleeps. Nothing I needed do."

"Nothing?" he asked, flicking his tongue out to taste the air.

The hands gestured, one reaching beneath the fronds of drapery to his belt. He took something from it, and advancing on Kezule in his strange gait, he handed it to him. "Scent for pain only." He reached out and touched Kezule on the nose with a twiglike finger. "Here. Work on thinking. You more reproduce later."

Cautiously he sniffed the container. It hadn't been used. So where had the scent come from? Unless it was one they produced naturally themselves.

"Thank you," he said, pocketing it and following the TeLaxaudin back to the lounge door. "Release the doctor and the recorder," he said tiredly to D'haalmu. "And escort our TeLaxaudin visitors to their transport." Then he returned to the bedroom.

He stopped to look at the egg in its heated nest. Already the leathery shell was beginning to harden, losing its flaccid appearance and filling out. Colors were beginning to emerge on its surface, wisps of green and blue. Now it resembled those he'd guarded on Shola, though it was definitely smaller. Strange to think this small object that was a potential person could also have caused Zayshul's death.

He moved away from it, going round to sit on the bed beside her. Touching her chest, he found her breathing was slow and even. She was deeply asleep, and just as well, he thought, hoping she didn't remember what she'd gone through. The suffering of prisoners and soldiers wasn't new to him, but the sounds she'd made while giving birth to their egg had shaken him. It had taught him she meant more to him than he could easily admit to himself.

A curious numbness seemed to possess his mind as he sat there, waiting for her to wake. One thought did surface; now that this was successfully over, he was closer to leaving K'oish'ik. Now he could plan the assault on the Directorate headquarters and the capture of the Sholan hybrids.

the *Couana*, Zhal-S'Asha 21st day (October)

"So three of the Valtegan outposts we've found are on a plane just above Jalna," said Banner, studying the holocube display thoughtfully. "With our fourth way down here by M'zull and J'kirtikk, it suggests there should be more in both vicinities."

"That's what I think," he agreed.

"Aren't we getting cozy," said Dzaou from the doorway.

He looked up sharply, banging his head against Banner's as he did. "Sorry," he muttered, rubbing his skull. "What is it, Dzaou? We're busy, unless it's important."

Dzaou came into his office, looking at the holo-cube. "You briefing Banner?"

"Yes," he said shortly, standing up. "What is it?"

"Watch change is over. Banner's supposed to relieve Khadui."

He switched off the imager. "We'll continue this later," he said to Banner.

Banner nodded and headed off for the bridge.

"Anything the rest of us should know?" Dzaou asked.

"Not yet," he said, checking his wrist comm as he sat down behind the desk. "And not that. If you're off duty, you could do worse than check over your kit."

"You haven't briefed us yet. We don't know what we'll need."

"Personal weapons should always be kept ready, as should your first aid pack. Standard procedure—for us. I don't suppose it was any different in your time."

"You keep making references to my time," said Dzaou, hair beginning to rise around his face. "Just what are you trying to say, Kusac?"

"Captain," he reminded him quietly, leaning back in his chair and locking eyes with him. "You trained under Ghezu, I assume. I trained when Rhyaz was Guild Master. Now, unlike you, I've work to do. Dismissed."

Dzaou's hair rose further but he bit back his anger and inclined his head in a jerky salute before leaving.

As the door hissed shut behind him, Kusac let out the breath he'd been holding. It was going to come to blows between him and Dzaou but now was not the time. He kept Challenging his authority and leadership, and would need to be dealt with publicly—just as Kaid had once done to him. Resolutely, he turned his thoughts away from those days. They were gone for the foreseeable future, maybe for good. Banner was right, he had to finish working his way through his past before they reached their rendezvous, otherwise he'd never have the confidence to do what he had to do.

He got up, toggling the privacy lock on the office door before bending down to unlatch the chair from its floor restraints. Pushing it aside, he lifted the square of deck plating to reveal the safe. Inside was the padded case he'd placed there during the first day. Snagging it at either end with his claws, he lifted it up and placed it on the desk, then proceeded to close the safe and restore the chair.

Within the padded compartments were three items. A small gas-powered pistol, a clip of projectile pellets, and an aerosol spray. All were undetectable with standard scanning procedures. He checked the clip, making sure each of the ten pellets had been fed in properly, then loaded it, slipping the pistol into an inside pocket of his jacket. Picking up the spray, he held it tightly in his hand. It and the pellets represented months of work by the science labs at Anchorage and deep under Stronghold. Developed from the resinous green la'quo stones found on Jalna, this was a chemical agent that affected not only the Valtegan nervous system, but specifically targeted their Warrior caste. If rumors were to be believed, it destroyed several key chemicals and the glands that produced them, permanently affecting their ability to increase their speed, endurance and deep healing. It didn't kill them, but it did even the odds when they awakened.

By now, Rhyaz would have discovered it was missing, but he'd wanted some insurance that he and his team would walk out alive from what was obviously a Valtegan trap. He thought of his daughter in Kezule's grasp, and what had happened to Dzaka and his sister Kitra. This would redress the balance, not just for them, but for what had happened to him on the Prime ship. He smiled, tossing the spray into the air and catching it single-handedly. This could be administered covertly onto food, or drink, or into the air. It could even be sprayed on skin, just as he'd been drugged that last night on the *Kz'adul*. The thought of that night made him frown briefly.

He put the spray into a pouch on his utility belt, snapping the flap closed. Picking up the box, he shut it and headed for the recycler. Tossing it in, he unlocked the door and made for the bridge. He wanted to check on current fuel levels and consumption. If necessary, they could drop out of jump to refuel at the nearest gas giant. He was leaving nothing to chance on this mission if he could help it.

The rest of the day was busy. Off duty personnel worked on weapons and munitions, performing maintenance checks, running simulations. He ran command drills for each shift, making sure everyone understood not only their own controls and functions but each other's.

Everyone was exhausted when he finally stood them down. Putting the ship on auto and routing the controls to the mess, he gave the duty watch half an hour to take an extra meal break.

"Happier now?" asked Banner, balancing his tray in one hand as he slid into a seat opposite Chima.

"He's thorough," she admitted, taking a bite out of her spiced meat stick. "I haven't been worked so hard before a mission in a long time. Where'd he pick up all those skills? I'll swear he hasn't been in the Brotherhood anywhere near long enough."

"From Kaid. They're sword-brothers as well as Triad partners."

"I knew Kaid was training him up at Stronghold, but I hadn't realized they'd taken the oath," she said, watching him. "Unusual, considering there's Carrie."

"I told you, never make assumptions," grinned Banner, trying to stab one of the meat balls on his plate.

"Perhaps I owe you an apology. Just don't let it complicate what's at stake here."

Banner looked up, no trace of a smile on his face. "It simplifies it."

"Score one to you," she acknowledged quietly.

Ears closed and flattened to his skull, he let the hot water beat down over his head and shoulders, feeling the tension gradually leave him. He knew when Banner let himself into the room.

Reaching for the soap dispenser, he squeezed some into his hand and began to massage his hair vigorously. He was almost done when Banner came into the bathing room.

"Want a hand?" Banner called out over the sound of the water. "You got the only Sholan cabin with a shower."

He hesitated, aware his torc was within easy reach and decided to leave it where it was. "If you want," he said diffidently, moving to one side of the cubicle.

"Ah, pure luxury," said Banner, stepping into the shower. Tilting his ears to the side, he lifted his face up to the multijet outlets, running his hands over his ears and down the back of his head. He leaned his hands against the wall, twisting his shoulders under the powerful stream. "I spent three hours crawling underneath one of the magazines, checking the damned thing out because it was sticking," he said, arching his back to relieve the last of the kinks. "You have no idea how good this is!"

"Here's the soap," said Kusac, passing it to Banner as he turned around and braced his arms against the rear wall. As Banner rubbed the soap deep into his pelt in a series of circular motions, he clenched his jaw, tensing his whole body in concentration, trying to cut out his awareness of his Second's emotions.

After a few minutes, Banner stopped. "If you'd rather leave it, that's all right, I won't be offended. You're not enjoying this, are you?"

"I have my torc off," he said, resting his head on his outstretched arm. "It isn't easy."

He felt Banner lean against him for a moment, hands resting on his shoulders, mutely offering him comfort. When his Second moved, the full force of the jets hit his back.

"Put your torc back on, Kusac," Banner said. "That's long enough for the first time, especially when it was such a sustained contact."

He straightened up, reaching out to retrieve his torc from the bottom of the soap rack. Twisting the finials apart, he slipped it round his neck. The relief was instantaneous. As his muscles relaxed involuntarily, he stumbled, grabbing at the wall to stop himself from falling over. A hand caught him and the water stopped abruptly.

"You're clean," Banner said, helping him out of the shower and bundling him into a towel.

"I'm fine," he said, refusing to move when the other tried to urge him toward the bedroom. "The torc takes control very suddenly, that's all. You finish your shower."

"Are you sure?" Banner asked, reaching out to take hold of his face and turn it to the light so he could see his eyes.

He clasped his hand firmly over Banner's, removing it. His Second's gesture reminded him of Kaid, and that was one wound too sore to probe right now. "I know how the torc works. This is normal, and temporary. Go finish your shower."

He toweled the worst of the dampness off before putting on his bathrobe and fetching a mug of coffee from the dispenser. He was sitting up in bed drinking it when Banner emerged wearing his own robe.

"I appreciate the invitation to bunk in here, Kusac. I hope you don't mind but I brought my kit with me," he said, coming over. "You should have told Father Lijou what was happening to you before you left. I'm sure he'd have spoken to Rhyaz and set the mission back a few days."

"I decided when to leave," he said, feeling the sharp pain of his fresh loss. He'd hidden it quite successfully from himself until now. "I couldn't stay on Shola any longer," he added, seeing the other's curious look.

"I'd heard you and Kaid had a blazing row."

He pulled his knees up until he could wrap his arms around them, as if holding himself tight could help contain the grief. He thought he'd been doing well last night. Obviously he hadn't. "I don't see how anyone could know," he said, his voice husky. "It happened out at his place. Only the three of us and T'Chebbi were there."

"It was how you looked when you came back," said Banner, squatting on the end of the bed. "Maybe talking about it will help."

"No. Not now."

"What did Kzizysus do to you, Kusac?" Banner asked.

"You were never this haunted by the past before he operated on you."

There was so much he couldn't tell anyone about what they'd done to him. He knew some of it, but there were a great many questions they'd refused to answer.

PART 2

WAKING

CHAPTER 15

Valsgarth Estate, Zhal-Oeshi, 28th day (August)

"PHRATRY Leader," said Kzizysus, clasping his hands respectfully in front of his mandibles before entering Annuur's lounge. Through the transparency of the bulkhead, he could see dawn breaking. "You asked for consultation."

"Enter, Kzizysus," said Annuur, sitting upright on his couch to make a gesture of greeting to the TeLaxaudin doctor. "Growth of blood samples from Kusac taken when he had his fever show my bio-component has been effective. Fully sensitized by now he is. Neurological messages unhindered travel to regulator as we wish. New bio-component for final procedure is ready. What is your status?"

Kzizysus stalked over to the couch nearest the Cabbarran and, climbing up onto it, folded himself up comfortably. "Tests of converters and regenerators unnecessary," he said, large eyes regarding his superior carefully. "Have sample jeggets if Sholans wish to examine. All trace of procedure excreted from them, nothing will be found to show how was done."

Annuur's mobile top lip curled back as he smiled in pleasure. "Is good. And you have prepared enough nano-converters and regenerators for him?"

"Yes, Phratry Leader," he said. "When combined with your new bio-component, is ready. Regulator device for torc need to adjust. Toueesut must have in torc while we operate. Next day torc must be ready to wear or possibly calamitous for all. Once access to full abilities obtained, must be control, must learn use regulator. For treatment, two days be isolated from everyone but us. Three days here to relearn skills. Five days in all. Will perhaps be periods of violence and frustration. Need others of his species for restraint."

"We use your children to restrain him. Captain Tirak is ideal. We are lucky. Great loyalty to me he has, will do as we ask and keep own counsel. Also is trusted by Sholans."

"I do the Camarilla's will," said Kzizysus, once more making the gesture of respect with his delicate hands. "When is our work to be done?"

"Today. Will be much excitement here when known son of Jo and Rezac being born. This will divert them from us for one day at least. You did well saving her and child on *Kz'adul*. Not easily accomplished at short notice."

Kzizysus chirred with pleasure. "As I have told you, my only regret is I could do nothing to help you and your Rryuk family."

"You did much. When Camarilla relayed my distress call to you, you ensured Prime ship *Kz'adul* came for us. Plot of Emperor's counselor could not be known to us. You did well, Kzizysus."

Seeing Annuur in such a benign mood, he ventured more. "A question, Phratry Leader. How came about these hybrids? I am not privy to knowledge of the Camarilla, but I know history of U'Churians. Which of us developed these Human and Sholan cubs? Whose children are they?"

"Not for you to ask, Kzizysus," Annuur said sharply. "Go prepare for surgery, combine our treatments. I will call Tirak and tell him to bring Kusac here."

the *Couana*, Zhal-S'Asha, 22nd day (October)

"It began just before the end of Zhal-Oeshi," he said quietly. "After my fever, Kaid had us moved to larger quarters so he could look after me, but you know that."

"I know you were extremely ill," said Banner. "They were afraid you might die. That's why they sent for Kzizysus."

He nodded. Much of it was a blur, but there were moments when he remembered the aftermath of the fever. He'd wake in the deep of the night, still held in the jaws of the nightmares, clinging terrified to the one who slept beside him, not caring who it was, just that someone was there for him.

"When the need is there," he murmured. His Triad had been there for him. Kaid had been there.

"After the fever," prompted Banner gently.

Valsgarth Estate, Zhal-Oeshi, 28th day (August)

Kaid's wrist comm buzzed gently, waking them both. While his friend took the call, he lay there, unwilling to move, glad of their shared warmth in the chill predawn air.

Finished, Kaid rolled away from him and sat up. "It's Kzizysus. He and Annuur have found a procedure that will work on you. They want to see you now."

Still more than half asleep, he barely heard what Kaid was saying. A hand grasped his shoulder and shook him gently.

"Wake up, Kusac. We've got to get over to the estate. Kzizysus has found a cure for you."

He opened his eyes, blinking owlishly. "What?"

Kaid sighed. "Get up. Jo's having her cub. Rezac needs our support."

"Rezac? Oh, right," he said, rubbing his eyes and attempting to sit up. His head felt thick this morning; it was harder than usual to focus on anything.

"Hold on a moment," said Kaid, leaning over to untangle him from the sheet. "Try now."

He shivered as he got up, reaching hurriedly for his tunic and hauling it on. Stumbling across the room, he opened his chest and pulled out one of his black robes.

"What?" he asked, turning round as he fought his arms into the sleeves. There was a puzzled look on Kaid's face. "I'm cold," he said, shivering again as he pulled his robe closed and fastened the tie belt.

"You'll be too hot in a couple of hours," said Kaid patiently, putting on his own tunic then going to get his coat from the hook on the door. "These freak dawn winds from the sea usually lift by sunup. Don't forget your utility belt."

"I thought this would be over now we've found Vartra's tomb," he said.

"Lijou says it should be soon. It takes time for the Entities to be persuaded to open Their realms again. Even Vartra can't do it overnight."

Crossing back to his side of the bed, he scrabbled on the floor for it, finally finding it actually under the bed.

Muttering fretfully, he fastened it over the top of the narrow tie belt. It was uncomfortable, and he began tugging at it, trying to center it. Kaid's hand closed round his arm.

"It's fine," he said. "Come on, we have to leave."

As they reached the main lobby, the smell of food penetrated his sleep-fogged mind. "Hungry," he said, heading toward the kitchens with the single-mindedness of a sleepwalker.

Kaid lunged after him. "No," he said, steering him toward the exit. "We're going home, remember?"

"Oh, yes. Jo and Rezac. We'll eat there, though, won't we?" he yawned, wishing he could shake off his tiredness.

"Yes, we'll eat at home."

Their aircar was parked round the back. Nodding to the guards huddled in their winter coats, they threaded their way through the vehicles till they reached it. He waited patiently, smothering more yawns until Kaid opened the door.

"This is your worst morning yet," said Kaid as he started up the aircar. "I'm beginning to get concerned about you. At least you're seeing Kzizysus today."

"I'm fine," he yawned, reclining his seat and trying to curl up in it. "What's this about Kzizysus? I seem to remember you mentioned him earlier."

"He's been working on a procedure to help you. Tirak called Carrie to say he was ready to try it out."

He tried to make sense of the words but his mind refused to concentrate on anything.

"Kusac? Did you hear me?"

"I heard you," he mumbled, closing his eyes and letting the comfortable warm feeling inside his head spread through his limbs.

"Well?" asked Kaid, glancing across at him.

"I need to speak to Carrie," he mumbled.

"You're not thinking of turning him down, are you?"

He couldn't think of anything right now. "Let me sleep," he said. "I'm tired."

*   *   *

Kaid was shaking him again. "We're here, Kusac."

Stretching and yawning, he sat up, returning the chair to an upright position. "That's Annuur's shuttle," he said. "I thought you'd be landing at the villa."

"I told you, Kzizysus is ready to . . ."

"But I'm not," he interrupted quietly. "I'm not, Kaid. I need time to think this through. Take me home, please."

Kaid looked at him. "If that's what you want," he said, starting up the aircar again.

Carrie was waiting for them.

"You shouldn't have called her," he said, getting up out of his seat. "There's no need to make an issue out of it. I just want some time to think, that's all."

"What's to think about?" asked Kaid, turning round to stop him. "This is what we've all been praying for, a chance for you to get your life back."

"It's not that simple any more, Kaid," he said softly, pulling away from him. "There's more to it than you think." He turned and, opening the door, jumped down to the ground.

"I was expecting to meet you down by Annuur's shuttle," said Carrie, reaching out to greet him.

Time slipped back and he saw her not as she was now, but as she'd been when she was carrying their cub, Kashini. He swept her into his arms, holding her close, just breathing in her scent. To have his old life back, his Talent again . . . But he could never regain his old life. She was Kaid's Leska now, even though this far into her pregnancy, her own Talent was sleeping because of her unborn cub.

"Gods, I love you so much, Carrie," he whispered, almost crushing her in his need to hold her close.

Her hands closed round his face, pulling it up from her shoulder so she could kiss him with all the fierceness he'd missed. His torc vibrated gently, letting him hear the sounds of her mind.

Slowly, their lips parted. "You aren't going to . . ."

He touched his lips to hers again, silencing her before letting her go. "Thank Kzizysus, but say I need time to think about it. I'll let him know as soon as I can."

She nodded slowly.

"Stop looking so worried," he said, flicking her cheek with his fingers. "I'm only going to walk in the garden, nothing more,

I promise. You take Kaid to Jo and Rulоc. They need your company more than I do right now."

He left her there and headed toward the small stream that ran through their land, thankful that the cold wind had indeed gone. The presence of open water had always helped him relax and concentrate. Right now, his mind seemed to slide away from anything that wasn't of the moment.

The sound of running water chuckling and gurgling as it tumbled over its bed of stones came to meet him as he got closer to the stream. Almost immediately, he could feel its soothing influence touching something deep inside him. Across the Nazule Bay, he could see the brassy disk of the sun beginning to clear the horizon. As he headed inland along the bank of the stream, the day's heat began to build.

He had a particular spot in mind, where the stream usually widened, its flow slowing as it formed a pool overshadowed by the trailing branches of trees. Last year he'd picnicked there several times with Carrie. It was just inside the woodland that marked the original boundaries of the villa's land.

He stopped at the edge of the clearing. Someone was already there, crouched on his haunches at the edge of the pool. Beside him lay the silver bodies of three medium-sized fish.

Moving quietly off the path, he concealed himself behind a group of trees and waited.

The stranger sat as still as if carved in wood, casting no shadow on the pool's gently moving surface. Forearms resting on his knees, body tilted slightly toward the water, he watched and waited. Suddenly, he plunged his arm into the pool, flicking a silver shape high into the air. Sunlight glinted off silver scales and droplets of water as the fish arced upward, flipping over and over before falling slowly downward again to land on the bank beside the other three.

"I've caught our first meal. I think it only fair you should cook it."

Startled, he looked back at the stranger. He'd been so focused on watching the fish that he'd forgotten the fisherman.

"This is private land," he said, stepping out from behind his cover. Head bent, the stranger was gutting his catch on a large, flat stone.

"I know. You aren't going to let that bother you, are you? No one's going to miss four fish that didn't belong to them anyway."

Now he was in the clearing, he could smell the fire.

"I know how to set a fire safely," said the stranger before he could speak. "Anyone ever told you that you worry too much?"

"Who are you?" he asked, hand resting on his pistol butt as he advanced on him. "What are you doing on my land?"

"Making a meal for you. Forget your weapon, you won't need it," he said, looking up. "I'm no threat to you."

The fisherman's body was totally relaxed, no sign of tension, even in the set of his ears or the tail that lay still against his ankles; he wasn't prepared for trouble. There was something familiar about him, but he couldn't quite put his finger on it. Deciding to trust his instincts for now, he walked around him and squatted down on the other side of the small fire.

"Here," the stranger said, passing him four long greenwood sticks. "Put the fish over the fire to grill."

Putting the sticks on the ground, he reached out for the first of the gutted fish. Small slits had been cut in the sides for him to push the stick through, and a makeshift rack had been set up on either side of the fire. He pushed the fish onto the middle of the stick then balanced it across the rack.

He was reaching for the last one when the stranger caught hold of his wrist, turning his hand over, revealing the still tender scars that ran the length of his palm.

"Ah, bonding scars. You were thorough. Perhaps it was a new marriage?" The fisherman looked up at him briefly, his thumb stroking gently over the scars. "No, an oath. It was important to you."

He pulled his hand away. "My business," he said sharply. "You've told me nothing about yourself."

"It's been a long time since I went fishing," said the stranger, mouth opening in a grin as he reached across for the remaining stick and threaded the last fish onto it. "I used to enjoy fishing when I was younger."

"Who are you?"

"A friend," he said, then pointed to the fire. "I'd check your meal if I were you. Sounds like they need turning."

He hadn't been aware of the gentle hissing and spitting coming from the fish until then. To his surprise, he found they did need turning. Hot juices splattered his fingers, making him wince and yelp as he attempted to turn them. With much blowing and sucking of his fingers, he finally accomplished it.

The stranger sat there laughing gently at his antics.

"What the hell are you burning in that fire?" he demanded, turning around to swill his tingling fingers in the pool. "I've never known food to cook so quickly!"

"Just wood." Leaning forward, the fisherman flipped the last fish over and sniffed audibly. "Smells good. Nothing quite like eating food you've caught and prepared yourself, is there?"

"I'd have liked it better if it hadn't burned me," he replied caustically, taking his fingers out of the water and wiggling them experimentally.

"Have you ever gone fishing?"

"Once or twice, but not like this, without a line or net."

"And cooked like this?" The stranger gestured to his fire and the grilling fish.

"I haven't."

"If you'd stayed in your garden, we wouldn't have met and your fingers wouldn't be singed. But here we are, trying something new. Worth a couple of lightly broiled fingers, don't you think?"

"I did cook like this once," he said, suddenly remembering. "When I met my life-mate. We were on Keiss, her world. I hunted for chiddoelike creatures and baked them in clay."

"So you have an adventurous side," the stranger said, reaching for two large leathery leaves. Taking two of the fish off the fire and placing them on one leaf, he deftly pulled the sticks free. "And you weren't burned that time." He held the leaf out to him.

"How d'you know that?" he demanded, accepting the rustic meal.

"You'd have mentioned it."

The smell was mouthwatering. He didn't care that the fish couldn't possibly have been cooked so quickly, they smelled as if they were. Putting the leaf on the ground in front of him, he extended his claws and carefully spread the fish open. Pulling off a few flakes, he nibbled them experimentally. They tasted as good as they smelled. He picked up the leaf and began to eat, keeping his eyes on the stranger.

"You're so suspicious. Why can't you just accept something good when it's offered to you?"

The conviction that there was something familiar about the stranger was growing stronger, but his hunger demanded to be satisfied.

"Nothing comes free," he said, scooping up more. "There's always a sting of some kind."

"Not always. This, for instance." The fisherman's gesture took in the campfire and them. "This is pleasant. I'm enjoying talking to you as much as I'm enjoying the food."

"Your point being?" He scraped up the last morsels before putting the leaf down and beginning to lick his fingers clean.

"Life is full of risks. There are no certainties, no guarantees. To achieve anything worthwhile, you have to take risks. You don't always burn your fingers."

He removed his fingers slowly from his mouth, looking carefully at the stranger, taking in the brown tunic, the tan pelt and tall thin ears—all features typical of one with desert tribal ancestry. "I know you from somewhere," he said. "We've met before, haven't we?"

"Once or twice, but I hate formality. I've enjoyed getting to know you like this." In one fluid move, the stranger got to his feet. "I have to go now, but before I do, remember one thing, Kusac. You have only one choice to make today. To be yourself. Everything else will follow because each of you is bound to the others by oaths, by blood, and by love. Trust that strength in your Triad to see you through what lies ahead."

"Wait!" he called out, leaping to his feet as the stranger turned and began to walk down the path. He ran after him, turning the corner to collide with Kaid.

"Where'd he go?" he demanded as Kaid grabbed hold of him. "Who?"

"The male who just went round the corner!"

"No one came round the corner, Kusac."

"He must have," he said, pulling free to run a short way down the empty path. He ground to a halt, looking round frantically, but even the dry scrubland on either side of the path was empty. Turning round, he went slowly back to Kaid. "I don't understand it. He *was* here. He was fishing in the pool. We cooked and ate the fish he'd caught."

He saw the disbelieving look on Kaid's face and pushed past him. "I'll prove it," he said. "The fire's still there."

"The stream's too low for fish because of the drought," Kaid called out after him.

The clearing was empty, with no scent or sign of a fire. "I don't understand," he said, looking round in bewilderment. "He *was* here." He bent down, scratching at the sun-baked earth where the fire had been, but there was nothing—no ashes, no heat in the ground except the heat of the sun beating down through the parched leaves of the trees overhead.

Kaid stepped past him, walking over to the side of the shallow pool. Stooping, he picked something up from the water margin.

"What is it?" he asked, looking over at him.

"A flower," said Kaid. "A nung flower." He held it out to him. "You've been gone three hours, Kusac, that's why I came to fetch you."

"Impossible!" he said, taking the still fresh flower from him. "Half an hour at most."

"Check the sun's position when we leave the clearing."

They walked back in silence until Kaid asked, "What did Vartra want?"

"To talk. We talked about how much he enjoyed fishing."

Kaid said nothing more until they were in the family garden. "Have you made a decision about Kzizysus?"

He looked at the nung flower again. "What did Kzizysus say?"

"It was Tirak I spoke to. The procedure's been tried out on several jeggets who all recovered completely, including having their psi abilities restored. At the worst, says Tirak, it'll remove the tendrils. You won't need to take psi suppressants and the pain you feel when you're angry will be gone permanently."

"And the risks?"

"He didn't mention any."

"I'll talk to Kzizysus," he said as they reached the open doors of the den.

Before leaving the villa, he'd spent a few minutes with Kashini, then gone to the suite he and Carrie had shared to call his parents.

Kaid found him there, taking off his black robe.

"You were right, I'm too hot now," he said, making an effort to fold the robe and failing because his hands were shaking.

Kaid took it from him and flung it onto the nearest chair. "Accept the chance Kzizysus is offering, Kusac," he said, taking hold of him by the shoulders. "I told you from the start that what matters most is getting you cured."

"I want to, but I need to know what Kzizysus is going to do. I need to be me again, Kaid," he said, dropping his gaze. He was finding it difficult to look him in the eyes, aware, through his torc, of Kaid's emotions. "I have to find myself, just as you needed to when you discovered you were from the past. But at least I know where to start from."

"Where's that?"

"I'm a member of the Brotherhood, and your sword-brother," he said, looking up. "It's not who I was, but it's who I am and want to be now."

Kaid clasped him gently round the neck, his thumb rubbing the edge of his jaw affectionately. "You'll do," he said, his voice low. "You've come a long way since Haven."

He leaned into the caress, grateful for his friend's steadying touch. "You and Carrie gave me the strength to do it. Without our Triad, I'd have been lost."

"But you weren't," said Kaid, holding him close and rubbing heads with him. "Thank Vartra you weren't. Carrie's here. Will you see her?"

He laughed shakily. "Of course!" Then felt her arms around him too. "Take care of each other if anything should happen to me," he said, flicking his tongue across both their cheeks before pushing them gently, but firmly, away. "We'd better go. I've kept Kzizysus waiting too long already."

Annuur greeted them at the air lock, and led them through into the shuttle's lounge where Kzizysus was waiting.

"I forget the need to be with family first," he said apologetically, gesturing to the floor cushions and couches. "Sit and ask Kzizysus what you need to know."

In deference to Carrie's pregnancy, they sat on a couch, the slope adjusted into a flat plane by Annuur.

"Kusac's been bothered by headaches and unable to wake properly in the mornings," said Kaid. "Will this affect the treatment?"

"No. Brain fever made him ill. This expected during recovery."

"Does the treatment involve implants?" he asked, looking at the TeLaxaudin. "I won't have an implant of any kind." He felt Carrie move closer, take hold of his hand, squeezing it gently in reassurance.

"Understanding this. No implants," Kzizysus' translator assured him. A prolonged burst of static followed, then silence. The TeLaxaudin mimicked a Sholan gesture of apology.

"No translation," explained Annuur, settling himself on his own couch. "Nearest to your medical terms is drug therapy."

"What's the procedure?" asked Kaid.

"Two drugs. Infuse tendrils, as you call, to kill. Test you for damage, then next drug. It increases neural connectivity, reconnecting what was lost. You practice skills to reinforce."

"Damage?" asked Carrie sharply. "What damage? From the tendrils or because of their removal?"

"Both," said Annuur succinctly. "Need diagnosis at that stage to determine next. Cannot do earlier. This procedure I contribute to also. You call it joint effort."

"Could this leave me worse than I am now?" he asked. "I've managed to find some peace at last."

"Unlikely," said the TeLaxaudin, tilting his head to one side and regarding him thoughtfully. "Degree of cure depend on damage, no more."

There was so much he needed to know, but he didn't know what to ask.

"Can you restore his psi talent no matter what the damage?" asked Kaid.

"Yes," said Kzizysus. Once more static issued from the translator.

"Again, degree of restoration depends on damage, but speak with mind and hear he will again," assured Annuur.

"Side effects?" asked Kaid.

"Some fever anticipated. Difficulties during period of adjustment, then no problem," said Annuur, not waiting for Kzizysus to reply.

He took a deep breath. "When do we start?"

Annuur sat up, mouth curling into a smile. "Good! We start now. One thing. We do here, not in Vanna's hospital as suggested. Equipment here, we here."

He nodded. It didn't matter to him where he was. "How long?"

"Five days you be here. Need isolation, no visitors."

"I'm staying with him," said Kaid, his tone uncompromising.

"Apologies, Kaid. You cannot," Annuur said firmly. "You not know equipment or procedure. Your medicals skills no use for this. But need Tirak's help. He be your eyes, tell you how it progresses."

He glanced at Kaid, aware of his friend's body stiffening when Annuur had said no. "I'll be all right," he said. "You trusted Tirak before."

Kaid's ears had rotated sidewards in anger but now they began to lift slightly and swivel back. "You're sure? Five days is a long time, and there's the fever. If you have more fever dreams . . ."

"We treat," interrupted Annuur. "Patient distress not acceptable. Knowledge of Sholan physiology we have, and Sholan medical database."

"I'm sure," he said. "I'll be fine."

He didn't want to watch them go so, after giving Kaid his pistol and knife, he left with Kzizysus before they did.

Tirak was already in the sick bay, sitting at the far side of the room on the edge of a bed designed for a non-Cabbarran. He got up, shutting off the comp pad he'd been reading, and stowed it on the night table.

"Welcome to the torture chamber," he smiled, coming over to him. "With me as your nurse, it will be, I'm afraid."

He managed a weak grin in response. At least there was no smell of antiseptics.

The room was small, with walls and floor a uniform off-white color. Immediately to his left was a door into a room within the room, and on his right, the nursing station with a work surface and sink. As he ventured farther in, he saw two low Cabbarran sleeping couches next to the bed that was to be his. It was almost stark in comparison to the sick bays he'd been in recently.

"That's the operating theater," said Tirak, pointing to the internal room. "The head's next door, in case you were wondering, but you'll be staying in bed for the next few days."

"Prepare him, Tirak," said Kzizysus. "I return shortly with Phratry Leader Annuur."

"Phratry Leader?" he asked, glad to have something to talk about.

"Annuur's important among his own people," said Tirak, taking him by the arm and leading him over to the bed. "Equivalent to one of your Clan Leaders. You undress while I get things ready." Tirak left him there and went over to the work area by the nursing station.

Now he was beside it, he realized the bed was also an IC unit. Like a douche of cold water, he remembered Tirak's reference to the head. "Tirak, we've different anatomy from you."

"It's been taken care of, taiban," the U'Churian said gently, turning round. "I've been working with Annuur since Kzizysus arrived. I've also passed Kaid's and Vanna's paramedic course as part of my training here. We studied both Sholan and U'Churian physiology." His tail began to move gently. "Trust us, Kusac. You'll be all right. I'm not really that bad a nurse. Just stow your clothes in the night table there, and don't forget to take off your psi damper."

He took off his wrist comm, then undressed, putting everything in the cupboard. Perching on the edge of the bed, he wondered idly how beings as small in stature as Kzizysus and Annuur could treat him on a bed this high. He presumed that was why Tirak was involved.

Tirak returned carrying a metal treatment tray which he placed on the bed beside him.

He flinched away, remembering his time on the *Kz'adul*. The cold sweat of fear was beginning to gather on his palms and back as Tirak began unsealing an antiseptic wipe.

Tirak looked up immediately. "Kusac, you're in the heart of your own Clan here," he said. "I swear you're safe. And you're in the care of more than just our navigators. Annuur's no ordinary sept leader, he's leader of all the septs that work with our family. That's nearly a thousand Cabbarrans. They're more than navigators as you'll find out while you're here. Trust us."

"It's not that," he said. "There's been too many sick bays and hospitals recently."

"I understand. Hopefully, this should be the last of them. You'll need to be sedated during the treatment," Tirak said, parting the pelt on one side of his neck before rubbing it with the antiseptic wipe. "So you won't even be aware of me fitting the catheters."

"I ate first meal," he said, remembering.

"Doesn't matter with this drug," he said, picking up a hypo spray.

A brief sting and it was over. Almost immediately he began to feel relaxed and drowsy. He clutched hold of Tirak's arm as the U'Churian eased him back onto the bed. "Don't leave me alone," he mumbled as his consciousness began to fade.

"I'll be with you the whole time, Kusac," Tirak said. "Just relax and let us do our job."

Tirak flicked the sheet back over Kusac's feet when he'd finished clinching the ankle restraints into place. "Are you sure this is necessary?" he asked.

"Positive," said Annuur. "Must not move during treatment, especially head. Cause brain damage otherwise. Is anesthetic feed connected?"

"I did that after his pre-med."

"Good. Take torc to Toueesut. Say need it day after tomorrow. Then collect blood for him from Vanna."

Tirak nodded, triggering the mechanism to lower the bed to a more comfortable height for the two doctors before picking up Kusac's torc from the night table.

Annuur examined the controls on the bed's side panel, then activated the body imager. A transparent panel, the length of Kusac's body, began to extrude from the lower part of the bed, curving upward and over him. As it did, an image of his internal organs and soft tissue began to form on the surface.

Kzizysus approached the open side and peered down through the panel, trying to locate the precise point to insert the catheter into his patient's neck. It had to go into the original site of the implant. "Prime scent marker, what do about it?" he asked as he checked the head restraint before gently inserting the needle under Kusac's ear.

"Leave marker. Has purpose later," said Annuur as he tapped the feed line from the drug delivery unit set into the side of the bed, making sure there were no air bubbles.

"Catheter ready," said Kzizysus. "Wait. Is something else here." He studied the image carefully. "Need scalpel. Has biomonitor implanted."

Annuur picked up a scalpel from the trolley behind him and passed it to the TeLaxaudin. Moments later, Kzizysus stepped aside. "Done. I destroy."

Annuur connected the feed line to the catheter, then bent down and switched the device on. "Now we watch and wait," he said.

the *Couana*, Zhal-S'Asha, 21st day (October)

"It can't have been an easy decision to put yourself into the hands of the surgeon who'd been involved in fitting the implant to you in the first place," said Banner, handing him a fresh mug of coffee.

"Kzizysus didn't fit it," he said quietly, accepting it. "It was Chy'qui. Kzizysus only adjusted it to my system rather than a Valtegan's."

"I thought only the TeLaxaudin could fit them."

"Normally, but Chy'qui wanted me implanted and he knew Kzizysus would refuse."

"You know that for sure?"

He nodded. "No other reason for Chy'qui to fit it himself."

"What Tirak said about Annuur leading a thousand people was rather an eye-opener."

"Kaid almost worked it out. Tirak's mission to Jalna was vital to them, they wouldn't just send some trading crew to do a deep cover mission like that. And if Tirak was important, then it followed Annuur would be too. Annuur was their medic, but when you manipulate certain kinds of matter on a cellular level for medicine, space travel and planet regeneration, it kind of takes you out of our league of paramedicine, doesn't it?" Even as he said it, he stopped, wondering how he'd known.

"Completely. It's getting late. Perhaps we should think about getting some sleep soon."

"No. I need to talk about it," he said slowly, taking a sip of his coffee. Banner was purposely downplaying what he'd just said. Why? "I know what's ahead tomorrow. I need to get this out of my system now."

Banner leaned over his side of the bed for a moment, then reappeared with a pack of cookies. "Take a break for a few minutes, then. Have one of these. I brought them with me."

"Thanks," he said, taking one. How could he know what was obviously highly classified Cabbarran information? After Annuur's surgical procedure, he'd been with Naacha, but when he tried to think about the blue tattooed Cabbarran and what he'd been taught by him, he found his memories blurred and vague. But he did know that his knowledge of the Cabbarrans capabilities must remain secret—for now.

Stronghold, Zhal-Oeshi, 28th day (August)

"Alex! We have to go now!"

"You don't need to yell," said Alex as she bounced across her bed to where he stood impatiently by the door. "I heard you the first time!"

"This isn't a pleasure trip, Alex," said Rhyaz sternly. "We should have been in Lijou's office for the briefing five minutes ago."

"I needed my comp pad. You're the one wanting me to study on this trip!"

"What the hell are you wearing?" he asked, actually seeing her jeans and T-shirt for the first time.

"Something wrong with your eyesight?" she muttered mutinously. "I'm not wearing that black outfit."

"You should be wearing gray, we're on active duty," he said, irritated. "Get changed and join me at the briefing. I'm not keeping the Father waiting any longer." He stalked out of the bedroom and headed down the corridor for Lijou's office, meeting Kha'Qwa on the way.

"I'll handle this," she said placidly. "You go and start briefing Lijou."

He nodded his thanks, allowing himself to relax slightly as he passed her.

Five minutes later, Alex, wearing an oversized gray uniform jacket over the top of her fatigues, preceded Kha'Qwa into Lijou's office.

"Problem solved," his mate said as Alex made her way over to join them. "Seems you didn't think to offer her a jacket, Rhyaz, so I gave her one of yours for now. She can pick up a couple of her own from the duty office on your way out. And you have no objection to her wearing her own clothes when she's off duty, do you? I've sent them downstairs with one of the juniors."

Rhyaz didn't get the chance to answer before Lijou sent to him.

Think of it from her point of view, Rhyaz. She was running away from enforced military training, now she's in a relationship with you. Uniforms are our choice, not hers. Compromise with her.

I'm constantly compromising with her! Including her in this briefing is one!

She's making concessions too.

"Hey, stop talking about me when I can't hear you," complained Alex, sitting down in a chair.

Rhyaz sighed, knowing Lijou and Kha'Qwa were right. If only she didn't make life so difficult for him, it would be easier for him to make concessions. "You can wear what you want when you're off duty, Alex, I should have told you that. And if you wanted a jacket, why didn't you ask for one?"

"Didn't know I could," she said, exploring the multitude of pockets.

"Anchorage," Lijou prompted him.

He gathered his thoughts again and looked back at Lijou. "We have four Valtegans in custody," he said. "We've used the Prime idea of encounter suits. They never see or smell us at all. Our scientists are ready to start limited trials of the drug when we arrive. We know what to expect from the computer simulations, this is our final field test."

"How many tests are they planning to do?" asked Lijou quietly.

"As many as necessary," said Rhyaz, standing up. "I like it as little as you do, Lijou, but it needs to be done. I'll call you as soon as I have any news. You're in charge until I get back. Yaszho can help you if necessary."

Lijou got to his feet. "Take care. You, too, Alex. Remember, it's your first time as a representative for Stronghold. Please be careful when you're in public."

"Like he'll let me forget," she muttered, getting up.

Lijou put his hand on her shoulder as they walked to the door. "You said you wanted to get out more," he said. "Not many folk your age go on any missions, let alone one of this gravity, you know."

"I'm only exchanging here for a ship," she said. "Big deal."

Rhyaz could appreciate her point, and decided to tell her what he'd planned to keep her amused—and out of his hair—during their voyage to Anchorage. "Your skills seem to lie in handling data processing and information systems. I thought you might like some time training on the bridge of the *Chazoi*," he said, following them out into the corridor.

"You're kidding!" she said, twisting round to see him.

"I'm serious. I had intended to tell you when I came for you this morning."

She stopped, turning to look back at him. "Thank you."

See? sent Lijou. *Kha'Qwa and Ruth were right. Stimulate her, catch her interest, Challenge her, and she'll stop fighting you. We do it all the time here when we try to motivate the juniors.*

I know, but it's not so easy when you're involved with one of them! replied Rhyaz as they made their way downstairs.

News of their Guild Master's acquisition of a Leska had stunned the community at Stronghold, but as Lijou had predicted, it was a short-lived topic of gossip, surviving for only a few days after they reappeared. The news hadn't yet penetrated beyond their mountain fortress, but it was about to, with this, their first public outing.

They stopped at the duty office for Rhyaz to collect extra ammunition and to pick up Alex's two jackets. He handed them to M'Azul, his adjutant, along with her off duty clothes and told him to wait for them on the aircar.

"Issue her with a stunner and belt knife, Chaddo," Rhyaz said to the duty officer as he stowed a couple of extra power cells in his belt.

"You're trusting me with weapons?" she asked, watching the elderly Sholan return to the safe.

"All Brothers and Sisters are armed when they leave here on a mission," he said. "Your scores on the shooting range are more than adequate."

Chaddo handed her a pistol and a black-bladed knife. "Here you are, Djana."

Rhyaz came to her aid, helping her position the weapons comfortably on her belt. As he was about to straighten up, Alex looped an arm around his neck, holding him back. "Thank you for not treating me like a kid," she said, kissing him.

Startled at the show of affection, he nonetheless returned her kiss. He might not have wanted this Link, and though he found her aggravating for much of the time, he wasn't blind to her charms. Her lips were warm and soft, and as he touched them, he could almost taste the magic of the Link they shared.

We have to leave now, Alex. Our Link day's starting earlier than I thought. We must be on board the Chazoi *before the compulsion starts. Make sure your psi damper is on full.* He stepped reluctantly away from her, just catching sight of Lijou and Chaddo exchanging indulgent smiles.

"Don't say a word!" he said, arching an eye ridge at the elderly Brother.

"No, sir, not one," Chaddo said, schooling his face into a neutral expression. "But it's good to see you've found someone to keep you interested, if I may say so. Always were a lively lad, not unlike the young Djana herself."

Rhyaz huffed in mock anger as Alex began to snigger. "You get away with murder, Chaddo," he said. "Be thankful it's the start of our Link day or I wouldn't be so amused."

"Yes, sir, absolutely. Won't happen again," Chaddo murmured, exchanging another glance with the head priest as they left.

Lyand had a speeder waiting for them in the courtyard. "We're a little behind time, Commander," he said as they climbed in. "I'll need to make it up now or we'll miss our window for Chagda Station."

"Do it," said Rhyaz, nodding to Nezyk and M'Azul before sliding into his seat and helping Alex buckle her safety harness.

The walk through Shanagi Spaceport was very different from the one she'd made the last time she'd been here. This time, she was very aware of being with the Guild Master of the Brotherhood. Flanked by Lyand, M'Azul, and Nezyk, the crowds melted in front of them as they headed straight for the military entrance to the landing field. Checkpoints were a matter of Lyand flashing their IDs while the other two did their bodyguard bit and then they were through. No prolonged questions or delays, just crisp salutes, even from the Forces personnel on duty.

Even so, people stopped to look, not only at Rhyaz, but at her, wondering what a young Human female was doing with the Brothers.

The short flight up to Chagda was in one of the regular shuttles, but in First Class. She'd never traveled in such style. It was laid out like a lounge, with comfortable seats arranged in pairs. There was even a personal comm screen she could access if she wanted.

Life was certainly looking up, she decided, thinking of the prospect of flying lessons and more on the *Chazoi*.

She stole a sideways glance at Rhyaz. He was leaning back in his seat, eyes closed for now. The last ten days had been difficult for both of them as they came to terms with their relationship. The last thing she'd wanted was a permanent boyfriend. Getting so much attention from the young Sholan males at Stronghold had been exciting. She'd been aware of Rhyaz' interest in her, and had enjoyed playing him off against the students, but she'd never actually considered responding seriously to him, until he'd kissed her in the temple and things had gotten out of her control.

For one thing, at forty, he was a lot older than her, even though his people lived longer than Humans. She'd had to revise her opinions of him, however, and was still doing so. Compared to him, the students were just kids, too young and unsophisticated for her. Not Rhyaz. On the two Link days they'd had so far, there had been nothing old about the way he'd made love to her. He'd been telling the truth, he was experienced. And he was good-looking, for any species of male. Kha'Qwa had been right about him having a great body, and he was hers.

"Finished assessing my virtues?" he asked quietly, his voice rich with amusement.

She flushed and looked away. His hand covered hers, his fingers curling round into her palm where it lay on the chair arm beside him.

"I know you're a free spirit, Alex, and I'll try to make sure you've room to spread those wings of yours, as they say in your language, but you need to work with me. I run the Brotherhood along with Lijou. A great many lives depend on our decisions. As you found out, you can make my life very difficult, or you can help me. I don't want us to be adversaries."

"Did you mean what you said that first night?" she asked abruptly.

"Excuse me?"

"You said I'd succeeded in teasing you beyond my wildest hopes."

He laughed quietly, releasing her hand to lift the dividing chair arm and pull her against his side. "Haven't I just said so? I was ready to strangle you, or . . . Well, let's say I got what I preferred."

Pleased, she leaned her head against his chest, enjoying the gentle flow of thoughts and energy between them, and dozed for the rest of the journey.

Lyand fell back beside him as they walked across the docks to the *Chazoi*'s berth.

"General Raiban's up ahead, sir," he said quietly.

"I see her. Contact the *Chazoi*. Backup might be useful if she decides to get stroppy." *Alex, Raiban is . . .*

I know. Found the information, no need to brief me, she sent. *Say nothing and let me handle this.*

She glanced at him. *Of course. You're the Guild Master.*

"Commander Rhyaz," said Raiban, stepping in front of them as they drew level with her. "What brings you here? And with a young protégée. Recruiting from among the Human cubs, now, are you?"

Rhyaz winced inwardly. He'd forgotten how young Alex looked. "Like you, I'm on business, Raiban," he said.

"A domestic run, perhaps? Aren't you going to introduce me to your young—Companion? Wasn't she one of the two illegal visitors that the Humans were attempting to return to Earth?"

"It's thanks to them we know Earth was breaking the treaty regarding recruiting their telepaths."

"Very altruistic of them to come all that distance to bring it to your attention. But you still haven't introduced me."

"Alex," he said, "This is General Raiban, President of Sholan High Command, and this is Alex Ward, my Leska. Now, if you'll excuse us, Raiban, I have pressing business to attend to." He took advantage of Raiban's stunned surprise to draw Alex with him as he neatly sidestepped her and continued on down the dock-side.

"She doesn't like you," said Alex as they headed up the gang-way into the *Chazoi*.

"The feeling's mutual," he said as Nezyk retracted the ramp and began closing the air lock behind them. "She threatened Kha'Qwa and Lijou while I was on Haven. Distressed her so much she fell and nearly lost her life and her cub's. This way," he said, leading the way to his office. "Tell them to disengage and break orbit now, M'Azul. I'll be—we'll be—in my office if I'm needed."

"Aye, sir. Captain Fyshar says they've picked up a Striker in stealth mode standing off Chagda. It's his opinion they plan to follow us."

"Tell him to put the station between us and them and initiate our chameleon shields. It'll give us the opportunity to test them against the best Raiban's got. I'll be damned if she's following us to Anchorage or any of our outposts."

Valsgarth estate, evening, the same day

"Stop worrying," Kaid said quietly to Carrie as they sat in the small waiting room in Vanna's hospital. "Tirak told us all was going well with Kusac. Rezac's been fretting enough for everyone."

Carrie sighed and rested her head against his shoulder. "I can't help it. After all he's been through, it seems cruel to leave him shut away on his own. How's Jo doing?"

"Almost over, from what I can tell."

"She seems to have taken a lot longer than I did."

"You had an accelerated pregnancy because we went back in time. It usually takes at least this long according to what I've read. I've studied birthing, I don't intend to get caught like that a second time."

"This time I want security and a soft bed," she said.

"You won't find me arguing with that," he said. "Here's Zashou."

Carrie looked up, seeing Zashou through the transparent partition between them and the corridor.

"I'm not too late, am I?" she asked as she came in. "I had to block Rezac out for most of today, but I picked up the change in his mental state a few minutes ago."

"No news yet," said Kaid. "But I think it's over."

Ten minutes later, Vanna opened the door. "You can come and see them now," she said. "Noni delivered their son ten minutes ago. He's healthy and hungry!"

Jo was sitting up, looking tired but happy. Rezac came toward them, holding the tiny cub carefully. A bemused grin was spread across his face.

"We have a son," he said in a hushed voice. "See. Isn't he beautiful?" He tilted his arms so they could see him.

"He's just like you," said Carrie, touching a gentle finger to the tiny dark brown cheek. "Have you chosen a name for him yet?" she asked, looking over to Jo.

"A Sholan name," she said. "We're calling him Rhion."

"A lovely name for a lovely boy," she said as the cub began to mewl.

"He's hungry," said Rezac, looking slightly startled. "He sent to me!"

Carrie laughed. "Give him to Jo," she said, shoving him gently toward the bed. "All our cubs touch our minds when they're born, but it usually doesn't last."

"Everything about newborns surprises their fathers," said Noni from her chair beside Jo. "The novelty will soon wear off, more's the pity!"

Rezac handed his son carefully to Jo, then pulled up a chair to sit beside her. "Not for me," he said, reaching out to stroke Jo's cheek. He looked over his shoulder at Kaid. "I missed my first son, I don't intend to lose a moment with Rhion."

"Go and have a look at him," Carrie said to Kaid. "He won't bite you—yet!"

"Be your turn next, Tallinu," cackled Noni. "Only eight weeks now, isn't it, child? Now that'll be a sight! You wearing the idiotic grin of a new father!"

Kaid smiled gently as he went over to look down at the cub. "I'm sure I will. I couldn't spoil your fun, could I, Noni?"

Noni laughed as she got to her feet. "In that you're no different from any other male, Tallinu, as I've no doubt you've been discovering lately. I've seen the way you look at Carrie. You're already as proud as any father-to-be over her pregnancy. Mark my words, you'll melt when you hold your own newborn. Then there's T'Chebbi due just before midwinter!"

"He's lovely, Jo," said Kaid, gently touching Rhion's head before leaning down to press his cheek against Jo's. "Congratulations."

"Stop teasing him, Noni," chided Carrie, going over to her. "Time we got you back home. Zhala will have hot food ready for us."

"Aye, I must admit I'm tired, child," she said, leaning on her stick as she made her way slowly to the door. "I'll see you tomorrow, Jo. You make sure you get some rest tonight! No sitting up looking at your berran all night. He'll still be there come morning."

Jo laughed. "I can't promise I won't, but I'll try to get some sleep as well. Good night, Noni, and thank you."

Kzizysus had placed the imager over Kusac's unconscious body again and was watching the progress of the nano-virus. Tirak was at the nursing station, trying to read his comp pad. The regular tone of the monitor was lulling him to sleep.

"Take meal break, Captain," said Annuur, sitting up on his haunches to look at his U'Churian friend. "Rest a few hours. Come back later. Nothing happen here tonight."

Tirak yawned and put his pad down. "Can't, Annuur. I told Kusac I'd stay with him."

"He not know."

"But I would," he replied. "I can get Sheeowl to bring me something, if you've no objection."

"Can, but still have to leave here to eat it. Must take nourishment. Sokarr will make something for you. Ask him. Quicker. I be here."

Tirak nodded and got up. "Do you or Kzizysus want anything?"

Annuur considered it for a moment. "Yes. Make meals for all of us. Tell when ready."

When he'd gone, Annuur joined Kzizysus. He didn't like lying to Tirak, nor to Kusac and his family, about the procedure they were using, but there was too much at stake for scruples. Getting the TeLaxaudin's attention, he tapped his translator, mimicking turning it off.

Kzizysus did as he was asked then returned his attention to the imager. He pointed to the area displaying Kusac's brain tissue. "Active tendrils show green," he said. "Inactive area is now red. Process almost complete, very little green left. Check anesthetic levels. May need replacing now. Also hydration fluids." He glanced up at the life-support monitor. Satisfied by the readings, he returned to watching the imager.

Annuur did as he was asked. Kzizysus was the expert here, his part had been developing the virus used to sensitize Kusac to the biological component in the torc, and the carrier for the nanos.

"Will he develop a fever like the jeggets did?" he asked.

Kzizysus turned round, eyes swirling. "Will be, but when I not sure. Could be soon, could be once we start next drug. No seizures though. Is good. You get regenerator drug now. Want it set up ready to switch on when this finished."

"Is there enough inactive material for regenerator nanos to transform?" he asked, trotting over to the cooler to fetch the drug pack.

"Plenty," affirmed Kzizysus. "Any excess will be excreted with nanos. No trace be left of our procedure."

Returning, he placed the pack in the second delivery unit and set about unsealing a fresh feed line.

the *Couana*, Zhal-S'Asha, 22nd day (October)

"The treatment took two days," said Kusac. "Tirak told me that. They were destroying the implant tendrils on the first day, and on the second, using a neurotransmitter virus to redirect the connections that had been lost or misconnected because of the implant. I remember coming round with one hell of a headache and fever."

Valsgarth Estate, Zhal-Oeshi, 29th day (August)

He was burning up and his head ached as if a vise were trying to crush his skull. Trying to move, he found he couldn't.

"You've got a fever, Kusac," he heard Tirak say. "They've had to restrain you. Try to lie still."

He felt hands touching him, and smelled a strange alien scent he half remembered from somewhere else. All he could see was an expanse of white above him. Memories of torture and pain came rushing back and he began to struggle frantically.

Cold, wet cloths were placed on his body, making him cry out in shock, but it eased the fire and the aching in his joints.

"Increase sedation," he heard a translator say and within moments, the whiteness began to fade as he passed out.

The fever was gone the next time he woke. Experimentally, he moved his head and saw Tirak sitting on a chair beside him.

"You're awake," the U'Churian said, leaning toward him. "Do you remember where you are?"

He licked dry lips before speaking. "Annuur's sick bay?"

"That's right. You had a fever and woke sooner than expected."

"I couldn't move," he said.

"You were restrained because of the catheters. Would you like to sit up?"

"Please."

As part of the bed began to rise, he attempted to pull his arms out from under the cover. They felt heavy, as if they were made of lead, but by the time he was sitting up, he'd managed to get them free.

Tirak held out a glass of water and he accepted it gratefully. Kzizysus and Annuur came in as he was handing the empty glass back.

"How you feel?" asked the Cabbaran.

His head was clear, and though his body felt physically exhausted, he actually didn't feel that bad. "All right," he said. "Hungry," he added as his stomach growled.

Kzizysus came over to the side of his bed. "Reach out," he said through his translator. "Reach with your mind."

He looked at the TeLaxaudin. "The pain," he began.

"Is gone. Try."

He looked at Tirak who raised his eye ridges expressively.

"Lower mental shields," said Kzizysus.

He turned his thoughts inward, gradually lowering his shields one by one until they were all down. He listened, then shook his head. "No difference," he said.

Tirak got up and went round the other side of the bed, opening the cupboard and pulling out his wrist comm. "You left the psi damper on," he said, passing it to him.

Sighing with relief, he turned it off and passed it back to Tirak, waiting for something—anything—to happen.

"Nothing." Dispiritedly, he lay back against his pillow.

Annuur and Kzizysus began to talk rapidly, the conversation going back and forth for some time.

"Maybe you just need to get used to having that ability again," said Tirak eventually.

"It's either there, or it isn't," he said.

"Take off torc," Annuur repeated.

"Why?"

"Do it!" the Cabbarran ordered.

He reached up and removed his torc. Suddenly his mind was flooded with sounds and emotions and the hissing of white noise. Keening in pain and shock, he dropped the torc, clapping his hands to his head.

"What the hell?" exclaimed Tirak, lunging to catch the torc before it hit the floor.

"Replace torc," Annuur ordered the U'Churian.

As soon as the torc touched his neck, quiet returned. Shaking, his eyes streaming, he let go of his head and looked up at them.

"Is no doubt treatment worked," he heard Annuur say. "Problem is with regulator in torc." He looked across at Kzizysus. "Need adjusting."

"What happened?" he asked, blinking and rubbing his smarting eyes. "What was that?"

"No shields to protect you, you hear too many minds," said Annur. "Is like ability new again. Have to relearn, Kusac. Torc regulates what you sense, more sensitive than your dampers. Not need damper after this. Rest now, Tirak get you food. We scan you after. Time for adjustment is needed."

He nodded his understanding, but in truth, he'd taken in little after Annuur said he'd have to relearn how to use his Talent.

Valsgarth Estate, Zhal-Oeshi, 30th day (August)

The bed beside him moved and he opened his eyes to see Annuur leaning on it.

The Cabbarran's crest of stiff hair was tilted toward him and his long top lip, the whiskers on his nose almost touching his hand, wriggled as he began to speak.

"This you must know. Scans and tests we did last night while you sedated confirmed many things. Psi abilities restored, neural damage caused by pain collar mostly repaired, torc recalibrated. But anomaly showed too. Not told us of sensitivity to la'quo and experimenting with temporal gates. Sensitivity affected neuroviral regeneration, cause memory problems."

"What kind of problems?"

A burst of static, then, "Like memory loop. Must find and

reevaluate affected memories. If not, then they keep replay, night-mares follow. Likely most recent ones affected."

"If I've lost them, how can I find them?" he asked, confused.

"Family help. They remember for you. Try see from outside, objectively. Bits of memories will come, cannot be avoided," he said firmly.

There are some memories I could do without, he thought. "But my telepathy? You said I have it back." That was more important to him than memories.

Annuur dipped his head once in a nod. "Is back. You get up now, eat. Practice you must. Naacha help you. His ability this is, not mine."

"You have telepaths? I didn't know that."

"All are, is like, not same as telepathy. Much you learn here will not be remembered, Kusac. Rise. Dress. I take you to Sokarr for food." Annuur got down and trotted over to the nursing station, climbing up on the chair to access the comm terminal there.

He pushed the cover back and swung his feet to the floor. He was a little unsteady perhaps, but that was all. "My family, can I speak to them?"

"Apologies, no. Three days it takes to stabilize you. Tirak will have told them all is well with you."

"Where is Tirak?" he asked, going round to the night table for his clothes.

"With his own family. No nursing you need now. Only us."

It dawned on him that he was alone with them. "Tirak said he'd stay with me."

"He did, while you needed nursing," confirmed Annuur. "Now, need practice new skills."

Anger flared. He felt his pelt starting to rise. "Dammit, Annuur, that wasn't part of what I agreed to," he growled. "I wanted some contact with my family!"

Annuur looked across at him, tilting his head from one side to the other as he surveyed him. "You angry. No matter. We set conditions, not you." He looked away and began speaking into the comm. The translator remained silent.

He began to snarl low in his throat, the need to get out para-mount in his mind. Grabbing his tunic, he hauled it on. Fasten-ing his belt as he went, he headed past Annuur and out into the corridor. They thought they could keep him locked in here, did they? Well they could think again! The air lock stood opposite. He was leaving here now.

His field of vision narrowed, focusing in on the access panel as he strode toward the exit. His mind was automatically thinking of numeric combinations even before he was within reach.

"That's far enough, Kusac," he heard Tirak's voice say from behind him. "No need to leave. Annuur was testing your responses, nothing more."

He stopped, his pelt rising about his face till it rivaled any U'Churian mane. *So Annuur had lied, had he? Even more reason to leave,* he thought, reaching for the panel.

A jolt of power surged through him, flinging him backward till he collided with the wall. Cold rage overtook anger as he turned on Tirak. He found himself looking down the short muzzle of a pistol.

"You trapped the panel and didn't warn me," he snarled, furious.

"To stop you leaving," said the Captain. "Think, Kusac. Think of your anger. There's no pain."

He began to advance. He wanted that gun.

Tirak fired.

Something hit him in the shoulder, distracting him enough to glance at it. The short, brightly colored tuft of a dart protruded from his black tunic. His knees buckled under him and, as he fell against the wall, he looked back at Tirak in shock. He'd hit the deck before the U'Churian reached him. Anger evaporated to be replaced by confusion.

"It's only a trank," Tirak said, hauling him up to his feet. "We needed to demonstrate to you that the neural damage has been cured." Tirak slid his arm under his shoulder and began leading him away from the air lock. "You've got one hell of a temper there."

"Hell of a way to demonstrate your point," he said, trying to control legs which refused to support him. "Where you taking me?"

"To the mess and Sokarr. You haven't eaten in two days."

"What day is it?"

"The thirtieth, and just after fourth hour."

*   *   *

The food was good, though mainly vegetarian. Out of deference to him and Tirak, Sokarr had cooked a couple of meat accompaniments.

"You going to work hard next few days, need your meat," the Cabbarran said, jumping down from his work platform to the floor.

"Have you spoken to Carrie and Kaid?" he asked Tirak as he sipped the strange cold malted drink.

"I told them everything was going well," he said. "Sorry about the trank dart," he began.

"I'll survive," he said ruefully, rubbing his shoulder where the tiny puncture wound still smarted. "I don't understand why I got so angry. Everything about it was odd. I was using huntersight, but with unusual clarity."

"Tell Annuur," said Tirak. "I know nothing about this."

He didn't know what made him look up at the door, but when he did, he saw the third member of the Cabbarran crew, Naacha.

He was older than Annuur and Sokarr, his sandy pelt liberally shot with gray, as was the upright mane. It was the tattoos that drew Kusac's attention. There were the usual ones of sept and rank, but those on his cheeks, executed in a bright, almost electric blue, were less formal, more swirling and free-flowing. They captured his gaze, drawing him into the pattern until he felt dizzy.

"Morning, Naacha," said Tirak without turning round.

"Captain. Come, Hunter," Naacha said before turning and disappearing into the corridor.

the *Couana,* Zhal-S'Asha, 20th day (October)

"Naacha took me to the cargo area and started teaching me how to use the torc and what remained of my Talent again," he said quietly.

"You told me the torc mimics psi skills. Now you're implying you got your abilities back. Which is it, Kusac?"

He realized he'd said too much. "The torc is a tool, a device to amplify others' thoughts," he lied. "I left Annuur's shuttle afraid to trust it despite Naacha's teaching." *Or was it because of it?* he began to wonder. "Father Lijou knows this," he said, glancing at Banner. "I needed to know how far I could trust you before telling you more. This mission hinges on the fact that Kezule assumes I'm no longer a telepath."

"So that's why he sent for you."

"And possibly revenge for what Carrie did to him."

"What did she do?"

"We were trying to get him to tell us how he called Fyak back to the past. She humiliated him through his fear of telepaths. In the end, she had to force a contact and read him, and even then we didn't get what we wanted."

"Annuur said you'd forget much of what you learned. Did you, or did Naacha make you forget?"

"There was a lot to learn, Banner. Mind skills aren't like learning a new craft. You can't see someone else do it then copy them." Banner was being too astute for his liking. He drained his mug and put it on the night stand. "There's little left to tell you. I was afraid to use my torc-enhanced gift because when I did, it was erratic. I went to Stronghold because the dampers there made me feel more secure about trying to practice what I did remember of Naacha's teaching. Lijou helped me as much as he could, but the nightmares and flashbacks had started by then. I found it difficult to cope with them, and couldn't face the thought of reliving the past again."

"So the memories and dreams were caused by the la'quo you'd taken to go back to the Margins reacting with the TeLaxaudin and Cabbarran treatment."

"That, and the dose they'd given me on the *Kz'adul.*" Annuur had been right, he'd forgotten much of Naacha's teaching, but every now and then, tiny portions would return. Like now.

He glanced at his wrist comm. "It's late, we should get some sleep," he said, stretching out his legs and taking off his bath robe before sliding down into the bed.

"Hadn't realized it was so late." Banner got up, taking off his own damp robe before climbing into the other side. "Good night."

He lay in the darkness, unable to sleep, listening to Banner's breathing gradually slow until he knew the other was asleep. Another thing he'd just remembered was how to control the torc.

Mentally, he reached for it, trying to find the active bio-component, attempting to turn it off. It wasn't easy, taking all his concentration, but he knew instantly that he'd been successful when he could sense Banner's dream thoughts.

Their discussion of the Cabbarrans was still at the forefront of his Second's mind. He thought how easy it would have been before for him to just reach in and make Banner forget, except then his own ethics would have prevented him. . . . With a start, he realized he'd already instinctively reached out and grasped the memory and was destroying it—just as he'd been shown. Moments later, it was gone, as if the conversation had never happened.

Shocked, he pulled away from Banner and focused instead on reaching beyond his room to the whole of the *Couana* herself. It felt like he was detaching a small portion of himself and setting it free to wander around the corridors. Where it went, so could his mind.

He could feel exactly where each member of his crew was and whether they were awake or asleep. Satisfied, he pulled back and began concentrating again on the torc. Gradually, his awareness faded as the torc once more took control.

Annuur had been right about the memories. The closer he came to completing and accepting them, the easier it became to use his Talent, and the more stable it was, though what he'd done to Banner had been on such an instinctive level that he doubted he could reproduce it at will. He fell asleep determined not to think of the row he'd had with Kaid before leaving on this mission. He couldn't yet face that final memory.

Valsgarth Estate, Zhal-Nylam (month of the Hunt) 1st day (September)

"Phratry Leader Annuur, we received your report on the hunter. Concerned because of error we are. How long will it delay his full use of abilities?"

"Cannot say, Skepp Lord Aizshuss," said Annuur. "Effect of la'quo on hunters not anticipated because not known it interact like this with temporal displacement. Not something we could have tested for."

"This understood but Camarilla needs a time scale. Extrapolate."

Annuur looked at Kzizysus.

"Eight or nine weeks more. Depends on him."

"I heard," said the Skepp Lord, mandibles moving agitatedly. "Not pleased. Too long."

"When discover anomaly, tried to correct. Could not affect actual memories but corrected problem. Is stable now."

"Have to wait, then. What of training? Have enhancements worked?"

"Yes, Skepp Lord, have worked well." He hesitated, unhappy about admitting to further delays. "Lessons are blocked for now until he has dealt with memory problems."

Annuur winced while Kzizysus made soft noises of distress at the Skepp Lord's reaction. When Aizshuss had calmed down a little, Annuur leaped into the first lull in his tirade.

"If we hadn't done this, disaster results! His mind affected by dark memories of time on *Kz'adul*, creates imbalance. Damage he did to our lab here. Chance of discovery of augmentation high if he continues practicing in this state. You and Camarilla say avoid this at all cost! All this was in our report to you."

"He have no time left to practice skills! Your decision flawed!"

"Skepp Lord, I am also of the Camarilla," he said icily. "I am in field. I make decisions. You disagree, you leave safety of Council Chamber and do my task. More important our cover be kept and he survives to practice later. Laws here prevent killing using mind powers. In his state, could happen had I not made this decision. No use to us in prison or mind-wiped. I have work to do, Aizshuss. I contact you when we have more news." He cut the connection and turned away from the screen to look at Kzizysus.

"Can do no more than our best," he said.

CHAPTER 16

**Valsgarth Estate, Zhal-Nylam, 1st day
(September)**

CARRIE and Kaid were waiting for him as he emerged from the shuttle. Shielding his eyes against the glare of the morning sun, he nevertheless saw them exchange glances. He felt Kaid's concern.

Holding up his hand, he backed off a little as they came to greet him. "No, don't touch me. Everything's too new, too raw," he said. "I can sense you faintly, Kaid, but nothing else for now." He laughed gently. "All the disadvantages, eh?"

"How do you feel?" asked Kaid.

"I feel all right. You're wondering if they told me what's gone wrong, aren't you? Yes, they did," he said, coming off the ramp onto the ground beside them. "That la'quo's been more far reaching than we thought." He reached out and touched Carrie's face tentatively, then sighed with a relief tinged with sadness as he cupped his hand briefly around her cheek. "I can't sense you because of the cub," he said. He'd wanted to feel her mind so much, yet part of him had been afraid of what he'd find.

"They shaved your hair again," said Carrie, distressed.

He put his hand to his neck, feeling the small patch of bare flesh for the first time. "It'll grow back soon," he said. "I'd like to go home, if you don't mind."

"Of course," said Carrie. "Your parents are waiting. They're very anxious about you. Everyone is."

"There's no reason to be," he said, reaching for her hand and beginning to walk toward the village main street.

"What did they do to you for five days?" asked Kaid, falling into step beside him.

"I don't remember anything about the treatment because I was sedated the whole time. After it, well, there were tests and one of the Cabbarrans, Naacha, he showed me how to use the torc."

Kaid frowned. "Use your torc for what? I thought you already knew how to use it."

"They had to remove the Touiban device to put in something else," he said. "Annuur described it as a highly sensitive psi damper. It's keeping nearly everything out right now. I have to be next to someone, or touching them, to pick up anything."

"What happens if you take it off?" asked Carrie.

"I collapse in pain," he said simply, glancing at her. "I'm swamped by the emotions of everyone around me."

"Do you regret having it done?" Kaid asked.

He stopped. "No, not at all. I have some of my Talent back, Kaid, and by Vartra, that's better than the nothing I had till now! Annuur says it will improve, once I've dealt with the memories."

"How do you do that? Just sit down and remember what happened to you? And for how far back?" asked Carrie.

"I wait until the memories come to me. A few weeks, Annuur said." He looked from one to the other of them. "I know it's not as much as you'd hoped for me, but without the torc on, I can't cope. I need to grow into my Talent again, just as I did when I was a kitling. I think it's worked out better this way," he said. He'd have time to gradually get used to being aware of her mentally while still being excluded from her Link to Kaid.

Training center, evening, the same day

Kaid excused himself from the group around the table and followed Banner into the training center mess.

"Can I have a word with you?" he asked him quietly as they stood at the bar.

"Of course," Banner said, collecting his change and drink before accompanying him over to one of the empty tables. "What is it?" he asked, sitting down. "Must be serious to want to speak to me in here. It's as hot as an oven."

It was, but there was less chance of being overheard than around the crowded tables outside in the cooler evening air. "I need someone to help me keep an eye on Kusac. I saw the fine job you and Jurrel did with Brynne."

"Not me," said Banner, taking a drink of his ale. "That was Brynne himself, with some help from Jurrel."

Kaid raised an eye ridge. "I was still at Stronghold when you and Jurrel got together. I remember how he used to be."

Banner grinned. "You rub the corners off each other's personalities over the years. But I thought you and Kusac had gotten close. Why do you need me?"

"He's changing again," said Kaid, looking at his glass. "I'd gotten him over the worst while we were working at the Nezule estate, but Kzizysus' cure wasn't all we hoped. Wanting to come down here tonight, this isn't like Kusac at all. He always preferred to stay in with Carrie, or with friends." He lifted his glass and took a drink. "He needs to have his freedom, obviously, and I can't follow him around like his keeper. So I need someone covering his back. I want you to do it, not least because he seems at ease in your company."

Banner looked at him thoughtfully. "Do you want an undercover bodyguard, or someone to befriend him?"

Kaid shrugged. "Up to you. Play it any way that works. I just don't want him getting in over his head. Pick another two for backup in case you need them, but keep it low key."

Banner nodded. "Anything else I should know?" he asked.

Kaid looked at him. "Like what?"

"There was talk a few weeks back," he said diffidently.

"Oh?"

"T'Chebbi getting hurt."

Kaid sighed, idly turning his glass round on the tabletop.

"Don't worry, it was dealt with," Banner reassured him.

He hesitated, wondering if it was necessary to say anything. "J'koshuk was a torturer priest, head of his Order of Enforcers on Keiss. They were dedicated to rooting out any heresy among their people, heresy being defined as anything their Emperor wouldn't have approved of. He was a specialist in pain, bred for the job, and as you know, he had Kusac for three weeks."

"Ouch," said Banner, with feeling. "At least Kusac got to kill the bastard."

"J'koshuk's overuse of the pain collar caused Kusac neural damage, which is apparently now cured. But it also caused psychological damage. T'Chebbi invited him to her room, and got hurt by accident as a result."

"You don't need to say any more," said Banner. "I can imagine."

"He should be over it," said Kaid, looking up at him. "There may not be a problem, but he might want to find out for himself. If he does pair up with someone, just make sure you're near enough to intervene if necessary. I could be wrong. He might just be coming here tonight because he was shut up in the shuttle for five days."

"I'll shadow him, Kaid, don't worry. Are you going back to Nezule?"

"No. It's getting close to Carrie's time, I don't want to be away from her, and Kusac needs time to recuperate. I don't want to leave him alone either. Hopefully we'll remain here for now."

"When do you want me to start?"

"Ideally, now. I know it's short notice, but it's late and I want to get back to Carrie. She gets easily worked up these days. I'm going to suggest Kusac comes back with me, but if he doesn't want to . . ."

"I can manage tonight. Do you want him watched overnight as well?"

"Again, use your judgment. We've an attendant on duty at the villa all night now. If he can contact you on your comm if Kusac leaves the premises, that should be enough."

"You go on home. If he doesn't go with you, I'll have him covered. Do you want regular updates?"

"Just tell me as and when. Thanks, Banner," said Kaid, getting up. "I appreciate it," he said, touching him on the shoulder before going outside to rejoin Kusac.

"It was good to get out for an hour or two," he said as they opened the front door. "I found I could cope easily. The torc's sensitivity is set so low that I could barely sense anything."

"I'm glad it's not proving a problem. Having a bar down there a couple of evenings a week was a good idea of Garras'."

"There's a small inn on my mother's estate. I saw no reason why we shouldn't have one when Garras suggested it. Kaid," he said, stopping at the foot of the stairs. "I'll be all right alone tonight. I managed when I was in the shuttle."

"Are you sure?"

"I'm sure. I've had my things put in the nursery where I slept before. It's not that I don't want to move back in with Carrie, but you're sharing this cub with her. You should be able to be together when you want."

"Carrie comes to me when she wants to, Kusac. We don't make a habit of using your rooms," he said quietly.

"I know," he said, looking away from him briefly. "Truth is, I'm afraid of hurting her if we get too close. I'd never forgive myself if anything happened to her or your cub."

"If you need me, call me on your wrist comm. Don't lie there having nightmares alone," Kaid said reaching out to touch his cheek. Then he remembered and pulled away. "Sorry. I forgot."

He caught hold of his friend's hand. "It's all right, Kaid, I don't mind your touch. I wasn't sure when I came back this morning, but I'm fine. That's one of the reasons I wanted to go down to the training center, to find out if I could handle being jostled and touched. It's difficult, but I can cope."

Kaid nodded and clasped his hand. "You know where I am if you need me," he said before letting him go.

The quiet of the night was shattered by Kusac yowling in fear. Kashini woke, shrieking her head off inconsolably. Carrie, in the suite next door, was first on the scene, closely followed by Kaid. He smelled the sweat and the fear the moment he arrived.

Kashini's high-pitched cries, and her mental distress, cut through his head like a knife, making it impossible for him to think clearly. When Yashui the nurse arrived, he pounced on her with relief.

"Get Kashini out of here," he said, propelling her toward Carrie, who was frantically trying to hush the struggling and screaming child. "Take Carrie with you, and for Vartra's sake, turn on the psi dampers! I can't think straight!"

"This room is designed to keep her mind contained, Leader Kaid," said the nurse frostily. "None of you should be in here. Her father's the one causing the problem."

"I'll see to him," he snapped, feeling his hair beginning to rise in aggravation. "Just do your job and silence the cub!"

Shooting him an angry look, she went over to help Carrie. As soon as they left, the decibel level dropped dramatically. Before he'd taken a step in Kusac's direction, the door behind him burst open again.

"What the hell is it now?" he demanded, spinning round, then he saw T'Chebbi.

"Only me," she said, holstering her gun.

"Nightmares," he said succinctly. "Go reassure the rest of the house, T'Chebbi."

"Aye," she said, closing the door quietly.

As his hair settled down around his shoulders again, he rubbed his aching temples then headed over to the bed where Kusac was cowering, still not fully awake despite the noise.

Sitting down, he wrapped his arms around him, holding him tight against his chest. He'd done this so many times over the last few weeks at Nezule that he knew now what worked. Resting his head on Kusac's, he began to rock him, waiting for the shaking to stop. His time, he kept a tight rein on his emotions, aware that Kusac was now capable of sensing them.

Gradually, Kusac grew still and as the tension began to drain from his body, he was able to lessen his hold.

"It's all right," said Kaid soothing him as he'd seen Carrie soothe Kashini. He lifted his head up so he could stroke his friend's. "It's not real, only a bad dream. I'm here." He relaxed his own mental control, hoping a light contact would help.

"I know," said Kusac, his voice muffled against Kaid's chest. "I can feel you."

"I thought these dreams were over," said Kaid gently.

"So did I."

"What was it this time? Memories of J'koshuk again?"

"Yes. I could see him, Kaid. It was as if he was here in this room."

Kaid could feel the memory of it forming a picture before his eyes. The green-skinned face, almost human, with its huge yellow eyes, and the mouth, smiling, showing dozens of tiny pointed teeth. He shuddered, shaking his head to dispel the image of that smile.

"Don't, Kusac," he said sharply. "You're projecting him. The more often you remember him, the longer it'll take for you to forget what happened."

"I'm not trying to remember," he said, voice breaking. "Do you think I want to go through that again?"

"No, I don't think that," he said, letting Kusac go and taking hold of his head, forcing it up till they were eye to eye. "You can't sleep here, Kusac. Kashini saw it too. You'll have to come in with me again."

"I can't," Kusac said, taking a shuddering breath. "What about you and Carrie?"

"We'll sort it out tomorrow, but you're not sleeping alone— for now at least. Now get up. Kashini needs her bedroom back."

T'Chebbi called him on his wrist comm as he left Kusac in his shower. "Get someone to freshen the room up for Kashini," he said, heading for the desk comm in his lounge. "Tell Carrie it was a nightmare. He's fine now, she can relax."

"He in with you?"

"Yes. You get back to bed, T'Chebbi, there's nothing else needing to be done tonight. And thank you. I'm going to call Annuur and find out what the hell this was about."

It took a few minutes before his call was answered, not by Annuur but by Sokarr.

"I get. You wait," Sokarr said when he heard why Kaid was calling.

Annuur looked as rumpled as he felt, Kaid thought with satisfaction. "What the hell have you done to him, Annuur?" he demanded, trying to keep his voice low. "He's just awakened the whole household with a nightmare."

Annuur blinked sleepily out from the screen at him, rubbing his hand over his eyes and ears. "Had nightmares before this, you told us. Nothing new. Why wake me for this?"

"He couldn't actually project his nightmares into an external form before," said Kaid. "You imagine going through what Kusac did then seeing J'koshuk with you in your cub's nursery, Annuur, then ask me again why I'm calling you!"

That woke the Cabbarran. "What?"

"You heard me. I saw it happening again when I was with him. His daughter saw it, and felt her father's terror! What's happening to him, Annuur?"

"Not our treatment, Kaid, assure you," said the Cabbarran with obvious sincerity. "Has he projected like this before? Must be existing skill."

"Something similar," admitted Kaid. "On Keiss, he and Carrie broke into a Valtegan base. He projected an image of himself as a Valtegan then. But what's that to do with this?" He wasn't going to let the Cabbarran off the hook that easily.

"Before dreams are in his head. With psi ability back, even reduced as is now, can externalize it. Maybe easier to deal with for him. Maybe in dream he think if J'koshuk not in head, he can kill dream-J'koshuk again. This time for good."

It made some kind of sense, he admitted grudgingly to himself.

"Warned you we did memories needed to be faced. Not so soon we thought, but not our fault."

"What do we do, dammit? He can't go around externalizing everything he went through!"

"He wear your design psi damper too when he sleeps until this over. Is only suggestion I can think. Is temporary. Will go."

"Can't you turn up the torc?"

"No! What point? Has to learn to live with Talent again. My apologies it being so difficult for him, but is fault of la'quo, not us. It alters brain chemistry. Fixed what we could, these memories are side effect of it. Rather we left it alone? Cause worse damage that way."

"Of course I'm glad you fixed it," he said, his anger beginning to dissipate now he understood some of the reasons.

"You need watch him more than we thought. Obvious he cannot cope with this alone. Has you, so no problem. We go back to beds now, Kaid. Your psi damper with our torc will work. Good night." The line went dead.

"Great," he muttered, sitting back in his chair.

"Maybe I should go to Stronghold," said Kusac. "They've got psi dampers there and Lijou and Noni can help me."

Kaid turned around to see him standing in the bathing room doorway, wrapped in a towel, still dripping. "Don't even consider it," he said forcefully, getting up and going over to him. "We're in this together, the three of us," he said, taking hold of him by the neck. "We're family, Kusac." He rubbed his thumbs gently along Kusac's jawline. "Family means a lot to me now I have one."

Kusac returned the gesture, resting his forehead on Kaid's shoulder for a moment. "Me too, Kaid."

"You're dripping onto the floor," observed Kaid, letting him go. "Let's get you dry and into bed."

*   *   *

He surfaced, aware of the warmth of Kaid's body curled around his back, and of something else. Still hazy with sleep, he jumped when a hand touched his face. Carrie's hand.

He caught hold of her, aware of her scent surrounding him because of the warmth of the bed.

"It's only me," she whispered, moving closer. "I wanted to be sure you were all right."

"I'm fine," he said quietly. "Another nightmare, that's all."

She disengaged her hand gently and put it on his neck. "Nightmares are not little matters. I know. I've had my own of J'koshuk."

"I didn't realize," he said, reaching automatically to comfort her. His hand touched naked skin; he froze, confused. Then her lips touched his.

"You need something good to dream about," she murmured, gently catching hold of his bottom lip then releasing it to tease him with her tongue.

Something other than her presence seemed strange, slightly off true. Unsure, he responded cautiously, aware of her hand stroking his chest, working its way slowly across his ribs. As their kiss grew deeper, he slid his hand up her side until he reached the soft swell of her breast. It had been so long since he'd touched her like this.

Desire flooded through him, making his heart beat faster and his groin clench as his genitals descended suddenly.

He felt Kaid stir and move away, felt a light caress travel down his back. He pulled away from her, unwilling to go further now he knew Kaid was awake.

"Hush," she said, clasping him again. "We've done this before. Just relax."

Too stunned to stop her, he let her lips close on his again. Memories from the *Kz'adul* deep in his subconscious began to wake as gently she urged him onto his back. Ruthlessly, he pushed the memories deeper.

"Carrie," he began, turning his head aside from her, but her hand closed on his erection, making him suck in his breath with a low moan of pleasure and reach for her again. Sensations coursed through him, and as wisps of more recent memories began to return, his mouth sought hers, kissing her frantically, Kaid's presence forgotten.

She teased him for a moment then let him go. Cool air hit his pelt as she sat up and threw back the cover. There was just enough light for him to see the glow of her eyes and the faint outline of her body as she leaned over him. Her fingers trailed patterns of fire across his side and belly, making him ache even more for her.

"I can't," he said, even as he reached for her, pulling her down. "I'm afraid of hurting you."

"You won't. Kaid's here, just as he was at Nezule," she whispered between kisses as her hands pushed through the longer pelt on his chest.

"Kaid's here," he said, the remembered wisps solidifying as he realized the hand touching his belly was Kaid's.

The hand withdrew as Kaid reached across him to help Carrie slide between them.

Then her hands were caressing him, working her magic, making him forget everything but the need to hold her and touch her. His hand cupped her breast, his tongue gently lapping at it, playing with her nipple until his teeth closed on it, nipping gently.

He felt Kaid's breath warm on his face and looked up to see his sword-brother's eyes glowing down at him. Lowering his head, Kaid began to gently lick at Carrie's shoulder. Her fingers twined in his hair, drawing his attention back to her.

"Don't stop," she whispered, arching toward him as a shudder of pleasure ran through her body.

He returned to teasing her breast while sliding his hand over the taut swell of her belly. In his mind, Kaid's presence grew stronger, his friend's arousal making his own more intense. His hand moved lower, running the tips of his claws over the softness of her thighs. She moaned softly, the sound muffled when Kaid began to kiss her.

Darkness held them close, gave them anonymity. Once more he neither knew nor cared who caressed whom as the barriers between them blurred. All that mattered was that they shared the love they felt for each other. When they joined, he tucked against her back, she holding Kaid, he knew that they'd come together as one.

Valsgarth Estate, Zhal-Nylam, 2nd day (September)

He woke first, finding himself partly entangled with Kaid, both of them wrapped protectively round Carrie. He felt Kaid's presence in his mind before his friend began to stir. It felt different, not as harsh as he'd remembered it back in their early days at Stronghold.

"Morning," said Kaid lazily, looking at him with half open eyes across the sleeping form of Carrie.

"You've changed," he said quietly.

"You know I have." Kaid slid his leg free.

"I meant mentally. Your touch is gentler."

"With you and Carrie," he agreed.

"This is what should have happened when we become sword-brothers, isn't it? Not you and me, the three of us."

Kaid nodded. "Neither of you were ready for this then. As it was, I was afraid you'd misunderstand what I feel for you."

"I did, until we took the oath. You didn't make it easy for me, you know."

Arching an eye ridge, Kaid grinned. "Garras didn't make it easy for me. Why should I have done different for you?"

"No reason. How did we first . . . ?" His gesture took them all in.

"It was while you had your fever at Nezule. The dreams were so bad we both slept with you. The night the fever broke, you were the one who turned to us—and to me. Other Triads have found this solution, Kusac. We're not alone."

"No wonder Triads need to be close." He moved closer to Carrie, placing his hand over the curve of her belly, feeling the cub inside her move.

Carrie stirred, putting her hand over his. "Got a kick like Kashini had," she mumbled. "Maybe it's a Sholan thing. Maybe you two got more in common than you know." Her wrist comm buzzed in a short, rhythmic pattern. She groaned. "I gotta go see to Kashini." She reached out and pulled him close, kissing him before turning to Kaid and doing the same. "Would one of you get me my robe? Unless you want to lose this sheet."

Kaid laughed and untangled himself. "I'll go. Kusac doesn't know where it is."

When she'd gone, Kaid went over to the dispenser. "Coffee or c'shar?" he asked.

He was about to say c'shar when he realized he hadn't had coffee for some time. "Coffee, please. Kaid, I think I should go to Stronghold."

"You're kidding," said Kaid, swinging round or look at him. "Why? Not because of last night?"

"No, of course not," he said, getting up and sitting on the side of the bed. "Well, sort of," he amended. "Look at it logically. Where do I stay here? With you? What about you and Carrie? I can't stay in the nursery after last night's nightmare. Carrie can't, she needs her sleep, not a bed in the nursery where she's awakened bright and early by Kashini."

"I'll sleep in the nursery if necessary," said Kaid, turning back to pick up the first drink. "I don't want you leaving us, Kusac. You don't need to go through this alone."

"I wouldn't ask you to sleep with Kashini," he said with a smile. "I know how uneasy you are with cubs. No, the more I think about it, the more sure I am that Stronghold is where I should be until these new nightmares stop."

Kaid picked up the second mug and headed back to Kusac with them. "Wait a few days, see what happens. There's a guest suite still unused here, and some staff rooms downstairs. I'd rather go there than have you leave." He held out the mug of coffee. "It's your home, Kusac."

"Our home." He hesitated a moment then nodded, taking the drink from Kaid. "All right. I'll wait a couple of days, but if I have another night like last night, I'm going to Stronghold."

Prime world, the same day

Kezule watched the civilian females training with his daughters in the barracks gymnasium. According to Zayshul, several of her friends carried the extra organs his caste had, and could pass them on—to their daughters. He'd been working with them for a week and already he knew that only these females of all the civilian Primes that had tried their hand at his combat training, had the potential to be Warriors. But why them? And if only them, was it a modern trait, a mutation caused by the Fall, or were they regressing to what they'd been before?

Alone, he'd even considered the unthinkable—were Warrior males like him the aberration and females like these the norm? Were the females of his time kept feral because of this? His thoughts had been fueled by the racial memories he had of a time before the Empire, and Zayshul's success at learning to use bio-feedback. Not only did she have the organs, but they worked. And that augured well for these females he was watching.

"General, your wife called . . ."

A bell rang out, drowning his words. Below them, the class stopped and, bowing to the instructors, the females filed off to their locker areas.

"Your wife called," he continued. "She said you should return immediately."

He looked thoughtfully at his aide, wondering why Zayshul hadn't used his personal communicator. "How did she sound?"

"Frightened, General." He hesitated.

"Go on."

"The tone was, but not her choice of words."

Kezule began walking toward the exit. "Take it further, M'kou."

"If it had been really urgent, then her guards would have called in. They didn't. She didn't use your personal communicator. That leaves the possibility she thinks her call to you could be overheard, and was expected."

"It also means she might have lost her communicator," he said, pushing the swing door open and heading out into the courtyard where his grav floater stood under guard.

"Yes, sir," said M'kou, crestfallen, before running forward to open the floater door.

Kezule took the controls, taking off before M'kou had finished sitting down. "Don't be so hard on yourself, M'kou," he said, glancing across as the young male recovered his balance in the seat. "That wasn't a bad assessment of the situation. Had my wife lost her communicator, there was still no reason for her to call me over the public line."

M'kou brightened visibly, his crest rising a few millimeters before settling down again.

"Call in and tell them we've gone home, M'kou," he said, dodging the vehicle round a slow moving goods floater.

"Shall I contact her guards, General?"

"Yes. Ask for a report from them. Imply they're late calling in." He concentrated on driving for the next few minutes.

"Nothing to report, sir. They didn't use any code words to warn us of trouble."

"Curiouser and curiouser," he murmured.

The doorkeepers had noticed nothing strange over the last few hours, and there had been no unusual visitors. Impatiently he waited for the elevator to reach his floor. The corridor was clear, except for the two guards on the door. They snapped to attention when they saw him.

"Two visitors called, sir. One left, the other remained."

"Carry on," he said, unlocking the door, more intrigued than worried.

Zayshul leaped to her feet as he entered. "Thank the God-Kings you're back! Come with me," she said, grabbing hold of him and hustling him toward the bathing room.

"The visitor," he began.

"In here," she said, opening the door. "Look. What the hell do we do with her?"

Lying curled in a ball on a pile of cushions was a small gray-pelted shape. Kezule moved closer, bending down to get a better look. She was asleep, nose tucked under her tail tip, thumb in her mouth.

Kezule backed out, drawing Zayshul with him, and shut the door quietly. "She's the Sholan hybrid cub I told you about," he said, gesturing M'kou over. "Sweep the apartment for recording and listening devices," he ordered quietly.

"I figured that out myself," she said.

"It's a trap, whatever we do," he said as he guided her by the elbow to the sofa. "I didn't expect her so soon. K'hedduk said he'd give her to me after the coup, not before. What's he trying to do? Compromise me by reporting her presence to the Enforcers?"

"He gave me this," she said, handing him a slim crystal data card. "I didn't recognize him."

Taking it from her, he changed direction for his desk reader. Switching it on, he fed the card into the slot in the side. The screen remained dark as a synthesized voice began to speak.

"As requested, General, here's your little companion. I'm sure she's a shade young for what you have in mind, but enjoy her, and your revenge. We'll talk again soon."

Kezule hissed, his crest rising to its full height in rage. "She's a bribe! He's sent her to buy my loyalty, and ensure my destruction if I betray him!"

"What's he mean about revenge?"

He pulled the data card out and turned to her. "He assumed I wanted her for sexual reasons for revenge against the Sholans. How dare he think I'd use a child! I'll have his hide for this, Zayshul, by the God-Kings, I will!"

"Let him think what he wants," she said. "What do we do with her?"

He saw M'kou hovering out of the corner of his eye and swung his head around. "What is it?" he demanded.

"The apartment's clean, General."

"Good. There's a Sholan child in the bathing room, M'kou. Warn the guards they must on no account let her be seen by anyone visiting the apartment, and they must not speak freely in front of her. She could be an agent in a coup against the Emperor."

M'kou's eyes widened as he nodded his understanding and disappeared again.

Kezule headed for the sofa, taking Zayshul with him. "What's due to happen in the next few days?" he demanded. "Any royal events?"

Zayshul looked dubious. "There's the Festival of Fruitfulness in about ten days to celebrate the harvest, but what has that to do . . ."

"They'll move then," he said, trying to remember the few occasions his visits to the Court had coincided with festivals in the past. "We'll be providing the honor guard for the Emperor. What better time to turn on him then when we celebrate rebirth?"

"What do we do?" she asked grimly.

He glanced at her, surprised and pleased by her attitude. "They'll be watching us to see how we react. I need to mobilize our forces now, before they contact me with their plans." He checked the time. It was midafternoon. If he didn't head back to the barracks, it would be seen as odd by his own people. Another twenty minutes or so would be a reasonable time for him to take to deal with his new arrival, then he could leave.

"M'kou!" he called. "I've got a job for you," he said when

his aide came running. "I want you to log a flight plan for the *N'zishok* at the orbiting station. Backdate it by several days so it looks like it was planned weeks ago. Can you do it from my communicator?"

"Should be able to, sir. What's the flight plan?"

"You word it. I intend to put out tonight for a series of four one-day maneuvers. We'll redock each night. Following this, we'll leave on a three-day weapons' skill exercise out by that asteroid field—you know the one I mean."

"Aye, sir. Anything more?"

"Yes, put down that personnel will be arriving in several units at various times over the next ten hours. Make sure our ship gets a copy. They aren't our people so spin them some yarn about us doing undercover ops so if questioned they can say they knew about the exercise. Tell them to have the ship fully provisioned with munitions, fuel, and food. They're to expect me the day after tomorrow but my wife will be arriving tonight."

"Aye sir," he said, going over to the communicator and sitting down.

"I'm not going up to the ship without you!" she said.

"I want you and that egg up there in safety. What I've got to do is dangerous. I don't want to be worrying about you when my mind should be focused on what I'm doing. And you can take the Sholan child with you."

"How am I supposed to do that? I can't just walk about with her in full view!"

"But you will. She'll be sedated and packed in a kit bag over the shoulder of one of our guards."

"She'll suffocate!"

"Not if you get one of those oxygen breathers and put it on her first. She'll have her own air supply."

She stared at him. "You've got it all worked out, haven't you?"

He looked away.

"You were going to take me like that if I hadn't agreed to go with you."

"I hoped it would never come to that," he said. "You're valuable to me, Zayshul. You've got a good mind." He saw the look in her eyes and added hastily, "And I'd have missed your company."

A door opened and they turned round quickly to see a small gray face peering in. The gap widened and the cub, dressed in a short tan-colored tunic, edged slowly into the room and stood there, looking at the floor, hands held behind her back.

Kezule got up, preventing Zayshul from rising. "Let me," he said. He approached the cub and stood in front of her. She was smaller than he remembered, her head reaching only just above his waist.

"Look up at me, child," he said. "Have you a name?"

She looked up, pale blue eyes serious. "Yes, Seniormost, Gaylla."

The voice was quiet, her Valtegan surprisingly understandable. He took hold of her chin and tilted her head up. A metal collar circled her neck. He let her go.

"I seen you before," she said slowly, tail flicking from side to side.

"Do you know why you're here?"

"I yours, Seniormost. Stay here with you." Tears began to flood her eyes, spilling over onto her cheeks. "I vassal of Prime Empire. I go where told," she said, hands going up to her mouth, pressing it closed in an effort not to cry.

Before he could blink, Zayshul was there, sweeping the cub up into her arms and holding her close. "She's lonely and frightened, Kezule! Leave her alone! How dare they tell her she was a slave!"

He looked at her, a pained expression on his face. "I was the one who asked for her to stop her being harmed, Zayshul," he pointed out as she retreated to the sofa carrying the now sobbing cub. "I'm not trying to frighten her."

"You'd frighten any child the way you look at them!" she said tartly. "Just remember, we don't keep slaves or pets in this time, Kezule. Now do something useful. Get Gaylla something to eat and drink. She must be starving."

"She doesn't look starved to me," he murmured, going over to the drink dispenser.

"It's done, Commander," said M'kou from his desk. "Your flight plan is logged in for two days ago. I contacted the ship and passed on your message."

"Well done," he said, choosing a bland herbal drink. "Go fetch something from the kitchen for her to eat, would you? You're young, pick something a child would like."

M'kou rolled his eyes at Zayshul as he passed her.

"Here," he said, putting the drink on the table. "I have to get back to the barracks. Don't let anyone but me or M'kou in, hear me? With her here, everyone coming to the door is suspect right now. And pack. You'll be leaving in a few hours."

"I hope you're not going to be as unfeeling when our child hatches," she said, eyes flashing at him over the top of the cub's head.

"Ah, that's something else entirely," he said, backing away from her. "Never liked the smell of mammals, you know."

"Kezule!"

"I have to go now, Zayshul," he said firmly, checking over his shoulder to see where the door was.

"I know, but you'll find breathers for fire drills at the barracks."

"Good point," he said, beating a hasty exit.

M'kou ran back with a plate of spiced meat balls on sticks which he slid across the table to her before disappearing after Kezule.

There was an air of suppressed excitement in the lecture room. All one hundred of his sons and daughters were here, security being provided for the time being by the fifteen M'Zullians. He waited till the gentle buzz of conversation died down.

"You've been training for this day since the beginning," he said. "It's what we, as Warriors, do. We protect the God-King and his royal family, and the people of the Court of the City of Light. From today, those words become actions. The days ahead will test your loyalty to me, but hold firm, play your part in the whole, and all will go as planned."

He paused, letting the importance of his words sink in as they looked at each other with a mixture of emotions.

"Because of my close relationship to the royal family, it isn't practical for me to remain here. I am taking some of you with me, you all know who they are. I wish it could be more, but the Emperor needs you. The security of the Court and the royal family depends on you remaining here after we've destroyed this attempted rebellion." He stopped, looking around at them once more. It wasn't going to be easy to leave any behind. He could have made a life for himself among these children of his—had it not been for the rest of the Prime culture.

"I've chosen Khayikule to replace me. As of this moment, he assumes the rank of Captain. You will obey him in all things.

Unit leaders, remain here, the rest of you, return to your dorms and await further orders. Dismissed."

He waited till all but eleven and M'kou had gone. "Come to the front," he said, gesturing them closer. They left their seats, taking new ones in front of the table he leaned against. He looked at their fresh, eager faces, the flush of excitement staining their skins a darker green. Two were female, the rainbow-colored skin surrounding their eyes standing out among the plain faces of the ten males. They were the one weak link, weak only by virtue of their gender. As small as the females of this time, they still had the necessary characteristics of a Warrior.

"There is a threat against the Emperor from a group calling themselves the Directorate," he said. "I expect them to make their move within the week, at the Festival of Fruitfulness. We, however, are moving now. Zhookoh, you and Shartoh have been shadowing members of the Directorate. Zhookoh, you'll leave immediately after this briefing and position yourself to pick up your target as soon as you see him. Take him to the designated holding place and keep him there until you hear from me. Shartoh, your team is going undercover for the next two days, employing diversionary tactics against the other three Directorate members. You have your brief. Target them in their homes, their offices and on the streets. I want them good and paranoid. Remember, you've done it half a dozen times as exercises. All that's different is that you set off your charges and fire a few shots. Try to locate K'hedduk this time. When you're done, proceed to the main rendezvous and hand your units over to Kayikule. You'll proceed to the orbiter with the second group of civilians."

"Yes, sir," they murmured.

"Zhalmo, your unit's with me the day after tomorrow at 01.00 hours. Stay behind after this briefing and we'll go over the plans of the Directorate. Our target is the headquarters itself. You're based at the barracks till then."

"Yes, sir," said Zhalmo.

"Shezhul," he said, looking at the other female. "You'll hold the main rendezvous area, making sure our people have safe access to the transport out to the shuttle port. You'll also join the last group for the N'zishok."

She nodded.

"The rest of you will be picking up your civilians in three stages, just as planned. The first group will go up to the orbiter platform with Noolgoi. We're using your plan to take command of the *N'zishok,* Noolgoi, therefore you should implement it." He stopped for a moment before continuing. "There will be an extra piece of luggage with my wife, Noolgoi. She'll tell you about it, but it will require handling as carefully as the incubator. It's to stay with my wife at all times. Once the ship is yours, secure the crew in the brig. I'll deal with them when I arrive. First group of civilians go tonight, second tomorrow night, third the night after. Remember, we want to create the impression that we're rotating personnel from here to each of the four one-day training missions."

"Aye, sir," said Noolgoi.

"Finally, Khayikule," he said, turning to him. "Yours is the most difficult task of all. That of staying behind and leading. Only someone I trust implicitly could be given that responsibility. I know you'll fulfill your role with honor. I know you all will," he added, looking round them again. "Now check your kit and move your units out. Dismissed."

Chairs scraped on the floor as they got to their feet. "Yes, sir," they murmured, saluting him before filing out.

Zhalmo joined Kezule at the table as he opened the large floor plan of the Directorate. "I found this in the library," he said. "It has two levels below ground. The first is the labs where the doctors work, the rooms where the captives are held. The level below is the staff and troop sleeping quarters."

"Captives?" she asked, leaning her hands on the table as she looked at the layout.

"There are eight young Sholans—seven," he corrected himself. "Three adult Sholans in cryo units—we may have to leave them, but there is certainly one Sholan female in a cage in this lab," he said, pointing to it on the plans. "There are also several of our people in this room here." Again he indicated it on the map. "I want all of them out alive, but if any Primes give you trouble, kill them. We're shipping the Sholans directly up to the *N'zishok* by rendezvousing with it once they've undocked from the orbiter. The Primes we help above ground and leave. I want this place destroyed," he said, looking up at her.

She nodded.

"Each of you will have two of the M'zullians as your team, one guarding you at all times, the other working with you. They are expendable, you are not, remember that. The main entrance is a heavy steel door, guarded by two males. It leads to an elevator. Two more males guard it. The first level down is ours, below it are living quarters for their guards and staff."

"There's another entrance here, above ground, a stairwell. It covers both levels," she said, poring over the map. "If we send a fire team in there with a couple of grenades to drop down the stairs to the lower level, it should block off their access. They can then guard our exit point. We approach the main way, through the elevator. If we brace that open on our level, rig it with a remote charge, we can forget the guards below and detonate it as we exit. Same with the stairwell."

Kezule nodded, pleased she'd noticed those features. "We'll do it that way."

"We'll need thermal explosives for the steel doors, timed charges for the elevator and stairwell, stun grenades, and long and short-range weapons, General."

"Calculate the amount of explosives you'll need, and get the charges made up. Run some simulations on the assault course while we're waiting."

"Aye, sir. Permission to ask a question, sir?"

Kezule nodded, folding the map.

"Why choose my unit for this mission, sir? Females were only considered as feral breeding stock in your time, so why entrust this to a female unit leader?"

Kezule looked thoughtfully at her for a moment, then decided she deserved no less than the truth. "The military considers all its members as tools, parts of the whole, or weapons to be used if you prefer. Part of your value is that you are female. Your brothers will fight harder to defend you. But you also got this mission on merit as a unit leader." He handed the map to her. "You'll need this. Dismissed, Sergeant Zhalmo."

the N'zishok, later the same evening

Ghidd'ah glanced anxiously at the door as the sounds of marching drew closer.

"Ignore it," said Zayshul calmly, unzipping the large carry bag their escort had placed on the sofa for them. "We're safe in here. You know Noolgoi has two guards posted outside the door. We need to get Gaylla out of this bag."

"Gaylla?" her friend asked, her attention diverted back to the task in hand. Then she gasped in shock as the still form of the Sholan cub was revealed.

"Stop panicking!" said Zayshul, pushing the sides of the bag back and slipping her hands under the cub's shoulders. "She's perfectly all right, just drugged. Now help me lift her out so I can get the breather mask off."

"Drugged? But why? And where did you get her? I didn't know there were any Sholan children on K'oish'ik!"

"Officially, there aren't," she said as they lifted the cub free of the bag and placed her carefully on the sofa. "She's one of eight that the Directorate bred from samples taken from the Sholans and Humans we had on the *Kz'adul*. That's where the General and his Warriors are now, trying to free the others."

Ghidd'ah grabbed the bag and pushed it onto the floor to give them more room. "I thought there was a plot against the Emperor, not the Sholans. What are you going to do with them?"

Zayshul sat down beside Gaylla and began to carefully remove the breathing mask fitted over the cub's mouth and nose. "The plot is against the Emperor, and our treaty with the Sholans," she said, being economical with the truth in the interests of brevity. "They'll be returned to their own people when we've found the base my husband's looking for. I need you to check her over, make sure she's comfortable. Get a blanket from the bed and cover her up for now. She should sleep for another hour or two. I need to find out where the incubator has gotten to."

Leaving her friend seeing to the cub, she headed for the door.

"Sergeant Noolgoi said you were to remain here, Doctor," said the taller of the two guards as she stepped out into the now deserted corridor.

"My incubator hasn't arrived," she said. "I intend to find out where it is."

The guard took hold of her arm, stopping her from leaving. "A moment, Doctor. Let me use the communicator, it'll be faster. We're not sure all the crew has been safely rounded up yet."

She nodded, waiting impatiently while the guard contacted his control.

"It's in the lab area, Doctor," he said at last. "They thought it would be safer there."

"Safer than with me? Who's guarding the labs? What reason

would they have to guard them?" she exclaimed, starting off down the corridor at a run.

"Doctor!" the guard called out as he raced after her. "It'll be guarded! They won't have just left it there!"

"I'm not prepared to take the risk," she said, avoiding his outstretched arm as she increased her speed. "My child is in that incubator!"

She rounded a corner, skidding to a halt as she came face to face with a patrol. Guns whined, coming up to bear on her instantly, then were turned aside as she was recognized.

"Doctor Zayshul," said Noolgoi. "We were just coming to see you. The ship has been secured, and . . ."

"My egg! Where is it?" she demanded. "Who left it in the lab area? I want it right now!"

"We were bringing it to you," said Noolgoi, standing aside so she could see the soldier carrying the portable incubator. "The labs were closed and locked when we arrived, so I detailed four of my team to guard the incubator there. Being close to the entrance, I decided it was safer there than carrying it through an unsecured ship. I'm sorry if my decision had you concerned for its safety."

Zayshul leaned against the wall, suddenly drained of energy now that she knew her child was safe. "Thank you," she said. "You're right, it was wiser."

"We didn't have time to tell you," apologized Noolgoi, taking her gently by the arm and leading her back the way she'd come. "Everything went as planned. We're undocking in a few minutes. You and the incubator need to be safely stowed in your suite."

Zayshul insisted on checking the incubator unit thoroughly, making sure the temperature hadn't fluctuated and that the grips holding the egg in its cradle hadn't worked loose or slackened off during the trip up to the *N'zishok*. All the while, Noolgoi stood waiting patiently.

Eventually, he spoke. "Doctor, we're ready to disengage from the platform. We must leave now. Every minute we delay increases our chances of being discovered."

"In a minute," she said, touching her fingertips to the transparent domed cover. Inside, the egg sat firmly in its cradle, the light glowing off the shell, highlighting the iridescent swirls of

green and blue that covered its surface. It would be a female,
she knew it by the colors, and in her heart.

Ten weeks still to go before it would hatch. It was so long!
What would their daughter look like? Like her, with the Prime's
lighter skin, or dark like her father? And what of the TeLaxaudin's intervention, how would that have affected their child?
How had they known to have the device there, waiting for them
to arrive? Why had they let them continue using the growth tanks
when there was a way for them bear their own young? Were the
TeLaxaudin breeding them for their own purposes, just as they
were trying to breed from the M'zullians?

A hand touched her arm. "Doctor."

"All right, Noolgoi," she murmured, reaching for the switch
that would engage the safety shield.

As the dome became opaque, she turned away from it, her
mind still troubled. Kzizysus had worked on Kezule, had taken
samples from him to extract his racial memories so they could be
edited and then transferred to the growth tubes for his offspring.
At their request, he'd done more, he'd adjusted the memories
Kezule would pass on to his naturally born children—children like
hers, so they'd also carry no memory of their father's captivity
by the Sholans. At the time, none of this had troubled her. Now
it did, especially when Kezule spoke about the memories only he
had of their people long before even his time.

Anchorage, Zhal-Nylam, 3rd day (September)

Alex glanced at her wrist comm as she dashed along the crowded
corridor heading for the interrogation area. Five minutes late.
Damn! She'd attempted to block Rhyaz out, but she wasn't too
good at it yet and she was still aware of him demanding her attention at the back of her mind. And he was hopping mad.

She slid to a stop at the security door, digging in her pocket
for the ID card she never remembered to leave clipped to her
jacket.

"It's all right, Sister," said the Brother on duty. "You can pass.
I recognize you." He pushed his own pass through the locking
mechanism.

"Thanks," she said. The door slid open and she slipped inside, praying Rhyaz wouldn't yell at her in front of everyone.

"I'm glad you could join us, Alex," Rhyaz said, glancing in her direction. "Please continue, Captain Ghadde."

Alex tuned out what was being said. What Rhyaz knew, she knew, there was no need for her to pay attention to this, but she was curious about who was there. She glanced around, seeing a medic sitting at a table with a comm unit against the far wall. Mentally she ticked off the captains of the five larger ships berthed around Anchorage as well as the captain in charge of the outpost. And Vriuzu, the telepathic Brother, and Rhyaz.

A movement on the far wall drew her attention. What she'd assumed was an opaque wall was gradually becoming transparent. In the room beyond, she could see a green-skinned alien held in a chair by restraints. She recognized it as a Valtegan. Fascinated, she threaded her way closer. Apart from the Sholans, she'd never seen another alien species. Curious, she let down her shields and stared at him, trying to read his surface thoughts without actually probing his mind.

"The gas is being released now," a voice was saying.

She could just feel him, and his determination not to show fear in front of the captors who chose to hide behind armored suits. He sniffed the air, and she saw his expression change rapidly to one of terror. He began to struggle, pulling at the wrist restraints in an effort to get free.

His terror filled her mind, dominating it until she felt the pain start. She opened her mouth to scream, but suddenly something clamped itself around her mind and she was frozen to the spot, unable to move or speak.

Foolish child! You had no business touching the prisoner's mind! You were warned about this!

Vriuzu's mental tone was angry beyond anything she'd experienced before. A hand closed on her shoulder like a vise, keeping her facing the window. Her body was released, but not her mind. As she went limp in his grasp, he jerked her upright.

Stand up! You will not let the Commander down any further!

The prisoner had collapsed, a trickle of blood coming from what passed for his nose. She shut her eyes, not wanting to see or hear any more.

"He looks dead, Ghadde," said Rhyaz, concerned.

"Bio-monitor confirms that," said the medic, checking the readings on the comm unit.

"I want the autopsy report in two hours," said Rhyaz, turning to those in the room. "Find out what killed him. The simulations showed the drug to be safe at this dosage. I want to know why it wasn't. Dismissed," he said.

She found herself being propelled toward Rhyaz.

"Commander, she was reading the Valtegan's mind," said Vriuzu quietly as the room emptied.

Rhyaz didn't even look at her. "Was it enough to affect him?"

"I don't know, Commander. She was doing a passive scan so it's possible that it wasn't a factor."

"Thank you, Vriuzu," he said quietly. "I'll take it from here."

Vriuzu inclined his head and let her go, turning to leave.

"My office, now," said Rhyaz tersely, walking past her.

She followed him, trying to think up as many excuses as she could in an attempt to find one that would be acceptable. She wasn't looking forward to this.

Lyand was at his desk catching up on some of Rhyaz' paperwork. He looked up as the door opened, and got hurriedly to his feet.

"Wait for me outside, please, Lyand. See no one comes in until I call you."

"Aye, sir," he said, leaving.

As Rhyaz walked over to his desk and sat down, Alex tentatively lowered the barrier she'd erected between them, but she could sense nothing from him. His mind was closed to her.

"Where were you this time?" he asked. "The mess? Or the viewing room?"

"The landing bay," she said.

"This trip hasn't exactly been a success, has it? There was the music you uploaded to the ship's comm that blared out in the middle of the night. The several tons of unprocessed fuel you somehow managed to vent while we were in jump. You've been late three times to meetings, and now this. You realize you could have caused the prisoner's death, don't you?"

"What?" She looked at him, shocked by what he'd said.

"Valtegans have a racial memory of us that makes them go catatonic or into seizures at the touch of a Sholan telepath's mind. You were fully briefed, along with everyone else as we left Chagda Station, yet you still touched his mind. Why?"

"I didn't mean to harm him," she stammered. "I was only curious."

"You're bright, and undoubtedly talented, Alex, but there's an arrogance about you that's not justified, and very unattractive. I know you don't bother listening properly to briefings because you know you can get the knowledge from me. I can feel your attention wandering. Just because I've said nothing about it to date doesn't mean I'm unaware of what's going on, or that I condone it."

She looked at the floor, thinking about the Valtegan. "You were going to kill him anyway! And I'm not a Sholan so it couldn't have been me."

"I wanted him alive, Alex! Yes, we were testing a chemical weapon on him, but a disabling one. It would be easy to use a gas that kills, we have several already. They also kill Sholans and Humans. What we want is a chemical that will disable them, attack that which makes them so determined to destroy us. As for not being a Sholan, have you read any of the Mixed Leska data you've been given? Actually listened to Father Lijou or Tutor Kha'Qwa when they talked to you about it?"

"Of course I have," she said.

"Then you should know that you're no longer what's considered Human, you're also part Sholan. Everything about you has been altered—your mind, your body, and your genes. You're no longer compatible with your own species, only with other gene-altered Sholans and Humans."

"What do you mean?"

"That if you can't settle down within the Brotherhood as an operative, then perhaps you should think of having cubs. We gene-altered people need to breed the next generation, Alex."

"Cubs?" she said, horrified. "You mean like Kha'Qwa's?"

He nodded. "Maybe it's time I had a family. You'd still have to come with me on trips like this, of course, but you'd bring our cubs with you."

"You're joking!" she said, horrified. "Even if what you say is possible, I'm only a kid!"

"Are you? You're involved in a military Order that is responsible for the lives of thousands of people, Alex. Your decisions affect us all, your incompetence too. The music can be laughed over as a prank, not so the venting of fuel. We were lucky there was someone on the bridge capable of handling it rather than other trainees. As for this latest incident, need I say more? I'm sending you to our room to reevaluate your career options, Alex. You'll stay there until I send for you. I'm also cut-

ting all access from the comm unit. You've got your comp pad,
I suggest you spend the time reading up on several topics, including the Mixed Leska data."

The door opened and Lyand entered. "Yes, sir?"

"Escort Djana Alex to our room, please, and arrange for a
guard outside the door. She's to remain inside till I send for her.
Tell the bridge to isolate the comm unit until I give orders for it
to be restored."

"Aye, sir."

"And Alex, give your wrist comm to Lyand."

Lyand turned to Alex and gestured to the door. "If you please,
Djana."

"I can't believe he's doing this to me," she fumed as Lyand
and a Sister escorted her to their room.

"You're lucky," said Lyand. "If it were anyone but you, you'd
be in the brig in solitary until you could be posted back to Stronghold for a disciplinary hearing."

"What would they do to me?" she asked in a small voice.

Lyand looked at her. "Habitual lateness, failure to attend to
briefings, disobeying an order relating to a prisoner, endangering
the life of said prisoner? Assuming you didn't cause his death,
a prison term, or a posting to a very lonely place. Given that the
prisoner is one of only four, and they were obtained at great risk
to the whole Alliance, you could face a death penalty if proved
responsible for his death as a direct consequence of not obeying
orders."

She stopped in her tracks, eyes wide with terror.

Lyand took her by the arm and drew her onward. "However,
Commander Rhyaz couldn't do that, Djana. You're his Leska. If
you die, so does he. It's the nature of your Link. You have to
realize we're a military Order, we depend on discipline. It isn't
like ignoring a teacher at school or in your guild. Your age is irrelevant, we have juniors younger than you who don't break half
the rules you trample every day."

"But they grew up at Stronghold," she said, tears starting in
her eyes. "I haven't! I've been thrown in and been expected to
pick it all up from thin air!"

He stopped at the door to her quarters. "That's not true, Djana.
Commander Rhyaz doesn't expect from you what he expects from
the rest of us. All he wants is that you do what you're asked."

He took his pass card from his pocket and inserted it in the lock, standing back for her to enter.

"My advice is if the Commander told you to do anything while you're in here, do it, and do it well. That's all that will impress him. Good day, Djana."

"What do I do with her, Lyand?" Rhyaz asked when his aide came back. "I take it you talked to her on the way to our quarters? I don't want to frighten her too much. She's quite capable of trying to run off. Look at how close to Shola she got when she and Kai decided to leave Earth."

"She's very resourceful. I have a suggestion, something that came up as we talked, sir."

"What?"

"She's no idea of what's expected of an ordinary junior. Why don't you twin her with one of the ones here of her own age for the next three days? Let her see how much hard work it really is, and how little's being asked of her in comparison. It's difficult for her, sir. She's halfway between a life-mate and a colleague. If you'll excuse me saying, neither of you know where she belongs."

Rhyaz ignored the implication and eyed him thoughtfully. "It might work. Set it up for me, Lyand. Would it be better if the junior was attached to you?"

"There's a lot to be done here, Commander. Yes, the help would be worthwhile."

"If you run out of tasks, I'm sure you can invent some," sighed Rhyaz.

Anchorage, Zhal-Nylam, 4th day (September)

"We've almost got it right, Lijou," said Rhyaz to his colleague back at Stronghold. "We lost two of the prisoners, unfortunately, but have hopes that the modifications we're doing today will solve the problem."

"What will you do with the survivors?" asked Lijou.

"They'll be kept here for questioning. Our scientists would like to find a way to target their inherited memories, see if we can find something to neutralize their fear of us. If we could sit down and talk to them like we can the Primes, it would be a start."

Lijou sighed. "I can say nothing useful, Rhyaz. You know my opinions. How is Alex doing?"

It was Rhyaz' turn to sigh. "Don't ask. She's working off a punishment detail. I've got her twinned with a junior her own age running errands for Lyand and anyone else who needs them. I have to say, she's sticking with it, doing what she's been asked to do quickly and politely."

"We have Kusac back. The TeLaxaudin came up with a cure for him, but unfortunately there were side effects. He's come here for help from me and Noni."

"What side effects? Nothing dangerous I hope."

"A memory problem that has to be resolved before he can use his Talent properly. We can manage between us, I'm sure."

"Keep me posted. I'll call you tomorrow, let you know how the experiment went. Until then, Lijou."

"Till tomorrow."

Prime world, Zhal-Nylam, 5th day (September)

Shaking with exhaustion and hunger, Director Zsiyuk stumbled out of the abandoned warehouse into the street, blinking in the bright sunlight. Clinging to the doorframe, he looked around frantically. The street was a cul-de-sac, and deserted. The buildings surrounding him looked as ancient and unused as the one he'd been held in. He had to get back to the safety of the Court! His kidnappers could come back at any time, might be watching him even now!

He didn't recognize this part of the City, but then what reason would he have to come to such a run-down area? Pushing himself away from the support of the wall, he staggered down the street toward the exit.

A foul smell began to fill the air, getting stronger as he neared the opening. Now he could recognize it! Manure—the smell of mammal dung. And the greeny gold ahead of him wasn't the grassed area he'd thought it to be, it was fields. He was in the southeast agricultural area on the outskirts of the City!

His corpulent frame wasn't geared toward endurance and by the time he reached the entrance to the City proper, he was soaked in sweat and barely able to stand. A public grav floater came by, and he hailed it, shouting and gesticulating until it pulled to a halt to wait for him.

Face flushed almost black, he hauled open the door and collapsed into the vehicle.

"Office of Naval Architecture," he wheezed, ignoring the driver's exclamation of disgust at the smell that surrounded him. "And fast!"

"I don't carry farm laborers," said the driver, turning round to look at him, his nostrils flaring several times in disgust. "Get out and walk. I'm not having you stinking out my vehicle!"

"Do I look like a farm laborer?" demanded Zsiyuk angrily, wiping his forehead on his jacket sleeve. "Get moving at once!"

"Now look, I don't know who you think you are," he began.

"Obviously," hissed Zsiyuk, digging in a pocket till he found his ID card. "Here! Take me to my offices! I've just escaped a gang of kidnappers! My life's in danger the longer I stay here!"

"I'm not getting involved in any of that! Get out, right now!"

Zsiyuk sighed. "There's a reward in it for you," he said, slumping back against the seat, grateful for its softness. "What day is it?" he demanded.

"It better be enough to pay for cleaning your stench out of my vehicle," the driver muttered, turning back and starting the engine. "Today's the 5th."

"I'll pay your damned cleaning bills!"

Fifteen minutes later, he was being fussed over by his secretaries and aide as he attempted to call the Office of Science.

He swiped the ministering hands away and ordered them out as he waited for his communicator to connect him to Zhayan's office.

"What do you want, Zsiyuk? I'm rather busy right now."

Zsiyuk frowned. "Is that one of the Palace guards I see behind you?"

"Yes, it is. What do you want? I told you I'm busy."

"I was kidnapped, Zhayan," he said. "Snatched by armed people as I left my office three days ago!"

"Were you? Then you were fortunate to escape. Ghoddoh wasn't so lucky, but I expect you know all about that."

Noticing the note of sarcasm in the other's voice for the first time, he narrowed his eyes, staring again at the guard behind him. "What's going on, Zhayan? Why wasn't Ghoddoh lucky?"

"You know well enough what happened to Ghoddoh! He was found slumped dead at his desk in the Palace yesterday morning, and a letter intended for me exploded shortly after it was delivered yesterday afternoon."

"Good God! What about Schoudu?"

"Don't bother pretending you don't know anything about it, Zsiyuk, you're not that good at dissembling. Your absence these last three days has been very convenient."

"Someone's targeting us, aren't they? Who's behind it? What happened to Schoudu?"

"Have it your way, then. You usually do," hissed Zhayan. "Schoudu's in hospital recovering from his injuries. His grav floater was attacked by armed people last night."

"Hospital?" That stunned him. "I'm not behind this, Zhayan. I'm a victim myself!"

"You're the only one unhurt. Like I said, you were nowhere to be found while the rest of us were being attacked. I call that very convenient. That's why I asked for a bodyguard. You won't get me, Zsiyuk."

The line went dead. He sat and looked at the blank screen for several minutes, mind working overtime as he tried to work out his best course of action.

Directorate headquarters, the same day

Zsiyuk found K'hedduk in his office at the end of the corridor. He was packing papers into a large briefcase. He looked up, frowning as he entered.

"Zsiyuk! What're you doing here? It's past midnight."

"Looking for you, K'hedduk. Seems like I found you just in time," he said angrily. "What's going on? Ghoddoh's dead, Schoudu's in hospital, Zhayan's gotten a Palace guard assigned to him as protection after a bomb wrecked his front office, and I've just escaped from kidnappers!"

"Nothing to do with me, Zsiyuk," said K'hedduk, closing and locking his case. "I'm just leaving. I suggest you do the same."

"For where?" demanded Zsiyuk, placing his bulk in front of

the other. "I want answers, dammit! Zhayan thinks I'm responsible for this!"

A muffled explosion shook the room, making the door rattle and the loose objects on the desk move. It was immediately followed by another, fainter one.

"I really do suggest that you leave," said K'hedduk, picking up his case and moving round the other side of his desk.

"What's happening?" demanded Zsiyuk. "What was that noise?"

"Someone attacking us, I suspect," he said, taking advantage of Zsiyuk's shock to walk unheeded to the door. "The same someone who kidnapped you and shot at the others."

Zsiyuk paled, then came suddenly to life as his innate instinct for survival cut in. "Where's the nearest exit?" he demanded, following K'hedduk.

"The explosion came from this end so I suggest the elevator," he said, checking the corridor.

As the elevator doors began to open, M'kou lobbed a grenade out then plastered himself to the wall like the others, turning his head aside. It detonated instantly. When the doors opened fully, Kezule sprayed the area outside with a burst of energy from his auto rifle. A brief scream from behind the nurse's desk confirmed he'd got her.

"Guards down," confirmed M'kou.

"Cover me," ordered Kezule, diving out and vaulting over the desk opposite.

Perfunctorily, he checked the nurse while glancing across at the two supine guards. From their injuries, he doubted they'd be a problem. She was dead. One less to worry about. M'kou was already checking the guards. Two of the M'zullians were hammering wedges round the elevator's doors and between it and the floor, jamming it in position. A third planted a charge on an inner wall.

"Dead," came the quiet confirmation.

He stepped over the nurse's body and moved cautiously to the corner of the reception area, peering carefully down the corridor. It was empty. Briefly he wondered where the guard on the hybrids' room was. He gestured the rest of the unit out.

"Clear each room then destroy it," said Kezule. "Treat any

Primes moving in a zone of fire as a potential enemy. I want the Sholan captives alive. Move out."

Zhalmo gestured the first team toward the door on the left, the other on the right. Cautiously they moved into the corridor, two covering as the third tried the door, then they were in. They'd no sooner disappeared from sight than from farther down the corridor, three guards dived out, one hitting the floor and firing at them while the other two dashed for the room opposite.

Three bolts of energy hit the guard as Zhalmo, M'kou, and one of the M'zullians fired on him simultaneously. A scream of pain and it was over. He saw Zhalmo murmuring in her link, warning the others.

The two in the ward doorway began sporadic fire, attempting to halt their advance. Kezule pulled a stun grenade and lobbed it down in their direction. It detonated, but moments later the shooting resumed.

Zhalmo motioned the M'zullian with the grenade launcher forward, directing him to the opposite wall. Covering fire lit up the corridor as the youth dodged his way down, ducking into the doorways until he reached an optimum position and stopped to fire. The grenade shot out, shattering the transparent wall.

"There go the Primes," murmured M'kou.

"Less to worry about," said Kezule, watching as the wall exploded outward in a shower of fragments.

Two teams rushed past them, heading for the devastated room and the mess area opposite as the soldier with the launcher fell back.

Zhalmo led the rest into the corridor. Kezule and M'kou began to follow. At the far end, two figures emerged from a room, one with his hands in the air. Zsiyuk.

"Don't shoot!" he called out. "We're unarmed!"

Kezule could feel those around him relax slightly and opened his mouth. As he did, Zsiyuk stumbled, half turned to look in shock behind him; then a shot rang out and the second figure dodged into the exit.

The M'zullian in front of him cried out and dropped to the ground. Instantly the corridor lit up again as five energy weapons took Zsiyuk out.

"Burn it!" snarled Kezule, angry that they'd let themselves be fooled. "Check every room! We take no prisoners! Only the Sholans have value!"

"Mess and ward rooms are clear," said Zhalmo in a subdued voice as their Warriors reappeared. "No survivors."

"There's at least one guard in the room with the hybrids," he said. "I'm going in first. I want those cubs alive!" He gestured to M'kou and his team. "You're with me. Clear the rooms opposite," he ordered his own two M'zullians.

He waited until he had the all clear. "Cover us, Zhalmo," he said, and began to edge forward. There was no time for subtlety. He pulled his pistol and shot the lock open, gesturing them to force the door.

It gave under the rain of kicks, slamming inward to bounce back off the wall. M'kou caught it, holding it open. A quick glance told him the room was empty. Fanning out, they ran in, taking up defensive positions behind the furniture. Kezule kicked the chairs on his side of the table aside, and toppled it on its edge before ducking behind it.

"Surrender now and your life will be spared," Kezule called out.

"I've hostages here. You try to get in, I'll kill them one at a time," came the reply.

"Gas gun," suggested M'kou's voice in his earpiece. "We're wearing plugs. Interior walls are thin enough."

He raised his hand in agreement. A firefight risked all the cubs, this way, only one, two at most, would be sacrificed, maybe even none. "Aim high," he whispered. "I don't make deals," he said loudly. "Surrender."

The shot rang out, the pellet punching a neat hole in the wall. There was an exclamation of shock then the sound of coughing, followed by a single shot.

"Move!" hissed Kezule, diving over the table and heading for the door.

Through the faint mist of the gas, he could see one child lying on the floor, a dark-pelted one. The others had scattered, cowering behind their beds. The guard, backing up to the far wall, was coughing violently. Gun waving aimlessly, he held a child in front of him by the neck as a body shield—another dark-furred one.

Kezule hesitated briefly. Which was the one he wanted? This, or the one already lying in a pool of blood? With gas in the room, he couldn't risk tasting the air to be sure.

The guard had reached a pocket of clean air and was recovering slightly, his gun now moving toward the cub.

As Kezule fired, so did the guard. The child yowled, a high-pitched sound of terror that stopped abruptly as he hit the floor and the guard fell on top of him. He was there in an instant, the dead Prime sent flying aside as he examined the child for signs of life.

M'kou was at his side moments later, his emergency aid kit already out. "Let me, sir," he said.

Kezule got up, checking to see the children were being rounded up before going over to the one lying bleeding.

"That one's dead, sir," said M'kou, glancing at him. "This one is seriously injured."

He knelt down to turn the small body over, and sighed with relief. It was dark, but dark brown, not black.

"I want that one kept alive, M'kou," he said, getting up. "What's the extent of his injuries?"

"Minor energy burn to the shoulder, and one, maybe two broken ribs. He's bleeding from the mouth and having breathing problems—punctured lung, I think. That guard was heavy. He needs more than trauma treatment. How're we going to get him up to the ship?"

"Stasis units," he said, remembering what K'hedduk had said about the adult Sholans. "They have stasis units."

"That would stabilize him till we reach the *N'zishok*," agreed M'kou. "But how do we get a stasis unit on board?"

"General, we've got the other three children," said the M'zullian.

"Three? There should be five including this one! Find the missing one!" he hissed.

"There's another one dead. We think the gas pellet hit it on the back of the head as it rebounded."

Kezule hissed angrily. Two dead and one on the verge of death were not good results. "Get them to the exit," he said. He toggled his comm. "Zhalmo, call the shuttle and get it to pick us up here. Tell them we're bringing a stasis unit. M'kou, can you move this cub into the other room? The gas can't be helping him any. I want the bodies of the dead ones completely destroyed. Incinerated to ash," he ordered the M'zullian.

Carefully M'kou picked up the limp body and headed for the other room.

By the time Kezule joined Zhalmo, the area had been secured.

"We've two adult Sholans in cages in a lab area," said Zhalmo, her face taking on a look of distaste. "The male's in a bad way, General, not likely to survive if we move him."

"What happened?" he demanded.

"Not us," she said. "We found him like that. He's burning up with a fever, got sores on his body that have gone septic too. I'd say they've been conducting experiments on him. He's got a device implanted on his neck, and another on his skull. Shaved his head to do it. Not a pretty sight. We left them where they were till I could speak to you about them."

Kezule, crest rising in anger, stalked off toward the lab. Why was this simple mission turning into one so troublesome?

"Let her out," he ordered as soon as he saw the Sholan female standing holding onto the bars of her cage. "I want your word you'll do nothing to harm my troops," he said to her in her own language. "I'm giving you your freedom if you cooperate with me. Understand?"

"Yes, Seniormost," she stammered, standing back from the bars in shock as one of his warriors aimed at the lock. As the cage door swung open, she grasped hold of the bars with one hand and took a first tentative step out into the room. "I remember you. You helped my mate. Why're you here, Seniormost?"

"To rescue you and the children they've been holding," he said. "I need your help. One of them is badly injured. You have a child in stasis, don't you?"

"General!" Zhalmo called out from the doorway. "Got another problem. Some of the stasis units have been sabotaged."

"My cub!" she whimpered, putting her hands to her face in fear.

"Continue, Sergeant."

"The adults are dead but the child's unit at the back is untouched. It's occupied, but large enough for the injured cub if we wake the infant. We're taking it to the surface now. And we're getting noises from below, as if the guards and staff are close to digging their way out. Advise we leave immediately, sir, and detonate our charges to be sure of containing them."

"Free me and give me a gun before you leave," said a male Sholan voice from behind him. "I know I'm not going to make it, but I want to take a few of them with me before I go."

Kezule spun round. He'd forgotten the male in the cage. Seeing him sitting slumped against the bars, he vividly remembered the last one.

Eyes glittered feverishly from a face damp with sweat. On his head, dark skin showed where there should have been fur, and he could clearly see the implant devices Zhalmo had mentioned, implants identical to those used on the volunteer Palace guards until his Warriors had been birthed. The devices were surrounded by angry, swollen flesh. Several other wounds on his scalp looked equally infected. No attempt had been made to dress them, nor the wounds that liberally covered the rest of his body.

"I didn't want to cooperate," the male said, with the ghost of a smile as he attempted to sit up.

"He has seizures," said the female. "The implant had failed, they said. No point in treating him when he was going to die anyway."

"General," urged Zhalmo. "We must go."

Kezule looked at the male, remembering his time with the Sholans. Alone, an exile in time as well as space, when the opportunity to escape had come, he'd taken it. "We're blowing the exits when we leave," he said. "There'll be no escape. The guards below may not make it up to this level."

"But if they do, I'll be here. They won't escape me," he said. Groaning, he pulled himself upright by hanging onto the bars.

Kezule stepped to one side and sliced through the lock with a burst from his gun. The door swung slowly open. Stepping away from the cage, he took the female by the arm, drawing her with him. "I'll leave a gun and a grenade on the lab bench," he said. "Good hunting, Sholan."

"And to you, General."

Their transport was waiting when he got above ground. As he pushed the Sholan female on board, he felt the earth beneath his feet vibrate and heard the dull crump of the charges detonating.

"Captain Khayikule reports that the Enforcers have emerged from the hospital after questioning Director Schoudu," said Zhalmo, heading for the rear of the vehicle where the stasis unit and the injured child had been taken. "Guards have been placed outside his room. On the other side of the city, his people are reporting seeing Enforcer vehicles stopping outside the apartments where Director Zhayan lives."

"Was Zsiyuk's body brought up and left for them to find?"

he asked tiredly, leaving the Sholan female with one of the officers before following her. "And those of the dead children?"

"Zsiyuk's body was placed above ground near the stairwell, and all the dead Sholans were destroyed, sir," said the young female. "To ash as you specified."

Kezule watched Zhalmo as her fingers flew confidently over the stasis unit control panel. The unit had been opened and the infant within was already beginning to wake.

"Where did you learn those skills? Not from me, I know nothing about stasis technology."

She glanced up at him. "Sleep tapes, sir. They gave us access to any we wanted in the days before you came for us."

"Ah." He turned to M'kou, grabbing hold of the seat back as the shuttle took off. "How is he?"

"I've got him stable enough for stasis, sir, but it'll be touch and go if I don't get him in within the next few minutes," his aide said, securing the dressing on the unconscious child's shoulder.

"I'm nearly there, M'kou," she said.

Out of his depth, Kezule said, "Carry on. I'm going up front. Let me know if he makes it into stasis, M'kou."

"Yes, sir."

CHAPTER 17

N'zishok, **the same day**

"GENERAL on board," said Maaz'ih as Kezule, followed by his unit, debarked from their shuttle.

"General Kezule," said Maaz'ih, saluting him crisply. "Seniormost Doctor Zayshul is waiting in the sick bay for your patient."

"Sergeant," said Kezule, returning the salute as he stood to one side and watched the grav loader for the stasis unit being rolled into the shuttle. "Have all the Sholans escorted to the sick bay for medical checks. See the adult is allocated suitable quarters and is given what she needs for her infant. And put the cubs next door to her," he added as an afterthought.

"Aye, sir."

He walked to the wall communicator and switched it on. "Take us out, Captain Zaykkuh. Follow our official flight plan for now. I'll give you our new heading later. I'll be in the sick bay if you need me," he said, flipping it off without waiting for a reply.

He headed for the grav lift up to the next deck, M'kou following in his wake. He eyed him with a frown. "M'kou, get yourself freshened up, you're covered in blood. Then debrief the unit leaders for me. Send your report to my quarters. Tomorrow, I want you to mingle, get the feel of our new people, find out their mood."

"Understood, General," said his aide. "General, why's that child so important to you?"

"Because he's the son of my enemies," he said quietly to Zayshul when she asked him the same question.

"You can't know that," she said, drying her hands.

"I know he's Kusac's son," he said. "And the son of the Human female, Carrie. I remember their scents. I won't easily forget how she treated me."

She leaned against the sink, watching as the child was transferred from her operating room to an IC bed.

"Will he survive?" asked Kezule.

"He's in no danger now," she said. "I've put a chest drain in and he's on a drip and a course of anti-infection agents that I know his species can tolerate. The ribs and the lung will heal by themselves but he'll be sore and uncomfortable for some time. The burn is minor, it'll heal within a week or two. Just what do you intend to do with these five cubs, Kezule?" She indicated the far side of the room where Zhookah and her friend Ghidd'ah were still examining the Sholans.

"Use them and the adult female to buy help," he said. "But not him," he indicated the small unconscious body. "Him I'll keep."

"What for? To torment and torture him?"

He looked shocked. "I don't make war on children!"

"Then why keep him from his own kind, away from his parents?"

"He's never known his own kind, or his parents. They were programmed to be content to serve the Prime Empire. He'll do well enough here with us."

"I'll not be involved in this, Kezule. He should be returned with the others. Have you thought what this could do to our treaty with the Sholans?"

"I've done what you asked of me," he said, his voice taking on a hard edge. "I dealt with the plot against your Emperor, and protected your treaty by bringing the embarrassing evidence of what the Directorate had done with us. I also left most of my sons and daughters behind to protect the royal family. As for the treaty, both sides need it too much to be affected by this. You keep your part of the bargain, Zayshul. Treat the child as you would a guest. And his collar remains on, same with the others. It only prevents them from stealing our thoughts, nothing more."

She nodded reluctantly. "Why do we need help? Who do you intend to buy it from?"

"The Sholans. You said Kusac is no longer a telepath, that his ability was destroyed by the implant that Chy'qui used on him, didn't you?"

"Yes. What of it?"

"The twenty M'zullians on the Sholan world are being trained by him and the third one who brought me to this time. They haven't degenerated the way my twenty did, and there have been no deaths during training. I need to know why. I told you, we can't just put a Warrior caste into Prime society and make it work."

"Then what do you intend to do?"

"The Sholans have no castes, they're one people. Their Warriors are trained not born. Once we were the same. Your female friends have performed as well as my daughters—better than the civilian males, and they're not even Warrior caste females."

"We aren't representative of our people. We've got no Workers here, Kezule, only Intellectuals with some drone ancestry and your Warriors."

"Then we'll combine the castes we have into one and *train* those who show promise as Warriors, not try to breed them!"

"You want Sholans to come here and train us, don't you?"

"Only Kusac. I won't have mind-stealers near me. For his help, they can have these children, and the adult female."

"You're mad. After what Chy'qui and J'koshuk did to him, there's no way he'd come!"

"Oh, he'll come," said Kezule softly. "For several reasons. I've seen Sholans who've been entertained by the likes of J'koshuk return voluntarily to captivity after they'd been rescued by their own people. The pain twists their natures. It becomes like a drug that they can't live without. And if that isn't enough, I know how to make him come to us, and how to keep him. His son is only part of it, Zayshul."

the *N'zishok,* next day, Zhal-Nylam, 6th day (September)

Next morning, after she'd breakfasted, Zayshul left Kezule debriefing M'kou and went to call on the Sholan female and the cubs.

As soon as she entered, the cubs stopped what they were doing and got to their feet, heads bowed, looking at the ground. The female, feeding her infant with the milk they'd managed to synthesize the night before, stood more slowly, obviously ill at ease.

"Seniormost," she said as her cub began to mewl hungrily.

"Please, sit down, all of you," she said, going over to the cubs. "Finish feeding your infant." Bending down, she put the box she was carrying on the floor and opened it before getting up. "They're yours," she said, gesturing to the box. "Toys for you to play with. Go on," she urged when they didn't move. "Have a look at them."

"They don't know what toys are, Seniormost," said the female quietly as she sat down again. "They've never played before, only studied."

Tight-lipped, Zayshul went to the door and spoke to someone outside then returned. "I don't know your names," she said to the adult. "I'm Doctor Zayshul."

"I'm Rraelga, and this is N'Yua, my daughter," she said. "I can't thank you enough, Seniormost Doctor, for giving me back my cub."

"Please, don't use the title Seniormost," Zayshul said. "Doctor will do."

The door chimed, then opened to admit Gaylla, clutching a soft toy tightly to her chest. As she saw her one-time companions, her mouth opened in a slow smile. "I missed you. Where others?"

"There was an accident, Gaylla," said Zayshul, kneeling down beside her. "We had to rescue your friends from the nasty people just as we rescued you, but before we could stop them, two of your friends were hurt badly, so badly they died."

Gaylla blinked and nodded solemnly, then her mouth dropped in a large grin. "Toys!" she said, looking to Zayshul for permission. When she nodded, Gaylla ran quickly over to the box. Her toy, a Prime doll made of cloth, was dropped to the floor as she grabbed hold of the box and tipped it on its side, spilling the brightly colored contents onto the floor.

She picked up a ball and threw it on the floor to a shocked exclamation from the largest of the cubs.

"No, is for throwing," Gaylla assured him earnestly as she picked up another doll and thrust it at the other young female. "Vazih, you play with this doll." She scrambled across to the other side of the box to retrieve a book, which she handed to a brown-pelted male. "Book for you, Dhyshac." She looked up at Zayshul. "Dhyshac like books, Aunt."

A sealed container was next, and she attempted to open it. The remaining male reached out to help her. The lid popped off suddenly, spraying bright building bricks everywhere, much to the distress of the young male.

"Bricks. You put together and make things, Zsayal," said Gaylla, grabbing a handful and showing him.

"Why do we do this, Seniormost?" asked Zsayal, looking up at her.

"To enjoy yourselves," said Zayshul, getting up. "And call me Aunt like Gaylla. You're children, and children should have fun and play with toys."

He looked perplexed, but obediently began to gather up the bricks and start fitting them together.

"Is Shaidan dead, too?" asked Gaylla, sitting with Vazih and showing her how the clothes on her doll fastened.

"Shaidan?"

"The one who was hurt," said Vazih.

"Shaidan's fine. He's in the sick bay right now, but you'll be able to see him later today if you wish," said Zayshul, going over to sit with Rraelga.

"Want to see Shaidan," said Gaylla firmly.

"Then you shall," Zayshul said, leaning over to look at the infant. "That's a newborn child!" she said in surprise.

"They took her from me as soon as she was born," said Rraelga, putting the adapted bottle down on the table beside her. She lifted her cub up and held her against her chest. "She was put in stasis."

"But you have her back safely now," said Zayshul, hiding her anger as she looked at the tiny furled ears and the tightly closed eyes. She reached out and gently stroked the cub's head as it snuffled at her fingers. "She's so soft." How could they have taken this infant away from her mother and put her into stasis?

"What will you do with us, Seniormost?" Rraelga asked, a worried look on her face. "Where are you taking us?"

"Home, in a few weeks," she said, watching the other's look of incredulity. "We have treaties with your people, Rraelga. The ones who held you captive were a renegade group who wanted to break our agreements with the Sholans. Thankfully, we stopped them."

"Home? To Khyaal?"

"To Shola," said Zayshul, not wanting to get drawn into an explanation of the destruction of that world by the M'zullians. "I came to see if there's anything you need or want. We've tried to find clothing for you and the cubs, I hope what we gave you will do."

Rraelga looked down at the large pull-on shirt she was wearing. "It'll be fine, Seniormost," she said, mouth opening in a small smile. "They didn't give me clothes at all."

"That's all changed, Rraelga," she said, getting up. "You're no longer slaves, but you will have to be confined to these rooms for now, I'm afraid. Is the food in the dispenser to your liking? Again, we tried to choose food that might be familiar to you."

"It's fine, Sen—Doctor," she corrected herself.

Zayshul nodded and called to Gaylla. "Do you want to stay here for now?" she asked.

Gaylla nodded her head enthusiastically. "I stay for now," she confirmed.

"Then I'll come for you after your midday meal and we can go visit Shaidan."

"Have the original crew been dropped off at the relay station?" asked Kezule, settling himself into the weapons station on the bridge.

"Yes, General," said Zaykkuh from his Captain's seat. "We disabled the communicator in such a way that it'll take them a day to fix it, giving us time to disappear first."

Kezule pulled out a crystal data card and handed it to the navigator. "Well done. Your new coordinates, Maaz'ih."

"Aye, sir," the officer said, taking the card from him and putting it in the data reader slot.

"We're heading for a deep space outpost called Kij'ik," said Kezule, raising his voice so all the bridge crew could hear him. "Hopefully it'll be still there and operational, but if it isn't, I know the location of several more we can try. The odds are that at least one is still there and usable. If it is, it'll be our base for the time being. The outpost is one of many that made up an early warning network that spanned the Valtegan Empire in my time. It's in an asteroid belt, large enough for our needs and not far from fuel sources—a nearby sun and a gas giant. Kij'ik was one of the main ones, large enough to house over a thousand people. It was self-sustaining, having a hydroponics area and even small herds of food beasts. Though after fifteen hundred years, I doubt they'll still be viable," he added dryly.

"New coordinates loaded, sir," said Maaz'ih.

"Hyperdrive engines ready," said Shartoh.

"Chameleon shields up, Captain," said Zhalmo.

"General? Do you want to give the order?" asked Zaykkuh, turning around to look at him.

"No, you may give the order, Captain."

"Engage hyperdrive," said Zaykkuh.

Stronghold, the same day

"Ah, Kusac," said Lijou, gesturing him over. "Just the person I wanted. Banner, I'm sure you don't mind Kha'Qwa and I kidnapping your friend for the rest of the day, do you?"

"Hardly kidnapping, Father Lijou," smiled Banner as they strolled over to join the head priest and his mate. "And we weren't doing anything important."

"Thank you," said Lijou, taking Kusac by the arm. "We're going up to the pool on the Dumiyat Peak. You swim, don't you?"

"Silly question, he lives on the coast," said Kha'Qwa, tucking Chay'Dah into the carrier she wore.

"True," admitted Lijou, drawing Kusac along with him. "Do you know it? Now the weather's getting back to normal, it'll be worth the visit. I love that part of the burn, it's so clear and cooling at this time of year. I want to catch it now before autumn comes. Do you realize it's officially only two weeks away? Once the weather starts to turn, that stream becomes icy."

"I haven't seen much outside Dzahai village, Lijou," he said. "I'd love to come but I don't have a towel."

Lijou let him go and held out one of the two bags he was carrying. "We packed one for you. Here, you take it. I'll take the important one—the food and drink!"

Feeling a little nonplussed, he took the bag and fell in step with them.

As they climbed up the track, conversations centered on the bizarre weather patterns that had swept over Shola because of the Entities and how relieved everyone was it finally seemed to be over.

He found the countryside beautiful, and quite different from that around his home estate. The grass here was bleached almost straw-colored by the sun and the wind, and beneath his feet, the soil was so hot he could feel its heat rising like warm breath around him. The air was full of the scents of the mountainside— the faint tang of pine resin from the distant trees, the clumps of dark green brackens, the thorn bushes with their yellow blossoms. Against the outcrops of lichen-covered rocks, the brightly colored petals of mountain flowers stood out vividly. In the distance, he thought he could hear the chuckling of the stream. He sniffed, smelling the dampness in the air.

"You can smell it already?" asked Kha'Qwa, holding her hand out to Lijou for help over a small hillock.

"Yes, can't you?"

She shook her head. "Too far."

He stopped a moment, looking down the way they'd come, seeing the village spread out below him, as tiny as a cub's toy. "It's beautiful up here."

"And peaceful," said Lijou. "Usually," he added as a group of laughing Brothers and Sisters came into view, pelts still damp, towels thrown across their shoulders.

"Father, Tutor Kha'Qwa," they murmured, inclining their heads in courtesy as they passed.

"I hope it's not too crowded," said Kha'Qwa as they began walking again. "I want to take Chay'Dah into the pool. He's old enough to start swimming. Does Carrie take Kashini in the sea?"

"Yes, but we have a lake for swimming in now that we train so intensively on the estate. The sea's too cold except in high summer."

"Do you take picnics there?"

He remembered the pool where he'd met Vartra. "No. We went to a pool on the edge of the woodland in our garden. But that was last year."

"You should try to go there as a family before the end of the summer," said Kha'Qwa. "Memories of the summer help keep you warm when the wind's howling round the house."

"It doesn't howl so loudly down in their peninsula," said Lijou with a laugh.

*   *   *

The pool was large, measuring a couple of hundred meters across, and bounded for most of its margins by soft green grass. The remaining edge was a sand and gravel soil.

Groups of people were playing in the water or lounging around on the grass. A few low trees and bushes provided spots of shade, but he could see none near the water that were unoccupied. Further back, three or four small aircars were parked.

"Can you see them?" asked Kha'Qwa, looking round.

Despite the torc, Kusac felt a gentle mental touch he recognized instantly. "If you mean Master Sorli, he's over by the bushes there," he said, pointing.

"I'm impressed," said Kha'Qwa, taking hold of his arm and gently squeezing it. "It must be so good to have your Talent back. I know what it felt like when I got back what little I have after Chay'Dah was born. Until then, I hadn't realized how much I relied on it and how blind and deaf I felt without it."

He looked away, aware his eyes were showing his innermost feelings. "I don't like being set up, Kha'Qwa," he said, hiding behind indignation. "You should have told me."

"It isn't a setup," said Lijou. "We're genuinely having a family day out with Sorli and Mayoi. I saw it as an opportunity to get all of us together in pleasant circumstances. You've enjoyed the walk, haven't you?"

He nodded, having to admit he had.

"Then come on," said Kha'Qwa, tugging him onward. "We've the whole day before us."

He didn't get the opportunity to feel awkward at being with two couples as Kha'Qwa immediately handed him Chay'Dah.

"I wouldn't trust him to just anyone," she said with a grin, "only another father."

Now four months old, he was a wriggler, trying instantly to squirm out of Kusac's grip. When he found he couldn't, he started playing catch-the-finger, managing to give a couple of nasty nips before settling down to chew on his thumb while pulling at his other fingers with both hands.

"Am I going to have to suffer similar indignities?" Sorli asked, gently patting Mayoi's hand.

"What's dignity?" asked Kusac wryly, wincing as one of Chay'Dah's teeth nicked him.

"Dignity goes out the door never to return once you're a parent," Lijou agreed with a rumble of amusement as he placed the insulated food bag in the shade of the bushes. "But you wouldn't have it any other way," he added, sprawling down on the grass and rescuing Kusac from his son. "I'm sure Kusac agrees with me."

He smiled, thinking of his daughter, forgetting all else for the moment. "She made us complete," he said. "She loves so unconditionally, it's humbling, the trust she puts in us."

"A spiritual experience," agreed Lijou, letting his son clamber over him in his attempts to catch his tail tip.

"If you males had to put up with being chewed by those sharp little teeth six or so times a day for three weeks, you'd not call it spiritual," said Kha'Qwa, rolling her eyes as she pulled a harness and play leash out of her bag for her son.

"Not really?" said Mayoi, sitting up, a concerned look on her face. "Oh dear, I hope I'm not going to regret this."

Kha'Qwa laughed and leaned forward to grab Chay'Dah. "You won't even notice it, trust me! You'll be so busy looking down at the tiny face of your newborn that you'll see nothing else."

Kusac watched in admiration as with a couple of deft twists, she had her son fastened safely in. He'd never found it that easy with Kashini. Putting him down on the ground between herself and Lijou, she gave her mate the other end of the leash.

"Now even you can't lose him!" she said.

"Lose him?" asked Sorli. "I'm intrigued."

"I didn't lose him!" exclaimed Lijou, bracing himself as the cub pounced on his tail, mouth wide and paws spread. "I only put him down on the chair in my office for a moment . . ."

"And expected him to stay there like one of your comp pads," added Kha'Qwa, pulling off her tunic and folding it up neatly. "Of course, he didn't. And we were expecting Dhaika from the Retreat over for a policy meeting so the table had all the pastries and so on set out for them."

Mayoi began to laugh even as Kusac began to grin. The picture Kha'Qwa was managing to project was amusing.

"What happened?" asked Mayoi.

"Dhaika was already late and I was in the middle of clearing up the mess when Kha'Qwa came in to ask where Chay'Dah was."

"They ate packaged cookies," said Kha'Qwa, "and Lijou got to sit up all night with Chay'Dah and his belly ache!"

"It was a bit more than a belly ache as I remember it," grum-

bled Lijou, with an embarrassed grin. "He was throwing up and
. . . other things as well! And I had an early class that morning."

Mayoi leaned weakly against Sorli, both of them unable to
stop laughing.

"Where was Chay'Dah?" he managed to ask, holding aching
sides.

"Under a chair stuffing himself," said Lijou. "Dhaika arrived
to find us pulling my office apart looking for him. Rhyaz had to
take him off to see Vartra's tomb for the next hour. The joys of
parenthood," he said, then yelped and grabbed his son to prevent
him from shredding his tail. "When do they get some idea of responsible behavior?" he demanded of Kusac.

"Not for a long time, I think," he laughed. "Kashini's about
nine months now, and when she met Prince Zsurtul, she tried to
eat his fingers. Wait till he starts talking. Then he'll embarrass
you even more!"

Kha'Qwa got to her feet, still grinning. "I get to have the first
swim on my own, so who's coming with me? Kusac?"

The heat, coupled with the swimming and the meal, had them
all lying dozing contentedly in the sun. Even Chay'Dah was
flopped out on his stomach fast asleep.

"Talk to me, Kusac," said Lijou, rolling over on his back until
he was close enough to speak quietly to him.

"Hmm?"

"You've been with us for three days now, and though you've
given me the medical information on what Kzizysus did, that's
all. What's troubling you? I can feel something's not right."

He lifted himself up, leaning his chin on his forearms. "Nothing's wrong, Lijou," he said. "I'm just tired, that's all. Not sleeping well."

"You and Kaid," Lijou said, shielding his eyes as he turned
to look at him. "So alike in some ways that you could almost be
brothers. He had periods where he was plagued by visions and
nightmares."

"I didn't say it was nightmares."

The priest rolled over onto his side, looking seriously at him.
"To have learned so painfully to live blinded and deafened by
your lack of Talent, and the loss of your Leska, only to have it
set aside now with this cure must be unimaginably difficult. It's
not something anyone can cope with alone, Kusac."

"It's not been easy," he admitted.

"And there's Kaid."

"What about Kaid?"

"I know the Gods guided you when you chose him as your Third."

"I think Kaid chose us," he murmured, eyes unfocusing as he seemed to step back in time until he could see Carrie and himself through the eyes of a small cub. He felt drawn to them, and when Kaid appeared, the presence of his adult self triggered the searing mental fusion of child and adult. Suddenly, he was filled with unconditional love for them.

"Kusac." His shoulder was being shaken, a damp cloth wiped across his face.

Unsteadily, he batted it away with his hand, finding himself looking up into Kha'Qwa's concerned face.

"Sorry," he said, trying to sit up. Other hands supported him as she sat back on her haunches, studying his face.

"He's fine," she said.

He smiled, then began to laugh gently.

"What is it?" asked Lijou, touching his neck to check his pulse.

Instantly Kusac's hand covered the priest's, holding it still. "I'm fine," he said, his grin gradually fading. "I just solved a puzzle, that's all." The vision had explained the bond between their Triad.

"You passed out," said Lijou as Kusac released his hand.

"A vision?" asked Sorli, sitting down beside him.

He shook his head. "An explanation."

"What did Annuur and Kzizysus really say was wrong, Kusac?" asked the Telepath Guild Master. "Why are you here at Stronghold, and how we can help you?"

He looked from one to the other. "I should have expected this," he said with a crooked Human smile. Then he told them.

"You were right to come back to us," said Lijou, reaching out to touch his shoulder compassionately. "Not many realize that helping our Brothers and Sisters come to terms with missions that go wrong is one of the major roles I perform at Stronghold."

"We may be able to force the memories to return, Kusac," began Sorli.

"No. They told me the memories must come to me. I'm going

to have to just sit it out and hope it happens sooner rather than later."

"There are ways we can teach you to cope with them when they do come, and with the nightmares," said Lijou.

"The nightmares are bearable if I use my psi damper at night," he said, resting his chin on his knees. "Somehow I was making the dreams real, like holo images that Kashini and Kaid could see. I couldn't stay at home because of that and . . ." He stopped abruptly, realizing he'd said more than he wanted.

"Because of Carrie and Kaid's Link," finished Lijou. "Surely Carrie's telepathic abilities are silent now because of her pregnancy."

"You do realize it's quite possible that once she's had the cub, your Leska Link to her could be reestablished, don't you?" said Sorli. "Or is that the problem?"

"How can I hope to have our Link back if it means Kaid losing what he shares with her?"

"Then leave it to the Gods to decide," said Lijou gently. "Meanwhile, we'll help you prepare to deal with the memories and with relearning how to use your Talent."

Anchorage, Zhal-Nylam, 6th day (September)

Alex sat slumped in the mess, her punishment detail finally over. She had barely enough energy left to pick up her mug of c'shar. Nezoa, the junior she'd been twinned with, sat opposite her, equally exhausted.

A shadow fell over them, then the chair next to her was pulled out and Rhyaz sat down.

"Excuse us, Nezoa," he said. "This is private."

"Aye, Commander," she said, getting to her feet and leaving.

"Have you eaten tonight?" he asked quietly.

"I'm too tired to eat."

"You should try," he said. "You need the food for energy."

"I'm too tired, Rhyaz—or is it still Commander?" she asked with a touch of her usual acerbity.

"Rhyaz. We're both off duty now. They've got rather a nice soup you could have."

She looked at him. "You don't give up, do you?"

"Not if I think the person has some saving graces, no."

"I'm too tired for this. Did you want something?"

"I came to tell you I was impressed with the way you've worked hard these last three days, harder than you did at Stronghold."

She looked at him, checking the set of his ears. "Praise from you? I think this is a first," she said.

"Perhaps because this is the first time you've actually put any effort into the work you've been assigned."

"It was interesting, most of the time. Studying at Stronghold is boring, especially when if I look for it, I can find the knowledge there already."

He sighed. "You can't rely on our Link for everything, Alex. Apart from anything else, even if you have my knowledge, you have to practice it to acquire the skills."

"I don't have to do it all day, every day! Give me something interesting to do as well."

"You enjoyed being a messenger?"

"Some of it. The juniors all gossip and speculate about what's going on." She shook her head. "They're way off! They think it's something to do with the Primes." She stifled a yawn and got to her feet. "I'm going to bed unless there's anything else you want."

"I came to walk you to our room."

She eyed him tiredly. "I'm sleeping down with the juniors, or had you forgotten that?"

"You can sleep there later if you want, Alex," he said. "You're probably too tired to notice, but our Link day is starting."

"Yeah, well I'm too tired for that. Do you want me to come with you?"

She watched him hesitate, weighing up the possible answers, and turned away. If he had to think about it, then he was only interested because it was their Link day.

"Actually, yes, I'm inviting you to my room," he said, getting up. "The dispenser there has protein drinks if you're too tired to eat."

She glanced at him again, surprised at the concern she was feeling from him. It was genuine concern. In her experience, most people were only interested in being seen to make the right noises, it didn't go deeper than that.

"Have you missed me, then?" she asked lightly as they began to walk out of the mess. She could see the few off duty personnel surreptitiously looking at them as they passed. Granted the Guild Master's presence alone was reason enough, but though everyone knew she was his Leska, few had actually seen them together. That much she had found out from Nezoa. She glanced at him, seeing the broad jawline and the tips of his wide pointed ears just showing above his shock of darker brown hair. Wherever he went, he'd draw admiring glances.

He turned his head to her and she knew he'd picked up on her thoughts. Before he could suppress it, she felt him wish she'd missed him, not the attention he brought her when they were together.

"I've been busy, Alex," he said, opening the door into the corridor for her. "I haven't really had time to worry about anything but the work we're doing here."

She could hear the tiredness in his voice now, and felt a pang of guilt that she'd asked him. It wasn't as if she didn't know how busy he'd been; she and Nezoa had been running around for him and Lyand after all.

"Being honest, I could do without losing tomorrow," he continued, "but asking you to let me work when I can during our Link day wouldn't be fair to you."

For the first time, she began looking through the memories she'd inherited from him, trying to find those that related to why they were here. Through his eyes, she saw the military vids he'd seen of the devastation of Khyaal and Szurtha, the liberation of Keiss and the questioning of the Valtegan on the *Khalossa*. Then from him, she picked up his worries on the setting up of the Watchers and the relative positions of the Valtegan planets in relation to Earth, Shola, and its remaining colony, and the two Touiban worlds. She suddenly realized just how much danger they faced, and it appalled her.

Too preoccupied to notice her thoughts, Rhyaz stopped and opened the door to his small lounge area, letting her enter first. Following her in, he unfastened his belt and stripped off his uniform jacket, throwing them both onto the nearest chair as he headed for the dispenser that had been set up on one of the drawer units. Pushing his thoughts of work aside, he concentrated on selecting a drink for her.

Now that he'd begun to relax, Alex could see how exhausted he was by the set of his ears and the way he was letting his tail hang down close to his legs.

"I want you to try a protein drink," he said, waiting for the tall glass to fill. "Our energy levels can affect each other, you know."

"I'd forgotten that," she said, glancing round as she ventured farther into the room. Apart from the clothes he'd just discarded, it was spotlessly tidy and clean.

"Not me, I'm afraid," said Rhyaz, picking up the glass and bringing it over to her. "Lyand sees it gets kept tidy. I don't have time to do it. Here, try this. Don't force yourself to drink it, but at least try it. Make yourself comfortable, I'm going to have a shower."

"Rhyaz," she said, reaching out to catch his arm as he turned away. The touch brought more information; he didn't like what he was doing to the Valtegan captives, the shower was as much to wash himself psychologically as physically. And the drink was for her, because she was tired, not just because her tiredness was Linked to his. With everything that was on his mind, he was still thinking of her.

"Can I help? I didn't realize how important what we're doing here is. I don't mind if you need to work tomorrow. I'm sure we can manage it somehow."

His expression changed briefly to one of surprise, then relaxed back into tiredness. "Using the last three or four hours of our day would help," he said. "That's more than enough, thank you, Alex."

"I did what you said, I looked at your memories," she said, taking a mouthful of the drink and finding it quite pleasant after all. "I saw how close to the Valtegan worlds we are. I know the danger we're in. I meant it, can I help?"

"You really want to help? Then please give me one less thing to worry about," he said, touching her face. "You. I'm not being unkind, just practical. If you want constant attention, take a lover, Alex, someone younger than me. Young males under thirty, ideally one around twenty, are focused on finding a mate. One of them would give you all the attention you want. You're entitled to have a lover, just as I am. Being Leskas doesn't mean we have an exclusive relationship. And try to find something in the Brotherhood that you want to do so I can get on with the job of running it." He turned away from her and went into the bathing room, closing the door quietly behind him.

She stood there, looking at the door, too stunned to react. The light rapport he'd allowed her was gone now, closed off as firmly as the bathing room door had been. Finishing the drink, she returned the glass to the recycler at the side of the dispensing unit and began to take off her own jacket, thinking through what he'd said. It hurt that he saw her as shallow, but then she supposed she could see why. She hadn't exactly made an effort to dispel that impression.

There must be something she could do to convince him that this time she was serious. His memories scared her. In coming to Shola, she and Kai were in far more danger from the Valtegans than they'd been on Earth. Why hadn't she thought it through properly before they'd sneaked onto the merchant ship? On Earth, the Valtegans were a distant threat, no more. Not here. Rhyaz was one of the few leaders who stood between them and certain death. And she was disrupting his life so much it was affecting his work.

Tears started to her eyes and she began to cry. She didn't want constant attention, all she wanted was someone to care about her and let her lead her own life. Rhyaz had offered her all those, and a fresh start, and she'd messed it up by not taking him seriously.

Wrenching the bathing room door open, she ran inside, flinging her arms around him as he stood in the shower.

"I don't want anyone else," she sobbed, plastering herself to his wet body. "I want you for yourself, not because of who you are!"

Rhyaz staggered back, grabbing for her as he tried to keep his balance. "Alex! Vartra's bones, you nearly had us both cracking our skulls on the tiles!"

Shoulders heaving, she clung to him, winding her hands in his slick pelt when he tried to break free. Abruptly, the jets of water stopped.

"Alex," he said, giving her a shake. Then he felt her terror at the images she'd seen. This was something neither he nor Lijou had even considered, and they should have. "It's all right, Alex," he said more gently, putting an arm around her and stroking her wet hair. "The danger is there, yes, but not imminent. The Valtegans don't know we exist. They think they killed us all when they destroyed our two colonies. They're at war with their own kind right now, they aren't interested in us."

"I should have looked at your memories like you said, learned about you and what you're doing. I didn't mean to kill the Valtegan prisoner!"

"You didn't," he said, then when she looked up at him, blinking the water from her eyes, "We found out it was the chemicals. I'd forgotten just how much I've seen and done that you shouldn't be aware of, Alex. You're too young to be exposed to all my experiences. All I wanted you to do was to understand the importance of the Brotherhood and the work I do and not— behave like the kid you are," he sighed, holding her close, realizing that despite their caution, he'd still expected too much of her.

"I really want to help, and to understand you and what you're doing," she said earnestly.

"I know your intentions are good, but you forget them, Alex. You can't help it. We get the odd youngling like you who's not grown up with the discipline of the Warrior or Telepath Guilds before they come to us. It takes them a long time to settle in. They have to grow up fast to do it, and I don't know that you could do that. Or that I'd want you to," he added truthfully.

"You're afraid I'm like Mara was."

Reaching behind him, he unfastened her hands and gently propelled her out of the shower cubicle. "Mara's doing well," he said, feeling guilty that she'd picked up on that. "She has a Human Leska now, they're the only pair we have. The problem wasn't really her, it was Zhyaf. He was too staid for her, couldn't adjust to having a young Leska."

"And I'm younger than Mara, that's what worries you," she said, shivering now as the wet clothes drew the heat from her body.

"I'm not Zhyaf, Alex," he said firmly. "If you would only make an effort to work with me, we wouldn't have a problem."

"I just said I would. I can do what I've been doing with Nezoa. Lyand said we were helping you both."

"It's a possibility, of course," he said, the cold she was feeling beginning to affect him. "But now isn't the time to talk about it. You need to get out of those wet clothes."

Miserably, she nodded, hands fumbling with the fatigues as she tried to stop shivering.

He sighed and began to help her. What harm would it do to tell her he cared about her? She probably knew it anyway. "All right, yes, I did miss you," he admitted. "I don't know why, but I did."

"I do want you for yourself, Rhyaz," she said, concentrating on what his hands were doing. "Sure, I like it that folk look up to you because of who you are, and are envious of me, but is that so wrong? You used me to make Raiban mad when we were at Chagda Station."

"You're too observant," he growled, struggling with her clothes and giving up. "And this has too many buttons. When we get back home, I'm getting you a more practical uniform made, a Sholan one, with sealing strips."

Frustrated, he tugged sharply at the fastenings, sending the remaining buttons skittering across the bathing room floor. "Till then, you can borrow some Juniors tunics and enjoy showing your legs off," he continued, peeling off her soaking garments. Gathering her close, he drew her back into the shower with him and turned the hot water on again.

"My bed was empty without you," he said, catching her earlobe gently with his teeth. "Was yours?"

"Yes. I missed you, Rhyaz."

Prime world, the same day

"Majesty," said Khayikule patiently, "the reason there was no attempt on your life is precisely because General Kezule foiled it by attacking their headquarters!"

"Very convenient. And the reason there's no evidence is because, according to you, he blew the place up!" said Counselor Q'iou sarcastically.

"We can only take the facts into consideration," said Counselor Chysho slowly. "And the facts we have are that Science Director Zhayan accuses the late Naval Director Zsiyuk of attempting to murder him by sending him an explosive parcel. And that Treasury Director Schoudu was injured during an attack on his life and he lays the blame at the door of the same person, who, incidentally was found dead at the site of the claimed secret establishment. Finally, the General has left Prime space, taking a valuable ship and assorted personnel with him. It bears all the signs of a plot."

"We know all that," said Q'iou testily. "What we don't know

is how loyal these offspring of the General are! They claim to have stopped a coup, but this could be part of an elaborate plan of their own to put Kezule on the throne!"

"Captain Khayikule is here and he's sworn allegiance to you, Majesty," said Shyadd. "Our orbiting platform is capable of performing a scan that will reveal what's below the ruins of the Directorate headquarters, and Khayikule knows that. I suggest we have this done."

Emperor Cheu'ko'h stirred, looking over at the carmine-robed priest that sat to one side of the conference table. "M'zikk, have your Enforcers question Schoudu and Zhayan but warn them I want no forced confessions, I want the truth. In the meantime, Shyadd, order the scan of the ruined animal breeding center. If secret laboratories existed there, they will show up and the guilt of the two Directors will be confirmed."

"What about the General?" exclaimed Q'iou. "You can't leave him out there somewhere with his own private army!"

"He only took fourteen of his sons and two of his daughters, Majesty," said Shyadd. "And the fourteen troublesome M'zullians. The rest were friends of Doctor Zayshul. Hardly a personal army. I'd be inclined to believe the reasons the General gave. Namely, if he remained here, he was a focus for discontented citizens to rally round. I think we should be trying to find Doctor K'hedduk. As the leader of this group, he is the most dangerous one. If he remains free, then he could well try again."

Emperor Cheu'ko'h picked up the letter that had been left for him by General Kezule and read through it again, especially the portion offering him advice about his counselors. *You can't rule by committee, Majesty. Have one trusted adviser and fire the others—they're too conservative for the changing times in which you now live. And learn to trust your own judgment more.*

He'd rather liked the General. A powerful and charismatic male, Kezule had managed not to make him feel intimidated or threatened by his presence. And unlike many of the courtiers that surrounded him, he hadn't wanted to make use of their connection, except in one thing. His choice of wife. Kezule had offered him a bargain—he, the Emperor, had actually haggled with one of his subjects—and he'd quite enjoyed the novelty. And Kezule had kept his word. Standing before him was Kezule's son, the new Captain of his Palace Guard, a guard that the General had promised would be loyal to him alone.

And live in changing times they did, which Shyadd, the replacement for the unlamented Chy'qui, seemed to be the only
one to appreciate. His son Zsurtul was on the Sholan world, training with those who'd proved to be their deadliest enemies in the
past, at the General's suggestion. Bridges were finally being built
with the Sholans. An adviser like him was too valuable to let go.

Empress Zsh'eungee leaned toward him. "Listen to Shyadd,"
she said quietly. "He's the only one speaking sense. I told you,
Kezule spoke to me in the gardens about the danger from the
M'zullian Warriors a month ago, before Director Zsoyshuu told
us. I trust him, and his wife."

He looked at her, seeing in her eyes a glow that reminded him
of their early years together, before the loss of children had taken
her youth. That look that had been there since Kezule's wife had
visited her only four days ago.

Cheu'ko'h folded the letter and put it down on the table in
front of him. "I have spoken, let it be done," he said. "I disagree
with General Kezule's concern that he could be a focus for the
discontented. I wish him found and brought back to K'oish'ik.
His talents are too valuable to be lost to us. Captain Khayikule,
you will assume the position the General held, that of commander
of the Palace Guard, with the rank of General. I wish this K'hedduk found. I am also raising Councillor Shyadd to the new rank
of Prime Counselor. Henceforth, only he will attend me at the
daily briefings unless I specify otherwise. You will attend us in
our office in fifteen minutes, Prime Counselor Shyadd. This council is dismissed."

He rose, holding out his hand to his wife, pleased that his decisions would evoke a furor among his councillors. General
Kezule was right. It was time he did more than just listen to
them.

It had taken him a whole day, but when he pushed the final
chunks of masonry aside and the night air hit his sweating face
and cooled his aching lungs, K'hedduk finally rested. He tried to
stifle his coughs, but the fine dust caused by the explosions was
cloying, coating not only him, but the inner surfaces of his nose
and mouth. He rubbed his hands in the damp grass, using the

moisture to scrub at his face. It gave him some relief, turning the dust into streaks of mud, but at least he wasn't breathing it in any longer. Pushing his briefcase through the gap, he hauled himself out of the ruined building.

That he'd survived at all was a miracle. After pushing Zsiyuk into the path of the attackers, he'd turned and raced for the exit, throwing himself down the stairs toward the lower level where the explosion had been. There he'd scrabbled among the still settling rubble, managing to burrow a cavity large enough to conceal himself in until Kezule's soldiers had detonated the final charge.

While he'd hidden there, he'd faced not only discovery from them, but also from his own guards and staff trapped below. He'd heard them pulling at the rubble almost as soon as he'd taken up his hiding place. They were within feet of him when Kezule had left. Taking ex-Directorate employees with him was not part of his escape plan.

They had made the mistake he'd narrowly avoided himself. They'd gone back into the main corridor, heading for the elevator in the hope they could get out that way. Gunfire, followed by screams of pain and raised voices, had ended with another explosion, then silence. One of the voices had been Sholan. Kezule must have released and armed the male in the lab. He shuddered at the memory of how nearly he'd fallen into that trap. He had a score to settle with Kezule.

K'hedduk started walking. Dawn wasn't far off. It wouldn't be long before the Palace Guard and the Enforcers returned to start excavating the ruins. Checking the time, he calculated how long it would take him to reach his destination, allowing himself time to change into the coveralls in his briefcase. He'd be late, but only by a small margin. It was regrettable, he didn't like turning up late for his shift, the Palace chef had a foul temper.

the *Couana*, Zhal-S'Asha, 22nd day (October)

"You look preoccupied," said Banner, strolling over to his table in the mess and sitting down. "Worried about the briefing?"

"No. I know how that's going to go. More memories," he said.

"What's it this time?"

"Zsurtul's visit to the estate."

Banner frowned. "But that went well."

"On the surface, perhaps it seemed so. I'd gone home for a couple of days and they suddenly sprang the news of his visit on me."

Valsgarth Estate, Zhal-Nylam, 14th day (September)

"I'm not happy about Zsurtul coming here," he said, sitting patiently on the sofa as Carrie lifted a hank of his hair and began to run the brush through it. "His presence will upset too many people, me included."

"Your hair is really long now. I can see the blue sheen in it."

"Don't change the subject. Why do you want to invite him here?"

"He entertained us and I said we'd return the favor," she said patiently, moving the length of his hair aside to brush the shorter ones that grew down the sides of his neck. "Would you have us be less hospitable than him?"

"I can see Kusac's point," said Kaid, coming over with a drink for each of them. He put theirs on the low table beside them. "It might be better to leave it for a week or two." Going over to an easy chair he sat down, sipping the cold drink.

"That's too near my due date," she said. "Anyway, I've already set it for tomorrow. Your parents think it's a great idea. They're coming too."

He stiffened. "You did what?" he asked quietly.

"Kusac . . ." began Kaid.

"No. I want to hear what Carrie has to say." He could feel his hair and pelt begin to lift.

The brush stopped moving. "You told us Annuur and Kzizysus said you had to come to terms with what happened to you. The meal with Zsurtul went so well that I thought this would be an ideal follow-up. Surely the more you see of them in normal nonthreatening circumstances, the easier it'll be for you to get used to them."

"I don't want to get used to them!" he said angrily, turning round to look at her. "You know how I feel about all Valtegans, Carrie. In the God's name, they tortured your twin to death—and nearly killed you! Have you forgotten so quickly why our Link formed?" His torc began to vibrate gently, warningly, against his neck. Too angry to wonder why, he eased it away from his throat with one hand.

"Of course I haven't," she said, sitting down on the sofa beside him. She put her hand on his knee but he pushed it away.

"I won't have a Valtegan on my estate. You'd no right to make that decision without consulting me!"

"I knew what you'd say and thought . . ."

"Thought what I felt didn't matter," he said, releasing his torc before getting up and moving away from her. "They set my teeth on edge, Carrie. I don't like them near me. Get on the comm and cancel it now."

"I can't, not with your father coming too," she said quietly. "It'll look like an official snub."

"And entertaining him will look like I'm endorsing their presence here and on Shola! You should have thought this through properly—spoken to me!—before arranging this. Call my father, get him to find you a way out of this."

"I think you're getting things out of proportion, Kusac," she said. "The Primes are totally different from the Valtegans. Yes, all three of us suffered because of Chy'qui's experiments, but he's dead, it's over, and most importantly you've got your Talent back."

"Have I?" He swung round angrily on her, feeling a jolt of pain surge down his spine. He gasped, grabbing hold of the chair back beside him for support, but the pain was short-lived.

"What is it?" asked Kaid, instantly on his feet in concern. "I felt that!"

"It's nothing. Leave me be," he said, waving him away. "I have a form of empathy, but that's all. I can't communicate with you or anyone! Their treatment wasn't as effective as they said. I can't forget or forgive what happened to me on the Prime ship, and they were directly responsible for it. How could they claim we were supposed to be guests and yet hold us captive the way they did? There's no way the Sholan Forces would have allowed

Chy'qui the kind of access he had to us for his experiments! They failed to protect us. I won't have him here, Carrie!"

"That pain should be gone," said Kaid. "If you've got it back then something's wrong. You need to see Kzizysus."

"No, I've had enough of doctors to last a lifetime!" Then he stopped. "I'll see him if you cancel this on the grounds I'm ill."

"No," said Kaid before Carrie could speak. "If you want to gamble with your health, then do so, it's your right, but the visit goes ahead as planned. Primes on Shola are a fact of life now, Kusac. You have to learn to live with it, we all have to."

"Then I won't be here," he snarled, stalking out of the den into the garden. "Nor will my daughter!"

"Kusac!" Carrie called out after him.

"Let him walk off his anger, Carrie," said Kaid, calling Banner on his wrist comm.

"I see him," said Banner's distant voice.

"How's he been at Stronghold?"

"Patchy. He seemed to settle in, went for a picnic with Father Lijou and his mate, and came back to start specialized training with them. He's gotten increasingly short-tempered over the last few days, though. If I'd have to guess, I'd say it isn't working out as easily as he'd thought it would."

"Any of the pain attacks?"

"Not that I know of. You said they were over."

"We thought they were. He just had a minor one."

"I'll watch for them now. He's on his way to the village from the look of it. Gotta go."

The link went dead.

"What do we do?" asked Carrie. "I didn't think he'd react this badly. I really thought that with him getting back his Talent, he'd be more willing to let the past go. Only it doesn't seem to be working out like that," she sighed, leaning forward slightly to ease her back.

"I did say I thought it was a little too soon," he said, going over to her and starting to rub her lower back gently. "If he doesn't go to see Kzizysus, then I'll haul him bodily there myself. I want to know what's happening even if he doesn't. As for tomorrow, leave it as it is but talk to Konis and Rhyasha. Kusac can stay away if he wishes, but I have a feeling Kashini won't want to, and if she's where Zsurtul is, take my word for it, he'll be there." He stopped, leaning over her shoulder slightly. "I hate to say this, but I don't remember you being this large last time, Carrie."

"Don't start! I'm not going through an accelerated pregnancy this time, Kaid! I'm fine. Second cubs are often bigger."

the *Couana*, Zhal-S'Asha, 22nd day (October)

"I know you went to the Cabbarrans' vehicle," said Banner. "What did they say?"

"Not a lot," said Kusac, shifting his position on the hard mess seat. He picked up his coffee. "Only that nothing was wrong, that it was just taking me longer than they thought to come to terms with the past." He remembered the visit now; there had been a surreal quality to it that even its memory evoked. He let it play through in his mind, saying nothing to Banner this time.

Valsgarth Estate, Zhal-Nylam, 14th day (September)

Surrounded by crates, Naacha was waiting for him just inside the air lock of their shuttle. He reared up on his haunches, folding his short forelimbs across his chest. Sunlight coming through the entrance fell on him, turning the swirling blue tattoos on the alien's face almost luminous.

He stopped, eyeing the Cabbaran warily, his anger suddenly dissipated. A vague, half-remembered memory of Naacha warned him to tread carefully.

"The pain came back," he said in answer to the question he knew the other was asking. "I thought I was healed."

Rapid quadrupedal footsteps sounded from inside and Annuur appeared, nosing his way past Naacha. "What matter, Kusac? Why here?" he asked, sitting down.

"I told him. Why doesn't he answer me?" he said, unable to look away from the swirling tattoos. He could swear they were actually moving.

"Naacha talk rarely," said Annuur, glancing obliquely at his crewmate. "Very spiritual, like your priests."

He was aware of what Annuur said, but his whole attention was focused on the patterns as they began to grow larger, gradually filling not only his field of view, but his mind as well.

"Not here, Naacha! Too visible he be here!" he heard Annuur say as if from a great distance. "Bring him inside! Sokarr, Lweeu, get crates moved immediately!"

"Must keep calm as possible while your system adjusts, so collar still warns when not. Is temporary," Annuur was saying.

He nodded his head, then blinked, slightly surprised to find himself sitting with Annuur on a pile of deep cushions in the Cabarrans' lounge.

"No reason for pain, must be psychological. Anticipating it, you feel it. Again remedy with you."

"Makes sense," he heard himself say.

"Take another drink, Kusac. Still are swaying a little. Sun very strong today. Lucky we got you in here before you passed out."

He'd passed out? Confused, he finished the drink he found in his hand, suddenly anxious to leave.

"When your system settles, then nightmares stop. Bits of memories will become memories you can look at and understand. Then you let go of them. When this done, Talent return. Is as we said before. Nothing changed."

"Thank you, Annuur," he said, looking around for a place to put the glass.

Annuur reached out his broad four-fingered hand and took it from him. "You find own way out? Too hot for me today in corridors."

"Yes, of course." He remembered the blue-tattooed Cabbarran. "Where's Naacha?"

"Naacha working in lab, that why he first to hear you arrive."

He nodded, and took his leave, hesitating before stepping out onto the landing pad. There was something not quite right, something he was missing, but he was damned if he knew what it was. Shaking his head, he went down the ramp.

the *Couana*, Zhal-S'Asha, 22nd day (October)

"What changed your mind about Prince Zsurtul?"

"Kashini. She refused to come with me to Vanna's. There was no way I was leaving my daughter alone."

"She had her mother and Kaid," said Banner reasonably.

"You've never shared a cub, have you?" he said with a smile. "She's my flesh and blood."

His mind, however, was still on that visit to Annuur—or was it Naacha? He was the spiritual one of the four, *Like your priests,* the Cabbarran had said. Their priests were all telepaths. Was that why Naacha's tattoos had fascinated him? Were they designed to make the viewer susceptible to mental manipulation? Was that why he'd passed out? And the way all his memories had suddenly started to fuse together was another mystery. Was it waiting for Carrie's and Kaid's daughter to be born that had caused it?

They'd certainly started returning at a convenient time, just before setting out on a mission where he'd need his Talents, and when everyone still believed he had none. More questions, and not one answer.

Valsgarth Estate, Zhal-Nylam, 14th day (September)

"No. 'Shini stay," she said firmly, reinforcing it mentally.

"We're going to Aunt Vanna's. You'll have Marak to play with," he said, tugging on her hand.

"No. Stay."

He bent down to pick her up.

"No! Stay!" she shrieked, anchoring the claws on her toes into the carpet and going limp in his grasp.

"What're you feeding her these days, Carrie?" he asked, bending down to unlatch her feet and scoop her up into his arms. "She weighs a ton."

"She doesn't want to go," said Carrie calmly, leaning on the end of the cot watching him.

"Stay! Not go Aunt Vanna's! Stay party!" she screeched, her body galvanizing into life as she began to squirm and kick.

"Stop it, Kashini," he said firmly, turning her around so she was kicking thin air. "We're going and that's that."

The shrieks became louder, peal after peal of them till he flattened his ears to his skull trying to close out the noise. She brought her feet up, scrabbling and clawing with them and her hands at his arms. Then she started sending the screams mentally.

The noise brought Kaid out of his room to see what was going on.

Grim-faced, he left the nursery and began walking along the corridor. He got halfway to the stairs before she bit him.

His yowl of rage could be heard as far as her shrieks. Taking advantage of the moment, she slipped from his grasp, hitting the floor running. She didn't stop till she'd reached her mother and was hiding behind her.

Sucking his bitten forearm, he glowered at Carrie. "You put her up to this, didn't you?"

"Me? No. I wouldn't do that, Kusac, no matter how much I disagreed with you," she said, trying not to wince as Kashini's needle-sharp little claws dug into her leg. "Kashini is just as strong-willed as you, and as able to make up her own mind."

He stared at her peeping round at him from behind Carrie's leg, an anxious expression on her small face.

"'Shini want stay," she said, regarding him with enormous damp eyes, her bottom lip trembling.

Beaten, he sighed and examined his arm. It had only been a token bite, but her teeth had broken the skin. He glowered over at Kaid who was trying extremely hard not to grin.

Carrie bent down and picked her up. "You bit Daddy," she said sternly, looking her in the eyes. "That hurt him and was very naughty. You'll apologize at once, then you'll go quietly with Daddy to Aunt Vanna's." She put her down again and gave her a gentle push toward him.

Kashini resisted, looking at her mother before looking up at him. "Want stay," she whimpered, ears flattened and tears filling the amber eyes as she pulled at the bow on her tabard belt. Her small tail hung dejectedly to the ground. She hiccuped.

"All right," he sighed, bending down and cuffing her lightly on the side of the head. "We'll stay, but don't you ever bite me again, or next time you'll be a sorry cub!"

"'ank you Da-Da!" she said, flinging herself at him and scrambling up his leg and chest to hug him. "Sorry hurt Da-Da. Not do 'gain."

"You'd better get changed, then," said Carrie, turning back to the nursery. "If you come in here first, I'll put some antiseptic on that bite."

He could hear the laughter in her voice and decided to ignore it and keep what little shreds of dignity he had left.

the *Couana*, Zhal-S'Asha, 22nd day (October)

Banner didn't bother hiding his amusement. When he'd stopped laughing, he said, "I'm sorry I missed all this! Go on. What happened next?"

"You know, you were there at the parking area along with all the others," he said.

"But I only know it from my perspective. I want to know what went on behind the scenes."

"Getting to be quite the voyeur, aren't you?" he said, lifting an eye ridge humorously.

Valsgarth Estate, evening, Zhal-Nylam, 14th day (September)

He stood beside Carrie, holding Kashini's hand, watching Prince Zsurtul's aircar approach. As it drew closer, he could see it was the Prince's own aircar, the exterior resplendent in the blues, reds, and golds of the Prime royal family. On its side it bore the emblem Zsurtul wore tattooed on his chest—an open eggshell hatching a fire of light, the symbol of the Enlightened One.

Already his hair had risen to the point where his ears were almost invisible. It framed his face like a U'Churian mane, cascading down his shoulders and back for several inches. He resented Zsurtul's presence, and was still angry with Carrie for forcing this onto him.

Like Kaid, he'd put on his black Brotherhood tunic, his belt knife prominent since, this being a peaceful visit, he couldn't justify wearing his gun.

As the vehicle hovered prior to landing, Carrie moved closer to him.

"Look, I'm sorry, Kusac," she said, leaning against him and stroking his cheek. "I really did think this would be for the best. The Prince is only a youngling, probably about Kitra's age in our terms. What possible threat can he be to you or any of us?"

Her scent, mingled with Sashti's oils, filled his nostrils and he found himself leaning into her caress as he put his free arm round her. He understood the very real concern for him that had prompted her to arrange this visit. Maybe she was right. What threat could Zsurtul pose to them, one youth alone among so many of his Clan?

"He'll be Emperor one day."

"And how we treat him here today will affect his attitude to us in the future. Even more reason for him to visit us, and you to welcome him with at least a semblance of goodwill."

"I'll do it this time, but this is a one-time event. Don't put me in this position again, Carrie."

She said nothing, content just to rest her head on his shoulder, and he to let her, knowing that this time he was there to protect her and his daughter. Gradually, his hair and pelt began to settle around his shoulders.

The engines changed pitch and he turned back to watch the vehicle drop gently to the ground.

"Shall I greet him for us?" asked Kaid.

He nodded briefly, grateful to his friend for sparing him that duty, suddenly aware of the crowd of Sholans and their alien friends that was gathering to watch at a respectful distance. He felt torn in two directions as one part of his mind asked him what was one alien more among so many, while the other, more primitive part attempted to flex his claws.

The door opened and Zsurtul stepped out, resplendent in his court finery. It shocked him, making Zsurtul appear at once more alien, yet less like any Valtegan or Prime he'd ever seen.

"Think of Kitra, dressing up to impress Dzaka in their early days," whispered Carrie as Kaid moved forward to greet him.

the *Couana*, Zhal-S'Asha, 22nd day (October)

"But the meal itself went well, didn't it?"

"As far as Zsurtul was concerned," he agreed. "Though I did leave them to it as soon as Kashini started to get sleepy."

"Is meeting with Kezule going to be a problem?" Banner asked after a short pause. "I knew the visit annoyed you because the next morning you left without warning for Stronghold."

"Not for me," he said, picking up his mug.

"How long till the briefing?" asked Banner, changing the topic.

He checked his wrist comm. "We leave jump in about six hours. With another half day to slow down to reach the rendezvous point, I'm scheduling the briefing for fifteen hours from now."

"Cutting it fine, aren't you?"

"I don't think so. Leaves us two hours for final preparations."

"You're the Captain," said Banner, getting up.

Stronghold, Zhal-Nylam, 15th day (September)

"Lijou, Kusac's on his way back to you and he won't reply to my calls. I got up this morning and he'd gone!"

"Calm down, Carrie," said Lijou soothingly, seeing her red, swollen eyes and damp face. "Tell me what happened from the start."

"I invited Zsurtul over for a meal yesterday and we fell out over it, but I thought he'd gotten over it. He says he feels threatened by him, insists on calling him a Valtegan. I thought having Zsurtul over would help since when we went to him for a meal, it seemed to go well. But it didn't and now he's gone and he won't talk to me! And Banner's not with him." Tears welled up again and she scrubbed her hand over her face in a determined effort to stop them.

"Is Kaid there? What does he say?" asked Lijou, knowing

Carrie was too distressed to give an objective view of what had happened.

"Yes, he's here, but Kusac's switched off his wrist comm and the aircar comm!"

"In that case, I'm afraid you'll have to wait till he gets here, my dear. I'll talk to him when he arrives and call you back. Meanwhile, can I speak to Kaid?"

Kaid's face replaced hers and Lijou instantly revised his opinion of a storm over nothing.

"We didn't expect him to leave before morning, Lijou. He did get extremely worked up about Zsurtul's visit earlier but seemed to calm down during the evening. His attitude to the Primes is bad, very bad."

"Primes as in Zsurtul, or the M'zullians?"

Kaid's ears flicked back. "He doesn't like the M'zullians, but Zsurtul seems to upset him more, now you come to mention it. He knows what we owe the Prince, but it doesn't seem to make a difference."

"How does Zsurtul take this? Is he aware of it?"

"Must be. The youngling can be hard to read at times, however he's been very understanding over the odd incident."

"I wonder if the Prince knows more than he's telling us. Could there be something about him that's setting Kusac off?"

"His scent, you mean? Kusac can certainly tell Zsurtul from the M'zullians by scent, we can't. According to him we're supposed to smell like the officer caste to the M'zullians, that's why they don't have problems with us. They're more Valtegan than Prime, though."

"Leave that for now. You can always ask Zsurtul if you get a chance, though don't make an issue out of it. I'll have a word with Kusac when he arrives here and get back to you. Meanwhile, be patient with Carrie for the next few weeks. It might feel like you're living on the edge of a volcano now and then, but it's as bad for her, if not worse. I take it Banner is on his way here."

"You sound like you're speaking from experience," Kaid said with a wry smile. "Yes, Banner took off after him. By the way, Kusac had a pain episode while he was here and went to see Annuur about it. He told us Annuur says his Talent is restricted to empathy for now. Is that right?"

"Essentially," said Lijou. "Kha'Qwa and I have been teaching him various meditation skills to help him calm himself and get a peaceful night's sleep. What else did Annuur say?"

"Kusac wouldn't tell us. I had to go ask Annuur myself. Apparently the pain is psychological—he expects it so it's there. As for the rest, his system is still adjusting to the treatment. When it does, then the fragments of memories causing nightmares will come together and he'll be able to deal with them. Sounds a lot like he's suffering from a form of partial amnesia."

"Nothing new, then. That's good at least. Leave it with me, Kaid. I'll get back to you when I can."

"I appreciate it, Lijou. I know you're busy right now. Tirak tells me they move out tomorrow for Anchorage."

"Does he? Then he must be getting one of the new ships. I know we took delivery of the first six scouters a week ago. Rhyaz stayed on at Anchorage to see the trials. They went well, he said. Our Watchers will be up and running within the next two weeks. We're moving the last of our Brothers and Sisters up to Haven today. Stronghold will soon seem very empty with only us and the juniors here."

"You'll be handling the six monthly training rotations, though."

Lijou looked startled, knowing Kaid was referring to the Sleepers. "You're remarkably well informed," he said. "As usual."

Kaid shrugged. "You know me. Kzizysus has asked to stay on with us when Annuur and his sept leave tomorrow with Tirak. He's going to be working with the Telepath Guild hospital for the next few months so he'll be here if we need him for Kusac."

"Good. I'd hate to be without any support for him if we need it. Oh, before I go, I meant to tell you. One of our Brothers died in fight at a Warrior Guildhouse in Shanagi a couple of days ago."

"Oh? Not our old friends Jebousa and Vikkul?"

"The very same. Seems Vikkul turned on Jebousa with a knife. He was killed and Jebousa's been hospitalized. He's due back here in a few days."

"A falling out of villains. I don't think he'll be mourned, Lijou."

"I thought I should tell you."

"Thank you. We'll hear from you later, then."

N'zishok, the same day

Shaidan was awake and sitting up in his bed reading when Kezule entered the sick bay. This was the first time he'd visited him when he was awake. His other visits had been conducted in the dead of night when he'd been able to sit at the bedside and study him. The rounded childish features already had an unmistakable look of his father about him, and some indefinable quality of his Human mother. He found it difficult to comprehend that this child was only two years younger than his sons and daughters yet was still so very much a child.

The Sholans obviously invested far more time in raising their young, but then they lacked the ability to pass on memories from generation to generation. He suddenly thought of his own child safe in its shell in the heated incubator. How could it know his past with no drones for him to give his memories to? Only drones could secrete the memory-carrying chemicals—but drones no longer existed as a separate caste. And did he want this first real child of his to know all he'd been through, inherit a knowledge of a faded Empire that was no longer relevant? Perhaps the lack of drones was a good way to ensure a new start for his people, to forget empires and God-Kings who were no more godlike than he was.

He pushed his introspective mood aside and stepped into the small ward. Now it was time to meet the person behind the child's sleeping face.

Immediately Shaidan saw him, he closed the book.

Kezule pulled a chair up to the bedside and sat down. "You're Shaidan," he said. "Do you know who I am?"

"The General," he said. "You rescued us from the place we were in."

"Do you know why you needed rescuing?"

He frowned, eye ridges meeting, ears tilting back slightly as he considered the question carefully. "Aunt said they were unpleasant people who intended to harm us."

"They intended to use you for tests to see how your mental abilities worked," he said, pleased to see Zayshul had managed to train him to make eye contact.

"Do you like the book?" he asked when the cub said nothing more.

"Yes, General."

Again Kezule waited, but Shaidan remained silent. He was answering only what he was asked. Good.

"In a few days, you'll be leaving here and coming to stay in our quarters. Your injuries will be painful for some time yet so the doctor wants to look after you herself."

"Yes, General," he said quietly.

"Is there anything you'd like to know?"

"No, General. I'm a vassal, I do what I'm told. Curiosity is not acceptable."

"Who told you that?"

For a moment, Shaidan looked confused. "The Seniormosts where we lived until you came for us."

"They were right. You'll be told what you need to know, Shaidan," he said, getting up and putting the chair back against the wall. "When you talk to anyone but the doctor or me, you must remember your training and keep your eyes on the ground. Vassals may not look others in the eyes. Since you now belong to me and the doctor, it is permissible for you to do it with us unless told otherwise. Do you understand?"

"Yes, General."

"Goodnight, Shaidan."

"Goodnight, General."

Zayshul was at the other end of her sick bay, working. "You were right about Shaidan," she said, studying the images on the monitor. "He is Carrie's and Kusac's son. Those data cards Zhalmo took from the Directorate lab had all the breeding information on the cubs. She said she didn't see any stasis storage area in the lab, did you? Or it could have been in the stasis room itself."

"No, why?"

"Because going from what's here, Chy'qui accelerated the females' egg development with hormones and was able to take five from each of them. He only used eight of the ten. Mind you, he'd have to leave one for Carrie to become pregnant," she mused, before looking up at him. "He could have one more egg and all the males' samples."

"The team at the top of the exit didn't see anyone trying to get out. I think we got him, Zayshul."

"He's slippery, that one. I wouldn't depend on it. He posed as Chy'qui's steward and when he died, I found he'd been reassigned to me. I remember him trying to sniff round my lab on the *Kz'adul*. You told Khayikule that you'd lost him."

"I was being cautious," he said. "Who do the other cubs belong to?"

"Dhyshac is Kaid's and Kate's, Gaylla is Kate's and Taynar's—Chy'qui aborted her mother's existing embryo to study it in order to get the growth tank medium right. I think Gaylla's slow because her mother wasn't allowed time to recover from the aborted fetus before being forced to produce more eggs. Vazih is Rezac's and Kate's, and Zsaya is Carrie's and Rezac's."

"Kaid was the third one who brought me to this time," he said. "Point this child out to me."

"You're not thinking of keeping two of them, are you? Because I'll tell you . . ."

"No, only Shaidan."

"Good. I've prepared sleep tapes for them, Kezule, to get rid of K'hedduk's programming. They can't go back to their families thinking they're slaves to the Prime Empire. That could really harm our treaty with the Sholans."

"Use them on all but Shaidan. I want him left as he is."

"What? Kezule, that child has done nothing to you! Why in the name of the God-Kings do you want him to behave like a slave!"

"Not for me. I want his father to see it."

"I don't understand you. You want Kusac's help yet you're willing to antagonize him by dangling his son in front of him as a slave."

"As he is, Shaidan asks no questions, he obeys me instantly. That's what I want, the obedience and the lack of curiosity. Just bear with me, Zayshul, I know what I'm doing." He got to his feet. "We'll reach our destination in a few hours. Finish what you're doing and come back to our quarters. I want you to get some sleep. We'll all have more than enough to do once we arrive at the outpost."

CHAPTER 18

"Fan out," ordered Kezule, gesturing to the far side of the landing bay in the heart of the asteroid called Kij'ik.

The light beams set on their helmets pierced the darkness, as, guns powered and ready, they split into two flanks, each moving to one side. Kezule led the right flank while M'zynal, the weapons officer, led the left.

Movement was easy in the powered armor, and the visibility was superb, far better than anything they'd had in his day, thought Kezule as he turned his head inside the helmet to check on M'zynal's unit. They advanced slowly, picking their way around the long abandoned containers and drums, debris of his vanished people.

"At least they left the grav plates on," he heard someone murmur.

"Hold the private comments," he ordered sharply, scanning walls lined with levers, power sockets and clip-in racks for tools no longer there.

"Where the hell is the main breaker?" he muttered to himself as his flashlight played over the standard warning messages for loaders and mechanics.

He almost missed it, surrounded as it was by posters advertising upcoming fights and athletic competitions. Angrily, he grasped hold of them, ripping them from the wall and letting them fall to the deck. Now he could clearly see the small screen with the keypad below, and the faint glow of the stand-by light.

He gave a sigh of relief. So far, so good. The main power source was still functioning—at least enough to feed this master

control panel. He began keying in his personal ID, praying that
they hadn't changed their system in the last days before the outpost was abandoned. Only senior officers like himself had the
clearance to activate or deactivate such a facility. As he punched
in the final digit, he remembered that he'd been taken off active
service several months before the Sholan Telepaths had struck.

For several heart-stopping seconds he waited, then the panel
lit up.

"Identity accepted," responded the station computer. "Additional password required."

Additional password? He didn't have one! What the hell was
it on about? He thought furiously, trying to figure out what the
damned machine wanted.

"Maybe all it needs is a command, sir," said M'kou.

"Worth a try," he muttered, and punched in *Reactivate.*

"Password accepted."

He could feel the humming through the soles of his boots.
Gradually it built in volume until it was audible in his suit speak-
ers. One by one, panels in the ceiling began to illuminate until
suddenly, the landing bay was flooded with light.

The visor in his helmet polarized instantly, cutting out any
glare and preventing him from being momentarily blinded.

"Force field's coming on at the entrance, sir!" yelled one of
the males near their shuttle.

Kezule glanced behind him, seeing the faint glow building
round the edge of the bay doors. As he turned back to the panel,
a flicker of movement caught his eye. One of the posters he'd
pulled off the wall was slowly traveling across the floor. On the
control panel, he could see a rapidly advancing counter. Atmospheric pressure. Air was being pumped into the bay. He wasn't
going to rely on the station display alone, his suit would confirm
it for him. Flicking his tongue out, he toggled the appropriate
key on his helmet interior and turned to survey the rest of the
landing bay while keeping an eye on the faint holo display projected onto the inside of his visor.

It was vast. Two *N'zishok*s would fit in with plenty of room
to spare. And it was empty, stripped clean, apart from the abandoned drums and containers.

"Stay alert," he ordered. "I want this level cleared before we
proceed further. Assume there could be sentients or animal life
now alerted to our presence."

He turned back to the panel—the counter was still running.

"Display status of life support on all levels," he ordered.

"Life support functioning at optimum performance on levels one through four."

"Recycle atmosphere on levels two through four."

"Initiating atmosphere recycling procedure."

"Report life signs on any deck."

"Cannot comply. This terminal cannot access that function."

Damn! "Locate main command center."

"Main command center is located on level two by elevator A."

"Locate elevator A."

"Elevator A is located to the left of this terminal."

"Landing bay secured, General," said M'zynal. "There's nothing of use here."

"Regroup on me," said Kezule. "M'zynal, delegate guards for the elevator, the rest of us are going to the command center on level two."

"What take so long reach here?" demanded a translator as the doors to the command center began to open. The TeLaxaudin perched on the Commander's chair unfolded his limbs and stood up. His space suit, lying on the chair beside him, resembled a discarded skin.

"Why am I not surprised?" Kezule murmured to himself.

Six hours later, tired but jubilant, they returned to the *N'zishok*. Once on board, Kezule headed for the bridge to address the crew on the PA.

"Kij'ik is inhabitable," he said. "The *N'zishok* will land at 21.00 tonight. All systems are functioning at optimum performance. Levels one and two have been secured and the rest of the station isolated for the time being. A team has been left in the command center on the second level and will be relieved by the third watch in two hours time. On arrival, those designated command staff will crew the center while the rest will start making the living quarters habitable. It will take a great deal of hard work to make this outpost operational again for our needs. You know your watch designations, and your officers. Each watch will be eight hours long. Those of you who are off duty now, ensure that you've had enough sleep before you're due on again." He hesitated briefly before continuing. "Finally, we have an unexpected guest. A TeLaxaudin called Giyarishis. Treat him with all respect and give him what aid he requests. General Kezule out."

When he returned to his quarters, he found Shaidan lying in a makeshift bed on the sofa watching Gaylla play. Zayshul was working at the table on her comm.

"You found Giyarishis waiting on the station, didn't you?" she said, looking round at him.

Kezule pushed aside his niggling thoughts on her perceptiveness. "Yes. What's he doing out of sick bay?" he demanded quietly, joining her.

"He was scared. I brought him here to free the nurse for watch duty," she said, looking up at him. "He's too young to be left in there on his own, Kezule."

Kezule grunted, seeing the sense in her reasoning. "It's time Gaylla went back to the others. I don't want any problems when it comes to handing her over to the Sholans."

Zayshul sighed. "Very well. Can she stay tonight? She's unsettled too because of all the frantic activity."

He hesitated. "Tonight's the last night," he said. "She goes in with the others tomorrow morning." He yawned. "I'm too tired to go to the mess to eat. Can you get them to send our meals here?"

"Aren't you worried about there being a TeLaxaudin on Kij'ik?"

"No. Should I be? Didn't they help your people survive the Fall? It pleases me. I want you and Giyarishis to do some research into what made you females feral in the first place. It may be possible to undo it. I'd like something in my back pocket in case we end up facing trouble from the M'zullians or J'kirtikkians. Not that I expect us to," he added, seeing her face take on a worried look. "And see about giving our females the same drink you were given at our wedding so they can breed."

"It has to be a matter of choice, Kezule."

"Of course," he agreed.

She nodded, and began keying in the communications interface. "How well preserved is the station really?"

"Remarkably," he said, taking off his jacket and putting it on the back of the chair. "But then it's fusion powered, few moving parts, not a lot to go wrong with the basics. However, we've only seen the landing bay, and command area. The outpost has drifted some in fifteen hundred years, but that was to be expected. I want to nudge it a little farther into the asteroid belt just in case your people come here looking for us."

"How long are we staying?"

He sat down at the table opposite her. "Six months to a year at least. It could take nearly that long to get this place up and running, but it does make a good base of operations from which to go looking for the other resources I need."

"When are you going to contact the Sholans?"

"When I'm sure this place really is habitable and there's no hidden faults in its systems. A week or two at most." She was as unsettled as the young ones he realized. And working herself up to saying something important.

She turned away from her comm to look at him properly. "Kezule, Kusac was scent marked by one of the females on the *Kz'adul*," she said quietly.

He sat back in his chair and regarded her carefully. He'd wondered when she'd tell him. "Was he now? Scent marking. We didn't have that in my time, not with feral females. As I understand it, it's placed by a female to mark a male out as a desirable partner, isn't it?"

"That's right. Chy'qui sent a female to Kusac his last night on the *Kz'adul* to collect breeding samples from him. For some reason best known to her, she scent marked him. Chy'qui had her killed so she couldn't betray him."

"Then I don't see the problem."

"Kusac thinks it was me who went to him that night," she said, looking away. "It affected him differently from the way it would one of our males. We'd be able to tell which female had done it, he can't." She glanced back at him. "As a Sholan, he shouldn't even be able to smell the nuances in our scents. The pheromones must have heightened his sense of smell. I had to agree it was me for fear he'd tell his people what had happened and they'd figure out about Chy'qui taking breeding samples. Keeping it secret is academic now that we're giving the cubs to them."

"So he thinks you came to him that last night. This is better than I'd hoped." He began to smile, a plan forming in his mind already.

"What?" she asked, surprised.

"I knew he'd been marked in some way as soon as I smelled his scent on that chair on the *Kz'adul*. I'd intended to use it to bring him here, but to find out he thinks he's spent the night with you is even better. We'll use your scent on the message, along with his son's, as the main lure."

"You can't do that!" she hissed, trying to keep her voice down. "That marker attracts the male to the female who placed it! He's focusing on me as a desirable sexual partner!"

"We can deal with it," he said urbanely.

"Kezule, he has to be released from it!"

"Why? I have his son, and I have him attracted to my wife. He's in my power already, he just doesn't know it yet. And anyway, how can you release him from the marker placed by a dead female?"

"It can be done. He's suffered enough, Kezule! He lost his telepathic abilities because of Chy'qui and his damned priest, and he lost the mental link he had to his mate! Have some compassion! He's a decent person, I won't have you tormenting him! What you plan to do to him through his son is bad enough!"

He raised his eye ridges at her. "Do I detect an affection for him?" he asked quietly. "You'll do what I tell you to do, Zayshul. Don't forget he and his companions kidnapped me and brought me forward to this time! I need him and his skills to train our people. When he's done, I'll let him go. I'm not that vindictive."

"What about his son?"

"Ah, Shaidan," he said, looking over at the young male. "Now he's another matter. That depends."

"On what?" she asked angrily.

He looked back at her. "On how well you perform your part."

"You bastard! I won't lead him on!"

"I don't intend to ask you to," he said coldly. "There are plenty other females here who can do that if necessary. Let's just get him here first."

the *Couana*, Zhal-S'Asha, 22nd day (October)

The last few remaining memories clamored at the edges of his mind despite his best efforts to stop them. Somehow he managed to make it through the remainder of his shift, grateful that he'd shortened them for today. He headed back to his room and privacy, only to find the lock on the door no longer worked, a legacy of his suicide attempt.

Sighing, he settled himself on the bed prior to trying to relax and let the memories return. This time, following some instinct, he took off his torc.

Stronghold, Zhal-Nylam, 20th day (September)

"So this is where you're hiding! Come you here to me this instant, boy! How dare you make Noni come traipsing round this labyrinth of a bird's nest looking for you!"

He stiffened, outraged at being addressed like this in front of the juniors he was teaching, especially the young Human male, Kai. The shouted command was almost immediately reinforced by a mental one that gripped his mind like a vise as it delivered its imperative.

"No sweat, Kusac. I can finish showing you this another time," said Kai, glancing over to the library door where the elderly Sholan stood.

"I want to continue," he said through gritted teeth as he fought against Noni's control of him.

"Uh, if you don't go, she'll start on me next, and no offense, but it's you she wants. That's one tough old bird there." Hurriedly he saved the program they'd been working on onto a data crystal, grabbed it and got to his feet. "See you later."

He barely heard the youth as his mental barriers began to fall like toppling dominos before Noni's onslaught. With a roar of rage, he flung the chair back and leaped to his feet, making the juniors gasp in shock.

A reserve of energy deep within him he hadn't known was there suddenly flared, enabling him to throw her out of his mind and snap his barriers back into place. But it was too late: she'd gotten what she wanted from him.

"That's better," she said mildly, standing her ground as he advanced on her, hair out like a mane and tail lashing from side to side. "Thought you'd turned soft on me, Kusac. Go get the elevator for us. We're going up to my surgery."

"You meddlesome old crone! You have no right to go into my mind like that!" he snarled, afraid of what she'd found.

"I haven't, haven't I?" she said, grasping him by the forearm and latching her claws into him. "Tell me, when you were in the military and on the *Khalossa,* did you have regular medical checkups? And did the Telepath Guild Mentor send for you every now and then?" She drew him inexorably with her as she turned to leave the library and head for the elevator.

"You know we did. What of it?" he demanded, unable to pull away for fear of knocking her over.

"This is your checkup. The Brotherhood is older than the Forces, they copied us."

"I don't believe you!"

"Your privilege. I'm ordering you, as Stronghold's Healer, to accompany me to my surgery," she retorted. "Refuse that if you dare, you arrogant cub!"

He snarled softly, aware of the futility of arguing, and went with her.

Noni's surgery wasn't what he expected, but then with Noni, nothing ever was. It was a regular white tiled treatment room with an examination bed and all the paraphernalia associated with it. The only difference between it and the standard ones was it was all laid out so Noni could sit, not stand.

Still smarting at her blatant disregard of his right to mental privacy, he sat down in the chair beside her desk. "I was medically and mentally examined three weeks ago by the TeLaxaudin physician Kzizysus, Noni," he growled. "There's no need for this."

"I think there is," she said, placing her walking stick in a holder beside the desk. "You been hiding from your life-mate for the last week, Kusac. You're distressing her needlessly. I'm telling you this as her birther: you risk her having the cub too early."

"Because of a row?" he asked uncomfortably. "You're exaggerating, Noni. She brought it on herself. She knew how I felt about Zsurtul. Why didn't she think of me before arranging the visit?"

"She did. She thought it would help bring those memories back for you. Why do you see Zsurtul as a threat? Tell me, what harm can he do to you and your family? You're not thinking this through properly, Kusac, you're just reacting like a youngling, not a mature male."

"Letting him visit my estate made it look like I'm endorsing his presence on Shola and I'm not!"

"No one gives a damn about how you feel about the Primes," she said tartly. "You're the one who's left the trail. Everyone but you has accepted the Prime presence on Shola."

"The Telepath Guild has been using Attitude Indoctrination through the media and you know it, Noni! I can see them for what they really are."

"You want Father Lijou to send you for a course of that yourself?" she demanded. "Or worse, have them think your mind's not recovered from being programmed by Chy'qui?"

"What?" He looked at her, hardly able to believe what she was saying.

"You heard. Carry on like this and he'll send for a Guild Telepath to adjust your thinking for the public good."

"He wouldn't," he said, hearing the note of uncertainty in his voice.

"Wouldn't he? You're risking your Triad cub's life—maybe even Carrie's—with this attitude, and you're endangering interspecies relationships by antagonizing the Prime Emperor's son!" She looked at him from under meeting eye ridges. "I'll say this for you, Kusac, you never do things by half! So tell me how this youngling Prime is a threat to you or your family."

"His people were responsible for me losing my Talent! That's reason enough!"

"Is it? If not for the Prince intervening, Carrie would have been more than raped by J'koshuk. Zsurtul fought for you to be released as soon as Carrie was fit to travel. You'd never have been found either. Zsurtul didn't have to do any of this, he did it because he knew it was right. So what does he threaten? Your mate? I think not. He has his own female with him at the Embassy. Your liberty? He's the one who has to be protected from the Valtegans on the Nezule estate!"

"His scent sets my teeth on edge!" he spat at her, knowing she knew this already.

"Ah, his scent," she nodded. "You don't like how he smells. Funny, I hear that mammals smell very different to the likes of him, yet for all he's a youngling, he can live alone among us and put up with our scents. And when you gave him a beating in the exercise hall at Nezule, he was prepared to let it go rather than make an incident out of it. Time you measured yourself against this Prince, Kusac. He's acting more like an adult than you are for all he's only lived ten years! You going to let your senses rule your head, boy?"

She was making him angry with her comparisons. "His people were responsible for our welfare on their ship! They claim we were supposed to be guests, yet they didn't prevent Chy'qui from using my Triad for his experiments, didn't stop J'koshuk from torturing me!"

"Zsurtul went out of his way to save your lives when he knew what was happening," she said. "He is a civilian, not a Court employee. He had no responsibility for you at all! In fact, he has more reason to hate you than you have him!"

"What the hell are you talking about?" he demanded. "I never did anything to him!"

She sat back in her chair and surveyed him. "Apart from beating him up, you tried to kill him during the hostage exchange at Haven, Kusac."

He opened his mouth angrily, then the truth of what she was saying dawned on him. "That wasn't me," he muttered. "That was Chy'qui's programming."

"So?" she countered. "He sees you personally try to kill him at Haven after blasting this J'koshuk with mind power, then attack him during a training session. He has never raised a hand against you. Think this through, Kusac. Keep up this attitude to Zsurtul and the Primes and just maybe they'll look closer at how you killed J'koshuk, especially now you have your Talent back. Use your brain on this for once!"

Her talk of how he killed J'koshuk worried him. It had been mentioned briefly between himself and Kaid but with no one else, and there had been no official enquiry into it.

"You know the penalty for using your Talent to kill, don't you?" she said quietly, leaning forward in her seat. "They destroy that area of your brain. We're talking about your attitude toward the Crown Prince of the Primes here. The ally who can talk to the M'zullians when we can't because of their psychopathic hatred of us. We're talking possible interstellar war if you harm him. Those who knew what you did at Haven covered it up because you'd lost your Talent then, they knew it was unlikely you'd ever be able to do it again. Now you're in the process of regaining it. You keep this up and they'll be forced to do something drastic, Kusac. You're in AlRel, you know they can't ignore it. You want to lose everything you're in the process of regaining just because you don't like his scent?"

As she spoke, fear had hit him like an icy shower, shocking any vestige of anger from him. "I hadn't realized," he stammered. "Have they . . ."

"Nothing's been done yet," she said, patting his arm reassuringly. "Nor will it be if it's up to me. That's why we're having this talk. Carrie had a good intuition of what could happen if you didn't overcome your dislike of Zsurtul, that's why she did what she did. Though she'd not be able to tell you that's why."

"What do I do, Noni?"

"You call that mate of yours and apologize. Tell her she was right, that you're on your way back to see her. Stay a couple of days, maybe even visit the Nezule estate and see Prince Zsurtul—you suggest it! Just remember what's at stake, Kusac. We Sholans are more than just our base instincts, you know. And when you come back, come to me and we'll see if I can't do something to start those memories resurfacing properly."

He got to his feet, barely noticing that her steadying mental influence had stopped his shaking. "I'm in your debt, Noni," he said quietly.

"No," she replied. "We're family, Kusac. That's why I'm here."

the *Couana*, Zhal-S'Asha, 22nd day (October)

He could see how blind he'd been to reason and that he should have realized what was happening to him. He'd been too close to the problem and everyone else had lacked the piece of information only he had; that he'd spent a night with Zayshul and somehow it had changed his perception of Primes.

Going back to the estate to see Carrie and Kaid hadn't been as difficult as he'd thought, but visiting Zsurtul had proved impossible. When he'd returned to Stronghold, Noni had not been pleased. As she'd said though, better he came back than made a fool of himself if he couldn't handle it.

Despite Lijou's personal objections, he'd gone to stay

with her at the cottage. He'd learned all he could from them,
it was time to let Noni try.

Inside her home, with the psi damper on, he'd finally
been able to access the beginnings of his returning Talent
and start retraining. It hadn't been much, because nothing
could be done to help his fragmented memories become
whole, but she'd helped him overcome the fear that reaching out for her mind and trying to send to her would trigger the pain.

Yawning, he closed his eyes for a few minutes, unwittingly drifting into an uneasy sleep.

Shola, Governor's Palace at Shanagi, Zhal-Nylam, 21st day (September)

Falma ushered the Prime Ambassador into Konis' office and indicated the less formal chairs round a low table.

"I'll be with you in a moment, Ambassador," said Konis from
his desk. "I'm nearly finished. Falma, take this to Father Lijou,
will you, please?"

"I'm grateful to you for seeing me at such short notice, Clan
Lord Aldatan," said M'szudoe, taking the seat indicated and settling himself comfortably. Curious, he looked around. This was
the first time he'd visited the head of Alien Relations in his office. Usually his business was conducted in council chambers or
informally over a rushed meal in the refectory.

Two fans, one at either end of the room, spun lazily in the
high ceiling, circulating the cooler air that came in through the
open portico that formed one wall of the AlRel office. It was beside this that he was sitting. Brightly colored murals depicting
the various Alliance species meeting and conducting business on
all their worlds covered the office walls. At the far end, he could
see the section where his people had been added. A portion of
the wall still remained blank, painted the almost impossible deep
turquoise blue of the Sholan sky, so that other new species could
be added one day.

"You indicated it was important, Ambassador. Unlike some
representatives, you've not been one to take up my time without
reason." Konis held out an envelope and a hastily scribbled note

to Falma. "Tell Lijou it's the funding he's been waiting for," he said in a low voice. "Say I advise him to bank it immediately, before Raiban gets to hear about this."

Falma smiled. "Yes, Master Konis."

As he left, Konis got up and joined the ambassador. "I see you're admiring the murals," he said, sitting down opposite him. "Beautiful, aren't they? I have to admit I'm glad I work in AlRel and not in Transport or Industry. I couldn't live with industrial scenes. These constantly remind me of the wonderful diversity of our universe."

"Beautiful, indeed," said M'szudoe. "It has been educational for me coming to Shola. Until now our contacts with other species have been mainly limited to our TeLaxaudin allies, and they don't permit Ambassadors to their world."

"I'd noticed," said Konis, choosing a widemouthed glass for the Prime and pouring out a drink of lightly flavored water. He offered it to the Ambassador then poured one for himself. "Glad it isn't just us. Anyway, Ambassador, what can I do for you?"

"Emperor Cheu'ko'h has asked me to approach you on a matter of great delicacy, Clan Lord," said M'szudoe, taking a sip. "General Kezule has left K'oish'ik taking with him one of our small destroyers, the *N'zishok,* and a number of our people."

"Regrettable, indeed, Ambassador, but hardly an Alliance matter," said Konis picking up his own glass. "Do you know why he left?"

M'szudoe hesitated, his forked tongue just flicking beyond his lips as he returned his glass to the table. "As I said, this is a matter of great delicacy. It seems that the dissident Chy'qui who so grievously injured one of your people on the *Kz'adul,* was not alone. They tried to recruit General Kezule to their cause and failed. He dealt with their center of operations, giving us the names of the leaders to pick up for questioning, then left immediately afterward. He claimed if he remained, he'd be a further focus for the discontented. The Emperor does not agree. He wants the General back. He is, after all, family."

Konis, the tip of his tail beginning to flick gently against his ankles in agitation, watched the Ambassador taking another mouthful of his drink. "Does Emperor Cheu'ko'h believe that the General is himself a dissident?"

"Oh, no. You misunderstand me," said M'szudoe hastily, putting his glass back on the table. "The General is held in high esteem by his Majesty. He values his counsel greatly. It is due to the General that our Enlightened One is now living on your Warrior Estate."

"I'm afraid I don't see what we can do to help you," said Konis. "When did you say the General left K'oish'ik?"

"Just over three of your weeks ago. We don't expect you to go after the General, Clan Lord. What we were hoping is that if your new Watcher security patrols out in the Anchorage sector had a sighting of his ship, you'd send word to us."

"Anchorage?" repeated Konis, his expression freezing.

"Clan Lord, we're aware of what your Brotherhood calls our old outpost." M'szudoe allowed himself a small smile. "Will you contact us if your Watchers see the *N'zishok*? We don't want this matter widely known, you understand."

"I'll certainly pass your request over to the Brotherhood, Ambassador," said Konis. "Have you any idea where the General is bound?"

"None, I'm afraid. If you can let us know if there's a sighting, Clan Lord, we'll handle the rest," said M'szudoe, getting to his feet. "Thank you for your time."

"He came after my son and his family once, Lijou, could he be doing it again?"

"If he is, then he'll be picked up long before he reaches Shola, Konis," said Lijou. "We've got the Watchers and there's the home fleet ringing our solar system. I really don't think he's headed for here. We were aware the General and his wife had disappeared, but not why. They've a—hatchling I think they call them—on the way, and they took it with them. Hardly the kind of thing you do if you're bent on revenge. I'll have our people at the Embassy updated and see what more they can find out."

"Are Kusac and my bond-daughter aware of this? Or Kaid?"

"No, we thought it wiser to say nothing for now. Carrie doesn't need this worry so near her time. It's already a priority with the Watchers. We look after our own, Konis. Trust us."

"I expect you're right, Lijou," he sighed before heading slowly back to his own office.

Kij'ik, the same day

Silently, like a shadow, Shaidan padded behind Kezule. The General was pleased, he could feel it despite the collar he wore. As he'd been trained, he was beginning to learn the range of Kezule's moods. Following him into the lab, he found himself an out of the way niche near the entrance and crouched carefully down on his haunches to wait.

"The hydroponic area is up and running, Zayshul," said Kezule. "The seeds we brought with us are growing well in their accelerated stasis fields. And Maaz'ih has gotten the protein vats started. We should have fresh food within a month."

"Kezule, in the name of the God-Kings, if you must take Shaidan everywhere with you, send him to sit somewhere more comfortable! This is his first day out and about, his ribs are nowhere near healed yet," said Zayshul, looking up from the screen where she and Giyarishis were working.

"He's fine," said Kezule, glancing back at the cub. "He's not complaining of being in any pain."

"He wouldn't," she said. "You've left him with K'hedduk's programming. Unless you ask him a direct question, he'll not tell you anything."

Kezule sighed. Ever since the child had been able to get out of his bed, he and Zayshul had argued over him.

"Has pain," said Giyarishis suddenly, breaking into their conversation.

Kezule turned to look at him, surprised at the interruption.

"There you are," said Zayshul, turning around on her stool. "I'm taking him to the sick bay, then back to our quarters to rest."

He was beginning to recognize when he was beaten. "Tell me about your work first. Shaidan, go to the sick bay and wait for the Doctor there," he ordered.

"Yes, General," said the cub, pushing himself slowly to his feet.

"Tell Ghidd'ah she's to give you something to eat," Zayshul called out after him.

"You spoil him," said Kezule, frowning. "You treat him like a pet."

Zayshul stiffened. "I treat him as I will treat our child."

He didn't want to go down that corridor right now. "Talking

of which, have you had any success encouraging our females to breed?"

"Some, but only among those already in a relationship, and they're not too sure about bearing their own eggs. You need us too, Kezule. With so much needing to be done to the station, you can't afford to lose almost half your people to egg-bearing."

"True. I'm not used to counting females as part of my forces," he said. "What about your research on the feral females of my time?"

"We're finishing analyzing the data now. Giyarishis' family was one of those involved in bringing us females out of the breeding rooms after the Fall. We think that their situation was exacerbated by their food and the slave collars. The raw meat was heavily laced with la'quo and the collars had the resin in them. They were being slowly poisoned every day of their lives, just as the Jalnians were so long ago."

"Jalnians?" The name sounded familiar, but he was more interested in what she'd said about the TeLaxaudin.

"The indigenes of Jalna, the world near which we picked up the M'zullians and the Sholans. Around the time of the Fall, our ancestors were farming laalquoi on that world but it mutated into a toxic version that sent locals and Valtegans alike into uncontrollable rages. A version of that plant might be what they're still using to control the females on M'zull and J'kirtikk even now."

"I always assumed the slave collars were to control them as we controlled the telepaths." He stopped, thinking over what he'd just said.

"Perhaps it wasn't intended they become feral, it was just a side effect," she said.

"No. I told you," he said automatically. "There was a coup led by a group of Warriors. They took the power from the females and imprisoned them. Surely they'd have noticed the contaminated la'quo products from Jalna and stopped using them?" Pulling up a stool, he sat beside her. "And you females were kept in breeding rooms for at least two hundred years before the Fall. Ask Giyarishis."

Zayshul looked at the small being perched on her other side.

"Is true. Memory he has," agreed Giyarishis.

Her small silence made him look back to her, catching the strange expression on her face.

"When they discovered what it did, yes," she said hastily. "I can't see any reason why they'd make the females feral in the first place, nor why you males didn't refuse to go near them at all."

"You're female," he said absently, reaching out and taking hold of her hand. "You wouldn't understand the sheer physical drive to reproduce that the ordinary male Warrior possesses. It can rob them of all reason. We had to lace the water supply with la'quo to suppress it or we'd have had riots for the use of the drones on the ships. The only thing that kept them away from the true females was their ferocity." He looked up at her, wondering again about her uncanny knack of following his thoughts, wondering if it could be the reason the females had been put in slave collars in the first place.

"I visited my own wife only four times in as many years because she had to be sedated to the point of unconsciousness before she could be brought out of the breeding room. Then there was the fear she'd waken before I was done."

"There were the drones, though."

His mouth twitched slightly at the corners. "True, but they didn't smell female. When all was said and done, I preferred my wife."

"And the Sholan pets?"

He put her hand back on the bench. "Mine was a male telepath," he said, getting up, the moment shattered. "A few of our people tried mating with the Sholans. Several court officials were savaged—Sholan females are as ferocious as our own when taken against their will, and none submitted willingly—a few succeeded but had to inject sharroh poison with their bite, chemically binding them to the female until they'd mated. It was a practice I found abhorrent." He remembered the Sholan female that had shared his captivity and how he'd had to bite her in order to heal himself after a beating by the Sholan interrogator. It was yet another grudge he had against Kusac and those who'd brought him forward in time.

"It must have been a very strange culture," Zayshul said. "I can understand your reluctance to marry again."

"Marriage is to breed, nothing more," he said. "We've spoken of this before. Now go and see to the child, I want to talk to Giyarishis."

He waited until she'd left. "What else do you know about the time before the Fall?" he asked the TeLaxaudin.

Giyarishis began to hum, mandibles opening and closing gently. "Little. Before me. Can process stored memories."

"Mine?"

"Yes. Answer in you."

"Do it. I need to know more about our past."

"Tomorrow come. Test take."

"I need you to do something else for me. I want you to mark the Sholan child who was here so he gives off a Prime scent as well as a Sholan one."

"Make Sholan seem Prime? Why?"

"I need him to be thought a Prime hybrid."

Giyarishis hummed and the translator made a few untranslatable sounds. "Impossible! Too different. Why do?"

"I need to bring someone here, a Sholan. The child's father. He's more likely to come if he thinks his child is also part Prime."

The TeLaxaudin was silent for a moment. "Need samples both."

"What kind of samples? I'll get them for you."

"I do. Who else?"

"My wife, the Doctor."

The humming grew louder as the alien's hands began to twitch. "Not like."

Dammit! Surely the TeLaxaudin wasn't getting moralistic on him?

"Why? Tell or not do."

"Because I need his cooperation. I need to make him think this Sholan child is his, and my wife's."

Eyes swirling, Giyarishis looked away. "Go. I think. Maybe do."

"I need it done soon, Giyarishis," said Kezule, getting to his feet. "I have to send a message to him within the next few days and I need the scent to go on it."

Valsgarth Estate, Zhal-Nylam, 23rd day (September)

The beginning of autumn had brought a welcome coolness to the air after the long, hot summer. As Kaid approached the tables outside the training center mess that evening Garras looked up, catching his eye. His friend's mouth split in a Human grin, showing white canines against his dark brown pelt.

"Your drink's waiting," said Garras, pushing it toward him as he slipped into the seat they'd kept for him.

Gratefully he picked it up, taking a large mouthful before putting the glass down. Slumping forward, he rested his elbows on the table and his chin on his hand and began to relax.

"Let me guess," said Rezac, his voice full of amusement. "You've been moving furniture all day. Jo was just the same in her last month."

Kaid turned his head fractionally so he could see him. "That was yesterday." He sounded tired even to himself.

"She wanted to go for a walk," said Garras. "I know, I saw you. Vanna did that a lot too. She'd get some food from the kitchen then drag me off into the woods on the pretext of a picnic and spend the time searching for the ideal spot to eat. Except she was looking for a den."

"That's a Sholan trait," said Brynne. "Not a Human one. Keeza hasn't started nesting yet."

"It's exhausting," said Kaid. "I never thought I'd see the day when I'd be hovering over any female so protectively, especially one as independent and capable as Carrie. She must have dragged me on a five mile hike." He flicked his ears back slightly in an equivalent of a shrug. "I don't know where she gets the energy."

"Nervous energy," said Garras, taking a drink of his own ale. "They're psyching themselves up for the birth I've always reckoned. At least for most of the last month their bellies are too big to walk upright comfortably so they stay in."

"Not Carrie," said Kaid as Rezac echoed him with a "Not Jo!" They shared a grin.

"Humans are different. They're designed for upright walking," said Rezac. "Jo had endless energy. It was me that got exhausted. She had me reorganizing the kitchen store cupboards, the linen cupboards—the nursery room was redecorated three times . . . I could go on for ever."

"But there's something good about it," said Brynne quietly, a gentle smile on his face. "I wasn't ready to be a father when Marak was born so Vanna didn't involve me much. This time it's different. This time I'm sharing it with Keeza."

"You're just being sentimental," said Jurrel with a laugh. "You moan like mad to me when Keeza can't hear you!"

"I think we're entitled to moan a little considering what our females put us through," said Garras. "Don't you, Kaid?"

He smiled vaguely. He'd learned a lot from hearing the problems the other males had and were facing, but none had mentioned what Carrie was going through.

He felt a hand close over his wrist and looked up to see, and feel, Garras' concern.

"What's wrong, Kaid?" his friend asked quietly. "I can sense it. What's worrying you about Carrie?"

Aware the others were trading grumbles in a lively fashion, he decided it was time he asked Garras' advice. "She wakes crying most days," he said quietly, moving his head till it was only inches from his friend's. "And the walking, it's not just nesting, she's distressed about something, deeply distressed. Even Kashini can't make her smile the way she used to. I've tried everything I can think of to cheer her up, but . . ." He shrugged, then gave a wry smile. "I've even taken her to Valsgarth to go around the stores for toys and such for the cub when she's born. Can you imagine that? Me going round infant shops?"

"You're no different from the rest of us, Kaid. You're as proud as any of them," said Garras, flicking an ear at the group around the table. "Us," he amended with a large grin. "How long have you wanted to share a cub with Carrie? Since you were three! That's well over forty years, Kaid! I'm glad to see you enjoying this with her."

"But is she when she's so distressed? I think she's feeling torn between me and Kusac, even more so now the birth's so close and he's staying up at Noni's."

"I thought that row was over."

"It is, but he's still staying away. I miss him too, Garras."

"I heard you two had become closer. It must be very difficult for you all at this time."

"His lack of Talent makes misunderstandings between us easier," sighed Kaid. "He experienced an emotion similar to what the Humans call jealousy over T'Chebbi being pregnant, but that lasted a very short time. He's looking forward to our cub almost as much as we are, and is pleased for us. But it doesn't really help."

"I know. No matter how much they both love you, memories of their sharing Kashini are bound to be affecting them, particularly now. The villa is full of reminders of what they've lost."

"Perhaps I should take her to my home up in the Dzahai mountains," he said. "There are no memories of Kusac there."

"I think you should. You'll be nearer Noni for one thing. These last days should be yours to make your own wholesome memories, ones not touched by what's been lost, only by the joy of waiting for the daughter you're sharing. You take her there. I can manage here, you know that."

He thought about it seriously for a few minutes and nodded. "You're right. I'll suggest it to her when I get back tonight. She should be more relaxed. Vanna and Sashti are visiting her and T'Chebbi—they're having a females only evening testing Sashti's new blends of oils," he grinned. "I got thrown out on my ear."

Garras laughed. "Let's hope T'Chebbi's not giving Sashti any Consortia recipes, otherwise we'll all have to watch out!"

"T'Chebbi was a Consortia?" asked Jurrel, pouncing on this tidbit of information about the enigmatic Sister.

"It's all right, Garras," said Kaid, feeling his friend's embarrassment at giving away information about his Companion. "If she told you, then she's not wanting to keep it quiet any more. T'Chebbi was training as a Consortia to be her foster-father's hostess. He was a merchant in fine arts."

A strange look crossed Jurrel's face. "Not . . ."

"Yes," said Kaid. "That one. That's why he was murdered and she was taken by the packs." He turned to Brynne, pointedly changing the conversation. "Have you found homes for all Belle's kits yet?"

"Father Lijou sent a Brother over to pick the last young female up this afternoon. He said Stronghold couldn't be without one of Belle's kits when Vartra Himself gave her to me."

Kaid shook his head. "Jeggets as household pets," he said with a faint grin. "Whatever next?"

"Ruth says they're helping the young Humans adjust because they're telepathic too," said Rezac, sipping his drink. "The Telepath Guild sent us another twelve people from the last group of Terrans. A couple of them are young enough to need her help adapting to our culture."

"I thought the sleep tape technology from the Primes combined with our own telepathic transfers was making life easier all around," said Kaid.

"It is, but it's no substitute for personal experience," said Brynne with a wry smile. "As I know only too well."

*   *   *

When Kaid got back to the villa, only T'Chebbi was still up.

"She's fine," his Companion reassured him. "Sashti's massage made her sleepy so we put her to bed and left her."

"I'm thinking of taking her to my house in the mountains until our cub's born," he said, sitting on the sofa beside her. "Get her away from the memories of here. Would you like to come with us?"

"Is good idea," she said, pleased that he wanted her there too. "Can help with Kashini and birthing if necessary. Besides, never been to your home."

He glanced away briefly, embarrassed. "Carrie's only been there once. With us based here, there's never been the need for me to go home."

She patted him gently on the knee. "Is all right, Kaid. No reason why you should take me or anyone there. Was your retreat, all you had during your ten years exile."

His arm went round her shoulders, urging her closer until her head rested on his shoulder. "Those years seem a lifetime away," he said quietly. "Now I have a family, a life-mate, you, and two cubs on the way. So many changes in such a short time takes a lot of getting used to, T'Chebbi. I would like your company tonight if you've no other plans." Gently he stroked her cheek.

"I've no other plans," she purred.

the *Couana*, Zhal-S'Asha, 22nd day (October)

Caught between dreaming and waking, he was powerless to prevent the last memories beginning to play. He whimpered, trying to move, to force himself to wakefulness, but it was useless, he was unable to do anything but endure.

It had all begun with the arrival of the message.

Stronghold, Zhal-S'Asha, (month of Approaching Darkness), 13th day (October)

"Brother Kusac, got a message for you."

He looked up to see Kai and grunted around his mouthful of food.

"Master Rhyaz wants to see you in his office."

"I'll be ten minutes," he said when he'd swallowed it.

"He said it was urgent," pressed Kai.

"I'm eating!"

Kai shrugged. "Hey, I only pass the messages on. Up to you if you want your ear chewed."

He frowned at the Human youth. "Watch your tongue, youngling, or it'll be your ears that get chewed! Go hand my meal into the kitchen and ask them to keep it warm for me," he said, holding out his plate as he got up.

As he entered Rhyaz' office, he was surprised to see his father sitting with Lijou in the informal area. Crossing the room to join them, his eyes were drawn to a cylindrical container about eight inches long lying on the low table. Intrigued, he sat down, nodding a greeting to his father. "I didn't expect to see you here, Father."

"This arrived at Haven three days ago," said Rhyaz, picking it up as he sat down. He held it out to him.

"For me?" Surprised, he took it from Rhyaz, turning it over to examine the exterior. His name had been etched into the metal casing. "What is it?"

"It's the contents of a deep space message beacon. It emerged from jump by the outpost and began emitting a signal guiding our people to it."

"Who's it from?" he asked, turning it round, looking for a way to open it.

"Twist the top," said Rhyaz. "It's from General Kezule. I apologize, but we had to open it for security reasons."

Surprised, he unscrewed the top and shook the contents—a sheet of paper and a data crystal—into his lap. As he did, a familiar scent drifted up to his nostrils. Lifting the cylinder to his nose, he sniffed. He recognized it instantly—Doctor Zayshul's. A jolt of anticipation mixed with fear filled him as he dropped the container to his lap and picked up the message, praying that this meeting wasn't because it contained references to his night with Zayshul.

"We opened it because we couldn't take the risk it was trapped, Kusac," said Rhyaz.

He stared at the words, hardly taking in them or what Rhyaz was saying. On the paper, her scent was stronger, but he was picking up another, more elusive odor. Not Kezule's, which was there; this was Sholan—not Rhyaz', the scent was too immature for that. A sense of horror flooded through him: it was the scent of a Sholan cub. His ears began to flatten; hurriedly he forced them to remain upright.

"Kezule wants you to meet him," said his father, breaking the silence.

He read the words, written not by Kezule, but by Zayshul.

I have something of interest to you, Kusac Aldatan. Meet me on the fifteenth day of Khazuh at the coordinates on the data crystal. When you arrive, transmit the given ID code. Bring no telepaths and do not come in force.

"Kezule's left the Prime world," Rhyaz said. "He's taken a ship and some sixty people and disappeared. Our intelligence tells us that an anti-Sholan dissident group tried to recruit him for a coup against their Emperor. He exposed the plot, but the ringleader escaped. The message he left behind claimed he was leaving K'oish'ik because if he remained, he'd always be a focus for dissidents."

"What could Kezule have of interest to you, Kusac?" his father asked.

Even though he heard their voices, his mind had shut down, was refusing to take in what they were saying. There had been more to the cub's scent, another layer that struck fear into his heart.

"What could he have, Kusac?" repeated Rhyaz more sharply.

"I don't know," he replied through lips that felt numb. How could he tell them what had happened between him and the Valtegan doctor? That night was branded on his soul forever.

"We need to know what Kezule's up to," said Rhyaz. "Why he really left the Prime world. We need you to keep this rendezvous and find out what he claims he has on you."

"He could be laying a false trail," he heard himself say.

"He could, but we don't think so. Why expose the dissidents and then leave K'oish'ik if he wanted revenge on us?"

"The political situation is very tricky, Kusac," said his father quietly. "This is the second time in five months there's been an attempt on the lives of their royal family. If the monarchy is destabilizing, we need to know about it now. We don't know how widespread this anti-Sholan feeling is and our operatives can't get permission to leave the City to find out. This meeting with Kezule may be our only chance to discover what's going on outside the Royal Court."

He nodded, barely aware of what he was agreeing to.

"If he has something of interest to us, get it and bring it back, even if you have to use lethal force," said Rhyaz. "One other thing: because your father's been asked to pass on any information concerning Kezule to the Prime Ambassador, you have to be seen acting independently of us—a renegade. Unfortunately, you've too high a profile to just disappear."

That caught his attention. "What?"

"We can't take you off Shola secretly on one of our ships. You'll have to steal one."

He looked from Rhyaz to his father in disbelief. "Steal a ship? You sanction this, Father?"

"It's the only way we can do it without getting drawn into an incident with the Primes. If there was any other way, believe me, I wouldn't agree to this mission," his father said.

Pulling his thoughts together, he folded the message up, putting it and the crystal back into the container. "The penalty for stealing a ship is mental readjustment and imprisonment in a correction facility. You want me to risk this? And who'd believe I'd steal a ship and leave Shola for no reason?"

"You have a reason," said Rhyaz. "At the time of the Cataclysm, Sholans rescued after being questioned by Enforcers like J'koshuk often returned voluntarily to the Valtegans because they'd become dependent on their captors. We'll make sure it's known you've been similarly affected. It should give you some protection if you're caught."

His thoughts returned to the scents. Had he somehow sired a cub on the Valtegan doctor despite his fears that the Prime implant had left him sterile, and despite the fact that the Valtegans were so different from them? Were it not for his own hybrid daughter and the half-U'Churian cub still to be born, he'd have dismissed the idea instantly, but not now. Not when he knew Doctor Zayshul headed medical research on the *Kz'adul*, and not after smelling the cub's scent on the message. His blood ran cold as he realized he wanted to see her again, not because—the Gods forbid!—there might be a cub, but because her scent had evoked memories that were pleasurable.

Wrenching his attention back to the conversation, he rammed the lid on the container, tightened it, then all but threw it on the table in front of him.

"What happens to a renegade Brother, Rhyaz? Will you set all the others to kill me on sight?" he demanded, looking at his father again, scarcely able to believe he was part of this mad scheme.

"He has no jurisdiction over you," interrupted Lijou. "Only I have, and no, that will not happen, I promise you."

Rhyaz looked at the priest. "Lijou, be realistic! I don't want Kusac killed either, but how am I to stop them without it looking like complicity? What reason do I give?"

"You'll find one," said his father harshly. "He can't go alone, you know that. Even Kezule admits there will be others present. He needs an interstellar ship and a crew."

"You already gave a reason for not pursuing him with force. He's ill, suffering from trauma caused by his captivity," said Lijou.

"I'm not leaving before Carrie's cub is born," he said suddenly, taking hold of the situation.

"You need to leave within the next ten days to be sure of meeting his deadline," objected Rhyaz.

"It's not negotiable," he said, getting up and beginning to pace the room.

"Agreed," said Lijou.

"Lijou!" exclaimed the Warrior Master, ears tilting forward and eyes narrowing. "This mission is vital, even Konis admits that!"

"So is the birth of my son's Triad-daughter," said Konis. "The En'Shallans are my concern, not yours, Rhyaz. You can ask him to go but he's under my jurisdiction. He has a right to know his life-mate and the cub are doing well."

"Very well," said Rhyaz suddenly relaxing.

"I'll need a fast ship—one capable of doing it in three days," he said, wondering why Rhyaz had capitulated so suddenly. It mattered little, he had no option but to go and find out the truth about Zayshul and the second scent. Let them think they were sending him, he knew differently. "I want the *Couana*, Rhyaz. It's capable of being crewed exclusively by Sholans."

"You'll have it. One other consideration, Kusac. You have to ensure Kaid won't try to follow you. If you don't, you'll put him and Carrie, to say nothing of their newborn, at risk."

He stared at Rhyaz, suddenly realizing the full extent of what he was losing by heading out to meet Kezule and Zayshul. Once Carrie had given birth, her mind would Leska Link again—perhaps back to him despite his Talent being suppressed by the memory problems. Even if this mission went well, he'd not get the chance to Link to Carrie again until she'd born yet another cub, a cub he might be unable to father given the damage the Prime's implant had caused.

"You can't ask him to alienate Carrie and Kaid!" exclaimed Konis, rising to his feet in distress. "In Vartra's name, Rhyaz, we're asking him enough of him as it is!"

"I'm only pointing out what could happen if he doesn't," said Rhyaz reasonably.

Anger surged through him. "I'll do it, but you organize the *Couana*," he snarled, snatching up the message cannister. "And choose me a crew who have nothing to lose if this goes wrong and we end up branded traitors and renegades by the whole Alliance!"

He went straight to Kaid's home. This had to be gotten over with before he lost his courage. As he approached, the security system automatically began to interrogate his craft.

"Kaid, it's me, Kusac," he said. "We need to talk."

"Kusac? Hold on. Let me disable the security," came Kaid's voice over the craft's comm. "You can land now. What's the matter?"

"Meet me outside," he said shortly, cutting the link.

When he landed, Kaid was waiting for him in front of the house.

"It's good to see you, Kusac," he said, coming forward to greet him.

"This isn't a social visit, Kaid," he said, avoiding his sword-brother's outstretched arms. "I want Carrie to go home to have the cub. You shouldn't have brought her here. She's a Clan Leader, her place is on our estate."

"Carrie's free to go where she wants, Kusac," said Kaid, frowning as he stopped short. "She's closer to Noni here, that's all. What's wrong? This isn't like you."

"Carrie being here is what's wrong," he said harshly. This wasn't easy. It was hurting him far more than he'd imagined to speak to Kaid like this. "Neither of you thought to ask me how I felt about her leaving home." He caught sight of T'Chebbi and Carrie through the large front window. "I see you brought T'Chebbi here too. Quite a little hareem you've gotten yourself, isn't it? I thought there was something special between us, Kaid, but there isn't, is there? Bringing Carrie here is about you and what you want, not her safety."

"You know that's not true," said Kaid, his voice low. "We're sword-brothers. You're as dear to me as Carrie is. If you stopped to think, you'd realize that. What's gotten into you? Why, after we've been here three weeks, are you suddenly coming here to complain? Have the memories started? Is that what it is? I know this isn't you talking right now."

Why did Kaid have to be so understanding? Couldn't he tell this was tearing him apart? Mentally, he retreated even further into himself, walling away the hurt he was causing them all, reminding himself he had to do this—or risk them following him into Kezule's grasp.

"Dammit, Kaid! Listen to me for once!" he said with genuine anger. "You're too damned used to everyone looking to you for leadership because of your age and experience! You don't see me as an equal, do you? You've never even considered me a real sword-brother! After all, I forced the relationship on you, just as you forced . . ."

"Kusac, don't!" interrupted Kaid coldly, hair beginning to rise and his ears swivel sideways, folding down ready to fight. "I forced nothing on you at any time. The opposite in fact. You turned to me."

As Kaid seemed to grow in stature, he remembered just how dangerous a person his sword-brother was. Fear clutched him low in his belly and he retreated a few steps till he hit the side of the aircar. "I should have expected that response from you, considering your background," he said, hearing his voice breaking. "I can see through you now, Kaid. Our Triad means nothing to you except as a way to get all that you wanted. I'm just an inconvenience to your plans now, aren't I?"

Kaid's low growl deepened, becoming a full-throated roar as he leaped forward and grasped hold of him with a swiping motion. The sharp burning pain across his chest faded to unimportance as he found his face inches from Kaid's mask of fury.

"Any other male I would have killed for saying what you just did," he snarled. "I told you once before never to question my loyalty to you. You have. Repeat what you've said today to anyone else, and by Vartra, Kusac, you'll wish you had died on the *Kz'adul*! Now get out of here! Carrie can return to the villa when our cub is old enough to travel if that's what she chooses. I will not. Until you apologize for what you just said, I want nothing more to do with you!"

He was lifted and flung bodily into the aircar, careening off the far bulkhead as Kaid sealed the door.

Shaking violently, he caught hold of the pilot's seat and pulled himself to his feet. He opaqued the windows, knowing if he looked back, he'd change his mind and rush out to apologize and tell Kaid everything.

Mechanically, he started the ignition sequence and took off, the pain in his chest when he stretched across the console feeling good because it reminded him he was still alive. He didn't notice the tears rolling down his cheeks.

Aldatan Estate, Zhal-S'Asha, 14th day (October)

Konis had learned the hard way that trying to keep anything from his life-mate was not a wise decision to make. With their twin cubs due in four weeks, however, he was afraid to tell her about Kusac's mission lest the news cause her to go into premature labor. Not telling her and letting her hear the public version on the newsnets was not an option he relished either. And there was no one he could ask for advice beyond those at Stronghold, each of whom had a different opinion.

When he arrived home, Rhyasha was resting. Too gravid to walk upright comfortably, she rose late and spent her days conducting estate business in her upstairs office from her day bed.

She looked up as he entered. With her hair unbound, framing her face and cascading round her shoulders like a cloud of sunlight, he was reminded of their early days together, when she'd been expecting their firstborn, Kusac. Then she'd flown in the face of convention, rejecting the marriage arranged for her by his predecessor, ensuring she'd become pregnant by him, knowing that the Clan Lord and her family would have to accept their marriage.

"What's wrong, Konis?" she asked. "I might be brain-dead now because of the cubs, but I can tell when all's not well with you. What did they want at Stronghold?"

Before he could answer, she'd pushed herself upright in her nest of cushions. "It's about Kusac, isn't it? Tell me!"

He shook his head, Human style, and joined her on the day bed.

"Carrie then! In Vartra's name, tell me, Konis!" she said anxiously.

The decision was made for him. "They're fine, Rhyasha," he said, putting an arm round her and drawing her back until she rested against his chest. Then he told her it all.

She listened in silence, but he could feel her rising anguish and fear for their son.

"How could you ask that of him! Don't you realize that if he leaves, he won't get back his Link to Carrie?"

"That's not very likely, Rhyasha," he said gently. "We had no option but to ask him to go. We need to know why Kezule left K'oish'ik. There's unrest on the Prime world and it might affect our treaty with them."

"But to send him into Kezule's claws, Konis! What were you all thinking of? He eats living creatures! He tortured our bondson Dzaka, kidnapped Kashini! It was a miracle Kitra and Dzaka were able to stop him trying to return to the past to change our history! Vartra knows what Kezule will do to our son!"

"We need to know what's happening on the Prime world," he repeated firmly. "Kusac's in the Brotherhood, missions like this are what they do. We didn't put any pressure on him, I promise you. It was almost as if he wanted to go."

"Want to go? Why would he *want* to go?" she demanded, pulling away from him. "What could Kezule possibly have that would interest our son? And is it really so important that he has to steal a ship and be branded a criminal and a traitor? Who's going to believe that rubbish about returning to the Primes because of the torture he suffered?"

"Everyone will," he said quietly. "Because that's what Rhyaz will tell the newsnets when they find out."

"The 'nets?" she moaned, closing her eyes and slumping back

against the back of her daybed, clutching her belly. "Not the 'nets, Konis!"

"Because of her feud with Stronghold, General Raiban will try to use this as an argument to have us integrated with the Forces."

"Then make Lijou play it for sympathy, Konis! He's our friend, he can do it even if Rhyaz won't! You realize they'll all be looking for Kusac? The Forces and the Brotherhood? His life could be at risk!" She stopped abruptly, her arms tightening over her belly as her eyes widened in shock.

"What's wrong?" demanded Konis. "You haven't gone into labor, have you?"

As she doubled up moaning, he held onto her with one arm while using his wrist comm to call Vanna, inwardly cursing himself for telling her.

Behind him, the door opened as Taizia came in at a run, her mate Meral remaining hovering outside, waiting to see if he was needed.

"Mother? Are you all right?" she demanded, leaning over her.

"It's too soon!" Rhyasha whimpered. "They can't come yet! I've a month still to go!"

Taizia beckoned Meral in as her father finished speaking to Vanna. "Father, we need to get her to Vanna. Let Meral help you."

As soon as Rhyasha came round from the anesthetic, they took her from the recovery room to the infants' IC ward to see her cubs. Lying on the soft bedding of the incubator, attached to drips and ventilators, the tiny cubs looked fragile, as if not long for the world.

Supported by Konis, she rested her hands on the transparent cover, tears running unheeded down her cheeks. "They're so small, and I can't even touch them!"

"They're not as bad as they look, Rhyasha," said Vanna gently, stroking the older female's hair. "They'll only be on the ventilators for a day or two as a precaution. Although they're premature, they're both healthy."

"You've two grand little lads there, Rhyasha," said Jack. "We wouldn't lie to you. The next day or two will be worrying for us all, but there's no reason for anything to go wrong."

"They'll be fine," reassured Konis, folding her close. "Come away now. You should be in bed resting. You've just had major surgery." He tried to urge her away and when she resisted, he solved the problem by lifting her carefully into his arms. "You must rest," he said as he carried her out of the room. "I'll stay with you."

His heart ached for her as he shared her distress. She felt beaten, knowing there was nothing she could do for either her cubs, or Kusac. It cut him like a knife to feel her brought this low.

Noni's cottage, Dzahai village, Zhal-S'Asha, 18th day (October)

The room seemed to lurch as he looked at the newborn cub in Noni's arms, unsure what to do or say.

"She's yours, Tallinu," the familiar old voice said. "Your daughter. Take her from me, for Vartra's sake! Let her know you accept your child!"

He reached down to take the child from her, holding the little one awkwardly in his arms.

She gave a soft mewl, mind and hands reaching out for him. He offered her a finger and she took it, holding onto him firmly as she began to purr. He was totally unprepared for the flood of emotions that rushed through him as he stroked the tiny brown-furred hand. Gathering her closer, he laid his face against her tiny head, taking in her scent, bonding to her. Suddenly, this cub he'd tried so hard to avoid conceiving because of his love for her mother, was even more precious.

"A daughter," he said, looking over to where Carrie lay, exhausted from the birth. "We share a daughter."

Dawn's light, streaming in from the small window in Noni's main room, blinded him.

"I know," she said, her voice tired but holding a purr beneath the words.

He moved his head out of the autumn sunlight in an effort to see her clearly. As he blinked, his vision cleared—and the images he'd seen so many times were gone, replaced by reality.

Lowering his face to hers, he gently licked their cub's cheek. Their daughter stirred in his arms as he moved closer to the bed, sitting down beside her. Leaning forward, he passed her to Carrie, watching as she cradled the still damp mewling cub against her breast.

"She's beautiful," he whispered, stroking the hair from her sweat-drenched forehead. "Which name shall we choose, Dzinae?"

"Layeesha," she said, her voice faint as her face creased again in pain. "Noni . . ."

"Hush, child," said Noni, pressing gently on her still distended belly. "Tallinu, take the cub from her and clean her up, if you please. 'Tis only the afterbirth, child."

"I'll do that, Noni," said Teusi quietly, moving closer. "You go call T'Chebbi, then Stronghold to tell Kusac the good news."

Noni glanced at her apprentice and nodded. "Aye, it's about time you did more, Teusi," she said, turning and heading for the sink to wash her hands first.

"What did you want me to do?" asked Kaid.

"Just take the cub before she drops it," said Noni tartly. "Clean her down and wrap her in the blanket you'll find in the crib. Dammit, Tallinu, you did it with Kashini, didn't you? And here I was believing you when you said you'd studied birthing!"

"I did," said Kaid, carefully taking the slippery cub back from Carrie. "But that was books and vids, this is our daughter." Even he could hear the pride in his voice.

Noni looked over at him and laughed. "Ah, you have the same besotted look on your face as any new father! Long is the time I've waited to see that look, Kaid Tallinu, and be made a grandmother again by you!"

He grinned sheepishly as he took the soft towel Teusi held out to him. "Would I spoil your pleasure, Noni?" he asked, spreading it across his lap then laying his daughter on it so he could gently wipe her face and body.

Stronghold

"Konis is here, Noni," said Lijou when she called him. "Would you like to give him the news yourself?"

"What's the Clan Lord doing there?" she asked, surprised. "With two new sons of his own, I'd have thought he'd be home looking after them and that pretty life-mate of his!"

"Business," said Lijou briefly.

"Let me speak to Kusac."

"I'm afraid Kusac's in a strange mood and won't speak to anyone right now. He's shut himself up in one of the seniors' common rooms. I really think you should talk to Konis."

"I'll tell Kusac," said Rhyaz, getting up. "It's me that's sending him on this mission."

"I should be the one," said Konis tiredly.

"You've already done more than enough," said Rhyaz. "I know how difficult this is for you."

Noni's cottage

Teusi joined Noni at the table, leaving Carrie to feed her cub in peace. "She's still very large, Noni. Is that normal?" he asked quietly, accepting the cup of coffee she handed him.

"You think so too? I been wondering about that myself these last few weeks. Thought it was just she was carrying a lot of fluid. Let's wait and see what happens, shall we?"

"Should I get the aircar ready to take her to Stronghold?"

"Might be a good idea," she said. "Have your drink first, though. Depends how immature the second cub is. I'll warrant it's not from the same pairing as Layeesha."

"If we go to Stronghold, will Tallinu be a problem, given that Kusac's there?"

"He'll be too worried for her to care, which is as well because he's still mad as fire about that row they had." She wagged a finger at him. "When neither of them will talk about it, there's more to it than meets the eye, my lad, you mark my words."

Kaid sat on a chair beside the bed, holding Carrie's free hand, her fingertips pressed gently to his mouth, just enjoying the mingled tastes of her and their daughter.

Carrie laughed gently. "You're so different," she said, easing her hand from him so she could cup it round his cheek. "I've never seen such a softness in your face before."

He turned his head, touching his lips to her hand. "I've never had so much as I have at this moment," he said. "You didn't suffer too much pain, did you? Noni's potion worked? I felt very little at all, not like it was with Kashini."

She nodded, then her face creased in a mixture of surprise and pain as she bit back a cry.

"What is it?" Kaid asked anxiously, sitting up.

"Noni! Something's wrong! I think I'm bleeding!" she called out in fear.

"Take the berran from her, Tallinu," said Noni, getting to her feet. "Go put her in the crib, if you please, then fetch me some clean towels and a sheet from that pile on my bed. Teusi, you know what to do."

Kaid lifted the cub away, hushing her when she complained with small mewling sounds of distress.

Teusi was at the bedside almost instantly, moving the chair aside and pulling back the covers.

"It's all right, Carrie," he said, helping her lie down. "It's not blood, only a little fluid." He moved aside for Noni.

"Don't you fret, child, this is nothing to worry about," said Noni. "I had a feeling there might be another cub in you. Tallinu, I want that clean sheet now if you please," she said, raising her voice.

Kaid came running in from the other room as Carrie began to moan again. "What's wrong?" he demanded, handing her the folded sheet.

"There's a second cub," she said briefly as Carrie doubled up with a shriek of pain. "You see to your mate, I'll see to this cub."

It was over in minutes. As Noni gently eased the dark furred cub into the world, she looked up at Carrie. "No guessing who this one's father is, child. Kusac has a son."

"It can't be his," said Carrie, trying to lean forward against Kaid and see as Noni wiped the cub's face clean. "We've only paired once since we got back from Haven."

"You don't need me to tell you it only takes once, child," Noni said dryly, carefully handing the newborn to her.

Carrie held him close, looking at the tiny black-furred face as it crinkled up and he began to wail in a thin voice. "What's wrong with him? He's so small. He's sick, isn't he?" she asked in a trembling voice.

"Not sick, premature." As she severed the cord, Noni glanced at Teusi. "Call Stronghold, tell them why we're coming in, then get the aircar started," she ordered. "Tallinu, get two towels, one to clean him off and the other to wrap him in after."

Stunned, Kaid did as she asked.

"How could he be Kusac's? I was pregnant with Layeesha!"

"You just lie still and let me finish off, child," said Noni. "How long after you got pregnant did you pair with Kusac?"

"Just over two weeks," said Kaid as he tried to clean the tiny cub. He whimpered unhappily, head searching blindly for his mother, tiny hands waving aimlessly. "Noni's right, this is Kusac's cub, Carrie. I can sense the difference. We have to tell him."

"Kusac's left Stronghold," said Teusi quietly, looking up from the comm. "His father doesn't know where he's gone, only that he left after a row with Master Rhyaz."

Tears began to roll down Carrie's cheeks as she took the cub back from Kaid and clutched him close, burying her head against the towel he was wrapped in. "He's going to die, isn't he, Noni? He's too small. Why didn't anyone tell me I was carrying two babies?"

"Because we didn't know," said Noni, handing the soiled linen to Kaid as Teusi ran out to the aircar. "Your daughter masked the presence of the second cub and you refused to have scans done. And there's no reason why the cub should die if you can start him feeding!"

"Then why are we going to Stronghold? And where's Kusac gone?"

Noni reached out to stroke her cheek gently. "We're going to Stronghold because I want him to have every chance, child. It's a precaution, nothing more. Now try to get him to suckle while we get ready. And think of a name for the wee mite! Make him feel he's wanted too!" She said, glaring across at Kaid as he returned from the wash house in the back garden.

"Of course he's wanted," said Kaid sharply. "How could I turn my back on Layeesha's twin?"

"Considering the row you two had, I was wondering," sniffed Noni. "Twice a mother in one day! A reason to celebrate when you're better, child," she said to Carrie.

"The row's between Kusac and me," he said stiffly. "Nothing to do with his cub."

"Kusac should help choose a name," said Carrie, tears still rolling down her cheeks as she parted the towel round her son's face so he could suckle. "I can't choose it alone! Where's he gone? Why has he left Stronghold? You shouldn't have let him row with you, Tallinu, you know he's not himself."

Kaid grunted. "It wasn't me, Dzinae. From anyone else, his

insults would have been unforgivable. Let's leave it. I don't want to spoil this time with you."

The cub began to whimper, resisting Carrie's attempts to feed him until Kaid sat down beside her again, reaching out to try to soothe the crying infant. At that moment, Carrie's mind exploded within his, reestablishing their Leska Link. Seconds later, scared and frightened, the cub's mind joined theirs. Fretfully, he squirmed his arms free, searching with his hand until his fingers closed on Kaid's. Only then did the tension leave his tiny body and he began to suckle.

Startled, they exchanged glances over the infant's head.

"If you want your son to feed, then stop getting him all worked up with your worrying," said Noni tartly. "You'll all suffer for it later with a colicky cub yowling the place down! Tallinu, get moving, lad! I want this cub in the infirmary today, not tomorrow!"

CHAPTER 19

Stronghold

KONIS and Kha'Qwa were waiting for them with Physician Muushoi to help unload Carrie's floating stretcher from the aircar.

"Twins!" said Kha'Qwa in surprise as she saw Kaid emerge carrying Layeesha. "Noni didn't say she'd had twins. And so different," she added, seeing the dark pelt of the cub Carrie still held cradled in her arms.

Konis, ears held back in distress, went to Carrie's side. "Shall I take him, my dear?" he asked. "It might be safer while they move you up to the infirmary."

Reluctantly, Carrie let Konis take her son.

"It's Kusac's cub," Konis said quietly to Kha'Qwa as they followed them up the front steps into the main building.

"In Vartra's name! He doesn't know, does he?" she said, shocked.

"No one knew," he said, gently parting the wrappings to look at his grandson's face. "He's so tiny, Kha'Qwa! Almost as small as ours!"

"He's early," said Noni from behind them. "Thankfully not as premature as yours and Rhyasha's were, Konis. There's nothing to worry about, but given his size, I want him in an incubator being kept warm till he gains a bit of weight."

"What's she calling them?" asked Kha'Qwa.

Konis called out to Kaid who stopped and waited for them as Carrie was taken into the elevator. "My grandchildren, Kaid, what are their names?"

"Dhaykin," he said. "We've called him Dhaykin, and our daughter Layeesha. Where's Kusac gone?"

"We've just had word he's left Shola," said Kha'Qwa. "Vartra knows what he thinks he's doing, or where he's going!"

Kaid stared at them. "I know where he's gone," he said quietly. "Rezac was right. He's headed for the Prime world. Whatever you do, don't tell Carrie. She's enough to worry about right now with his cub being so fragile."

"I told you," began Noni as Teusi helped her up the steps, "There's nothing to worry about."

Kaid rounded on her, holding his daughter close. "You don't fool me, Noni."

"He needs his father, Kaid, just as your daughter needs you," she said quietly. "Only Kusac's gone. You'll have to fill that role till he returns. Can you do it? Can you be as much a father to Dhaykin as to Layeesha?"

"Sometimes you're an old fool, Noni," he said quietly, distress flitting briefly across his face. "If I didn't love Kusac, what he said wouldn't have hurt so much."

She smiled, reaching out familiarly to touch his neck. "Then Dhaykin will be fine."

Lijou looked up as Rhyaz came into his lounge.

"Didn't expect to see you for a while yet," said Kha'Qwa from her position curled up in front of the fire at her mate's feet. "Where's Alex?"

Rhyaz' eyes glazed over for a moment before he replied. "She's over in cryptology with Kai, working on some project of their own."

"Has Konis gone to his room?" asked Lijou.

"Yes. He's lying down for an hour or two before joining us for second meal," said Rhyaz, taking the chair at the other side of the fire and leaning forward to warm his hands. "His pilot hasn't enough experience of our weather patterns to risk flying home tonight. It's begun to snow quite heavily now."

"Did you go to see Carrie and the cubs?" asked Kha'Qwa.

"Not yet. I didn't want to disturb them. I'll visit them tomorrow."

"How was Konis?" asked Lijou. "Has he gotten over seeing Kusac off?"

"I don't think so," said Rhyaz, holding his hands out to the blaze. "He wasn't happy at all."

"I wish we hadn't needed to involve him but he knows the current political situation with the Primes better than us. Knowing he's got to go back home and publically condemn his son for treason must be the hardest thing he's ever done."

"I didn't want to send him either, but it was the only way we could send Kusac without being involved in accusations of treason ourselves, Lijou. No one can hold us responsible for the actions of a renegade who's known to be mentally unstable."

"I wonder why Kezule left the Primes," said Kha'Qwa, filling the silence that had fallen. "And why he wanted to meet with Kusac. You'd think the last Sholan he'd want to see again was one of those responsible for bringing him forward in time. He should have been glad to be back home among his own people. He'd married the doctor from the *Kz'adul*, hadn't he?"

"I believe so, but why he left is just one of the many answers we hope Kusac will find," said Rhyaz. "When I went to tell him Noni had called to say the cub had been born, he already knew. I wonder if he would have gotten his Link to Carrie back if this message hadn't come."

"I know he would," said Lijou. "His Talent was back, it was just sleeping. Her mind would have awakened it, and he knew that. I'm concerned at the wisdom of sending anyone, Rhyaz, I still think it would have been better put in the hands of the Prime Ambassador."

"Kusac wanted to go, despite every other consideration," said Rhyaz uncomfortably, remembering Kusac's threat. "He knew what was at stake."

"You're wrong, he didn't want to go," said Lijou. "It was as if he were driven. I still fear this is a trap and the General will try to kill him."

"I made sure Kusac can kill Kezule if necessary," said Rhyaz, his hands now thawed out enough for him to lean back in his chair. "I left one of our prototype chemical guns and a spray available for him to take, and he took it."

Lijou looked at him in shock. "He's got the la'quo gun? Are you mad? I thought you wanted information from Kezule! And if he gets hold of them from Kusac, he's got a way to buy his freedom from the Primes by letting them know we've developed a chemical weapon to use against them!"

"He won't get it from Kusac. If he's threatened with capture, all he needs is one shot into the room, or one spray of that chemical and all Valtegans, or Primes, will be out cold for a couple of hours. When they wake, Kusac and his crew will be long gone, and those like Kezule will no longer have that aggressive edge over us. I've also taken other measures to ensure none of our people get captured."

"Chima," said Lijou. "Yes, I know about Chima, and I've sent someone too."

Rhyaz looked startled. "You knew?"

"Don't underestimate my mate, Rhyaz," purred Kha'Qwa, leaning back against Lijou's legs and looking up at him. "He's as much Brotherhood as you for all he's more compassionate. He is the other side of your coin, after all."

"Apparently," said Rhyaz dryly. "You briefed Banner, didn't you? What's his objective, Lijou?"

"Only to ensure fairness," said Lijou. "Kusac doesn't deserve this, Rhyaz. He's not unstable. I know that when it comes to it, he'll do the right thing. I couldn't in conscience let him go on this mission without someone he could rely on, considering you foisted Dzaou on him as one of his crew."

Rhyaz nodded, a very Human gesture. "I'll concede that. Dzaou's presence is designed to test his patience and stability. Banner's a good operative. He'll be there for him but won't let sentiment get in the way."

"He'll be scrupulously fair," countered Lijou. "This mission is fraught enough without sending someone as xenophobic as Dzaou on it. Hell, Kusac's bad enough over the Primes!"

"Again, insurance. Chima isn't likely to be fooled by Kezule, and controlling Dzaou's xenophobia will help Kusac control his own. I picked the crew carefully, Lijou. I want Kusac to succeed. If his team fails to return, we get no information as well as losing several good people."

"I hope when he gets back that the row between him and Kaid can be patched up," said Kha'Qwa. "You realize he's lost almost everything he had here, including his freedom, don't you? At this moment, he's got nothing to come home for—except his daughter, and a son he doesn't know he has."

"It was necessary," said Rhyaz. "No one but those involved must know about this mission, including Kusac's Triad-mates, otherwise his supposed treason won't be believable. We're relying on their assumption that he's become psychologically dependent on the Primes because of what happened to him on the *Kz'adul*."

"What if it's true? What if he is dependent on them and that's part of the reason he hates the Primes?" asked Kha'Qwa. "What if that's why he knew he had to go to the rendezvous?"

"Then as I said, we have the rest of the team. They know what to do," said Rhyaz, his voice taking on a touch of hardness.

"Vartra help him," murmured Kha'Qwa, pressing herself closer to Lijou.

Lijou looked over to the empty place on his shelves where a certain wooden casket had rested until he'd given it to Kusac. "I pray that Vartra will," he said softly.

Stronghold, later that evening

"I can only apologize, Toueesut," said Konis. "I don't know what has gotten into him lately. The Physician here at Stronghold thinks he's headed for the Prime world."

"Why going Prime world when not tolerating Primes on Shola, Master Konis?" demanded Toueesut. "Not making sense. If Primes looking for him warn them we not wanting *Couana* damaged nor Kusac. Cannot believe our Clan Leader would do this after his Talent returned even if taking time to manifest itself for him again." He sighed gustily, shaking his head. "We will not be pressing charges against him, Master Konis."

"You have my thanks, Toueesut. I'll make sure the Primes are aware of the need to call us rather than attempt to take back the *Couana*," reassured Konis. "I'll be in touch as soon as we have any word."

The connection closed, he turned to Lijou. "Can't we get word to Kusac? Tell him he has a son?"

Lijou sensed Rhyaz about to speak and sent him a private imperative telling him to leave the matter to him.

"Konis, it's been hard enough for him to leave Shola as it is," he said, getting up and going to his friend's side. "Telling him of the birth of a son he didn't know he'd conceived would be cruel at this time. Believe me, he's better not knowing."

Konis sighed and slumped back in his seat. "How long be-

fore Raiban starts jumping up and down?" he asked tiredly. This
had been one of the longest nights of his life—as long and worrying as the night the twins had been born.

"Soon," began Rhyaz as the door burst open to admit Alex.

"How the hell could you do this to Kusac?" she demanded.
"I just figured it out! You've thrown him and his crew not only
to the Primes, but to Raiban and the military! I thought you were
a good person, Rhyaz, someone I could respect, but this stinks!
Kusac isn't a renegade, he's ill!"

"Alex," Rhyaz said warningly, getting to his feet. "I've told
you before about not interfering in my business."

"Don't try to shut me up," she said, slamming the door behind her and stalking into the room. "And you, you're his father!"
she said, pointing at Konis. "You should be supporting him, not
helping these two sell him out!"

"Alex, be quiet!" thundered Rhyaz. "You've no idea what
you're talking about!"

"Then explain it to me," she said, glowering at them all. "Justify it, if you can!"

"He's on a mission, Alex," said Konis from his seat at Rhyaz's
desk. "We can't officially send him out to meet with General
Kezule. If we did, it would cause a bigger incident than the one
that we're letting happen now. Do you think I'd let them sacrifice my son if the safety of Shola didn't depend on it and he
hadn't agreed to it?"

Alex looked at the Clan Lord, seeing the anguished set of his
ears for the first time. Uncertainly, she looked over at Lijou.

"You know what's at stake here, Alex," said the priest. "Rhyaz
and I have to make decisions like this all the time. It's what we
do for the good not only of our species, but the Alliance as a
whole. As Rhyaz' Leska, you'll have to get used to the fact that
sometimes individuals have to be sacrificed for the good of many
more people. Kezule asked for Kusac by name. He had to go.
Believe me, when he comes back, we'll do everything we can to
see any charges against him are dropped. But we must know why
Kezule wants him."

"He agreed to go?" she asked in a small voice.

"He agreed," confirmed Rhyaz. "But even if he hadn't, I would
have done my utmost to persuade him. There's unrest on the
Prime world and we must know more about it."

Lijou rose. "Konis, perhaps we should go visit Carrie and her cubs in the infirmary," he said. "Noni should have them settled by now. Alex, you must keep this information to yourself. Only we four know they are on a mission for us. Carrie and Kaid must not find out. Do you understand me?"

She nodded mutely.

Konis stopped to put his hand on her shoulder as he went past her. "Your heart's in the right place, child. Thank you for defending my son."

"I'm sorry I jumped to conclusions," she said quietly. "I should have known better. I apologize, Clan Lord, Father Lijou."

"No harm was done. The Brotherhood needs another conscience, Alex," said Lijou, stopping by the door. "Sometimes I feel I'm in a minority." He smiled as he watched Rhyaz go over to her, knowing his friend was going to take the time to explain the situation to her. "Perhaps you should brief Alex more often, Rhyaz. She's surely shown she can be trusted now with sensitive information. It would save misunderstandings like this."

"I know she can be trusted," said Rhyaz, putting an arm round her shoulders. "I was trying to spare her the less palatable side of our work, that's all."

"It takes time to adjust to having a Leska," said Konis. "But despite the disparity in your ages, it'll be easier if you work as a team."

"What disparity?" asked Alex, giving Rhyaz a sideways glance. "You should see him when he relaxes."

Rhyaz cuffed her gently, making the other two males smile as they left.

"Nicely done," said Rhyaz, stroking her cheek gently. "You made them forget for a moment."

"I still want that explanation," she said.

The comm buzzed discreetly and Rhyaz sighed, letting her go. "Raiban," he said.

"Has Speaker Toueesut pressed charges?" demanded Rhyaz.

"You know damned well he hasn't," snarled Raiban.

"Then this is an internal Clan matter and outside your jurisdiction."

"What do you mean, a Clan matter?"

"Speaker Toueesut considers his swarm members of Kusac's Clan. They applied for permission to live in the Valgarth Estate village and Kusac granted them that right."

Raiban's growl of anger almost made him wince.

You got her good and mad this time, she sent with a mental chuckle.

"There's still the matter of an unauthorized take-off from Lygoh space port and the disruptor he and the one called Dzaou planted! It put communications out for over an hour!"

Rhyaz shrugged. "What can I say? We're not responsible, Raiban. Whatever they're doing, they're doing it independently."

"They've gone renegade?" Raiban pounced on the news.

"We're dealing with it, General," he said coldly. "You confine yourself to matters that concern you, like last week's laundry bill for the Forces."

"Don't take that attitude with me, Rhyaz! If you're dealing with it, you catch them then! I've issued warrants for their arrest. They all face several years in a correction facility and I intend to see they serve out that time in full!"

"Noted, General. Now if you'll excuse me, I've matters of my own to see to."

"You shouldn't have fought to remain independent of us, Rhyaz. Had you been part of the Forces, we could have kept this quiet. As it is, it'll be splashed across all the media nets by tomorrow. Doesn't look good, you know, the founder of your En'Shalla Clan going renegade on you like this. Still, your choice." She grinned widely and broke the link.

"She's right," he murmured, sitting back in his chair. "They'll have a field day at our expense."

"It must be worth it or you wouldn't let him go," said Alex.

"We won't know that until after Kusac has returned from his rendezvous with Kezule."

"He's done what?" said Kaid in disbelief when Lijou told him later that night outside Carrie's room in the infirmary. "He's damned lucky Toueesut didn't press charges! At least Banner is with him. Do you know who else went?"

"Not yet. It won't be difficult to trace them, though. Very few senior Brothers and Sisters are left on Shola now."

"I noticed how empty Stronghold was," said Kaid. "At least if he turns up at K'oish'ik, the Primes will return him to us." He stopped and looked sharply at Lijou. "They will return him, won't they?"

"So long as he doesn't commit any crimes against them."

Kaid shrugged. "Then let's hope he's retained some shreds of common sense. You'll excuse me, but I've wasted enough time talking about him. My place is with Carrie and the twins at this time."

Troubled, Lijou watched him leave. Kaid might affect uninterest in Kusac's situation, but he knew better—he could feel the pain the other male was trying desperately to hide, even from himself. Whatever Kusac had said to alienate Kaid, it had worked only too well because the hurt had gone deep, very deep.

Teusi helped Noni over to Vartra's tomb then left her there, standing guard outside the main doors of the temple.

Angrily, she rapped on the edge of the sarcophagus with the head of her stick. "What you doing, Vartra?" she demanded. "What in Hell's name do you think you're doing to my Triad? They did everything you asked of them, dammit!"

She waited, listening to the silence until she could hear the sound of the flames flickering almost silently in their braziers. Then, leaning against it for support, she rapped on the tomb again, harder, sending a spark flying from the stone.

"Answer me, dammit!" she snarled. "I got the right to call You several times over! We're linked by blood, my family to Yours through him! What You done to Kusac, You moth-bitten, maggot-ridden corpse! Wake up in there!" She hit it again and again until the metal head knocked off a shower of chips.

"Hardly that, Old One," His voice said gently from off to her left. "I believe My remains are in better condition than that, what's left of them that is."

She stopped, lowering her stick to the ground and leaning on it before turning round to face the gentle glow that came from Ghyakulla's shrine. "I got him settled," she said harshly. "Started training his mind again, looking to the future. He hoped to get his Link back with her—and he would have but for this fool's errand! This talk of him going renegade is a crock of jegget shit and you know it! Get You out here where I can talk to You face to face and explain Yourself to me!"

"You did your job well, Rhuna," He said, His tone still gentle despite her insults. "It's out of My hands. He's where he was meant to be. I can do nothing, tell you nothing more."

"Since when?" she demanded, peering between the pillars for a sight of the Entity. "You manipulated them all these years and suddenly You claim you got nothing to do with it? Why the switch to Kusac? What really took him off Shola? Don't you know you're risking the lives of all three of them?"

The glow was obscured briefly and she could see a dark shape coming toward her.

"Ghyakulla's Realm is open again, Old One, as are the others," He said, coming to a stop in front of her. "I'm keeping My word to you. The pledge is renewed."

"Been open since the first rains four weeks ago," she snapped. "Answer my questions, dammit!"

"This is something over which I have no influence, Noni. Forces are being brought into play that have nothing to do with Us, and Kusac is one of the people at the core. This must play itself out."

"What forces?" she demanded. "Nothing is more powerful than the Entities on our world!"

He mercly touched her face with His fingertips. "I can do nothing," He whispered. His image faded in front of her eyes.

Vartra's realm, Zhal-S'Asha, 22nd day (October)

In the distance, thunder rumbled, low and menacing. Vartra shivered, moving closer to the flickering heat of the braziers. The storm wasn't here in His realm; it prowled the mortal world of the Dzahai mountain range around Stronghold. Since the Brotherhood had found His tomb, the veil between His reality and theirs had grown increasingly weaker. He glanced sideways at the dark shape of the sarcophagus, unsettled by its presence in this mirror image of His temple. It reminded Him too much of a mortality that was beyond His reach.

Thunder pealed overhead, shocking Him from His reverie. A jagged shaft of energy split the darkness of the temple, tearing apart the very fabric of His realm. Deep in His bones, He felt the humming begin to build as roiling clouds of blue and silver poured through the rent, pushing the edges apart, reaching out for Him.

"No!" he shouted, trying to back away even as the maelstrom engulfed Him.

Consciousness returned. Darkness, relieved only by pinpoints of light, surrounded Him. Rising to His haunches, He crouched there, waiting, flicking His tail tip gently on the ground beside Him in a display of unconcern He was far from feeling.

I thought I was done with you. Why have you called Me? He sent.

We have work for You.

Haven't You plagued Me enough?

The Balance is shifting again. All must work to restore it.

He stilled his thoughts, knowing it was the truth.

The Hunter is ready. You must awaken him.

Knowledge of who and what the Hunter was came to Him. *You place too great a burden on him!*

The choice was not Ours. He's Your kin. Only You can reach him, prepare him for what comes. You must wake the Hunter.

Leave Me in peace! I've done Your bidding long enough!

You cannot refuse. It's your geas. Wake the Hunter!

Falling, the lights spinning crazily round Him, He tumbled end over end until finally He was hurled into the void between the realms.

the *Couana*, the same day

The memory of his row with Kaid finally released him and he came to curled in a ball, arms wrapped protectively over his aching chest. Tears were flowing down his face and the pain he felt wasn't dimmed by the nine days that had passed since then. He felt gentle hands holding him, stroking his head as he attempted to calm himself.

"You did what was needed," a soothing voice said. "If your Triad built your relationships on rock, then it will survive, Kusac. This was the last of the memories. What have you learned from them? How can they help you in what lies ahead?"

"I've learned how many people I've hurt," he whispered, rubbing at his eyes to wipe away the tears.

"Not you. That person was the one J'koshuk tried to beat into submission," the voice whispered, its breath warm against his face. "In these last three days, you've learned that by seeming to bend to his will, you did survive. He did not win."

Banner didn't talk like this. Confused, he raised his head, blinking as he tried to see the speaker but his eyes were still too swollen and gritty. He smelled nothing recognizable and opened his mouth, flicking his tongue tip out to taste the air.

A hand gripped him tightly by the scruff, forcing his head down again. "Listen to me, Kusac Aldatan! What did you learn?" The voice was hard, commanding him to answer.

Nung blossom! He tasted nung blossom. "I survived," he whispered, beginning to believe it. "They tried to destroy me and my Triad but we all survived—until I . . ."

"You did what had to be done," repeated Vartra, loosening His grip and letting him move. "What else did you learn?"

He uncurled, feeling his chest for the deep scratches he knew had already healed before looking across at the male crouched by the side of his bed. "That until now I've been driven by memories of the past, of what happened to me on the *Kz'adul*. I need to go beyond them. I need to face Doctor Zayshul and find out the truth."

"Good," purred Vartra, sitting back on His haunches, eyes glowing as they reflected the dim light of the room. "You progress well. It's time your Talent awoke again, but before it does, I give you one piece of advice. Tread warily with the Liege of Hell, Kusac. Remember my prophecy to Kaid. There must be an alliance between you." In one fluid move, Vartra rose to His feet, the dark gray of His tunic filling Kusac's field of vision.

He felt a hand touch the top of his head, then agony exploded inside his skull. Crying out, he clasped his hands to his head, keening softly as he curled up on himself again, barely hearing the Entity's last words.

"The pain will last only a short time, Kusac. Use wisely what's been returned to you. Remember, the only boundaries are those you create yourself."

Anchorage

"The Hunter's awakened," said Naacha, stopping in front of Annuur and Sokarr. "I feel him."

"At this distance?" asked the Cabbarran, long thin ears and stiff crest tilting forward in concern. "Not possible."

"Warned you of hidden power sleeping there." The tone was censuring. "Is greater than what we did. Only needed awaking, not enhancing. Balance be overturned if he destroys sand-dweller."

Annuur regarded his mystic. "We did what Camarilla ordered," he said. "A Skepp Lord is with sand-dweller. Little as possible being left to chance. They *must* combine."

Naacha grunted. "We suffer if Camarilla wrong. If war happens, all will be engulfed as four combine against rest."

"Camarilla is aware. You not only one to see this potentiality." Annuur quashed his personal worries, trying to convince himself that the Camarilla had, indeed, foreseen all possible futures.

"I see maybe we created something cannot control," grumbled Naacha, dropping back to all fours and turning to leave.

"Concealed Camarilla weapon fully installed in *Watcher* ship," said Sokaar helpfully, breaking the silence that had fallen.

"Good," said Annuur absently, his mind on other matters.

the *Couana*, the same day

Showered, pelt brushed as best he could manage, he made his way to the mess. Banner and Chima were already there, sitting at one end of the largest table. Stopping to get a coffee and a pastry from the dispenser, he went over to the command panel in the wall and toggled the ship's comm.

"All hands to the mess. Briefing in five minutes," he said.

"I tried to call you half an hour ago but the door was locked," said Banner as he joined them at their table.

"I fixed the lock," he said, taking a sip of his drink and concentrating on his pastry. "I was meditating and didn't want to be disturbed."

Banner gave him a long look over the top of his own mug before putting it down.

The other three arrived together, grabbing drinks of their own before joining them. Their intense curiosity and expectation battered at the edges of his mind, threatening to pierce his mental shielding. He regretted turning down the torc's sensitivity, but for a wonder, his own shields held.

"General Kezule has stolen a small destroyer class ship and left the Prime homeworld with some sixty people. The Primes are searching for him. However, several days ago, a message was received from Kezule at Haven, telling us to meet him at the coordinates I gave you at the beginning of this journey. He claims he has something of interest to us. Our mission is to meet him, get whatever he has, find out why he left and what he's planning to do, if we can, then head for Haven."

"Why steal the *Couana*?" demanded Dzaou.

He turned to look at Dzaou, waiting for a moment before replying. "It would jeopardize our treaty if we were seen meeting secretly with him."

"Do we report his position to the Primes once we've gotten what we want?" asked Khadui.

"No. Our priority is to get what we've come for and take it to Haven," he said.

"Why are the Primes after him?" asked Chima. "And why send you?"

"They say the Emperor values Kezule, he's not being hunted for any crime. As for why me, Kezule asked for me in person."

"It strikes me this could well be Kezule's revenge on you for bringing him forward to our time," said Jayza thoughtfully.

"Too complicated, and too obvious," said Chima. "Sixty people on a destroyer: if they had warriors, I'd assume it was a raiding vessel, but they don't. I wonder what he's up to."

"We should have brought a telepath," said Khadui, then looked stricken as he realized what he'd said.

"Kezule specified no telepaths, that's why he asked for me," he said, ignoring it.

"Do we negotiate with Kezule for whatever it is he has?" asked Banner, filling the silence.

"No. He gives it to us or we take it, with lethal force if necessary," he replied. "We reach the . . ."

"Hold on," said Dzaou. "I'm not happy with this. No negotiating? I don't think so, Kusac. I'm Challenging your judgment on his mission. It's well known how much you dislike the Primes, and given that Kezule had your sister and daughter captive for several days, I think you could be twisting this your way to get your own revenge on him. I don't trust you to be objective. I believe you should stand down and hand this mission over to Banner."

He looked at Dzaou, seeing through his newly awakened senses that the male's hatred and paranoia seemed to surround him with a dark aura.

"You're entitled to your opinion," he said, fascinated by the effect, even as it faded. "You have, however, been told the mission objectives and you will follow your orders exactly." He returned his attention to the group as a whole. "We reach the rendezvous in just under two hours. Chima, Banner, check your personal weapons, armor and air supplies. You have until the twentieth hour, at which time, in full combat armor, you'll relieve the bridge crew. I'll meet you there. Dzaou, Jayza, Khadui, you'll then do the same and report to the bridge at 20.45 hours, when we'll take up our battle positions for the final approach. Dismissed."

"Just a damned minute," said Dzaou, getting up. "I said I don't trust you—I want Banner in charge . . ."

He didn't get the chance to finish as Kusac lunged across the table and grasped him firmly by the throat.

"You are Challenging me," he said, his tone almost conversational as his claws tightened in Dzaou's flesh. "Leadership of this mission is not open to discussion. You've been given your orders, carry them out or face the consequences." He flung him backwards, watching in surprise as Dzaou traveled the length of the mess, hitting the wall by the entrance before sliding, stunned, to the ground. Unconsciously, he glanced at his hand, remembering how Banner had been sent flying the length of his cabin only a couple of days before merely by touching him when he'd been sleeping without his torc.

He turned back to the others. "Anyone else want to Challenge me?" he asked with deceptive mildness.

"No, sir," said Jayza, getting up and going to help the stunned Dzaou to his feet. Angrily, the bruised male pulled himself free, stalking out of the mess, tail flicking angrily. The others followed, leaving him alone with Banner.

"The memories are finished, aren't they?" Banner said quietly, getting to his feet. "Your Talent's returned. You used psi power to throw him across the room, just like you did with me the other day when you were asleep."

"We're about to go into combat, Banner. You have your orders," he said quietly, sitting down and lifting his mug. "I'll see you on the bridge in forty-five minutes."

The rendezvous was on the edges of a small uninhabited solar system. After Kusac had transmitted the ID, they parked in orbit around the second world's moon. They weren't kept waiting for long.

"We're being scanned, Captain," said Khadui.

"Incoming transmission," said Jayza.

"Play it," ordered Kusac. "I want that ship located now, Khadui."

"*M'zayik* to Touiban vessel. State your purpose in this system." The Prime spoke perfectly accented Sholan, with only a trace of a lisp.

"Got it! It's hiding just on the edge of the horizon of this moon, Captain. Small vessel, well armored. Their weapon ports are open and they're powered up. Eighteen life forms, Primes from the looks of them, but there's an area that's showing up blank. The scanners won't penetrate it."

"That isn't the ship they took from the Prime world," said Dzaou. "That's only a scout ship."

"Acknowledged. Open a channel to them. Get me a vid link. I want to see who we're talking to," he ordered. The voice wasn't Kezule's, or Zayshul's.

"Establishing vid link. Channel open, Captain."

The main screen now showed the interior of the vessel hailing them. Lighting was at a lower level than theirs, and sitting in what he assumed was the Captain's chair, was a Valtegan. A Prime, he corrected himself, hands clenching on the arms of his chair as he recognized the sandy green skin of the male looking out at him.

"This is Kusac Aldatan of the *Couana*," he said. "We received a message to meet General Kezule here."

"Captain Zaykkuh of the *M'zayik* at your service, Captain Aldatan. The General requests that your crew remains here in orbit and you transfer to your shuttle and join us."

"You'll understand if I decline your invitation, Captain Zaykkuh," he said. "My appointment was with your General. Call me when he's prepared to talk to me himself."

"I wouldn't be so hasty if I were you, Kusac Aldatan," said

a voice he recognized. Another male came into view, peremptorily gesturing the Captain out of his chair.

Kezule had changed. The face that regarded him from the comm screen was relaxed now, his confidence echoed in his body posture as he lounged back in the command seat. "I see you're dressed for combat. That's not why I sent for you. Our mission is peaceful."

"I'm sure that as a warrior you'll appreciate our caution," he said. "Why have you dragged us all the way out here?"

"Patience, Captain. I don't think you want me to show you what I have on an open ship to ship channel. You have a shuttle. Join me and find out."

"Bring it here, Kezule. I'm not leaving the *Couana*."

"Then unfortunately, you'll be none the wiser. My offer is nonnegotiable. If you want what I have, come to me." The General's tone had sharpened, grown colder. "I take a great risk meeting you like this."

"True, but then so do I. I've no way of knowing that we want what you have."

"Oh, you'll want them," said Kezule softly, making a slight hand gesture to someone off-screen. "Shall we say that I want to return some items acquired the same way you were by the *Kz'adul*?"

"Does he mean other Sholans?" asked Banner in an undervoice.

"I'm picking up Sholan life forms, Captain," said Chima quietly. "Two."

"Send them over, Kezule," he said, claws extending until they punctured the padded arm coverings.

"You come to me, Kusac," said Kezule, the sibilance suddenly noticeable in his voice. "They cannot easily be transported. The shock of contact with you will be too great."

He frowned, wondering what Kezule meant.

"You may bring one other crew member with you," Kezule said abruptly. "And you may carry weapons. If you delay any longer, I may change my mind."

He got up. "We'll be there," he said, cutting the connection. "Chima, take the bridge. Banner, you're with me."

"You're playing into his hands," warned Banner as they powered up the shuttle.

"He's got two Sholans over there, maybe more. Vartra knows what state they're in. We came here for them and if this is the only way we can get them, so be it," he said, letting the shuttle drop down out of the *Couana's* bay doors.

Ten minutes later, they emerged into the cargo bay of the Prime scout ship. Their eyes took a moment or two to adjust to the dimmer light. When they did, they saw the black-clad Captain they'd spoken to earlier. He was accompanied by two soldiers in green fatigues, energy rifles slung across their backs—all Warriors, if he read their scents correctly.

"Only one's a Prime," said Banner quietly, resting a gloved hand on the butt of his pistol. "And they're armed."

"I know," he said briefly, lowering his mental shields just enough to send a gentle questing thought out toward them.

Immediately he sensed the psi dampers fitted to the ship. Retreating, he opened his mind, allowing himself only to absorb passively for now, not that he'd be able to sense much. If they were using psi dampers, they'd be alert to any psychic activity and he didn't want to let them know that his Talent was functioning again. His hand went to his weapons belt, unconsciously checking on the loaded la'quo pellet gun hidden there.

"Captain Aldatan," said Zaykkuh, inclining his head slightly. "My name is Zaykkuh. You may leave your helmets here if you wish. You won't need them."

"We'll keep them," he said shortly, adjusting his grip on the lightweight vacuum helm.

"As you wish. Please follow me." The Captain gestured to the door behind him.

After his time on the *Kz'adul,* the smells were familiar to him: the distinctive odor of their recycled air, the dry leathery scent of the Valtegans themselves. As he fell in behind the Captain, memories of his captivity came back to him, but now that his fear of them was gone, they held no power over him.

The metal-floored corridor was cool beneath his feet as they followed the Captain down the main corridor to an empty recreation room.

"General Kezule will join you shortly," said Captain Zaykkuh, gesturing them to enter.

There was an appearance of age about the room, a faded look

to the paintwork and a faint mustiness in the air at odds with the pristine condition of the landing bay. Cupboards lined two of the walls and in the third was set a large vid screen. Several worn easy chairs were grouped round low tables. It was obviously a recreation lounge. And like the landing bay and the corridor, it was fitted with psi dampers.

"Rather well worn, isn't it?" said Banner in a low voice.

He'd no chance to reply before the sound of approaching footsteps drew their attention back to the door.

"You can relax, Kusac," said Kezule, as he strolled into the room, hands in the pockets of his black fatigues. "Unlike you, we're unarmed." Behind him was Doctor Zayshul.

"You've armed guards outside the door," he said, eyes on the Doctor as, hesitating in the doorway when she saw him, she followed Kezule in.

"A precaution because we allowed you to retain your weapons. I believe you know my wife," Kezule said, walking past them toward the chairs and sitting down.

"Yes," he murmured, forcing himself not to taste the air for her scent. He experienced a jolt of surprise to hear she was married, and to Kezule. "Doctor Zayshul."

She nodded, passing close to him as she joined her husband. Her scent hit him then, making his senses reel briefly as it brought back memories of their night on the *Kz'adul*.

"Sit down, Kusac," said Kezule. "It's been a long time since I saw you. How are your delightful sister and her mate? And your daughter, of course."

He clenched his jaw, then forced himself to relax. Kezule was only trying to wind him up. "They're fine," he said. "Let's forget the pleasantries, Kezule. We know you've got two Sholans. Just give them to us and we'll be gone."

Kezule lifted his chin slightly. "I thought we could make this reunion a little more pleasant, but if that's what you wish," he said, gesturing to the soldiers standing at the door. "Fetch her," he ordered.

Minutes later, a female Sholan carrying an infant entered, stopping abruptly when she saw them.

"It's all right, Rraelga," said Zayshul. "They've come to take you home to Shola."

Clutching her cub closer, Rraelga looked from the Valtegans to them. "Home?" she said, voice barely audible, ears flattening out of sight in her short tan hair. "You're from Shola?" The hope in her voice was frightening.

Banner stepped forward. "We're from the Brotherhood of Vartra, Djana, and yes, we're here to take you home."

"The good Goddess be praised!" she whispered, stepping forward impulsively. She stopped, looking fearfully again at Kezule and Zayshul. "Not that we haven't been well treated by the General and his wife."

"They understand, I'm sure," said Banner, taking her by the arm and drawing her closer, into his protection.

He turned to Kezule. "How did you get them?" he demanded.

"They were picked up some time ago from a M'zullian vessel," said Kezule. "Their presence on K'oish'ik only just came to my attention. They were victims of the same people who held you."

"You could have returned them through our Embassy. Why call us out here? Whatever you want, Kezule, you're not going to get it."

"So discourteous. I want a little of your time, Kusac, nothing more," murmured Kezule.

"No deal," he said. "Under the terms of the Treaty, they would have been returned to us anyway."

"Why don't you wait and see what else I have before being so sure you won't help me." Kezule got to his feet and left the room.

Seeing Banner talking to the Sholan female, he took the opportunity to approach Zayshul. "What's this all about?" he asked in a low voice, trying to ignore the effect she was having on him. "It wasn't their scents you put on the message. There was the scent of a cub older than that infant. What happened between us that night, Zayshul? What did you do to me—and yourself?"

She looked away. "Kezule will tell you," she said, her voice almost inaudible. "This is out of my hands, Kusac. He's the one in command."

He opened his mouth to speak again, then stopped dead, suddenly sensing the presence of four minds, minds that even as a telepath he shouldn't have been able to pick up. Forcing himself to continue, he said, "We need to talk privately, Zayshul. I know you did something to me that night and I want to know what."

Banner's exclamation of shock made him turn around. He

could only stare open-mouthed as four kitlings, barely ten years old, crowded into the room.

"Vartra's bones," he heard Banner say. "Where did *they* come from?"

"These are yours too, I believe. As I said, Kusac, I want some of your time. Call it a gesture of good faith for our return of these children," Kezule said quietly. He looked over to Banner. "Remain here with your people. Your Captain and I have private business to discuss."

"I don't think so," said Kusac.

"I've more to show you, but it's for your eyes only." Kezule looked over to his wife, raising his voice slightly. "Tell him, Zayshul. Persuade your Sholan he needs to come with me."

Annoyed at being referred to in those terms, he looked back at her. Zayshul stirred but refused to meet his eyes. "Go with him, Kusac."

Her voice was still barely audible, and he could smell her apprehension. Whatever it was Kezule wanted to show him, it worried her.

"Not afraid, are you?" said Kezule, his tone gently mocking. "If I intended either to kill you or keep you captive, I'd have done it as soon as you got off your shuttle. You have my word you'll be allowed to leave safely with your people. You're far more use to me alive than dead, Kusac. Zayshul, come with us. Your presence may reassure our guest."

"Captain," began Banner.

Throwing him his helmet, he followed Kezule. The General's behavior had him puzzled.

They didn't go far, only a matter of a hundred yards or so further down the corridor. An armed guard waited ahead of them, and as Kezule approached, he leaned forward to open the door, following them inside. More Primes, and these Primes were Warriors. Where had Kezule gotten Prime Warriors from?

The lounge was small, with two worn soft seats and a low table in front of them. It was obviously a crew cabin. Yet another guard stood at the room's inner door.

"Wait here," ordered Kezule, heading for it.

He waited impatiently, annoyed that the presence of the guards prevented him talking further to Zayshul. He looked across at her, studying the face that had haunted him for so long, noticing features he'd taken for granted before. Like how the color of her eyes was enhanced by the rainbow hued skin surrounding them, and how her close fitting gray coveralls did little to conceal the muscular body beneath.

He heard the door opening and, with an effort, turned back to look at it. The General stood in the doorway, his hand on the shoulder of a fifth Sholan cub. He blinked, unable to believe what he saw.

The cub's pelt was so dark that even in the reduced light of the room, it shone with the distinctive blue sheen peculiar to the Aldatan family. He felt the pull of blood between them, and knew in one terrifying moment of revelation that this was his son. As his eyes met Kezule's, he realized that the General did too.

Kezule's nonretractile claws tightened on the cub's shoulder. "This is Captain Kusac Aldatan," he said in his own language, bending his head to speak to the kitling. "It's my hope he'll be joining us on Kij'ik. You may look at him so you'll know him again."

As the kitling raised his head, amber eyes looking incuriously at him, he could see that round his neck nestled a close-fitting metal collar.

"You can come closer, Kusac," said Kezule.

Like a sleepwalker, he stepped forward. It was like looking at a younger version of himself. He remembered to breathe, opening his mouth and flicking his tongue out to be sure of catching every nuance of the cub's scent. Biting back a small noise of horror, he looked up at the General.

"Return to your cabin," Kezule ordered the cub.

"As the General commands," the kitling said in the same language as Kezule released him. Turning round, he began to walk back into the inner room.

"Wait!" Automatically he reached out to stop him, but his son left the room without a backward glance.

"What have you done to him?"

Kezule closed the inner door. "I've done nothing to him, Kusac. Like the others, he was a prisoner of the Directorate. Take the Sholans I've given you back to your outpost at Haven, then return here in six days or you'll never see him again."

"You bastard," he whispered, hands clenching at his sides, all thoughts of revenge vanishing. "Give me them all, then we'll talk." His voice was harsh with emotions he didn't dare show. Like the others, the cub looked to be about ten years old—how could he possibly have a son of that age? And what had Kezule done to his son to make him turn away from his own kind?

"No, Kusac. That cub is my surety you'll return. The Primes are a dying race, and the M'zullians and J'kirtikkians are psychopaths, equally as flawed as the Primes. If my people are to survive, we need to change. And you're going to help me by training them."

"You think you can blackmail me?" He wanted his son— whether or not he was part Valtegan, he was still Sholan. "You think that I'll help you keep your kind alive after what you've done to my family?"

"You know what I'm holding," said Kezule. "And you know the price I'm asking—your time as their trainer. Now go, take the children and the adult. Return here in six days, prepared to stay for as long as I need you or you'll never see him again. Zayshul will escort you to your shuttle." Gesturing the warriors forward to guard the door, he strode from the room, leaving them alone.

Unslinging their weapons, the warriors made it clear he had no option but to go. Like an automaton, he let himself be escorted by Zayshul and one of the guards back to the room where Banner and the others waited.

Just before the entrance, he stopped, glaring at her. "You're allowing this?" he demanded in a low voice. "You'd let him hold the cub and force me to return?"

"Captain, we should leave," Banner said from within the room.

Zayshul took hold of his arm, pulling him out of sight of his Second. "You must go," she whispered, gesturing the guard behind them to wait. "And don't even think of going after Kezule. He'll kill you before he'll let you have the cub."

"Kusac!" Banner's tone was sharp this time, making him look round. His Second was leading the cubs and the Sholan female out of the room. "We have to leave."

He nodded and pulled himself free of Zayshul, following them down the corridor toward the landing bay, Zayshul walking silently beside him. This close, her scent was too strong, was making him too aware of her as a desirable female, and the mother of the cub he'd just seen. His thoughts were in a turmoil; he wanted to stay now, never mind leave and return later.

The fresher air as they neared the landing bay helped clear his mind. He turned to her again. "How?" he asked quietly. "How can I have a son of that age?" Now was the time to ask the question he'd been dreading to have answered. "Who's his mother, Zayshul?"

"Why should you think Shaidan is your son?" she whispered. "How could he be?"

He stopped dead, anger surging through him as he grabbed her by the arm. "Don't lie to me, Zayshul!" he hissed, keeping one eye on Banner and the others walking ahead of them. "I know he is—his scent, his looks—everything about him tells me he's mine! His blood calls to me! Who's his mother?" This close, he scented and felt her panic as if it were his own. "Are you?"

"Your armor, you're hurting me," she said, face creasing in pain as she tried to pull free.

He let her go. "Tell me the truth, dammit! I trusted you!"

"He's your son," she whispered, not looking at him. "I was only trying to save you from becoming Kezule's pawn."

"Tell me who his mother is!" He needed her to admit that she was the mother.

She glanced at the soldiers behind them. "I can't speak now, Kusac. You *must* go, but when you return . . ." She left the sentence unfinished as the guards moved closer.

He bit back an angry retort and nodded once, briefly. "Don't betray me again, Zayshul," he warned.

Several containers lay on the deck near the entrance to their shuttle.

"What're they?" he demanded of Zayshul.

"Their toys," she said. "Open them if you want. I swear they've not been tampered with."

"They stay behind," he said unequivocally.

She looked at him, her wide mouth parting in a slight smile. "You've never travelled with bored children, have you? Don't take your anger out on the cubs, Kusac. The toys are only toys. It would be cruel to deprive them of amusement on their journey home."

He hesitated, remembering the sheer number of toys they had for Kashini, then gestured to Banner. "Check them out once our passengers are on board."

"Where we going, Aunt?" asked the small gray-pelted cub, catching hold of Zayshul's hand. "Are you coming?"

"No, Gaylla," she said, bending down so her face was level

with the cub's. "Speak in Sholan as I taught you. These are your people. They'll take you home to your own parents."

"But I see you soon?"

Zayshul ruffled the cub's ears gently. "I'm afraid not. It's time for us to say goodbye."

Gaylla began to sob, throwing her arms round the doctor, her doll falling forgotten to the deck. "I not want to leave you!"

"She's a hybrid!" he exclaimed in Valtegan. "Vartra's bones, how in Hell's name could you find hybrid cubs?"

Equally distraught, Zayshul stood up and thrust the sobbing cub at Kusac. "Take her and leave! Go now, before they stop you!" She turned and fled into the interior of the ship, leaving him holding the screaming child.

Shocked, he heard the distinctive sound of Valtegan energy rifles powering up and saw the soldiers begin to advance. Bending down, he scooped up the doll and ran up the ramp where an equally shocked Banner had just looked up from his toy inspection.

"Go!" he ordered, aiming a kick at the box his Second was examining and sending it skittering through the airlock.

Banner dived in after it, slamming the hatch shut behind them.

"Get us out of here, now!"

"Aye, sir!" Banner was already halfway to the cockpit.

The access ramp was still retracting as Banner accelerated out of the *M'zayik*'s bay. Staggering, his arms still full of the struggling and sobbing cub, he was trying to come to terms with what he'd seen.

"Give her to me, Djani," said Rraelga, passing her infant to the young kitling in the seat beside her. "She's not as bright as the others, she takes things more to heart."

With relief, he dumped the cub on her lap. He stopped, his enhanced sense of smell bringing the scents of the others to his nostrils. Unsealing his glove, he reached out to touch the cubs one after the other, barely aware of the few words of comfort he murmured to them. They were all hybrids, and the scents of two of them were disquietingly familiar.

Unlike Shaidan, they didn't wear collars and he was able to absorb the feel of their minds—the mental signature that, like Human fingerprints, made each of them unique but also held a flavor of the parents. Deeply disturbed, he headed up front to join Banner.

"What happened back there?" asked his Second. "What did you say to the doctor?"

"She got twitchy," he snapped, patching a link through to the *Couana*. His son's existence, and the fact that the others were hybrids, was something he wanted kept quiet right now.

"*Couana*, code 3, 9, 0, Red. We have passengers, four cubs and an adult Sholan female with her infant. Lay in a course for Haven. We leave immediately." He cut the connection in the middle of Jayza's startled acknowledgment, concentrating on his piloting.

"What did Kezule want from you?"

"Me. He wants me to train his people, and he's keeping one of the cubs as a hostage to make sure I go back."

Banner glanced at him. "You're going to return, aren't you?"

"What option have I?" he snarled angrily. "I can't leave that cub with him. Kezule kept a telepath as a pet, Banner! I can't leave him there!"

"Rraelga says they've all been well treated by Kezule and his people, especially the doctor. They were rescued from some experimental facility on the Prime homeworld."

That could explain the hybrids, but not his son. "Did she mention the fifth cub, say anything about him?" he demanded.

"Shaidan? Only that he was hurt in their escape. Doctor Zayshul kept him with them, nursing him back to health herself. Rraelga says she treats him as if he was her own child. He's not in any danger, Kusac. We should inform Stronghold, let them decide what's to be done next. Our mission's over."

"Not till I have Shaidan. I'm going back for him, alone if necessary," he said in a tone that brooked no further discussion.

Shaidan. His son was called Shaidan. At least it was a Sholan name. If the Primes could breed M'zullians and Shaidan, then they could breed Sholan hybrids. He found the thought of the Primes taking genetic samples from his Triad terrifying, as terrifying as the fact that the resulting cubs were now ten years old. Obviously Zayshul had been deeply involved in the whole procedure—and for reasons of her own, had made his contribution one of a far more personal nature. At least she'd not left their son in the experimental facility. Maybe that was why they'd left K'oish'ik.

Kaid's home, Dzahai Mountains, the same day

"I want us to go home today, Tallinu," said Carrie. "All of us, you included. Before the winter storms really start. I can't cope with Kashini and the twins without you."

Kaid got to his feet and began to pace the lounge restlessly. "I'd prefer to stay here until we hear more about Kusac," he said finally, stopping beside the recently acquired sofa on which she lay. "I told him I wouldn't return to the villa until he apologized, and I won't."

"He isn't there, Tallinu, but your daughter will be, and she needs her father," she said gently, pushing her own pain at what Kusac had done aside, aware that Kaid's anger and hurt went as deep. "Dhaykin needs you too. We're a family."

"Then stay here with me. Let's be a family, yes, but in my home."

She held her hand up to him, tugging him down beside her when he took it. "You know that's not practical. You've only one bedroom and this lounge—thank God T'Chebbi and Kashini went home several days ago. The nurse has to be flown in by you from Dzahai village every day because there's nowhere for her to sleep, and I miss Kashini and T'Chebbi. I love my cubs, Tallinu, but now Dhaykin is in no danger and is gaining weight, I need time to myself. I know what Kusac said hurt you, but you're not the only one he hurt. He left without coming to see me and our cubs—before he could be told he had a son."

"That's just as inexcusable," he said, attempting to withdraw his hand from hers as his tail began to flick angrily. "He's become a renegade, Carrie, turned his back on us all, stolen Toueesut's ship and headed off to cause the Gods know what trouble!"

"I can't believe he has," she said. "He'd no reason to do it. Kzizysus had operated on him, cured the damage the implant had done and given him back his Talent. Why would he want to risk it all again by going to the Prime world to find torturer priests who no longer exist?"

"Then he's headed for the M'zullian home world," said Kaid, his tone dismissive. "In which case the Watchers will pick him up before he gets close. I won't be on the estate when he gets back, Carrie. I meant it. Until he apologizes, I want nothing more to do with him."

"I don't believe he's looking for them," she said. "It isn't like him to leave like this."

"He's changed completely since we came back," he said, trying again to dislodge her hand. "At the end of the day, he has to take responsibility for what he says and does. We can't all go around excusing him for the rest of his life. If we do, there'll be no need for him to change. I'm sorry you can't see it the same way."

"I'm not saying he shouldn't be held responsible," she said quietly, tightening her grip on him. "I'm saying there has to be a reason why he stole a ship and left, and the one you've given me just doesn't fit the person I know. What does Noni say? He was staying with her up until a few days before the cubs were born."

"How should I know what she said? He's gone over the edge, Carrie. Raiban has a warrant out for his arrest and Stronghold has issued instructions he's to be apprehended and brought in. It's probably the best thing that could happen to him. His treatment will be taken out of our hands once and for all. Maybe the Telepath Guild medics can straighten out his mind. We couldn't."

"What?" Letting his hand go, she sat up suddenly—too suddenly—and cried out in pain.

His anger instantly forgotten, he was all attention and she was hard pressed to stop him calling the nurse in from the other room.

"I'm fine! You didn't tell me he was being treated as a criminal, Tallinu! I assumed that since Toueesut wasn't pressing charges, that would be the end of it! We've got to do something!"

"What do you suggest?" he asked sarcastically. "Because of our Link and the cubs, I can't go out looking for him, even if I wanted to. Besides, looking for the *Couana* would be like looking for a needle in the wilderness."

"Speak to Father Lijou! I thought Kusac meant more to you, especially after those nights together!"

"Don't you start doubting me," he said, a touch of coldness creeping into his voice as he pulled back from her. "You know what I feel for him. He was the one who turned to me, Carrie, then accused me of . . ."

"I know what he said," she interrupted, clutching him anxiously, afraid she'd gone too far. "Can't you see that's proof he wasn't in his right mind? Would he do that and then accuse you like he did if he wasn't disturbed? Maybe there's something else behind his actions. When did he leave Noni's? Before or after he came out here? How did he persuade those who went with him to go? Why choose the *Couana,* and how did he manage to steal it from the middle of a busy spaceport?"

"You're looking for excuses for him," he said. "I want to end this conversation now. I don't want to argue with you over this. You know how I feel, what I think, let's just leave it."

"He's our Triad partner—your sword-brother! You can't just assume he's guilty and do nothing about it, even if he did hurt your feelings!"

"This is more than hurt feelings, Carrie. My sword-brother, who swore my honor would be as dear to him as his own, accused me of dishonorable conduct! I could have Challenged him on the spot, and not to first blood either!" he said angrily.

"You're both Telepaths, Challenges are illegal for you," she said frantically, grasping him by the hair at the sides of his neck as he began to get up.

He snarled at the unexpected pain and attempted to free himself.

She leaned closer, kissing his forehead, trying to hold back her tears. "I know it's more than hurt feelings, I didn't mean to trivialize it. All I'm asking is you think about it, Tallinu," she said, resting her cheek against his. "I know how important your honor is to you, and to me, but Kusac didn't repeat his allegations to anyone else, and within days he left Shola. I just don't think this is as straightforward as it seems."

As he stopped trying to pull her hands away, gently she began to nibble the outer edge of his ear the way she knew he liked. "Please," she said persuasively. "I need you both, Tallinu. I can't stand the thought of him being jailed, or hurt as they try to capture him. And I know you feel the same."

Letting his hair go, she slipped her arms around him, working her way across his cheek. The tension was leaving his body and she could feel his anger dissipating as he began to respond to her.

"Dzinae." He sighed, turning his face to kiss her, the word both his nickname for her and an affirmation of her affinity to Vartra's heavenly tormentors. "I'll think about it," he said between kisses. "I'll take you home tomorrow."

"You'll come too?" she asked, slipping further down the sofa so he could stretch out beside her.

"Do you think I'm going to let you or our cubs out of my sight at this time?" he asked, nosing her chin up and kissing his way down her throat.

CHAPTER 20

Anchorage, Zhal-S'Asha, 22nd day (October)

ANNUUR was in his quarters on the shuttle when the call from the Camarilla came in. "I come, I come," he grumbled to Sokarr as he uncurled himself from his sleeping nest and staggered to the comm unit in the next room.

"Phratry Leader," the Cabbarran female said as he settled himself in front of the screen. "The sand-dwellers in sector four are mobilizing. Imperative you monitor situation from close hand."

"No sign of movement we detect, Leader Shvosi," said Annuur calmly. "Area constantly patrolled by we Watchers. All is quiet."

"Are mobilizing," insisted his colleague, her nose wrinkling in agitation. "Have seen it from imager in their sector. Must observe their destination. Fear we have they take offensive action against second world. Imager scanners indicate presence of chiro isotope particles."

"Means not control activator is present. Sand-dwellers consumed available resources destroying hunter worlds, no more have they."

"Potentialities indicate they found more. Now move against second world. Camarilla orders that you go, observe, and destroy activator if present."

"Presume Camarilla sends vessel to accompany us," said Annuur sarcastically. "We only one scout ship, small, vulnerable. How get in center of their fleet and escape afterwards? Cannot affect outcome, can only attract sand-dwellers's notice to ourselves, present Alliance as target. And draw attention to ourselves among other Watchers," he added.

"Enhanced shields and drives have you if used what Camarilla put on your *Watcher,* and sent you on Shola. Hides you. No need of our presence."

"What of children? Do this and they discover us. Tell Alliance. This not wise," he said, shaking his head. It wasn't the Camarilla's way to take direct action like this. And how had the sand-dwellers's acquisition of more resources escaped the Camarilla's notice in the first place?

"Must go. Naacha can make children attack, make them forget after. Shields hide you, other Watchers not see. If activator deployed, destruction of second world is inevitable."

He considered the situation dispassionately for a moment or two. "Destruction halves our problem, Leader Shvosi. Less of violent ones is to be wished for. Let them destroy each other, make our task easier. Camarilla say intervention should be always minimal. Better we do after attack second world."

There was a short silence. "You mistake your mission, Annuur," said Shvosi carefully. "Hear me. Skepp Lords only say objective is destruction of ship *if* carrying activator."

A klaxon began to sound, relayed into their shuttle from the landing bay by the outpost's communications system.

"Maybe you right and sand-dwellers do move," Annuur murmured. He didn't like this mission at all but Shvosi was giving him room to maneuver. "Is what Sholans call Battle Muster—urgent call to go to ships ready for takeoff. Who speak for Camarilla in this?"

"Azwokkuss spoke for all. Must persuade children to attack. You have made prescribed modifications to ship?" Shvosi asked anxiously.

He should have known it was one of the TeLaxaudin. "Yes, yes. Done. Must go now, not be late at posts. Unwanted attention we draw to ourselves otherwise."

"Annuur! Move your furry ass and get your sept on board now! We got a M'zullian fleet on the move!" yelled Tirak over the ship to ship comm.

"Must do, Annuur," said Shvosi anxiously. "Must do."

"I do." Annuur broke the connection and jumped hurriedly down from his couch, heading for the corridor as fast as his short legs could run. Rounding the corner, he almost collided with Lweeu.

"I help with harness," said Lweeu, rearing up on her hind legs and holding out Annuur's belt and shoulder retainers.

Thrusting his arms through the loops, he fidgeted impatiently while she quickly fastened the buckles then handed him his side arm.

"We go," he said tersely, dropping down to all fours when they finished. "Where Sokarr and Naacha?"

"On *Watcher 6,* starting up systems," Lweeu said as they began to run for the airlock.

"What kept you?" demanded Manesh, hitting the retractor as they clattered up the *Watcher*'s access ramp.

"Might wait till we're in before ramp closing," complained Annuur as he leapt the last few feet onto the cargo deck.

"No time," she snapped. "The M'zullians' fleet is gathering off their space platform. We're being sent to observe."

Hooves skittered on the cold metal flooring as the Cabbarrans turned sharply to reach the elevator up to the mid-deck.

"Annuur on board, Captain," she called out, running after them.

"Take off in thirty seconds," came Tirak's voice over the ship's comm.

The high-pitched whine of the engines increased as the elevator came to a stop, spilling out the two Cabbarrans and Manesh. One at a time, the Cabbarrans dropped out of sight down the grav shaft to their specially adapted avionics unit while Manesh clambered nimbly up the wall-mounted ladder into the bridge section.

Like a Sholan bird of prey with wings held upward ready to swoop, *Watcher 6* rose into the air and began to move forward. It gathered speed quickly, shooting out of the asteroid's landing bay as Annuur and Lweeu joined Sokarr and Naacha on the form-fitting work couches that spread out in a cross shape from the central navigation unit.

"Routing avionics functions from bridge to your station, Phratry Leader," said Sokarr, looking across at Annuur.

"Accepted," said Annuur, spatulate hands flying over the pressure sensitive keys to either side of him as he checked their heading on the small screens. "De-opaque avionics hull."

"Done," said Sokarr.

"Turn off lighting units."

The darkness of space surrounded him like black velvet, relieved only by the faint glow of their control panels and the pinpoints of light from the distant suns.

"Initiating neural net," said Lweeu.

Annuur reached for the metal bands lying in the recessses on either side of him. Slipping one on each wrist, he glanced at Naacha. He didn't know how the mystic managed to drop so suddenly into the requisite light trance. Already Naacha's head and neck were lying stretched out in the support. Checking the others, he waited until they were ready before lowering his head to the padded rest and squirming around until he had an unhindered view of the darkness of space that surrounded them.

He took a deep breath, tensing himself. "Activate neural net relay," he said.

The world around him changed abruptly as he found himself mentally linked through Naacha to the rest of his sept and the *Watcher 6*'s nav system. Concentrating on the grid of faint green lines that now bisected the darkness, he located the other five ships. The lines, guided by Naacha, moved, seeking out the shortest route before converging on the J'kirtikkain sector.

"Jump engines on-line," he heard Sheeowl say through the comm.

"Chameleon shielding activated," said Nayash.

"Course plotted," Annuur said. "Updating nav headings."

"New headings locked in and relayed to the other *Watchers*, Captain," said Sayuk.

"Initiate jump engines," said Captain Tirak.

J'kirtikkian world, Zhal-S'Asha, 26th day (October)

They emerged in the J'kirtikkian solar system three days later. In the shadow of a small moon, they sat silently watching the main M'zullian fleet fighting off the defending J'kirtikkian ships while the remainder deployed itself over one hemisphere of the world below.

At first, the disposition of the Valtegan ships seemed random, but not to Annuur and his sept. They'd seen it before in recordings of the destruction of the two hunter worlds. With surprising swiftness, the M'zullians took up their positions, creating a grid. In and out wove their fighters, dealing with any incoming fire from J'kirtikkian ships. Then suddenly, they pulled back high above the grid. From the main fleet, a fine mist began to fall.

"What *is* that?" asked Sheeowl.

"Nothing I can identify," said Nayash. "Dammit! I could have done with Giyesh on the scanners right now!"

"Belay that," snapped Tirak.

On their main screen, they watched in growing horror as the particulate cloud seemed to home in on the hulls of the remaining J'kirtikkian defenders, dissolving the very fabric of the ships, aware that they were witnessing the destruction of a world and its population.

"They're descending," said Nayash eventually, breaking the silence. "Dropping down into the planet's atmospheric envelope."

"Why we not try to stop them?" Sokarr asked Annuur. "You say Camarilla orders us to do this."

"Needed confirmation they had activator. Now have. No chance to target lead ship earlier without risking us," he replied. "We wait. Sand-dwellers will regroup to return home. Soon as lead ship is isolated, we go. Main drives accessed?"

He wanted to do this alone, without involving Tirak and his crew, no matter what Shvosi said. This was the Camarilla's problem. They, as its representatives, should solve it, not their U'Churian family. It was his private opinion that the TeLaxaudin were often offhanded in dealings with the child-species they'd created.

Sokarr looked offended as his narrow ears flattened themselves briefly to his skull. "Of course," he said stiffly.

"Dangerous," ventured Lweeu. "Not easy to do small jump."

"Concentrate on weapons, leave nav and piloting to Naccha and me," Annuur said sternly.

"What of Tirak? We family. Not right to . . ." she began.

"Balance must be achieved. What sand-dwellers stole upsets it. Already two worlds dead, now this. Must do minimal intervention. Destroy lead ship and activator, then cannot use again."

"But other *Watchers* see us, Captain knows what we do . . ."

"Not," said Naacha unequivocally, touching his controls. "I fix *Watchers* after. Remodulating shields, none see." He stopped to check his display again. "Fleet dispersing."

"Initiate lockout sequence," ordered Annuur, checking his wrist bands. "Disconnect power from upper bridge section and start separation sequence."

The muffled bang as the explosive bolts detonated echoed throughout the ship. They experienced a slight dropping sensation as the two sections of the ship parted, then their own power source kicked in.

"Activate neural net."

"Wait till I get my hands on Annuur," snarled Tirak angrily as he paced the length of his bridge. "Have you found out how the hell he managed to separate us from the lower section of the ship?" he demanded of Sheeowl. "It shouldn't be possible! How much longer until you get the drives back on-line?"

Sheeowl glanced over her shoulder at him. "We don't," she said shortly. "He's blocked me completely. I can't bypass it, Captain."

"I'm getting a jump point forming in the M'zullian fleet," said Sayuk.

"Where?" demanded Tirak, spinning round to face the main view screen.

"Above the main battleship, Captain. But I'm getting no readings from it . . . no ships. Nothing."

Space seemed to fold in on itself, then spiraled open in a swirl of blue and silver. As swiftly as it had formed, it was gone, but nothing they could sense emerged.

"That's like no jump I've ever seen," murmured Sheeowl as they watched the battleship's shield flare each time the same nothing began to strafe its way along its length.

Fighters began to veer toward the battleship as its guns moved ponderously, beginning to track its phantom attacker. When the M'zullian fighters opened fire, Tirak spat out one word.

"Annuur!"

"We're going to lose him!" said Sheeowl, her voice hushed with fear.

As each hit drained more power from the huge battleship, the flares caused by Annuur's weapons intensified, each one sending larger surges of energy through the battleship's weakening defensive shield.

"He'll do it," said Nayash, standing up. "He's going too fast for them, and he's too close to their hull—they'll hit their own ship before they hit him!"

Light blossomed suddenly, and a piece of debris spun out of the nothingness where Annuur's ship was.

"He's hit," moaned Sheeowl.

"Silence!" ordered Tirak. "Can you pick up anything on the sensors?" he demanded.

"Only the debris," said Nayash, sitting hurriedly down at his post again.

Suddenly, their blacked-out consoles lit up again.

"Drives back on-line, Captain," said Sheeowl, her voice shaking.

"Comms back, Captain. I have *Watcher 1* demanding information," said Sayuk.

"Ignore them, we're on Silent until we're out of scanner range," he ordered, staring at the chaos at the heart of the M'zullian fleet. "There's nothing we can do for Annuur."

"Upper port battery hit," reported Leewu as the ship lurched violently to one side. "Weapons gone."

Annuur cursed silently. The M'zullians' targeting systems were better than he'd anticipated. They couldn't afford another hit. He had to finish this now, no matter the cost.

"Bringing her around for second run. Deploy integrated pulse weapon," snapped Annuur as he banked the ship sharply to the other side.

"Energy levels too low to sustain . . ." began Lweeu.

"Do it!" snarled Annuur.

In the belly of the ship, concealed bay doors opened and a weapon known only to the Camarilla was lowered.

"Weapon deployed," said Lweeu, her voice subdued.

"Lower shields and transfer all available power to Weapons."

"Transferred," said Sokarr.

"Fire," said Annuur.

Energy beams from the remaining weapons located on the body of the *Watcher* pulsed forward to intersect with those from the starboard guns and the newly deployed one in the belly. Where they joined, the beam thickened briefly before surging outward in a continuous stream.

"Twenty seconds to burnout," said Sokarr, and began counting.

This time, the M'zullian battleship's shield was easily penetrated. A trail of exploding debris followed their path as Annuur dived down to skim only a few meters from the surface of the hull.

"Three, two, one. Burnout complete," said Sokarr as the beam stopped abruptly. "Energy cells depleted. All weapons now offline."

"Naacha, open jump," ordered Annuur as he pulled the ship sharply up from the crippled destroyer. "We leave."

A jump point opened up ahead just as the M'zullian fighters converged on them.

A warning sounded discreetly on the bridge, startling everyone.

"Proximity alert. Jump point forming to starboard," Nayash called out, looking away from the long-range screens to his scanners. "Initiating evasive action!"

As they lurched to one side, the lower section of *Watcher 6* suddenly emerged several hundred kilometers from them, spinning wildly, both upright wings and gun emplacements gone. It was closely followed by three M'zullian fighters.

"Kathan's beard! He made it!" swore Mrowbay.

"So did the M'zullians," snarled Tirak.

"Target enemy fighters?" asked Manesh.

"Yes! Relay that order to all *Watchers*!"

"And Annuur?" asked Sheeowl.

"Leave him," he snapped. "He chose to leave us stranded and take his own risks. We have ourselves and the Alliance to protect first."

"At least he's heading for deep space," Sayuk murmured to her.

the Camarilla, TeLaxaudin homeworld, at the same time

Dusk was already falling outside the main chamber of the Camarilla as Shvosi hurried over to the Speaker's dais. As the one in charge of Annuur's mission, it was her duty to keep the Camarilla informed of developments, and there had been developments, possibly disastrous ones. In preparation for her report, the lights that hovered among the internal trees and bushes dimmed until she could see the faint luminescence of the path under her feet. Despite her haste, as she passed the small fountain, she paused briefly, taking comfort from the gentle spray of water before stepping up to her place on the raised Speaker's dais.

Sitting up on her haunches, the Cabbarran leaned on the lectern and activated the image player. Behind her, the three-dimensional projection of a battleship under attack began to take shape.

"The lost matter compiler activator was located," she said quietly. "Phratry Leader Annuur has done as ordered and neutralized the ship carrying it. But as you see, not in time to stop death of second world." With a gesture of her hand, she stopped the image replay. "He had to know activator was there before he could attack."

On his cushion, Hkairass stirred. "Show us more. The *Watcher* ship, where is it? When this happen?"

Shvosi looked down to where the TeLaxaudin sat, just beyond the dais. "Happening now, Hkairass. Not necessary see more. Task has been completed. Useless compiler is without controller. More pressing matter do I bring to . . ."

"Show sequence for confirmation," insisted Hkairass. "Including *Watcher* ship."

Sighing, Shvosi gestured again and the lower section of *Watcher 6* came into view, its outline shimmering because of the enhanced chameleon shielding. She should have known he would cause problems. He was leader of the Isolationist faction who believed they should withdraw totally from the affairs of the other species.

"That not *Watcher*," objected Hkairass, rising up from his cushion and beginning to walk toward the projection.

"Is," insisted Shvosi, heart in mouth, turning to watch as the

TeLaxaudin stopped at the edges of the image. "Looks different because imager is reading shape of shield, not ship."

He studied it, walking round the limits of the projection, waving his hand over one of the floor-mounted projectors to enhance the size of the battleship.

"Your point, Hkairass?" asked Khassiss from her seat among the TeLaxaudin Elders.

Hkairass turned to look at her. "Is not *Watcher*. Kouansishus send images of ships Primes build with us and Cabbarran aid. This not it. Different."

"Different?" asked Aizshuss, unfolding himself and stepping down from his couch before making his way over to Hkairass. "I look. Augmented shielding show blurred image of ship at best."

Shvosi reached out surreptitiously with her spatulate hand to touch the other as he passed her.

Not do this! she sent. *Troubles has Annuur, needs aid. Divert them from ship configuration. Must stop replay now before too late!*

The slight faltering of Aizshuss' stride was the only sign he'd heard her as he continued on the path, coming to a stop beside his TeLaxaudin colleague. Stopping, he peered at the small ship, watching its shields flare as the uppermost port gun battery was hit and destroyed.

"Outline matches *Watcher* ship," said Aizshuss quietly.

Concerned humming from the TeLaxaudin and the soft chittering of the Cabbarrans swept through the chamber almost like a sigh. Shvosi took the opportunity to reach out and grasp the mood, trying to enhance the Camarilla's sympathy for Annuur. Then Aizshuss' mind joined hers, adding to her strength until the noise died down, then he was gone. At least he'd been willing to help. If only she'd had time to edit the recording before having to bring it in front of the council!

"Damage has it sustained," Aizshuss continued, turning to look at the assembly. "Enough I have seen to know task completed and our Phratry brother needs help."

"Is bit missing," insisted Hkairass, pointing with one slender hand to the blurred image of the swaying *Watcher*.

"I see no bit missing," said Aizshuss, looking back to the projection.

"I also call for aid for our Phratry brother," said Kuvaa as she reared up from her place among the Cabbarran Elders. "Shape of ship irrelevant. Safety of Annuur and his crew matters."

Thankful that at last one of her own people had spoken up, Shvosi reached out to turn the imager off. They hadn't yet come to the portion she wanted to conceal.

"Leave," said Khassiss firmly. "See to end. Hkairass is right. Where rest of *Watcher,* Shvosi? Our order was to have our children attack ship."

"Annuur take only his part, not whole ship," said Hkairass. "Disobey our orders. If all ship used, then this stopped sooner, before world destroyed. His actions cause death of this world."

Shvosi swung round to address the Elder responsible for the order. "Skepp Lord Azwokkuss, Camarilla order was only to destroy sand-dweller ship if carrying activator, was it not?" She asked with icy politeness, her long upper lip curling back in anger. "Annuur carry out that order."

"Phratry Leader is correct," said Azwokkuss with equal formality, speaking for the first time. "But was intended whole ship used . . ." He stopped, his translator falling silent as he began to hum with anger of his own.

Heart heavy, Shvosi turned round, knowing what she'd see. In the projection, *Watcher 6* was now clearly visible as its remaining weapons' fire linked together, forming a single beam of energy focused several hundred meters in front of where the bow of the ship should have been.

As angry voices broke out, Shvosi dropped down onto all fours in defeat. She'd hoped to be able to hide that portion of the recording from them. Annuur's misjudgment in not taking the whole ship was compounded by using Camarilla enhanced weapons when they could be seen by everyone.

"Attention has he drawn, from sand-dwellers, from children, from other *Watchers.* This course of action not wise I said at time. Now I proved right," said Hkairass triumphantly.

Surely not giving up now, Shvosi! came Aizshuss' acerbic thought.

Who fight for Annuur if we don't? came Kuvaa's.

She reared up again, putting all the arrogance and contempt behind her eyes that she could muster. "So Annuur has affection for your children, Skepp Lords!" she said, glaring round the gathered Lords and Leaders of the Camarilla. "Tried to save them, he did. Take risks only on himself to carry out our orders. Not a crime! Look how he succeeded!"

Annuur's damaged craft was darting along the surface of the battleship, searing a path of devastation before it. The replay had run to the end now, and the distant imager's AI had taken over, transmitting the current situation direct to the Camarilla. As they continued to watch, Annuur's energy beam died. The ship pulled up sharply, heading for the jump point that opened ahead of it, three fighters converging on it, weapons blazing.

"Succeeded in drawing attention of Alliance to us," said Hkairass sarcastically. "Trusted him we did not to do this. All intervention should stop now. This I have been saying since sand-dwellers first began to die after they were beaten by hunters! Like then, nothing has this positive achieved. Balance still upset—directly endangered are we now! Withdraw we should, find new worlds, before Alliance demands we give them our knowledge, before sand-dwellers take war out to all Alliance—and us."

"Potentialities showed victorious sand-dwellers will wait until second world stable again, then spend much time looting," said Aizshuss dryly, joining Shvosi on the Speaker's dais. "Death of this world anticipated, hoped to prevent. Likely they think *Watcher* is from world below."

"When fighters fail to return, what then they think?" asked Khassiss, gesturing toward the projection where Annuur's stricken ship was tumbling end over end, still pursued by the three fighters.

"Lost in jump," said Kuvaa promptly, getting up from her place to join her two colleagues on the dais. "Who in right mind believe Camarilla Lord Annuur's ship capable of escaping? Who in right mind follows such a ship into jump? Escape remarkable in first place without getting lost in jump!"

Hkairass stalked over to them, eyes swirling angrily, the broad scented strips of his clothing discharging the harsh perfume his body was now exuding. As he began to talk, his mandibles clicked rapidly. "What now you want? Want Camarilla to order Anuur's retrieval? Draw even more attention to ourselves?" he demanded, oval eyes swirling with anger. "How we hide this—disaster—from anyone!" He gestured to the projection where they could see the upper section of a *Watcher*, accompanied by three others, intercepting the fighters. "Better Annuur and crew die than aided to be questioned!"

"Why give Annuur weapon if not to use?" countered Aizshuss.

"To use covertly," said Khassiss.

"Discovery inevitable," said Aizshuss. "Routine maintenance at hunter outpost could expose it any time. This I said when decision taken to fit weapon before sending to hunters' Alliance. I overruled. Blame not Annuur for having it and using."

"Annuur in unique position. Much we have learned since he went to hunter world," said Kuvaa. "Aid him we must."

"Kzizysus with hunters," said Hkairass. "No need for another if we must have people outside."

"Kzizysus young, not of the Camarilla, nor will be for many hundred of years," said Aizshuss. "Has not mystic abilities. Annuur left voluntarily, gave up the rapport of Camarilla to serve us in the field. Much has been asked of him that he has accomplished against odds. He still has value, to us and among children and hunter Alliance. We owe him same loyalty he gives us."

Hkairass hummed his contempt, flicking his hand to one side in a gesture of dismissal while behind him the fight to destroy the sand-dweller fighters played itself out. "Annuur hasn't mystic abilities! Are overrated in my opinion. Technology can do all you can."

Shvosi's eyes narrowed and under the blue tattoos, her cheeks began to itch. Beside her, she felt Aizshuss and Kuvaa stiffen in anger.

Hkairass looked away from her. "Do not use that trick on me, Phratry Leader Shvosi," he began.

"Enough!" said Khassiss, raising her voice as she stood up. "Aizshuss speaks the truth. Camarilla need eyes and ears outside as provided by those like Annuur's sept and Kouansishus. Combined our two people are for many millennia, each using own skills for common good. Shvosi, show potentialities if Annuur not retrieved," she ordered. "Decision must be made hastily if the Phratry Leader to be successfully aided. Consequences of our actions are not of concern at this moment. Later will we look at them."

Hkairass hummed his displeasure. "I ask the Camarilla to say if this necessary. Annuur has attracted too much attention over this matter. Further intervention now will lead to our discovery. We must leave him to his fate."

A murmur of disagreement ran round the chamber and with

an angry clicking of his mandibles, Hkairass stalked back to his cushion.

Stopping the projection, Shvosi reached mentally for Aizshuss, then beyond him to Kuvaa and the assembly, joining with all the other mystics of her people and the TeLaxaudin. The telepathic net formed, she touched the control on the lectern to activate the neural interface. Now the rest of the TeLaxaudin joined them, as did those of her own people who were not mystics.

Forming where the Camarilla had watched the image of Anuur's attack on the destroyer, another began to emerge, one of shades of light and dark, swirling and weaving themselves into an intricate pattern of potentialities that spread outward to fill the Camarilla chamber. It could only be experienced, not seen, and it was a pattern that boded ill if aid was not sent immediately.

Their decision made, Khassiss spoke for the Camarilla and aid was dispatched to intercept the Camarilla Lord's crippled ship.

When it became obvious the M'zullians had no interest in their three missing fighters, against his better judgment, Tirak allowed himself to be persuaded to follow the trail left by Annuur. It was only the fact that Nayash was picking up life signs that convinced him. The other *Watchers* had complained but he'd overruled them, sending two back to Anchorage to make their report and ordering the other three to accompany him.

It was several hours before they had the missing section in visual sight. Not only had it slowed down, but the chaotic tumbling had been reduced to a slow rotation. Matching velocities, they circled it, examining it for damage and the possibility of reintegration. The hull, though battered, seemed intact, and damage around the couplings was minimal. Of the strange weapon Annuur had used, there was no sign, though on the lower surface of the hull there was a badly scorched and fused area.

With the help of two of the other ships, they'd docked. The couplings hastily welded together to reinforce them, they waited by the airlock down to the cargo level for Sayuk's report on the state of the hull.

"Atmospheric pressure's holding, Captain," he said over the ship's comm. "Hull integrity now confirmed."

"Copy," said Tirak as Nayash opened the hatch.

Latching it back, they climbed down into the lower section. Save for the sparks caused by severed power lines, they found themselves in total darkness. And it was cold, deathly cold.

"They're down in avionics, Captain," said Nayash quietly, his breath coming out in white clouds as he checked his scanner. "But I'm only getting three life signs."

Tirak grunted, giving nothing of his feelings away as he shone the powerful flashlight around the cargo bay then across to the grav lift heading down to avionics. The beam showed debris had been hurled everywhere—the tool crate had been torn free of its lashings, tumbled back and forth, splitting and spilling its contents.

Overhead, the severed power lines spat and sizzled briefly as a dim light flickered several times then stayed on.

Sayuk's voice sounded over the comm. "Emergency lighting restored, Captain. Sheeowl's working on the elevator now. Mrowbay's on his way down with the canvas stretcher."

Tirak ducked under a bunch of dangling cables and picked his way over to the grav lift.

"Nayash, give me a hand here," he said, taking hold of a crumpled stanchion that had been thrown across the access iris.

Pocketing the scanner, Nyash joined him and grabbed hold of the other end. Between them, they pushed it slowly aside, then cleared the iris of the remaining debris. Sticking a claw tip under the edge of a recessed panel, Tirak flipped it open to reveal the manual wheel.

The iris opened, they waited for Mrowbay. When he arrived, Tirak went down with him.

Naacha was brought up first, unconscious and with a deep gash on one shoulder. Lweeu was next.

"Careful with her," Mrowbay called up. "I think her skull's fractured."

Annuur was last, followed by Mrowbay as he helped guide the sling safely through the iris.

"Sokarr?" asked Sheeowl as she and Nayash eased Annuur's cut and bleeding body to the deck.

Tirak shook his head as he hauled himself out. "Ceiling strut fell on him. Didn't have a chance. We'll get him later. Looks like a strut caught Lweeu a glancing blow too. Annuur had been thrown off his couch. He's in a bad way."

"They all are," said Mrowbay as Annuur was transferred to a rigid stretcher for his journey up to the sick bay.

Its navigation system too damaged to use, the other three ships cradled *Watcher 6* between them as they prepared to jump. Without the Cabbarran navigators it would take them twice as long to get back to Anchorage.

"We've put Annuur and Lweeu in the stasis units, Captain," said Nayash, taking his seat on the bridge. "Their injuries are beyond our resources to treat. Lweeu's skull is fractured, and Annuur has severe internal injuries. They'll both need surgery. Naacha got off very lightly. He's only got a cut and bruised shoulder. Mrowbay's tidying him up right now. I couldn't ask him what the hell they were doing because he's still unconscious."

"Annuur better make it," Tirak growled as they headed for the jump point that had opened up ahead of them. "He's got a hell of a lot of explaining to do and I want to hear it!"

"Captain," said Sheeowl, her voice tight with fear. "That isn't like any jump gate I've ever been through!"

the *Couana*, Zhal-S'Asha, 26th day (October)

Broadcasting the signal of a Watcher ship, the *Couana* emerged from jump at the Haven cluster then made its way to the secluded parking orbit given him by Rhyaz before he left. He called L'Seuli's personal comm from his office, taking off his torc first and adjusting its sensitivity manually.

"Commander," he said, inclining his head briefly. "Is the line secure?"

"As secure as it gets for the Brotherhood, Kusac," L'Seuli said. "I hadn't expected you so soon. I assume everything went well?"

"Yes. I have both the items and the information. I'll need a shuttle to transport them over to you."

"What did Kezule have?"

"Sholans, rescued from a dissident Prime facility on their homeworld," he said. Despite the distance, he could feel L'Seuli's shock.

"Sholans? What kind of dissident facility?"

"An experimental one, run by the same group that were on the *Kz'adul*. They were taken from a M'zullian ship the same way we were, except their presence was kept secret from their authorities. There are four cubs of ten years and an adult Sholan with her infant. I'll send Chima with them."

"I'll come over in my own shuttle," L'Seuli said. "I'm off station right now. Kezule must have found them when he overthrew the coup against his Emperor. But why give them directly to us, why not through our Embassy? Did he ask for anything in return?"

He'd already decided what his answer was going to be. Banner knew the truth was otherwise, maybe he'd even told Chima, but he intended to be gone before they could inform L'Seuli.

"No," he lied, gently reaching for the Commander's mind. He needed to find out where the *Venture II* was berthed. "Doctor Zayshul was there. I believe she influenced him into giving us our people back quietly like this. Fewer awkward questions to answer than if it had been done through official channels."

"Do they need any medical attention?"

"None," he said, looking away as his head began to ache with the strain of trying to reach L'Seuli and filter out the psychic noise of those on the *Couana*. Dammit! He was too sensitive! He needed to be able to target only the mind he wanted without picking up all the mental white noise around him.

His eyes glazed briefly as he encountered L'Seuli's mental barriers, the ones every Brotherhood operative was trained to use. Because the Commander was capable of receiving mental transmissions, he had to be sure his touch was light enough not to draw attention to his presence. With all the distractions around him, it wasn't going to be easy.

"I'll have them all sent to Stronghold for debriefing," said L'Seuli. "We aren't equipped to handle kitlings."

"No!" he exclaimed, trying to focus his attention on his torc to reduce his sensitivity. "No, they're Telepaths. Send the cubs to my estate, L'Seuli. Let Carrie and Ruth handle them. They've been through a lot, they need the gentle handling of a mother."

Gradually, as the noise began to abate, he knew he'd been successful. Surreptitiously, he wiped his sweaty palms on his thighs, feeling the band of pain around his forehead begin to lessen.

"Everything all right, Kusac? You look strained," L'Seuli said.

He put his hand up and rubbed his ears back. "I've a headache, that's all," he admitted as the Commander's surface thoughts suddenly began to fill his mind. "I have a package for the Shrine from Father Lijou," he said slowly. Gods, he hadn't realized how hard it was to keep his mind on the conversation we well as listen in to L'Seuli's thoughts! What had once been second nature to him was a thousand times more difficult now.

He sensed the surprise before it crossed the Commander's face. "Not Vartra's . . ."

"Head," he interrupted. "Father Lijou said I was to place it in the concealed niche left for it under the statue so it could be permanently sealed in."

"I'll tell Jiosha. She'll be pleased. The Shrine's almost finished. With His—relic—in place, she can hold the dedication ceremony. It's on the main level opposite the elevator. Take your shuttle out and land disguised as me as we arranged. I take it someone on board has a priest's robe?"

Vartra be praised! He'd found the location of his ship! It was in Haven's landing bay, waiting fueled and ready for him to take home. "Yes, I have one," he said.

"Good. I'll meet you on board the *Couana* when you're done."

L'Seuli's decision complicated matters. He headed for the mess where the rest of the crew were waiting. "Chima, get our passengers ready to debark. Commander L'Seuli himself is coming over in a shuttle for them. You'll accompany him to Haven." He handed her a comp pad. "Give him this, it's my report. Tell him it includes my debriefing of the female, Rraelga. Dzaou, you can help her get the cubs ready. Banner, you're in command. I have some business to conduct for Father Lijou on Haven. The rest of you, make sure the ship is presentable for the Commander."

Banner was waiting for him on the cargo ramp by the airlock into the shuttle. "I'll come with you."

"I can manage. What's the matter? Don't you trust me?" he asked, his tone faintly mocking. "Only I can do this, Banner."

"Just like only you could meet with Kezule? I saw no reason why you were so vital to our mission. What's so important to the Father—and Kezule—that only you can do it? He said nothing to me about you conducting business for him on Haven."

"And you're his special operative, aren't you?" He smiled

lazily. "No special operative is special enough to take this to the Shrine, Banner. Trust me. Only someone of Vartra's bloodline can deliver this." He displayed the box hidden under his sleeve, projecting an image of a skull, barely covered in dried flesh, with wisps of tan-colored hair still attached to it, glaring out at him from empty eye sockets.

With a cry of horror, Banner stepped hurriedly back.

Laughing softly, he opened the airlock. "L'Seuli knows what I'm doing. You know, imagination is a dreadful master, Banner. Vartra's head doesn't look nearly as bad as you seem to think it does," he said gently as the airlock door closed, sealing him in the shuttle.

Swearing, Banner headed for the sick bay where he punched a line straight through to his contact, Jiosha, Mentor of the Brotherhood priests on Haven.

"Banner. How can I help you?" she asked. "Where are you?"

"Here, sitting off Haven," he said. "Are you expecting Kusac with an item from Father Lijou?"

"Yes. It's a relic from Vartra's time. Why? Is he on his way over?"

"Yes. Where's the *Venture II*? I think he's heading for it after he leaves you."

"Hold on, I'll find out," she said, moving out of view.

A hand moved across the keypad, putting his call on hold. "Don't alert Haven," said Dzaou quietly. "We want to talk to you."

Banner looked up to see Khadui and Jayza standing in the doorway.

"We're going back with him," continued Dzaou. "You can come, or you can stay here, but we're not leaving that cub alone with those Primes any longer than we have to. Find some way to put Sister Jiosha off the scent and get her to send us some transport. We need to be on the *Venture* before Kusac is."

Thinking fast, Banner weighed his options. "Does Chima know you're here?"

Dzaou gave him a contemptuous look. "How stupid do you think I am? I know why Chima's here, and she'd stop him going. You won't. Now get back on to the Sister before she gets suspicious."

"You'll have to trust me," he warned, then hit the hold key. The screen cleared to show Jiosha just returning.

"It's in the landing bay. What's up?"

"I need to get over there before he leaves Haven."

"I thought your mission was over when you got here."

"Ours is. He's heading back because Kezule is holding a cub hostage to force him to return." Out of sight of the screen, he felt Dzaou's hand close over his arm, claws pricking his flesh warningly. He ignored it.

"Then I'll have the *Venture* put under guard," she said calmly. "He has to bring the relic to me first, Banner. I can't have him apprehended before it's in the Shrine."

"We'll see to it, Sister Jiosha," he said. "It'll be easier. Just get us off here before the Commander arrives. There'll be four of us. We can wait for Kusac in the *Venture*."

"Give me your coordinates. I'll send the nearest hopper over for you and I'll try to delay Kusac as long as possible at the Shrine."

"I hate hoppers. I'm always afraid they'll run out of air before they land."

She smiled. "They're perfectly safe, and they have priority for landing. You'll be here with time to spare."

His call finished, he turned round to face them. "I'm coming," he said.

He could tell Banner was plotting something even before he left the *Couana*, and admitted to himself that his Second would be failing in his duty if he didn't attempt to stop him. Trying to read him was out of the question with the cubs on board. However, Banner didn't expect him to be posing as Commander L'Seuli.

He'd been practicing using his newly awakened Talent over the last three days, but it hadn't been easy. For a start, he'd had to adapt his personal psi damper, turning it into a room damper. The Talent he had now was very different. It was disturbingly more powerful and he'd made some disastrous mistakes—though none as bad as when he'd sent Banner and Dzaou flying across the room. Learning to separate his subconscious thoughts from the task at hand was more difficult than he would have believed, even though it was the second time around. But it had kept him from thinking about Zayshul and his son.

He'd also been listening passively to the minds of the cubs. He hadn't dared spend much time in their company, though. As far as he knew, they hadn't been aware of him, but then they used their Talent rarely, which was unusual for cubs with newly emerged skills. What had surprised him was their level of understanding of their Talent and how to use it. That was way beyond their years. And all the time, he'd been dodging Banner's increasingly awkward questions.

His projection into Banner's mind had been so successful that his Second hadn't realized it wasn't the product of his own imagination. Not for him the spray-on dye that Rhyaz had given him to change his pelt and hair color to match L'Seuli's, he felt confident enough to use an illusion, just as he and Carrie had done so long ago in the Valtegan garrison on Keiss.

Thinking of her made him remember the small tissue-wrapped package he'd left in the center of his bed for her. He hoped Banner would have the decency to see it was passed on to her. He should, it wasn't as if anything he'd said openly violated his cover, but he had managed to insert a coded message about the cubs being hybrids.

The *Couana*'s shuttle, unlike the garishly colored ship herself, was of a generic Alliance manufacture and would cause no problems. The approach codes were accepted by Control, but there was a short delay before he could land—an incoming hopper had priority.

He'd crafted the illusion carefully, drawing on his own memories of the Commander—memories that he'd found to be much more detailed and vivid than he'd thought possible. He could even remember the Commander's stance and gestures. Nonetheless, he still took the precaution of pulling his robe's hood up.

The box concealed beneath his wide sleeves, he walked down the short ramp onto the landing bay of Haven.

There was an air of anxiety and suppressed excitement among the people working there that he could feel despite having reduced the sensitivity of his torc again. It intrigued him, but his time was too short to allow himself to be diverted.

"Commander, we didn't expect you back quite so soon," said Captain Kheal, stopping beside him. "I see you're holding the briefing at fourteenth hour. Worrying business. Thank Vartra we got everyone but the regular crew off Safehold before the M'zullians made their move."

"Worrying times as you say," he said, turning his face partially away from Kheal in shock. "What's the latest news?"

Kheal gave him an odd look. "There is none. We're waiting to hear from the Watchers at Anchorage. The M'zullians are still sitting off J'kirtikk like a flock of carrion eaters. I thought you'd have heard something because you're calling the briefing."

"Not yet," he said. "But I expect to before then."

"I'll see you at the briefing, then, Commander. If you'll excuse me? I have matters I must attend to."

"Carry on, Captain," he said and began to walk toward the elevator, pushing all thoughts of M'zullians aside. He couldn't allow his concentration to lapse for anything.

The Shrine was a simple place, brightly lit at this time, with the half life-sized statue of the seated Vartra placed just in front of the usual red velvet curtain. The plinth on which it rested was made of rough hewn rock from the asteroid itself. To either side stood the obligatory braziers, fed not by charcoal as they were on Shola, but by a gas mixture coming through fireproof blocks. In a small room adjacent to the main one, he felt the presence of Jiosha.

The door hissed closed behind him, alerting her to his presence. As she came in from her office, he dropped his illusion, reaching mentally for her, grasping control of her mind and body. He misjudged the strength of his sending, and with a gentle sigh, she fell to the ground like a sack of vegetables.

Swearing under his breath, he ran to her side, checking her pulse and breathing. He sighed with relief—she was only unconscious. Then he swore some more as he realized he couldn't leave her lying here like this. Putting the box down, he picked her up and carried her into her office, laying her down on the worn sofa he found there.

Returning to the Shrine, he retrieved the box and went around to the back of the statue, looking for the recess. It was open and waiting for him. Carefully he put the box into its niche, feeling around the outside for the trigger that would close the secret panel. A faint click, and a small slab of stone slid out from one side, sealing in the box containing Vartra's head.

Getting up, he spent a moment reestablishing his illusion before striding confidently out.

*   *   *

Looking like the outpost's commander, access to the *Venture II* was easy. What he didn't expect as he sealed the airlock door behind him was to find Banner waiting just out of sight.

A surprised look crossed the other's face. "Commander? I thought you were still on the *Couana*."

"I sent my aide instead," he said shortly. "You're supposed to be there. What're you doing on the *Venture*?"

"Waiting for our Captain. He was delivering something to the Shrine for Father Lijou. He plans to take the *Venture II* to go home."

A warning klaxon, relayed through the ship's comm, went off outside.

"Damn! Get off now, Banner," he said, dropping all pretense of being L'Seuli as he pushed past him into the ship's interior. "I'm going back for Shaidan."

Banner coped well with his revelation. There was shock, of course, but then his Second felt a sense of satisfaction that his suspicions had been proved right.

"I know. I'm coming with you," Banner said, following him. "So are the others."

He stopped dead. "Others?"

"All but Chima. I managed to make sure she's busy elsewhere. You didn't want a female with us after what happened to Carrie, did you?" Banner raised his wrist, turning on his comm link. "Start her up, Khadui," he said. "Captain's on board."

"Aye sir."

"This mission is unauthorized, Banner. If you come with me, we'll be branded renegades for real this time."

"We know, but the M'zullians have destroyed the J'kirtikkian world with the weapon they used on Khyaal and Szurtha. If we don't go now, they'll leave the cub with Kezule."

Shocked, he stared at Banner, then beneath his feet, he felt the deck begin to vibrate. He began to run for the bridge.

"Head for the jump point, Banner," he said flinging himself into the command chair as the other leaped into his own seat. "I'll take over once we're off Haven."

"Incoming message, Captain," said Khadui.

"Ignore it." The *Venture II* began to rise and head for the force field that protected the entrance to the landing bay. "You all realize what we're doing, don't you?" he said. "This isn't a rescue mission. We need to do what Kezule wants, play for time if we're going to get that cub back."

"We understand," said Banner.

"At least this time we can't be accused of stealing a ship," said Jayza, glancing over his shoulder at him.

EPILOGUE

Haven

L'SEULI was in a calmer mood when he debarked from his shuttle. It was with relief he saw Jiosha waiting for them with Physician Vryalma. Once more, Chima was given the job of looking after their guests, this time taking them to the sick bay for obligatory health checks.

Taking his co-ruler by the arm, he drew her toward the elevator, waiting for it to return. "Thank Vartra you're all right. Did you have Vryalma examine you?" he asked.

"No need," she replied with an amused glance at him. "I only passed out, that's all."

"It's how you passed out that worries me. The thought of anyone controlling your mind . . ."

"L'Seuli, I'm fine. Kusac didn't try to control my mind. He was as surprised as I was when I passed out. What worries me is that he did it. I thought he'd lost his Talent."

"He had, but Kzizysus, the TeLaxaudin, developed a cure for him. Father Lijou told me it would take several weeks before he was able to use his abilities again, though. Are you sure there's been no damage done?" he asked as the elevator doors slid open and they got in.

"Why don't you ask me what's really in your mind, L'Seuli?" she said, leaning against him as the doors closed. "I've been aware of your interest for several months now, and I'd be happy to spend time with you. This evening will be fine. Now tell me what you're doing about Kusac."

L'Seuli stared down at her, speechless and embarrassed.

She laughed gently, resting her hand on his shoulder as she

watched his ears flatten down out of sight. "Come on, L'Seuli, I'm a telepath. You've been very good trying to hide it, but I noticed, and I'm flattered. One of us had to bring up the subject and I've waited long enough for you to do it!"

"I sent half a dozen fighters after them to force them back, but they jumped before we could reach them," he said in a slightly strangled voice, trying to back away from her, but he found her grip surprisingly strong. "I've reported the matter to Commander Rhyaz."

"Are you sending ships to the rendezvous coordinates?"

"No. The Commander agrees with me that we might as well let them go. Given the current crisis, we can't afford to get involved any further. Our treaty with the Primes is even more vital now. Besides, it's likely Kezule will have changed the rendezvous."

"Makes sense," she nodded, stroking his neck briefly and intimately before moving her hand to link it through his arm as the elevator doors opened. "It's no different from before. We can't risk showing up in case it frightens Kezule away."

"Fright isn't a word I'd associate with the General," said L'Seuli, his mind on her as she escorted him out into the corridor. His surprise at her acknowledgment of his interest had worn off enough for him to consider the situation between them now.

"So it's a matter of waiting until tomorrow to debrief the female Rraelga, then send them all home. Where are the cubs going? To Kusac's estate as he asked, or to Stronghold?"

"Probably the Telepath Guild," said L'Seuli as she drew him inexorably through the busy corridor toward his office. "Master Sorli is well equipped to debrief them there, and if it's appropriate they be sent to Ruth and Carrie, they're close enough to do so. We can send them back to Shola on the *Couana*." He imagined everyone they passed was staring at them and speculating on what would happen between them

They're far more interested in news of the M'zullians and the arrival of the cubs and Rraelga, she sent, opening his office door and propelling him inside.

"I suppose so," he murmured, enjoying the warmth of her hand resting on his arm and her scent mingled with the faint smell of nung incense. He'd dreamed of this opportunity for so long that he didn't quite know what to do now it was here.

"So we've got perhaps half an hour to begin to get to know

each other better before your briefing at the fourteenth hour." She
stopped and turned round to face him expectantly.

"I should . . ."

"What?" she interrupted him. "You never struck me as the shy
type, L'Seuli."

His ears flattened again. "I'm not! I just want a relationship
that will last with you, not something . . ." Seeing her surprise,
he ground to a halt.

"You're serious about me, aren't you?" she said quietly. "I
hadn't realized. Look, I can't cook, so I can't offer to make a
meal for you . . ."

"I can," he interrupted, ears rising. "So will you come to my
quarters tonight for third meal?"

She began to laugh softly, reaching out to touch his face.

"What's so funny?" he asked, slightly hurt.

"Nothing," she chuckled, stepping closer, and closer still when
his arms opened automatically for her. "Just that I hadn't realized I was so lucky. Not only do I have one of the nicest and
most old-fashioned males I know, but you can cook too!"

"I don't know if that's a compliment or not," he said as she
tilted her face up to his. He felt a rush of light-headedness and
his heart began to beat even faster as their lips touched.

My fault, I'm sending to you. I'll stop if you want.

"Don't even think about it," he murmured, hands closing round
her shoulders. "One of the nice things about having a telepath
for a lover, so I hear, is the sharing."

Jiosha began to purr with amusement—just as the comm began
to buzz.

L'Seuli let her go and answered it with a sigh. "L'Seuli here."

"Commander, it's Vryalma from the sick bay. Are you alone?"

"Apart from Mentor Jiosha, yes."

"Those cubs—they're hybrids, not pure Sholans."

"What? Are you sure?" he asked, glancing across at Jiosha.

"Positive. On a hunch, I got the main comp to cross-check
their DNA against that of our people who were on the Prime
ship *Kz'adul*, and I got matches. These are the cubs of those
Brothers and Sisters, Commander. And they're ten years old."

"On my way up," he said.

Stronghold, the same day

"Take them to Tanjo," said Rhyaz. "And get Jiosha to speak to those who've been in contact with them. I don't want word of this getting out to anyone until we've decided what to do with them. Use Attitude Indoctrination if you have to, but ensure this story dies now. How do we explain the presence of ten-year-old hybrids without shaking our treaty with the Primes to its very foundations? With the M'zullians on the move, we need that treaty, L'Seuli. Kusac needs it."

"What about the needs of the cubs, Master Rhyaz?" asked Jiosha. "They've known nothing but an experimental facility and the renegade Primes. They've had no childhood—from what Rraelga says we think they're actually only twelve weeks old— they don't deserve to be put in cryo for the next nine years."

"No decision has been made, yet, Jiosha, but if they were, they'd know nothing about it. For them it would be like a night's sleep, nothing more," said Rhyaz.

"You wouldn't be sending them to the Instructor if you intended to return them to their parents."

"Did Kusac's report—or Banner's—say why Kezule left the Prime world?" asked Rhyaz, changing the topic.

"Nothing in Kusac's beyond what we already know," said L'Seuli. "His was very brief. It was Banner's that said that Kezule wanted Kusac to train his people and had kept a cub back to ensure he returned."

Rhyaz sighed. Once again he had more puzzles, not less. "Have Tanjo question the cubs closely, but carefully, L'Seuli. I'll inform you both of our decision regarding them when Father Lijou and I have discussed the matter. Keep me posted on any developments."

"Yes, Commander."

"Have you any idea what Kaid will say and do when he finds out you've put his and Carrie's sons, and Rezac's daughter all into cryo?" Kha'Qwa asked Rhyaz, obviously aghast at the thought.

"I haven't put them in cryo yet," Rhyaz said, irritated. He should have remembered Kha'Qwa was too newly a mother to be able to view the problem of the cubs dispassionately.

"But you will," said Lijou, placing more logs on the fire. "Because right now, regrettably, we haven't any other option."

"Until Kusac returns to us," said Kha'Qwa.

"If he does," said Rhyaz. "Now Kezule's got his claws into him, I doubt we'll see him again. He probably holds Kusac responsible for his treatment on Shola. But why didn't Kezule keep him when he had him? Why lure him back with a cub—unless the cub's his."

"Not possible," said Lijou. "The implant made Kusac sterile, just like the M'zullians."

"Then how come Carrie had twins, one of them Kusac's son?" asked Rhyaz reasonably.

"The implant had been removed by then," said Lijou. "I'm beginning to wonder if Rezac was right all along and that despite his hatred of the Valtegans, Kusac is suffering from the same dependency as the Sholan captives in his time."

"What about the female and her infant?" asked Kha'Qwa. "You can't put them in cryo too."

"I'm having her brought here so you can adjust her memories, Lijou, then we'll take her to Noni. She can find her a place in one of the villages looking after a Brotherhood family."

Lijou flicked an ear in agreement. "A nice solution. I wish it were as easy for the cubs," he sighed.

"Kusac left something on the *Couana* for Carrie," said Rhyaz. "A pair of birthing bracelets and a data crystal with a message. Could he have known about the twins? When I went to tell him Carrie and Kaid's daughter had been born, he already knew. Has his Talent started returning?"

"Not to that degree," said Lijou. "He might have picked up the birth of their daughter, but that's all, and he had to have bought the bracelets some time before he left Shola, when he was on his estate. You can't get them out here unless you go to Ranz. I know, I tried." He glanced over at his life-mate with a gentle smile. "Likely the second one was for Kashini."

"I'm not so sure," said Rhyaz uncomfortably, remembering his last conversation with Kusac. "He was anxious to leave immediately, said there was a very strong risk of his mind Linking to Carrie's now she'd had the cub, and if that happened, he couldn't go on the mission."

"He was right," said Lijou quietly. "I'll take the bracelets and data crystal to Carrie. We owe them that at least. From what I hear, with the worry over Dhaykin and Kusac, her health is fragile at the moment."

"Not the crystal," said Rhyaz. "I want to check for any coded messages. We can't risk him telling her about the mission and the cubs. It isn't as if she'll know there was a crystal in the first place." His eyes glazed over briefly and he got to his feet hurriedly. "Alex is on her way up. Will you explain about the cubs to her, Kha'Qwa? She gets on well with you."

Kha'Qwa sighed. "I'll try, but I don't like your decision in the first place."

"Just do your best," he said, heading for the concealed exit from their lounge. He stopped and looked at Lijou. "May I?" he asked.

Lijou waved his hand. "Go," he said. "We'll speak to Alex."

Valsgarth Estate, Zhal-S'Asha, 29th day (October)

Carrie sat looking at Lijou, unable to take in what he was saying. First Kusac's apparent defection from Shola, now this.

"This is what Kusac left for you," said Lijou gently, putting a tissue wrapped package onto the lap of her long woollen robe. She could feel his hope that this would bring her out of her state of shock.

It was something concrete in a world suddenly gone even more insane than it had been for the last eleven days.

"What is it?" Kaid asked the priest sharply.

She caught Lijou's negative gesture and automatically closed her hands round the package. It was hers, from Kusac, perhaps the last communication she'd ever have from him if this latest move by the M'zullians led to war. It—no, they, she could feel two curved items—felt hard, the coldness from them drawing the heat from her hands.

An image began to form in her mind and frantically, she tore the wrapping from them until they tumbled, shining brightly, into her lap.

Kaid was squatting on his haunches at her side in an instant. "Birthing bracelets!" he said, looking up at Lijou, as surprised as she was. "But they're only given by the parents."

"He wanted her to know he welcomed your cub," said Lijou quietly.

"But two of them? How could he know about his son?"

"Where's his message, Lijou?" said Carrie, her voice tight and brittle. She looked across at him. "He left me a data crystal and I want it."

"There was no crystal," he began.

"Don't lie to me!" She was on her feet now, towering over him, the bracelets clutched tightly in one hand, the tissue wrapping cascading to the floor around her. "Why have you kept it from me? What's in it that you need to hide?" Her eyes glittered with unshed tears.

"Nothing's being hidden from you, Carrie," said Lijou. "I kept the crystal back only so as not to distress you. I can tell you what it . . ."

"I want the message my life-mate left for me." She needed it, needed to see him and hear his voice again! "How did he know to buy two birthing bracelets? He could have bought Kashini one at any time, but he didn't!"

"When he left, his Talent was still suppressed," began Lijou.

"Take these!" she said, thrusting the bracelets at him. "Feel them, Lijou, then tell me his Talent was suppressed! I can *feel* him in the bracelets!"

"I believe you, my dear," said Lijou, sitting hurriedly back in his seat. "You don't need to convince me."

"Then why keep it from me? Can't you realize that with him gone, anything he's left for me is precious? Or are you punishing me for what Kusac's supposed to have done?"

"No one's being punished, Carrie. I felt the message might distress you, that's all."

She laughed, aware she sounded more than a little hysterical. "Don't patronize me, Lijou. What I can't handle is knowing nothing about where he is or why he left."

"Carrie, I promise that first thing tomorrow, a Brother will be sent from Stronghold with it," said Lijou, standing up.

"You can trust Lijou, Carrie," said Kaid gently, taking her by the elbow and urging her to sit down. "If he says the crystal will be sent to you tomorrow, then he'll see it's done. Can we offer you something, Lijou—a drink, or a meal? It's a long way to come just to deliver the bracelets."

"No, thank you. I must get back. I felt you deserved to have the bracelets delivered in person," said Lijou. "And it doesn't take too long in the speeder."

"I'll walk you to your vehicle," said Kaid.

Taizia was hovering outside the den and as they left, Kaid nodded to her and she slipped in.

"I take it there's been no news of Kusac beyond his visit to Haven."

"None, I'm afraid. Carrie seems very fragile," said Lijou, choosing his words carefully.

"You've seen her at the best she's been since we got home," said Kaid. "As you know, thanks to Raiban, the news hit the Infonets the same day it happened. When we returned, we were besieged, not only on the estate's perimeters by reporters but by our own Clan, all of them clamoring for the truth." He glanced at Lijou as they passed out through the side door into the vehicle park. "He's lost it, Lijou, really gone over the edge to walk out on her at this time. He needs finding and hospitalizing for his own good. What was on the crystal, anyway?"

"A love letter, that's all," said Lijou "I should have listened to Kha'Qwa and brought it with me. So much for hoping not to distress Carrie."

"Everything distresses her just now. She's convinced herself that Kusac's innocent of the charges against him, that there's some other reason for him leaving Shola than returning to the Primes. Vanna's coming to see her later this afternoon to try to persuade her to take some medication."

"They say love is blind, it sees what it wants to see," murmured Lijou, stopping beside the speeder to wait for Yaszho to open the door. "How are the twins doing? I promised Kha'Qwa I'd ask about them."

"Fine. Layeesha's thriving, and Dhaykin is beginning to slowly catch up with his sister," said Kaid, smiling for the first time that day.

"That's good news," he said as the door slid open. "Keep us posted on how Carrie's doing, Kaid. We're all most concerned for her."

"I will. Thank you for bringing the bracelets over."

As the speeder took off and began to climb over the bare branched trees, Lijou sat back in his seat and sighed. He'd have closed his eyes if he could, but he knew if he did he'd see four small bodies lying rimed with frost in cryo units.

Yaszho reached into his door pocket and passed him a can. "Try this, Father. You look like you could do with it."

"What's this?" he asked, taking it from him and turning it round, trying to read the alien script.

"A U'Churian hot beverage with sweetener in it. Pull the tab and wait thirty seconds for it to heat up, then it's ready to drink."

He pulled the tab and waited. As it began to warm, the interesting smell that drifted out of the opening made him realize how hungry he was. "I don't suppose you brought any food?"

"Tutor Kha'Qwa wouldn't let me leave without enough to feed a household," he said. "It's in the box behind you, Father. Don't blame yourself about the cubs. Master Rhyaz is right. It was impossible to give them to their parents without word of what the Primes had done getting out. Then we'd have had all Shola baying for their blood. That would mean the collapse of the treaty and Brother Kusac stranded in hostile territory even if he did get away from Kezule. If the cubs hadn't have been hybrids . . . but when the oldest is only a little over a year old, how can four ten-year-olds suddenly appear from nowhere? It just isn't possible to give them to their parents right now, Father Lijou, not when we're poised on the brink of war."

"I know," he sighed. "It doesn't make it any easier to lie to people I consider my friends."

APPENDIX

Ancient Brotherhood records

It was the end of an age, a time of terror and fire, when two suns shone briefly in the heavens. The lesser one hung fiery red in our sky, searing the land with the heat of its breath as it drew ever closer to our world. Across forest, plain and city, fires raged, devastating everything in their path. It brought the beginnings of hope as the flames drove the invaders forever from our soil.

Those who could run fled, heading for the high lands, praying their Gods hadn't forsaken them, watching the blazing orb as it grew ever larger before finally disappearing beyond the horizon.

The very earth trembled at its falling, shaking even the temples to their foundations. Then the sea rose up to wipe the face of Shola clean, washing away the taint of the occupation, and the debris of what was now past.

Darkness fell across the face of Shola. For two years, rain and clouds hid the face of the sun. In their mountain lairs, the people of Shola survived, and grew stronger. We watched and waited for the return of the sun, praying to our Gods for deliverance, never dreaming that a God already lived among us.

When that first day came, Vartra Himself emerged from Stronghold, sending His followers out into the spring sunlight to find and reunite all the people of Shola. The Brotherhood we were called, sworn to protect the weakest among our kind but particularly the telepaths.

Guilds were formed so that no knowledge or skill could be lost, and slowly the work of rebuilding began. To this day, that time of year is named after Mellasha, the Goddess of Rebirth and Spring. And lest any forget the second sun that brought about our deliverance, or our joy at seeing the clouds finally part, our calendar was rewritten on the sun's cycles with each month bearing a portion of the name of Zhalwae, the Sun God.

Sholan Months of the Year.

Shola has 12 months, 11 of which are 31 days long, the twelfth being 33 days long. It has two moons, the larger one called Agalimi, the smaller one called Aduan, and their orbits are 19 and 16 days long respectively.

The Sholans have a pantheon of Gods and Goddesses not unlike the Greek one on Earth. Each deity has helpers, called dzinaes, who embody lesser aspects of their patron deity.

Human Month	*Sholan Month*	*Meaning in Human language and associated deity*
January	Zhal-L'Shoh	Winter's Hellmouth—L'Shoh is the God of Hell and Consort of Kuushoi.
February	Zhal-Mellasha	Spring Hope, 16th day is First of Spring—Mellasha is Goddess of Spring.
March	Zhal-Arema	Month of Love—Arema is Goddess of Love.
April	Zhal-Ch'Ioka	Month of Hearth—Ch'Ioka is Ghyakulla's female dzinae of Hearth and Home.
May	Zhal-Zhalwae	Month of the Sun God, 6th day is the First of Summer—Zhalwae is the Sun God.
June	Zhal-Ghyakulla	Month of the Goddess—the Green Goddess, the Earth Mother.
July	Zhal-Vartra	Month of the Consort, 8th day is Midsummer Festival—Vartra's month, a fertility festival as He is both Son and Consort of Ghyakulla.
August	Zhal-Oeshi	Month of Harvest—Oeshi is Goddess of Harvest time.
September	Zhal-Nylam	Month of the Hunt, 18th day is First of Autumn—Nylam is God of the Hunt
October	Zhal-S'Asha	Month of Approaching Darkness—S'Asha is L'Shoh's

		female dzinae of Dusk and Darkness.
November	Zhal-Rojae	Month of Snow, 4th day First of Winter—Rojae is Kuushoi's male dzinae of Snow and Frost.
December	Zhal-Kuushoi	Month of Winter, 26th day is Midwinter Festival—Kuushoi is the Winter Goddess and the festival is when the birth of Vartra, Her Son, is celebrated.

GAYLE GREENO

GHATTEN'S GAMBIT
In THE FARTHEST SEEKING, a new generation of human Seekers and their catlike Ghatti companions journey into a dangerous wilderness, while in the tunnels beneath Marchmont's Capital a deadly piece of long-forgotten technology is about to be rediscovered. . . .

☐ **SUNDERLIES SEEKING Book 1**   0-88677-805-0—$6.99

☐ **THE FARTHEST SEEKING Book 2**
                                  0-88677-897-2—$6.99

And don't miss:

THE GHATTI'S TALE

☐ **FINDERS, SEEKERS Book 1**   0-88677-550-7—$6.99

☐ **MINDSPEAKER'S CALL Book 2**   0-88677-579-5—$6.99

☐ **EXILES' RETURN Book 3**   0-88677-655-4—$6.99